PRAISE FOR

SUNDAY JEWS

"Calisher's impressively dense novel resembles the family room: crammed with arch dialogue, bulging with baroque narration and long setups for quick jokes, stuffed with chatter about tribal customs as practiced from Asia Minor to Central Park West.... The wit and insight of these intertwined character studies doesn't let up for 694 pages, but neither does the self-conscious marvelousness."
—*Entertainment Weekly*

"Calisher provides social commentary as dense as the Torah commentary that Zipporah's family, centuries ago, must have studied."
—*Los Angles Times Book World*

"All Calisher's signature complexities, idiosyncrasies and pleasures are on full display."   —*The New Leader*

"Calisher has created an impressively complex family tableau in her nonagenarian novel. Her ability to construct a work of fiction is still as evident as her linguistic gifts, proving yet again why she has been a literary force for almost half a century."
—*Richmond Times-Dispatch*

"Like Edith Wharton and Henry James, Hortense Calisher finds the drama of fiction as much in the analysis of motive as in the various excitements of action.... Majestically persistent, with an old-fashioned faith in the novel's ability to make worlds."
—*Publishers Weekly* (starred review)

"*Sunday Jews* is a summa, and a triumph. . . . This incandescent elegy to age, change, and acceptance burns with an urgency that seems to have pared Calisher's often-reviled ornate style down to taut, focused simplicity and purity. She has often before written as fervently, even as generously, but she has never written better."

—*Kirkus Reviews* (starred review)

"Calisher, Jamesian in style and intent, traces the meshing of inner and outer worlds with voluptuous precision. Truly a grande dame of letters, she remains intrepid, demanding, and indefatigable in her fifteenth novel, a riverine family saga. . . . Subtly and incrementally powerful." —*Booklist* (starred review)

PRAISE FOR HORTENSE CALISHER

"When American writing of the twentieth century is summed up—perhaps in the twenty-first—Hortense Calisher will be seen to stand vividly with Cather and Fitzgerald. In the meantime, even before the Long Perspective, the body of her work (and the perfection of her prose) is here to complicate, enlighten, startle, and delight us."

—Cynthia Ozick

"Via a geneology that include Henry James and Edith Wharton, Hortense Calisher inherited and, today, uniquely embodies the vision of an author as the natural chronicler of her age."

—Allan Gurganus

"Her tales are all a form of amber, sealing unforgettable moments in time. And Hortense Calisher is better at this sort of sealing than any other writer I know of." —Anne Tyler

SUNDAY
JEWS

SUNDAY JEWS

HORTENSE CALISHER

A HARVEST BOOK • HARCOURT, INC.

Orlando   Austin   New York   San Diego   Toronto   London

www.HarcourtBooks.com

Library of Congress Cataloging-in-Publication Data
Calisher, Hortense.
Sunday Jews/Hortense Calisher. 1st ed.
p.   cm.
ISBN 0-15-100930-9
ISBN 0-15-602745-3 (pbk.)
1. Jews—New York (State)—New York—Fiction.
2. Women intellectuals—Fiction.   3. New York (N.Y.)—Fiction.
4. Jewish families—Fiction.   5. Jewish women—Fiction.   I. Title.
PS3553.A4 S+   2002002517

Text set in Dante MT
Display set in Charlemagne
Designed by Cathy Riggs

Printed in the United States of America

First Harvest edition 2003
A C E G I K J H F D B

For my granddaughter, Katy May Spencer,
transcriber of this text

SUNDAY
JEWS

In her mid-sixties, Zipporah Zangwill, born in Boston to long-time residents of that name, for over forty years married to Peter Duffy, who teaches philosophy in New York, and herself well-known as a "social" anthropologist, has informed her family, a large clan, that from now on she wishes to be known as Zoe—sending out cards to that effect, along with an invitation to a celebratory party.

To Peter, who has perhaps been aware of her progress toward some decision that will mortally affect their lives, if not this one, she has merely shown the cards, ordered from the same stationer who had always supplied the formal announcements the years had required: engagements and weddings of the children, anniversaries of all kinds, plus bids to those coveted "theme parties" she threw when some professional or affectionate interest erupted. And of course the two change-of-address announcements, of yore.

These newest cards, thinner than any of those and modest in size, say simply "One of our Sundays," giving the date. The time would be known by custom as afternoon, the eats to straggle along with individual noshing, and focus hard as dusk falls. A footnote, lower left, in small but legible print, says: "From now on Zipporah asks to be known as Zoe . . ." It's not certain whether the reason for the party is this.

Few phone to inquire. For some grateful elders in the circle, she is their only fount of surprise. The Duffy children—Gerald, Charles, Nell, Erika, and Zachary, all grown now—do mildly mention it, in no order of age status except whoever had the smarts and the sass to speak up first. They chat constantly, over a sibling network maintained either coast to coast from their homes or now and then from sites no longer as strange as those their mother had all their young lives gone to. Their feeling on her travels had long since been expressed by Mickey, a former youngest son, whose age was fixed, he having died at twelve: "She never really leaves us. And she always comes back."

The network isn't kept out of duty. All the Duffys have the kind of family feeling that filches away their attention even from those they are married to. Charles, an academic always somewhere in the middle of the country, is also their median voice. "They're so close a pair. They never skimped us. But it helped us close ranks." His puns, as a part-time lawyer as well as a physicist, make Nell sigh. "A pun should be more illegal, Chuck. But I hear you."

Nobody in their immediate family is a naysayer, though Erika tends to marry them. "Maybe Ma just wants to shed her identity. I do now and then."

Gerald, who has a wife who does that constantly, keeps quiet.

Zach, now the youngest, speaks for all of them. "Hope not."

Peter, when shown the cheaper cards, merely quirks: "Wise of you, not to jump to Tiffany."

"One hundred sixty-four of them? Would've cost the earth."

"Will you tell them why?" He's looking at the footnote.

Her answer, with her handsome eyes wide: "I don't have to tell you."

"No."

They kiss. She's as intense, he as genial, as on the day they met in front of the Alma Mater statue on the Columbia campus, where she'd lost the very high heel of one shoe, and he'd picked it up. The legend is that in trying to fit the heel on her shoe again, he'd knelt, but saying carefully, "This means nothing." Yet then offered his arm, so that she could hop to the shoe-repair shop across Broadway. Instead, she ran barefoot across the hot macadam, he following.

Waiting for the shoemaker, they exchanged:

"Zangwill? Any relation to Israel Zangwill who wrote the *Melting Pot*? English Jew, 1914."

If they were, her father had said, they were very collateral. "No. But we did come from England, and are Jewish, of course . . . You in History?" . . . "No. Philo." By that time they were outside the shop door. "And you?" he'd said . . . "Anthro. So I can travel." Three years older than she, he had already done some, promising himself more . . . "You're Catholic, of course," she'd said; "'Duffy.'" . . . A smile from Peter. "Of course. Lapsed." Wiggling the foot in the repaired shoe, she'd said to that, half-smiling: "Lace curtain?" A Boston term he hadn't known, having grown up in the Bronx. "We're 'lace curtain Jewish,'" she'd joked. "Still morally Jewish, though we don't go to synagogue more than once a year. And we don't say 'lapsed.' Our word for it is 'reformed.'"

Before they slept together that very night, a fact not in the legend, they'd agreed that whatever their families had or had not declined to, it was impossible for either an anthropologist or a philosopher to believe in God. "Not a personal one," Peter had said. "We must leave ourselves some room. For—uh." He'd meant to spend the rest of his career defining that "uh."

"Oh sure," she'd said. "Impersonality is in."

The family, as all within refer to it, is now very large, but considers itself to be the opposite of that chill term "extended."

The outsiders' opinion of the Duffy-Zangwill ménage is: "Close. Ve-ry close. By joint intention, no doubt. But the flavor is Jewish. Peter's the one living son of a stray Irish couple emigrated from Dublin. Had a brother who died. After Peter's marriage, the two older maiden sisters wouldn't speak to him. But you know Zipporah." Or Zippy or Zee. "She's won them over, don't ask me how . . . Ever been to one of her and Peter's Sundays? Friends welcome."

"Not a lot of our Duffys in the States when I was your age," Peter says to his youngest grandson, Bert, on one of those Sunday afternoons. "All must have stayed back home. You might see your very earliest ancestors in some remains at the British Museum. Called 'the Sutton Hoo treasure,' if you really want to check."

"But there're lots of us Duffys now," Bert said.

"Did my best." She and he had had four early on, then two more, when near that age called "menopause" by the less sexually interested.

The Boston Zangwills had been amused. The Long Island and Westchester ones, younger connections in Roslyn, Manhasset, Mamaroneck, had been appalled. Such large broods were out of fashion, and not practical if a woman wanted to keep her waistline or a man hoped to send his kids to private school. And hadn't past generations of Zangwills done well enough? Since Zipporah's own maternal grandparents had had nine, she'd had nearly that many surviving aunts and uncles and fourteen first cousins. Her own children were providing young Bertram with nearly the same.

"If we still did math with multiplication tables," Bertram says, looking over the crowded living room he has known since a toddler, "I could just multiply cousins. But that wouldn't be very modern either, would it."

"I'm leaving room for you to say what's modern, m'boy."

"You never called me that before." Bert is now past sixteen.

"Seen it coming," his gramps said.

When Bert got his card from Zipporah, some weeks before the party, he'd brought it to Peter's attention that next Sunday.

"You seen this coming, Gramps?" He never uses first names for his elders in the informal style parents like his encouraged. He had campaigned to attend a public school, but had lost.

"You know the story, brother. Your grandmother runs. She can't hop."

"'Brother'?" Bert says. "I find this family very confusing. But reading the Bible has helped." Although he had said, "Nah, never mind," when the possibility of a bar mitzvah was faintly dangled, he has elected to go to Hebrew school, which some in the room consider odd, or even retrograde.

"Old Testament or New?"

"Both. On my own. Hebrew class, they just do the commentaries."

"Just like at my university," Peter sighed. "And?"

"The New Testament? Very late stuff. The Old has the bang."

"The creation, yes," his grandfather says. "Uh."

"Anyway, I hear Grandma, I mean Zoe, is making the party just a real one. Not a potlatch, like when she tried to let us in on Amerindian ethic. Or that icky German one. *Turnverein*, Munich, 1939."

"She still feels guilty about the Holocaust, Bertram. She had no one in it . . . And anthropologists try to live what they teach and vice versa." He grins. "S'helped me no end."

"Oh, her real parties are great, yeah. Last year, that big down-town warehouse, some of the oldies took sick so they wouldn't have to come to—great. I got to lay a girl. Only a cousin. But a girl."

"Oh. But that friend you brought, you always bring—"

"Oh yeah, him. The Shine."

"Bertram. That's a racial epithet." Though the young man they can both see across the room, leaning against a wall and talking languidly to a couple of his contemporaries, isn't very black.

"Not with him, it isn't. It's what he calls himself. Capitalized. The Shine. He could call himself The Sheeny, he says, for the other half of him, but it wouldn't have as much dash. He likes to refer to himself in the third person. Told Granma—Zoe, it's because maybe he's gay. She was very empathetic. Told him she does that third person stuff lots of times, even though she's not. Not gay."

"Ah. No, I guess not."

"Nor me. I'm like you and her. Not even bi. Not even wor-ried—that I'm not worried. About sex, that is."

"But the family confuses you?"

Bert stands tall. Gilt blond, with Zipporah's thin, not quite

Roman nose, he is intermarriage's finest product, with his father being Peter and Zipporah's eldest son, Gerald, and his mother a Jewish Finn. He has only one flaw, the crooked pinkie often called a baseball finger. "How come a Jew got that?" the rabbi joked at the confirmation Bert did go through, "But it'll keep you from being a Jesuit. I understand they have to be perfect physically."

"I'm yeah tired of having such an open mind. And you know what? I think so is Granma."

"Funny," his grandfather says. "An open mind is what's kept me going. But about her—mmm. She's a bit . . . lost her breeze . . . Oh, not physically."

Bert grins. "Those high heels. She runs for a cab, she looks like a chicken with its head cut off. But fast."

"Bert. You grew up in Westchester. You go to Dalton. Or is it Riverdale? Where would you see a chicken with its head cut off?"

"Voodoo garage, out in Queens. I go there with The Shine, he comes to the Yeshiva with me. We're on a project, see?" He can't control the grin. "At Collegiate."

On the double, they are both yakking. Bert goes pink, Peter slaps his knee. "Voodoo. That's where you saw Zippy go for the cab," Peter gasps. "And where she and The Shine talk third person? Wish I'd been there. But your grandmother won't ever let me on location with her. She says Jewish mockers are a dime a dozen any cocktail hour. But Christian ones anywhere are a serious proposition. Pit-bulls, she calls us. Trailing the cathedrals behind us."

"No more 'Zippy,' gee," his grandson says. "I always liked to hear you say it . . . Zoe, Zo-ay? Fooey." He looks uncomfortable. "But yeah, we think something is like serious with her."

"Bert. Spill."

"It's creeping around the school too. That's how we recognized it."

"What is creeping around your bloody school?"

Bert looks about to cry. "We think Granma is beginning to believe in God."

"Ho-lee," Peter whispers. His hand goes to his cheek. "Haven't said that since I was your age." His tall grandson stands eye-to-eye with him but is avoiding this. "So. You make a show of feeling small before the Lord, so you can feel big before everybody else? I remember that . . . And are you and that con man friend of yours her messengers? Or is this a private observation, courtesy the sixth form?"

"Seventh, Gramps . . . No, it's just—like you recognize it on somebody."

"I see." He puts a gentle hand on the boy's shoulder. "Let's go have a Coke. No—a beer."

In the kitchen, which is always immaculate and quiet during a normal afternoon hour, when both mistress and the long-term maid, Jennie, maybe taking their naps or walks, are elsewhere, Peter says, "Cookie jar?"

"Jennie will have a fit."

"Your grandmother didn't want to have any help at all, once we could afford. Professionally, she already had to have so much ethnic tenderness. 'I could never keep a maid in her proper place,' she said. So I told her I'd do it for her. Not that we've succeeded . . . Take as many cookies as you want. It's Jennie's job."

"In our house, the maids come and go."

Peter is not fond of his oldest's son's wife, Kitty, a woman who changes her clothes five times a day. But he'll forgive her anything for having had Bertram. "Generations differ. In mine, even middle-class kids had an obligation to steal from the larder. Yours, there's all kinds of silly food lying around." He rubs his fingers free of cookie. "Now, let's discuss this immortality business."

"Is that what? I thought it was her we—"

"Uh . . . By the way, do I seem to you vaguer than usual?"

"Not so I noticed."

"Thanks. My trade, we get away with murder . . . But I must be getting older. Can you believe, yesterday at the florist's, having the new assistant send my sister a birthday plant, I couldn't remember my own name. Then the owner breaks in, 'Why Mr. Duffy, you've an account with us'... And at my age, seems we also get obscure little rages... Or can't recall what trousers are for."

Bert bursts out laughing. "Wear jeans."

"Used to. They gave me up... Listen, kid. Your age, you believe in your own death? Oh, not by war. Or motorbikes. Your own natural death. Like everybody is supposed to expect?"

"Funnee." Bert's voice is wee. "No, I don't. I know it's— crayzee. And I don't think of it much. But when I do, it's like I'll beat the rap. An exception will be made."

How great he looks. Nothing will ever dent that cheek.

"Not crazy, sonny. It's strongest at your age. But everybody believes the same. Right until the blinds pull down, maybe... Even those who never stop thinking about dying. Hypochondriacs."

"You're not one of those."

Both voices tremor to what's being said. To the wonder of its being said between them.

Peter clears his throat, has a little trouble with it. "No."

"Nor Gran."

"Zipporah?" Just saying that lifts his grandfather's head, as the Sunday crowd often marks. "Half her folks live past ninety. She's convinced she'll take after the right half. And means to carry us along with her. Her mother's half had a saying: 'Just keep out of sight of the Lord's eye.' Even for Brookline at that time, they took the prize for being invisible. You bump into one of them and it was like to a squeak, with a shadow. As for money, pots of it, some had. But like the Chinese, never on display. Gave your grandmother the subject for her dissertation. *Primitive Images.* She went to Melanesia for it. Said she could have stayed right at home."

Jennie can be heard on her way up to the kitchen.

"I should look it up," Bert says. Going down the book-lined hall, they pass the shelf of works written in this house.

"Yes, Byron. Do."

Byron is Bert's older brother.

His grandfather is checking his watch. "No, it's Sunday. This is not the office." The watch is upside down on his grandfather's wrist. It does not have the days of the week, surely. No, same old watch. He sees that Gramps's slippers, fancy velvet ones Bert's own mother had insisted they give for Hanukkah, are on in reverse.

His grandfather's uplifted palms seem to adhere, then part to bang his thighs. "My ideas...the rest of me won't handle them." Then a whisper. "Last time this happened...there were flowers." His face supplicates.

What put the right words on Bert's tongue he can't explain, he tells The Shine later.

"Your name is Peter Duffy," he said.

And there Peter was again: former commander in the Naval Reserve, holder of a chair in semantics and head of this household—Gramps.

As the time nears for Zipporah's "nameday" party, as some are calling it, most family members intend to address her as usual, until instructed otherwise. "Front-face," they say to each other. Why would a woman who has been Mother, Mom, Ma, Cousin, Aunt, Grandma, as well as "a distinguished byline" want to sink herself under a name most likely a monosyllable, at best stretching to two? Outsiders are more careful, citing only the opinion first given them by some relative. Cousin Grace thinks the name change must have to do with Zipporah's not yet looking like a matriarch. But Grace is such a flirt. Two former brothers-in-law of the Duffy daughters, men who are still familiars here and still rivals, chat each other up. "Bet you it has something to do with copyright." The second one counters, "I have it otherwise from Aunt Bee." That great-aunt, applied to, is careful not to roll her eyes, which might suggest she thinks Zippy has a lover, so speaks to her own lap. "Alice says"— her elder sister in Brookline—"Alice says we must be grateful for any family theme."

Attendance is perfect, down to second cousins once removed and the brood of step-grandchildren whom the several divorces and remarriages of the Duffy children have brought into the fold. Even for some minor public functions this would be a fair crowd, but the rambling apartment gently accommodates, as family rooms of any size seem in the end to do, with children squeezed together or on the floor, grown-ups perched on the arms of chairs, bathroom doors flapping. The men, too proud to do anything but stand when in close quarters, and the half-asleep nodder on the best sofa give the whole scene a mulling ease. For the younger parents there is that sense of the plush or at least settled comfort that generational quarters provide, combined with irritation at the bric-a-brac, and covert glances at pieces possibly choice.

All present have lived some part of their lives here. Schooldays lurk in the bookshelves; the mantel photos will earn the same old comments and stories. The feeding will be enormous. Old jokes have begun to pop. Norman, the Duffys' next-door neighbor and lawyer, has obliged with some variant of the one he brings out at Christmas: "Who are all these Yid Duffys? The Pope will want to know."

To Norman, the synagogue is "a social infrastructure," not a vision. He never goes to *schul*, plays cards with those who do and violin with those who don't; gives generously to "charity," among those the Jewish ones; but never excuses his lack of religious observance, his stated attitude being: "We Jews already know who we are." Yet it is rumored that he has left Temple Emanuel a considerable sum, with the stipulation that they give him a proper burial. Some have heard that he has offered to pay the tab for Zippy as well, if she wishes the same. She has never indicated.

Since the death of his wife, by whom there were no children, he has had two quiet mistressess, one Jewish, one not, both of whom ultimately married other men but kept Norman on, for lawyer and friend. As to clubs, he claims himself "unclubbable," with acid comment on most. A coveted weekend houseguest, often accompanied by some woman of appropriate age, he refuses dinners where invited as an extra man. "I don't need that career." Any matchmaker has long since given him up.

Since he and his wife had no kids, there's no way of knowing what schools they might have sent their children to—as yet one of the surest ways of measuring how far a couple might be straying from Judaism, and toward what. Surely, however, he has made certain familiar adjustments toward the mainstream? Yet nothing angers him more than the word "assimilated" as applied either to him or to Jews whose habits resemble his. When a young California associate, referring to rich Jews in his state who contributed largely to Israel "so that they never have to go there," added cannily, "Half-and-half does it, eh? Out here, unless you observe, you hardly feel Jewish at all," he wasn't rebuked. But he got no more business.

None of the Zangwill side, either back home in Boston or in Zipporah's own later household, has espoused Israel, on the grounds that it was now as much of a national state as a religion, and with too much dogma pimpling the original holy tolerance. In Zipporah's middle years, invited to lecture there as "a prominent Jewish woman," she had finally agreed to be presented as an "anthropologist interested in national customs worldwide."

Her first address, touching lightly on tribal rituals and structures all the way from Mesopotamia to Maine, had engendered enough warmth, and the pleased laughter spouted from silly customs reported from elsewhere, so that when she'd ended with a firm inclusion of the tribe of Israel, "which has variously permitted or stipulated that women serve in the army, but does not grant them equal divorce legalities," courtesy had prevailed. While at the mayor of Jerusalem's reception, certain women had flocked to her side from the pool of those who stiffly had not, and even a few men had veered toward her, if only to teeter at her elbow to "explain."

At her second lecture, enticingly dubbed "Slavery and the Camps," all went well as long as she stuck to Greece and Africa—and the U.S.A. Then had come her "unfortunate peroration," as one report called it: "Of course, refugee camps like yours are not death camps, except perhaps for the young. And our U.S.A. Indian reservations, like the Palestinians', are merely 'colonial.'"

"When I sat down," she told the American press, "I could hear the intake of breath. Then there was silence. Somehow, that's worse than being shot at." As she once had been in Kurdistan, when interrogating too near some poachers. "You hear a whole hall draw breath through its teeth, it's like they're casting a rope. Then one man got up to shout that I was a blot on 'Sacred be his name,' the author of *The Children of the Ghetto,* of whose blood I could not be. I said, no, I wasn't kin to him, but I rather saw him standing up to wave. Then a couple near me rose in the aisle, the woman screaming she had lost two sons on a schoolbus blasted by terrorists and didn't have to listen to assimilated American trash."

The worst, expressed only to Peter, was how she had felt for that couple, though from the whorl where you fully see how little the right opinion counts. But that man's face had purpled exactly the way Norman's did at the hated word, prompting her to quote him exactly, this being what had engaged the American press. "Why is it that we Jews never think of it as *us* assimilating *them?*"

In the lore of the Duffy-Zangwills, this rejoinder is repeated at least once at every such gathering.

Along the bookshelves are copies of a philosophical review to which Peter has for forty years contributed his essays, saying, "It's the kind people subscribe to out of virtue, and put aside 'to read later.'"

Next to these, a few copies of Zipporah's one book: *Images of God.* Begun as that dissertation, and pursued, she suspects, from preconscious images of her own that will neither surface frankly nor let go, her study, parlayed through the decades, has enabled her to travel in the field, on a slim but continuing staircase of grants and awards. She feels no guilt over that connection; energy of pursuit is real, whatever it springs from. "Funny," she once said to Peter, "how Jewish a child can be, even with the parents scarcely being it. We were never denied we were. Maybe that was it . . . There is an edge of conduct where you can simply not mention it. We always did, though. So for me, and I still feel it, being Jewish is being sincere." Why should that be? In the mess of ethic-babble everybody

was now living in, why does that "sincerity," often not voiced, give
her such relief? "Even power," she'd said.

Peter is careful to say he's no longer a Catholic, if the situation
arises, but gets no such boost. "I may even cherish that identity. But
it doesn't carry the same weight. I'm just saying what I'm not."

"You are what you are in those." She points to the line of magazines here and there including a special issue devoted to him,
where the cover of the end one, 'In Search of the Double Vision,'
was just visible. Then comes her array of single publications, from
articles to monographs, and finally, the book.

"Well, it hasn't hurt the children," Peter had said. "What we
are and what we aren't. Not at all. Though we probably shouldn't
say."

Rather, their bit of diversity, mild when you come to think of
it, had endowed their offspring with an all-over-the-lot confidence.
That could give trouble and had, but could be said to have finally
weighed in to the good for all of them, if in predictably diverging
styles.

Why had she and Peter kept this vanity-row of their work on
display, and in that particular cranny of the library wall? Some
must wonder. Answer: the children had demanded it. As backup?
In any case, the lineup was low enough on the wall for a child to
reach, and over the years one or the other had been seen doing so,
even throughout the gangly years when they'd had to kneel.

She doesn't need to squint to see Mickey there, the lost one. A
dead child never dies, not at any age. One loses them, one's nails
scrabbling for them in the dirt of memory. Or, almost sighted in
some white Alhambra of dream, you feel them nearly with you,
your throat swollen with the news, though you must not open
your eyes. Mickey has his back turned, just as he used to; she won't
have to see the blank face. He and his pal from the fourth grade are
just home from school with their sacks of after-hours books.
"Here's where they got married," he's saying. "This shelf." The pal
traces the spine of her book with a forefinger. "Gee, oh, dee—" he
says. "God."

Having one subject only can work to make a scholar heard. And of course that one: "Gee-oh-dee." Much of her zealous accumulation from Asia and Africa already being "in the canon," it was her zeal that was first lauded. Her allegiance to one side of the never quite outmoded anthropological argument still brings her flack. For she believes that religions, cultures, had originated in sites around the globe, not in one sacred place, from which dispersed.

"Naturally, this offends everybody with a probable Eden in the pocket," Peter had said to Norman, shortly after they had met. "At least in the religious camp."

Not to his surprise, Norman responded, "She will learn that is where we Jews still are."

"Catholics don't pay much attention to image talk," Peter had said. "Too used to them. Every little plaster saint assures us of one registered vote."

To which Norman had said, "Us? We?"

Then both of them, smiling at Zipporah consolingly, clapped each other on the shoulder and made for the Duffy bar, whose liquor supply was always ecumenical.

But "the chosen," as all Jews, reformed or not, must still consider themselves, remained the most offended. "Graven Images!" headed the review in an obscure periodical (later reprinted in a daily edited by the reviewer's brother-in-law):

Anthropology is not Judaism. Interfaith can only go so far. Ms. Zangwill-Duffy's handsomely illustrated volume pays deference to the observed connections between say, Renaissance Madonnas and African fertility goddesses. But her untoward interest in what she dubs "the eyes of God"—"from the blind eyeballs of stone sculpture to the wide-eyed stare of Asia Minor terrazzo, and on to the bas-relief whose sidelong stare is surely Egyptian"—is a silly iconography, which in fact dares to see "God's eyes" even in Jewish bridal-headpiece designs.

Any Jewish schoolchild knows that Jews do not make idols, golden or otherwise. As with the God of Israel, the Jehovah of the Desert, whose name was never to be taken in vain (the word *adonai,* or *Lord,* being substituted when reading the scripture), so the *image* of the Lord our God cannot be lightly invoked. Nor can the spiritual be *assimilated,* into casual, latterday scholarship."

Seeing the book, two of her daughters-in-law-to-be, one a stormy young woman of Irish-Catholic extraction and renegade rather than lapsed, the other from staid Cleveland Jews whose faith had long since been subsumed into philanthropy, asked Zipporah eagerly, "You using the two names now, married and maiden, maybe should we?" and, seeing her taken aback, "Oh, as women, y'know, not religion-wise."

How lightly she had answered them. Had dared to? For even a modern Jew will pay attention to the old superstitions. Name the Lord God in his own right, as simply God? Many a backslider will. But put a lien on the future, with some remark the little demons who handle providence are always lurking for? Even in her own family, faded mildly toward the secular, the adult heads would have nicked back in a hush quickly over with, and sealed with an abashed smirk. Jews don't cross themselves. But a child at the proper level can see them hide thumbs and be warned.

"Oh girls," she'd said, laughing, "I'm coming not to *want* to be watched."

No guardian angel clucked. Jews don't have those either.

"Oh you're so right," Agnes, the elder of Peter's two sisters interposed, safe in just such protection. "Like for one's stocking seams."

The two younger women stare. Where on earth, these days, do these two old biddies get those heavy-duty stockings, with seams to be sure, straight up Agnes's thick calves?

Theresa, the younger sister, who has a skittish air to her, maybe because of that, says, "Altman's. They went out of biz, we stocked up, Agnes did. Took all they had." She wears a virginal crown of braids, from a constant touching of which her fingertips come away black. "Hard," she added, while the two swanlings waited, their pretty beaks raised. "To be watched."

On this, her nameday, as each wave of memory rolls in, Zipporah is holding herself in plain sight, the way an aerialist does, just before swinging from ring to ring. Ordinarily, she wouldn't have dreamed of making herself visible. This is family, and after the first greetings and embraces at the door, the invigorating Sunday mood takes over. As hostess, she has normally been free to prowl unassumingly behind the busy façade while people chatter, catching up.

Today, they're ostentatiously carrying on as if all is as usual. She finds herself taking a fierce pride in them for that, meanwhile nursing her own sense of shame. The worst that can happen to a devoted couple except death is happening to her and Peter; some would call death preferable. She's trying to stage-manage destiny, all the time knowing that the play is going on the rocks.

Meanwhile, the change of name will be seen by many here as no more absurd than her other pretexts for these parties, all of those excused and even relished as part of her eccentric professional life.

"Lovely to have a look-see," a relative might gush, leaving a potlatch, but with a headshake, "when you yourself keep such a fine household." Which often meant such a generously Jewish one.

Norman saw these parties as a canny solicitation to the young who thronged them. "All parties are schmaltz, when you come down to it." In his mind he has never given them, beyond passing out cigars. Wives took care of the sentiments. He's sure to see the shift to "Zoe" as a silly one. As it may be. She has never disliked the stern, semi-biblical sound of Zipporah. Peter teases that it has helped her to act accordingly.

At the time, the name-change had seemed such a simple ruse to keep the family scrutiny on her, not him. And she had wished to keep the Z. But why had the idea of the shift come so quickly to her? From what buried niche in her psyche? Perhaps the discomfort she now feels is specifically Jewish? Because one tenet of her lax up-bringing had been upheld without compromise. For a Jew to change his last name, no matter how ill-awarded in the past, was to commit an indignity against Jewish history. And the first names must chime in tune. In Brookline, there had been few "Christian cop-outs" or "country-club monikers," as her father had dubbed them. At least not in his generation. Names acquired by intermar-riage, as with her children, were quite acceptable. His sneers were against Jews of the blood only. As so much of Jewish morality is? Perhaps there are ukases against name-changing in the Talmud? Or more likely, jokes? She must ask Bert.

Perversely, she's savoring the last of the Sunday afternoons likely to take place in this house. (She alone knows that it is a pre-amble to what she prays to keep dark for as long as may be allowed.) People will still be wandering in. Not to be subjugated to the formal limits of "cocktails at six," or "supper served From: __ To __," is a joy confessed to by many. The oldest cousin, deaf and given to loud remarks to her companion from that solitude which the deaf think they own, will at some point punctuate the buzz with her, "Take heed, Mariella, you don't see a get-together like this anymore. This is an At Home."

So it is, and nowhere near its height. A couple not seen for years, now living abroad, may suddenly drop by. The pair around the cor-ner will surely be as late as they are faithful. Her own son Charles, marooned in his physics lab by a universe that stares at him like a basilisk, but who claims to share an extrasensory perception with his mother (he doesn't, that was Mickey), may fly in, on a schedule whose regularity he doesn't seem aware of—the last Sunday of al-ternate months. Peter no longer invites students on Sunday; they are a different sort of family. She has learned to fend off strays from her travels, like the Chinese pair who, confused by the warmth here, re-turned later that night with their bags. Friends of the family's young are always welcome, however, sometimes staying overnight.

When she herself was hovering on the cusp of the teens, the grandparents' Sundays had worse than bored her. She and her cousins, briefly and loudly adored, then squashed under the press of adults, had been consigned to sneaking about unnoticed, or else to making alliances in the kitchen. Yet was it "down in the teen dump," as her cousin Eustace, an older gangler of like temperament, had called it, that she'd acquired a lifelong habit of feeling always more the observer than the observed? Even the only one?

This will vary in degree of course, with where she happens to be, and she has been teased by Peter or a suddenly astute child as to how this connects with her profession. One of the pleasures of their marriage, almost the deepest, is that he too is an observer, though the solitary or even troublesome aspect of that doesn't occur to him, and his and her verdicts of what they see, even if together, are never the same. At a concert, seeing her inspect those in the seats ahead before the music begins, he'll analogize, "Royal Opera House, Copenhagen," but she'll answer, "No, this is a cathedral audience, a provincial one." Or at a public session in which members of the Senate of his own university are performing in clacking euphony, she'll mutter, "I wouldn't insult any ethnic rite I've attended, by comparison: oh, maybe the parrot house at the zoo. Where are you?" His answer, eyes closed, "At Chulalongkorn University, where they held a lecture in Thai in my honor . . . I'm being most careful not to cross my legs or point the toe." Where to do that would have been insult. She'd whispered, "Go ahead."

When had that kind of interchange all but stopped? Don't scratch among the bygones, Zipporah. Try not to watch him so, Zoe. Look at your crowd.

Here in the long double living room they are disposed as in a painting, a woman's head turned over a shoulder toward another, men sitting by age with their natural confreres, there the women's legs crossed at the ankle, there one draped along a sofa. Some of the men hold cigars between their spread knees. Only a few are standing formally, yet the room suggests one of those genre pictures of a family, perhaps English and knee-breeched, of some minor grandee or local patriarch; though there are no characters like that here, surely. Nothing royal—if even that Goya comes suddenly to mind, the one with the dwarf princess in it, she can laugh; the children here are all sturdy and fine. And she herself is not hung with jewelry. But yes, she's a matron surveying what her loins have made, and upheld for the ages to contemplate. There's even a border of painter's greenery visible in the background, though not from a royal preserve, or English county, but from the west side of Central Park, in which there are no hinds or hares.

She and Peter, once he'd been awarded tenure as professor, had managed to buy a run-down single residence on West End Avenue, once a very minor "mansion," two floors of which they had rented out to other faculty—a tetchy arrangement, not lasting well. That the street was known as the residence of choice for rising middle-class Jews hadn't consciously swayed them, yet a chance meeting with the broker who'd had it for sale would have to be counted in. She had been a client of Norman's, who later enabled the Duffys to sell what they had bought from her very profitably, in time to buy that "very good deal" from another client of his, which had brought them here. So, once again, if only by according to "the way things were," they had made the recognizable trek of Jews of that sort to Central Park West, bringing their mixed mores with them. For what Peter brought, acknowledged subversively by some of the Jews themselves as "less flashy," was always to be reckoned with.

How is it then that their style of life, though relaxed, is still recognizably Jewish, to both outsiders and themselves? Domestically so, it would be said, because of the wife; yet where the husband was the Jew, the wife the shiksa, the bias could be even more pronounced. While at the Duffys, a couple whom some would consider too exotic to account for any statistic, could religion be coming back, with Bert?

Or does all of this fix on sequestered strains of blood and conduct only serve to romanticize what her traveling trade blasts at? In Tierra del Fuego, that symbol of the inaccessible, where a few castaways had produced the entire small population, new blood was now yearned for. Else one saw either too many vacant angel-faces, or extraordinary mariners for whom the modern world has little use. Can't the rabbis who mourn the rise of interfaith marriage see that one way to atone for the ravages of the Holocaust is to tolerate that more and more people might have a bit of Jew in them? Even if not adopting the motto she had early affixed to all her position papers on tribal practice, whether exotic or nearby: *Since it's going to happen anyway* . . .

She sneaks around the periphery of the crowd. What better way to clean out scrambled thoughts than to go into the kitchen?

From a see-through in the pantry, via which she can survey all the living room, she stares out on her own tribal heath. This small aperture, whose flap can be unobtrusively slid aside, had endeared the apartment to her, even beyond the view, which after the first shock of ownership and the compliments of visitors, one rarely stops to scrutinize. The possession of a view seeps into the consciousness, both psychic and financial, and only lastly into the visual: if it were denied her, claustrophobia would surely ensue. But in truth, a view always there is a perspective one gazes at most when thinking of something else.

This biddable little pass-through window, set in at eye-level in bookshelves that bear the true library on the outer wall, and cookbooks on the inner kitchen side where she is standing, performs a function never confessed even to Peter, though no doubt he knows. It keeps her in her place. Her ordinary domestic one, in fact unopposed to her professional one. Rather, embedded there. For what is anthropology except the study of the slots people are born to, and of how little or greatly the people and the slots may seem to diverge?

Behind her, in the large, homely kitchen, the young people of the family, teens to twenties, are helping to set up the "spread," provided by her but always augmented by what some will insist on bringing, in a convention that shouldn't obtain for family. Underneath lie certain long-persisting statuses, even guilts. Wine, from those who must have their vintages, no matter what. The richest cousin's yearly jar of homemade jam; the poorest's costly store-bought chocolates. The Duffy sisters' Dundee cake, made from an inherited "receipt," and as rock-hard and durable as their faith. Testimonials all.

And here she stands, seen clearly through the spyglass of her own profession: ZZD, as the monogrammed wedding presents, not yet redistributed, still say, a woman of a generation now more than midway along a calendar almost parallel with its century. One who has remained "domestic" in spite of her sporadic encampments along what some scholars have called "an undigested itinerary" or worse: Bessarabia, Melanesia, the Kalahari Desert, an India nowhere near Agra or Kashmir, and Spartanburg, North Carolina (to investigate a curious Gullah maladversion of "cross-eyed"). Who remains ever more domestic than many would require of her? Who insists on remaining the fulcrum of this—? This long-house, log cabin, dacha, tent-for-a-night . . . cave. In which occur whatever ruttings, carnivals, or masses said privately or in unison, to godheads not necessarily divine. This—house.

Which, if it is typical, will harbor some inmate or habitué who keeps the scabs of evasion raw. Who won't allow dogma to rest easy. Or, as in this case, the lack of one.

And there he is, seen through her aperture.

Not a resident, nor yet only a visitor, though he may not turn up for years at a time. One who whether he's met those here seldom or over the years seems to know the very brand of their socks. And can speak, as if idly, to that small or swollen throttle of the heart in all except the youngest here: Are we still Jews?

Even if she hadn't seen him, she would know he'd arrived, by the scent of packages always delivered by some minion to the back door, and now being opened with "ohs" and "ahs" of recognition behind her: sturgeon, whitefish, sable, smoked salmon, cold cuts, matjes herring, pickles, and special dishes not always definable... There he is. Lev. And still alone? Before she has a second look, he passes out of sight.

His shaggy black head, not so much barbered as sprouted, will yet be visible somewhere in the palely comfortable room, at first sight of which he'd murmured, "Almost 'decorated.' But not quite," and on seeing Peter had overheard, adding, "Saved by the books."

"Oh yes, Lev can smile," Peter had said that time, almost a decade ago. "But we may never be sure whether for us or against."

Lev has adopted them. Without a by-your-leave, which is clearly how he does everything, even perhaps how he had married Libby, the shyest granddaughter of "the Boston Z's." All that those here know of their romance is whatever Libby had chosen to say, up until her death from breast cancer when their twin boys were nine: "We met when I was at N.Y.U. studying film and Levi was in a business course at your city college."

Lev would smile. "*The* City College. I don't know of another one."

This slight playfulness, as between the two cities, was the only tension ever observed, Peter said after Libby's death: "She was really a girl more likely to be single. In a past generation she might not have been allowed out alone. Film must have been the way she could remain quiet, and still have a life. He grabbed her out of that. Never regretted. But the physical side of her may have known best. She did die."

She had been the only one who called him Levi. "Otherwise," Peter dared to say to him when they first met, "you might be dubbed Leviticus, far as we know." But even Peter got nowhere as to the facts.

"Only the rumors, Zip." In Boston, where Peter shortly went for an academic conference, he had stayed at the college; the two branches of the family were not that close. A lunch at the Harvard faculty club had been mutually agreeable. "From your cousin

James." Uncle to Lev's dead wife. "Seems it was rumored, at the time of the marriage, that Lev had once studied for the rabbinate, no one could say where. 'More likely in the provinces,' James said. And had either not qualified, or had left . . . 'But to go from that to being a diamond merchant? And in your town, Peter, where we understand that can be quite dangerous?' . . . You know James."

"All of them—" she'd said. Apparently the Z's up there have let things be. Libby's parents, who have many grandchildren, see the boys occasionally, who Lev always posted up there on their own.

"But Peter, you'll have imagined more. I know you." When she and Peter estimated others was when their trust in each other's confidence reached its height. In a kind of variation of love, she thinks now. But can it now go on?

"Lev is too savvy about New York not to be from here," Peter had said. "And about one area. I would guess, or rather I see him, as a Hasid. Who maybe got out. Somehow, I don't think he was pushed. Not Lev. I see him . . . slicing off his forelocks, saving up to buy some cheap normal pants and jacket he wouldn't steal, and lighting out."

"Still won't," she'd said. "Steal. And in his trade to be honest— yes, maybe dangerous. How he'd earned college: 'he was "a runner,"' Lib said. Not saying for what. But I could see she admired him for it."

"Like maybe such a quiet woman would admire risk. And after school maybe, he went back to it. And for the money."

"That huge diamond engagement ring he gave her? He told me once, how to divide that between the twins would be worse than the dilemma of King Solomon over that baby."

"Hmm. He's always referring, isn't he," Peter had laughed. "Maybe that's why he's chosen us for second family. Or you, rather. And brings you all that kosher-style food. I think, Zipporah"— when Peter called her that, he was always serious, "that no matter what Lev did once, or maybe because he did it, he still wears, maybe only in his head, what a man of his faith does. That leather thing with the strings, that has the Jewish law inscribed on it."

"On vellum," she'd said, quick as a flash. "Though actually I've never seen one . . . Not worn on the Sabbath. Every other day, at morning prayer."

"Funny—how you speak of your tribal habits, as just that: from a tribe."

She'd grinned. "One of the many dealt with in my profession? Maybe that's why I chose it. Women can't wear the phylactery."

"And I've done the same. The tribe of Duffys. As exemplified by my sisters. A place in heaven assured. Where they can arrive in their Dobbs hats. Or, if death isn't quick, but dirty, a Monsignor of influence will surely get them into the Mary Manning Walsh Home."

"No—the one true way isn't ours."

It had been her turn to say that. Peter often made other scholars sore by always finding new ways of asserting this. And saying it so well. "Funny, too. How it was your sisters discovered Lev packs a gun."

"Faith recognizes faith."

"They call him 'the mobster.' Not to his face."

"No. But they will manage to let him overhear. That much is owed to God."

A word he's easier with in company than she. Because she might be asked to define it?

And what precisely do the Jews owe?

"Lev never again brought the twins here," she said. "After that once."

"A big family group—it attracts. But also affects."

And that time, he had first brought the food.

"To get the sons started on it, d'ya think? On kosher. Or to keep to it. He knows that we don't." Not for generations, in her case. She wouldn't know how. "But in a family setting." She giggled, a habit only when with him.

He waited for it. "Or," he'd said, "to convert us?"

They had been standing together at this very opening, the better to see the assemblage of those they had given birth to.

"Peter, look. He has brought them again. The sons."

They'd been in their early teens then, dressed to the nines in boarding school jackets, and hanging back foolish, though they were nice-looking enough.

"Lev's a truthster," Peter had said. "You just watch."

She had. Though not recently with Peter. For weeks she's felt him to be avoiding their usual chatter. All the years before there has been a babble of talk between them. "Like the talk you would get in the best society," he'd said. "If you could find it." She adding, "If it were limited to two."

Underneath, allowing them to be superficial, silly, and light-hearted, were what he'd hailed as "the great ordinaries": birth and death, say, and whatever might be etcetera to those. Those facts to which one must say "Um . . ." These they don't bother to discuss. It seems to her that they have paid tribute enough in their happy, almost musical, fleshy dialogue. "Especially do you do that, pay tribute, when you conceive a child? Whether or not you know?" she'd once asked while in his embrace. "Perhaps," he'd said. "Could be that's why we've had so many of them. For these times." As with everybody they know, "the times"—the decade, the year, the century—are always in mind, as the largest fact of all, other than being alive in them.

Behind her now she hears the kitchen talk of the young as they unwrap Lev's packages, the older teens and college-age grandchildren, nieces and nephews, hooting at a recognized specialty, and instructing the younger young.

At first Lev had patronized a delicatessen, both the food and its wrappings impersonal. As the menu evolved, he must have enlisted a subcommittee of Orthodox housewives.

Now she imagines perhaps one unsung, elderly genius who cooks, wraps, and marks each package and dish in her odd script, saying to her own flesh-and-bone scrambling round her, "Here:

take this. Leaves only eleven to the dozen, but those backsliders will never know. And this—taste! Made only for the high holidays—but what's that to them?"

Some old granny, bending her wig over the feathery dumplings you must prick while cooking to keep them light, although which of her sons, wives now bothers? Even the wigs they wear now, so polished, like shiksa hair. And the names they call their male children, names for the outside, no longer the given ones from the prophets: Abraham, Isaac, Jacob, the old Hebrew ones that can be properly chanted over a circumcised squawler or a patriarch's wooden coffin. "Here A-aron—what's your other name yet—Ah-len? Here, Ikey, you'll never be Ir-win in this house." The old woman's daughters-in-law would also go more easy on the girls, for whom husbands must be found: maybe not so many Esthers, and the Leahs now smartly called Lee. What are the names of the two boys Lev has now and then brought over to sniff her household, from the branched menorah to the mezuzah over the door? The old woman maybe doesn't want to hear. Or about what is said of the father. "A good man, Levi, not a Beelzebub, only lost to us..." You have to cook for such a man, you use dishes separate from even separate ones. And say over each dish the prayer for the prodigal son...

Behind her in the kitchen, the girls, names are rather plain at the moment—Janes and Annes, the Sarah that can straddle either New England or the Bible, milkmaid Nancys or Sues. Among the boys, the Simons and the Adams are demi-British, rather than from the Testament (doesn't matter, my loves, I merely observe)... and Lev out there is still alone, the sons in a kibbutz in Israel. Whatever he does about women—he would do something—he doesn't bring them here. Just as well. Not that she wouldn't accept; this house is built on acceptance.

Meanwhile, he's her bit of mystery. The great eternals are changeless. You may either worship at that status quo, or ignore it.

The small human mysteries—as you experience your life, there's less of them. But what remains of them between people you can still see evolve, thrilling to the endless combinations.

To which Peter had once said, "Um, yes, Zipporah. But Lev, as you imagine him, is the mystery you do and don't quite want to solve." When her husband looked smug, it was because, regretfully almost, he could state an opinion. "Lev stands for your Jewishness. Or the remnants thereof."

She was almost angry, almost as angry as Norman would be.

"Oh it's the same for me," Peter had said quickly. "At sixteen, when I was leaving the church, I had dreams. Of punishment. Until one cured me. I was on my deathbed, and the Pope himself was giving me an extreme unction. He was wearing a Dobbs hat."

When they'd stopped laughing she'd said, "Lev does treat me—with a kind of intimacy. As if there's something we share. But it's the flirting courtesy to older women that Jewish men used to have. Like my father used to tease my mother's ninety-six-year-old grandmother, who lived with us. That if he'd been around when she was young he would have asked for her hand . . . she loved it. Saying, 'Ah, Moshe—excuse me, Maurice. You could still carry me off.'"

"Ah. Maybe that's why my sisters, whom Lev is always nice to, worry about his gun."

When they'd chortled again—what fun they've had in their time!—he said, "Lev respects orthodoxy. Like many an apostate." And then, teasing, "Saw him examining your linen closet."

"He spied it out as the only closet we keep locked. 'Not even the liquor. Why this one?' So I showed it to him."

"You showed him? You never show anybody, even women. You're ashamed of your fix on all that embroidery. On towels. Lace-edged napkins. Linen tablecloths nobody uses now—even for banquets, the caterer for Marcy's wedding said." Called "niece Marcy" because there was also an aunt.

"The bride wanted pleated paper. But was afraid to say . . . And I do use the pillowcases. Not often the monogrammed ones. My mother's dozens. Linen so soft on the cheek you can't get any-more. And I put out the guest towels, just to remember. Nobody uses anymore, except now and then one of the oldies, to show she's still a lady. Usually some guest. The family, they know you can't get home laundresses either.

"We used to have Idas. All of them black and all of them named that."

"They recommended each other. Maybe it was their joke on us."

And now, Jennie, herself a woman of color, won't allow any-body else "in my kitchen," which she feels to be identical to the whole apartment, almost.

"So now, you go to Zimbabwe, and anywhere else you can get in?"

"Ah, you sly."

"Looking for conclusions. Of what you know in your heart never concludes. Same as me . . . So why're you ashamed of that closet?"

"Didn't say I was." But she'd been caught, half wanting to be. "Men don't have that fix. Only in the garages, stuff they'll never again use. Here in the city, maybe a drawer—for the old baseball they caught at a game, the compass they used on hikes. A T-shirt with a letter on it. A clutch of ties that are too narrow or too wide . . . All the padding that we use to get through life. That's what that closet is to me."

"Not because you're a professional, and ashamed to be domestic?"

"I didn't know you thought so little of me."

"I don't—" he'd said.

Down on the floor then, clasped from ankle to mouth. Not a Sunday, a Saturday. Jennie out on her day off, their brood grown, and what she and he do here will no longer breed. This is the golden mean of sex, when the genitals converse one step beyond the conversation, the hips idle and jolt, mouths punctuate in time with knees, and a breast is a lure for the head only. While stream-ing from between the legs, thoughts murmur, retreat.

"Early on, I was kind of hiding that closet. Not now. Because in what I do abroad I see the padding, worldwide."

From the shaman dances one has never before seen, to the sacred garments these hallow . . . The carved penis sheath a headman showed me, kept in six wrappings, the last bit of cloth "six fathers back." The rare kimono hung on a wall, never worn, nor likely to be. . . .

"Now I can't help knowing how the padding links up." With the ceremonials. "And when I get home, I see it again every time."

Open your closet, Zipporah, and see the padding a bride was entitled to, that a matron accumulates. What's hiding under your neat piles of huck towels, linen sheets forty years white? Maiden lives unraveling in the old hope chest language: hemstitch, drawnwork, trapunto, appliqué . . . "In the old days, Jewish families ran to a lot of spinsters," my mother said. "Will you look at this work? And we don't even know their names.". . .

"Because early on, the padding is joy, an occupation," she says, sitting up. "Like money-making is, to some. But the older you get, and the more I see of it, what you have is how you've passed your life. It's not just what you'll leave behind. It's what you'll have to answer for."

He too had sat up. "To whom?"

Always that question they'd thought solved the day he picked up her shoe.

"Who indeed? You and I cut off our forelocks long ago."

When the unbelievers hang their heads so, whom are they honoring?

It's so often the woman who breaks a silence, she thought now. But that time, I held out.

Some one of the young ones has brought her a kitchen stool, slipping it under her so deftly, then vanishing, that she doesn't see

who. They know her habits. "Shh—Zipporah's in her tower," had
she heard one of them say?

A phrase picked up from Charles, overheard saying it to that
scamp, his first-born son. By her watch, Charles is still to be waited
for. Also several from Boston, who surprisingly had asked to come.
Has she been asleep? The chair, counter-high, raises her above her
window, but she can see what she is after, well enough.

Sometimes, she isn't sure of the progression of Sundays. Part
of their strength is that they blend. But the day she remembers
couldn't have been long after that Sunday.

It's again a Saturday, actually. The big room, empty of people,
has again the dusk that comes post-love. Savoring it, they haven't
yet been to the shower.

"So what did Lev think of your closet?" Peter says.

"He said—oh Peter, he looked aside for the longest time. Then
he said, 'Shelves that pull out. Libby would have gone down on her
knees.'"

"Ah-h? Remember what James told me?" Once she'd died,
James had said resentfully, up in Boston, Levi had never again mentioned her name. Not even to the boys.

"And then Lev reached in the closet and touched one pile, the
one that has my mother's banquet cloth. We never in our lives had
banquets, but she made one. And I swear, Peter, it was like he was
smoothing a woman. And he said, so I could hardly hear it: 'Libby
claimed any Jewish woman worth her salt was a linen freak.' Then
he took the key from me and locked the closet himself."

"He sure knows how to get round you all right, all right."

"Ah yes, love. I've always been an easy mark."

"Come on. I didn't mean—"

"No, you're on the ball," she said. "He did ask me to do him a
favor."

"Oh?"

"It was the week after he'd sent the boys back to Israel again,
remember?"

"Do I. Even Norman said, 'For once I feel sorry for that tight-mouth. He adores those boys. And they him, I hope. But that line he's in—even a tough cookie needs a little relief.'... Um. Don't tell me Lev wants you to act for him as a—what do you call them—a *schatchen*? He want you to find him a wife?" Peter seems to find this uproarious. "All those candidates you could supply. Six-armed sub-goddesses from south India. Those doctoral students you say are so elegant, from Senegal via Paris. Or those Polynesians you said yourself they wear their bare skin as if it's their mufti..."

Was it as far as back then that she'd first noticed how pink with the effort to speak his forehead could be? Not sexual, surely. Though he has never talked like the boys in the back room, he and she are free enough on that score. But there will now and then be a slippage of language that eludes her. A repetition, often of where they'd been and what had been said—in order to pin it down? Odd analogies? He and she have a taste for them, though conceding that the lingo of many a scholar they know can sound like Tibetan on a fast-forward tape. Yet recently his jokes, puns—comparisons— seem insufficiently on the mark.

"*Mane,*" he'd said to her, in the bathroom one morning. "Carousel horse." She'd turned to see him holding puzzledly the tufted English toothbrush, made of real bristle, that she always bought when passing through London. "So it is," she'd said, long since accustomed to traveling and arriving in a scurf of foreign odd-ments. "Hard to tell Mom's own ratpack from her artifacts," her own girls had agreed. So, when recently he had said, staring at the dining-room mantel, laden with her trophies, "We are so—so—; we are so—," expelling it finally: "so—*gourd*," she had later quoted him. "Clever, was it?" he'd asked. He couldn't recall saying that.

But he'd remembered to twit her about Lev. "Marriage broker, are you? Well, this house was built on brokers: a real-estate one, a lawyer—and now a diamond dealer? Don't tell me he's speaking for one of our girls?"

His quips had never before been aimed at what she was. Now was there a touch of what her aunts and uncles had called *rishus*, a Hebrew word she was not even sure how to spell?

"No. I won't tell you," she'd said. "You never told me—that dream."

What Lev had said as he closed the closet door, testing it with a pull, was, "Would you keep something here for me, if I bring it? For the boys, that is—just in case? I don't want to keep it in my office safe."

Just in case. A phrase familiar to anyone reared in the depths of family, and in hers still that Oriental tag of the Jewishness. Their care to refer to both God and disaster sidelong.

"Of course, Lev," she'd said.

Yet months would elapse before he came again. Only last fall it had been, the first Sunday of the holiday season, when all the family gathered, even from the distant grade schools and colleges, and she took it upon herself to reinvite those hangers-on who might be too humble or shy. He'll turn up whenever, she thought in passing; he's not one of those.

This time he brought no delicatessen with him. Only a small brown paper bag he'd handed her as they stood again in front of the opened linen closet. She'd felt the flattened bag, whose contents, wrapped in cloth maybe, seemed scarcely to expand it, but hadn't peered inside. He'd watched her enclose the bag in a white one of her own, which she'd marked MOTH CRYSTALS—DO NOT OPEN, and place it well behind the stack of banquet cloths. If those reminded him, this time he didn't touch. But when the door was locked again she'd seen his tremble of relief and said, "Let me give you a cup of tea."

They'd gone to the kitchen for it. "Jennie's on her annual," she'd said. "She always has to be pushed." He'd said, "I figured." And he had come early, before the crowd.

When they'd had a cup, and a slice from the stock of home-mades Jennie always left, he'd brought out the tiny, domed red plush box whose function was all too clear. "No, Lev—" she'd already said before he had a chance to open it. On Libby's engagement ring. "Not moth crystals," she said. "No, Lev. You can't pass that problem on to me." It had been her acknowledgment that he'd already passed along something.

"With luck, the boys will come into the business when they're of age. Otherwise, businesses of their own." He'd swallowed, then gone on. "Here's their address."

A man's name in Tel Aviv.

"He lives there now. I knew him from here; we were students together. I would trust him with my life." He swallowed again. "I have. He's their guardian."

She stared down at the address, the name. And they had been students together. "A rabbi...yes." And from her too, Lev was wanting a pledge. She'd held out the fourth finger of her right hand.

At once he'd said, "Send them what we locked away...in the event that anything should happen to me."

"Or to me?" she'd said, but only as a formality. At merely a young sixty-five, she wasn't yet thinking about that. Let it remain *that*, with a hush for others gone ahead.

"Oh you, you'll live to be a hundred."

The phrase has been said to her before. Crushing a sugar cube between her teeth she'd corrected him. "Ninety-four. All on my mother's side went about then. And always with some smart crack between their lips. You wouldn't believe they'd have the breath for it."

"You will." When he smiled you could well see what Libby had seen in him.

"My trade's a gabby one, Lev. But it's the stones that really speak." Jewelers call diamonds "stones"; had she meant to pun or hadn't she? Looking down at the two rings on her fingers she'd said, "I can't really wear yours, you know. People will ask. And it quite outshines my other one." Chosen by Peter and her, the smallest carat stocked.

He'd cast it a glance. "Pure enough." Lightly he'd flicked the bigger stone. "Got it on discount, else I couldn't have afforded. Wanted to impress her crowd. But they weren't."

"Hoo. Cousin Charlotte? Never called Lottie. Token lady on half a dozen boards, pioneer on a couple never before 'mixed.' Shirtwaist manners. Atoning for all the rest of us Jews who mightn't have those."

He'd mimicked: "'We run to the plain Tiffany setting, Lev. And not the platinum. The gold.'. . . So pass the ring on, Zipporah. Or sell for charity. It's good enough for any of God's altars. Or your favorite."

"Mine are not always God's," she'd said. "You still believe?"

She has had to be professionally quick on gesture. For those body movements that aren't the sign of the cross, or the palms pressed to each other, but grow from other hallowed pasts. The way a "primitive" foot turns inward, then slyly stomps. Or a thumb rubs an amulet, worn in the proper place.

Or smooths the place where it should have been. Lev wears no sideburns, or the briefest possible. A fingernail had flicked, if not caressed, where that long braid would have been.

"I got Him too on discount," he said.

He'd left before the crowd arrived. Her and Peter's crowd. He must know he's an object of gossip there. But in a way, so is everybody else; that's half why they come.

"Off to the office," he'd said this time, as if he now owed her that.

"On a Sunday?"

"Weekends are the danger time, in the district. I check. But also, I phone the boys from there. It's like a quiet we share . . . And I have all my goods around me . . . I give them pointers." His voice trails.

"Lev. You must be hungry. You—look hungry. Stay to eat."

The classic mother-cry that women of their race were mocked for? She shrugged. So did he. He kissed her hand.

Seeing him to the door, a ritual of the house, they found Peter and his sisters there. For a minute, standing there in phalanx, they seem to be barring Lev's way. Tipping an imaginary cap to them, he'd lit out.

Strange how, seen in this sudden, half-hostile phalanx, the three Duffys still resemble. She has a flash of the three young auburn heads they once were, as seen through the rain of the past: Agnes, Theresa, Peter: milk-white skin, rose-hip mouth, the boy as much as the girls. She can smell the meal, often quoted, that they'd be going to: fresh pork, soda bread, a sweet with a cuddly name. The mother's a fine cook. The two girls, rising to be office managers, will mostly eat out. The brothers will have escorted them to dances in vain. No man will be good enough for them, except the round-collared ones they can't have.

But as kids, were they as pouter-pigeon-breasted as now? Peter, shifting his glance to her, retracts his lower lip. The "girls" pull in theirs; has she caught them at something?

"Peter wouldn't let us in the door," Agnes, the elder sister says in a shuddery voice. Terry, her follower though smarter, says low, with a glance to the living room beyond, "Actually tried to slam the door in our face."

"Blather!" Peter says. "You two been rushin' the growler?" His voice is far-off. She knows the old term for going for beer, but has never heard him drop his g's. There's a kind of coarse, greedy-eyed luminosity uniting the three of them. Like might collect in one of their churches when the congregation filed in to worship a saint, after a Saint Patrick's Day brawl.

And so help me, what crossed my mind then I'll spend any time we two have together atoning for. I thought I saw the color of his soul, and that it was nothing like I had really ever seen before. And I thought: This man's too Christian for me . . .

Then Terry skreeks, "Watch out, Ag—he's going to hit us— like Mam did Dad."

While under her own blistered stare Peter turns into himself again, or half himself. Saying, "Come, Sis. You are welcome here. But take care milady here doesn't marry you off."

When there's grace in the young, one swears it will abolish all creeds, all flags. For here came Bertram to our side. There's no shadow on him yet, of what he may become. Just a decent sixteen-year-old, with the slow stalking gait of one who may already have had to mediate at home. So has staunchly fixed his sights on what and whom to adore.

"Gramps. Come and sit with Norman and me . . . Here you go."

Everything is always happening at once.

"That's axiom," Peter has always said to her, and of course it is so in his works. "The world is an organism. It's only us—the 'not very inhumans,'" a phrase he'd substituted for the word "people" in his bedtime stories to the children, "who make events seem like soloists crashing into one another... Take the 'us' from the random, and what do you have?" And she, answering from her store of human variation, would always reply, "Us."

Since that episode at the door, Peter hadn't further acted in any way she must either refuse to admit, or must ignore. Settling on those alternatives is as far as she will go.

A mild surprise has been a card from Lev, from Israel, saying: "No nation can be a religion. No religion should be a nation. So why can serving in the army make wonderful women? Boys feel the same. But want to stay in the kibbutz for this year. If I can ever get her to New York, prepare to break out the banquet cloth."

"Typical," she'd said, handing Peter the card, which has a view of Antwerp, though sent from Tel Aviv.

"Typical of you. What do we know about him that we can judge?"

"The jokery. And maybe a certain fear of the facts. But why the Israel bit?"

"Hardly I know—what's typical for me."

"I'll tell you," she says slowly. "That when you're too long on an essay—or as long, say, as you've been on this one, your words invert." They are both digging the toes of their shoes into the prayer rug that Norman's wife had willed them, with a warning that it should stay hung on a wall, which it was until Jennie, who believes in luxury and thinks this house hasn't enough of it, said, "Mr. Norman, he says it's time it could come down on the floor."

"Unless," she says slowly. Hoping against hope, she chooses the best alternative, "it's some new philosophy you've—slowed up for."

He doesn't answer for a sec. Then only, "Zipporah." Then, picking the words slowly, "I . . . find it harder . . . to keep to . . . the logic." Then a pause. Then—"What did I just say?"

She tells him. Behind his back, as he turns without a word and goes to his studio, her mouth stretches wide with all the words and logic she can command but must stifle.

She managed to cover it with her hand, and not to follow him.

Next, that call from Agnes. Who wants to have tea "outside the house." As happens about twice a year, and means it is to be her treat. "No more Schrafft's," she always sighed. The Duffy sisters have a history of tearooms, most of them gone, and some— Huyler's, the Happiness Candy Stores—their mother's or their grandmother's, so far back that they themselves could only have attended them in childhood, or not at all. "How I miss them!" And this time she adds that at the department-store tea shops there's a risk she might start buying. Would Zipporah mind the parish house of their church?

It is cool, sparse: old oak dados newly shellacked, and white walls. The floridity of devotion is elsewhere, except for Mrs. Loftus, the housekeeper from the priests' residence next door. Sister Terry has been left at home, though she'd always taken time from her job before. The Father himself, hovering; this is serious. For saying nothing much at first, tea is the best beverage. The tea itself isn't

China, but is strongly itself, like the whole domicile. Wherever this is true of a religious one, Zipporah feels no antagonism. Rather the natural alliance of a person bred to the same. Though she is well aware that among the holy men of most religious venues she has encountered, from the muezzins of Islam to the pork-complexioned clergy of the Palatinate, she would not be believed.

"Miss Duffy tells me you and her brother met on an archaeological dig."

Already living together, Peter and she had opted for the trip as a kind of middle-ground between their lifelong interests-to-be and the Romeo-and-Juliet story, Peter's idea, which was what the family had been told. Yet it was the trip that had decided them to marry.

"Yes, Father." A glint of surprise from Agnes, at the priest being properly addressed. "Kitchen middens. In the Euphrates valley. Just a student-study trip. Not a real dig."

"My sister-in-law runs a fine household," Agnes grudges stiffly.

Peter's early account to his sisters of what Zipporah "did" hadn't helped. "Belly-goddesses!" he'd crowed, stuffing his thumb in an ear and finger-wiggling, while waving a photo-study of Indian temple sculptures, the lingam everywhere. "She do study what the dark peoples do." Long since, he'd apologized for that juvenile teasing, saying his sisters were stupider than he'd thought.

"Way to a man's heart, kitchens," Mrs. Loftus smirks, sliding a plate of cakes on the table. "No disrespect." But her eyes and Agnes's have met; they're buddies.

"Mrs. Loftus has been here twenty-three years," the priest says. "Here when I arrived. The Misses Duffy knew her before I did."

That's it. Those two have commiserated. Six children, mind you, Mrs. Loftus, that deep in the sex those two are. And none of them promised to God.

Yet to posit only that Punch-and-Judy line of prejudice is to clamp down on another vibration. That chill shimmy of some central cell in one's own flesh, alerting to the exchanged glances, the corner-of-the-mouth murmurs: A Jew.

"Ah, er, a midden is like what the ancients leave, Mrs. Loftus.

Shells of mollusks they ate, animal bones." The priest pushes the cake plate forward. "You won't get that here, Miss Zangwill. The Loftus maple-sugar patties are famous...But we had digs in Canada I've seen. Tell me more."

"Actually, we went on into different fields. My husband into philosophy. Excursions into the theory of randoms." Peter's own phrase for those essays...To her, the beatific flights surely near to genius, in which the lucid expanded on wavelengths that held you in a sea of light, in anticipation of a source yet to be explained. "And I got hooked on the—on the living. People's nowaday middens, you might say." She's never said this before, scarcely thought about it. If she can prolong this tea conversation until it's polite to go, she can delay the terror of hearing for sure why she's been asked here. And why, without a word, she has come.

She has choked; she has been given water. "Hooked on the living," the priest says. "So are we. So Miss Duffy here has asked my help."

It's the nauseating maple sugar. If her throat were clear of it, she could deny that yes, she'd heard, and could have stopped her ears, and watched, turned her back on those repetitions, those not quite "where-am-I?" wanderings.

"A mind heretofore so precise, so superior, Miss Duffy tells us"—is the priest saying?—"that the decline would scarcely be credited. Except that—"

"Peter is—the least absent-minded professor there ever was." Is she confirming, or denying? Worse than the Inquisition, this arraignment by this good Samaritan. Not a fat holy man, with a wine list high on the sumptuary budget, nor a bony abstainer with a sacrificial stare. Nor a mesmerizer. He has the careworn sweetness that comes from local burdens pursued.

"E-lusive, de-lusive, yea." Is he chanting a spell against an incubus? "They're saying it's a new disease. That you can get from cookpots made of aluminium." The word, pronounced in the British form, somehow soothes. "Nonsense, m'dear. Alas, it's the oldest disease in the sacerdotum—senility. But the progress in some can be especially sad. And Miss Duffy here says she recognizes the symptoms. Their mother went the same."

She can hear Peter's saucy comment, when in full command: You go. You have went.

"Mother wasn't a good person. Did awful. And at the end, the soiled sheets we dealt with, and worse—excuse it, Father. We didn't deserve it, the Dad either. He knew she ran around."

The priest orders her to hold her tongue. "We aren't in judgment here."

Aren't they? Can a Jew ever be sure they are not?

"Thank you, Father." With an effort she adds, "And you, Agnes." She will seek medical advice.

"Now, shall we pray?" His brows go up—would she mind?

She nods him to go ahead. She's on firmer ground now, via the habit of noting forms of worship anywhere. An activity one early mentor had warned might be "a psychological defense," making her furious, though her degree depended on it. "Well—if you too worshipped," he'd said, "one might better understand such zeal."

The four of them bow their heads. Mrs. Loftus, clearly seeing this as a laying on of hands, stands well behind.

Zipporah knows all the responses to their most elaborate solicitations of God. The wooden table has an oval flaw in it, toward its center. As good an image to focus on as any. To their surprise, she joins in the prayer.

At the end, not unusually, she is a little shamed. "Thanks, father. 'May He make his face to shine upon thee.' That's what we say too."

Father Coniglia, his name was. He escorted her and Agnes to the curb, to get them cabs. As Agnes took the first to come, she threw up her gloved palms. "My brother, he may attack you. You had to be warned."

During the following week, Peter seemed so much like himself that she dared not broach anything. How terrible to hint at breakdown, much less that grim collapse beyond, were she proved wrong. Then one morning Peter says, "I've been going through some tests. Those times you thought I was at Dr. Wexler's." Their dentist. "I get the results today. They won't be good, I'm afraid. Will you come?"

They hold hands while the doctor explains how little is yet known. A patient's decline is steady. Focus will go, replaced by endless repetition. Interest may flicker, but not wholly revive. As the brain freezes into stasis, so will the body, unable to keep its own location in mind. Rage is a common reaction. Incontinence to be expected. Death? The doctor seems almost surprised to be asked. "As with any ordinary person," he says. "From whatever organs happen to fail." There is no rescue for the intellect.

"You'll have to play it by ear," the second-opinion neurologist says. "Like every illness it can depend on the individual. Some may act fairly normally, for a time. Or intermittently. But I believe in informing both patient and family that it will worsen. So that planning may occur?"

"Curious," Peter had said, as they emerged from the hospital onto an East River corner bright with spring. "How he said that last sentence like a question. Not only to us. Tell you what, let's go buy me a pair of rubber pants."

Next morning she found on her desk a note from him: "I know I am blessed. You will deal with me as I would deal with you."

Tucking that into her heart, she waits. But he does not again refer to it—and she cannot bear to ask. In case he doesn't remember. He's always been slow to answer questions, but patient, even when the children, teasing, would begin to clap and drum. Now any query irritates.

She's dragging her feet toward enlightenment. Then, one afternoon, as she passes the closed door of his study, it comes.

All down this hallway, the doors have glass transoms, long ago stuck fast with paint even before the Duffys arrived. Against advice that the delicate gray glass would shatter, this one has been pried open to air the windowless study and a certain habit of Peter's. An odor of tobacco is now coming from it, identified with both her father and her husband. As a kid, she'd been nightly awarded a paper ring from a cigar of just this brand.

Twisting her marriage ring she stands, happily poised between the two men. Her father, after a session with her "fiancé," had clapped Peter on the shoulder, saying, "You two were made for one another. Remember Jesus was a Jew. I don't know for sure about Miz Mary Magdalene here—." And had hugged her to a fare-thee-well. "I hated all her other suitors." It was the first she realized that he'd known all along that they had not been merely suitors. "Sure I knew," he'd smiled at her, on his deathbed, not too many years later. "But him I could take."

In his honor Peter had opted for the same brand of cigar. Even before they had money enough for such luxuries, the slow pace of his work had made those affordable. His habit is to smoke one of those Havanas only after he completes an essay. "Never finished to my satisfaction, natch. So why not wreathe my head in satisfactory cloud?" If, rereading in that haze, he finds his pages have worth, he will smoke another after dinner that evening.

At her insistence they had this day once again visited a doctor, this time an old friend who had received the first report, and now the second. "No apologies. Come along." Once again, a prognosis only, of what the future will likely be. He had spoken to each of them separately. Saying to her, "I can lie. But not to him."

The transom, unsealed like a mouth, wafts toward her its blessing. She breathes in that blue, generational smoke. Now she can plan.

Peter is completing his life.

Coming out of the study, he had found her there. Taking her hand, he led them to a sofa. "I want now to get away from people who know me. And stay away. Can that be arranged?"

Here her work will serve her well. In more than one enclosure she knows of, by custom the elders or the mortally ill remove themselves to a certain distance as much moral as physical, a kind of apartheid of the soul. This being quite separate from those whom the community itself casts aside. What man like him would wish to pace out his time like some aging polar bear caged in a zoo, no longer free on the ice floes of the imagination? And in his case, cribbed up within the sight of all those who have held him dear?

"Of course," she says. "You won't want that audience. Except for me," and when he doesn't answer: "People who know you? That doesn't include me?"

His nod says it does. Then his voice.

"No!" She shouts it. When she screams "No, No, No," Jennie comes running, to find them sitting down, not quite turned to stone.

"I thought you was being hit. You all right, Mrs. Duffy? I never hear you and him even foul-mouth each other, all these years, fourteen." She dares to step between them, to survey Peter. "You all right for sure; I smell that seegar. But what's with her?"

Thank Jennie, wordlessly but forever. For the flash solution.

She, Zipporah, will be the one they're leaving for. Zippy, the intransigent, to some even the greedy husband-and-child eater, always sot on walking her road. She will cast herself in an exaggerated version of what the family half thinks of her, or can be persuaded to believe. And starting with the Duffy sisters, who, basking in Jennie's mock-deferential address, "Miz Agnes, Miz Theresa," think they have a secret alliance with her, based on her telling them the worst.

"I want to sell this house, Jennie. I want him to go round the world with me, seeing all the places where I've done my—my work. And I want us to live out there somewhere. For good."

Jennie cocks her head; maybe she's been studying up Norman, who does have an in with her, though she clearly thinks of it as the other way round. "But it was you, Mrs. Duffy, who yelled no."

"Because he won't. He won't do it. He won't go."

And Peter at once played up to her, God bless him. "We would all three of us have to leave this house."

It's impossible not to take a house-servant for granted, in spite of all the proper instincts. But men don't usually bother with lady-of-the-house confusion. "So, Jennie," he says, "what say?"

She doesn't answer at first. Often doesn't. They wait.

Jennie was born during World War II, of a Viennese mother and a black American GI. If the two bloods roil, there's seldom any sign of it. Any identity problems have been transferred to her self-styled "talent," cookery. She's had two husbands, one white, one black, and has tired of both. "Didn't like to eat." As an artist, she'll never have enough audience, though for a private family the Duffys do fairly well, and she can refer to her mistress and herself as both "women of talent." On home ground she'll try anything, and is usually superb, if moody. When down in the dumps her meals go pallid and dry, half-white. She considers soul food not a cuisine but "a history." Once she left them to be a Harlem chef, but returned pronto. "You know that niece of yours who does plays, one got done downtown, then she got hexed? I did the same as her. Got 'blocked.'"

"You go on in and have my supper," she says at last. "Then we'll talk."

The meal is rijstafel, a lengthy meal she has never served for less than four, six to eight being preferable. Now all the courses have been set out at once, for their privacy.

"So we can talk," Peter says. "Uncanny how she knows." Ordinarily they're careful never to refer to Jennie as "she."

"Jennie—takes the phone calls. Can't help knowing where we go daily." But would never listen in.

"Jennie—" he falters, with that drowning look, to let her understand that yes, he'd forgotten the name. For how long, though, will he be able to clue her as to his condition?

"We're going to eat this," she says. "A lot of it. Nothing wrong with our digestions. And pretend to still be settling our differences. Though we already have."

He likes the sweet side dishes best, she the hot.

Halfway through, he says, "In the beginning, God created ritual. Then, only then I'm sure of it, He leaned back and created the world."

"Funny," she says. "How in travail even we nonbelievers invoke God."

"Call us backsliders, rather."

He is flushed. Does food maybe help with the words? Or any stimulus?

He is waving a hand across the half dozen or so mounded dishes. Above his tightened lips his eyes seek hers, reminding her how with marriage one stops looking into those. "Way to a man's heart."

Not a phrase they ever use. Now and then, he'll drop a tidbit from his former world, though never as freely as she'll lather up a chat with her background. Jews coddle memory more, he's said.

"You been to Father Coniglia's?" That has crossed her mind.

He shakes his head. "Mrs. Loftus sent me a get-well card."

No reply.

"Laugh," he says. "Let her hear."

Marriage, that long earthing, will it save them yet?

They are laughing when Jennie comes to the dining-room door.

"Women of talent, both of you," Peter rallies. "We are just planning our i-tinerary."

"Mr. Norman's stopped by," Jennie says, grinning. "Just in time for dessert. I put him-and-all in the living room."

As Peter and she go in he says behind her, "Him-and-all, and-all" in odd singsong. Her spine freezes but she doesn't turn.

The coffee is set out, along with one of "the gooeys" that Jennie knows Norman looks forward to. Does she alert him? The Duffys have never asked.

The ugly cigar stand, seized on by Peter when her father's furnishings were doled out, and a fixture in his study, is being brought out also, to no one's surprise. Norman's breastpocket bulges with two Perfectos, or whatever they are, in their tin cases.

But Norman is staring down at one of the two brass cigar rests on the stand. "Peter," he says, in the strangulated rasp he reserves for scoundrelism in the stock market, "you finished something? But you don't like?" Upper lip retracted in distaste, he bends over the stub left in the oval prong, his cigar cutter swinging on his watch chain. It has a turquoise set in its top, which he deplores, but was given him "by a person for whom I had regard." Plainly a woman, and not his wife. "Peter," he says again. He makes as if to pick up the stub resting there but cannot bring himself to do so. "In all the years we are friends, I ever seen you *chew* a stub?"

So they have been released to tell him. What indeed she intends to spread far and wide—in her version. Which she must shortly work out in detail.

"Sell?" Norman says. "With me living next door? Not on your life . . . So Zippy wants to go round the world, does she. With you schlepping along."

These men. Men like him. Not all of them Jews by a long shot, but a recognizable parcel of them. Who divide women into those who can be dangled on a watch chain, and those—like his teacher-wife probably, whom he refers to gravely as "such a fine woman"—who will not so allow.

"So you'll have your way for sure," he says. "I know Peter here." He forswears saying, And I know you. Full of yourself, with that profession of yours. That lets you act like a man.

But loyal he is. This is our mutual bond. One by necessity known to us Jews.

"So go and sell," he says. "I'll buy it back and keep it on. For—for the family. While you're gone." He squints, into the purchaser's horizon. "And maybe Jennie will do for me and this place both. For the whole shebang."

Jennie has sidled in. *"Entschuldigen-Sie . . .* Excuse me." She usually drops these German politenesses only at Christmas. Swiftly
she tidies the cigar stand and is out again.

Norman snorts into the upper air. Pats his breastpocket. Decides against. Looks a little lost. Then straightens, chin tucked in.
Someone will help find him.

Peter speaks. Has spoken. In all the woe to come, will there be
these insights he drops? Lighting up his mind like the elf lanterns
that glow along the dark copses in stories for children? She will
treasure them.

"We amuse Jennie. We Jews."

For the time intervening, before she had gathered nerve enough to
send out those cards, the family is like a gauge she watches. A clan
may be lackadaisical on phone calls, private about its other interests, but only let it gather and it will instruct. Until now, she has
taken for granted how much this place is their center. Some members must be pressed to come, reassured of welcome; others consider it their duty, of which they are fond; all arrive on schedules
differing according to their life situations, and these being known
are a double intimacy. No-shows send bulletins as to why; attention
is paid. They show their gratitude for this time clock in different
ways, the older women showing off their new clothes, the older
men swapping tales of cigarette brands they kicked or bicycle-
exercise models they now use. Even the collegers like to meet again,
often to play instruments. Or they barge in in tennis whites, trailing
a new partner. Or with none, but still in company. All come because
the place is one more bulwark, in the city they happen to love.

As yet she has told them nothing. What are they thinking,
maybe saying, as Peter drifts in their midst, quiet and hostly still, if
not quite dependable? His manner has always been quirky, with a
wit delighting some, perplexing others, according to their lot in
life. To all he is the academic, celebrated for his loftiness even in
that quarter. He is "the professor." He is gramps.

Norman, noting Peter's "absent-mindedness," ascribes it to "the aging process" for which Norman himself is now a self-scrutinizing candidate. "I tell you, every man needs a daily lode-stone." His now being ballroom dancing, where he has joined up for instruction and is twirling respectably, though he means to keep away from the competitions, where you met the heavy-breathing widows, stringy middle-aged athletes, and too many over the hill like yourself. "In class you get to hold a nice girl like you did at your first prom—not too tight, plus a pat and a smile later, if you did good." And you always did, of course; you were paying for it. "That's enough."

The one who seems always to be watching his gramps is Bert. Quick with the chairs, as if he expects Peter's legs are failing him, though so far there's not been that kind of decline. But once, when Peter's conversation to a younger group slowed abnormally, there was Bert at his elbow, neatly supplying him, engaging them. She'd had a moment of pure agony, for them all—all here who love him. And a yearning new to her. To confide. All the more painful because of never having needed any other except him. But Bert's too young to lay that on. The poor boy has discovered enough.

She has put the note Peter wrote her in an old wallet of his, but does not need to look at it. One day, direction dawns on her through that durable old leather. Peter has told her what to do. Or as nearly as a life-mate can. "Deal with me as I would deal with you." Meaning "if you were no longer you." She won't be herself anyway, not without him. So why not discard what she can? A name, for instance. What she will be is yet to discover. But it will be for him.

The Duffy kitchen midden is still a live one. Paper wrappings crackle, serving dishes clatter; the air has a cereal warmth; some-one's dropped a spoon. Five hundred years hence will some sifter detect the fume of salt fish? But not the buzz, ripple and hum, cicada talk-talk that is the oratorio of the young. Surviving only as it repeats. They have small need as yet for her see-through window. At which one leans toward memory, as from a sill.

When she takes her turn on the other side of the wall, this particular society-of-the-Sunday will begin to crumble.

Step on it, Zoe.

Surveying the big room from just inside the pantry door, she does not see Lev. Only now she remembers he keeps Sunday office hours when he's in New York. Though the food he sends heralds him, he prefers to escape thanks. Some in-laws comport themselves like blood relatives. He has always remained apart from the ensemble, though one with a lively sense of the histories here. Politely attentive to the gossip run by him, but not being on the local seesaw, he is excused from response. Yet he's chosen her to rid him of Libby's diamond, and to hold the just-in-case keepsake for the sons. She is already his confidante. No wonder she's been dwelling on him so. He will be hers. She can tell him about Peter. The prospect eases her. Whatever Lev is apostate from, he must know what it feels like to have to get out.

Scanning the crowd, she sees the person whom, standing with his back turned and at a distance from her window, she'd mistaken for Lev. That other black shag-head, less swarthy than Lev actually, the long-legged harlequin who calls himself "The Shine." When sending him the invitation, she'd learned from Bert that his full name is Wole Thorvaldsen, and that he lives on Park Avenue with his mother, member of an African delegation to the U.N., and a stepfather whose last name Wole has taken, who, like Wole's own father was, is white. "No dope," she'd teased Bert, the young having long since laid their slang on her, "so that's why he talks of himself in the third person—what's his real father's name?" But this, Wole has never told Bert.

She likes having him here. The room can stand some anomalies. One burden her trade has left her with, also her travels. She is no longer at ease where the crowd, the meeting, even at times the dinner party, is—not by chance—all white. Here in this room, though, it's not merely a matter of skin. Even the young here, though they verge, marrying at will, doing vigorously whatever their parents did not, are still traceably from this city, this neighborhood, this class—the ever-climbing and one-step-back middle middle.

In toto, a clan still best described by that word which fires up Norman—as applied only to them. Because it is true? She sees it in every corner of this room, no matter how many here are descended from a Duffy or other merging. If it's not in the face, it's in the attitude. Assimilated, yea, but always with an edge to it, of race. The race.

People can be hardest on their own tribe. As she'd once said to Peter, she'd feared that she was one of that kind and could only hope it was out of love. "No," he said. "It's because they're nearer. I can't help knowing my sisters' politics is exactly like their dowdy underwear."

He is over there with the two boys, Bert and his friend. But not sitting; is that good or bad? When standing he can sometimes seem more irresolute. Dread is constant with her now, at the same time amorphous and binding; she is to expect disaster but not in precise shape. Yet the three over there are smiling at each other. She feels the grace that steals over her anywhere she sees the young attending. She moves toward it.

"You'll never guess—" Peter says, without slur. If he halts, it's the natural pause, when one says that. "You'll never guess what these two have told me. Bertram here. And Wole." He pronounces with gusto, as one does when names jump to the tongue. When he sees her brows raise questioningly toward "Shine" he is quick. "He's allowing me to call him that. Seeing my preference."

"Ah, Gramps," Bert says adoringly. "Ah, Gramps."

Peter has linked arms with them; perhaps he too feels the grace.

"Guess what?" she says incautiously.

To silence . . . But how was she to know? She will learn. A question is a threat. A statement just issued cannot always be pursued. Direction has shifted. Or been lost . . .

But he regains it. "Guess—?" His arms sag. The boys hold

on—a team. They must have done this before. His shoulders square. "Ah-hh, this." He's flushed, gloriously regained, and knows it. "These two cussed believers want to study to be—rabbis."

Then all four of them are laughing.

"Rabbi Duffy—" Peter gasps. He's enjoying his brain again, riding out the curse. "And Rabbi—?"

The boys look at each other. "The Shine" draws himself up, hook nose flaring. "Silverstein." Bertram blinks. Then the two of them race to the kitchen to stuff themselves, before everybody else gets down to it. And before the talk goes public. They know she is obliged.

There must be more than thirty people in the room, of all ages, sizes, and faces, maybe more than forty; she will not count. "Never count the persons in a room," her mother warned her, half laughing at this one of her family's sayings, handed down among them like secret jewelry. "It alerts the Lord."

Her father, snorting, "The less religion we Reform Jews have, the more we treasure any bit of superstition," did not mind counting. But on the one day he went to service, the Day of Atonement, Yom Kippur, his fast had to be broken by a vinegary, even bitter herring from an old shop far across town. "Yah, my father, blessed be his name, stocked for his father the holy days," the new owner said. "But how many customers bought? 'The Zangwill herring,' we even called it. If people don't keep kosher, leastways their atonement smells of the right fish. But we don't anymore have call for it."

Not all of the folk present are related. Some, like Norman, are what Peter calls "the dear barnacles." He has loved this atmosphere of their house. "Anybody notice how outgoing people can be, when they don't have to believe in heaven?" And he'd not been too surprised to find that to Zippy, though she had been brought up conventionally, among Jews sex did not appear to be anything for which you must atone. Their bed was inventive from the first. Only when they married, shared a house, had they become analytical, as coupledom will. "Forbidden fruit?" she'd teased, and he: "Well, at *our* Orthodox weddings, not just the men dance. And I haven't required you to shave your head."

Yet he could be sharp on the mildness of this ingrown company. "All passion not being spent. And no longer priceless. Or gone weedy with smaller argument...Where heresy doesn't exist, does energy take a dive?" Any such strictures are always in confidence. Once in the company he is always honestly charmed.

When Norman is seen drifting toward them now, Peter stiffens. "These days Norman is always drifting toward us."

"We're his relatives, now. Accept it." Then puts her hand on Peter's. The last thing she wants to be is sharp with him. She has seen the kindest of nurses be sharp with the sick—with her mother, her father, out of sheer weariness.

"What's our host smiling at?" Norman says. "Let me in on it."

"The Jewish venial sin," Peter says. "And as important here as ours were to us."

"You don't say." Norman looks uncomfortable. On Jews, he does the kidding. "So what is it, this sin?"

"Gossip. Lovely gossip."

"Hah. That you got right." Norman's upper accent sometimes deserts him. But when it does his manners take up the slack. "Lovely. Like they're saying about this lady." He kisses her hand. "You don't look one day over, say forty-eight. And the figure. Nell's saying she had to make you buy that dress."

"I get out of touch." She hadn't wanted the dress. But the one thing her daughters get together on is her.

"No, the real gossip. Sly in the women, openly commercial with the men." Peter isn't looking at either Norman or her. His eyes are sometimes spoken of by his students. "Double cones of perception," one had elaborated to her. "Professor Duffy can make a seminar feel bare. But he's not like some of the others. He won't

let you sink. He just doesn't want you to fall back . . . But where forward is, he's not saying. Guys say it's because he doesn't know. I say
that's what he's telling us. You agree, Mrs. Duffy?"

"So what's the real gossip?" Norman says. "Give."

"The lowdown of anybody on the rise here. Where nobody
plans to stay where he began. Not even the rich." Peter is still smiling. This is what he says to the students maybe, and to her. Who
does agree. But never to anyone here. "It's maybe why you do so
well in America, uh? Of course as Jews, you want to be safe—and
that's why you're more in the swing here all the time. Because in
America everybody wants to be safe; that's why we're here."

"You don't say, professor." Norman sweats white and icy.
Not red.

"Norman," she says. "Understand, please. It's what he'll say to
me, when he's amused by the family. He's not saying 'you Jews.' He
says 'We.' And—and I agree."

She's thrust aside with a low, "It's maybe you we have to stand
by." Norman fumbles at his watch chain, first at the cigar cutter,
then the Phi Beta key, then the watch. "Is that the sort of thing he's
putting in that essay? I never did read them; maybe I should." He
turns to Peter. "I never heard *rishus* from you before."

Peter has heard Norman use the word once and had asked her
what it meant, being shy of asking Norman such pointers. "I know
the common Yiddisher New Yorkisms, but not that." As a kid she
had heard it once, from an ancient aunt, and had picked up what it
must mean: "I think it means the small slights. Not the ace-brand
prejudices." He had marveled at the hairsplitting . . . If, she thinks,
she has got it right?

For Norman is turning on her. As she has postulated may happen, to Peter's good, and now hopes she can bear.

"All those underdog harmonies you hear so well on your travel,
Zippy, whyn't you apply some to nearer home?"

Peter is a tall man. In the last weeks he hasn't seemed so. Now
he's leaning some. "Harmonies, Norman? We forget you play the
violin. But who's the underdog?"

Norman cocks his head. A specialist in landlord-tenant relationships, he's said to be good in court. "Maybe a better word is 'schnook.'" He points to Peter's study. "In there all day, with her out making a brave safari, you develop that temperament? She takes you away from your habitat, you could develop a real bias." His head cocks at Zipporah. "Any marriage is a mix. Yours is a special one, baby. I'm just reminding you, Zipporah, you're *his* Jew."

They watch his back as he makes for the front-room fireplace, where the older men gather. The dance class hasn't unbent those thick, rounded shoulders. The fireplace is on the south wall, commanding the room. Leaning on the mantel helps a man survey down through the second living room to the small center hall, leading one way to the studio, the other down a longer hall to the strung-out bedchambers and baths. Peter and Zipporah are standing in the small hall. Norman, turning to face the other men and the view, leaves the two in shadow.

Peter takes her hand. If he gobbles a bit he can still speak. "Help me. To be me."

If the fingers that clasp his tremble, they accept.

"Peter. Our plan." She won't further challenge his recall.

His neck swells red, the jaw juts with his effort. "I . . . remember." His eyes gain the familiar depth. Only the mouth is awry. "We—go forward." His tone is as light as a whistle.

And I will help you, she whispers to herself. To stay you.

This is a "step-down" living room, with one triangular interior corner raised. On that haven the piano flaunts. Along the steps leading down to floor level, people have seated themselves in a jumbled line, of all ages except the old. These and the rest are scattered on sofas, settees, wing chairs, or on the hummocks bought for her children, some of whom now hold theirs on their laps. A couple of teenagers have wound themselves on a set of library steps. When the nervous heel of one jitters against wood, he is shushed.

A bulbous armchair, one of those hand-me-downs that cling to a householder rather than the reverse, has been skewed into a hoped-for center, half facing the steps and the fireplace. She has always disliked it but goes to it, laughing, "It looks as if it's at sea."

"Can't be. It's a camelback." Son Charles, who charts the cosmos, has a furniture hobby that could supply it. From whatever locus, he has arrived. She sends him a tremulous mother-smile. Grown-ups who were once your children can make you uncertain. You are confirmed by love, but perhaps no longer by opinion?

"Chuck can probably find a saddle for it." Nell scorns the chair not because it is ugly, but now scarce enough to tempt some tastes, and valuable. Her flaming liberalism seems altogether out of synch with the perfect if conventional American Beauty Rose face inherited from Peter's mother. Neither takes over fully, perhaps fortunately.

Erika, whose wit rescues her from her own gloom, at least to other people, says, "I like that chair. But of course I wouldn't dream of saying so."

Gerald, busy in the world of finance at the mantelpiece, doesn't look up.

Zach, in whose loft one lolls on an inclined place or sits on the floor on one's bones, in order to suffer the immutability of design, looks down.

For once they all agree: who talks about chairs? As for what Mickey would have said—she hasn't the time for that just now; disaster has for the moment cured her of him.

So, all her children have registered in; they always do. What she is going to take away from them, and from those around them, is the place where she and they all have earned such perspectives. She scoops up the three toddlers, one after the other, into her seat's ample lap, leaning with them against its fleshy arm.

"What I love about this family—this crowd—" She must not cry—"is that we're always too many for the chairs."

So, she has told them. Their faces suspend before her, in that sinkhole from which someone willing to be the monkey must speak. Only memorials, toasts, mild send-offs have ever caused any stoppage here, when for a moment the little personals, asides, and powwows must give way. Impatient with the ceremonial, one still does one's duty, even returning to the previous huddle with refreshed zest. But to be caught when drinking the champagne that always distinguishes the parties here from the Sundays—only to have that very rug, one of such familiar pattern, all but whisked from under one's feet?

On the steps, in the lowlands of the sofas, heads turn around to fix on that praiseworthy view. So rooted in one's own archive, almost owned. Already congealing into "the last time."... *They're going to sell. Can they really be allowed to? And to leave. How can they leave? Us.*

Let some elder deal in. They always do; they relish it. Reminding us we're still an old-fashioned family. Which means strong. All the kitchen smells don't have to be Orthodox.

"That card. I knew there was trouble. To the family—who sends out cards?"

Cousin Nanette, in the solitary voice of the stone-deaf. At her side, the paid companion emits a groan from her collection of utterances.

From the three nearest adult children—Charles, Erika, Nell— a bouquet of coughs, gasps. "Why?" and "Where will you go?" As if no other "where" exists, for this. A couple of whistles from the steps are quelled by a father. At Zipporah's knee, Erika reaches up to touch her mother's wet cheek. "Mom."

I'm crying because no one is noticing your father. And because it is all going according to plan.

"Where?" Nell cries. "Where did Mom ever go we didn't need maps? As for why, maybe it's time. A mother gets fed up." Nell has just again become one.

Keep it up, my girls—the silliness expected of women. Or have I taught you too well?

At the mantel Gerald, her eldest, clears his throat. This doesn't always mean he will speak, but he does. "Sell?"

Around the room, a sigh of relief. It has been said.

But who's this raising his cupped hands, as if he holds all their bewilderment? That young man who never sits, always standing one leg in front of the other, a pointed boot resting on its toe, in electric communication with the earth. A born leader, according to his and Bertram's school. Though one not born to the properly humble circumstances. At his feet, of course, is his buddy. "That boy with the good singing voice." To annoy Bert's fashionable mother, just add, "Bert could become a cantor."

"But Miss Zipporah—beg pardon, Missus Duffy, you don't mind my special interest?" The Shine says. "Wha-at about the na-ame cha-ange?"

She had wholly forgotten it, this ploy conceived in the first shock and designed, she'd thought, to keep Peter and herself anonymous on their trek. Particularly him. His quiet pursuit, in tune with certain physicists, of what he has called the "neo-random," is opaque here to all except Charles. Peter is revered in his own nest of scholars. But a reputation might well be axed by reports of this disease.

When in the bush, quickness can save the day, or lose you your head. Looking at the faces circling her, she remembers Mindanao, those upheld student faces hungry for long circular explanations, both to soothe and counterpart the confusions of living in at least three languages. She has to choose among her own.

"I'm used to—peoples who... have new names for different stages of their lives. So... why not me?" She sighs, that long Semite arrrchh which others here, though born in the U.S., have like her inherited, its source unknown and never questioned—a token sound, exchanged as birds do when in flock.

"You're right." Cousin Nanette's hearing aid squawks an endorsement. She'll never learn not to put a hand to her ear. "Your mother, all our side of the family. After sixty, why let God single you out? I feel the same."

A titter, not quashed fast enough.

"So laugh," she says. "Myra hears me say it every day. Tell them what." But Myra, who also answers to several other names, is by training irremediably out of sight. "She's shy. So I'll tell you... Genealogy isn't to make us big. It's a get-together. For what's coming." Her tone hallows that as much as it fears. This is the tone that all present have been accustomed to hear from elders like her since childhood. She even grasps Myra's skinny elbow, which may have scarcely any genealogy worth a cent. "It's a show of stren'th."

Not all here are as ready for death as that.

"But you'd be crazy to sell right now, you and Peter," a man says. "The forecast for the nineteen-eighties is that these old-line places will double, maybe triple in value. Also this avenue. Forget Park, leave it to their millionaires." By which he means the WASP ones.

This is Wallie, a cousin-in-law, born on Central Park West and still there by inheritance. In the decade to come, he hopes to sell his family place for a big wad—though one by then perhaps minor to him—and will cross to the Park's other side, to join those billionaires who, like him, no longer need to be WASP. He is one of several here, money-market men or ad men, in their late forties, some fleshy, some wiry, for whom the academics of the family, of the same age mostly, have a disaffection, or out-and-out scorn. "And look . . . at . . . that . . . view." His spread hand, the Rolex gleaming from the starched linen, displays that arcade of treetops, frail from traffic gas maybe, but a sky is a sky.

A ripple from the college crowd, not quite suppressed. More and more of these ripples will not be. Wallie, thanks to ever upgraded cuff links from wives—including his current one, Zipporah's dizzy or dotty Cousin Bea, named for her mother, a senior aunt—is known to them all as The Cuff-shooter.

"I will buy," Norman says, soft as a purr.

The market men, whose venue here is the fireplace, for stock tips as well as cigarette ashes and elbow-leaning, turn their collective stare at him.

"At a price to be arbitered by an outside party, of course," he says quickly. "Nah, better still, by you boys."

A hoot from one of the collegers, a grandson who has won a scholarship to M.I.T., "in physics, yet" the elders say with pride. "And works, too; won't let his father pay a red cent."

The father is her oldest son, Gerald, named at her insistence for his Catholic grandfather, that cuckolded and probably henpecked never-met father-in-law, for whom she has a certain sympathy. Because of Gerald's Christian name, Peter's sisters had half adopted him, at any holy day of theirs they could find an excuse for, and in his teens, with the purchase of his first car, as their steady escort to church. The result, which had filled Peter with glee: Gerald is a pillar of his synagogue; at the kickoff of its annual drive he is always the first to rise and pledge. Gerald knows better why his son James, middle name Ezekiel, won't let him fund him; he despises the men at the fireplace.

Now he accepts James's hoot with a shrug and a half salute. The days when he would have thundered to his son, "Respect your father!"—a phrase tossed at any renegade youth of her own youth—have drained away. Among the many households attached here by blood or even friendship only, most are honorable and moral, and the young still good as gold if you look close. But there are no more thunderers.

"There's far, far more to 'assimilation' than loss of religion," she'd said to Peter, on her return from an anniversary trek around some of the sites she had visited early on. "And not just the disappearance of the artifacts. There should be funding, museums even, for the really endangered," she'd mourned, not quite fooling. "Persons who die out for lack of function. Or habitat."

Yet, even in these family jamborees, where the whole of her clan is displayed before her in what most would call their steady ascent into the general American likenesses, she's never thought of any of that professional lore in connection with the home.

"Why, there's a mezuzah over our door," she'd have joked if any such connection between her "anthro" and her life had been posed to her. "Over the house door." Adding that Peter had put the thing there, an artifact she did not even know how to spell.

In the room in front of her the financial hum of the men, always the underground z-z-z of this hive, has taken over. Both her daughters are sitting on the floor at her side.

This is the division here to which she is most used, even accepting that "head-of-the-house versus the female" separation as natural. As just a mild version of that bold orthodoxy which sections off women to worship as second-class untouchables (some of whom might even be unclean enough to be menstruating) in the pure and scholarly house of God.

None of that, surely, threatens these three women here. But each, in the style of her generation, can be viewed perhaps as belonging to the "dispersed." In the modern style, her daughters have taken their attitudes, even the physical ones, from everywhere. Nell, the lawyer, sits in the lotus position taught her in college

dance; the moodier Frederika crouches on her heels. One has currently left a Jew to live with a Christian; one has divorced an Iranian to marry a Jew. Nell's children have at times attended Reform
Jewish Sunday school, but also were carefully exposed to ecumenical lectures around town. Frederika-Erika, whose name-changes
come from a bit of psychiatry, nothing too serious, often works as
a well-paid executive director for nonprofit organizations, then
quits out of guilt, to serve as their volunteer. Early on, she and her
former husband had subscribed to that doctrine "We won't bring
children into such a parlous world," which had appealed especially
to "enlightened" liberals of their sort. Secretly Zipporah judged
them, and their friends, as perhaps lacking the confidence to have
children like them.

This she, Zipporah, would never say. The more children you
have, the better you get along with them. Swathed in mother history, she sees in each of her thirty-odd-year-olds *their* hearts at thirteen. Frederika, for instance, who has the childless woman's severe
tenderness for other people's kids. Just now she's prying a small,
sharp-edged silver object from a three-year-old's fist. "Whatever is
this; what's its mother thinking of? Why it's from that tea caddy on
that low table in the pantry? It's the top."

"I thought for a minute it was the mezuzah," Zipporah says.
"Jennie says it's just hanging by a thread."

Both sisters burst into laughter. "Ah, Jennie."

Nell has been quiet, for Nell. "Jennie has such respect for
what's hung here. I used to love to watch her dust around the
permanences."

"Remember when your father hung that mezuzah?"

She's struck a bell. Immuring them in that nucleus of voice-
over charm-talk women can manage anywhere.

"An apartment door's not exactly the required doorpost," he'd said,
the day they had moved in. She can see him on the ladder, a paterfamilias in his forties, speaking down to kids also ranged in steps.

To Frederika, who'd had a sibling jealousy over Gerry's being favored by the aunts: "No, this is not a crucifix. Nor a saint's medal either." He'd hung the little case carefully. "A kind of blessing. Or an asking for one. For such smart kids . . . Has some rules, on a piece of parchment inside . . . So maybe it's a kind of bargaining—like all luck-pieces are." And it had, he'd said, one of the divine names on the other side. "Buddy Devine?" their youngest, Zachary, born after Mickey was gone, had said. "No, not him, stupe," Nell, the next one up, had snickered. "It's for God . . . Mom's, I think."

And one hand on the ladder, she, Zipporah, had said, "I can't give you that holy name, there are a lot of them. But I can give you the first rule; it's from the Bible, Deuteronomy, I looked that up. Yesterday." She was always honest with them. "And it was the first text we learned in Sunday school . . . After all, I was confirmed. It's called, or we called it, the *Shema*." Raising her head, hand on chest, she'd declaimed it. "*Shema Yisrael, Adonai Elohenu, Adonai, echad* . . . Hear, oh Israel, the Lord is our God, the Lord is One."

From the top of the ladder Peter said, "The name on the other side of the parchment is *Shaddai*." He'd spelled it out. "I looked it up."

How this story, well-known to all denizens here, would have got around must have been from cousin to cousin; she and Peter never told smart-aleck tales on their kids. But Zach, the grown man, and a heavy one, can still be teased at family meals, having said, "What's a 'potchmunt,' Dad—is it to eat?" And Nell, very pretty Nell, for having blurted what is also still teasable: "No. silly, a 'potch' is what my friend Mary Selig's pop says when we're noisy: 'Get outa here or I'll *potch* you in the behind.'"

She watches Nell sneak out to the foyer and return. "The mezuzah, it's still there," she says, "Hanging by a thread." She's still not smiling. "When you and Dad leave, where will it go?"

There are legends and legends. Theirs have shrunk to this? Whatever, she, Zipporah, does not intend to be one. Not yet.

Nell and Mickey were the most Irish-looking of her children, and the most complex. If of an age, they could have been a twinship;

sometimes in the sway of the genders, one can speak to her as once to him. Nell is pretty enough to have swung on any of the red-velvet swings that were the epitome of easy vice in her grand-mother Duffy's day—with the men of that era craning up at the cutpurse crotch arcing in and out of eyeshot? She considers herself "not sexually permissive but generous," with two bastards she has legitimized by other means than marriage. She is an attorney, who patiently explains to both the "mouthy divorcees and the anti-male femmes" who want their alimony "drop by bloody drop" that she is "basically a criminal lawyer," specializing in the corporate, "which is where all the discrimination really is." Her father has twitted her with putting the random really to work, she answering happily, "I get good money. And I'm really working pro bono all the livelong day." That last phrase being a quote from Cousin Net-tie. Nell is the one who has most "worked" the clan, not only for pragmatic help recommendations, summer jobs, etcetera, which they all do, but for additions to her own personality. "Her own mother most of all," Peter had remarked, at the party they gave her when she passed the bar. "Neither of you sees it, of course, and better so. But Nell's doing what you might, were you young now."

Had he meant that the study of man, as she practiced it, was outmoded? Now and then she herself has thought so; the study of man in terms of race, habitat, customs, gender, might now be more akin to a savant's Rhine Journey, in the age when almost all one's flying machines were words. Or, before the age of molecular biology, physics, and that lot, the kind of final travelogue wealthy dying men gave themselves. "No, Peter," she had said, "and yes. Outmoded internationally, anthropology as we've known may well come to be. But never so at home."

Nell has sent her boy and girl to such Sunday schools as her city and suburb arrangements have dictated; after the Dutch Re-formed, then a Reform Jewish, then an unsatisfactory Quaker group, "on Thursday afternoons; no wonder doctrine was lost track of." Then a Catholic Sunday school, "Over whose power I was truly scared. It's so watertight, which I too love. But it was okay; the kids had had Buddhist instruction in between. And of course history in regular school. So when time came for the Easter Passion play—Gethsemane, what else?—they busted from the crowd saying they were monks from the Inquisition. Dressed accordingly, and holding up two instruments of torture, homemade." Their inspiration, a Swiss artist who worked with burlap and iron, the Modern being round the corner from their flat.

"They weren't expelled, Mother; they never are." Winsomeness is inherited; she is her father's girl, the American Girl, saved by the intelligence now slowly thinning her hair. "The kids are eager for new fields," she'd said, after the Catholic episode, "but the Hasids, they refused. Really it's time for a lull. So I think next it will be back to plain old Congregationalist." One of the two fathers of her children is that. Both fathers are an influence, she reports. "And remain highly interested."

Peter, who has since had each to lunch, confirms this, adding that both men, willing donors of sperm and the agreed-upon limited paternal service that Nell stipulated, have a healthy fear of ever fully meeting the family, which they have heard is formidable. "Heard from whom?" Peter joked to his daughter, saying later, "She just wants her own life, Zipporah. Everyone separates from family in his own way. My way was scarcely distinguished. But I did ask her wasn't she afraid all those religions would mix the kids up? She says it is the business of each new generation to mix up the preceding one, and that Thelma and Derek are already very satisfactorily confounding her. I told her, 'Nellie, you swallow every new line of talk, but don't regurgitate well.'"

Peter fancies he's concealed from Nell and everyone else except Zipporah that though Nell comports herself as his favorite, Frederika, the moody listener, is his lamb. "If she can ever whip those moods into line, she'll originate." Zipporah recalls how, at one of the many times she was leaving her household behind, Erika said to her, "Nell will miss you for herself. I'll miss you for you."

No one ever takes Erika and Nell for sisters. Erika has a great mop of the Brillo-like hair which from generation to generation signifies that some one of Zipporah's mother's ancestors had stopped over in Egypt, and the nervy, slightly llama profile that goes with. No wonder she feels herself to be the most Jewish of the Duffy brood. She has a Ph.D., gained in her late twenties, of which she is ashamed. Charles says of her, "She picked art history like you pick a chance at a fair. And because she hadn't a hope at any prizes." She feels closest to Charles because he prefers planets to people, but while he and all the other Duffys spout their innards to the general huddle, you will not find Erika even in a tête-à-tête.

Starting as a volunteer in a corner of the Jewish Museum, she now works as curator of a large private collection of Judaica, actually a small behind-the-scene museum specializing also in authentication, whose bon vivant owner lives mostly in France, where the collection is kept. "She's like your mother," Peter has said to the others, defending Erika's bristling solitude. "Oh, not in warmth. But she's on the world scene in her own style." Generally the Duffys' free-for-alls take place honorably, when everybody is there to hear. But their sister worries them. "What's that prize you say she wants, Charles, and can't have?" Nell said. Charles, crinkling eyes as blue as his father's, always surveys his family like a galaxy he knows all too well. "She wants to be all Jew."

They no longer discuss her, their unsettled star. Gerald, sniggering, had closed that subject: "Let her convert."

Now she draws up a chair behind Zipporah and sits there, almost but not quite tête-à-tête. This is often her habit, always calming to both of them, to Zipporah confirming their physical link. This is me, your daughter, the breath at Zipporah's nape seems to be quietly saying; let me inherit you. Sometimes she will rest her chin on your shoulder, so that the two of you are almost eye-to-eye on what's ahead. As if she's saying, In this company I can confide . . . What happens is that you do. To get Erika's opinion, a collector of Jewish art will do anything. So will a mother.

The men at the fireplace aren't in a back-room huddle; that would be unseemly here. But the taller ones are leaning over the shorter, who pat their thighs and are talking out of the side of their mouths. All except Norman, who, gazing at the ceiling, is clearly listening to whatever he has started. Commerce, surely. For in that part of the room the conversation is no longer an even buzz, but the slightly elevated, jerky artifice when money talk is known to be going on. The women chatter absently; this is a scene they know well. We know how our bread is buttered, their slight smiles say . . . And how we're loved?

"Bracelets," Zipporah says wickedly. The reference is to a cousin, long since assumpted into the lore, who had informed a Sunday, "A diamond bracelet he's giving me. And it's only our silver anniversary."

A puff of laughter at her nape. She's emboldened. "At least Norman isn't on his usual bugaboo."

"Assimilation? No. You've boosted him otherwise . . . But, Mom? What do you think about it?"

"About what?" Does she mean the sale, the real reason for it? She's been in France, called back suddenly by the absentee whose museum she directs.

"About orthodoxy. And—people like us."

"Strayers, you mean? And whether we should go back? Whether we could."

"You never said."

Why would I? How could I? Is Erika thinking of what Gerald said about her, which she must know? Carefully, Zipporah doesn't turn around. "We never thought of our children as half and half, you know. Or watered down. You were ours. And whole."

"Of course." The voice at her ear is firm. "It's my boss. He was brought up Orthodox but hasn't worshiped for years. Now he has liver cancer, and the rabbis he chums with over there are urging him back. He's tempted. He thinks it might ease him at the end. To be among friends. But he doesn't want to be led by the nose. The museum collection is safely positioned, of course. But he's always buying new, there's a lot they could still have in mind. Anyway, he asked me what I thought. And to ask you; he thinks very highly of you. 'She collects,' he said, 'the word gets around.' I suppose, Mother, he means the stuff in the spare room?"

"If a couple of pieces of Judaica is collecting."

How shall she answer this child?

All around her is her crowd. Though she honors no mind among them especially, laughs at or disapproves mildly of some of them, and knows she is understood by few, their genes pool in her blood, her feet share their earth.

"When I rocked you, I first thought about what Jews are. And with each babe-in-arms. I'll never forget that rocker."

The high-backed, cane-seated pine rocker had been bought at an up-Hudson roadside auction Peter had chanced upon while on a fishing trip. An old patroon family gone to seed, he was told. The two sons two versions of "not quite right." The mother a huge dropsical creature with hair on her chin. Every time an article was knocked down, the three of them giggled. The chair's viciously short rockers could kick you out of spite. But the perfect curve of the back atoned, guardian to the gentle mother-hunch nestling there. Reflection had poised like a falcon on her wrist.

"After you give birth. There's no time quite like it. When you've been submerged in the depths of the body, yet must emerge. Once again, a mind. I wasn't mulling intermarriage. Your father and I moved from absolute choice. I'd have done the same if I'd married a Jew. I was mulling our history, as any modern Jew must. A baby held tight is the globe of the world. Very soon it's a question mark. To answer a child shakes one's foundations. What would I be saying to you, about the me in you?...And you all came so close together. With each child I thought of it, refining what I would say. For myself, of course. My theology. But I thought it was for you."

"But you never said." When her daughter's eyes are wide, her mouth parted, she is one to be proud of; all moods disappear.

In front of them, all are chatting sotto voce; there's no doubt as to what's cooking among the men at the fireplace. On the steps the kids are in a huddle. Nell's two, Thelma and Derek, appear to be showing them a sort of game, harmlessly Buddhist, one hopes.

She seizes her daughter's hands. There's such a lightsome secrecy in what one says in a crowd. "If you can pass theology on, you're already Orthodox." They laugh. "So tell your boss . . . tell him—" She rocks back and forth, though her chair doesn't rock. For a moment she can't speak. Erika's hands are still in hers. "The desert *is* orthodoxy. Wind and sand demand it. And the stars in that hemisphere—like pinholes to God. I saw all that in Israel. You can see it in the Bible as well."

But the city disorients with its free-range suggestions, and splayed streets leading ever back to the maze of oneself. And we were all there once, as immigrants. Sticking together at first, on those mean streets. But where the milk doesn't sour to vomit, the meat doesn't have to be sun-dried. Where the young marrieds see a golden image in every shop. In this great autocracy of the casual that a democracy always is. Where no one God is watching them. And the stars aren't always visible.

With each child suckling warm in her arms, parenthood further descending on her like the colorful sash swung over the head of an academic inductee, she had brooded further on her obligations. Saying to Peter, "I'm getting my Ph.D. in breastfeeding. You don't mind if I slip them a little kosher mix?" He'd said, *"Mazel tov."*

She's too beat now to say it all. "We Jews ooze toward the secular. It's not going to stop."

They are still holding hands. "I see it in the museum, I told my boss," Erika says in a stifled voice. "Orthodoxy is a scholarly ethic. One belongs, like to a regiment. The women are the camp-followers."

"Ah, you saw that?" Zipporah breathes. When you and an adult who was once your child find yourselves in sympathy there is a kind of brilliance in the chest. All breeding being spent. But this I have bred.

"Until he got sick we used to fight about it." Erika's tears are blinked back. She was the one who never cried. Pull my hair, she'd say. Go on.

"How old is he, this boss of yours?"

"Jean André? Only fifty-two."

Her girl, this woman, looking straight at her from the same platform of life. Soon to slide.

"Ah, daughter. Ah, baby."

But Erika had turned. At the other end of the room Norman has bid for attention. Behind him, the other men shift in uneasy phalanx. He's managing to look shorter than any of them, though not actually so. "When Norman's angling for something," Peter has noted, "he shrinks to less than his normal size. Like that cigar deal he got me into. I have enough to last me the millennium."

"I'm to have the museum," Erika says softly. "When I was leaving France, and not to see him again—he wanted that—he said to me, 'The rabbis, they'll give you a hard time. Just remember, we're most of us bourgeoisie now. And the bourgeoisie ethic is to buy. And to sell.'"

And our homes still bedouin? Zipporah says to herself.

"He said I was to think of him as just leaving the country also. 'A personal diaspora,' he said. Before France, where his family had only been for fifty years, they had been in two other countries they knew of at similar intervals. 'It's in our bones,' he said. 'Even if we only do it from the bed.' So no matter what kind of Jew he decides to be at the end, he'll still be one. 'Jews always leave.'"

That's true. Across the sea, a flash of empathy. "We have no paradise, he means. Can I call him up?"

But Norman is clucking. That catarrhal peremptory which comes from rolling in the mouth what you can afford to buy. "My friends here agree to facilitate. So, Master Peter—what say?" He flirts a glance at Zipporah. But Peter is the owner, for tax reasons Norman himself has set up.

"Eh. Peter? You'll consider the proposition?" Norman's voice is slightly raised. "Ah, no mooning off, you sharpie." Does he suspect something; do they all? Rumor spreads like fleas here. In the ghetto, rumor was once a godly duty, which might redound to one's profit or even save a life. Now that precious mouth-to-ear has been reduced to mere scuttlebutt. But is still part of one's racial rights.

All eyes are on Peter, their soldier-scholar of the intellect, and pet Christian. "He'll be the one to make your marriage work," her own father had said. Meaning the intermarriage, back in the days when such alliances were new to clans like theirs.

"Eh, Peter Duffy?" Norman's smile is tolerant, lenient, his spread hands affectionate. They are used to Peter's stately pace, part of his luster, even.

Peter's hand is pressed so hard on the knob of his chair arm that the whole arm trembles. He rises. Nothing wrong yet with his knees... Couldn't it be M.S., Parkinson's?—she'd wooed the neurologist, rattling off that common litany. "Or 'Lou Gehrig's disease?'" he'd answered. "One of those that won't so plainly affect the mind? No, Mrs. Duffy. Alas, no."

Peter is looking at her. That axis between their glances, so palpable to both that a ruler might have drawn it, will it fade at once or only by degrees? She's shaken by the rage that she's been warned may foment in him, attacking those whom the patient may hold most dear. Hers can't be against him. But may be as irrational. Being against whom?

"Trust—" Peter is saying. "The... the greatest emotion." He has written that it is maybe the supreme Jewish one, but never said that here, where maybe he learned it. His accent is so of the clan, also so simple a statement of his complexity, that she wants to put her arms around him, to protect.

"Arrrh, no tisn't. Not for-r some of us."

Who's that who's piped up? Can it be? It is. Theresa, the other Duffy sister. The gold cross glitters at her neck. "Surely it's Love." A hand clutches the cross. She is speaking for it.

Next to her, Nell's teenager, Thelma, half-named for this lesser great-aunt, and like her mother once Theresa's pet, slides out from under her aunt's arm, head down, and makes for the kitchen.

Excusably, she's an earnest helper there. But she's also plainly about to burst. Her new crony, Mitzi, a sly outsider who'll have much enlightened her, tails after her, to that haven where they can safely clutch their stomachs and whoop.

Faces scattered here and there confirm. They too know that Theresa, that skinny maiden of fifty-five, whose only open rebellion against Aggie is her ebony-dyed crown of braids, has for years been "seeing," "keeping company," or even "secretly engaged."

"To a 'spoiled priest,'" Peter had said. Though his younger sister has never breathed a word, he has theological connections everywhere. "'Spoiled priest'—what a sour phrase." Not Aggie's. Who is presumed not to know. Or blinks the other way, for the sake of their joint low-rent apartment, Theresa's salary, and all the other primped-up benefices of a life bound to the sodality as much as to the Trinity?

These faces: the white, fallen chaps of the old ladies, swart old men who no longer need to tan, bloom-bud girls and their handsomely assisted mothers, fathers imprinted on sons at their side, whether by the adoring copycats or those sullenly escaping. Pensioners, and snugly happy with that. Or those who assert, some with truth, some not: "Sollie, I left him," or "My only boy, God be thanked, he's no loafer." These, these are Zipporah's "view."

They all think, the clan, that Peter and I are leaving them, specifically. Simpler to see it that way. It absolves the younger ones from the guilt that a new generation must always carry—that as nature dictates they themselves have already left. It salves the drear of the old ones, whose leaving will be soon.

Someday, to tell them the facts. How? Not yet. The kitchen door slams open.

Theresa's stringy neck quivers behind its sacred ornament. Peter, too far down the crowded living room to soothe his sister with a pat or a grasp, as always when she flares, struggles to speak. He can't.

The embarrassed, I-told-you-so faces slide in front of Zipporah like those masks at a fun fair, at which you aim.

"I'll tell you what a mixed marriage is—" Zipporah squawks.

Words you've never used before won't trill. "You never know whether to laugh or cry. And everybody's right . . . Come on, Peter. Lead the way. Let's eat."

What a released trooping, what a joy! Like a garden, marching.

"There should be music," Peter murmurs. He has got to her side.

At the kitchen door Jennie, her arms outflung, is backed against it, Jeanne d'Arc in an apron, over the gray silk armor she wears on feast days. What's gotten into her? Born in a Vienna dulled by the war it had lost but espoused. Steeped in that cuisine which whoever cooks it mixes meat arrogantly with cream. Willing captive of these, "her family," and of its love and trust. There's no telling what danger she thinks may have pursued them here, even to America.

"Two policemen at the back door. Mr. Lev, he's been shot."

They go at once to the hotel, she and Peter, in this blurred, transitional time, when he and she can still be referred to as "they." Before their flight, but when the two of them have begun to move like clockwork toward what is coming. She sees herself and him, two figures under the bell glass of doom. But no artificial snows of the past will prettify them, as the cab rushes them past the concave porticos and Egyptian pillars of their avenue, along the southern border of the park. The hegira she plans to begin in Europe, if never reaching to Asia, will be better than that, and worse. A journey silvered with the kindness of others, if a steady progress toward those last slops and sawtooth screams that extinguish the spirit, it will have the sore, transcendent touches known as human. It will be real.

This day, he will still help her out of the cab. At the hotel desk, asked to identify themselves and who they are visiting, she has to prompt. But the halo of the ordinary still encloses them. As they ride up to meet Lev's poor bride, from whom the police had obtained their name, in turn informing them as to her existence, Zipporah sees the society she lives in, her portion of it, as mirrored in this hotel.

Toward the last quarter of the century, people who can afford the St. Regis, the Pierre, and the Plaza are further identified by which one they choose. The first two, even now, do not appear in the Hotels classification in the telephone directory, being content with single-line listings as the preferred "in" places for those who expect to be sequestered in the way of guests who won't require status from where they stay. Or those who know Paris well enough to want a French gloss. The Plaza, as perhaps the best known, and the supreme for those who cluster at once-in-a-lifetime wedding receptions, has the somewhat trodden, even dusty aspect of an establishment that will take anybody. Of course by law now, all hotels must. But should you detect the faintest tinge of racial preference in all these discriminations—only of course as to where people feel most comfortable—you will not have been wrong.

As they ride up to a good high floor, her nostrils expand, sniffing out, wherever she is, the tactic of a society. The shards and piecemeal of what was once savagery. And may be, still.

This is where Lev Cohen, diamond broker, has brought his Israeli bride.

"In the money, eh?" Nanette rasps in her ear. "When I was a girl, for the announcements the Waldorf Astoria looked the best when engraved. But to whom would *he* announce?"

It's a suite. The empty array of overstuffed beige armchairs, sofas, poufs, is instantly adaptable. Meeting her, they seem to mourn. In the bay an iron-and-leather dinette set, speckless, testifies to what will never be.

Debra is bronze. A well-cut, solid face, long eyes planed toward the temples, high cheekbones, straight nose not a millimeter too near the full mouth, she is a woman, not a girl. What will prove most memorable in the many moments when Zipporah will think of her after their time together is over is those bare calves, long-muscled, brown, not manly, but with a competence seldom seen here on the female leg. She is wearing khaki shorts and shirt, her old army uniform. "Only I bought new," she will tell them, later. This is her honeymoon dress.

The three double-kiss, dare to embrace. In the Duffys' grasps, she submits, head bowed. It is half a prayer, half the European formality that elders are paid. When they all sit down her hands are clenched. They see the diamond on one, large enough to notice.

Smaller diamonds in the ears. She sees Zipporah's glance skitter there and away, puts her fingertips to the earrings. "I did not want. It is not our style. But he wanted. So I let." The hands are slim but dimpled, a rare conjunction. One sees Lev's black shag, trimmed for this day, bent over them. In the heat of a wedding guest's imagination one sees the pair grappled and complete, in the nuptial dark. These curtains, flounced with neutral drapery, have not been drawn. Nor will they be, for him. He is at the morgue.

Debra is staring at her nails, which are not added to, but long, curved, white at the tips—her own. "They aren't my style either. We laugh at the magazines. But I see he likes. So I grow them." She's biting her lip. Is it that she won't cry, or that she can't? "So now—it will be my style." It's not that she doesn't speak good English, but there's an intonation, downward, rather than up.

A knock at the door. They blanch. The management has sent afternoon coffee, tea. "Eat," they whisper to one another, "Eat."

There is a note from the manager. The police are cooperating, and will not identify the hotel in any news story. The hotel will appreciate it if she will do the same. The reception desk will protect her from the press. She may stay the week without charge. "Compliments of the Management."

"What gall," Zipporah says.

"Nah." She shrugs. "So I'll stay for free. Where I grew up, there's always a catch; we're used to it. But not Lev."

He was shot in the back, sitting in his office, doing bills, writing the boys. "The reb, their guardian; he's a stickler. In the Likud." Do they know what that is—the Conservative party? She does not wait for their reply. "But he stood by Lev once, through thick and thin." She does not further explain. "So, every Sunday, Lev wrote." From Antwerp, where she and Lev had stopped on the way, so he could show her his diamond-cutters. "So I could see that there was more than money to his business, maybe even art." And in London, they stopped also. To show her that his connections were still Jewish. Even if not him much anymore. "And to pick up the mail." Though the boys did not always write back. "That gave him *tsoris.*"

"I don't know how to spell it," Zipporah said. "But I know it means sorrow."

Today Lev had planned to skip the office. "Not to leave me, on my first Sunday in America, he said. It should belong to me." But she had encouraged him to go. "It's a dangerous business: he didn't want the boys to be in it. Even in Tel Aviv, everybody knows what Forty-seventh Street means, here." The reb made Lev promise never to carry any goods on his person. And he had not. Deposits were made at the office, everything with armed guards. The thieves had bored through the office wall from the next building, at dead of night. "Shabbos. Saturday." And had come back for the loot. "They surprised each other, maybe?"

Peter got up and put his arms around her. She beat her forehead against them. When Lev hadn't come back she had phoned the police.

"You will come home with us," Zipporah said.

No, she has to go to the morgue. "To say—who Lev is. To—claim."

It's then those calves begin to tremble. She grasps her thighs above her knees, stilling them. "In the army. We went afterwards to the battlefields. With the tags."

"I'll go with you," Peter growls.

Alone? How much must he be monitored? When should it begin? It won't be like it was with the children. Where one mustn't neuter them with over-care.

"No, Peter. Give me the phone."

At home, guess who answers? No, the party is only half dispersed. Those who've gone will get back to her. From Connecticut, from Boston, from the plane. "Who's stayed on?" The suburbans, the ones who live in town, a few elders. The women. Her children are coping with theirs. Any would come running. But who would be the best?

"No, you come, Bert. You. Go in my bureau, take all the twenties there. Couple of hundreds too . . . And listen, Bert. Come alone . . . What? . . . No, it's not to take Grandpa home . . . Just come."

So he's seen, he knows . . . I thought so.

"Soon as he can get a cab," she says, as she sits down again. She doesn't have to tell Peter whom. He doesn't ask.

They each go to the bathroom. Nobody eats.

When Bert enters, he is wearing a fedora. On the hall tree in the Duffy foyer there is always a collection of hats, in change with the seasons. This one, left by an unknown party and never called for, hangs concordance all the year. It's a serious piece of headgear, suede-black, suitable for one's first brush with mortality. Too large, though—size 27½—for most who have tried it.

Under its shadow one sees that its new wearer's skinny neck is not yet a man's, but the head is big enough not to be swamped by the dipped brim. Bert is tieless, but he's found a dark jacket in the spare room's catch-all wardrobe, which everybody raids. His shirt is white, the jeans black. In a pinch has he dressed for that prayer referred to by the bar mitzvah trainees as the *Yiskadal veyiskadash*— the *Kaddish*, quorumed only by men? The service for the dead.

"Our grandson Bert, Debra. He knows the city like a book." Always they hug, he and Zipporah. This time not. "Bert, this is Mrs. Cohen."

"He is our rabbi." In the ordeal to come, will Peter interrupt more and more? In the voice of a child? The voice of all of us in our dotage, but here like rompers on a man of sixty-three. Will she learn how to tolerate? Will he come to seem to her not an adult in decline but a precocious child, only now allowed the full virtue of his simplicity?

The woman, Debra, turns to look at him. There is a bubble at the side of his mouth. Her gaze travels to Zipporah. Quite suddenly she is in command—a familiar one, but where met? Turning to Bert, she brushes mischievously at his shaven sideburn. "A Jewish rabbi?" Her lashes lower. She could be still in her mid-twenties, a crucial ten years older than he. "Forgive me. A joke from home."

When she and Zipporah go to the bedroom for their coats they have a moment alone. Debra huddles. "That boy. The same age, give a couple years, as Lev's boys. But not lightweight... What's the matter with me, already to see this? Already to think—better that Lev did not see? When only two hours ago I am thinking that man in the morgue is not Lev."

"Nothing is wrong with you. Women make these leaps." These wild, sure conclusions that come of year-by-year watching by the hearth... But she had long since learned never to assault lay people with her references. "And you will come home with us, please. Bert can help you check out."

"You know nothing about me."

"Except that Lev chose you." Looking into this woman-girl's clear, almost mocking eyes she knows this isn't enough. "And you, him."

"What a family you must be. And to Lev—what? I think he was using you in his head for something, but I don't know how... When the police came, 'Who does he know from here?' I said: 'Friends. A *hamish* place to go.'... But not one word from Lev ever about the trouble you're in." She gestures with her head toward the room. "Him."

"We only just found out."

"Ah-h-h. Just." Her mouth sets, jaw forward, with pity.

"Who are you? I mean—what?"

The long, suave coat she swings from the bed, where it has been lying, has a small pouched collar of fine leather, as yet unsullied. Anglo-Indian bearers used to carry the "chitty," their certificate of passage, in pouches of such shape. In Zipporah's desk at home she has a cherished one still containing its small document.

This coat has the same mien. Of the finest material, it will wear like iron, in the service of military romance. Under it, Debra's khaki shorts, a shade darker, are mountain or desert utility.

Women wearing both these garments are a common sight in Zipporah's travel world. Intense sojourners, they go from break to break, and crave this as others do permanence. Finding jobs or men, or both, to feed their need for hazard, risk, jeopardy. In their company the token fashion photographer, hung with her black boxes, peering from "shades" and aping the dangerous, is mere farce, for hire. The true adventuress may carry little of record in her multi-pockets, and need not be beautiful. And may well be honest. Transactions are not the point for these quondam journalists, mountain climbers, self-starting roamers; each is waiting for her next ship to arrive. Men and women alike flock toward these persons, who of course have their male counterparts—was Lev too such a follower? The attraction being more than sexual. A sense of compliancy, one to the other. Tracking the scent of the eternal campfire, and of burning meat.

Debra, picking up what appears to be a leather briefcase or sectioned handbag, checking its contents, does not answer at first.

Be sensible, Zipporah. Her own wardrobe adjusts to her sites, *kepi* helmet to desert boots, to leg warmers, to cottons from West Africa, gauzes from Chieng Mai—and even to what her girls used to dub "Mother's smarts," for Central Park West. Whatever Debra is or was when Lev found her—for given the disparity in their ages, countries, plus Lev's needs, this surely was the way it would have been—this handsome, somewhat remote creature is still one on whom tragedy has fallen.

Yet who, delaying answer to Zipporah's question as to who and what she is, can reach out a sinewy brown hand to soothe this other victim with a touch at Zipporah's breastbone, a light pressure on Zipporah's cheek.

"I went into the army a doll-baby hairdresser. I came out a nurse."

When the four of them stand at the hotel's wide flight of steps waiting for their two separate cabs, Debra is interested in the scene

before her: the doormen, more than one, scurrying or loftily signaling while a bill is slid into their other palm; the line of limou-
sines parked without drivers; silent hearses for hire, waiting to
come alive. The stream of people, ever coming down the steps,
ever plodding up. One can imagine a man at her side, watching
how those eyes record this American crossway, this huge sinkhole
of a nation that swallows all religions but chooses none. How goes
it, her honeymoon with America?

She's wearing a battle jacket whose khaki is the same as the
shorts. Heavy for this mild day, the sleeves creased with duty and
covering half her hands, it bristles on her like a statement. She is
not wearing the coat.

When Bert comes into the apartment lugging the two heavy bags,
with Debra behind him, he is no longer wearing the hat. He must
no longer need it. He does not say whether it hangs now on a hook
over a bench in the morgue, to passersby the hat of someone who
went in to claim a body, or the hat of one who will never emerge.
Nor does he expect to be asked. There are no twigs in his hair or
slashes on his cheeks, but he is now akin to the young men who are
sent for a night into forest dark, or escorted to a mountaintop,
where, for whatever interval, they will be initiated into all the burdens of sperm—and with these secrets will return.

Debra, pale as a wraith with what has overtaken her, glides
past him like one of those white-smeared Kabuki women-ghosts
who in the legend are both the haunter and the haunted. If Zipporah had not put out a hand to stop her, she might have passed into
and through the wall.

Zipporah leads them first to the spare room, a long, large divided space cobbled together from several unneeded maids' rooms
and a connecting hall, and here and there half-partitioned. Although
it is on a level with the rest of the apartment, it serves almost like
an upper floor, eccentric as an attic, in its outlook both a guest
wing waiting for arousal and a childhood's rainy-day retreat—roller

skates here are not unknown. Zach's "loud records" corner, sound-proofed in his teens, is at one end, and opposite it at the farthest, her own storage house and retreat.

At the entry end, the spare room's closets and walls, hung with hand-me-downs too cherished to be sent off to "the thrift," are a home thrift shop for family pickers of every age, pawing for properly faded jeans or glittery tunics for a costume ball. Under the bagged garments there is a row of discarded luggage, leather now too heavy or outmoded for the airlines; hatboxes, one or two of those 1950s carry-on "vanity" cases that were once standard shower presents for brides, several Boy Scout packs, and a wicker creel.

Lev's suitcase, the heavier of the two Bert is bent under, is set there.

"You need food, Bert. See you in the kitchen."

Gratefully he goes off. She knows better than to offer to Debra. When you come from a morgue there is a clamminess in your clothing, in your marrow a chill that only the rosy sight of living flesh will annul. She leads Debra to her own bathroom, a well-stocked haven the girls did up for her one year, "for when you come in from the wild." The "wild" is scarcely that anywhere these days, or hers has become tamed, but the girls often pop in to adore their handiwork, and to the gabfests that they can easily persuade their mother to join, extra housecoats, bath tools, and a Jacuzzi being provided. To the senior Duffys, a Jacuzzi is both a middle-class show-off for those who don't have the wit for real decadence, as well as a functional bust—but there's no denying the pink-bulbed glow of affection that greets her here.

"Take a good long soak." Three white housecoats hang there, identical—another joke. "And put on one of those." She leaves Debra there. "I'll take forty winks myself—in that other room. The dorm."

Where she never sleeps, in spite of its lineup of beds. But always communes. At times still a professional visitor from abroad, suddenly immersed again in the dearest tatty details of her domestic life. Sometimes the housemother, sitting at the rolltop desk that

keeps her professional records in focus here, and staring at that
other archive in its farthest corner—those "primitives." Which
even the chastely honorable of her colleagues sooner or later bring
home. As weird as that huge canoe or that mongoose bench may
seem to the so-called civilized eye, the family rejects that survive
here, mild-mannered nothings at first glance, are weird enough
also, if scrutinized. To her they testify to both the campsite temper
and willed intensity of apartment house life.

She often posits what an Iranian and a Japanese might well whisper to one another, "Why do these Westerners so insist on getting
themselves off the floor?" For, with the exception of that side table
whose top is a chessboard, missing too many inlays for it to be sold
and pressed on the kids by Wallie's wife ("See, it's a game"), and the
heavy wardrobe in which Zipporah as a child had once hidden and
as a mother wanted to see her kids do the same, the center of the
attic is lined with beds. Former family ones, happily dumped on the
Duffys, "in recognition or reproof?" Peter joked, "of our decision
to breed? Too bad, though, they haven't been able to send us the
double beds in which, up to our generation, a lot of them would
have been conceived...We could have labeled them, for the kids."

She recalls telling him otherwise. "I think the first Jew peddlers
over here must have bought elaborate double beds the minute they
could afford. Dynasty being intended. Some families we knew still
had them." Victorian monstrosities, or later ones bought at Lud-
wig Bauman. Then they slimmed down, the people and the beds
both. But the old beds—if they could, those they kept. Even
Cousin Nettie, creeping round the huge walnut headboard crypt in
her one bedroom. "She saw her grandmother die in it. And hopes
to do the same."

A few of the beds here have identity, like that folding "salesman's cot," wood-slatted and metal-framed, with which Peter's star
salesman father barnstormed his "territory"—"up among the cold-
bottoms, upstate New York." And the Swedish pallet that had kept
her uncle Arthur's bad back in kilter, until he married a young girl.
All of the beds here are single. That's why it's a dorm.

"Mixed marriages lack legends," a rabbi her father played poker with advised her, having heard hers was imminent. "Or the division waters them down. Oh, I'm for Reform as much as any in my flock, believe me. But the Conservatives have all the legends— from the Red Sea on. They got in first. And can those sons of Israel make you feel it!" In the new rabbi's congregation, a rump group that had walked out of one of the oldest synagogues in the area, al- most every member was older than he; their choice of a spiritual leader had been limited. The assignment had been his initial one, and the verdict of the elders, "Not dry behind the ears yet, but a nice boy."

"We Reform Jews must make our own legends," her father had replied to him, "in fact here we have already begun one. It's about a rabbi who's so smart at poker you can never lose to him." He'd let this sink in. "So—you can never win." Then had touched the young rabbi on the shoulder. "David, if, as we are taught, God is omnipresent, who gets in first?"

On her way to the airport—she'd been visiting during an ill- ness of her mother's (ridden like a wave while her father's went unnoticed)—she had said: "It comes and goes, in little nudges, doesn't it. All that kind of argument." And will never be settled.

"Noodges!" her father had exclaimed in delight. "That's how it's said, how Samson Haas, our Men's Auxiliary president says it. Born in Boston, from Jews who came to Idaho no less, before World War I—and he still says to me, 'Can't we noodge you to come to the synagogue more than once a year?'. . . And how the hell do we Jews keep those intonations? I'll tell you. The same way we keep those arguments."

Just then, in the gaunt of his cheek, the waxy fixity of his eyes, was when she acknowledged how sick he must be, knowing that she was not to say. What she said came quite without thought: "The bitter herring. That was a legend we had, wasn't it?"

"The bitter herring," he'd said in wonder. "Our bitter herring, yes. A sure path to the Lord's grace."

The plane was being called. They held each other. "You have a Jewish memory," he said to her. "That will be Jewish enough."

It is still the best said to her on the subject, by anyone.

Meanwhile, down the years this room has gathered its own apocrypha of sorts from the transients who have flitted through, from school-vacationers linked to the family's out-of-town branches, to Peter's scholar visitors from abroad, to the "temps" who had subbed for Jennie when she'd had her varicoses fixed in the hospital—one of which substitutes had broken into Jennie's own sanctum next door. As excuse, that "temp" said she had been "voodooed" by that stuff heaped in the far corner, whose "power" had beamed into her head when she lay down. "When I felt a twang in my curlers, I pulled out."

A family collects such anecdotes, for airing, say, at holiday time. Perhaps to convince themselves that hilarity is what they have gathered for. The Duffys have never had that trouble. Yet Zipporah is not sure that "the helper," as that woman preferred to call herself, was altogether wrong.

Throughout her own long tenure here it has been her habit to steal in now and then, always on a particular bench, one rejected for mere storage in that far corner of known and special objects.

Spotted by her when she and Peter were on a snorkeling trip to Hawaii in their early days, it is wooden, seductively carved by tools surely primitive, has a long, uncomfortable back curved in the shape of a mongoose, and one similarly carved arm, and has remained unclassifiable, neither the wood nor the mongoose being indigenous to early Hawaii, that isle of bamboo, cattle, and deep sea. Or in this particular combo, to anywhere else. Possibly, after a lifetime of seeing how footnotes can downsize mystery, that's why she has singled it out. "Probably," Peter has said, "it was carved by a retired anthropologist."

Seated on it, she is opposite that storage where the artifacts of her devotion steadily pile, some en route to museums, some permanently hers—that is, until she gifts them to their proper place; she never sells. All have been identified. Masks are hung, their snouts, curved and snub, quietly singing to her of what they are. The largest object, a life-size carved canoe with full crew, is half upended at the prow, so that its oarsmen, alternatively hunched and upright, seem to be paddling air. Sometimes, as with any who pursue one trek, one grail, she wonders whether she is in their same situation. Sitting there, downcast or exalted, the mongoose under her arm like a mutt's muzzle comfortable for stroking, she can study whether or how she may have voodooed her life.

Once, settling in two of Peter's visiting scholars—a married couple, the man a Basque, the woman from Brittany, the pair collaborating on a critique of Jacques Maritain the Catholic philosopher—she had found them standing dubiously in front of the array of beds, of various vintages but all with new mattresses and neatly made up, as the two had just then discovered. They'd been studying how best to push two of the singles together, to make what the Italians call a *matrimonia*, their practice wherever hotels didn't provide doubles. "We do not rest well otherwise. Nor does the critique."

Raiding the linen closet for her mother's old double sheets, she had helped them make up the *matrimonia*, learning in the process that their subject, Maritain, never met and recently dead, had taught in the United States, this necessitating their stay for some months of research. Would they have to deal with such bedmaking everywhere? She had reassured them, "Just order ahead." In the discussion they had been enchanted to find that there wasn't a double bed in her house. "Never thought. We didn't have too much money when we began. And six kids." Both Peter's folks and hers had had twin beds. "We inherited them." In any case, Peter's and her nocturnal habits were different. "He reads, waking at times throughout the night. I sleep like a log." He likes a soft bed. She, hardening herself for deserts, pallets, shakedowns that must be slung well off the ground, can manage anywhere. As for sex, it was none of this pair's business that the Duffys thought a total in-bed style dull.

"Ah, you must visit us in the Midi," the man said, adding coyly that the area itself was their compromise. "Doubles in every chamber."

By then they had finished making up the grand expanse, which the old linen covered handily. "It is all a collaboration," he says. "I am a Thomist. Madeleine is not. She, like our Jacques, was born a Protestant. I am born in the faith. You would not believe what tussles we have, over the domain of reason in one's existence."

Which does not prevent them from wearing identical rings with seals as large as acorns.

"Sometimes she kicks me all the way to the edge, on my side."

"Sometimes he rolls me onto the floor, on mine."

"But it will make a marvelous book," he'd said with a grin. "Its bed is so broad."

His Madeleine had giggled. "And Jacques Maritain sleeps between."

The children had grown up with these stories, not necessarily the kind told on holidays. There is both a nakedness and a mystery to family life; its members are always balancing the two, not always unwittingly. This "nothing room," as the kids had taken to calling it—you could tell from the fondness in their faces that for them it at times held everything. In the rear, with its own back entry, and, high over the next roof, it has the apartment's one glimpse of the river to the west, as prized as if this was their porch. At times they and their friends had camped out here, bringing a supply of sandwiches, battery radio for the night, blankets, and opening the window to the east-west wind. "Hah—that's what a wind-oh is," Mickey had said. His collection of shells and meticulously cured fish skeletons is still on a stand near its sill. The final meningitis had been acquired on a Scout hike. Whenever she is at a campfire anywhere in the world he creeps toward the warmth, the flame, and sits with her.

That too is why the Duffys have stayed here, when other families with less of a brood were moving them into that spacious greenery guaranteed to produce "roots." Often so for persons like Bert's mother, who hopes by this means to wriggle out of those roots bound round her ankles by reason of birth. Have you told your mother yet, Bertram—she so pleased with my son, your father's "watered down" half Jewishness—that you may want to be a rabbi? What Bert's mother has been pushing for years is for her husband and her father-in-law to buy land in Connecticut and erect two houses on it. "Family compounds are the latest thing." And the earliest, Peter had muttered. It was Zach who had taken up the cudgels. Grown man though he is, having taken his brother Mickey's place as the youngest, long since, does he still see himself as posthumous? "We were all born in this apartment, Aunt Kitty." Although this was not strictly true, the two eldest, Erika and Gerald, had not spoken up.

All habitation is drained of history with each departing tenant, even houses that have their feet in the ground, or better yet are part of communal or legal memory. They have a trail of ownership that any title search will supply. Apartments have far frailer personae. Even when freighted with possessions for decades, like this one, though you stuff the closets as you may, and train your young to be the troubadours of reflection, one night the moon will shine in on anonymous, empty rooms—if those had a moon. The view belongs to the city, once again. All amenities in life are leased; rain against a pane, sun on a rug. Here one but senses that anonymity clearer. In an apartment one lives in rented air.

And hunts for permanence (for which read eternity, for which read religion) somewhere else? As both she and Peter have done, in their separate ways, and in these very rooms even feeling more free? Even, even, even, she thinks, hearing her own thoughts, ever qualifying. But that is—isn't it—civilization? People like us. We are civil even to God.

While from those savage enclosures left to Him, from within the brains slaughtered so that the tribute skull may hang in the longhouse, or from those farthest palisades whose only temple is cloud, the Eye follows us? Or follows her—his left-handed disciple still?

The children have never begrudged her that corner there, over the years having become incurious over what collects here, even bored. A "Do Not Disturb" sign filched from a hotel hangs on the attic's entry door with its blank side up; when she wishes to be left to herself in here she turns it around. All the routines in the family are respected; this is merely another. When she is at her desk niche, her typewriter can't be heard; it pleases her that therefore neither can her silence be. Nell, in her raging teens, once did ask, having first secured the entire family's attention: "Mom, whatever do you do in there? I mean, when you're not doing anything?" She had struggled for a plain answer, for of course she was answering herself, grateful that Nell had pushed her to it. It had come slowly.

"When you're in a household, doing the daily, you're living a plot laid out for you. No matter what else you do, or how often you leave. Everybody has it, kings and queens and tycoons, when they shut the door on the equerry, the lady-in-waiting, the personnel poop. Daily life—we're all its pensioners. It's supposed to be the subplot only. Whatever else you do is the star."

To feel your own voice wavering, in front of your children, should humiliate. It's the opposite; she has enchanted them. The human condition, that perilous equipoise we go to the Greeks for the last word on, or to the Egyptians, Sumerians, Chaldeans, Aztecs—anybody except ourselves—for a moment it passes tangibly between her and the house of her flesh. Behind the children, Peter is also rapt.

"I'll tell you what I do there," she sings out, coloratura with joy. "I—I digress."

And then they all burst out laughing.

For that is her habit, her fault line, her high-heeled scramble-ramble from Day One of their first nursery tales. She's always qualifying. Quote Jennie, who said once, "Ma'am Duffy, this a recipe you saying? Or a prayer?"

That is how they understood. And why they ignore, or never parse, the images that confront them here, whether traced on silk, gouged in teak or lignum vitae, spelled out in mosaic, lapis, or cheap Mexican silver. Here a Tuscan ex voto, in silver also, in the shape of an a eye, meant to be hung in a church, to sue for cure of a disease, blindness perhaps. Here three photos whose images seem akin, one of Navaho sand designs, one of an incised wall supposedly Etruscan, and one of the bulging retina, two feet across, of a Siva in a famous façade. Under those three is a fourth, of a tiny, orb-decorated Tibetan sandal she was unable to buy, its child possessor having no substitute.

This is the array to which her mature study has narrowed. Are the images here the insignia of godhood, or merely her signature? Some have that calm we call innocence, others that threat we call primitive. On the prow of that Papuan canoe whose crew paddles air, there is a small, incised marking. Two knobs in the wood have been taken advantage of by an added stroke above and below, creating upper and lower lids for each eye, the pupils being already in the plank of the craft.

She will not call these wooden eyes "symbols," that easy-out term used by nonvisionaries to describe what they assume other people see. The people who build such canoes are excellent river craftsmen. She has always thought of her own profession as a domestic craft also, forever sifting and relating the means by which people plod on, in which a clay pot is as good as an illusion, any day. These river craftsmen believe that the second self, the spirit one, may leave the body at night. Who then is to give a person total direction, both for the city of pursuits that is daytime and the nightime canals one must navigate? Do the two small marks serve as a hint: to see the Eye that may be overseeing you, whatever its denomination, keep your own eye peeled?

Be practical. Not merely for herself, but for those partially in her keeping. Though Peter had been included there, he has had his own sanctum, and a "private practice" he had described humbly at a commencement, in thanks for an academic award. "A spider-work, spun of other men and women's ideas. In which you can sometimes snare your own. Or hang, hamstrung." Accordingly, for her this room, where religion can become housewifery. A dorm for that storage of vision, where children too can spend the night, on what is not a porch.

She used to sit and smoke here during the earliest years, at the children's nap times, after she and those dailies who preceded Jennie had fed them their midday meal. Though she'd had no academic affiliation, and had written nothing but her thesis, she would plan trips to come. Once those had begun to be real she no longer needed the smoke rings, and without effort stopped. Once, in a wartime, when Peter, a commander in the naval reserve, was away training conscriptees and home helpers were hard to come by, she had hired, perhaps sentimentally, an older Greek woman, fat, heavy-browed, and prone to sighing, as at the interview, over the loss of her own children, whether to war, accident, or mere adulthood was not said. Whenever she sighed, the younger children shrank from her, yet she swayed them. The older children, absolved from naps by school, had shrugged matter-of-factly when consulted. "She puts pennies on their eyes, to make them dream.". . . "Why, that's what's done when people d—" Zippy had shrieked, rushing in to rescue them.

When she had let the woman go, which after a nasty session had meant sending her packing, two stringy, heavy-browed young women came for her and her belongings—ugly, intelligent Athenas who worked for the Greek consulate. When introduced as her nieces, they half-smiled; were they in truth her daughters? "Sometimes, when she and we fight, she wishes to dismiss us from her mind." They both wore crucifixes, Maltese style. When Zipporah couldn't resist telling them what the woman had made the children submit to, one said hesitantly, "The folklore can be scary, yes. But it has to be taught." The other's face darkened. "She won't go to church. We have to get her there."

When they bore the woman off, Zipporah was ashamed. Had she and her children been dipped in a mystery whose nature she should have recognized? What's here in her Amen Corner, as Peter dubs it, but signs, tokens of the halting steps and ruses by which a tribe, hers included, honors it evolution? Go farther, too personally or too blindly, and a bible and a godhead comes of that. She can't quite make such a covenant. But comes back again and again here, to mystery's wall.

There have never been enough beds here to accommodate all her brood and their current friends, at any given time. As the college generations descend upon her during their breaks, she can hear them in the front hall totting up, and is proud. "This must be what keeps matriarchs lighthearted," Peter quips. "Allow a paterfamilias to feel the same."

One old iron bedstead, almost a three-quarter (hence the tease: "Room for one more"), is the favorite here. Today Jennie has made it up fit for a bride.

"Jennie, your interest in weddings passeth understanding," Peter had said, at one of their many home receptions for such.

He never simplifies his language, for Jennie or any subordinate. That's her beloved; he has no subordinates. Claiming his phrases aren't really elaborate, only culled from that theology which the Catholics have given the world. "With bloodstained hands like all the rest."

Anyway, Jennie always sparks to such treatment. "My pleasure, Mr. Duff." To drop the "y" is her intimacy.

"Maybe we should marry you off," he'd teased.

Jennie's reply has created yet another family anecdote. Maybe watching the balances here, she had copied those. The Duffys are nimble at avoidances. Or the half-breed children she had cared for had taught her their breezy language?

"Who'm I going to find the opportunity here?" she'd sparked. "At those churches?" The aunts, aware she'd been born in a Catholic country but not whether she'd been christened, had volunteered to take her to mass, her reply being that she preferred "the mix at home," which Aggie had received as insolence.

"Weddings?" she'd said this time. "I can see hands down why a man would marry a Joosh woman, neither having the religion too hard. What I can't see is any woman, me nor any, marrying a too good Joosh man." Then with a shoulder hitch reminding them how handsome she still is, "Find me a mix; that could do it. Maybe I'll ask that Shine to hunt me one up."

Beds. Statements, each of them. That silly French couple were right. No home is safe from such statement. Nor any family safe from making them. This Debra, who has been on the battlefield, what does she think of ours?

This bride, shot down to widow. Who is taking so long at her bath.

On the way there Zipporah doesn't let herself hurry. She is a mother who has had dramas. Though she's still slender and high-heeled, her breasts have swollen enough to hold the day a son was brought home with a baseball-mashed eye. To weather the moments a politically brash daughter had been under threat in a foreign jail, and other humdrum surprises. If her waist is still lithe, this is in part due to certain forest horrors she has bent to, touched, fled from, but carried inside forever after, in recoil. To counter those are the mountain niches stretched toward, which a body can sometimes hold onto, in recall.

So she walks measuredly down the long hall.

On the way, passing the living room, she sees Peter and Bert, asleep on the long sectional sofa at the far end, one on each side. The sofa is the recent gift of certain family members, in response to the room's lack of plushy chairs, and in louder tribute, "For your anniversary." Peter had at once dubbed it "The Cliché," and his prediction that the dullest conversationalists in the group would make it their haven had since been fulfilled. What she sees now is a cliché also: a man and a boy asleep, with over fifty years and their separate perils between them.

At her bathroom door she stops. Once the three bathrooms here had tumbled with cherubs at their water games, from which a ceiling in the apartment below had at Easter time fallen in. "On *Shavuot!*" the wife of the childless pair below had screamed over the house telephone. "And with our house full of California. Why don't you at least pack those brats off to *schul!*" The pair seemed not Orthodox, but of a kind known among the Duffys as "high-powered observers," a careful notch below the ultra-Conservative. On the high holy days they rode down in the elevator stiffly, "showing the satin" as Jennie reported—and the wide-rimmed homburg. Partners in a publicity firm for charities whose patron members must be nurtured, their use of their home for waves of business visitors at these times had already caused the co-op concern. Peter, remarking on the springtime consonance between Christian and Jewish holy days, had said, "I see the clients, Jewish like them no doubt, grouped at the mantelpiece like those expensively forced Easter flowerpots. And we help water them."

Strange, to stand at what is now her own bathroom, as Peter too has his, and wonder whether to knock. Reminiscent of the teenage and college periods when one had to monitor for serious smoke and even sex. She neither romances these periods nor feels relieved of them. Each is a stratum of her own riches. She knocks.

No answer. Knock. No answer.

"Debra? . . . Debra!"

She opens the door.

The young woman is asleep, her hair floating, chin just above the deep tub's waterline, the long, slender body lucid below.

At a touch she scrambles up and out, eyes mazed—a girl's. Then—how quickly awakened!—a woman's. "Dear God. I worried you. Sorry." A headshake, hands clasped at her crotch. "I couldn't. I don't drown well." A grimace, as if at fault. "But how to mourn him? How?" She slaps a cheek, then the other, both dry. Reaching out, she touches Zipporah's cheek, the left one, the right. "Maybe you'll know."

Above the thighs the naked body is a slope of white, the breasts pear-shaped. Once again, Zipporah sees Lev there, head bent. Or lying sated, agape.

"You don't ever know how. You go through it."

The head hangs. The knuckles beat the forehead, rapidly then slow, as if to learn.

Zipporah whispers, "But you never quite learn how."

She is embraced. This is a caring embrace, she thinks—one that has been learned. Yes, this is a nurse.

When she is released she says, "Maybe in Israel you will heal? Back among your beliefs?"

"No." A harsh one. "I came away from that. With him."

"Ah, we do," Zipporah says. "Any marriage. Is a coming away . . . And—" She stops short.

"And he, came away with me? That what you were going to say?"

She won't deny it. This one wants the harsh. "And you are left . . . Have some hot milk."

Her hand is taken. "Ah, you really are Jewish."

"Who said not?"

"Not—" Lev. She cannot say it.

"Here. Take a robe."

They pass through the living room. Bert's gone. Not home yet, not him. No doubt in the kitchen, following his insatiable body. In the young such a pure direction. Selfless later, it can change the world. If greedy—it can change the world.

Peter is lying there alone. The bedroom light is mostly soft. Here, with a ceiling light left on, it is cruel. He is a handsome man in the Irish style, or one of those, the aquiline, not the snub. And he has been a lucky one. From the earliest snapshots to the earnest high-school cabinet portrait, this is as plain as when she and he met. People don't resent Peter's good looks. Living with it she has seen how, with no conscious effort, and from more than his lack of vanity, he disarms. Not by a total goodness, which can irk. Nor from that bright arc of "soul," or "charisma," which can make one feel left behind. Whatever it is, looking at him, she prays that this will not be lost. He has never won by appearance alone. Now, may he have to?

What perhaps only she as yet sees is—a waning. A blurring. Though the outline of the lips is there, even redder, and the features the same, there's—don't think about it. This is not aging, or not as we know it. He seems as young, as he was yesterday? Younger. Displaced by that. Wrong. "Don't project," the doctor had said tersely, "what you fear his state will be. We—none of us— have data to do that. People differ, as to the state of decline. According to what they have been, some suspect. But to collate that with the physical, impossible. Don't lie in wait for it." His heavy brows connected like a verdict. He looked over his shoulder, as if about to counsel evil. Or, as she says to herself now, as if his ancestors were looking at him. "Don't feel guilty—when you can no longer stick with it."

But she will. Stick with it.

Debra is staring down at Peter. She looks up, searching. "You know?" At the nod her chin lifts, in the crisp remote manner the medical have. They don't adopt it. It adopts them. "I was in neurological once. Civilian cases as well. And in London once, before that, to train."

Peter has removed his shoes. Or Bert has. The soles of his feet are upturned. His socks don't match.

As she and Debra pass the linen closet she remembers that Sunday as if Lev stands there. Not his doppelgänger; no weird visitation. His smile, as if there are humors you and he share. One of those men who take women seriously. Or rather, arrowing straight to any person, regardless of sex. Was she herself a little in love with him? No, no aura of that. But there are those who enter one's life instantly. Who, if they absent themselves, will move in your mind like shades still flesh-and-blood, only at a distance that may at any moment dissolve.

"Lev—" she says.

The pale mask at her side opens, shuts. He is hers.

"He left something with me." Why must she tell this now? Of all times now.

"His wife's ring. He told me. When he gave me mine. . . . Diamonds. They kill people. I was always afraid for him."

"There was also a packet. Valuable. To be kept for him. But not

in a safe. 'Maybe for the boys? he said, 'when they reach twenty-
one. Or for that rabbi who keeps them. For him most of all. But
not now.'"

"Keep it without an address," he'd said. "It'll be my luck."

But that she can't repeat. Now that she knows his luck.

"Ah, him. Lev's mentor. And enemy." She could be looking at
that man across a room not this room. "If it is diamonds, yes, send
him." She glances at her left hand. "I am provided for."

"I was to hang onto it unopened. I have."

She looks stricken, like in the fairy tales, at some omen. "Always he bets on people . . . Oh, Lev." She puts her face in her hands.
Rock, rock. Yes, that's the way a lost name should be said.

In the dorm Jennie has already set out the milk, covered and
warm.

"Please drink."

Obediently she sips, staring at the turned-down bed sheet with
its unwieldy hand-crocheted border. "You have a house for brides."

"Those sheets always make me think of hymens," Zipporah had
said to her mother, when the pile of them was pressed upon her.
"These are top sheets," her mother had said coldly. "And pillowslips."

Two per bed. And Jennie has complied.

Some of her granddaughters expect linen dowry. Some reject.
Though they're putting her in her place, she's begun to favor the
latter—yet fears for them. Is it better to see through the artifacts?
Or best to accept them?

What Debra does will not be classified, now or later.

After setting her cup in the tray, her hands begin slowly to
wring, as if being taught this. The voice is not quite a wail but has an
edge and a rhythm, grudged. "The head not wrapped . . . He was not
shot there . . . Only the body . . . in the winding sheet . . . The face still
his own . . . but sealed . . . One ankle sticks out. Bare. Bare. Bare."

What's she intoning? The service for the dead, as allowed to
women?

She falls on her knees in front of Lev's suitcase. Smooth old
brown leather, what some call a valise. Big enough for much more

than overnight. The tassel of the borrowed robe's belt catches in its lock. She nods, as if this is in order. "Your ankle had a cord on it. They have tagged you, my love. You have been tagged."

What she says next must be in Hebrew. Her spread arms enfold the suitcase. Face pressed to one side of the lock she breathes, not a sob, not a moan, a rhythm . . . thm . . . mm. She is asleep. Or sleeping with him.

Zipporah pulls the coverlet off the bed and puts it over her.

Bert's in the kitchen, waiting for her. He's waited so long that he has washed whatever dishes he used and dried them. "I put him in your room to rest," he says in a rush. "He needed it. On his upper lip there's a smear of chocolate. He bites it away. "I mean, he needed to be put." Bert is a boy who corrects himself, a process endearing to watch. Sometimes heartbreaking. He's not referred to Peter in the usual way: Gramps. Mark him as the first to refer to Peter in that collusive way we do with the ill. But he has done it in her hearing, directly. In return, she will not lie to him.

"He is not well. Unwell, severely. Nothing we can change. Or operate for. We can only follow his needs."

When he has absorbed this, he says, "Is it from getting older?"

How soon, for this boy to ask.

"Partly. Sooner than some. And not pretty to watch."

"I would watch. But you are taking him away."

"That's why. You would watch with love. But not everybody would. Not for long."

He takes this in.

"So Bert, we'll make our getaway." She's able to grin at him. "Mine."

"Ah, Ma," he groans. He calls her that, now and then. His mother likes to be first-named.

"So this is between us."

"You—you aren't going to put him away?"

This is the family phrase, sotto voce. These days, the congregational voice also ... In her grandparents' day the family misfits were kept at home. The senile of course, as the ironclad duty that would be paid you in your turn. The crippled; this went without saying. (If you a little paraded your pity, in the daily wheelchair walk, or the waiting on at the table, who would gainsay?) As for the mild sweeties, not too hard to keep that covenant. Hard lines to keep the idiots, but even that was done, the public alternative not being possible for one of yours. One of ours. And this was done by rich or poor. In the days when Jews commonly referred to one another as "one of the faithful." When the interchange between family sentiment and communal approval was constant. When it was still taken for granted that these were identical.

So, Zipporah, humble yourself. The ego-shock is a blow, but bracing. Even a comfort, to have the past reach for you like a paw. You're not doing this crazy thing merely out of love.

"No. Not ever. Even if they say I must."

"I'll help," he says. "Promise to call."

She weeps on the shoulder of this tall child.

When that's over he says, "I better tell you about her."

As he speaks, a glow comes from him. Debra has leaned on him, but decently.

"You ever been in a morgue, Ma?"

"In France once, my junior year. Six of us went on a bike trip. My friend—my friend Cora was killed. I had to—"

"Identify." He chokes up.

"Coldest places on the planet. Even the Great Wall in the high wind isn't as." And in a morgue there is no wind. "But so well-managed—grisly. At least in France." What else had she expected? Bodies tumbled in a vat? As in accounts of the plague years?

"Here too, right. They didn't want to release. The body."

"Autopsy?"

"No. He was clean, they said. 'Clean.' And he was. They come down slow, motorized. Behind a window. I wanted to do it for her—identify. But she says, 'No. I have to see.' So then we both. He's like hanging there, wrapped, looking at us. One foot bare.

You kind of see what quiet is. And yeah, that anybody gets tagged. So then she goes to the desk. 'It's him.' And the sergeant there says, very respectful, 'You have your passport, Mrs. Cohen? Your husband had his on him.' And she says—Ma, she says, 'I am not Mrs. Cohen.'"

In shock, she looks over her shoulder. "Excuse me." Running back to the dorm, she cracks the door. Still asleep, the face upward now, one arm still sprawled across the valise. The coverlet has slipped to the floor. Creeping in, Zipporah pulls it over her, runs back to the kitchen. "Who is she?"

"Wait."

Bert's father, her son Gerald, raises his hand the same way. Works fine, in a court of law. Does the kid know he's doing it? She says what she said to his father at that age, and still does. "For God's sake, spill."

"'It's a shooting,' the sarge said. 'Sorry about it, lady. We don't pry. But we got to have solid identification. And not from nobody in the diamond trade.'... I volunteer. But he says what you all say."

"Ah, Bert. What's that?"

"'You're tall for your age.'... So, Debra, she's like on her high horse, y'know? But still in a dream. So I'm thinking, who in the family could fix this, with just one phone call?... Guess."

"Your father? Uncle Zach?"

"Maybe they could have. But Dad's in Washington. And Zach's not always easy to find. But who has the portfolio even, of the Pee Aye Ell—PAL?"

"Search me. What is the—PAL?"

"Policemen's Athletic League. Y'know, every year they solicit for their annual ball? And whose mug do you see in the papers, every year, at that ball? Who buys their tickets; they all do, lawyers, but like he actually goes?"

"I'm very tired, Bert. Who?"

"Wallie. With a couple of phone calls he fixed it. He didn't even have to come down."

Wallie. Of course. Whose "push" awes us, and annoys. She sees the starched cuff reaching for the phone.

"You did well . . . Ah, Bert."

"Yeah."

They smile.

"You're, yeah, tired," he says.

She sees he has more to tell, and his sweetness. "Go on."

"The route is—the body has to be picked up by an undertaker. I know the outfit our crowd mostly uses. But maybe not for her. She wants it plain, she says. Only not Orthodox. So I don't call the yeshiva. They would grab him, put him in the pine box, that same-day stuff . . . So I call you-know-who. He's like the ragbag of city savvy; he says you're like him, you have that advantage." Bert's eyes narrow, maybe with something of the same. "So I don't mind asking him, like for a family emergency. I did like that once, for him."

Bert is across a divide, in teenage country, those years when a friend and you know where each of you is every hour of the day. She used to keep track of her own brood that way; she knows it well: it's snake-path geography.

"The Shine," she says.

"He knew just where to go."

Lev is now at a mortician's in East Harlem. They had stopped for arrangements on the way here.

"It's plain, honest. I see myself it has the right tone." Bert is his mother's son there. "But it has to take anybody. It's poor. So Ma— I gave them your hundreds. All of them, except for the cab fare. Which was a lot." He is his father's son also. As her and Peter's eldest, Gerald has known the penny pinch; in spite of earned riches, he excuses himself on that score. "But Debra tips big," their son is saying. "She can well afford to, she says; she'll pay back. Lev settled money on her here; she only needs to claim. But Lev had all the real cash on him."

A marriage settlement without a marriage—why?

He's bursting to tell her.

"Never mind, Bert." This is not the time to pry.

"No, she told us. In the cab. Shine got her to. He says—if he's gay, it's his obligation. To be extra sympathetic to women. Where me, I come by it naturally." His mouth quirks.

Ah, he can laugh. Not all her brood can. She sometimes wonders whether those with the lack may get it from her. In the women's colleges of her time there had been a high seriousness, safely enmeshed in the Latin and Greek classics. Some of the New England places, early adulterated by sport in bloomers, were more median. As a "Cliffie," from a Radcliffe fatally linked to Harvard, how could she help having a streak of that high radicalism often accompanying the ethic that considers itself the best? Add to it the New England "commonness," a moral tone some Americans consider smug, or even staple comic. So it was that she only became aware of her birthright of Jewish humor in the sly company, always curdling with shrewd social fun, of some Jewish classmates from the South. "Yo' mental la-ahf so hah en mahty, up yere," the smartest one, Lee Esther, said to her. "We Hebrews down ho-ome jess as chosen as you-all; we jess doan shayah the sigh-em diptho-ong." Only pointing out to her the exalted seriousness the two of them shared?

Sleep assails her, as it always does when she's lulled by that dialect. Perhaps it's in the way they know how to say "home"?

"Have to close me eyes a bit, Bert. Forty winks." She does.

He knows her habit, that energy-saver. At Bert's age her Charles, whose fate would be to command full attention only from the planetary system, had complained: "She's not on trek; why do that here? We were talking about my major." She had dimly heard Peter say, "This is the family trek." She'd later apologized to Charles, whose need to discuss shouldn't have been scotched just because he'd had his "major" circled in red on his brow ever since his first telescope.

Bert, who pays attention to others—one can't be sure yet whether as a game or a grace—raids Jennie's cupboard, every dodge of which he's onto, and munches contentedly at Zipporah's side.

Slumbering now, yet not quite, she's out in the field, among tribes where sessions of ritually exchanged laughter are often in order. To show that neither side is a threat. Or to get something. At either of which she does quite well. It's not for nothing that after hours of bargaining, a headman can dig you in the ribs. Assisted perhaps by the local wine. And because they really do not consider her a woman. There's that of course. Rather, according to each region, a sibyl, a missionary, or the white devil's companion freak.

That threesome in the cab—extraordinary? Or merely part of what Peter dignifies as that stream of random events which can as powerfully affect life, or a universe, as those events in which we discern a cause? In her travels, the haphazard, brutal yet marvelous, is the amalgam she glimpses everywhere, that excuses what she is. Toward that day, ever accelerating, where there won't be anthropology anymore? Not as it now condescends to the "primitive," even as that vanishes. To clock the general amalgam will have to be enough. As maybe those three Raphael angel-babes awhile ago at her knee will be burdened with.

She's dreamed off a bit. Bert has waited. Trust. Peter has taught him that.

"So, who is she?" she says, sitting up.

He's brimming with it. "She's the wife of that reb who's the legal guardian of Lev's boys. An arranged marriage, when she was eighteen. After the army, she never went back to him. But she'd known the boys when they were little, and kept on visiting them. Where she met Lev...Now, she can't get her divorce. The reb wishes to remain the injured party. That's weird, isn't it? And he won't release the boys from his authority—but that she approves. Until they do army, she says...Then they can go."

And it's then, she thinks. That I'm to send the packet he left. Or when their service is finished? When they attain that majority we no longer ask of our boys.

"Must they?"

"Dunno. That reb—maybe he's brainwashed them. We kids here never got to know them. They were always stiff with us."

"Libby's kids," she says, with a flash of family ownership. "Surely the Boston side will have authority."

"Oh, can you?" he says with a rush. "Notify? We think she told us—because she hoped we'd tell *you.*"

She smooths his cheek. The haircut is quite ordinary, in these times a feat.

"'The Funeral Parlor,'" he says, "that's what it says above the door. They wanted to know which cemetery. She said no, to burn him . . . That's what she said. 'Burn him.' But to give her the ashes. They said that's routine. But she would have to wait for them. But Shine says, 'No. I'll wait.' Like he's the headman. And she bows, takes his hand, takes mine, like for a minute we three are in prayer. Then she says to bring her here."

So that was the ceremony. Her forearms are shivering.

"Is cremation legal with them over there?" he whispers. "The Orthodox? Or is it still the pine box?"

"Can't say." It may be the desert still. "It is with the—the rest of us." Which is how they over there make us feel. Or intend to make us feel. Her hostility surprises her.

"I have one more yeshiva class this term. I'll ask."

"You two going to keep on with it?"

"Not the Shine—uh, Wole. He wants to be called that now. He's thinking of crossing over."

"He is? . . . You don't say." To what? She considers. Not to Jesus, surely. "Oh. Bert. Not—skin."

"Him?" A chuckle. "Ma. He likes his skin. He says it works for him."

"So. So what's he . . . Ah."

"Uh-huh. Girls."

She mustn't laugh. During the teens it's not boundaries one sees, but alternatives. In the Philippines a seventeen-year-old with a fine tenor says to her again, "I go to Manila to be in the opera chorus, I must speak Tagalog. But down here in Cebu even the lizards speak Visayen. So maybe I'll be a biologist."

So she isn't monitoring herself and says absently, "Bully for him. Some of your girl cousins, aren't *they* a fast lot."

She's shocked him. They forget what she does; she neglects to license her tongue. "Sorry, it just slipped out. And Gramps—ordinarily he would never have mentioned your confidence."

He is pink. "I don't mind . . . Except—about him . . . Ma. Let me go with you two. I could be your legs, your go-for. And I'm already a year ahead at school . . . I want to help."

"I know." Is he to be one of those born with more pity than he will be able to handle in some worldly way? Dealt his lot by her son Gerald, the worldbeater, and a mother who needs nobody except everybody—a salon-keeper whom only the unwounded charm.

"Ah, Bert. What would be in it for you—I know. But for what life owes your age—what?"

"Travel."

He'd be such an honest rabbi. Performing hard at the altar of a dogma he only hopes to accept? She's always thought of him as Peter's heir; maybe he's part hers? "Where do you imagine we're going?"

"All the places you've been, like you used to tell us when you got home. Cape Horn, the Trobriands, the Prince Edward Islands. That village in South India with the endless name. Or Sikkim." He grins. "The folks think you make them up. 'The little kingdoms'— like you say in your book. 'Where the Eye of God hasn't shrunk to a squint.'"

He's looked them all up on the maps. As he names each place, spieling on in an alphabet of what to her is actual valley, familiar alp, she hears what is really sounding. A requiem.

"Bert. There's no place in the world now you can't get a guide to. Not always a courier, like the travel agents supply. But some linkage, from whoever's been there before. Which was sometimes— me. But all the noble savages, they're wired now. Or about to be."

That kind of "anthro" is dead. Where you blew into town, theirs, like out of their legends, working spells that stunned, and

with a news-gathering voracious appetite that could corrupt itself
daily. For which you, as well as they, would pay. By pretending it
was not all over. Or else saying it was—to academic grantland.

To be a science-killer, you don't get paid for that. So she had
later on funded her own trips. Peter had always been lavish with
the children, if only to establish them, they never questioning from
what cash reserve. Gerald's finances, she suspects, are always
stretched, on show. Zach, who makes all kinds of money from the
mergers of art, lets it purl through his fingers, endowing women
and other objects of virtue indiscriminately.

She wants never to ask anything of them, willingly as they
would all give.

Meanwhile the old apartment, lumbering along, all its joints
creaking like some outmoded ship of state, costs more and more
to maintain. At any moment she would be wise to sell; in the future she would likely have to. It's an ordinary story, happening all
along no doubt, and more indigenous to America than other countries she could name. And had less to do with money and wealth
than supposed. Or even whether a job or a profession dies.

Here the ship goes into dry dock once the young crew leaves.
Here the elders go out of the family, whose circle is no longer there
to tend. If there's money, to Florida, or the cruise; if not, to some
medical hilltop where one may neatly die. They go where you can
visit them. If you do.

How familiar it is, a kind of cultural annuity that at around age
fifty you are taught to expect. As the natural coming together—or
coming apart—of your "cultural" and your "industrial" life. Along
with a bit of news still classifiable as tribal? Those Semites—for
whom Honor Thy Father and Mother was once maybe the commandment most easily and formally kept out of all ten—well, it's
happened too, among the Jews.

"They have to sell the apartment," that group at the mantel
will have calculated. "It's time." Nobody's caught on to any other
reason for going, certainly not Norman, for whom their finances

will be prime. With luck, and if Peter and she get out soon enough, nobody will.

She wants to tell somebody; why not this boy, already endangered by family but enlightened too? "Depend on the custom of the country, Bert, if you have something to hide. Or somebody."

That agonized grimace on him, how shamefully it salves her. "I'll tell you what, Bert. To be fair and square, I'm going into hiding for me too."

"From what, Ma?"

"An ending." She shrugs it off like a scarf. "The ending, merely. Of my professional life." She manages to laugh. "Ah, that'll take another book to explain. Thanks for reading me, by the way. I never dreamed you had."

"We got shafted at yeshiva. Me and Wole. He's read a lot on that subject. Being him."

She can't help bridling. "And what's his opinion?" Being him."

"He says: The jungle—your crowd makes it up. According to what suits it best. You're innocents."

A jaw drop converts easily to a smile. Luckily she's done it often. Are those tears in Bert's eyes? "No sweat, Bert. Actually it's bracing. To have you interested. I did want to visit some of those places. Once again. And with him. But I've come to grips. He can't. So—a new itinerary. Starting out in Italy." Maybe they at home will write the two of them off like a travel agent would, as a pair of those late-in-the-day suckers for beauty. "We're going from spa to spa. I've begun to book." Hiding best among other seniors of dubious health. And if objected to in one place, on to the next.

"What's a spa?"

It's at the other end of life; you need have no truck with it. But she relents. "A health resort. And you? Still aiming for the seminary?"

He seems to grow an inch as she watches. Like one of those slowed videos on the growth of a flower. "The Theological? A great place. You walk there, you could even believe."

Though she had never walked there, that neighborhood, that

hill was once hers; she had been one of its denizens. To those, a university's air can smell like rows of lettuce plants with dew on them, even on a gassy city street. When what you are is half what you are going to be. And when any person met is part of your destiny.

She and Bert hug. But looking beyond her, shifting those clodhoppers, he doesn't go.

"She'll want to thank you, Bert. But right now I don't want to disturb her."

"Where will she go?"

"Who knows? . . . We'll try to keep her with us for a bit. I'm sure she'll want to thank you and . . . Shine. Wole."

He brushes that aside. "She was so decent to us. In the midst of it all. And so strong. She believes. You can feel that. She—" His eyes widen, looking past Zipporah.

Debra is there, the white robe clutched to her. "I heard voices. I thought . . . maybe your friend was back with the—."

"Tomorrow," he said. "They don't do it there."

"We watch our dead," she says. "I should go back."

"They got in paid watchers for the night. I saw them. A woman and a man."

Debra lays her right cheek on his right cheek, her left on his left, with a whispered thanks.

"Sh—Shine will call about the time tomorrow," he stutters. "I got to go somewhere with my brother. So . . ."

Half of Zipporah's brood knew early how to duck out of a situation; half never seemed to know how to leave. Whether it was merely a social talent, or had something to do with being Jewish and concerned about responsibility, she can't say. But Bert is surely of the second kind.

"Shalom, then," he says.

"Shalom." She is already gone.

What a useful word! With a host of meanings suitable to the situation. A greeting, a blessing. A good-bye.

He may not know for years that he had fallen in love with her. Or that she knew.

"Byron on probation again?" Zipporah says.

And Gerald, the father, on business somewhere, Kitty ready to flame with punishment. Or to subside to the usual intercessor, with a relieved sigh.

Bert grins. "Not yet."

She has an urge to call him "rabbi," but that would be to twit. "Just call me like always," she says. "To you I'm not Zoe."

When he goes, with a backward glance not for her, she is what she's never been. Least of all in those hamlets, arid or lush, but to her alertly footnoted senses already thronged with pre-beings. Before the actuals, the living populations, appear.

She's adrift. Arms hanging, feet uncertain. Alone. In her own house. He's right; she'll need company. Not just a go-for. A be-there. To turn to. To check with. Another witness.

What I need is a nurse.

W hat is this—this hegira?" Norman says to her three months later. "A trip you said once might be round the world for all you knew, but now has no itinerary that I can make out . . . So I bought this place from you. So I drew up a new will for Peter and you, leaving most not to your fine grown-up heirs, but to a boy who will just about attain his majority in a few years—when with God's blessing you two will still be extant. So I will put all the sale money not in investment but at the ready, for you don't know what yet . . . So I have done all this. But in order to cheat you—which I will still do, by God, to save you two from your own craziness—how can I, without knowing where you will be from day to day?"

She looks at him, this man who exorcised his sub-immigrant glottal vowels when he went to Harvard but when he speaks to her drops back into that New York lilt. One she never had, but finds herself joining. "Norman. Why do we use these words like they belong to us? Like we are their origin? . . . I looked up 'hegira.' Because you already said it to me. A word from my own childhood that I thought belonged only to us, and our wanderings . . . And want to know where it started? From the trip Mohammed made from Mecca to Medina, my dictionary says—six hundred something A.D. Mohammed, mind you."

But he is never dashed. "So try now Exodus. In the Old Testament. Out of the land of Egypt. Us Israelites. To some place we don't get thrown out. Took a long time."

"Israel. A place you give to, Norman. But have never been to. Now that you don't need?"

"You don't even give." Doing their small investments, a mutual fund here, a bond or two there, no stocks, knowing they will insist on paying him, he always slyly asks for a contribution to a fund for Israel of which he is the chair. She and Peter always switch it to a charity here. Nondenominational.

"No. We don't. Now that it's throwing other people out."

He is lighting a cigar. Three a day now, down from five. "I'm old-style, Zippy. Nonconfrontational." He snaps off the lighter flame. "Just leave us the capital *H* in Holocaust, okay?"

"Sorry. The O.D.—*Oxford Dictionary*, not the Old Testament, lists 'holocaust' lowercase. For a massacre by Louis the Seventh of France, of thirteen hundred persons. In a church."

The cigar hasn't lit. She has ruined it. "You. Must you live by looking everything up?"

Our life, he means. Jews who may not "observe," as the lingo goes, but are not yet lax about identity.

"I won't!" she cries. "That's partly the trip. I have a chance— maybe a last chance—to bring my life, and what I only know from study, in line."

Is it significant he doesn't ask how? So far, Peter hasn't too visibly declined. But Norman, who now presses his two extra daily smokes on anyone he can find, no longer does so to him.

"That Debra," he says. "When I offered my two extras around one night, but not to her, she said, 'I'll have,' and lit one. All proper. And smoked it to the end. Said she learned how in the army, but the habit didn't take. I asked her what else she learned that was out of the way; she said, 'To dare.' I said, 'I can't see you as only the hairdresser you say you were.' Though she's done wonders with Jennie's hair."

He's fishing. She's asked Debra not to reveal that she's a nurse.

"You don't approve of our asking her to come along?"

She's careful nowadays to say "we," "our." The one noticeable change in Peter, to anyone used to him, is that he avoids statements, lacks opinions, that wash of his commentary, smooth as pebbles one prized because they came from an ocean floor.

"On the contrary. Why not? Our age, we begin to crave the company of anybody from the young. To bring in what we ain't no longer. And she's got a head on her, that lady. The insurance? For what Lev had in the safe, and what he owned personally and what he didn't, she told us where to find. All that . . . And good intentions toward Lev's boys. She would only take so much of what Lev left her. Such a little. 'Because you haven't been around long enough?' I asked her. 'You're a wife in the courts, you're a wife in Heaven, too.' And she gave me the damnedest—" The second cigar puffs on. "She said, 'Jews don't expect a heaven. Good Jews, or bad.'" He sighed. "These Sabra women, the ones born there, they scare the daylights out of me. My dentist has one—the hygienist. I said to her, 'Seems like I spit an awful lot of blood, this process.' And she says, quiet as a mouse, or a cobra, 'You should.'" He laughs.

She does too. "Oh Norman. She had your number."

"Come on. To them, what's wrong with us is we never had any of those numbers on the wrist. From the camps . . . Anyways, I say to Debra, 'Lev wasn't maybe much of a Jew. But he wasn't a bad one.' And did she give me my come-uppance."

Cigars are anecdotal for men of Norman's generation—and fraternal, of course. "How?"

"She howled, 'Lev wasn't a bad anything' and rushed from the room—and then rushed back in. Like on a beeline." Norman is smoothing a glossy shoe-tip on the rug, though no ash has dropped there. "And snarls at me, 'Why don't you break down and marry Jennie?'"

The rocker she's sitting in almost dumps her. Keep the feet on the floor . . . Under our noses, that's the first shock. Then this immediate proprietary jealousy, as for a chattel thought to be owned. Think rather of Jennie, having to frolic all these years with this shrewd tub of pomp, its pomaded remnant of once-chestnut curls brushed forward from the crown. "My mother was one of those red-haired Austrian Jewesses," he would sigh. " 'Tales of the Vienna Woods.' How she enjoyed."

"All these years, Norman?"

He bucks, chin backed against his striped collar. "Of course not. Only since Sarah died."

These Sarahs, Rachels, Leahs, Hannahs—or those already as-sumpted into Carolines, Marjories, Dorothys, as the old nomen-clature faded along with orthodoxy—they had been wives secure in their pride. Whatever their solid wage-earner husbands did when they were "working late" or "at the Harmonie Club," it would be some concubinage that those achievers and donors of double-row pearl chokers and diamond dinner rings must be per-mitted; their cautious husbands would not be caught with whores.

"In our apartment, Norman, or yours?"

He rears again. "Mine, of course. What do you think?"

"What do I think? Only ... how neighborly. How Norman comes to us for dessert."

He flushes, but a smile edges both their mouths. She was raised in a circle of "uncles," related or not, maybe only merchants downtown, but in the family still seigneurs. Who, if they were increasingly subreligious in various ways, could be heard blam-ing this on a country where one could not—had best not—be aristocrats.

"So give me your opinion, man of experience. Why shouldn't we provide occupation to this suddenly bereaved young person? Getting ourselves a secretarial bargain, besides." She finds herself rocking to this rhythm; careful. Pull the wool over his eyes, maybe. But don't burlesque. "Or do you think—that Peter? Might get the hots for her?"

He is at once solemn. "You have such a good heart, Zippy." Which means he has never found her sexy. "I never seen Peter play the field, not in all the times you are away." A faint lip-lift of dis-paragement here. Of Peter? "But let me say—" His fingers make a steeple. "In your profession you get used to strange arrangements, that is all. No one in the family thinks for a moment. Only they are concerned that outsiders may talk. I tell them they are *meshugeneh*—nuts. That a top star in any profession gets it in the neck. Like that *Images of God* fuss."

"Mmm."

"That was pretty near the skin for some of your own family, right? Like the older cousins, your mother's side, I heard you yourself say: Only two generations Harvard, and already so paled out they could be direct heirs Ralph Waldo Emerson. Not that they would deny Jewish. Only they didn't like to be reminded . . . Or out on the Island. Where they like to keep a low profile."

"Mmm."

"Don't *mmm* me. Open your ears. I tell them, 'That Debra girl—she's just one of those—look at your own kids, these days. They come from good stock, they won't do just anything. They just want to do everything.' But that don't go down. Who was I to speak, I don't have kids." Norman is carried away now by his own rhythm. "Wallie was the ringleader; he said out loud what *ree-ally* bites them; you recall he's the head this winter of the Roslyn-area Appeal? Wallie said: 'She's like all of them over there, those young Israeli snots. One hand out for the mazuma we send them. A little back-scratching, even, when we bring. The other thumb up the nose.'" Norman thumbs his armpit, a relaxation not seen since old Nettie cracked at him, "You feeling for the scissors, Norman; your father was a tailor maybe?" He chuckles. "And you know, since that streak Wallie's on, the market boys are about taking him serious." He chuckles. "Only just before he thumbs his nose, he—" Norman shoots a cuff.

Saved by the gong, she thinks. Of our own jokes. Our ever-intramural jokes. Against ourselves.

From the kitchen there's the sound of chopping, then the blender; the door must be wide. Jennie likes to be heard. Especially when there are guests. This guest? "Tell me. Does Peter know about you and Jennie?" She's sure not. Disloyal even to ask.

What's with this sudden withdrawal, this glance away? "These days—maybe for some time now, hard to say what Peter knows." He regards the view, slaps his thigh. "You detach a man from his lifework, such a deep thinker, a college should weigh that responsibility. On the other hand, that honor he got—maybe a man retires best at the peak."

A silence. "Or a woman," he says then. "That name business. You want to pull out, you should be allowed."

So, the sly old fox. Into the grapes. Yet—a loyalist.

"Thanks, Norm. Knew you'd see it straight."

"You're welcome." Expanding, he starts to kiss her, thinks better of it. Not the right note. But he will have one.

At the door he pauses. "Tell me. What did Mohammed go to Mecca for?"

She shrugs, turning up her hands in the old immigrant posture. The old reflexes, the old locutions, how they survive. "Who knows, *Landsman*? Look it up."

A certain voice adopts us when we speak of folklore. It will chant like a cantor, and like him the syllables of a liturgy, rather than alight on one dry truth. It sneaks into the ear like a preacher, a mullah, a rabbi, persuading you that you have a soul. When it deals with the rural, it is like an old implement, making the tilling of the soil into tapestry. Under its sway, those kids in the choir loft trill to you like the very saints, and in the language of the larks. That basso, thundering on the page of the hymn book, is a voice from a cloud. At its most seductive the folklore voice issues as from beneath a helmet, addressing some martial art of hero-sport we were never near. Or soothes from behind a shawl, suckling to us that blood-milk we miss. Beware the voice most when it simples on about war.

But that is the voice Debra hears. As she tells her story, this will become clear.

If she had grown up in the first flush of a Tel Aviv being seeded with smart Western emigrés to whom Israel was both the promised land of their faith and a kind of retiree's Florida earning them religious merit as well, she might have been as modern as she looked. Instead, she had been the daughter of a couple of "proles" who had bounced from kibbutz to kibbutz, neither of them adept at rural life but forever romanticizing it, in order to keep it tolerable. Stalwart, handsome, a teacher and an engineer, they belonged to that legion of the miscast who found themselves among the fanatics of the homestead. They themselves had survived by deftly leaving one place for another, their aim being the savings, from extra teaching and consulting jobs, that would ultimately allow them to open a shop in the city.

She, Debra, meanwhile had a childhood in a land where every crevice held an old tale hiding from a bullet. The landscape of the Middle East, compounded half of sand, is one of the most ambiguous. Seas have a legend of turning solid enough to walk on. Hills at evening turn maritime. To settle such land, fierce orthodoxies have been required. And of the children, heroes, naturally. Or heroines.

Her parents' marriage had been an arranged one. A happy union, it had been the family's stability. They had had a son in each of their first three terms of kibbutz life; then, after a lapse of ten years, Debra. The three older brothers, finishing their army terms without casualty, had melded into conventional Israeli life, two businessmen and an engineer.

At eighteen, a girl's only orthodoxy may be her beauty.

"And a reb is a hero," Debra says, looking out on a Tuscan view from her lounge chair next to Zoe's. "Until you serve him." A word she means literally. If the kibbutz has taught her animal husbandry, being a nurse has coached her to deal plainly with the human. "At table, he was a lion. And on the throne. But in bed—not even a lamb."

"'The throne,'" Zoe answers, smiling. It helps: to be cheery in the company of a loss at the moment more severe than her own. "We, too, called the toilet that, at home. At least when my father was on it... You suppose it's only a Jewish expression?" From the arsenal of buttock jokes that our early comedians and their audiences in the two-a-days took such joy in? "Or worldwide?"

Debra is far from stupid. But she does not conjecture.

"He hid from me there. Because we did not make kids. He

could not do it. And would not get help. Because with a reb, every-thing is known. So I left." The solution her parents had taught her. "To the army. So he was not shamed. Until I did not came back. Four years. I took the blame. I said I was barren...How could I know? But I was willing to say. 'A reb should have a family,' I said. 'Let us divorce.'...But then came a peacetime. One of those. And Lev sent his boys to live in our house. I worked in a hospital away, but came home to be a mother...In Jerusalem you have no trouble being of two minds. I could neither get free of the war, or of home-duty...And then came Lev, to visit the boys."

The story gets told. Straight on, as it happened, and as if it is happening again. Debra does not interpret her life. That way, it re-mains hers only. So Zoe never feels herself a confidante. But for awhile after these view-sessions they remain silent, honoring the past. After which Zipporah may comment.

"You're still serving. That's how we got you, Peter and I."

"You know whom I serve, really." Sometimes Lev's name erupts from her, and she breathes better afterwards.

The view they face, as from the foreground of a pre-Renaissance painting, toward hills dropping away with towns somewhere concealed in their folds, is from the second spa they have been to. The first one, recommended by a client of Norman's and far more expensive, is now closed for the season. In such a fa-mous spot, each day had been a parade, almost a comedy, of all the ills of the fashionably tottering, with half the clientele merely seeking to sting and abrade themselves or drink emetics, in the penitential cures that calm the rich. A vacant or cynic face in a white linen pool suit, or framed in a fur collar on its evening walk, might be suffering either from what the nineteenth century had called "the vapors" or from some dread pox. Or was merely on its trendy once-a-year, to dry up, tune up, for the next. Back there, however, in that clutter of tremors, hacked spittle, collapsing limbs, or the eccentric swellings of the self-satisfied, Peter's mild lapses could still go unnoticed, except by a tolerant medico. And she, Zoe Duffy now, in a milieu far from her own, could be anonymous.

Here, where they have a two-bedroom suite and shared bath, with Peter at the moment safely asleep under his afternoon sedative in the larger of the two rooms which are theirs, guests "take the waters" from bottles; there is no famous spring, and no sea. Some appear to be small-town bureaucrats or landowners risen a step or two above the rural they can still return to here, this time with a retired doctor in charge. Mild heart cases, or arthritics, in this hill country they go for drives as their sole exercise. What they come for is the milk of Tuscan kindness, plus food to the very standard of what they may have been warned against but crave—here the only cuisine available. As well as to be able to say to a home circle returned to, as well as to any rumblings from the body's abyss, "Well, I've tried to do as prescribed. But you know how it is, when there is nothing else." The place caters also to weekend tours of provincials imitating their betters, or labor unions come for their annual reward. Meanwhile, the "staff" that does massages and mud baths is careful to tout that they have been to Rome for training, yet to maintain, at least for the Duffys, that lack of sophistication which they assume Americans hope to find.

The resident doctor, after "a little talk" with Peter, had at once prescribed the sedative. "For the siesta, very helpful. And at night when you, *Signora*, and the young lady are asleep, mandatory." His English, honed by years of visitors, is excellent. "We are not Montecatini. Our terrain is steeper, though some say, even more beautiful. But we have no all-night personnel to guard. And even in the day—" He'd been relieved to find that Debra could administer the drug, though he was left to assume, as Zoe and she had agreed upon, that she was merely an aide. "Has he a heart condition? Ah, no." He'd muttered to himself. Zipporah's Italian, though scholarly, was fair. A pity, he'd said.

Now, after the story just told, Debra cocks an ear. Listening for Peter. Yet for Lev?

Zoe does not have to listen for Peter herself. That helps. Nor will she ask Debra, "How is he?" Which would put him down. She fights to keep Peter level with her in respect. But waits for the account that a nurse may volunteer. "He still recognizes you," Debra may say. Or: "He recognizes you again. Though I have had to prompt."

Each morning now, and several times a day, Debra re-identifies herself and reminds him where they are, whether or not this seems to be needed. On good mornings, which are fairly frequent, he'll say, "I know." But no longer questioning the procedure, as earlier.

Zipporah can always tell when the news of him will be bad. One past evening now marks the end of the time when she could still be lulled by the status quo.

It had been the last night of their stay in the fashionable spa. They'd been served drinks on their own little opera box of a balcony, where every dusk they watched the *passeggiata* below. She and Debra were quiet, accepting with pleasure the ordinary male remarks Peter could still make: "That couple down there. A smashing girl, eh? He already trots on behind." Zoe, chipping in: "Want to bet he'll catch up with her?" A question, too late realized as one, gliding past Peter without drawing his frown.

That evening the couple didn't appear; perhaps they'd left. "Ah, so I'll never know if I've won my bet," Zipporah had mused, unaware, as she saw, that Peter hadn't a clue. He had begun beating on the table, as if searching there for a reference, just as the waiter was serving his drink, which had spilled. Too late to check herself, she bent to retrieve it. If there was hate in his eyes, she keeps telling herself, it was only a child's sense of his own inadequacy, at being a child. Peter had turned to Debra. "Who is she?"

When half-dreaming, she can convince herself that the difficult child, treated tenderly, will again see the light. When fully awake, the analogy won't hold. Repulsion fills her mouth, even at the prospect of such mothering, and at her own distaste.

Instead, there are morning miracles. Heartening as the opening of a flower in spite of the first frost. He is himself, marred only to the degree that he is at times painfully conscious of not always being that.

They could stay the winter here. Monthly rates are comfortably low. Here some physical failure or lack is acceptable, as long as confined to the "treatment," whose lack of progress can be glossed over by both parties, as long as payment is received. In a foreign language Peter's increasing vagaries, word fractures, elusive gaps don't register. Memory loss is more visible at home; abroad, people can't know what you were.

Oddly, Peter is more nimble with the terrain than either of the women. Debra has observed this in others neurologically damaged. "It comes maybe with the childhood. All the more we must watch." On their walks, one takes courage from a land too graceful not to be wholly true—as travelers have before. At table, Peter has now and then a minor mishap, swiftly accommodated by Debra. For witness they have the Italian kindness, rooted in a Catholic resignation to the embedded sorrows. Seeming to know that both these women have suffered loss. *Che serà serà,* a waiter mutters. "What's that mean?" Debra asks when they've left the salon. Zoe's teeth grind, answering, "What will be, will be."

But perhaps it won't. Outside, the tall man with the humorous expression, whom the staff call *il professore*— "He has that physiognomy you expect proverbs from," the doctor's poetic aide commented—is playing bocce with another "guest," and will likely win, this being a good day.

At night, when at last left alone for the toiletry with which women keep in touch with their bodies, Zoe is assailed with visions of those holistic stopping places she had at times dreamed of taking him to, after discovering his illness. Old haunts, among peoples where illness was spiritual or perhaps demonized, and there were routine ceremonies to cast out afflictions deemed not of the flesh. At the remembrance of cripples convinced by the shaman to dance and walk thereafter without knots, or of surgeries performed under the spell of an acupuncturist who claimed that anesthesia was more the result of his thought focus than of his needles, or of those bedside mantras that could relax terminal pain, all that is Western in her becomes a ragbag she must step from, the refuse of a world gone mad for medicines that perform quite apart from the ministering. She can't yet credit that a cancer might be dissolved by a laying-on of hands. But when the brain is sick, hope of the non-physical cure still loiters. Somewhere, not necessarily in the forest primeval, there might be a laying-on of minds.

Not in this hemisphere. Meanwhile, she creams her face with the current nostrum on the market, brushes her hair with the number of strokes mother advised. Vanity is a social history, and health for the ego; it can keep the personality juvenile, affecting even what one sees. Until her own mother's late eighties, that snub Hungarian and who-knows-what-else cat face had weathered like a small sundial the years could only streak, though she'd not had a man "for nigh forty years." Toward the nineties the skull asserts itself, a second lead at last able to show its talents. And now that the face lift is not confined to the films, on Zoe's own avenue, emerging from one of its great, exaggerated porticos, such a woman can often be seen, walking singly perhaps but floating on the hoop skirts of vanity pursued, and bearing above that pursed mouth the frightened eyes of a girl.

Her own face, a good enough combine of German, Hungarian, and Sephardic Jews, inherited mainly from her father, is not the question here; with the luck of the Zangwills, it has so far merely refined. Strangers at times take her for elder sister to her daughters, who chortle generously. "She takes a serum called 'anthro,'" Nell said to one such comment. "Keeps the figure trim. Plus our father whacks her often." Leaving the meaning of this moot.

A spa goes to bed early. All its woes lie under analgesics she doesn't qualify for. In these night depths she soothes her own widowhood. Reviewing her and his faithful, heterodox love life.

The sexual scene of a couple changes when there's even only

one extra person about, even if only a servant at a distance, or a young child to be ignored. And with absences. Unlike the common couple, he, not she, was the continuum. Yet not a house husband. As their brood grew, and her forays alternated more, she had once heard her youngest say to a buddy lying on the floor with him over a game of marbles: "When Mom's away? Sure I'll ask. Right now, she's here." The pal collected stones; though striving always not to make her returns into lessons, she'd brought him some.

Her brood seemed not to have felt that her being away—and in such odd or uncouth places—had damaged them; rather they had copied their father's pride in her. "Jonathan's parents are *paying* to go on a safari," Charles had jeered; the girls, when asked whether she had been missed much, had said, "Nah—there were too many of us." Reminding her how profoundly the lack of many siblings had changed the "Western," the "American" child. The Jewish ones.

Meanwhile she remembers how each time she returned, she and Peter had waited, half irritated, half excited, for the children to be in bed. She had had it brought home to her how among the "civilized," the hiding, the sequestering, the separating of parental sex from its very offspring had affected the lives of both.

There were primitives whose sexual tabus were far severer than Muslim ones, as well as those whom the old anthropology had recorded as having no idea that copulation caused birth, though of this she had always had doubts. There were others, from igloo to longhouse, who in the general rough-and-tumble might appear to hide nothing, nor have any constrictions that it should be done. Habitation, of course, often set the style. But the unease of hiding, where in everything else her Western world strove to be frank—the duality compounded by that still gives her pause.

"But there's risk to shocking ones's kids," she'd said, in bed with him, back on Central Park West, the night she'd arrived from a hut only twenty-seven hours away in one of the last subcontinents of the noncivilized. "Short of displaying ourselves, how do we act? One sees the other penalty. When openness becomes synonymous with romp." Often under the fancy wooing of the analysts. On both sides of the Park. "As for me," she'd said, "I have to be careful, Peter. Never to think of the family—as a tribe."

She had always been allowed her pomposity. He had buried his smirk in her neck. "No," he'd said. "Or not yet."

She screws the lid of the cream-jar tight again and discards the combings from the brush, in requiem. When the adult children had all left home, he and she were restored to their solitude, plus the freedom derived from her inability to become pregnant. She'd never really worried about conceiving, from time to time taking precautions when she needed to move professionally, yet accepting the unplanned, at times glorying in that. What has happened between us, is that we have been through all the stages, or most, including the one annealing loss of a child.

She and Debra have talked only around the edges, as primarily nurse-attendant with the patient's nearest. The worst has happened to both, but references to that remain sidelong, comparisons not being offered. Traveling together in the same scenery and accommodations has worn off some off Debra's silences, though only Zoe mixes with the other guests, if slightly. Peter does so solely in games; otherwise his lack of trust in himself is visible. More than once Debra has described her training at a medical unit in London as pertinent to Peter's condition. Conversationally they are also, if distantly, Jew to Jew. In Debra's recent stay at the Duffys', she met all the sons and daughters, so can talk of them. Now and then, if solicited, she will describe the parts of Israel Zipporah had not seen: mountainous, arid, both "beautiful."

They will never knit together into real friendship, yet live artificially close. Today's lounge-chair talk had come on gradually. Tomorrow's will be a retreat from intimacy, on both sides. They will talk of Peter, which is why they are here.

So it has happened, what never seemed possible. And for which there is no repair.

Peter is now the third person in her daily life.

He lies in the soft Italian featherbed across from hers, under his opiate. Their sexual play has been wedded to intellect; even their treasury of family had been incidental to that. Now the disease has cut between them, worse than any mortal woman. Worst is his diminishment in her own mind.

Memory loss, even as serious as his sometimes is, can be dealt with, a jokery we all come to. What's it matter even if a man forgets where a door is, or that he's passed through it, as long as one guards the doors? Eccentricity is what we all verge toward; one of her nonagenarian relatives, though capable of reviewing her bank statements up to the day of her death, had every dinnertime reported her morning's chat with her mother. Nor was one ever sure that she was not exerting a terrible cogency. Asked by an irreverent grandson in which part of the house his great-grandmother might be residing, she had replied fondly, "In me."

What's scarcely to be borne is that Zoe can't tell him the story just told her, for their whispered mutual judgment. That he won't predictably pun, "Well, poor Deb. What a debut." But his sympathy would have been real, for all parties. "In one of your huts, Zippy, the reb's secret wouldn't have stood a chance, eh. Well . . . Poor reb."

On a good day, new information will be acknowledged instead of turning him off, or angering him. But she cannot know when will be such a day.

Behind that slowly blunting, dear face there is daily less of any personality at all. Even a madman is still a soul. His is slowly being extracted from him.

Down on her knees, beside the bed, the night breeze blowing behind her, stirring hair uncut for the three months they have been away, she wills him back, creeps in with him to warm herself. She is lying there, suspended in a hammock of comfort, when his legs grip hers. Above her, while leaning on his left arm, his right fist pushes up her chin, a posture well-known to both; any pair long together has conventions of coupling. If she doesn't want him she will roll over and out from under him. She lies quiet. Normally his eyes would be wide, the lingering smile tender. His eyes are closed, the lips tense. His body is still strong; he could strangle her. In a wave of desire she wishes that he would—that in some opera born of this countryside, as her neck cracks he would fall on her hidden knife, and they would die, in a harness the audience can't see but knows the libretto for. "But we don't sing." Has she whispered that? His eyes open. They are what she remembers. Also the faint smile—a lecher's, saved from that by love.

How far off the mark, even obsessed has her estimate of him been? Do the attendants of disease fall victim to their own cruel need to be the survivors, whose organs are safe? Suffering, do we even so connive away from the doomed, to a safer distance?

He moves in her socket as always. They fall, fall—into health?

No.

But having lost a child, she can recall how little connection there is between what can happen and how we love. Peter, who when himself always teased at the assumptions that lay beneath the accepted social order, would not have been surprised.

Norman has sent him cigars. He can no longer be trusted with them. In plain sight, on the loggia while she and Debra wrote letters just inside, he had put a lighted one in his pocket, sitting there until they had smelled his wool suit smoldering. Luckily it had been a coolish day, with a throw rug handy to wrap him in, no one about in the siesta lull, and the owner gone to oversee the pressing of his wine.

They are surrounded here by the true connections, the hardy testimony of the land. The olives have been picked. The squat, gnarled ancient trees produce less, but the best. In the taller, queenly, newer ones the pickers, standing on ladders, have faces as gravely smooth as the ovals they reap. One picker, in a tree outside Zoe's uncurtained window, keeps his eyes lowered as she brushes her hair. She now wears it in a bun; some take her for Italian until she opens her mouth. In Debra's room next door, the window is high, the light like a chancel's. On a rod, her few clothes hang like a biography: khaki shirts to shift dresses, the long travel coat last.

Though she is not in black it has got about that she is a widow, perhaps from some male guest early on rebuffed. The Signor, as the doctor likes to be called, has seen the passport, but is discreet about all here. The maids admire the diamond but may have noted the absence of a marriage ring. Debra, in one of her bursts of confidence, had said to Zoe, "I cannot always wear the ring he gave me, not when I must be thinking of what to do with my life." Adding later, when she sees Zoe noting the ring's continued absence, "Forgive me. When I am ready I will tell you." Does this mean she is preparing to leave them? It must.

Outside, the *nebbia,* the fall mist, has come and gone. The three of them have an appointment with an English-speaking medical man recommended by the Signor, who had called in the two women and advised them that they must soon seek total nursing care. "Italy has a tradition of keeping the retarded and the mild mentalities in the home—but with this illness, we give in."

The consultant doctor, discovered snoozing at an outdoor table with a view of the hills dropping away in the distance, his binoculars near at hand, seems energized by his visitors, happily interrupted on a desultory afternoon. Excusing his lack of an assistant—"I am semi-retired"—he has the maidservant show Peter and Debra to an anteroom while he speaks with the Signora, whom he leads into a study lined with sets of books. No medical diplomas are visible. His English is circular, but clear.

There will be no need for an examination, he says; he and the head of the spa have already consulted, which he and the Signor do for all patients who need care beyond what can be offered. The verdict is already set. This doctor has a yet further suggestion, in case she and her husband, "or, rather, you, my dear," want to stay in Italy. "To avail themselves of some very special care, as foreigners often do." He and the head of the spa will be happy to recommend a place, and make all necessary introductions. "Not happy," he says, casting up his eyes. "But we do what we can. And now we will have some wine . . . No, no I am retired, there is no fee." But if she wishes, the local priest will welcome any sum, for his church. "To go to building repair or parishioners, as you may designate," he says with a smile that covers possible American crotchets or preferences. "And anonymous, or not." It is all so graceful that she feels herself participating in a dance.

When the maid ushers in Debra and Peter, he goes at once to the books, walking in that stiffly public gait he has adopted lately, as if to show he is not yet adrift.

"Ah, you were a philosopher, I hear," the doctor says. "I am myself a follower of Benedetto Croce's works, *The Philosophy of the Practical,* especially." He serves Zoe and Debra the wine, holding Peter's in abeyance. "*Vino santo*—but not too sacred, on a cold day." And sotto voce to Zoe, "I can refer you to an order of nuns, Signora Duffy, who are specializing in such care, in an excellent facility. The mother superior is a disciple of that analyst in England—the one who made a name by proposing we are all, hmm—*pazzo,* at times."

Debra is on a small, low chair. Under the dim lamp, her long, crossed bare legs have an opal shine. She leans forward, over them. "R. D. Laing? He used to advise the London unit where I was, after. We saw the video."

"Mrs. Cohen is a nurse."

He bows, his glance shifting. Debra's legs are perhaps not the best reference.

Peter is immobile, facing the kind of leatherbound sets of books he used to poke fun at, as mere decoration. But now, as she sees the angle of his neck and profile, stretched towards that shelf like a dog towards a bowl it can't reach, she is appalled at what she may have done to him. People should be allowed to vegetate like fungus, in the rooms they have inhabited. She should have managed that, no matter what. A man perhaps becomes stone, but worn by familiar touches. His head awhirl, but in the home place. His tongue stuttering, but to ears that once knew this man's flow.

He is pointing to the Croce set, set off by photos of the author at each side. "Min-is-ter. Of Edu-educa-tion." The words sound as if wrested from the depths.

"Good, good," the doctor crows. "Retired, yes, under the *Fascisti*. Always the idealist, Croce. And you, *Professore,* you were a philosopher also."

Zoe stands up. The rage is hers. She could slap. "*Is—*" she croaks. "Not 'were.'" To her surprise, Debra echoes, nodding. "Is."

"And now we must be off." Her voice is shaky. "Thank you for the wine."

On the steps, Peter, flushed with success, starts up again. "Min-is—" Debra presses a hard hand on each of the Duffys' shoulders. "Hush."

Peter's suit has been returned from the tailor's, the singed pocket neatly mended. Attached is a paper pouch, which Debra opens. Inside it is an elegant black leather gold-tipped American Express combination diary, travel information, and address book, about $3\frac{1}{2}$ by 7 inches, fittable in the jacket's inner pocket and apparently found there. Never used for its full purpose and several years out-of-date, it is not completely blank.

Here and there are jottings, on the pages helpful to travelers. On the page listing International Currencies, those for Gambia, Macao, Tanzania, and Uganda are checked; she learns that their coinages are the dalasi, the palaca, and the shilling, respectively. There are question marks next to—is it Malawi?—and Zambia, for both of whom the monetary unit is the kwacha. Both Togo and the Ivory Coast have been crossed out.

Finger on that, she recalls what Zoe had said of their at-first projected tour. "Thoughtless of me. Why would I make him accede at this point to what I had never asked of him before? I'll tell you. I must have been visualizing him—his state—as going back to the primitive. Which is not the case. What we call 'savage'—or used to—has its own basis, as much as you and me. They are in their own health."

"What they worship?" Debra had at once asked Zoe. "For me that is always a question burning." As she had phrased it to Lev when, looking forward to their marriage, he had asked her what ritual she wanted. He'd found her language quaint. Saying, "Ah yes, 'burning question' is not quite the same." Adding, "As for me, Debra, where I once worshiped, body and soul, there's now a scab." And she had answered, "I am used to scabs."

She knows what Zoe worships, no need to read her book, a copy of which is in the knapsack of Peter's writings, which travels with them. Zoe watches other people worship, and makes a religion of being on watch.

While to Debra, born to tenets scarcely less dislodgable than her perfect teeth, and still more in need of a demigod to admire than a modern Sabra should admit, Peter has become very nearly sanctified, a near-martyr whose fate she is entirely familiar with. Saints are beyond torture, and Jews do not have them anyway. But there is something of Job in every Jew.

Riffling through this elegant leather "accessory," a word she's learned from the American ads, she finds a couple of pages headed "Overview," with five-line spaces for each month of the year. This is followed by "Plans/Expenses—January," and so on for each month, with a line for each of a month's thirty or thirty-one days. That this gold-tipped notebook should be so precise for a man who no longer is might make her weep, were she a weeper. She is not. Wailing may once have been an approved ritual in the orthodoxy (and in that man Laing's treatment proposals, if she recalls correctly). These days the real thing is hard to come by. And you would want to be among your own for it.

Here's a page of *Weights and Measures: U.S. and British standards for Distance . . . a Hectare equals 2,472 acres. A gram, 15,342 grains . . .* And another page for conversions: *Bushels (long) or (short). To convert the latter to metric tons multiply by 9702.*

That such gabble should be the measure of a man. Pfui! She looks down at her ring. However many carats the diamond is, she never cared; those signify only the money it might have brought. The American Express, probably not interested in jeweler's weights, would not in any case know the stone's weight in loss.

Nor be able to say, line by line of this notebook's exquisitely de-signed graphic, what Peter Duffy is daily being converted to.

At the diary section's end, there is a columned page, *Time Around the World*, based on when it is Noon, Eastern Standard Time, in New York.

"Should cross that page out."

Peter, sneaked away from Zoe's side, is looking over her shoulder.

His reiterating speech is now a mild litany tolerated: *Brush my teeth—Have I?* His moments of clarity, running to excess, can ter-rify. Struggling, he will hone himself to a point beyond normal. Does he want to "cross out" time itself? The mentally confused can take great pains with themselves, her trainers had advised. Do your best to honor this. Treat what they say literally.

"You marked two places, see?"

"S-s-so I have." Not really a stammer. A sentence losing impetus.

"Read them out?" She keeps testing whether he still can.

He does, quite precisely. "St. Christopher, Nevis—Anguilla, São Tomé, and Principe."

"Why did you mark those?" Unlike Zoe, she's not afraid to question him.

"Never heard of them. Good place to stop . . . Stop." He palms his Adam's apple, with a grimace familiar by now, signaling: Here I am again—Me. "Where t-time is not of . . . the essence."

He's got a little beyond her. Yet she is oddly quieted. They swing in an abated moment, companion mourners.

In a minute will the mouth purse, the eyes blink? A child say-ing: You ask too much of me.

Instead that switch—to a man playing he is still adult. With the gesture, a salute, that had made Zoe turn aside, hiding tears. Whispering, "He was once in the R.O.T.C., National Guard train-ing corps. Before I knew him."

He clicks his heels. Touches the jacket lapel. "Nice suit." The syllables clog. "Civilian. Whose?"

"Yours. It's been at the cleaners, Dr. Duffy. We're in Italy, the three of us. With Zoe, your wife." She bends her head, praying. Please God, let him not say Who. Whenever he does, she feels the desertion. What she is now. Without Lev.

He doesn't nod anymore, from a stiffness not in the neck. Certain natural movements are gone. But he can still be positive. Like some of the elders in the kibbutz, imposing lay memories on those who were displacing the old ways? "I was a—lapsed. She a—reformed. We thought there was no difference. The children covered for us."

Anyone living with those two can see the difference—though if Lev hadn't remarked it, she wouldn't have known what.

Dr. Duffy has picked up the diary, scratching at the page marked. "She has to—" He starts to hit the side of his head, to urge out the rest. She thwarts him, smoothing down the attacking hand, clamping hers on his shoulders. All the hospital techniques return easily. One never finishes a patient's sentences. One waits.

But then, one doesn't live with them or with this one's wife, as she has. With this marriage, whose presence she has absorbed like a Bible lesson. According to which an agreed-upon conduct is the sole commandment. And the air is warmed, with an after-scent of ripe fruit. In her own way, she's helping them as they've helped her. She and they are neighbors leaning from either side of the same wall—each from a marriage half lost.

Debra has never communed with a patient. Medical forbearance requires that there be no extra-personal secrets between the brain-sick and the well. Sympathy must be primarily general, and publicly expressed. Nor can one ever admit to being, in some part of one's own life, a patient as well.

"Zoe has to believe, yes," Debra says. "You didn't, one thinks? Neither did Lev." She has no delicacy about putting them both in the past tense. They are there. "As for me, Peter?...I don't know." She has been wanting to say this to someone for months. Why not him? An oracle from which the spirit has flown.

One can't tell for sure what he has heard. But his eyes water. Like a child awarded a task beyond it.

The two of them are silent. Then he surprises her. "The letter."

"Letter? Which?" On the table a pile of them from dutiful family. There is a heavy pause, in which he can almost be seen climbing over the question as over a stile. He reaches out, touching the notebook. She's clipped his fingernails square, taking over the task from Zoe, whom this duty brought near to tears. For Debra it is performed for Lev as well; in the grave the nails grow long. She would have cut Peter's hair with the same linked piety, but he enjoys the local barber, who flourishes talk in time with his scissors and requires no reply.

"In the diary, do you mean?" There's nothing between those pages. But in the pouch that came with the returned suit? Yes.

The doctor's name on the letter is familiar to her from the minor prescriptions—for allergies, eye infections, antibiotics—that both Duffys carry. "Older than Peter and me," Mrs. Duffy had said of this doctor. "Did everything for us over the years except deliver the kids. It was to him Peter went, supposedly for the yearly physical. But was—sent on for more. My dear canny husband had expected to be." Zoe had bent her glance at Debra's as if over eyeglasses, though she wears none. "He still is canny, Debra, isn't he?" Debra had nodded, half to the plea.

He's watching her now, as she reads:

Dear Pete:

If it had to be me to tell you, maybe fate. I'm retiring, old friend, because of a similar diagnosis. Not me, but Helen, my wife. Our joint neurologist will be discreet. Dr. Green, my young associate, will be available to you if you wish.

I'm told that so far the decline seems to be case by case, high I.Q. being no guarantor. Cause of death being "normal," i.e., from whatever organ or system fails first. In that sense one may live out one's physical time for years.

Your cardiac report gives concern. Not quite the same as last year, when we agreed to bide our time. You may wish to consult Dr. Green or another, on medication, possible bypass surgery. On the other hand—you may not. Godspeed.

Ted

What Debra feels is what whelmed her during that harrowing training stint at the London clinic: she'd had to get out of that, the dealing mainly with what was inherited. She must get out of here too, where even the olives are genealogical. Back to my land of shotgun changes. And out from under this two-person vise, this thrall for which she cannot pay, except by continuing. Where to go is secondary. She must move on.

Dr. Duffy, as he still is to her—the first-naming is therapy—is trying to push the folded letter into the diary and the diary into his right pocket. She does this for him, then automatically takes his right hand in hers. He has a mild case of trigger-finger, the third one of his right hand, in which, if the swollen foreshortened tendon is left untreated, the finger may retract to the palm. One steroid injection has already been given him, though she had to suggest this to the local man. Meanwhile each day, hourly if possible, one holds the finger in prescribed pressure to straighten it, forefinger on the knuckle, thumb under the tip. One can do this for oneself with the other hand. Peter cannot remember to, so whenever near him she will absently do it for him. Zoe would also, but this he resists.

She gives him back the hand, absently, gazing out the window of the little salon where they are. The furniture is dark, spindly, unsittable, yet persists. "Like some relatives," Mrs. Duffy has said while opening the inquiries from home, which she has trouble evading. Peter's hand condition, begun before they left, had been blamed on his final spurt to finish that last essay on the old Olympia typewriter, of which he himself had long ago said, "Goose-steps like a Nazi. But I bark at it like our chief petty officer used to." Now the excuse for his not writing is convenient. Once in awhile he scrawls a postscript to one of Zoe's letters. Sometimes she has to prompt what he'll say, sometimes not. Zoe shows Debra these, explaining the context. On a letter to his son the "astronomer," Peter had written: "Chat with the planets for me, now and then?" To his favorite grandson, whose letters, read aloud to him behind their closed door, brought on a chuckling Debra could hear, he had dictated a reply Zoe had typed: "Found out the Hebrew for Paradise yet, son? A heathen notion. But the Jews would have a word for it." Underneath, in his own scrawl: "It is not here."

"Shall I let that be?" Zoe says, showing it to her. "I—I can't bear to."

"You Sunday Jews," Debra says half-fondly. "So much you cannot bear." In the kibbutz, "Sunday Jew," lightly bandied between her parents and their cronies, meant those who did not work hard enough. In Tel Aviv, where many of that crowd had become shopkeepers, the phrase was still used among them, but its meaning had changed. They no longer worked the land, but its dangers were still their crop, share-on-share. Though the city might not blunt your faith, it could teach the functions of money. Sneering that phrase meant you yourself were still kosher, still the crowd for real. And the children, riding buses with the guards on them, seeing lush foreign movies in the meantime, could scarcely be blamed for assuming that among those Sunday Jews there must be a lot of Americans.

But if you're a Jew, you're used to judgments that are often severe, yet affectionate. So when Zoe, at first blinking, dipped her head with a grin of recognition, neither she nor Debra was surprised.

She's in the owner's office now, settling the week's bill for the extras that can't be paid for in advance, like Peter's massages, at which he no longer balks, and their table wine. Two weeks have passed since they saw the consultant. There's been no further pressure, but still, this transaction is taking rather too long a time. At its end, Zoe will leave an extra sum on the table, "for the church." She has written to the nuns.

Soon it will be dinnertime. To Debra, the dining salon is the most homelike place in the *pensione,* and the sight of the white tablecloths is like some universal bandage, soothing the woes that one is silent on at table. At the farther end of the house, past the kitchen, is the pantry, where the cook beats the dough, baking the fragrant bread in an oven just outside the door. All processes here seem to have been in place since the beginning, whenever that was. And the balance of light and dark in the house is comforting.

But the landscape here, in spite of occasional, wild, flooding storms, is too easy, too graceful, seeming always to return to even keel. This is not the enclave she is used to, one still en route morally to the promised land. Even the violence that once went from tower to medieval tower here is said to be long gone. The small-town people in the village that houses the spa and the landowners dotting the hills seem to have settled into their allotted places like graduated pearls on a string. Lev had sometimes dealt in such as a sideline, but the smooth orbs with their buried Asian tints did not hold him. "I have to be nearer the source."

Dreaming still of what could have been their life, yearning to have him still influence her own, she's begun to say more than intended to this woman who is her last link with him. Like on yesterday's walk, when passing the town jeweler's window she had said: "When Lev and the Antwerp connection argued about how to cut a stone, what to call the color, it was like an argument out of the Torah." Such a hungry look on him. And not a care for how the verdict went, on a gem he had already bought in any case. It had been the snap and zest of the pro-and-con that burnished his and the other dealers' cheeks. "None of them wore yarmulkes. But it was like they did."

She and Zoe had ducked inside the church on the hot village square, both hunting in their handbags for Kleenex; it had been at the start of their inappropriate colds. "Maybe that's why we suffer so much respiratory trouble," Zoe snuffled. "Argument is the breath of life to us Jews." Above them a highly painted Christ hung on the cross, a crucifixion put up in place of a very old one said to have been sent away for restoration, but rumored to have been looted. "Not him, for sure," Zoe said, looking up. "He's too pink for it."

The priest, who kept track of the spa guests, nodded at them on his way to the vestry, genuflecting to the cross as he passed. "*Bello,* no? At last He is with us again. And thank you, *Signora,* for your donation."

"So he actually got it," Zoe muses, as they leave the church. "That consultant's fee. Or maybe they share?"

On the way to buy something for their noses, she says, "When they consecrated that restored crucifixion, in the news story, no picture of the old one appeared. Wise of them. And not to market the real one too soon. Unless a collector had ordered it."

According to her, aside from "bedroom opera" and family ones, crime here is not over belief, but for money, and taken care of by the syndicate. "Very calming, yes." Nobody else would have dared. "One can't assume the church is involved. They have too much taste." They would just keep mum. And that new job, which had arrived on the double, must have cost.

"My father was a Torah all by himself," she says. "Like many Jewish lawyers still are. He'd crack his own jokes, then criticize them. The year I was confirmed, he took me to my first cathedral, to a high mass for a business associate. 'So that's their Jesus?' I said. 'He could've been ours,' my father said. 'One of our messiahs; I don't hold with less than a full crew. And the best one so far.' 'So what did he do wrong?' I said. 'Convert?' And my father laughed, saying I was already a Jew and really didn't need to be confirmed. He'd taken me to Mass to show me the Gentile half of the world. I'd soon be a member of our half. And if we ever went to Palestine, which didn't interest my mother, he'd show me yet another half. When I said, 'Poppa, you can't have two halves of something, and then another,' he said, 'Oh? But we will.'"

They pass the bank in silence; it isn't open anyway. "I'm going to make a mathematical table of the hours before and after siesta and before and after lunchtime, when you can or cannot get to the P.O. or to the banks. Plus Saints-day closings. But Peter and I get our main exercise here. He loves the colonnades." She looks at her watch. He was getting physical therapy and then a massage; they'd have just enough time for the drugstore.

All the municipal services were under those colonnades, another evenness here. It was reassuring. Debra can see why he likes to walk here. You have a sense of being graded, held in, but in shade. These people have made friends with their climate by giving in to it. Following Zoe to the other side of the street under a lion-yellow midday sun, she could almost smell the musk and grit of the borders she had left, and held her head up proudly to the glare.

In the *pharmacia,* handsome with hung urns, and walled with wooden drawers marked in Latin script for potions Debra had never heard of, Zoe, greeting the courtly young owner, who as she had commented to Peter speaks English like a troubadour, says in a glinting aside to Debra, "Here's where they mix the medieval poisons." And turning to him, "But for us, just something for the nose." She points to the compartmented wall. "Maybe from one of those?" Delighted, he picks up on her rhythm, "Ah, no, *Signora,* they have not been opened for a century; we don't know what might fly out."

If Zoe sounds just the right interchange for these parts, it doesn't mean she's insincere. She is like that prism you're asked to turn in physics class, Debra tells herself. The one that breaks up light. The light you see through each one of her sides may be different, but still true. Is that what my Lev saw? How do I leave?

Plump-buttocked girls in skinny dungarees, buying lipsticks and trying eyeshadow on each others' great brown orbs, had glanced with curiosity at Debra's army getup. As Zoe bought a load of assorted cosmetics to send to the daughter hooked on a brand of Italian stuff not obtainable in the U.S.A., she did look sad, even forlorn. But in a minute, studying the minute print under a label, she has shifted again, almost giggling. "Look, Debra. Made in France, actually. Where my daughter lives half of the time."

At the door she says low, "How I miss them." Turning back as if she would find her daughter there. Grinding out, "And he does not."

Outside, Debra said, "Let's get a coffee. And a nosh."

She is smiled at so sadly, she knows her motive is spied.

"You don't drink coffee."

"No, but I nosh," Debra said.

Over the coffee Zoe talks a streak, reminding Debra of how soldiers sometimes did that the day after they'd lost a buddy in action. "Yes, most of the crime here is syndicated, Debra. Which must relieve them. The worst they do personally is to eat their own songbirds. You seldom hear any. Only see them in rows in the market stalls, on their backs, with their stiff claws spread like asterisks."

Animal torture had been the hardest to ignore on Zoe's travels. "Because on safari one is dependent. And in the field one must be accurate." As for tribal practices, to watch certain devilments acquiescently was bad, but one had to remind oneself that one had no influence, and in the name of knowledge was privileged to watch. And it gave one, alas, the full scope of what is so oddly called humanity.

She talked rapidly, another recognizable after-battle symptom, as if those left alive were trying to outrun their own flesh.

And all the time it is plain whose torture she has in mind.

"Queerly enough," she says, swallowing a spasm, stirring the coffee, putting the sugar in, stirring the brew she does not taste, "it made me a softie at home." At a dinner party once, when a show-off host had pulled the ears of his Great Dane in the guise of schooling it, she had left the table and vomited. "It was because the dog stood its ground," she said. "Letting it happen."

She looks up from her full cup. "You haven't eaten your nosh."

On the walk back, Zoe pauses at the bottom of the church steps; a few old women are going in. "The angelus," she says softly. "Morning, noon, and night they repeat it, at the sound of a bell. To celebrate the birth of Christ." As a few more worshipers straggle

up the steps, she might have been counting them. "Peter says—"
Again the spasm, familiar by now; again she swallows, goes on.
"Peter says Catholics post their intellectual bans early. And never
again have to look ahead."

That's it, Debra's thinking, scraping her sandal in the rubble at
the bottom of the steps, staring at Zoe. This is the way he talked to
me. This is why she reminds me of Lev.

So she replies as she had learned to answer him. Picking a detail, any, out of the bewildering talk offered her. "What's a—is
posting a ban something to do with government?"

Zoe looked at her then as he used to, as if Debra was suddenly
there. "Come. We should find some inside."

At the top of the steps she says, "Something tells me. You ever
been in a church before?"

"In England, once. A staff picnic; they wanted to do rubbings.
You put a long paper on the floor, rub it with a pencil, you get an
image of the saint? You roll it up. In London it wasn't allowed anymore. This was in the country. A ruin. There was only the floor."

"Come inside."

Inside, the pews are dotted with the old ones, murmuring.
Under cover of that, Zoe leads her from niche to niche, then to the
other side of the church, until they have in fact circled it. No priest
is up there where the ark should be, but the murmuring is contin-
uous; maybe this alone is the angelus. *Undercover, undercover,* her
and Zoe's sandals say; what are you seeking?

They find what they are looking for almost at the entry, on a
wall above where extra prayer books and announcements are, like
often in a *schul.* A line of notices, in Italian of course, each printed
in a set form, like on a legal paper. Or when a psalm is printed separately? Two names headed each, and are repeated in the text, a
man's and a woman's. She knows at once what these declarations
are for.

"Bann—with a double *n,*" Zipporah says. "Zoe" has for the
moment vanished. "Means 'to forbid.' Intentions of marriage
these are. Posted. In case anyone does want to object."

Two pictures were stuck above one of the banns. A middle-aged couple. Maybe someone had wanted to.

"There's always the chance," Debra says. In her and the reb's case, no one had.

Or there's that other declaration, toward a marriage canopy—with a wineglass to be broken, and dancing like pigeons on hot brick afterward—that you will never get to make.

While she weeps, Zipporah grips her hand.

"Ah, that's good. You hadn't yet, had you, all this time? Thought at first I shouldn't show you these. Then—that I should."

Leaving, they have to pass the center aisle leading back to the dead Christ-in-plaster whose birth in the flesh is being affirmed. As they come to the aisle, just before they must turn their backs to him, Zipporah dips her knee.

Out in the blinding glare, as they put their dark glasses back on, her face, too, is wet. "Couldn't make myself do that for years," she says. "Genuflect...It's just a thank-you." She takes out a Kleenex, only to wipe her forehead. Her mouth opens. "My nose has stopped running."

"Mine too."

"A miracle."

Debra makes as if to go back inside.

"Wait for the next coming, Debra. Before you give thanks."

Both smile weakly. The Jewish jokes have taken over.

As they start down the steps the priest comes running from the nearby restaurant, still wiping his mouth, and rushes in the church door.

"Ah, Italy," Zoe says. "Their God is comfortable."

"Some at the kibbutz said ours would strike us dead, if we ever did like dip the knee. But I wanted to check."

"He wouldn't. He would just let you remember it all your life." She sighed. "All the time I was getting ready to be confirmed, I was already sneaking into museums, my tongue hanging out...We Jews were not to worship graven images? I already knew I was going to spend my life at it."

That's it. When she talks like that, back and forth and between, is when she reminds me of Lev. Who swore me he would tell what was between him and the reb, not only the good blood, but the bad. "From which blood was it you sent the kids to him?" I said. He said he wasn't sure. And that's again when he sounded like her.

He said he would tell me everything about himself when we got to America. But God got there first.

"I brought a rubbing home from England," Debra says aloud. "Rolled, they're nothing. Unrolled, you have an eight-foot saint. Or just one of their monks, buried. But with every bump clear. On the wall it was like, I dunno, an eight-foot letter. Maybe a bann? The reb tore it down." The sound of paper tearing still sets her teeth on edge. "So then—I knocked him out."

"You punched?"

"Patients, sometimes you have to subdue them. You are supposed to do it without bruising. A six-foot man, you have your choices."

When you knee them, it's like sex. "Boss sex," the women at the hair salon used to call it, for when the woman leads. But for her, it was only the sex she had never had with him.

"Then I went." The boys had been away in the holiday camp.

"Back home?"

"To my parents? No. Too late for that."

The conversation ends. With Zoe thinking she went to Lev? No, I owe her, Debra thinks. So much I owe.

"In a hospital, I know I am a good person. I had to know. So I went back."

When they get to the spa gate, Peter is waiting behind it, roused and dressed for dinner, by himself perhaps but under the zealous eye of the staff, who have the spa's decorum to police.

He is rolling a bocce ball between his palms, though games are for mornings only. It is hard to tell which state of mind he is in, or where. He leans on the gate. "They tell me I won." He squints beyond the two of them. "That's because the world has gone flat."

Walking across the lawn to dinner, under the curious glances of some, the dulled masks of others, Zee says through her teeth: "A spa is a stage set, on two levels. He'll rid us of it yet."

Whatever is keeping Zoe so long in the spa owner's office? Could she perhaps be offering to pay double the rate? In one unit where Debra had briefly served, a nursing home that didn't normally keep chronic cases, one politician, a Parkinson's case for whom nothing further could be done, had been allowed to piece out his life there, by rumor on just such an arrangement, his rich family giving out that any special favor was due him for his "contribution"—not known to be military—in the Six Days "campaign" in Lebanon.

Like Debra herself, Zipporah won't lack for money. Their friend Norman has bought their apartment, planning not to attach it to his own but to keep it in abeyance, should the Duffys return. The sons and daughters also stand ready to provide, each according to his or her own circumstances.

In turn, Debra has inherited substantially from Lev, without hurt to the boys. Though she hadn't known of this prospect before his death, this too keeps his presence near, recalling those trips on which she was privy to his business, and at times even coached on "What more women should know." If in her heart she has come to see that in this oddly associating way he was keeping a kind of fond faith with his memory of the first wife, of whom he'd said, smiling tenderly, that "she never wanted to know more," such a joining was nothing to be jealous about.

Rather, didn't this mean that he tended all memory as carefully as the polished gems in his pouches? That he had been as faithful to Libby, and still was, so could he be to her, though this might have less to do with either of them than with that moral sternness she knows so well. Just so her father and mother strove even now to keep their Jewish morality simmering, though long since beguiled from the half-sacrificial kibbutz to the scramble of buy-and-sell. "Jews have the habit of faith," Lev had said. "No matter to what."

Now she may be embarking on a life where no one will have known of him, unlike that healing time in the Duffys' household. There a quiet sympathy had oozed about her, most refraining from mentioning him. After the woman introduced as Peter's older sister had dropped his name like a hot coal while crossing herself, and had been fled from without reply, Zipporah must have cautioned the rest of them. Honoring, or maybe understanding, how Debra needed to mourn.

What she'd wanted was to hear his echo in her head only. The silent way that whole family, even that old yenta Nettie, had swung like a phalanx answering a command had earned her eternal respect. Much else about their slack ways can amaze her. But in this they had reverted, as she had begun to see that in certain ways they yet do. Jews do not mourn the dead arisen. They mourn the forever departed. And knew she was doing that. They mourn life. That graven image in the church? This is what she would have said to it, if dipping the knee.

Zipporah, when asking whether Debra wished to come abroad with them, had warned her in the same breath not to feel "obligated," a word out of Judah if there ever was. Generous, but stern in its administration, a woman who will decree her own name and deny her husband's disease against the will of God, because to her the husband clearly is the deity she observes—Zipporah is that recognizable Jewish family figure, the matriarch whom women in Debra's generation are trying not to be. In Debra's family's nomad history, so much that was homely had been lost. Her own mother, a nervous shopkeeper subservient to the father, would never qualify, except for that other well-known role, the mother bowing down before her males. And marketing her daughter?

The Duffy daughters have been a revelation of how far the women descended of the diaspora can go toward disappearing further into the melting pot that their country of birth still vaunts. The Duffy sons seem more Jewish to her, maybe because of the mother. The Duffy daughters were the real half-Jews of the family.

Their mother has carried the Jewish gene with her, whether or not she admits. Though in her profession, according to her, they are bound to admit everything. A virtue to soothsayers only. Debra has no awe of her. These days she cherishes Zipporah for her injury. A poor statue, knocked off its pedestal into human woe, she still has her own Lev. Asleep in his lounge chair after his game, while Debra holds his hand.

Those lounge-chair conversations in front of that view? Debra will miss them. As two well-provided-for women who must manage their money, talk of how that will be is a mild relaxation in which Zoe, who along with Peter has always had some money counselor like Norman, is now the greenhorn. She went wide-eyed on hearing that Debra has learned about finances not only from Lev, but also from the reb, who was not one of those dreamers adrift in Talmudic counterplay, but a party economist.

"We should remind ourselves you are a business people," Zoe said wryly. "Which should not surprise those with our history, should it? Except that much of the world—and maybe our kinsmen who want it most—sees you, Israel, as a nonsecular nation. Still hanging by the nails from the Holocaust."

There was a minute of shock, all Zoe's, at what she had said. She had sworn, her whispered apology said, never to get into politics.

Debra had laughed. "Lev said far worse."

And saying so, her first spontaneous mention of him, she also felt the spark of home. That vibrant platform between dangers, in which she had breathed cold, hot, pure, or befouled, but always alive.

Now she again checks her watch, luckily on the wrist of the hand not holding her patient's. Inside the spa's main office the long-winded owner will be pouring his honey. Some medical men speak only in monosyllables, doling out themselves, for which there is no prescription. This doctor can't give a prognosis without taking you through his whole career. Nurses have to bear that, saying, "Yes, Doctor," or at best nothing. But the woman in there, who can say anything she wishes, will be attending with all her muscles, and that stare which trances you rather than her. And none of it put on. "Zipporah Duffy's a major listener," Lev had said. "Must have saved her skin many a time, in those jungles."

But the woman who doesn't always remember to sign herself "Zoe" can hang on you for something beyond your words, making you wonder what it is you have. She's not just paying you that envious tribute older people dart at any who are young. Besides, middle-aged men vacationing here and not always single have now and then made passes at Zoe, which she evades with practice.

"Women who've shared sexual love to the nth; it shows in the skin of their faces," Zoe had teased. "Like it's their beard." She's had that love, and the family scene as well, a bracelet encircling her if not entirely of gems of the first water.

Then why does one still want to shield her? Or offer her one doesn't yet know what? Smart as she is, she'll listen to anybody—the waiter, even that priest. What's her hunger? Debra has seen all kinds. Zipporah's is not professional. Nor connected with Peter even. She listens like some patients do. Or like one does in *schul,* for the answer that no one of us can give.

Bad for sure, the news being given her in there. And now, Debra thinks, I must tell her mine.

And here she is, standing in the doorway. In this ornate but not-so-old villa, the carved door frames seem to come forward as baroque only as people need that—as Zipporah herself had remarked. "Maybe so in all Italy." Her running commentary is like being in a museum with an expert ever at one's side. One learns that the info being slipped is not always over one's head—that there is a museum in oneself.

As she holds there, in the carved gilt frame of which only the ground-level bar is missing, she is dignity wounded, but as painted by a master. Debra might even have delayed telling her "I too must go," in spite of a resolve fostered slowly, in an odd calm she has begun to suspect may come from more than merely living in this backwater of nursery routine. But just then Zoe blurts in that coy way she's taken to when Peter is with them, "Ah, there you are again, you two. Holding hands."

There's no offense in it, either intended or found. But she has somehow vulgarized their threesome, like some ordinary patron. Releasing Debra to treat her like one of those. So without looking up, continuing to press Peter's middle finger, Debra croons in hateful imitation, "Doctor gave me a second steroid injection for that tendon, for when the month is up, which is about now. Before I leave, I'll show you how."

"Leave? Yes. End of the week. Our rooms are scheduled for someone else. Old customer he can't refuse." She's twiddling the sheaf of receipts she and the owner must have exchanged. Even when Peter is under sedation, as now, she never uses the sickroom voice—the visitor's hush that would collaborate with Nurse.

"He suggests again those nuns up north. A scholarly order, he says. The Mother Superior with a medical degree. Most of the sisters come of noble blood. Blonds, even, before they were shaved." She half laughs, shrugs. "The Italians. Well, what have we got to lose? Excellent part-German cuisine, he says, which Peter likes. 'And the terrain no worse for the *Signor* here, maybe better gardened.'... Of course it costs, fiendish, but so what?"

She breaks off, stuttering. "Before you leave ... is that what? And did I hear you say 'now'?" And when Debra nods: "What can I say, Debra. You have to get on with your life."

Debra releases Peter's hand, stares at her own. From behind her she hears steps; her hair is stroked. "You've been a godsend." To both of us. But we cannot expect."

It would be easy, to answer in their polite style. To say that she and he, the Duffys, will always be my family. But I would have managed, alone. And even my born family is no longer mine. That's my style. And I'll get on with it.

"We were each other's bargains. That's what a nurse is." She's not sorry to say it, if softly. Their world is so full of *schmier*.

And if the truth disappoints, do as the harsh bedside teaches one to do. Come up with more.

"So I'm going, yes." Nothing to do with you or him—or even Lev. She is at last able to raise her head.

"I have to be where there is a war."

So softly she said it, Zipporah muses, lying in Peter's bed, clasping his sleeping body from behind—like a credo. Which it is to her. To her I'm a gadabout, who has seen everything. And fought for nothing. So are all we Jews of the Diaspora, unless returned. To where we are once again a nation. Ten tribes of us, in all. Standing once again in our old footprints. Though those prove once more to be sand.

That must be how the vision is for them. For her. Rung by rung of the folklore, they have nailed themselves to the land. But to save that vision, must the sands be kept moist with bloodthirst, the heavens explode?

In her own imagination, which these days works like a second brain in service to her husband's, she is answered, as he would have done. Or as her jungles also had: No faith is as bright without holy conflict. Need an enemy? The gods will provide.

He slumbers on.

Hours later, unable to sleep for argument, thrashing between thoughts of the just peace that never comes for some Jews, and the peace of mind into which known deserters from that orthodoxy can fade, she goes back to her own bed.

Sometime later, he pads the cold floor to her bed and, slipping in with her, warms his feet on hers. Turning her away from him he clasps her waist as she had his, warming all his length. Whispering, "Let me go . . . Let me go," he takes her from behind.

All contradictions dissolve. They sleep.

They are in Venice for Debra's honeymoon, the one she
and Lev had planned to have. He would have wanted
them as witnesses, she said, insisting on settling them
with her in the *pensione* on the Zattere to which he had said she and
he would go.

The city is the fable he and she would have shared, distanced
from any war she is used to by its pact with the sea. Triremes are
half visible in the corner of the eye. If a flotilla of battleships were
to gray the horizon, the gunwales would sooner or later pour gold,
and beach umbrellas billow from the lifeboats. The dome of St.
Marks is the postcard royalty. And now that Zoe has followed
Debra's course they are equals, if only temporarily: both are traveling by metaphor.

Where their next destination will be is not mentioned between
them. For the moment they are kept on even keel by the routine
within which they strive to keep their charge. And people are extra
helpful here, as water-goers often are. Vigilant for the slow, elegant
stranger who might lose his balance on the *vaporetto,* tolerant of
this visitor struck dumb mid-gesture by their blown-glass light, his
hand raised *in hoc signo,* and forgotten there.

"Ah, thinks he's a cardinal," a vendor had joshed. Outside the
men's room of that hotel on the Grand Canal where she and Lev
would have had drinks, a man waiting irritably for Peter to emerge
had glanced askance at her, but at the sight of Peter's tranced exit

had muttered, *Scusi,* and had reached out to zip up Peter's fly. In the *pensione,* where Debra has engaged a parlor suite of two bedrooms and a sitting room, the forwarded mail had identified him as *il Dottore* or *il Professore,* at once allowing him any peculiar meditations—although the monitoring of the two women is surely observed. At the sight of a soupspoon paused in midair, the waiter will croon, "*Si, si,* . . . very hot." The *padrone,* leaning on the low wall that separates his establishment from the Zattere below, if suddenly joined there by the professor, who has slipped ahead of his watchers, slings his arm comfortably around Peter's shoulders: "Yes, isn't it beautiful?"

But midweek, when a chance overnight guest, noting their names on the list, touts himself in a note to them as a professor who knows his work, although Duffy and he have never met, he is fobbed off—and that night their trio does not dine in the salon.

"I don't want that crowd to know," Zoe confesses to Debra. "Or not yet."

"Ah, it's the same with cancer," she replies. "For some."

Is the girl cold, or deep? Zoe wonders. Were I sick, would I trust her to nurse me? Yes, utterly. Then what is it I must know about her? And why? Is it because I'm away from the studies that in whatever freakish setup—or maybe because of those—keep me a stable, even conventional citizen? How I miss that anchoring concentration, which can bewilder or even repel those without it. And that night-walking smile which honors something solved.

She hears a spectral sigh: "Eh, Zipporah. Those secrets with oneself that are the basis for all intellectual work."

The man who said that, one of those remarks he called his "old saws," had been amused at her treasuring them. She shivers with longing for that man.

Peter is at her side. It is after siesta—a time in the sitting room, her turn to watch him, with Debra out on her afternoon break. The room, one flight up, with a view of the canal, isn't lavish but has those half-awkward comforts the nineteenth century brewed: high, dim ceilings; a bay too wide to open, or fixed not to; a tall, dank cupboard with a new lock; a pile of old issues of an Italian publication called *Lady*. No rugs are provided, or wanted. And circulating like an old, forgotten amenity, the sweetish air that comes from wood, wood everywhere, teaching the nostril how breathing used to be, and the underarms to sweat.

In the downstairs salon, the guests tend to celebrate aloud the Venetian pulse-effect they are paying for. The American, "So relaxing," stretching its accent as wide as its yawn; the British braving the *"Chiarascuro!"* of light and dark the sunset induces in them. Debra's scrutiny turns from one to the other, as if they may be instructing her. Her presence registers strongly; perhaps they are.

In protracted hotel life one has dialogues with persons one never speaks to but may remember all one's life. The tension of such imperfect solitude may grow unbearable. It's possible that their patient, suspended in his stop-watch present—and not accumulating a past?—is tolerating this better than they.

On one end of the long table in the bay is a set of ten wooden letters, purchased in a children's toyshop here, which can be arranged to spell his name. At the other end is a folder containing a copy of his last essay, at which Zoe has never seen him look. Yet sometimes, passing it, he picks up the folder, presses it to him, and puts it down. In the middle of the table is a picture-puzzle with many tiny pieces forming a complicated, subtly graded scene, a parlor game he could always be tempted to. This one is a scene from *Der Rosenkavalier*, at which he is doing well. She blesses Bert for having sent it along. Watching Peter work at the high-glazed nuggets of vague color, she thinks it may be his fingers that somehow "psych" the shapes. His stints are short. Yet she must constantly remind herself that this man, monitored as he must be on the simplest daily actions, has a center still powerful, which can now and then break out. In pure sweetness still. In surely self-directed rage. And yes, like a man visiting his own language—with sudden intelligence.

Yesterday he quoted Dante. The familiar opening of the *Inferno,* at a slurred pace, but the words enunciated clear. He can translate lire into dollars quicker than she, though only when impelled, never on demand. After an earlier episode during which he quoted in Latin, unidentified source, she'd waited a few days, then cited the phrase, schoolgirl style. Her own Latin is limited. "Catullus, the old rip," he'd shot out. "Whoever put you onto that?" Then sat immobile, with a pinched mouth.

"I had a patient once; she would quote, quote, quote. But that was after shock treatments, too many," Debra says later. "And once a young man performed for us at the clinic. He could multiply in his head like a computer but was like stone otherwise; what's the name for them?"

"Idiot savant." Zoe had always disliked a term so cleverly apropos, that yet seems to cherish the dullness of those who don't otherwise exceed.

"So." Debra doesn't habitually read, even a newspaper. She has "earned her cap"—"Do your American nurses say that?"—Everything she does is—on site. That must be how she lives. Certainly that is why the two of them are here, though from impulses opposite.

To "Zee" (which is how Debra addresses her, as if in haste to another nurse), "Zee, catch him, he's just around the corner, I have to excuse myself for a sec," a "site" is where you go, in hope of a place sequestered in time and custom. Where one can trace, or even go back to, a hoard of how humans began. Slotting their life-in-the-now as if it is merely a mime of what life was once, in the long trek toward the present. For the civilized scientist, the "primitive" has a present of little significance except to himself. He and his kind are important artifacts, on their way to vanishing as soon as recorded, into an actual present that will only gentrify, and corrode. Since there is nowhere else to go?

Hard lines, Zipporah thinks. But this we admit.

Debra, on the other hand, the young Sabra—she and her kind must feel themselves to be instant history. The birth of a nation, that burden, is being carried forward on their backs, leavening their blood, turning it biblical when spilled. They are reared to walk, act, breed, and think as if in a pageant exposed to all—a modern testament. Their site is the now, and no matter their education or their bias, to watch them acting together can be marvelous: the human animal in concerted motion, toward what no one knows for sure is progress or doom.

Look at Debra there, lithe, beautiful example of that "now." Her own emotion, powerful as it must be, is a blend of rude health and how she has been schooled. Her devotion to those who need nursing may seem in a sense remote. Not less intense though because it is schooled, and maybe part of the nationalism that is ritual?

As for me, Zee whatever-you-call-me, don't I carry my site in history with me quite as consciously? People like me are "the old set" of each decade; even when speaking of the future, we have already given ourselves a place. Though we may try to be limber or to appear so, we, the "civilized," are always the status quo. Every time. No matter how smart we are about "time." Tricking it by accelerating our experience of it, examining it in reference to light, space, gravity, and all the while centering it. On us.

Across the table Peter, fallen into one of his spells of stasis, seems to have forgotten his puzzle. Yet his face isn't vacant but lonely, like some mild giant, victim to a pygmy illness. It has been her habit to be a collector of the specific only, to bring any question of theory to him. Now, if she could, she would ask him why the God-believers get most of the world's scrutiny. Why aren't the demi-agnostics like her, and presumably like him as he was, taken into the archives of study nearly as much, vague and unassociated though their numbers tend to be?

For surely Peter, we, the "assimilated," crowd the world, yet are churchless. And as "belief" goes, nearly anonymous. Tallied only insofar as the government dares, in that pitiful codex, the census, by where we live, on how much income, and to what categories, racial, political, social, we may belong. In other words, how we bank and transmute into generalized living, whatever we may believe.

It seems to her that Peter, in his anti-religion, may have in the end been more religious than she. It was he, knowing Greek but little Hebrew, who had hung the mezuzah. A couple of Hebrew hymns still ring in her head in syllables and tune, but not their English translation, which in the weekly Sunday school handout, when the Sunday school joined the "service," may have been underneath in wee script or not there at all. The *En-kel-lo-hay-ay-nu,* swelling to *En-kuh-mo-shee-Ay-nu,* she can hear it yet. But would have to ask a seminarian what it said. Says. Born in a Boston mayored by Catholics and suffused with that Irish energy-on-the-rise, she may even know more about Catholicism, its creeds an incense that penetrated others' corners, its Jesus a masque daily offered the rest of the populace.

When she was a child her country was in the main not merely Christian but, as one of her uncles had termed it, "Christian-out-loud." Her family, merchants and professionals when they had arrived here, had stayed that way, separated from the rest of the population only by pride of race and heritage, and of course "prejudice." A word mildly familiar in the dedicated gossip of a few synagogue-faithful elderly aunts or cousins, but otherwise not much bruited; though at the dinner table, when summer planning was discussed, one learned that one's family simply did not apply to certain hotels. Yet according to Peter, who'd met the elderly remnants of both her parents' clans, whose town and business acquaintance had already been wide, "Pride isn't what keeps them from joining those clubs and assemblies where they might at best be token Jews. Actually, they look down upon those types. It's a matter of taste. Though of course they can't say."

Laughing, she'd said, "Same when we intermarry, happy to say. Taste."

Now she is what? A once Sunday-schooled Jew who keeps, mildly, the same prides and tastes, but in no way as functionally? Nothing to do with having married a Christian. The word "assimilated" is still heard predominantly in the Jewish context; Italians and other white ethnics who depart from their backgrounds are in general seen as doing so nationally, rather than racially, or even religiously. It's the observing Jews themselves, as their numbers shrink, who most fearfully keep the term alive. Castigating their own apostates hardest, where known, but turning a jaundiced eye on all. Meanwhile covertly fanning what Peter, in that first meeting of minds with her father, had called "your famous sectarian differences, sir."

She had never heard of any such division. Her father had outlined them:

"The *schtetl*. From middle-European villages almost identical with the ghetto. Those are the most recently here. The German Jews who preceded them—also Ashkenazim, but middle class and huffier. The Sephardic strain: considered fancy, if from Spain and educated. Not so regarded, if Middle Eastern and poor.

"Though between your mother and me," her father had concluded with a grand sweep of the hand not usual with him, "You and your cousins are compounded of all of them."

According to him, every Jew had the ghetto in his or her ancestry. "Sooner or later. Used to be those of us who were 'sooner,' anywhere were the top of the hierarchy. Now the descendants of those who were closest to the death camps in geography hold the sway." He had bent his head to that in reverence, and also in the guilt of having been at a distance, comfortable and American, though he had done what he could at the time. "The Hitler Time," he'd said, was what his generation, already elderly, had called it. Only as the martyrdom solidified into history had it become the Holocaust to all. "With the State of Israel its natural heir. Though that can't last." Peter had asked why. "Because martyrdom is only for those who experience it."

Yet that day, such exchange had been preamble to the real business of the hour. Back there the sunlight, melding with the scholarly lamplight of her father's office-study, sheds a brown fatherliness. On her right is the bright column of destiny that is her lover. Her mother, that deep well of commonsense prattle, endless provisioning, plus an undoting loyalty that will rescue you if need

be but would rather teach you how to avoid such a situation, is upstairs awaiting the verdict on Peter. "That's what your grandfather
did about me and your father. Had him on the carpet. Looked him
over for fair."

The better truth was that she had banished herself, knowing
her own temper. Muttering, "I have no patience with male ma-
neuvers. Men are all hippos there."

"Smoke?" her father says to young Duffy, indicating a box of cigars from which he himself had not yet selected.

"Not yet," Peter answers. "I shall. But not today."

"Our fathers required that we smoke, after we attained majority. They weren't very athletic men. Too busy getting to be non-
immigrants. But hot on the spectator sports."

"My father, Aloysius Duffy, and his friends, were in the same
boat, you might say. On a different deck. Second generation, up
from laborers, they were busy being policemen, or if men of small
size, school caretakers, drivers, or conductors on the Fifth Avenue
Bus System, which was Irish to the core. The big men, Dad and his
friends, had biceps they had no time for. Their sport was to go to
the Yankee Stadium—and yell."

They had forgotten her. She might as well have been upstairs.
Here in Venice she is still the onlooker at their game. How both of
them had relished it! Her father, ready to sparkle, is careful not to
patronize. Peter is lounging informally but politely, in the posture
that will be his for life, but his sneakers, as if turned to iron, won't
give an inch.

"Ah, Duffy, your dad was second generation, also, like mine."

"We were refugees from the potato famine, sir. A minor diaspora. Can't compete with yours."

"For sure, we Jews think our diaspora cancels out all others.
With a capital _D._" Her father grinned. "From Deuteronomy
maybe, where that all started."

"Deuts twenty-eight, twenty-five, yes." Peter shot out the text
with an answering grin. "Father Lauder in our school, a Scots in a

nest of County Clares, took care to point out we Gentiles had our own Dispersion. But for safety's sake drilled us on both Testaments."

You were looking down at the box of cigars at the time, Peter, Zipporah all but says aloud to the tranced figure before her. On that same table now in your study. At home . . .

Back there, her father's glance is on him. "A little Cuban brings me those, every three weeks. More of his lot coming every week, he says. Mostly to Florida. His wife, a Basque and a housekeeper for a friend of mine, won't go. He got her through an agency. So did my friend."

"The whole world works by diaspora," Peter says, staring at the brown lengths in the box as if each is a Jew-boy or an Irisher setting out. "From atomic to racial. And random, underneath all the theology. I may well spend a happy life studying just that."

"Any interest in coming to Harvard?" Her father is not an alumnus. But the rising crowd of young Jews from the law school is well known to him.

The iron sneakers hold firm. "I plan to stay in New York."

The two face each other. To her father, in his youth an historian thwarted by family pressure into the law needed for her grandfather's business, scholarship is holy. In his law firm no junior partner has the nerve either to engage him with ideas, or to oppose his.

Peter sees a middle-size man, natty as to his profession but seemingly always dressed in the same worn suit, whose common expression of a severe intelligence is a chuckle, infusing the household with reassurance. Whose paternity is never a yell.

"Marry the girl," her father said. "Sir."

"I'll have a smoke on that," her husband-to-be said.

Why does she see only now how her clan may have assimilated him? A state of affairs never dreamed of as she watched him, often from her kitchen aerie, proud of his dignity and humor with her family, trusting most of all in his and her private dialogue.

But Venice, for all its rainbow illusion, is Shylock country still. Jews like me are never merely tourists here. While at my elbow is this half-heiress to the ages, battle witness of the new Judah. And demi-widowed of we don't know what.

Yet when Debra is here she is our intermediary. She dialogues with the disease. When he stalls mid-sentence, or loses touch with where he is, she hauls him back, sending forth the quietly stream-ing repetition that "the Neurological," that London clinic she sets such store by, has taught. "We deal with their present, entirely. Only the family can deal with their past."

And are relegated to it. She, Zipporah, is his memory now.

Ordinary people hunch over puzzles as if the solution of their lives is there. Peter sits erect and staring forward, like a blind pianist whose fingers are counseling him.

"Sunday school for the kids," she says aloud. "How you and I agonized." But more because for the first time we differed about them. He had wanted them not to go at all, to be taught religions secularly. She had prevailed, bolstered by the "group" emphasis in current child-rearing theory, but actually wanting to bequeath them those weekly mornings in fresh clothes, the warming bore-dom that comes of doing one's duty, and that slight, magical brush with the unknown, so easily sloughed off in life to come. Peter, silent and clenched as she had never seen him, had had no argu-ment except within. "You're right," he'd gouged out finally. "I'm not just 'lapsed,' apparently. I'm—what are the psycho-sages call-ing it? 'In denial.' And we must not teach them that."

Actually the free-for-all tone of the household had already turned the kids ecumenical.

"Let's choose," Mickey, peacemaker about to die, had volun-teered, sensing perhaps that he would never get to go? Nell, prag-matically herself, said, "Let's shop around." Gerald had already attended the bar mitzvah of a rich Jewish friend's elder brother, whose father took them for treats that Gerald had a mind to have again. Erika, his rival, may have started it all by wanting to be confirmed. Charles, as usual assuming himself diplomatic, said, "There's only a year or so between most of us. Shouldn't we all do them at once?" Zachary, early hippie and the best educated in worldly ways, had quipped, "Too late for me. They'd kick me out." In the end, egged on by interest, competitiveness, some serious craving for the spiritual, or the same social impulse that had acceded to dancing school, they had all of them attended several denominations, including the sexually precocious Zach, drawn in by one or the other girlfriend.

All of them have ended up adept at biblical allusion, a student lack of which had begun to be moaned by Peter's colleagues in the history and English departments. Always charmed by his children, he had made a game of that when they were young. Calling out, "Is this the company of Jehu?" when they were noisy, or even when they were near middle age, not above hinting to the divorced Charles, in love with an Asian girl like him an astronomer, but plainly needing a push: "Better to marry a Buddhist than burn for the planets only, eh?" Charles had replied in good family style: "Kindly inform St. Paul she is a Catholic," and had followed his advice. Though Peter might have noticed that the only two of their brood who had become religious observers had opted to be Jewish, he never spoke of it. Nor had she ever confided what Ruth Halle, a Jewish acquaintance deep in Hadassah, the women's organization, but once married "to a Mayflower descendant," had whispered to her at a funeral at Temple Emanuel, "It's we Jews who always win out." Another view had come from Peter's own departmental secretary, the dependable Maureen, who, wedded to the widowed Isaac, scholar-expounder of Wittgenstein, had asked timidly, after her second cocktail, "Mind if I ask you, Zipporah? You find intermarriage is shallow? Isaac and me don't ever talk about what counts."

Zipporah hadn't answered either of them as she could have, that in Ruth's case it was the massive weight of her family money that had marked out her children's path. Or that Maureen's lack of transcendental conversation might be sadly due to Isaac's estimate of her featherweight brain. Telling Peter about Isaac and Maureen, her own mother's "upstairs wit," as the family called the domestic or female kind, had come in handy. "Jews blame everything good or bad on being Jews. No wonder the Gentiles catch it from us."

For almost two decades prior to her death in her nineties a few years back, her mother, opting out of her role as the dowager supreme in the "cold Northeast style," had spent half of each year as the cherished houseguest of Edith and Opaline, who lived in Taos. Edith, widow of one of the noted editors of her day, and herself a former magazine executive both plaintively and assertively retired, had found ease in ceding up her sophistication in favor of Opaline, a Texan whose lean height and excessive shyness made her a personage even before you saw her grayed, leather-jerkined resemblance to the life-size subjects of her paintings, which lined the walls of one room. "Knights-in-armor, palely loitering," Edith said reflectively to each visitor, squinting one eye the better to see artist and subject simultaneously.

"I'm the child they're too old to adopt," Zipporah's mother had said. "When lesbians are WASP ladies there's nobody sweeter and more delicate to live with...And I can hold onto your father's memory better than in mixed company." She and he had been an affectionate couple. "An arranged marriage can be wonderful; when it works out there's an extra kick to it. No doubt mixed marriages can be the same—as I can see."

That last, reverberating like a blessing, had never before been said. Like many Jewish women, her mother had been intent on keeping up the family façade, while grimly critical of what went on behind it. "Edith and Opaline go in for harmony," she sighed, coming home to die. "I miss the Jews." And she had wanted to die well. "As I can *see*," she'd said, passing on the phrase like the jewel it was, since she had been all but blind, "Some people get last rites. We Jews go it alone."

———

Her own willed departure from her homeland had been meant to be merely that. Not this long séance in which, one by one, all those close to her appear, each in his or her unit of memory. No demons, djinns, or genie of the rubbed hunger-lamp. Just one's intimates, the ghosts as pink and white as those still living. Brooding so, her brain and Peter's, linked by their mutual past, seem to her a picture puzzle both are solving. Or else the puzzle, erupting from synapses made joint by time and love only, is solving them?

Which of its infinitely small pieces, each with an indented outline meant to be locked on all sides by others, will pop up?

T his time it's Norman, after a Sunday lunch with them, as often on those alternate dates when the relatives are not slated to appear. It's Jennie's day off from that, and similarly their's; the talk more lax, more personally linked. The kids, in from their various Sunday-morning denominations, after being gently probed on this by Peter, and in turn harking politely to adult exchanges whose worn paths they seem to expect, have gone to their usually separate destinations, which by rule must be marked on a calendar kept for that purpose in the kitchen, allowing them to clean up the remains of any dessert as they go.

"Saves the wear on the dishwasher," Jennie comments as she crumbs the tablecloth. "And you know, they never fight like most kids, over who gobbles what. Mebbe they turn out Quakers." She is privy to any dining-table conversation, but only comments as she crumbs. And quickly departs for good. Leaving what she's said to sink in.

Norman hoots. He and Peter are lighting up, as always before they repair to the latter's study. They know Zipporah enjoys the fragrance and its associations. In the study, Norm will impart financial advice they won't adhere to, and the worldly out-of-the-academic-loop confidences Peter and she enjoy. Among long-term friends, the one you don't agree with is often the spice.

"Quakers," Norman repeats. "All I know from them is they're peaceniks. But not too conscience-stricken they don't acquire banks." He likes to demonstrate how little he knows of most religions, including the one he was born to. Reverting also to the accent he grew up with, that being Norman's signal of what he considers to be close to his heart. Or what he wants people to consider as so. He plays the living-room version of the vaudeville comics whose "in our crowd" insolence he was brought up to admire. As with those, one is supposed to wonder whether Norm knows he's being funny, though he doesn't always get the same results. "Bear with your Uncle Benjamin," her father had advised, on a similar family commentator. "He shouldn't have taken off like that, on girls' miniskirts. Not with your friend there wearing one." As well as you, his sidelong look said. "But Ben's no fool." Her mother said, "He's our brother-in-law. And my sister reveres him; that's why your father wouldn't dress him down. Ben's kick is women. And somehow she falls for it."

In Boston, there was a bay window not unlike this one. Sit here long enough, and the spiders common to the crevices of both will weave the present-past, that enduring web.

"Free-run chickens, those kids of yours are," Norman is hooting. "All the young nowadays. Not only ours." He has long ago assumpted Peter into the category he calls Us. "Same with the giving. Used to be you could depend on Jews for Jews. Now it's all over the lot, to any charity comes along. Maybe a little token. It's mostly the rich Jews that still give to our charity. And mostly to Israel, which they seem to think is identical. Those boys do it in order not to be conspicuous. For not being very Jewish anymore in daily life." He smirks. "But sometimes in the old style also. To show off what they got." He can dwell on these analogies through half of one of Jennie's coffeecakes, to his credit not excluding himself. His own pet is the United Jewish Appeal, for which he fundraises steadily. You give at first, if not from conviction, maybe because you are beginning to be able to afford to. Your dead wife, blessed be her name, kept you up to the mark. Finally, you do it because it would be noticed if you didn't. Or, God forbid, if it was thought you had to stop. "You got to know the pitch."

On his last sip of coffee, he hands Peter one of the cheroots he imports directly from India. "With Peter here, what contribution I get is only from luck." He smokes in short puffs, while Peter, listening to him, forms a pale wreath of slowly exhaled blue.

"I check his tax returns," Norman says. "He gives only to non-Catholics. Otherwise, he don't discriminate, and him I don't blame. When he was already in grad school, one of the best brains to be in his field . . . Even if it is a cockamamie—hmm . . . And what does his family do but notify the dean of that nonsectarian college he got a scholarship over their heads to, that since their prodigy is still underage his grades must be sent to the parents first, not to him. And his course-list to their spiritual advisor. Just like when you went to St. Vincent Ferrer, hah, Peter? Or was it St. Vincent de Paul? . . . 'So will Columbia University, which has connections with a Union Theological, kindly oblige.'"

She had been shocked to the gills. "Peter. You never told me your parents did that."

"My mother. She was already a little—"

Senile? By the time Zipporah and Peter had met, the mother had been on her way to being institutionalized.

"*Meshugenah?*" Norman says. "Some our mothers get that way too, just from being a mother. That whadycallit string that goes to their navel; they never want it cut."

"Cord," she says. "To the umbilicus."

Peter had been smiling by then. "That point in any structure through which all its lines of curvature pass."

Norman had exploded. "The belly, huh? Never heard the ladies better defined . . . Or the non-ladies . . . But anyways, this wife of yours did all right by you. Gave you as many kids as a—." A cigar tops a gesture. He squints at it. "—as a Jesuit."

Their howl, joined by a blinking Norm, has brought Jennie to peer in the door, dressed for her afternoon off. Her destination never on any calendar.

"Dinner was so good, Jennie," Peter said, "that Mr. Norman

got his genders mixed." But all the way from Venice, she can see his strained face.

"Did he now." Jennie disappears behind the swing door, pops in again. "With what?"

"Theology. The church."

"'deed so? Maybe Miss Agnes could set him right." The door shuts.

How blind she and Peter had been about those two! Norman had grown quiet. Then had come down on her. "Your theology, Zip? I take it you scientists don't believe in a personal deity—personally. Yet you yourself run round the world like you got St. Vitus's Dance. Trying to get God to give you the eye."

Peter had said quickly, "Norm talks along with what he smokes. These cheroots have a windy draw. Being truncated at both ends."

That memory, of a November afternoon with gray clouds scuttling at the windows, pungent veils within, seems to her alive with habitation. The clash and runnel of intimate talk. The domestic chains of gentle ribbings and imposed secrets. Of affections and flarings that both last.

Here in Venice's rheumy pink-and-gilt air there's a waxwork silence, for which nobody's to blame. The silence of the rented room.

Which is her site?

She's brought that with her. She turns to Peter, speaking aloud. "Remember when I said, 'Norman, you're forever making analogies. It's the most Jewish thing about you.'" She chuckles. "And he said, 'So? So, watch out.'"

Peter has deserted his puzzle, but not as persons normally do, absently, its fret still in the head, the leftover pieces on the table regarded like insults. He's in that state early named by Debra, whether a medical term or one of her own sometimes stilted approximations is not clear. "Apathy."

The word has come to be a knell, of doom as yet stayed, of a time lapse the forces impose. The other Peter, rapped at for his habit of heavy musing, would have laughed it off: "Just give me a shake." Or would have brought up some treasure from his concentration. At times she fancies he still may.

This Peter suffers his state, breathing lightly, blinking to some metronome. There is no flutter, no hint of where he has gone to. At first she could not bear to be in the room with this. Now she's half charmed. Is he dreaming that he has absconded from a common dream?

Debra, if present, will clock his duration in this state. If not in the room when this occurs, she wants to be summoned. "Stopwatch!" Peter blurted the first time he caught her at that—he suddenly ordinary again, or in the state of consciousness that at the moment is so for him. In subsequent such moments he has been saying, "Stop. Watch." "One of his puns," she'd said to Debra, who either hadn't known the term or thought the event too insignificant for reply. He seems to bear Debra no rancor. Though sometimes when not in that state, he stares long at the heavy timepiece she wears. Last week he said suddenly, almost gratefully: "STOP." Nothing since.

Debra doesn't reveal why she keeps score; she doesn't have to. She's clocking the retreat of a personality, inch by cell-pinch, into the apathy absolute. To watch this while the physical body lives on, slackened but in familiar outline, now ruddy, now pale, is to be convinced once and for all of the existence of that beanbag of the psychologues, that exiled darling of all the philosophers—the soul. To know that souls exist you have only to watch one die.

And here Debra comes. From the window she can be seen crossing the *plage*, ending the long, lone walk she takes daily, without excuse. A nurse must have to remind herself constantly that she is also a person in her own right. And this nurse, surely. In this place.

Each evening, returning in time for the first sitting at dinner, and at the one hour when the *padrone* will not be found at his waterside post, she pauses to lean on the wall there, at which time one sees her as she must appear to the other guests. Perhaps it's because of the hour, that none approach.

Some, old clientele mostly, have a tender understanding of the Zattere, which runs more to shipping than to palaces, and can be counted on, in terms of both business and fashion, not to be the Grand Canal. Some of the British may have been coming here much of their lives. Even the American returnees seem to have escaped a status still common to U.S. travelers in European capitals— that awkward sense of having been just now added on. The few Italians are seen only in the salon, in family glut. Or else a stray commercial pair, like them impenetrably citizen.

For all of them, Debra's entry, quietly as she makes it into the old-fashioned spacious salon after having sent the spruced-up Peter on ahead with Zoe, is always an event. Polite as the diners may be, heads manage to swivel, to an undertone blur of comment. Clad in a dull dress bought only to supplement the shorts that would have affronted at dinner, eyes lowered, she still cannot be unassuming at will. She is young, a beauty, but no more so than many girls of these parts, though taller than most. If one sees her only from the side, is it the arch of her neck, her very stride, that makes one want to see her face to face?

Full-face, the eyebrows, though not heavy, arrest, above a clarity of pupil, brown, a plane of cheekbone, a wide curve of mouth. Now that you've seen the face, you want to see it move. As she speaks, not too often, not too long, all is as should be. This person's conduct will match that face. It will have convictions. That may make you feel comfortable, even happy, or uncomfortable, according to your lights. Whatever country you come from, nine times out of ten you're likely murmuring to your companion, "She's not one of us." It's her bearing, the men may say to their women. "Otherwise, she's no star." That confidence, the women say to themselves, "Does she have it at all times?"

These are median travelers. To the romantics among them she may be the hoped-for mystery. To the cynics, what they expect?

Zoe, watching her and the diners, thinks of the one female

confidence Debra has awarded her. An explanation, really. Or further apology for leaving?

After Debra and Lev had first slept together, he'd said, "Half expected to find the Star of David on your underwear." Confiding this, she had smiled like any female. And what had she replied? "There are dozens of us in our country," she'd said.

She's been washed clean with patriotism, Zoe says to herself. And what woman used to walking between the wounded and the dead wouldn't have that stride?

Her family name had been Cohen also, spelled the same as Lev's. In their travels abroad, hadn't that made it easier? He didn't know the kind of people who call you Mrs.". . . Raffish, but not criminal? One couldn't ask. "Warm," Debra had after a minute added on her own account.

At the time when she was still with them on Central Park West, while the legal calls over Lev's death were being fielded, the Duffys had been shy of bringing his name up personally. Yet in retrospect, perhaps to hear that name, if rarely, was why she'd stayed on, even to coming abroad with them. As well as from duty? Yes, in part. The Zipporah of old, immersed in children, could automatically spot—and not only in her own brood—those young birds who rush to serve, and those others who merely open wide their beaks. So what's happened to make Debra leave now?

There are people for whom life's actions are always a repetition, buying the same houses and clothes, and if circumstance thrusts, marrying again, over and over, the same woman, the same man. Then there are those who must not repeat, at least outwardly. Who fight shy of that. To whom each life-turn, beckoning, will appear to be grafted on anew. Where now is Debra's war?

What they know of her history before Lev has come mostly and first from Peter. Not that it was ever his habit to question. But as with his students, and perhaps arising from that occupation, he was, as they were wont to say, "always there for you." A fallow ground into which you might drop what you knew of yourself and what you wanted to know. "The young can be all-over acne inside, even though the skin is baby clear. And some of the smart ones are the worst off," he would say. "And sex is not the whole story."

His colleagues were jealous of what they saw as "being hot stuff in the student province." Isaac, the one who had married the featherweight he thought safely pillowed beneath him, could be snide. "You take 'how-to' lessons maybe?"

Waiting for Peter's answer to such digs, Zoe would often half resent his never capping hostility with the same. "My own adults were simply not my sort," he'd said that time. "To find that out when you're young, that's hard, Isaac. Lucky me. I found some who were."

Sincerity can unman the Isaacs, if not for too long. "And you found a vocation, huh?" The group around the two had narrowed in, ever ready for handouts from the "scholars' soup kitchen," as Peter had dubbed these regional conferences. At which the wives were admitted to the soirees, as being from no region in particular.

"One of his vocations," she had dared. The group veers toward her, not because she has status in their society or its language. Because she doesn't. She wonders if Isaac, whose field is semantics, knows that she and her husband call the expression on their faces "gnostic glee." "Hah, you read him too?" Isaac jeers. "On—I quote—'The ideas that remain unposed, forever changelings. As in the time before atoms. As now.' Unquote . . . No wonder, Peter, we call you the 'apostle of the in-between.'"

She dares a glance at Peter now. Is he back there with her, listening to his own music? Perhaps even to what he had said to her when they were again alone: "What's most misunderstood about the intellect, Zippy, is the animal fever that produces it. Quote. Unquote."

She's no more his real memory than the lily pad is the pool, that private tarn. Is she merely living her life backward, through him? Who cannot be questioned. Who these days can froth at any probing. A phenomenon she had seen at ceremonies the West would call hysteria. Foam bridling the mouths of those at the spectacle, who were themselves neither shaman, dervishes, nor Altaic priests in the Urals, but were being shaken into their own divinity. Spittle forms on the hairless nations as justly as a beard. On the swarthy it can be an extension of the teeth, part of the mask. On Peter, now when he pales in fury, the weak bubbles blend in, as if the impacted brain is breaking through. To form a second set of lips.

With Debra, by whom he had at once been recognized as the patient-to-be, who knows what in him most beguiles? When asked whether she would come with them she had at once agreed, even offering a sparse vita of her qualifications, the way a hospital nurse might present herself at a bedside—"You have come down from the Op. I am Nurse X, your night special."—giving the facts in short and immediately, while consciousness may still persist. Though she knows well that no Op will do.

For four nights before they left for Europe, Zipporah—as she still felt herself to be—had prowled the apartment, ticketing the last of the attic trove that was to be sent to museums, visiting the piled clothing to remind herself of how buttons and snaps and knee patches can hoard childhoods, are its medals. Then she had slept, as if drugged. While she slept was when Peter and Debra had had talks.

On the plane Debra sits alone by request, a few rows up ahead. The Duffys accept this. She is moving her story with her. They sit a few rows behind, Peter on the aisle for best access to the toilet, Zoe on his right, so that either way, if need be, he is bracketed.

Planes have always stimulated Peter. He becomes the gracious courier, lightly kite-flying his personal map of the world, picking you a travel bouquet. His brows quirk, as always before wordplay. "While you slept it out those nights, Zippy, she and I talked it out." They are aware that this may be the last chance to talk together separately. Already they are no longer alone. They are unaware that this will be the last time he talks fully consecutively.

"Her parents emigrated to Israel before she was born. 'When I was in the belly,' she said. One set of grandparents were already in Jerusalem. In either case, she didn't say from where. Poles, I sort of

recall, the elder ones. And late of Manchester. She's had some connection with Britain that counts with her. Maybe a training stint.
The mother may have been the Pole." He smiles as the reminiscing
do, overseeing his own recall, lending it authority. 'He is tall, my father; she is short,' she said. As if this was important. The father, by
then a haberdasher, moved them to Tel Aviv, where their store still
does fine. Her mother always helped in it, but wouldn't allow her
to. She was taught at home, through correspondence school. 'I
never saw boys.'...Her much older brothers left the family early.
'Then I was the one.' Then she shut up."

He'd told this haltingly, but at a pace ascribable to his manner,
rather than to his disease. "She tells what is necessary. Leaves it
there." He'd had the impression that the parents were not on good
terms with her now. "Either they don't speak to her? Or she to
them?" When he's the questioner his voice strengthens, as it will do
later, when he will have receded. "Debra wants to be without vanity," he asserts.

Idly Zoe had recalled the handsome long coat cast willfully
aside, in what might be the Sabra style. But had been more bound
up by Peter's new habit of digging in the ear with a fifth finger,
as if to penetrate the stubborn, ungiving skull. "She hasn't got
enough secrets," he brings out. "Maybe communal life...does
that. She is certainly...not sly." And then with a rush, which even
now can still happen to him, "I think she simply doesn't see that life
can be interpreted."

His head flings back triumphantly. They laugh together, complicit for the last time. Agreeing that for two zealous explainers like
them, this was just as well. "And we are doing what we are to help
her," they'd agreed.

The first pretense oils the tongue. Later ones stick in the throat
like gravel, grimly tolerated, as from an allergy to oneself...

At the window now, the Venetian evening steals in. Here each
hour of the twenty-four comports itself like the beauty it knows it
is. It's after dinner now. Let her dream that like her he is merely

musing with lids stark wide, on what only a sneak wife would
clock. That in a second he will say, "Let's take a plane back."

And here Debra is, down there on the *plage,* returning to give Peter
his dose. Each time she comes back after one of the breaks they
must continually observe for one another, Zoe must remind herself: This is a woman, not a girl.

"Wow, is she hip," the young gigglers of the clan had said, seeing only the no-frills cool. And the men of any age: "Those god-
dess legs." All the clan had dropped in, ostensibly to pay their
respects "after the death," actually "to see what the deal is." Old
Nanette had remarked, "So that's a Sabra? Very polite; she don't
stare down her nose at us, like all we got over her is good-time
schmier. But like she has ancestors came before genealogy charts."
Wallie had regretted that Debra would be off before the big Appeal
benefit of which lie was that year's chairman. During which the patrons vied with each other, rising from the festooned tables to
pledge what they would give. "But you have to keep them going."
She wouldn't have to agree to speak; he guesses she wouldn't. "But
just to look at such a creature, knowing the ache she comes from.
Who could say 'I already gave.'" Bert had come closest. Though he
wasn't yet officially at the seminary, he'd been spending time there,
letting it seep in. Maybe trying to free himself of an obsession he
must know some think inappropriate, or to firm it into place.
Whatever, though he keeps a grave distance from Debra, his
hunches have not deserted him: "She's the only one here who
doesn't have to keep saying she's a Jew." Or part Jew, as his friend
Silverstein had whispered to the girl on his own arm.

Over here Debra always carries the worn leather bag shaped
like a valise, with similar central top lock and side straps, but
accordion-pocketed and otherwise divided within. The bag punctuates their days.

Debra makes no bones about the variety of medications and
surgical accessories that she carries with her. "We had to. On call

you are, even when you're on leave." And never sure what might happen. Or to whom. Or where. On a bombed bus once, her friends Leah and Ari were the only ones for miles around with tourniquets and sulfa. And sterile gloves. No tools for what else Ari, a medical student, had had to do. "But what to improvise, he had that." Leah, a nurse, had had the instruments in her pack. "You learn to dispense. And to scavenge we took for granted. From the hospitals. From the free samples your American drug companies send the doctors. From the dead." Debra had toted her stash loose, wrapped only in plastic, until Lev. He had bought the bag for her in Milan. "It's called a doctor's bag." Or so the clerk had told them. "Must have small doctors here," Lev had said. For a moment she is radiant, a mistress recounting the small talk. The bag has the smug presence of an inanimate object that has outlasted the giver. Hung on its curved, suitcase-style handle is a tiny pouch containing its key.

Whenever Peter sees the bag he turns away his head, a child asserting it has nothing to do with him. Or he may shrink into himself the way a dog does when for some reason it doesn't want the leash. Or if he should be in that near normal state, which is still occurring, if less frequently, he will accept the pill with that false aplomb we all summon when medicated publicly. What he gets is a mild tranquilizer, for which Zoe carries dated prescriptions for the months ahead. While they were still at home, a blood-pressure medicine briefly prescribed had been adversely reacted to and stopped. "Just as well," their doctor friend had said. Some of these blood thinners hadn't been tested for the long haul. "And when the body signals, we must heed." Perhaps a quiet regimen would suffice, he'd added, embracing the two of them. "Your trip's openended? Ah."

Once, that time the three of them came down with the bad colds afflicting many at the spa just left, when Debra had dosed them with the same antihistamine, Zoe had briefly seen the bag's inside: rows of the same pill vials that drugstores issue, small stoppered flasks, a neat cache of first-aid supplies, bandage rolls and pins, and lying neatly lengthwise, a tray of small instruments:

syringes, alongside what was surely a pedometer, perhaps used on those walks?

What Zoe dwells on is that moment when, the three of them kneeling round the open bag as Debra had commanded, she had fed the two Duffys, then herself, the same two small red pills familiar as head-cold remedies anywhere. After swallowing her own dose she had rested an arm on each of the Duffys. Still kneeling, the three of them had nestled together as birds might, or as a trio about to break into *a capella* song. For a moment they were exactly that, a trio too far from home.

Zipporah had not had time to be homesick. Under Debra's lightly resting arm, the best word for that feeling, the German *Heimweh,* had floated through her head, in her ear its muted wail. In the next moment Peter, lodged under Debra's other arm, said in the spelled way he now has: "Cocoa time." That dusk when children all over the world come in from play. And she, Zoe-Zipporah, is wrenched by a sickness for that part of a mother's life which won't come again.

Either his hand had pressed hers in response to its clench or it had not. Either he knew who he was, who she was, where they were—or he did not. He's in the either-or land of mixed tenses, half-sentences, his feet on a ground that though firm for others is bearing him along.

Whether the word stuck in her throat had emerged with its full German sound, she doesn't know. Only that Debra, nodding, had whispered, "You too? This is not saving a person." Then two words not German enough to be *Geh zuruck,* not too Yiddish to be Hebrew. Gutteral words that must be nearly the same in all languages: *Go back.*

Tonight, down below nobody stirs. Beneath their window, on the walkway between the house and the seawall, the evening *passeggiata* will soon begin, people filtering along in the slowly dropping light. Through the open pane all day long have come the whorls of air and stuttering of voices that blow over any local waterway. The *padrone,* leaning seaward on his wall again after dinner, will be saying to anyone who nears him one of the heartfelt phrases with which he takes a guest into part ownership, "Isn't it beautiful, yes?" And whether or not you say anything, "Yes, our Venice is versatile, no?"

Boarding-house hours are not. There, stripped of all the grind and grist that citizens the hours for most inhabitants, and after an instructive morning walk to the drummed-up errands, you whelm yourself in the changing and choosing of clothes. A shirt or blouse fresh enough for lunch won't do for the evening apex, when you will once again be seen, even if only by people who do not quite know who you are. All the while, you are cherishing this sinking marvel of light and township that isn't yours, no matter its name and latitude. For even when lodged in the depths of your private room you are really traveling. Even a bath is a stagecoach stop in the long day. Any practical converse, with a laundress, a dry cleaner, must sub for the housewifery of old. Should you bend to chat with another guest, take care that it does not become a confessional.

While at dinner the permanent guest, of whom there are a few here, keeps his personal essence in the wine bottle the waiter sets beside him, the one with his name on it. It is at dinner that Zoe is happiest in her threesome, daring the exposure, grateful for being in community, even of those one will never get to know or be known by. Beforehand she'll have checked whether Peter need change his trousers, there being sometimes a slight odor of urine. His morning shave at the barber's will normally do. Though he can be trusted to a degree with body care and one cannot say that he forgets, he will sometimes glidingly desert one task for another. "In public" has less and less meaning for him. As for "private," who can tell?

Yet there are times—Zoe lives for these—when her mood swings from "how did I think we could live like this?" to what she hasn't enough phrase for: the dazzle of relief, sorrow, and love forced on her when the man once known briefly returns.

"We called it 'cell break' in the hospital," Debra has said. "That was only a word we and the interns made up. Understaffed like we always were, to report you need a quickie." They had used the term mostly for the psychotics and the shocked. But this disease is more like a replay, the brain reenacting some action it deeply knows. "Like we had an opera tenor once; he could be made to sing an aria perfectly. Only you weren't to suggest which one." Or require that he remember afterwards which one he had sung. "Or he would—." She had stopped short of saying what he'd done next.

Zoe had pressed, saying, "Debra, I want to know everything." And this woman whom she's come to admire, who in a way seems to belong to some Foreign Legion of women, had grunted, "So did we." Not "so did I." Never that. Of course, this is what a legion would mean to them. To us anywhere, if one has the guts to admit it. She had often seen this anti-rational, body-defying sisterhood in the bush. Among the Ubangi women, for instance, their lips stretched inches out by those terrible disks inserted since puberty or before and with growth, larger and larger in circumference, the bodies beneath meanwhile still in the lovely sculpture of nature, while the grotesque, dish-lipped faces lift toward each other in pride. Although she can't summon a male example as exaggerated, the men have their versions of this grim camaraderie, not merely with the slashed cheeks, but as she had suspected while out there, with secret accommodations that as a woman she had not been made privy to.

And this immersion of the single soul-body in the tribal canoe-body is what we still envy these people for. We, the civilized, never get the right balance. Nor believe fully in those we have. Never can decide how far a person may depart from the verdict of the crowd. Or must exceed.

Tonight, Debra too has dreamed off. This mutual quiet is actually when they two are most separate. They never ask each other what the subject of their dreaming has been. Because they know? This unspoken unity informing all their dealings with Peter has risen to a sentiment neither has moved to define.

On the morning when Debra had carried them off here, a hired car with driver had arrived at the spa steps. A packed lunch is trotted forth; reservations ahead are in hand. This is more than bedside practicality. Lev would have swept Debra across Europe this way. She is going, with witnesses, to meet him again. When Debra asks the driver to lift the hood of the car, her dark head leans over the engine. Just so Lev might have done at each station of their trek—their flight? There's no other hint. But Zoe knows that after a time those left behind sometimes catch themselves in the very gesture or cadence of the dead, in unconscious mimicry. Zoe's own father's cough used to replicate in her; now and then in the mirror, a gesture of her mother's had superimposed. But nothing of Mickey, never. The person can return in you only from the ultimate distance. Or when that distance is about to be accepted.

That's it, she'd thought, as Debra had raised her head from the engine, slammed down the hood, and stared toward the road that they were to take. Somewhere in her outline there had been a faint hitch and thrust of her arm. The body has its own recognitions. Is she letting him go?

Tomorrow, on a final sojourn before Debra leaves, they are going to do what Debra came for, but have been delaying. They're going to visit a synagogue, the most beautiful in Europe according to Lev, Debra had said, the one where they had promised themselves to be married. "If that became possible." Zoe wonders even now whether Debra really wants to go there, but it is she who has so proposed. As if she will keep what promises she can?

"Debra," Zoe says, "Don't feel guilty because you are leaving us. You and I—we've been a legion of two. Who could ask for more?"

Debra is staring at Peter, her brows knitted. Her long-fingered hands rest on her knees. The doctor's bag is gripped between them. Peter's eyes are fixed on the table, but one can't be certain whether there is conscious vision in them. The puzzle is center table. On either end are items just arrived in the mail. To his right, topping a small stack of identical magazines, is a new issue containing a portion of his last essay, on its cover a listing of his other works. To his left is the large, handsome envelope containing the letter of provisional acceptance from the order of nuns, its name in heavy black under a cross emblazoned on paper thick as cream; it is not a poor order. Payment of the considerable fee for a diagnostic period starts at once and is not returnable, "because of the medical atmosphere."

The convent is in the Apennines' *Gran Sasso d'Italia,* but is on a plateau. Relatives of a patient may be housed with him, or in a guesthouse, depending on the condition of the patient and at the discretion of the reverend mother, who has a medical degree from Canada. She has signed the letter and added a postscript. "Professor Duffy's medical record has arrived. At present you will be housed together." A choice of two arrival dates is given, with map and transportation agencies listed below.

Which of the objects on the table holds Peter's gaze is not certain. From weeks of obedient cathedral-going Zoe sees the three of them: Peter, Debra, and herself, a triptych to whoever might be standing at the room's door. She feels a chill, as if that observer has just said, "Look. At the three of them. And at the objects on the table. Three."

Debra's right hand shifts toward the lock on her bag, returns to her knee. As if the hand has received a message. So has Zoe.

Peter is "in apathy." If he is allowed to wake from his hibernation on his own, an energy results. Not normalcy, but as if a hand has reached into the storage of the brain and brought out a chapter of it. These are the "breaks" Debra refers to. But a touch too soon can annul that chance. This is why they clock him, each from her corner, holding her breath. Debra's hand is clenched, as if waiting for an aria to be sung. She's warned that these brief returns to awareness can be followed by despair, which can bring on rage. "But any emotion is therapy." Adding in a tone holy with precept, "In London we were taught to encourage them. To feel."

There's an air not nursely about her. She is clenched. What's she saying, in the small voice others use in the presence of the patient, but she never? "It's not for me to decide." Is it a question? To whom? Then comes a shrug. Nurses usually don't gesture that much.

Who of the three moves first? Peter, rising, shakes himself awake, stumbling toward the window. A boarding house this may be, but home to the Zattere and its festivals. A glare is now playing in on the worn sink, the maidenly tight, cotton bedspreads, on that bastard royal wardrobe and their own faces. A yellow glow comes from the huge birdcage floats, strung with hundreds of lightbulbs, sailing their caravans of dusky air to whatever church and canal. The route is always traditional, as any chambermaid will tell you, with the suggestive smile of the true church, that you are tourist even to the angels, unless you already know.

Peter stands in front of the bay, his back to them, a dark silhouette. If turned face-front, will he be the same, an outline of a man whose substance is now dark?

"Festa of the *Redentore*," his voice says. Two passing barges blind the room with gold, then pass on. Zoe and Debra can see each other in full; Peter has turned around. "Feast of the *Redentore*," he says, holding out a palm. "Redemption is at hand. So give me it, Debra. The international pill."

When the nurse in charge replies with a headshake, you hold quiet. Dosage refused. She wants him to stay awake. But all isn't safe. The *Redentore* was two weeks ago, the very night they came. And what does he mean by "international"? The same pill one may get anywhere, on a trip? The word "hegira," with its implied purpose, now fills Zoe with self-ridicule. Are he and she two antic cutout shadows cartooned against the great wall of true pilgrimages? Those that plod on in the march of history, long after the pilgrims are blown ashes, or bones.

Clio, the muse of history, is still putting her garters on, Peter said once. *All the others are fully dressed.*

What if she said that to him, suddenly? Or any one of the remarks that flew from his tongue like boomerangs worthy of return, but seldom made it into print. Would he recognize it? He has never hoarded his ideas the way some scholars do. Why should he be required to do so now? We allow the comedian, the poet, the known liar, to be scatterbrains, over and off the edge. From him must we have lockstep continuity, continuously demonstrated? To reassure us?

"We're going to the synagogue tomorrow, Dr. Duffy," Debra says. There's a sweet orderliness about her efforts with him, but a reserve also. "You told me the one near the Rialto must be the one Lev saw." She has crossed swiftly to the wardrobe and taken out a paper sack. "No pill just now. Have a chocolate?" She puts one in the center of a palm outstretched, hanging in space as if forgotten there. Zoe, offered one from the sack and taking it, holds her breath.

"Thanks...I will," Peter says slowly. He eats it carefully, without smear. "Yes, the Rialto was the nucleus of Venice, you know. That house of worship...most beautiful. Saw it as a young man." His eyes slide sideward, as if unsure of what age he is now.

"You loved chocolate when I first knew you," Zoe dares. "Not so much since."

"No...one enters...the realm—." He pauses. Realm is a favorite word. "—the realm of cigars...With one's first child, a father is obliged to hand them round...eh, Zip?"

She could weep. This is exactly what he said to her at the time. *The department expects it,* he'd added. *All the more because they're philosophers...Larkin did it. And he's only a humble assistant.*

"When you became Associate and Gerald was born, the same month," she says, trembling, almost with joy.

"Ah yes, Gerald. Bit of a windbag. But then, so's his old man." A chuckle is so normal. A soothing syrup in the ear.

Debra offers him the sack of chocolates.

"No thanks. Too near the...*pranzo.*" The pause now seems merely the slight emphasis on a word wrested from the tip of the tongue. "And they do us so well here."

She has to laugh. "That's what you always say, in any hotel." She smiles at Debra. "He doesn't like them, really." She can refer to him as "he" now, the way wives jokingly do, when the husband's right there. He is here. "That's why I—." She thinks better of say-

ing it. Why I thought instead to show him, one by one, my hotels
of the spirit. Those locales whose savage tolerance for the strange
might ease him, bear him along. Even swoon him away, and with
honor—as she was certain she had once seen a tribal ceremony do.
Though the man himself, cribbed in his leather-skin cage of ele-
phantiasis, had himself swallowed the deadly herb.

Honor? she thinks, as the barges pass, silent, in effect without
helmsmen.

Like all who grew up with the doctrine of the subconscious
she is accustomed to scrutinizing her motives for possible taint.
Even Jennie, schooled in Vienna, had the habit of saying to a pot
slow to boil, "See those bubbles not riz to the top yet? That's what
we all are down below," and to any of the kids caught marauding
her kitchen, "You full of bad bubbles today, for sure."

That man in the cage of himself had been fully there. Dipping
his horned head, to all celebrants in cahoots with him. As he'd
lumbered, swinging his head to each arc in the circle of those
around him, she had seen that eye encompassing all, and had
known that the spectacle, attended as such, was no charade. She
had seen him swallow; she hadn't seen him die. They hadn't let her
see the end of it. But his whole body had been his salute. For
honor, if there is such, the subject has to be fully there. What
honor accrues to the collaborator, she refuses to consider.

No, she dreams, I could never have managed it.

Bad bubbles? The phrase had become coin in the house. "But
we are not to patronize Jennie by making her into a character
only," Peter had cautioned the children. "Only indulge her." Yes, he
always saw between.

To date he hasn't mentioned Jennie, not once since leaving.
Nor will Zoe, for fear of that hollow "Who?" When letters come,
she identifies each—"Son Gerry; Daughter Nell; Cousin whoever"—before handing them on to him. When did he last nod? To
a letter from Charles, their academic, and perhaps his favorite of
the sons. He'd taken that letter to the toilet with him. To puzzle

over it, away from his watchers? It pains her that he must make such dodges for a bit of privacy. Yet encourages. A man who dodges is still aware.

Is he now?

She has to remind herself constantly now that he is here in the flesh. In the most crowded rooms of intercourse one takes for granted that each person's memory-lane is going on ticking, ticking, like in a Velasquez painting, where every face in a great convocation is cocked to its own opinion, so that what seems to be being most painted in that royal blotch of color is the silence of people thinking, of memory on the move. This is what he has forfeited. She's been denying him that citizenship. The progressively sick become nonentities, waiting at the borders of health. Worse off are the brainsick. We, the customs officers, are unlikely to let them in. Sanity has to be sure of itself.

Could she have been complicit enough to want to see him borne off in one or the other of those rites she has been privy to? Simple and jaunty as these jungle stompings and posed trances at first appear, in the end they depend on the ichor, not always deadly, that comes from the wounds and nail marks of the gods.

What would he have said if, when he was still enough himself, she'd proposed that they "go native," engage in those mysteries that might soothe, if not heal, on the long path ahead of him? Would he have seen, in that subconscious of hers which he'd likely known better from without than she from within, that in those depths we are taught to see as both sneaky and lyrical, orgiastic and innocent, but often with an unwashable bloodstain somewhere, that she'd harbored an unacknowledged wish to see him holding high a head already emptying on its own, parading it for the waiting skull-worshipers, walking with dignity behind his own open hearse?

Had she kept that buried wish from herself even as she issued the cards for that long-ago party? Changing her name—an impulse foreign to her no matter how glibly excused—like some absconding murderer? He would have known.

"Honor?" he would have said. "That's the kind widows arrange."

Instead he's here. Damaged, but with units of return. Hold the breath, while you wait, saved from being that murderess . . .

An ease invades her chest; it has no adult equivalent:

. . . She's home from Sunday school, sanctified, the house full of sun, dinner smell, and relatives. Everybody benevolent. Weekdays one can be scolded, but not today. God, that feisty old man, has taken over; even the elders don't remember to take care of you. A trickle of gossip runs two feet above her head. But topics are light; money doesn't yet intrude. Everybody has slipped from their burdens, along with this small seated person whose feet do not reach the floor. Way upstairs of the upstairs, beyond the roof, a holy aspect sees all, weaves the strings. Dinner has slid past and into the kitchen again. The box of chocolates is being handed round, reaches her. Her father's hand is poised. A motherly voice says, "Not one of the liqueurs." . . .

"Ah, Mrs. Duffy, Zipporah—you fell asleep. Good."

They lean over you like this when you've given birth. And the dream is the same. But her arms are empty. She starts up. "Where . . . ?"

"Over there."

He is seated at the long table that serves as the center of their boarding-house life. The left far end serves as an eatery. Debra is an addict to food she can bring back, from "little nibbles" to powerful salamis, deep-dish frittatas, and fruit. Even with peach juice dripping down her chin she's elegant, only spoiling the sleek picture with a Gypsy grunt: "Ahh. You like to nosh?" She buys and buys, stocking the windowsills as well, but keeping the food end of the table as neat as a nurse's station. Beyond that is the puzzle, kept on its board with an armchair facing it. The far right-hand corner is

for the mail, separately stacked for incoming and what is to be answered, as monitored by Zoe.

So far as she knows Debra receives no mail, all still being si-
phoned through Lev's lawyer in New York, with whom she checks.
At each of their moves, from spa to spa and to here, she has sent
cards, mostly to people that she met with Lev, a few to the staff she
had studied or nursed with in London. She writes these cards on
her lap, now and then characterizing recipients by what they do or
otherwise are: "A family business . . . The wife is very stylish. Their
designs one could die for . . . He and she were very good to us,
friendly . . . Jock is the best nurse in the field." In the table's center is
a personal space cleared for the patient, which she refers to as "Dr.
Duffy's desk." Each time she enters the room she checks the whole
table, as if this is her station now. In each place they've been she has
managed to create this same setup. That she'll have done something of the same as appropriate wherever she and Lev roamed
when crossing Europe together is as certain as—? As what women
are . . . Can Zipporah bear it, to be left behind, to nosh?

Peter is at his "desk," in front of two of the magazine issues
that have his name on the cover—one from years back, brought
with them, the other newly arrived. From the rear he might be the
very model of a senior professor bent over his publications. The barber has done well. The jacket is properly broken in. So may the face
still be, if he turns. Or with those blurrings that only the sharp-
eyed detect as not from mere aging. The head is a fine shape.

Does he miss his study? She daren't ask. Does he recall he had
one? It is she who returns to it in memory of him there . . . At her
approach he is standing at its door. A breeze from the park riffles
the papers behind him. He is pliant, welcoming, never grumpy. If
in that face you can see the boy, it's no discredit . . .

Not quite the case now, should he turn. But will he?

Debra is placing a shawl round her shoulders from behind, because she's been shivering. She hugs it close.

When the mail comes it's Debra who reads his letters to him,
in monotone. Her own reading, spiced with comment, warming

to news, disturbs him almost to anger. She is his widow prematurely, her memory serving them both.

Meanwhile she and Debra must hang on his every posture, every silence. In the ordinary sickroom it is the patient who is fixed, the healthy who revolve. But with this disease and its like, if you choose to live with and serve such, it's the caretaker who is fixed—and yet not. A compass needle, fast at one end, the point ever following, wavering.

Let her dream for a stolen respite, of when their lives were parallel, each drawn by the pole-star of accomplishment that beckoned. Compared to the aims of the average couple, the distance separating their stars had seemed to her negligible. If he'd never fully said so, that was because his goal was to study, in any system of thought, what was never fully said.

They are on that first field trip before they'd married. They've been watching a clutch of baby archeologists whom a professor has recruited to dig, in what he touts as the last undug corner of Crete. Meanwhile all but instructing his students on what they should find. As the shards are sifted, the best student, an Italian whose father is a curator, has indeed found the hoped-for pieces. "Planted?" she whispers.

"It's not necessarily true that he's not honest," that young Peter says. "We each of us to a degree find the food-for-thought that we're looking for. I'll probably be as bad as the rest."

Just then a vendor comes along, hawking small orbs of a yellow-green fruit new to them. Later, in New York, she will learn the rare season for them, and always seek them out. So that sinking her teeth again in the luminously pale skin of one of those she can recall how a stiff wind from the sea had ruffled the thick, brush-cut hair that would later help mark Peter as a student sympathizer. No later wind has blown away his words.

The autumn before they met, he'd visited a pal who had inherited an apple orchard. "We went to an apple fair. You might say I was instructed on the canon of apples. Or the accepted thought on the cultivation of the fruit of the roseaceous tree—at least in Washington State. Steve teaches logic out there. A canon is a body of specifics accepted on any subject—and by God, he hews to them."

Back in Crete, Peter is biting into the new fruit. "But I see how the theories rise and fall, some to last, others exploded and gone. What I mean to explore, step by step, is all the decisions that may have fallen by the wayside. What really interests me is those in-betweens. That not-quite-dead area always surrounded by the accepted." He hadn't yet used the word "realms" for it. Later, reading a galley-proof, he might carp, "That word's become my pet poodle. One should always scrutinize those one becomes too fond of."

But in Crete they are both bronzed, glowing with confidence. "I can't hope for Newton's apple to fall on my head, of course, Zip. But you know—the last word, even on gravitation, hasn't been spoke."

Just then, the professor, strutting by jubilantly, spots the fruit. "Ah, greengage plums." Copping one as his due and tossing one to the student in the pit, he goes on "to find out what the locals call it." "He won't," the student in the pit says, "he knows only Greek. Classical. The people here are Turks." Peter and she burst out laughing at this model of scholarly practice. Yet Peter plans to spend his life at the university, where ideas can at least fester. "Oh, never underestimate the academy. At least they identify the plums."

In the midden pit, the student, a short young guy whose head scarcely rises above its rim but whose knotted bicycle muscles and precociously lined grin seem to be ever mocking the Americans, brandishes the pale fruit just tossed him. He speaks several multicolored languages. "Green-a getch, is it? In Bologna, we call them nun's thighs." Later, in the night cool, "when it is safe for the wax," he will beckon them to hear contraband recordings of the monks at Grottaferrata on his one-horse gramophone; his passion is Gregorian chant. "Good for the honeymoon," he says, closing the machine in its case, the moon shining on a face gone serious. "Sleep well." When he's gone, she whispers, "He thinks we're legit. Married." "On the contrary," Peter whispers back, "He thinks we're not." And after a moment: "Those are the true Catholics."

Now and then in the obits one sees certain deaths among medical men that make one wonder. An oncologist specializing in lymphoma dies of it. A well-known orthopedist has a silly freak accident in which he loses the use of one of his legs. We're not talking, then, of the lumps and stresses caused by mere repetitive physical action, or of inaction merely, from the longshoreman's back strain to the pianist's tendonitis, to the dowager's hump. Or are we? Might a mental preoccupation, compounded with private longings too deep for notice, create a compensatory bias in the body? Could a brain be chilled into mimicry of the state of mind it is studying?

Peter sits now center table; he is at his "desk." The two periodicals containing his essays are in front of him. He could be intent on those; he could be rejecting them. The spine is ramrod, the wrists dangle. At times he seems an automaton, at others blobbed limp by the weight of what no longer connects. She had got him away before his lacks were noted professionally; to date there have been no hints otherwise. One citation for an honorary degree awarded two years ago does haunt, ferreting out as it had Steve's nickname for him. "The bastard," Peter had said with a grimace. The citation: "Can a man attain his ambition and fall victim to it? A man in between?"

Debra is watching him tensely. For the "break"? She herself seems tired, the fine oval of her face somewhat drawn. Watching her in turn, affection swarms. War may be her habitat, bound to it as she is by custom. But she can suffer from the peacetime emotions. She isn't cold, only not easily tender. Or trained to be bluff with those who are?

About to leave, Debra is exactly as attentive to him as before. And chatting with her, as woman-to-woman equals made so by loss and even the suddenness of financial circumstance, how can Zoe have ignored the solicitude directed at herself? One not merely extending to shawls. When Zoe, wanting much to thank her before their actual parting, however that is to come about, said,

"You have been our guardian angel," the measured reply had been, "I don't only leave him, I leave you. You two are one."

In the heat, the aquiline of Debra's body has blunted; sorting the morning's mail earlier, her long-fingered hands seemed plumper, less lithe. She's perhaps having her period. "How your children keep writing," she'd said. "And lucky so many." Her mouth quirked, almost with mischief. "I too am lucky. If I'd had kids with the reb, I'd have stayed. To be the *rebitzin*. Just some letters added on." She is impressed by the amount of professional mail Zoe is forwarded. She will nurse again, she says, and during their sojourn has put out feelers and gotten replies—by the envelopes, none from Israel.

"Realms," a voice from the table says, deep. "What the Sam Hill."

Debra's brows go up; what's that to mean? To date his lapses have been sequential—not knowing where he is or what he may have already said or done, and explicable when untangled. In this last hour he has demonstrated that he knows where he is. He hasn't seriously confused persons; that is, he knows who you are, though he might not be able to summon your name. "That's what a lot of us do when older, only exaggerated," she'd written Bert. "It gives one hope. We are pushing some new vitamin combos . . . Yes, when school is out perhaps come over. I'll write."

Bert is her other safety valve, in strict secrecy. She cannot bear to tell him Peter doesn't react to his name, so answers his letters herself, alleging the reason is Gramp's trick hand. "He gets in a rage now and then, against himself, really. Who can blame him? And many older people do; my mother's family was full of old crankies." But they'd been cranky about the modern world, whose details they could rack up like logarithms; and all except Etta, a hightailing drunk in her nineties, had handled their own dividends. ("My mind is perfectly clear," Etta had said. "I just don't want it filled with dreck." "So it's filled with lists of studs," her twin sister had snarled. "She calls an agency every night." Etta had liked the modern world.)

"Sam Hill," Zoe says dreamily, for a minute immersed in the

old support of being within the clan. Across from her, Peter is only
as remote as he had often been at home. Feast of redemption, she
thinks. Please Lord, let us sail for awhile on this gondola.

"'What the Sam Hill,'" she says again. "That's what people say
who haven't been allowed to mention hell, except from the pulpit,
eh Peter? It means 'What the hell.'"

This teasing has been part of their marital life. An openness
that the children enjoyed, settling them in their double heritage.
When at thirteen dazzling Nell was surrounded by gawky admirers, Peter had joked, "This ugly duckling. We'll someday have to
get a *schatchen* to take her off our hands. A marriage broker." Sensing a certain bravado in Peter's rupture with the past, Zipporah
had tempered her own jokes. The "aunts" had yet been fair game.

Once, when in a hospital for a minor op, she'd said to her gathered Duffy brood, "Hail Mary over the intercom every hour. We
saints don't get enough sleep." What Charles, ever the family observer, had answered had stayed with her and Peter both, one of
those parental moments when the heart is weighted with treasure:
"You and Mom—you admire each other's religion." The Hail
Mary just coming on again, the girls had chorused along, Erika's
alto blending well. "Ah, you're all full of grace," Peter had said to
his children, that solid front from which only one member was
missing. "We've assimilated you."

"Ah Peter," she sighs now, "remember St. Vincent's?"

He scrapes back his chair. That studio sound; she's missed it.
He would never allow a rug under his chair. Shifting back and forth
between the ideologies being analyzed, he'd worn a groove in the
floor. "Your pa's diggin' that ditch of his," Jennie would warn the
noisy kids. "Keep it down."

When he turns now he is taller than lately. As tall as once. His
eyebrows have shaggied; the forehead juts. "Ancient Jewish men
grow monkeyish," she'd once said to him, walking away from a
family funeral. He'd swung their joined hands. "We Irish of the
long upper lip can turn ape. The primates are strictly interfaith."

While she's been floating in stop-time he has found the nun's letter. Eyes don't burn; that's counter to the property of flesh. Sunken under their ridges, his do. The thick white paper, gold embossed, crackles in his hand. The long upper lip is tremoring. He understands what she has had to arrange. He starts toward her, a hesitant lover, his heavy boots ringing on the *sala's* tile.

"Ah, darling, you can read," she murmurs, arching toward him. When he reaches her, she will kiss that ridge.

Looming, he smells of the newly cleaned suit. She's never seen this face before, its animal misery. It can't speak. Tries. She must speak for it.

But we'll be together . . . Has she said it?

Under the clumsy blows, battering right-left, left-right, she hears the howl, from the lost zoo of a mind.

"Lucky your head didn't hit the tile. You fell easy." On Debra's face a new respect. There's a stress bandage on her own left wrist.

"You don't just visit the jungle." Zoe's voice is glottal. Once, falling down an incline, she'd almost been garroted by a plant. Sand accidents can be noiseless. The feet learn to listen, the spine to accede. She'd often delayed homecoming, in order to heal. But kids see adult bodies in close-up. What's with Mom's arm, lip, knee? Peter had always taken these knockabout injuries in stride. "Bruises from a pharaoh," he would answer. "Or maybe a sphinx's bite."

Though her head aches now, even after aspirin, she's escaped serious concussion; the puffed ear will subside. But in her head the man he once was will not cease his battering. The person who has succeeded him lies dosed in the next room. "How did you get him down, Debra?" A flailing over her head, cringing limbs, a chair knocked over. Then all still.

"We were taught wrestler's hold, jujitsu—anything. When you're left-handed it complicates." She taps the bound wrist. "You hit a neck artery wrong, you can kill; it's a risk. If you don't want to kill."

Have you ever? Wanted to? Their eyes lock. She leaves it unsaid.

Debra blinks, goes on softly. "I was able to inject." She motions to her bag, which rests again on the righted chair. "For manics we gave it, when they had an episode."

When one has met disaster before, one recognizes how smugly quiet the familiar objects remain. The quilt that has wrapped the dead child half his life lies there, so lucky to be only a quilt. In the kitchen drawer, the cutlery will perhaps neaten. Mud still tracks in the back door, merely from one less pair of boots. The inanimate survives. Can't lie.

Debra draws the Venetian curtains. They perform as asked.

From a small town in France, a drapery shop full of wonders, Zipporah had once flown home to New York with a bunch of magical hooks and screws, a valance tipped like a nostril, a weave of cloth. "Easier to bring me diamonds," Jennie had grunted, radiant, as the two of them dealt with her bedroom window, that still hangs so, as severe and translucent as one of the songs from the Auvergne where Jennie, detoured en route from Vienna with her bundle, courtesy a French boy, had been enchanted by its like. The French curtain, still in her room, hangs in the now otherwise untenanted apartment. "I dusts daily," she'd said on the phone. "All the furniture looks sad." She has it the wrong way round. What she's seeing is immanence. Looking at us.

"Life's all arrangements," Zoe grates now. "It's the nuns set him off. I never thought. I'll have to cancel."

"Anything may set him off, Zee. The brain is a warehouse. Or he could forget this altogether. They do. Once he gets there, he could be like in school to those nuns. Maybe for a while."

"Is he ready for a hospital?"

"None would keep him for long. And you could not be with him."

"There's no other answer, then."

Under the black kerchief Debra wears when they visit churches she might be one of their Madonna images, or a local sorrower from one of the pews. Not now. "Oh yes there is." She spits it. "Day-to-day."

"I won't have a nursing home." The very voice of the clan. *We never have,* her mother had said. But hers had been a clan as yet undispersed, with biddable spinsters at home. Not merely for physical help, which could be bought. For company. As in a hogan. A longhouse. An igloo.

"So?" The heavy brows go up. On her they are fashionable. "So then—so then—there's hell. I don't mind saying it." Debra leans forward. "Home."

Of a sudden, Zoe yearns for her daughters. Each now in a different city, and to be spared only briefly from their—arrangements. But to spare her from this rigorous woman. Who now shakes out Peter's rumpled jacket, laying it on a chair.

"No, we'll go north, as planned," Debra says. She pulls up. "I mean as you had planned. I cannot leave you to cope. And maybe the nuns here are different." A smile flashes. Hers are rare. "We don't have them at all, we Jews." She's smoothing the jacket, eyes hidden. "There was an old letter here I meant to show you—it's in my bag. On the way north I will." She listens, hand at ear. "Not that he's likely to wake now. He'll be sleeping it off."

Together they go in to check.

It's not like standing over a deathbed. Nor mourning afterward, bent over by a change common to all. Nor breathing over a sickbed. It's where he has brought her, battered her, to be with him. In between.

"And tomorrow—" Debra says, "—we'll go to *schul.*"

Since Lev left, Debra has been imagining other persons she knows in her shoes, her situation. Girls from school quickly vanish, as known too young. Operators in the hair salon then, also some of the customers. One or two girls from the kibbutz, though long ago. Those met in the military service, nurses mostly. After which her archive stops; it doesn't include America. Which is where he left. That's the way it still seems to her.

She picks those who had the strongest sense of their tomorrows. Rangy Leah, the dye expert at the beauty salon, who kept a print of Hokusai's great wave in her stall "to remind me never to go back to blow-dry," and in keeping for when she was going to open her own shop. Or their star customer, mistress of a government minister who could see her only when the Knesset was in session—or when it was not?—and when he could get away from his wife. Hedy lounged her golden body under the massage until it was pink, and iced her rosy cheeks until they were pale, all in his service, and ever a-twitter when, "ssshh-girls," he was due. Next, Batya, Debra's roommate in army training, a giantess bent on being a commandant in spite of her sex, and full of plots. And last, two smart nurse candidates from Debra's time in Britain: Sue, a plain, quiet hard worker from Leeds, and Daphne, a lazy, bubbly cockney, who'd kept chaffing each other into the future: "Sue needs to take a law degree in talking,". . . "Daphne slogs summers at the Greenwich Observatory. Gave her such a respect for the dawn that she never goes near it." If stuck in Debra's circumstance, what would each one do?

It hadn't worked, of course. One by one, no matter their personal style, in her shoes they all dead-end as she fears she might, doing what they'd have counseled her to do if she had asked.

Leah, her homemade cig drooping as she highlighted a client's back hair, would have one of her plots. "You have parents, real live parents? Get them to stake you to something—an office, an agency you can manage on your own. Keep your money, girl." Or while doing a silver-blonde rinse, which always made her feel daring, "Why not get your husband to inseminate artificial, then make public why." But what to do after this wasn't Leah's line.

"Never divorce," Hedy the mistress would say. "Go back to him, you rule the roost. I'll introduce you to a proper guy on the side." She'd give that little money-chuckle the salon found ravishing. The minister, of course, never gave her money directly. A rebate came from the dressmakers she patronized, a double-billing refund from the salon. All the luxury suppliers did this—part of the fun. Cash was only for her housekeeping, where her needs

were small, and as a little sweetening for her purse. "And if you had
a child," Debra could hear her say, "the reb might be glad to claim
it as his own, maybe even credit it. Men always do. As for the man
on the side, you're tall, Debra, a pioneer type. You believe in what
you do. A serious man could go mad for you. A short one. They
get power, there's no stopping that kind."

In the aftermath of sex, Lev had liked to hear such anecdotes of
her first youth, saying, "There's so little of it." According to him,
Hedy wouldn't have thought of herself as a procuress. "The state
of Israel talks like the West, thinks bottom line like the East. For
the women, it's all still stratagem." He winked." "That's why Israel
allows them to practice law . . . As for the holy Jewish mother, turn
that around. The honor comes from being mother of a Jew. The
minute she gives birth she's like those nebbish generals invalided to
the provinces, where they tyrannize over the commissary and get
their mugs put on local stamps. But never see action again." When
he saw he couldn't dampen her ardor for her country, he sighed.

"Stratagem?" The word was new to her. Lev had been to college. "Sneaky harem stuff?" Such spider webs wouldn't catch
zealots like the reb. "Bureaucrats for religion," Lev himself called
them. "Their sights are too low." Lev was sorry, though, to have
taken her from a former friend. "More than that. A mentor." But
the mighty had fallen, in the ways that counted with him. "That's
far worse." As for Lev and she: "We did not stoop to deceive."

When Lev gave her the ring, he'd said: "For a patriot."

One needn't get diamonds for that. Or ought not, for what she
had done, most people would think. One gives what one has the
power to give.

He's her spiritual advisor now. Nothing to do with life after
death, in her rearing not prophesied. Death is what hallows life
hard as that is to bear. All the people in the past speak, arguably not
always well. Listen to the best, or to what the judges say is so, and
you will hear the Law.

How many rabbi's wives, scholar's wives, hear the Law over the
teacups from behind the study door, from him at the telephone to

the acolytes, or carried into the marriage bed—and if they're lucky, incised on the penis of a male heir, on its eighth day?

No wonder, if instructed by what fate brings her, a woman makes her own Torah. When she confessed this to Lev he'd replied, "In the U.S. anybody is allowed to." Had his wife, Libby? She was too proud to ask. He'd kissed her. "On the tip of your tongue, that question, I tasted it. . . . Libby? I saw her as a haven. My troubles fascinated her. The Law was not involved." He had squeezed Debra to him. "So far as we can know . . . Or that I want to know."

On their flight to the United States he'd said, "The Duffys spend their lives looking for the Law. Not knowing they already have it. Anything happens to me, go there."

An instruction often given, in Israel. She hadn't liked to hear it applied to him. And on the way to the land of the free.

Touch wood. There being none handy on the plane, she'd teased, "Oh I will, though. Knowing what you gave Zipporah to hold for you."

"To hold—. I told you that?"

"Of course you did. Because of the boys, you said. You couldn't divide . . . Unless you give rings to every woman you meet."

"Oh that. Oh yes, of course. And no, I wouldn't," he'd said, slowly for him. "Give what I did to just anyone."

He must have been thinking of Libby. Debra respected this in him and kept silent too. After a while he returned to the Duffys. "She has her own Torah for sure, that one. Though I would bet she's not hip to all it contains."

"And him?"

"Onto everybody probably; it's his job. But he doesn't let it show." Like anyone, she could grow weary of talk about people she hadn't met. And dinner was being served.

What she would have liked to tell him is how in the battlefield afterward, or on a blasted civilian corner, separate disasters can strangely fit together—a woman's severed hand perhaps, lying across a male breast.

She, Debra, is here now not only because of what happened to
him, but because of what has happened to the Duffys, to them.

On her own account she would never have clung to them. It is
not her style. But on the battlefield where the Duffys now are, they
two are similarly tangled together. If a blast came while they had
been yards apart, if afterwards one were to find pieces of them
seeking each other, one would not have been surprised.

A good nurse learns to tend the sick for whom one is hired,
leaving the distressed healthy who haunt house or hospital to survive as they can. But with Peter and Zipporah-Zoe, she at times
feels as if, medicating the one, she should be giving of the same to
the other. This is a madness that all her training countermands. Except in some extremity—giving morphine, say, to the grossly
wounded—a nurse administers only on prescription. Exceptions
can occur in military action, or civilian bombings. There are none
in lay life. This is a nurse's identification, and her history.

The supreme rule being that you never medicate yourself.

In the bag's pocket for personal items there is Lev's passport, at
whose photo she no longer looks, and the key to their room at the
Plaza, which she hasn't returned. In the four months since his
death, Zoe, waiting on signal from her, had at first only dropped
his name in those business talks when they discussed the disposal
of Debra's increment from the estate. Zoe had left it to Debra to
mention him more. Slowly, gratefully, she has been able to. When
news of the boys comes, through their intermediary, Lev's New
York lawyer, or when once or twice this had included letters from
the boys themselves, she has left the opened contents on the table
to be read, as her share of the correspondence that in a hotel or
boardinghouse is a cherished communiqué from the outside. The
boys have opted for early military service. Though the reb is at the
moment their guardian, very soon they will be out from under his
wing. So long as she is out of Israel, so is she.

On giving Zoe notice she hasn't said where she is going, since
she doesn't yet know. Morning and evening she stands naked in
front of the long mirror inside her closet door, in order to find out.

She feels her breasts. Unswollen, neat, each would still fit in Lev's hand. She checks her waistline, which the army shorts would still fit unchanged. Lev had taken no precautions; once or twice she had not, betting which way she still isn't sure. In her army corps there had been other virgins like her, whose monthly bleeding became irregular or had altogether stopped, after too steady an attendance at what in the field and hospital gabble was called "blood-and-bones." A term meant to minimize horror, as all terse army slang was, but instead conjuring up human marrow and debris.

The corps' accompanying doctor, "Dr. Elise" they called her, a French Jewess whose parents, also doctors, had been sent to the death camp, the father surviving, had reported this menstrual reaction as also occurring there. And in some lower species, it was said, in killing season. "The body refuses to ovulate. There is then nothing to discard." Debra and the others must not assume any malfunctions of organs, and certainly not that they were barren; indeed powerful lovers, husbands were often the cure. "Or the lull of peacetime, which we cannot here provide." Two of the girls who weren't willing to wait for that lull had found the other cure as predicted—according to the gossip in the ritual monthly baths managed even when on campaign. "They must have those," Dr. Elise had said to the authorities. And sometimes she herself came.

During Debra's time with Lev, her own menses had indeed straggled back, though intermittent, not to be depended on. Mostly, she forgot to count. In Antwerp, Lev, at last noticing, had made her be examined. Nothing physically wrong, the verdict "Emotional." She recalled then what the French doctor had said. A small woman, clenching hands so dead-white clean that the skin itself might have served as surgical glove. "Women in an army have their own bonding, *mes amies*. Our bodies belong to the state. But the body fights to keep personal."

On that flight to the United States, Debra had suddenly found herself in flow again, though scantily. In the Plaza she and Lev had made love nevertheless, if not as violently as usual. In Europe she'd been the robber's bride. Now he was carrying her over his country's doorstep. In the morgue, as he hung behind glass, and in the funeral parlor, left alone with him in his pine box, she'd have touched his genitals, in promise, had this been possible. She would be his body's calendar.

Up to then her own body has been her sturdy engine, submissive to whatever is asked of it. Now it must be treated as delicately as one of those ostrich eggs Lev's jeweler friends imported from Africa, fitting them onto silver-filigree pedestals. No hot baths now, no climbing. She has been a swimmer; now she has been relieved to find the muddy Lido flats at lowest ebb. Venice's gliding pace has suited her purpose. If some soothsayer had advised her to search out Lev's ashes and smear her flesh with those, she'd have complied. Instead, each night lying with her arms above her head, eyes closed, limbs lifting, she dreams again their last motions. Mornings she drinks milk, abstains from coffee; their persistent evening waiter cannot persuade her to wine.

Meanwhile she cannot help remembering the reb. In her country the most avid microbiologist might feed his children only kosher, the safe diet of his desert forebears, so taking strength from both orthodoxies. The reb, hoping for potency, had permitted himself an aphrodisiac containing dried shellfish, forbidden shellfish, on the advice of his doctor, and had omitted saying *Jahrzeit* for his dead mother—on the advice of his analyst. In whose office, where sometimes the doctor could be seen only on the Shabbos, the rabbi, not riding there of course, had also to ignore the sign "Payment Requested at Time of Visit," not offending Yahweh by any money transaction on that day. The one time he'd done so, slipping the receptionist a tip to allow him to go in first, he had come down with an abscess on his thumb. "Superstition, as some call it, is very practical," he'd assured Debra. "Paper money holds germs; metal doesn't, but I couldn't just give her coins."

A dead man cannot inseminate, except in the lab. Yet on the chance that he might already have done so, she takes every care. And so far, so good; she hasn't bled. Even today, grappling with Peter to get him off Zee, she has felt oddly safe in her own cocooning flesh.

Invulnerable, the way gossip in the women's bath, instructing the younger ones, says you will feel. They crave each month's blood, those women, yet sigh with relief when free of it, when the virtue of motherhood is like a goose-down quilt. "I don't know which way to think," she had said to her mother at thirteen. "You will," her mother had replied. "The right man will teach you." And so— no thanks to her mother's choice—he has.

For days after they shot him she could not eat. So the body in the mirror is thinner, but still in a bloom that when first marked seemed specious to her, shameful. Yet may come merely from idleness? The routine that her patient imposes has been nearly that. Until today. From now on Zipporah can no longer keep up her brave charade of being Zoe, a wife embarking on that cruise ship, the "golden years," with her man. Already desperate, she will be dragged down by what is to come. Yet her Torah will never allow her to leave him to others.

What did you trust her with, Lev, besides Libby's ring? Me?

He couldn't have known about Peter.

Yet the dead speak.

With whom else is she arguing, splitting hairs the way the reb had done with his circle of students, his beard-fringed red lips like a sore? A pity he'd no longer been quite strict, acceding as he had to the more secular tide that had stocked Tel Aviv from the West. If she had had to crop her own hair—those thick black plumes, glinted with henna, that had been the pride of the salon—in order to wear the *scheitel,* the wife's wig, she would never have married him.

She can understand why the professor doesn't want to go to the nuns, though their nursing orders are among the best. Like Lev, he is a "lapsed." And like him, still wary of the Old World charms? All she knows of Lev's past for sure is that he came from the same New York neighborhood as the reb, "went West to make my fortune, didn't," and came back to a college in New York. "Where I got out of the argument for once and all."

In Antwerp, where most of the tradesmen Lev had dealt with were Jews and some were Sephardic observers to the *nth,* she and he had left just before the high holy days, but not before some home dinners, where one hostess had extravagantly admired Debra's beehive-styled hair, taking it for a modern *scheitel,* and had asked where to get one. Debra had been tempted to answer, "From God," but instead had given her the name of the salon—which had never sold such, but in any case had closed during a war. When she told this to Lev, he slapped his knee at her wit, though musing, "Why is it easier for women, to leave a religion?" She'd been astonished. Did he mean she had done that by leaving the reb? . . . *But I am Sabra. My faith is in the State. I may disagree with it, but I would never give up my passport* . . . But Lev is not from Israel. So she doesn't say it that way.

"What I left hurts me some, Lev. Just as what you left still hurts you."

He had stared at her. "So you've cottoned to that, have you."

She hadn't known that expression, but was learning fast. "When you tell me about the Duffys. What they are—and what they are not . . . And about the mezuzah over their door?"

A messenger had just then knocked. By instinct Lev had touched his gun, though over there things were as he said, "More regular." The messenger boy, very young for such an errand, and with yarmulke and side locks, had indeed been carrying "merchandise" from Lev's associate there. And roses for her, the wife. No card. Instead the boy had squeaked proudly in English, "Bun voyedge to you and your bride."

"It is maybe easier for us women to leave," she'd said, watching Lev slip the tip and close the door on the bowing boy, whose forelocks were still child's hair. But the boy would soon enough have a beard. "In so many religions the women have to make themselves bald." She hadn't meant it to be funny. Or for it to be a laughing matter. At his laugh she had buried her nose in a white bud. "And as you say—we follow the men."

Zipporah will be a survivor. Already is. Yet, a leader in her own right, she still follows a husband who no longer can lead. The children, grown now, have left her to it. Though she has put a false face on it by appearing to leave them first. Debra had watched both them and the rest of the clan come to say good-bye that last Sunday on Central Park West. The dutiful ones relaying phone calls from those who, in the forgiving family talk, were "too far away." Those who lived near would have helped with Peter, but not in any daily way, certainly not round-the-clock. None would come every night to check whether the windows were locked safe, or to walk Peter like a family dog. And later, to protect Zoe, spell her, during what must lie ahead?

They have no sense of the clustering, the blessed code of manners that can come with disaster, when the bomb's where you buy your onions, or hovering at night over the boys' beds. Nor of the keepering that must dress the wounds that won't heal. Lack of this is what happens in a country without war. That family had had the Sunday papers with them that day, chatting of this and that. They think they have wars. The American Jews think they have ours. But they do not.

Will she and Zipporah be able to handle Peter on the train north? There's no connecting plane. Or must they hire a male nurse? In the Jerusalem hospital a patient of just such mild appearance—and like Peter, still plausible—had stolen an ambulance, abandoned it on the outskirts of the city, and had not been found until the roadside eatery that had hired him as a kitchen helper had found him singing as he smashed certain dishes. He claimed to have recognized the elderly man who had eaten from them, a regular customer, as a former guard in the camps, the owner said. "A former dentist himself, you say? And never in the camps? Ah, but he is winsome, eh. Surely he knew something. There was something he knew."

So does Dr. Duffy. Sad survivor of himself.

When she has helped deliver the two of them, seen them safely to what will not likely be their last haven, where will she herself go?

In the mirror her belly is as smooth and flat an oval as when Lev last kissed her there, nuzzled below, and spread her. She closes her eyes.

In every household of her youth there had been one or another of the Hebrew commentaries, whether or not these were read, and regardless of how a family had defined its place in the religious scale. In her household, only a half-brother and his buddy, a cousin, had ever discussed from them. But even for the maidservant the presence of such books had sent a glow from the shelves. The maid's family, of little education, had owned only one such book. Debra and her brothers hadn't been especially encouraged to read theirs, but the oldest son, on bar mitzvah, had been given such a book. Now and then, Debra's father added to his own hoard, garnering old volumes from a secondhand stall near his store. His schedule, for lording over the store's array of ties jazzy or sedate, shirts made to order or wash-and-wear, and pebbly pullovers, prevented him from poring over these precious acquisitions, but like many secular men he'd had some handed-down opinions on the lore within them and looked forward to studying their contents when he was old, and would need them most. Now and then he took such a book down from the special shelf, cracked it open tenderly, ran his forefinger down the page, any page chanced upon, muttered over it, if not from it, and carefully laid it again away. On Kol Nidrei night, that rigidly taskless eve of Yom Kippur, when no one must touch piano, pots, cutlery, or phone, or any article tempting to action, he could be caught looking at the holy books, and once the day itself was over he oiled their leather covers, atoning. Likewise, when the boys were discovered to have left egg stains on some pages, Debra's mother's lamentations had lasted for days, though she herself did not expect ever to take part in what her husband and sons had been exposed to.

Though they had had their news almost exclusively from the television, a small amount of printed matter, including a weekly newspaper and the usual charitable pleas and thanks, had flowed through their existence; but it would have never occurred to any of them to seek spiritual guidance from these bulletins. For Debra, all manuals had been medical.

Suddenly now, half drowsing, almost ready for bed, she starts, rises on the balls of her feet, and huddles her nakedness into a robe. A vision impels her, of the two issues of Peter's magazine on the table in the next room. Small, white paper booklets, not old bruised brown leather, but to the Duffys maybe casting a glow, from modern print as open as a scrubbed face.

I want an Ark, she says to herself, almost out loud. For its door to open, on that scroll we thought we had a glimpse of every week, whether or not the rabbi really opened the Ark's door. Peter isn't a holy man; he isn't even a Jew. But he would tell what he too has seen.

As she tiptoes past the other bedroom the door is ajar, though the room is dark. They sleep on. How can she in there bear to sleep by the side of that dissolving man? Whose emblem—everyone in the family kept repeating it—had been "Trust." Whose children had given him as a going-away gift a wristwatch on the face of which letters had been substituted for ten of the twelve numerals on either side of the total circle: five on the left-hand side saying P E T E R from the top down, and five on the right-hand side say-ing T R U S T similarly. Meant to be read clockwise, but as the son Zach, its designer, had pointed out, when read counterclockwise was equally true. The daughter Erika had been crying, the one called Nell sniffling, son Charles blowing his nose. Son Gerald, the oldest, was presenting it. Everybody in the room was yearning to have some one of the grandkids who'd bent over it, lisping out the letters, ask right out, "What does it *mean*?" Gerald had grandly told them. "Because Dad, we trusted you—always—to trust us."

A wash of feeling had gone round the room. She was used to this, savoring the Jewishness of it. Even in that unbeleaguered room, with the early fronds of New York's park waving freely at the window, everybody in the gathering felt the same.

He had bent his head in thanks, strapping the watch shakily on his wrist. "Two numerals left to me—" he'd said, pointing to what must be the twelve and the six. "For luck."

"Leave out your name," the woman called Aggie said, leaning

over his shoulder, "and instead they could have put IN GOD." A baby-size cross of worn gold hung on a chain embedded in her neck folds.

"That's our great-aunt, Gramp's sister," Bert had whispered. "We Jews are her only family . . . You never met Catholics?" At her headshake he had explained them, or thought he had. Zipporah, overhearing, said, "Oh, that cross still hangs around my husband's neck, Debra. Though invisibly. He says so himself."

But back then, Dr. Duffy had been thinking with his head. Now his body thinks for him, mostly. But somewhere, a reflex is repeating. No wonder he won't go to the nuns.

Those magazines on the table. Maybe pieces from his Ark?

She picks up the smaller periodical. Thick paper, severely black and white, might it serve as a scroll? Of the kind scholars not too long ago had found in her country. Those had been ancient paper, outlasting stone, the very words of the prophets—if not all of those, some said, from the tribes of Israel.

Basics, this small book is titled, just as on the pamphlet given out in piano class in the kibbutz, where for a long while there had been no real piano, but keyboards handily made by the students themselves. A line at the bottom of this cover says it is one of a series on modern philosophers. She knows what they are from bringing in the kümmel and poundcake to those rousing late-night discussions that Lev had called the rebs' "musicals." Talmudists arguing with those absentees who didn't know they were, who couldn't be persuaded to Israel.

Inside, according to the flyleaf: Excerpts from Two Essays. She turns the pages. Each is headed with a summary. The first: *LOGIC: The reasoning field preempted by imagination. Ex.: Othello becomes Iago, the remote transition of the fierce . . . Ethics of Pain.*

This essay is listed as an early one.

The second essay is listed as his last.

REGION OF INDECISION: Random casual clustering. The realms between the "facts." What has not happened, powerful as what has?

Gibberish to her. But others understand. Like in her old gym class, the tumbling that her long, strongly articulated bones could not tuck into. Imagining Peter swaying to his own language until he shudders to a stop, as the reb and his visitors had, she's invaded with sadness, tightened in requiem. Begging the film to run backward for all three here. All four. What if Lev could be standing here—what would she be saying to him?

Naked, her abdomen presses against the table edge. Doctrine can seep from anywhere. Light from the Zattere falls on her. She still believes in dawns.

The sun is shedding on the Rialto like a general partner showing off the business quarters, as the member of the firm you can always depend on to come to work. Once it was all banks here; today it's fish. Zoe yearns to be carrying a basket, and only marketing. The passing shoppers, who include some trying to look like bankers, clearly know all the answers, carrying the solutions to their wants in sacks, on the shoulders of men and women alike. Saucy tams on young girls pepper the crowd like juvenile conversation. What any Italian wears is a statement, from an old vendor's sagging gray sweater, opened for comfort, to the pointed boot-toe of that slouching turtleneck who is not a gangster, to that curled blond with the paper-thin hips, who is not a movie star. And the voices; there's little Vespa buzz here, that locust sound of the city. On the carrying water the chatter comes like birdcalls one can almost identify, grackle to cardinal whistle, to evening thrush. Walking the Accademia bridge one is almost surprised to see people's feet not winged; everywhere twosomes and threesomes float arm-in-arm. No one will notice that each of the two women, one on either side of the strolling gentleman in a suit not of native cut, has his arm linked in hers.

And there's the Rialto bridge, its mother-arch centered in the brood of similar arches on each side. The three have made their way here first on foot, then by water, but Zoe has the sensation of having been wafted here on the waves of the crowd.

In the portrait gallery of a museum whose identity is lost in her childhood, never later identifiable as either the Gardner or the Fogg, eight-year-old Zee-zee (as reported by an uncle who had no small fry of his own and specialized in such Sunday afternoon tours) had said, "The pictures are looking at us," and could not be convinced that this was not the purpose of the tour. She still dallies with the notion that this reversal is the real heart of tourism. All the paraphernalia that *homo erectus*—and *mulier erectus*—have imposed on the globe, from the grand ruins to cheap-jack, is lined up to look at us, its creators.

Still later, she would find herself subject to another reversal. In museums, it's the crowd-in-the-aisles she can't stop looking at. Drawn there by art, they seem to fall obediently, even complicitly, into its categories: a tall, sculpted couple here, a skirt like a meadow ready for the wall, a babe-in-arms' snub pottery face. But in the end, the categories will be outdone. By the commonplace.

In the street, that museum of life, where the crowd is the great component, even to be jostled and swung there is her abiding joy. At times she censures herself. A crowd can be a revolution, a massacre; in such case will she be still on the spectator side? Today there's only the familiar delight, the empathy with the unknown faces, a panorama that goes on inside her, centering her, satisfying her, with the is-ness of what is.

They are traversing the path that Debra has taken daily. For her, as for so many, a walk may be the quietest healing. While for those like her reared in a commune, in a nation both flaunting its singularity and aggravating it, perhaps the only safe confessor is among those who walk past you, never again to be met?

So here they three plod on, in uncertain equation. One shortly to leave, for where she hasn't said. One who will be left; that can't help be the feeling. And one-half—say that brutally—on his way to the nuns. Peter's step is now and then masculinely ahead of the other two, who might at first glance seem to be his attendants; other times he seems a linkage between the two, whom he is gently guiding. Altogether a perfect rhythm, that cries out to be remem-

bered. And may well be. By each in a different way. They are going
to visit a deity, who is not the same to all of them.

To Zoe that's proper. She belongs to those Jews who see tolerance as a law. Debra was born of the soil that lays claim to the One
and Only: Hear, Oh Israel, the Lord, Thy God, the Lord is One.
That must help on the battlefield. But I'm not "righteous" anymore. A word that vibrated through the Sunday School's cubicles
and bloomed like tuba notes in the liturgy. Meanwhile at home,
for her thirteenth birthday she received bookplates of a head of
Athena on a pedestal; so soft we Jews had grown, on not honoring
graven images.

In an Italian city it is natural to trek the churches, and Debra
has followed along, tending to linger at the Madonnas, to stand almost knowingly in front of the Christs, though not bending the
knee; and once, buying a snack from a vendor who also sold carved
soap, she had lingered over some cherubs. "You miss the little
ones, the grandchildren?" she'd asked.

"I like them when I see them. And then I'm charmed. There's
a certain distance. One tends to love them more as they grow, become persons." Zoe had bought one of the cherubs—"Looks like
good soap"—and put it in Debra's bag. "There's a lot of traditional
fluff talked about the maternal instinct. Maybe to keep us in our
place? Of course, if asked beforehand, you always say you wanted
them—children. Most people say it, even the men." She glances at
Peter, who is looking at the fruit, or sniffing the sky slightly above.
"Actually we just had them. The fierce love comes when you do."

They walk on, arms unlinked, but she can't let go what she has
thought about so continuously. "In any tribe, children are status. A
barren woman is biblical. Nell, and my daughters-in-law who have
kids, they all have friends who are crazy to adopt. It's natural; they
want to join life. Or they want to—acquire, they're jealous. Or
spend their tenderness truly, on what they see in the headlines. All
very understandable. But maternal instinct it's not." She breaks off.
"There aren't many children on this street. Not for an Italian one.
Maybe that's why it came to mind."

Debra, walking head down, says softly, "I'm thinking . . . that's why I became a nurse."

They link arms again, walk on, past two side streets more. "Ah, there's a fish specialty here you really must try," Debra says. Stopping at a stall, they all have one of the little turnovers, Debra brushing Peter off afterward before they resume.

The crowd is heavier now, bearing them along in its current, and there are no more stalls. Whether Debra regards her dietary freedom as part of travel, or the reb's reportedly sly infringements have taught her how to judge the Orthodox—or more likely, Lev had—she appears to feel no guilt. Back home in New York, on that last Sunday, when certain of the elders standing in front of the spread and otherwise freely eating had alleged to each other, maybe as atonement for not keeping kosher, "Ham makes me sick, isn't that funny? Literally sick," Debra, munching contentedly, had said out of their hearing, "We had plenty of bad Jews who kept every law."

Or perhaps she belongs by temperament with those "Reformed" Jews Zipporah has met around the globe, who still consider themselves not mere adherents, but as tribally born, with a faith in the breast that cannot be dislodged. Zipporah's own father, soliciting and obtaining contributions to his pet Jewish charities from his WASP associates downtown, had crowed, "They know who I am, at the bank," and lunched with them at Locke-Ober, that haunt of theirs. The family's wives, saying, "Live in Boston and not eat shellfish?" though occasionally cooking whatever Passover delicacy had sifted down from maternal recipes, had served fish on Fridays like the Catholics, if only because it was then brought in the freshest, and agreed thoughtfully, "The *Boston Cooking School* book; it's really quite good to start teaching a child with." So stretching, they had achieved not a cuisine but a kind of holy enough home cooking that allowed them to travel at will, and patronize the best restaurants anywhere. That favorite uncle of hers, a stalwart always on call if the early morning *minyan* hadn't quite got its quota of males, called the synagogue merely "my place of worship," and quipped, "Millie and I eat ecumenical."

Debra makes no excuses. Listening to the Angelus, at a small church near enough to walk to after siesta, she'd said, "We Jews do not have to remind ourselves every hour of what we are." That's so, Zipporah had muttered to herself in surprise. We all feel we are the embodiment, no matter how we observe. But there was once another distinction, surely. We did not always need war for that purpose. Or am I wrong?

According to Debra, the synagogue they are heading toward is known as one of the three greatest here, and the grandest. She will be revisiting one of her last days with Lev. Perhaps it was there he gave her the ring? Or am I imagining for her, as I did on my girls' wedding nights? I've spent as much consistent time with her as I have with them, once they were grown. Yet she is no daughter to me. More than attendant, boardinghouse vigilant, half-friend? What?

Peter has stopped in the path. Hanging his head, he doesn't speak, but they know and are grateful. He is not yet incontinent. Sometimes he'll say like a child, "I have to go." But today, having stopped them in front of a convenient bar, he is triumphant. Since his outbreak, calmed with more tranquilizers, he has seemed to be more fully aware. Usually, in any public place, Debra will go along with him, to make it easy and adjust his dress if need be. Today he and she exchange looks. She won't question, which done unguardedly has once or twice tipped him into that stiff limbo which must be terror, or hate. Or merely—limbo.

This time she says, "We'll wait."

Jaunty, even swaggering, he goes into the bar, a scruffy one with a peeling front. Looking at each other, the two women wait, not long. When he comes out he is shifty-eyed. "All men. Nasty bunch. One foul hole in the floor. Had a quick one, a grappa, to get me out." He catches Debra's sharp look at the door. Lifting his chin proudly, Peter Duffy says, "I paid."

Zipporah swallows. Take pride in what he can still do. Pray

that this elation will last. Wonder not at what causes it. Don't, don't
tip the scale. Walk on.

Debra takes both their arms. Now she's in the center. "Not
far now."

One more street, winding toward what can already be seen to
be as entrenched as any of its neighbors—why should she think
otherwise? Because it is not a church? Outwardly, it is indeed more
modest than most sacred buildings here. Or more Moorish in extraction. On its façade, no cavalcade of ornament, no goblins,
saints, or archangels crowding in like communicants. Compared to
the towers and domes here, it rises only medianly, as most synagogues do. The better to prepare one, has she always thought, for
what is aspired to inside? Yet as one approaches, utterly satisfying
the hopeful visionary, with an architecture of roofline, sky, and
that unglittering madder brown—perhaps the tint of skin shed by
Eden's snake, of which so many "temples" are made. How wise of
the Jew, us Jews, whose reputation for red-lipped luxury is un-
abated, to ensure that our house of God is vaingloriously simple.

The door appears neither locked nor widely open, on a plaza
small enough for doubt to enter, broad enough for the exiting
faith. We Jews know how to compromise. Or once did.

As the three pause, passersby in the stream behind them see
the center person of the three slide her arm around the man, in-
clining her cheek to him. Perhaps the father? She then slides her
other arm around the woman on her left, again brushing cheeks.
Perhaps the mother. Devotion is always pleasant to see. In front of
a holy place especially.

Two of the watchers are priests, from Rome. "The Venetian
Jew is almost a Catholic," one says. The other agrees. "And from
the prices here, our Catholics are almost Jews."

The façade the three present themselves to is neither radiant
nor dowdy. Nor so soaring as to make them feel small. It is a testament. Sufficient to grip the three in pause. When Debra's arm
tightens, nuzzling Peter toward her, Zipporah thinks, Ah, that's
what can happen to the caretaker. She loves him. When the second

arm tightens holding her fast, bending Debra's side to her, My God. She loves me.

Debra stands tall, clasping her hands. "Be my guests." It is the parlance of the day, said when you cede a seat, or are offered the loan of a bathing suit, but her eyes are wide, her lips tremor. "My wedding guests."

Inside is an orb of space so quietly rounded it seems to have no boundary. So well arched between high and low that worship, though not on its knees, may both rock and rise. So poised between light and dark that this itself is a lesson. Shadows, black mixed with gold, are the only gesso. Behind the pulpit is that faintly traced wall which draws the gaze by the force within it: the secrets that are heralded every year by the sound of a horn. The soaring roof, gilded dully, is no heaven. A few cracks may serve as stars for the balconies that keep gender from gender. Hung here and there, the chandeliers, descending halfway to humans below, glitter like unshed tears.

This is the synagogue of which synagogues dream.

Even in the silence and empty as now, when as in any sacred place the spiritual flow is purged of the human sea of hats, the shuffle of boots, the grumble of prayers misting lenses bent over books, there's a reticence here not of churches. A forbearance. Not only of the knee-dip, or of that crisscross which will consign the body away. Wailing is permitted. Hunch sideways under the trials of Job. But stand straight under the lash of the Word.

No organ pipes visible? The sliding chant of the cantor must suffice. The childish piping of the hymns will swell, as on her own Sunday school mornings once, the emphasis on the downbeat like a knocking of heels, though decorum must be absolute.

En Ke-lo-hay-ay nu
En ke-mal kay-ay nu
En kah-do AY nu

And softly dying away,

En-kemosheeay-ay nu.

Another hymn, liked better for its short stops and starts, is long gone. What will never fade—some ethic, some godhead even for the apostate?—is surely here.

No sexton is visible. No chalices to guard? Should we expect Shylock? Candlesticks, that great spray. Other bric-a-brac traditional for certain uses gathers in Erika's museum, but here no service will exalt these for show. No poor box either. This faith was bred in the desert, its wealth and its Ark both swaying in the saddlebag panniers of the camel, its charity flitting from tent to tent. "They had to keep their treasure bedouin," Peter had replied to Mickey, who'd been troubled about moneylenders. "And the world helped."

The kids had always checked with Peter when they wanted an explanation of their intermixed selves. As if their mother's wanderings among all sorts of beliefs might have adulterated her own?

Out of the depths of habit she turns to him, that question half on her lips. He's looking at her as if he knows her. What's to be lost if she speaks memory straight? Summoning his the way the schoolmistresses of her grandparents once summoned their classes: "Come to attention."

"You had to explain 'bedouin' to him," she breathes.

A smile is so sane. So mutual, even when tenuous. He is looking up at a ceiling, at a high text bordering a wall. "Hebrew script. Even the shape of the letters teaches. Like shards." So here was her answer, in his old allusive style. Like an aside, to a boy just beginning Hebrew. Peter and she had never admitted to each other that the child taken was the favorite thereafter, above all others. Nell, sobbing, proclaiming it, had been swept up in their shocked embrace. Peter saying to her, "No child can be spared."

What's more aware than a smile? Between two people, a bridge.

"Be off—" Peter says to her lightly, "or I'll kick you downstairs."

Debra starts toward him in alarm.

"It's all right, Debra," Zipporah says. "It's only from *Alice.*"

"From who?" Are they both softening?—her face says.

"*Alice in Wonderland* . . . He used to growl that at the kids when they interrupted his work. They loved it."

"Debra doesn't approve," Peter says with just such a scowl. Neither had his sisters understood the rough-and-tumble style their nephews and nieces were allowed, along with their father's bombardment of quotes, seldom from any missal the aunts knew.

He is tremoring. Debra puts a hand on his wrist.

"That cuffing about—children crave," Peter says, staring past them. "Childless people take it for vulgarity, or worse. Their flesh hasn't stretched to that kind of affection. Never will."

Oh Peter, Zipporah whispers to herself. That's cruel. You were never that . . . No, he's glaring at Aggie. Not at this girl.

Debra has turned red. How odd that looks on her sculptured face. But she holds onto his wrist. "You're having a rapid heart-beat, yes?"

"Tack—" he says, uncertainly. "Tack—?"

"Tachycardia. Better give you a pill for it. They're small, re-member? You can take it dry."

When she opens her bag his hand dives in ahead of hers. She slaps it away, with the first irritation Zipporah has ever seen on her. "I've told you. You must not."

"Propan-olol," he reads, from the label of the vial of pills she's brought out. "Lolly lol. Pill for the jolly beat-beat . . . But this is not the international one."

"No. We're out of those. I gave you a substitute . . . Dr. Ted's prescription, Zee, the one he said we might try. What they give after-stroke patients for mental confusion. I gave him one last night." This is the first time she has spoken of Peter as "he" that baldly. She's looking at him, though. "Risky, maybe."

Zipporah sees him going from one landing to another, as the *vaporetto* does. Or treading from bridge to bridge just as the inhab-itants here do, but each of Peter's stops with its generic identity, pill to pill to pill.

"It did help," he says. "For instance, I clearly recall Zee said she needed to shop."

"I did, yes." Each morning, at Debra's suggestion, she tells him the day's schedule. And now and then during the day. It does help, or does one fancy so? Like with the pills?

"And you said you wanted to buy Byron a book."

Bertram. "Yes."

"At a little antiquarian shop on the bridge?" His nose is white with concentration.

"Right."

With each exchange they've drawn nearer.

"Clear as—what are things clear as?"

"A bell," Debra says softly.

"Bell." His face screws. "But I cannot . . . cannot remember . . . my children's names."

Zipporah grasps his hands. She will forge the chain. "Repeat after me: 'Gerald.'"

"Ge-Gerald."

"'Fredrika. Freddie.'"

"Fred-rika." He'd never used the *Erika* she preferred.

"'Nell.'"

"Ah, Nell . . . All those last names." He never liked any of his beauty's men. Even though she rarely married them.

"'Charlie.'"

"Charles. The . . . dignitary."

"'Zachary.'"

"Zachary. Our—what did we always call him?"

"Clown."

"He grew into it, yes, with a bang. What people meant to brand him with."

"And—" she can't say it.

He says it for her. The dead work their miracles. "Mickey. Our Mickey."

"Mickey," she says. As if coached. As hasn't she been?

With each link they have forged the chain. For now.

Debra has hold of his wrist again, counting. "Seventy-nine. It's coming down."

"And so am I?" he says. "What I said, Deb—I apologize . . . I'm a bad wedding guest."

"But you remember that you are one," she says boldly. Squeezing his hand, not for the trigger finger.

"Tachy . . . card . . . very tacky of me." His face is white, his voice tired. He lifts his head. "See, I can still pun . . . So, Z . . . , Z . . ." He can't bring it out. "So go shop."

They're giving her leave, the two of them. To slip for a moment from under the web they three travel in. Can that young woman understand how it is to flee the spectacle of the stricken lover, yet crawl in bed with him, holding the sick stranger as once, squeezing disease out of him? . . . Yes, this woman can. Remember her, flung on Lev's valise? "Bertram wants me to get him an old edition of the Talmud." And she must find something for Debra. A present for going away.

They nod. She is not to feel embarrassed. The language of buy-and-sell is never a foreign one. This hushed, gold-washed temple on the Rialto well understands that.

At the enormous, dwarfing outer door she turns. They look complicit, guardian nurse and man advancing into child. The cryptic shadow of this holy place dwarfs them also. Once you get here, no matter how or from where, you are lost to location, suspended in history. Destiny halts here. For the moment she can leave them. They are safe.

"I'll be back at two-thirty or so," she says. It echoes. I'll always be back.

When she is gone the pair sit hunched, as if they cannot straighten. In the current from the shut door the chandeliers waver, drawing a band of light across the two, and back again, a pendulum.

"One if by land, two if by sea," he says. "We might be on a boat."

She looks up. "Or under a clock."

"Yes, hear that ticking," he says swiftly. "It's not only for me you feel it. You have to . . . help her."

She's not answering. He looks down at his watch. "'Trust Peter.' They didn't know how dependable I am now, did they. How predictable." He seizes her wrists, waits. "Ah, you don't shudder . . . Why is my rage only for her?"

Her head is bent, her whisper low. "Because she is . . . like the other half of you."

He smoothes her hair, carefully an inch above. "How'd you know?"

She rears up. "It's what I feel against Lev, what else?" She spits into the air—*puh!* "Rage."

"Ah . . . and you can't kill him, for being dead. . . . But I . . . can kill her. . . . To be dead . . . along with me . . . Nor will any nuns prevent." For a moment he seems fuddled, sly. "I'd slip between their prayers, mind you." Hand pressed to mouth, his words clog, but she hears them. Between even my own.

Far in the recesses, an unseen sweeping. A sexton? No one appears.

"One of the crones who clean churches," he says. "They grow out of the walls for that purpose, then carve themselves back in, to watch us. Or so we young communicants told ourselves."

"This is not a church."

He stares her down. "No. No saints' niches. No ladies' chapels, where to tickle the sins in private. You Jews have a kind of Satan, but he's a second-class citizen." He peers toward the rear. The noise has stopped. "Where would she sweep up the sins? Scarcely any corners here. Just a circle of many circles, squared."

"My father belonged to a Workmen's Circle, before we came to Tel Aviv. They would bury us." Arms folded, she soothes her belly. "Now—I don't know." Tranced by this old-style gossip, she almost smiles.

He stands up. "And such a fine congregation we have here." He bows, nodding here and there.

She shrinks. "This is a monument. Not used. The floods weakened the floor."

He flourishes an arm toward the rows upon rows of empty pews. "They'll bear witness, Debra. The best in the world."

"To what?"

A question like a bullet report. Has she forgotten that she's a nurse? He'll clam up now, the deadening brain not up to the challenge, but still alive enough to be humiliated.

He stands up, yearning toward the audience of pews banked before them, "I meant to die a . . . a patriarch . . . All our grown children leaning forward . . . A Pietà . . . And their little children, the little heads, at the foot . . . footboard." His forehead is sweating. He seizes her hands. "Instead my life was like that. Who can complain?"

Through her hands she fancies she can feel his heart throb. "You didn't swallow that pill."

He blinks. "No. Not while, I am myself again almost, maybe not to come again. Not to . . . savor that? No . . . And I've had rapid heartbeat for some time now. You don't die of it."

"Not usually, no."

She could ask him. Whether he wants to die. She knows better. No one wants to, even if they gasp it out on the field of agony, hoping against hope for the painkiller, that angel of mercy, to float them instead into half-time in the universal game. No one can quite part with the unique misery of life. And the suicides? "They want rescue, really," her mentors in the British hospital had said. "Even if you have to fight them for it."

That's the conviction by which medics must live.

But if you could live on without that? You could try.

"If I let you see in my bag," she says, "what would you be looking for?" The silk of her voice surprises her.

His nose lifts, like a dog on the scent.

The inside of the bag greets her, its oilskin-on-leather pouches like propositions in a geometry for which she already knows the answers. Laid neatly side by side, the pills are in their places, the ampules in theirs. Antibiotics separate from the sulfas. Morphine

and its many-syllabled derivatives. Vaccines and their dispensers—
the old joke hovering. "For going into the interior." A tiny directory of drugs: which ones complement each other, which ones
should not be prescribed together. Long outmoded, but all she has.
These days the pharmacopoeia is computerized.

"It's like a bird's nest," he breathes, "But not eggs a boy would
find. And no magpie could manage to raid."

Pouch by pouch, he asks her to name the contents.

She complies with a few, then stops, dreamily. "Maybe I'll go
back. To nursing. It depends."

"On us. The patients? . . . No, it wouldn't, would it."

"No."

"What happens if I won't go to the nuns?"

Tell them the truth, was the counsel. Always the truth. The great
empty vault of the synagogue stares back at her. There's no counsel from the pews.

"Bedlam."

He turns from side to side, stares forward. Yes, up there is the
altar. There's that. "Not short for Bethlehem, eh?"

"We just said it so. At home."

The bag is open, lying unguarded on her lap.

"What's this?" His finger touches a gray metal pencil-length
case. She had opened it once, on a long syringe, colorless. "Some
of our pilots carried these. For if you came down in enemy territory. And couldn't hold out under questioning."

"Ah, yet another pill? A suicide one?"

She stares him down. "Not army issue." She picks up the case.
Steel, not just chrome. "And we women weren't in the front line."

When she'd told that to Lev he'd said, "These days a front line
can be anywhere. Where'd you get that thing?" From the dead,
she'd said. She looks down at her ring.

"I meant to give you away, you know," Peter says. "As a bride."

What can you answer him? the handbag says. Her ring flashes
in the shifting glow from above. "Thanks—" she says. They are
both staring into the bag.

"That pill you slipped me last night," he says. "Where are they?"

"Not last night," she says slowly. "The night before."

"What's the difference? You said it would help. You said that very strongly. You never did that before." He's fretful, not a good sign. "You know, not Dr. Ted's pill, that international one. Which isn't worth a damn."

"No, not that one. But you didn't take the one I did give you?"

"How did you know?"

She doesn't answer.

"This pill will help anyone, suffering from anything," the French doctor had said, handing each of the nurses a few. "Sometimes it will be all we have." She hadn't needed to tell them its name. Not a dose you have to repeat.

After a bit he says, "I'm not going deaf." A statement.

She shakes her head.

"Not in the ear." His face is bitter.

"Nor blind—not in the eyes. Nor mute—not in the tongue." His speech, rushing on, stops short. He looks down. "Nor weak in the hand." He clenches, unclenches them. "What did these do to her? I know they did something." He cups his head with them. Sits up, his face six inches from hers. "I'm not mad. The wires aren't crossed, not when they work at all. When they don't—a blank. A creeping blank. Sometimes . . . I can push my whole head back into its proper notch. Then out it slips again. Like that awful trick some people have; they can shift the scalp." He releases his head, folds his hands in his lap. "But with them it makes no difference to what they say. Or do."

He reaches suddenly for the bag; she grips it tight, but he's only scuffing it back and forth. "Nothing there for me, is there. Not for long . . . Yet I've had a . . . a day. And a night. At the back of my head here—" he raps it with his hand, but lightly, like you cuff a child. "So many quotes, last year's, last week's. But they're going."

There's a noise in the far back corner of the expanse behind the pews, which leads to the door.

"The caretaker," she whispers, half to herself, but he has turned round, facing the great entry door.

"The caretaker, yes," he whispers back. "You know. Z...Z... Z." The name bursts from his mouth, "Zipporah. Tell her not to trust my watch."

Is this a warning of more? She tenses, ready. A common danger, to be anticipated by all who treat those who decline in consciousness, is the emergence of the sly, as with any cornered animal. In her training hospital, warnings against a patient's violence were issued personnel on slips of yellow paper: Check Thompson's cupboard... Krauss will be off medication for three days... Smaldone's husband will visit; two staff must attend. And routinely, the suicide alerts: Griffin's been pleading with the therapist: Help me how to be me... We all know what that means.

They had been coached on that: Help me *not* to be me.

Peter Duffy's blue gaze, as with all like it, has a special meaning for us Jews. It is wide with Christian innocence. That traveled storekeeper, her father, has cautioned her on this. We must never allow them to be more honorable than us.

"I'm a guest—" he's saying. "In my own life."

Then, in horror, he slides down the pew, away from her. But she has already felt the warm urine, dripping from him.

"It's the grappa you drank," she ekes out. But they both know better. It's the beginning. He'll be that kind of guest in his own body, from now on.

By the honest numerals on her own wristwatch it's almost two-thirty. Outside, there'll be the afternoon languor, the shops closing, people going home or elsewhere for the interval, making the climate excuse, their need for home, love, rest. The steel watchcase is engraved on the back with her training dates and the name of that august hospital. Absent witnesses—better than these long wooden pews darkened with flood. Also the letter, still in the jacket of the suit that should never have to be cleaned again.

"You're in between," she whispers. "That's all." How many times has she consoled with something like. "So are we all." Ignoring the wet, she takes him in her arms. "You're still able to be yourself. That pill you didn't take. It was—only a kind of placebo. And you didn't take it."

"Between—" he whispers. "Where did you ever learn that?"

He means, where could such as she? But that doesn't matter. It's fitting now that he know who she is: staff assistant at all synagogues. Gathering him up in her arms, heavy as he is, she swivels him and herself so that they face the ark.

Raise your head, the French doctor had said to her, when she left the reb.

"Raise your head," she says. "You need not feel shame."

Swiftly her hand finds his shirt, opens it. "Hold still," she says. "That's our ark up there. No Bedlam there. And I am giving you away." The syringe plunges in.

Lev, the lost rabbi, standing beside her, surely approves. He too cut things short; she knows that story. No matter that she can see the mosaics of the walls here through his shade, he is at her side, as is her right. "Four months you been gone, or almost. At four months, my body reminds me, the first kick of life comes from those waters: a woman 'feels life.'"

When the high door behind them yearns open, letting in footsteps and a wash of that salt-sweet, clouded glass air, Peter lies stretched on a pew, his nurse bent above him, one hand on her belly, one on his heart.

Everybody has been so kind.

So here they three are, being driven to a Rome airport, an older woman and a younger, and a body legally and conventionally boxed. The family, reacting en masse, though each with a different reason, has pleaded that Peter be returned to them for burial. Cousin Nettie, their documentary specialist, though not consulted, when she heard the news had cabled to the effect that only a corpse in hand would get the proper notices.

Zipporah is not sure that she herself would have done otherwise. The soil of Venice, such as it is, is not easily augmented, much less by a foreigner. The *padrone* had been quick to help with the proper civic formalities, down to the very bills of lading. It would have been churlish to note that he might have in mind freeing his own establishment from any funeral rites.

Agnes had wanted her brother to be returned to Catholic America, whether or not he had died in the church being irrelevant. Father Coniglia had a straight route to the cardinal himself and could assure of a high mass at St. Pat's. As to cremation, she and Theresa, being unable to fund the alternative, would look the other way. But it must be done in the United States. Italy's runoff sewage was notorious. Despite the Holy Father, she will not leave her brother's ashes to the Wops.

Bertram and Jennie wanted to fly over. Jennie's "You needs me at your elbow," and Bertram's anguished "I want a last look now," had made Zipporah wish she could cry. But from the moment when, arms happy with gifts (the commentaries Bertram would prize, a miniature French copy of Flaubert's *Maxims and Thoughts* for Peter, who had a weakness for books one could nuzzle in one palm, and for Debra an old necklace of improbable date), she stood in the entry, blinded for a second by the temple's dusk, and then saw, down the long, knife-edged perspective to the ark, those two figures, Peter stretched out on a pew and Debra hunched over him, it had come to her with a thump of recognition that Peter's last journey should end as it had begun, with her and Debra alone.

World politics had influenced how they were to bring him home. The word "terrorist," until recently just part of general parlance, had in a rash of events jumped the barrier, freezing air passengers into attitudes new to them and denying even the most serious baggage an unexamined ride. Peter, who as his sons pointed out had taught them to crew their first fourteen-foot sailboats and later to race them, would have relished returning by sea, even if by engine rather than sail. Father Coniglia had found a colleague returning to New York by slow boat from the port of Ostia, whose holy charge the coffin could be. "If ever it has to be opened, during the voyage or later, he will be able to reconsecrate it," Agnes said. On the chance it might have to be opened at customs, Zipporah, gritting her teeth, had asked Bert to meet the body at American customs, adding, "Tell Jennie I'll fall into her arms the minute I get home."

Thanks to Norman, who had procured one of the flights at a premium because of the emergency—"The smart money is flying Air India"—and in spite of the long check-in lines delaying flights overnight at interim stops, she should arrive home before the priest's freight. In time for its disposal, which she might have to arbitrate. The phone calls from the children—that leftover term for these men and women she cherished for their wild departures and solid dependability—have come over the line like intimate music rattling at the wrong time. United suddenly by loss, they must want to signify that unity. A chorus of voices at her: "He should

not be further disturbed"... "Graves with bodies get visited"...
And finally, "You did that for Mickey, Ma."

She does not visit. But when abroad she had once witnessed an
incineration, and could have borne it again, if in the presence of
family and friends, as when a person is consigned to the earth. But
that Peter be pushed into the flames by handlers, like offal, and
with nobody to watch him go? "I wouldn't mind it for myself,"
she'd said, half to instruct them. "Yes, it's clean." And saves space,
on a belabored planet. "But we aren't witnessed to the end, like
they do on the Ganges... Yes, I agree, it's an avoidance the way we
do it... Okay, no." Avoiding what the physical endgame really is,
she'd thought. No wonder some religions oppose it.

Then had come the clincher. They wanted a memorial to be
held in a synagogue. "In deference to you," Charles said tactfully.
"And because he gave us most of the Jewish kick," Zachary, never
tactful. "And because he died in one," both daughters for once
agreed. Erika had found them beautiful photographs. Such
ceremonies.

Wallie, true to form, was the most practical. "I've secured you
a plot. Last ground for sale within city limits. After this, no more.
And only available because so long held. Now they want to finish
up. And cash in, of course. Hold onto anything, and how the value
increases!" He'd recently become a collector, of Americana. East
of St. Louis only. "Let it be my gift." When asked who "they"
were, there had been a hesitation. "Open to all; they're not questioning. And ground is ground... A churchyard."

When all the phones have rung off, she is still amazed. A house
divided we were, one that might have been thought to have no religion really. We would teach them to look out, in both senses. And
see specifically how they've gone about it. How tenderly. Unsup-
ported by all the public worship to which those who "observe" can
enviably cling. But maybe apostles on their own.

Throughout she has kept thinking how amused Peter would
be. "Apostles, no. Acolytes, maybe. You Jews lack a vocabulary for

these distinctions, bless you. Like your lack of statuary." Then he might give her a squeeze, held in which she would gasp, "Hope you didn't latch onto me for that reason." And he would squeeze again. "No. But it was a plus."

Already she expects that in the monologue called conscious-ness she will be forcing that dialogue for the rest of her life. His ab-sence will always dull her present. But will inform it.

In the hired car, driving to Rome, the two women are silent, ex-haustion in each face. Zipporah's high, firm cheeks are deflated. If at past sixty she has often been taken to be twenty years younger, that gap has now shrunk, although her long-limbed posture— "Your Granma's gams, wow!" the Shine had said—still keeps that illusion. As for Debra, her eyes now dominate an oval once per-fectly in balance. Because of the black circles under them, a mask appears to have settled there.

For part of the way they are on the Autostrada at a breathless pace, somewhere over ninety miles per hour, that is in itself a form of speech. On the back-road shortcuts, for which the driver must have his own reasons, the car takes the bumps in the same macho style. Hanging on the straps while the jaws click can preoccupy like exercise.

At a stop just past Bologna, Zipporah says, "He is still with me." Debra, watching the driver open the hood for oil check but step warily around the trunk of this vehicle, whose length is some-where between station wagon and hearse, says, "And with me." When Zipporah adds, "For life," Debra at first doesn't reply. When they start up again she folds her hands in pledge, "For life."

When they stop at Florence, Zipporah says, "In our attic, where you slept, remember? That long, wooden canoe with the men in it? They row alongside the spirits. I understand that even better now." When the car is rolling again, Debra says, "We never got to swim, Lev and me."

Some kilometers on, Debra takes an atlas from her knapsack. The *padrone* has suggested a stopover in Siena, where his sister-in-law has a restaurant, but they had refused. "You are hungry?" she asks. The answer is, "No." The book on her lap makes her appear to be in charge, though she does not open it. Always she has been the careful, deferent subordinate. In the ambulance, a dazzling motor-launch that had arrived at the synagogue on the double thanks to the old lady who swept, Debra had still been the attendant nurse, confirming with a quiet nod the Italian orderly's signal that there was no hope of resuscitation. And later, a comfort at the hospital, respondent to interns glad to rely on her qualifications. Dr. Ted's letter, found on the body and translated by one of the interns who'd served in New York on medical exchange—"Ah, the Mt. Sinai"—had made all easy. Arrangements for *imprenditore di pompe funebri* could be made at once. "Undertaker," the young doctor said softly.

Since then Debra has been a staff to lean upon, responsive when asked, never assuming, as even the telephoning family had noted. "She's certainly blossomed," Gerald had said. "My office could use her, I bet; what's she going to do afterward?"—his mother answering, "That we haven't discussed." When he pressed, saying, "Ask her," she'd pleaded a bad connection and had hung up.

Once all the interment and travel decisions had been set, including Debra's departure late this arrival evening, Debra had made a reservation, for herself only, for the coming night, in which room Zipporah could rest until her flight time. "At the Hotel Inghelterra," she'd said, not explaining her choice. Nor revealing where she would go from there.

If she had needed money, that could have been broached, with an offer to fund whatever her immediate plans. But of course she does not. Their almost chatty relationship on the subject of income now seems the patter of two other women. The Debra now next to her on the back seat is a statue of devotion from which intimacy has been drained. Or perhaps, as with that last remark about Lev, she is herself deep in memory, finally giving up a Europe with him. Yet pursuing in illusion—even to the *schul,* where in her mind she might even have been marrying him—that light-hearted trek which was to have been crowned in America.

At their trio's one trip to the Lido, the sight of that spread of water, almost mud and little more than ankle deep, had set her to laughing, a fit not seen before or again. She'd waded in barefoot, in her army shirt and shorts, and had gone quite far, the water-level below her knees, then had strode back to Zoe and Peter in their chairs, laughing all the way. When it was over, she'd bent to score the sand with one lax finger. "To the world, the Lido is still a treasure, no? In Israel we have hidden treasure, places to swim. But tourism will never be what we are known for, hah? Though we try." In former days Peter would have lit to this rare hint that she still took her country's political side, whatever her experience of its religious one, but lying in the chair under the weak sun, he hadn't lifted from his face the white beach hat that Debra had equipped him with.

Today she's wearing the dress she wore to the Rialto, the loose shift that in tan or black, cheap version or luxe, is the Italian street cliché. Since Peter's death, neither of them has worn black, perhaps offending the *padrone* and that small officialdom through which death has made them pass. But "going into black," as the old saying was, is not the way Zipporah wishes to mourn, and until today Debra had followed suit. Nor had she worn her army clothes again, even in private.

At the moment, Zipporah feels closer to her than to her daughters, who've not been involved in this fateful interlude. Even when again united with them, arm-in-arm, tears mingled or in sad drought, they will not be as close for awhile: they have missed out. Yet would she want Debra over there with her, a constant reminder? The grim answer is—no. Nor can she see her as Gerald's corporate employee. The blithe, new hardball style of American girls in business, in all relationship, is a topic for those sociologists who study the contemporary scene in a way Zoe herself does not. But precisely how hard Debra is evades her. One recalls Norman's comment. To say that she is a Sabra, a nurse, is not enough. Would Debra's own verdict on herself—"I have to be where there is war"—to Zipporah and all her kind a dreadful indictment—be the key? Had she looked to Lev to release her from all that? From all that the reb signified?

Yet, Zipporah reminds herself, the professional analyzers of society-at-large often have a poor score at tallying in the personal emotions, much less identifying those, either in other people or in themselves. Myself, she broods. That's my character flaw, whether or not those close to me have tolerated that, or even been aware. "You level-heads must always weigh the possibility that other people are cauldrons," her own father had warned—she seeing only the compliment.

Her mother had confided, "My side of the family pitches its egos like baseballs. Into the bleachers, more often than not. You have to learn to listen, like you learn to write thank-you notes." Her mother's listening had done its odd best. Supremely healthy herself, she had paid perhaps too many social calls on the unwell, simmering helpfully over woes that her friends and even her servants would have preferred to suffer in private. Meanwhile finding her own family as reluctant to being listened for as she herself would be to the end. "Maybe I'm not Jewish enough," she worried. "Worry not," Zipporah's father said. "I'll give you a certificate."

Such a worry had been voiced now and then among the other elders, or showed up tellingly in the compensatory conduct Zipporah can spot to this day in her coevals, not among the backsliders but among those Reformed Jews who may fancy themselves deep in that fold, whose word for each other is "co-religionist," but who worry, in the light of the Holocaust and the steely gaze from the state of Israel, whether to stand on one's liberalism, even one's Americanism, may be a dodge. Against being more Jewish?

She can hear Peter, on a word-fiddle to a colleague whose teenagers were opting out of Sabbath Eve Fridays to go to rock concerts, or horseback riding in the park on holy days, "when it's easier to get a horse." Should he and their mother have been stricter, gone kosher even? "Not to worry, Arnold. To worry makes you Jewish enough."

How Jewish she is or ought to be has little concerned her, as far as she can tell. What she has is a certain twinge of recognition at meeting a Jew, which she fancies all those of the birth do share. A response partly winsome, often secretly critical, or suddenly comfortable, and if admiring, arrogantly unsurprised. As if to say, not so much "one of us" as—"Here's another one." A vestigial desert-twitch may be its origin. Even an animal touching of noses, of flesh-and-bones that, since the Creator, has had the same scent.

"Was that because the Creator was taking special pains with his handiwork when he made the Jews?" Peter said. "Or because he was just negligent?"

She had giggled. "I think we can't make up our minds."

"I doubt that," he said. "I think the Israelites long ago decided to believe both."

Is she doing that now? In Debra's case there had been no time for such recognitions. She had been presented to their clan by circumstance, by the power of Lev, and had been enfolded. By the power of the clan, taking for granted its duty. But from the first she has seemed to them a foreigner. Not just in the natural gradations of different mores, climates, or even physiognomy that can separate, say, the French Jew, who has his mistress acceptably in tandem, from the American tycoon who hides his corporately, or the Scottish rabbi from the *schtetl* Pole, or the Ethiopian from them all.

Or the New England–reared Jew, often as Boston as Brattle Street, from the Southern "Hebrew" (as their elder literature still calls them) and their syrupy, mammy talk. In her travels Zoe has met all such denizens of the Jewish corner. Those united still, if only by a Talmud they have never read, by mothers in the mild glow of the Friday candles. Or by the fistfight on the corner lot, or the sneering hotel. Or by the royalty of Einstein, Disraeli, Freud. Or like dozens of New York City Lower East Side kids, in the kinship of having been forced to play the violin.

Debra is a new breed. Or an ancient one, protruding out of

history? Bred on the land, aligned by it. Bloodied by its communal-
ity, all of them; man, woman, soldier draftee, hairdresser, city teddy
boy, girl in middy blouse, both wearing the gas mask to study
God—or the storekeeper's girl in her turtleneck, riding the provac-
ateur buses over the rubbled middens of those-who-were-here-
once. Worship is by government rule, a steel prod to the divine
inner silver. Dancing the hora, heel-and-toe, in the sacramental
blood.

No wonder what I felt her to be and couldn't fathom why.
Remote.

What now links me so to her, even more now than when we
were in arm-in-arm daily-nightly service to him?

Simple. Like a plant rising from the floor and bursting into
bud, in the dusk of the old synagogue. Scarifying. An image one
knows one will keep for life is bound to be. It wasn't him I saw. The
low pew in front of him wouldn't have prevented me from seeing
him stretched in the death throe. She's saved me from seeing him
that way eternally.

What I saw, standing at the entry door, will see forever, across
the yards between us, is Debra bent over him, hunched over, trying
to save him. I know that despairing figure. A figure like it is always
at the bottom of any painting called The Deposition. The body
just off its cross will be—hard by.

As I ran, the distance between us three was like a yardstick
turning its length over and over. And when I got there we were already only two. I'll see her face, turned up to me at that wry-
necked angle so often painted—the angle that has just seen death.
The hands, palms up, empty, that say, "I could not save him."

Did I say, "Was it the heart?" If she didn't answer, there was no
need to. Nor did we broach his dignity by calling him "lucky." No
man leaving his life forever is that lucky, no matter what they say.
Those who have that impudence are the sacrilegious, who assume
what only the universe will decree.

"Oh my darling," I said to him. The nurse whose patient has
died while in her hands becomes a member of the family. Putting

my arms around her, though they seemed to remain empty, I said what family says to itself, to each other—We did what we could— only changing the "we" to "you." "You did what you could."

The woman now seated at her side, hands guardedly folded at her waist, stares ahead at some road other than the one passing under the wheels. Maybe it's a highway stretching forward. Maybe it's a path, leading back.

At Arezzo, another traveler boards. The driver, seating him on a jump seat that folds down to face the back-seat passengers, doesn't explain the man's presence in a car supposedly for exclusive private hire. But this is Italy, obliging and pragmatic both, a tandem Zipporah would normally enjoy. When the newcomer, smoothing his half-bald head and crossing his tasseled shoes, takes out a pack of cigarettes: *"Permesso?"* and she answers, "Please, no," he is affable. *"Capisco."* He would just as soon talk.

"You ladies are *Inglese,* no?" Ah, there are fabulous sights ahead! A businessman with a territory covering from Trieste to his native Rome, anytime he is near Arezzo he stops to see the Piero "—della Francesca?" he adds delicately. He has a passion for art, which goes well with his work as a contractor for special building supplies. "In fact I am not sure which is my real business, and do not wish to find out. It would be like asking myself how I chose my wife."

Having brought out that reassuring word, he stares unconcealed at Debra, measuring her slowly from head to toe. As the car curves, his shoe touches hers. When at the next curve he inadvertently braces himself on Zipporah's kneecap his apology is heavy, and his reprimand to the driver sharp. But as they swing on, and his fumbles and apologies alternate, she wonders whether there is some collaboration between the two men. The passenger is sleekly plump, well fitted out if not elegant, and has an urban pallor. The wizened driver is one of those taxi types seen the world over, with the nutcracker face that in turn has seen everything. The skittish car is winding between two hillsides, down whose slopes no rooftops are visible. But those bandits who prey on tourists are said to ply the rich coast, trafficked by foreigners who have their own cars.

Debra has opened the doctor's bag. Averse to opening it in public, she wears money and other quick needs in a purse on her belt also holding any small metal objects that might set up a cry under airport scanners. The metal wand she is bringing out from the bag is too long to be housed in the purse—is it a nail file? It is. She slides it down the side of a fingernail, the thumb's. When next the car swings, the man lurches away from its arc, just in time. He has narrowly escaped taking the steel point in his side. The file, nonchalantly in a horizontal line from Debra's belly, had not wagged.

A cackle from the driver, who can see them in his mirror. With a shrug the passenger settles back; he has poise. Or practice. Shifting sideways on the jump seat, bracing his feet, he buries himself in a folder of the kind in which artists stow drawings. Carefully guarding its sharp corner with his palm, giving them an encouraging smile—*Touché, but there's no revenge in me*—he bends to the folder's contents. How amused Peter would be. Many of the lighter essays that he wouldn't designate as philosophy had concerned those body movements so slight, deflections so common, that it had had to be noted that few note these. "Random" was merely a term for their less obvious existence, which would be found in counterpart for the physical, even the mathematical world. "We must find a better name for those 'randoms' that occur in human intercourse. They are the bell-charms of living. And the fun." When he went on that way she fancied she saw the Irish in him. Were these small doings akin to the logical mischief one might find in an academy of leprechauns—part of a rationale he had had to find?

She thinks she's figured out what may be involved in the loss of orthodoxy. One loses it, whether by flying in the face of it or gently loosening one's ties, to the very degree that one is also impelled to leave the family with whom one has been enclosed in that faith, those rites. He had had to leave God as he had had to leave "the porridgey mess and chill afternoons" of his natal household. His sisters, keeping to scripture, had really been keeping that household alive, ever tidying, denying, embroidering, with tongue as well as thread, as old maids can.

Zoe had managed her "flight out of Egypt," as it were, more tenderly, loving her parents, even savoring the clan, but as she lost the unswerving obedience of childhood to the scrutiny that came with adulthood, so with her subservience to God. To the very notion, concept of God. Nor had she ever had to go so far as Peter, in personal flight. Her parents, already free of the severer trappings of orthodoxy, had remained secure in their own heritage, sardonic on those "nouveau Jews," often but not always identical with the new rich, who took no pride in their Jewishness. Who would not deny what they were, but were flattered if you had to ask.

In each case, maybe in all, the little pawings of society conspire as well. We "reform" ourselves. Many, like her, link up only with the congregations of the intellect. "I changed my admirations," Peter had said. "It's little to do with psychology, which is merely the advice they give you to keep the package together."

Neither of them would forget their last Bible lesson, at Mickey's hospital bedside. Temporarily in remission, he had been wheeled off to visit the hospital's chapel, returning in hilarity. "The altar reverses," he'd crowed. "A Jewish star on one side, a cross on the other. I prayed to both...I'm entitled, no?" That last a sly quote from Norman, a family joke. "But I did pray more for Dad's God," he'd said, looking up at his mother in solemn apology. "He's the one got hurt." Outside the room Peter, his cheeks wet, said, "He prayed for God. Not to." Since then it has occurred to her to wonder whether the Jewish "character," seen even by some Jews as self-righteous, forms itself on the God who never gets hurt.

Meanwhile her own progeny have continued to follow that revolving altar, two of her three living sons in the habit of linking up with Christians, Gerald with a pretend one, and both girls favoring Jews. Yet all of them, after some religious picnicking, had sent their youngest kids to Jewish Sunday schools. Which may explain the preferred synagogue funeral service? She can hear Freddie-Erika rebut, "But Mom, our choice of temples is ve-ery ecumenical." Their respective choices being Gerald to Temple Emanuel, as to a good investment, Charles, until he moved out West, to the Spanish Portuguese Synagogue, which to his surprise wasn't as "dignified" as he'd thought such aristocrats would be (had he really thought all would be of that heroic Inquisition background?); Freddie-Erika, sending the child of a late pregnancy to a Russian emigré *schul* in Brighton Beach, because she herself was learning the language for a second Ph.D., while Zachary had packed off his two sets of loft-bred prodigies to a "New Wave" rump group with a woman rabbi. While Nell herself, whom one thinks of as eternally childless, though she has certainly had them, is now free to join a group called Sons and Daughters of the *Schtetl,* whose services are conducted in pre-Holocaust Lithuanian. Her reason being: "I prefer to love God in a language I don't understand."

To Erika, whom she prefers to call that, Zipporah, reflecting on all this, and on the funeral in particular, had finally said, "For your generation, maybe 'assimilated' has a new meaning? That's the first time I ever heard 'ecumenical' used by one kind of Jew to another."

And it seems to her that Peter, not clodded deep in the purple velvet and mahogany foisted upon her but lightly running alongside this patched cortege-for-hire, is listening even to what she does not say aloud, and answering her from her store of his responses. As a coveted after-dinner speaker at his society of mostly semantic "philosophers," he'd once entertained them with "The Language of Railroad Carriages," an insidious parody of the passenger mannerisms from that era, as these changed to autos, to air. Some of these usages currently fashionable, "although they haven't realized that yet," among those he'd addressed.

What does he think, say, peering in the window of this battered but still powerful vehicle, which at times must run cargoes not confined to the mortuary? There's a perfume to the leather that must be marijuana, an odor from the slippery floor that must be fish. An equipage heavy as sin, and carrying at times a mortal bundle of it, no doubt, from front to back, but with a wheelbase

not really long enough for the jump seat, surely not factory installed, whose front end is swollen with tape, as if the car is still
giving birth to it.

Once they are running smoothly on the straightaway, the salesman begins opening and closing his portfolio demonstratively—a
psalter he obviously wants them to see? Indeed the colors in a folder
of sacred pictures he thumbs, one by one, do hold the eye: ripe-fruit
reds, blackened leaves in a green containing its own shadow, mural
gold showing that crackle the centuries design, garments of peasant
blue crowding a deeper heaven, the cadaver-white of cut-off hill-
tops, of soldiers' helmets, and of the body on the cross. On the
folder's cover is a Deposition, the tiny red holes on the backs of the
Christ's hands seeming to bleed in streaks, as the salesman rapidly
lifts and lowers the cover to show yet another page.

"Duccio, I am mad for him. But Botticelli is what sells."

"Ah, you have a sideline." In Africa too, and all over Zoe's
other venues, this holy vending. On occasion from reverence,
somehow to atone for what else may be for sale. More often from
a shrewd sense, like this man's, of what the public will buy, feels
forced to buy?

"You sell them?" Debra's hand, innocent now of the nail file,
creeps toward the folder in his lap. "That first one?"

"Madonna and the Bambino—ye-e-s." A millimeter sniff. But
as a Navaho of that hairless breed once said to Zoe, "If your mus-
tached men of the West think to hide their opinions, they are
wrong." The man here seems fascinated by Debra's long, pointing
finger. "All you ladies like those. "Ma—" he ripples into Italian, but
pulls up. "E, scusi. But I stock all kinds prints, for your husbands
too." A snigger. Perhaps he mistakes their stare. "We get to Rome,
we have coffee, I show you." Perhaps their rings, nervously
checked, suggest they think him a cheapskate. Or he's seen that
Debra doesn't wear a marriage ring. "Or dinner. The funghi restaurant, where the government goes, maybe. You can still get there
the ... how you say?—tartufo?"

Truffles, Peter says, running alongside the window.—Oh listen to that, Zippy . . . to one of the sweet, small languages, of the railway carriage, the compartment, the jump seat. Detailing the fine art of the lunchbox, of a dozen dainty surprises bought at that shop near the Madeleine or at Demel's near the Sacher, and half-eaten in a confusion of the senses: What is nipped between the teeth, where have those crumbs fallen, what juices flow? . . . all the while the wheels below deliciously grind?

"Truffles," she says for him. From now on must she be his voice? "But thank you, I'm leaving Rome on an evening plane."

"Ah, you return to your *marito, e?*" His eyes roll. "Such businessmen, the Americans. And they let the wives travel alone . . . And you too, *Signora, scusi—Signorina?*" He sighs. "What a *disgrazione,* with all of my city to see—alone." He turns to Zipporah, "But for you, maybe the husband's picture . . . We will not let the *Signorina* see." He cracks a second folder, raising the wide cover.

For both of them not to see is impossible. The prints, a spread of two, are bad, even dog-eared, but recognizable: the "dirty" murals that the smirking guide, taking her and Peter to an upper floor of the tower at San Gimignano, on their first trip together, had offered for an extra fee. Not all the tour-bus passengers had understood his preamble, obediently following. She remembers his giggle. Copulating couples on those murals, as she remembers. "But they are married," the leering guide had said. "For this we paid extra?" two men said. Peter, smiling as she's smiling now, had said in her ear, "What they are doing up there is certainly not extra."

"*Sconto*—a deescount," the man at her elbow hisses. "Not in the good condition, but I see the *Signora* likes. Cold in America, no? A present for the *marito*. To keep him warm."

Peter is no longer at the window. Nothing between the glass pane and a slide of trees, dirt embankment, a flash of meadow, trees. The sob comes from her own icy depths. She is as cold as he.

An arm encircles her from behind. Debra's other arm crosses to meet it. She is held.

"We are widows."

The contralto words vibrate through Zoe, warming, an auxiliary heartbeat. So that's how Debra thinks of the two of us. Has thought, for how long?

"And our dead—" Debra's thumb jerks to the rear—"they ride with us."

"And alongside," Zoe whispers.

The man turns pale. "Who killed them?"

"One was shot," Debra says. "In the back."

"And one—in the head," Zipporah says. And lays her cheek on Debra's.

The man is already beating on the driver's seat, furious. Screaming, "Not in the contract!" in Italian, but so many times repeated over that the meaning penetrates. He must hitch on this trip regularly, selling to the tourists trapped in what they assume is their car exclusively. Giving the driver a percentage of what is sold. "The last time jewelry," he screams. "Your idea. We made nothing." But he has never bargained for this. "American gangsters? *Arresto!* STOP."

The word echoes, so recently said, and said. She huddles. Good, so good to break down. The Italian swirling over her head seems perfectly clear; who can be translating?

"Get rid of that cargo, you fool. I'm getting out of here." The car slows, starts on again. When she raises her head the man has decamped.

The outskirts of a town you want to get to are never bad. These still have majesty; the driver is singing.

In front of the hotel, the driver unloads their baggage from the cavernous trunk of the old car, leaving a toolbox, a grimy blanket, and the foodstuffs bought on the autostrada whenever he gassed up. "He will believe anything, my brother-in-law," he says, wrinkling a grin. Because he is the type who would do anything, if, excuse, 'e 'ad the balls. It is my sister who finds what to sell. But who could he be thinking we had in the back there, with one look at you two ladies?" He throws up his hands. *"E, la famiglia.* But what else can I do? He and she, they have no car." He accepts their large tip.

As the car recedes, it carries Peter with it, surely escaped from that airtight coffin but traveling now dutifully alongside on their way to the train that will deliver him to the ship. As cargo to the USA, the "America" to which a potato famine had in a previous century brought his family. A migration he never spoke much of. Out of modesty, perhaps, when faced with a clan propelled there not by the pogrom (for neither of her families has any such) but by the small scratchings of principle, ideas of freedom, engendered at such a times?

Perhaps, flying by her, alongside her, on some future train or plane, he will answer more fully, filling in the gaps in what he had let her see.

"Maybe we should—" she says aloud. "Believe anything."

Debra is shyly passing a hand over her new treasure. The Madonna's sloe eyes and long, straight nose echo only slightly in her face. The pinched thirteenth-century lips are nothing like that exuberant mouth. But the Madonna's hand, elongated so that it may seem to touch the child's navel, might be modeled on hers.

Behind her, the bellhop, ignored, waits for direction on the baggage. He has seen the car; are they really for this hotel?

Neither woman has brought much along. One has the frugality of those who travel lightly to the ends of the earth, trusting her bags to be heavy with wisdom on return. To date, the younger woman has had much of her baggage issued her. The shibboleth, that Hebrew word once used to detect foreigners by their lisp—and to identify what must be excluded or forbidden—she has a heritage. A costly coat flung on the one backpack looks unworn, but is baggage too. The rest of her trousseau still awaits. The bellhop's gaze goes to the beat-up dress, sneaking to well below the armpit, where maybe she's carrying what's most precious to her.

When one is as exhausted as this, as Zipporah rarely is, one's vision fractures, multiplies, bringing out the images always lurking under sense, even suggesting that these are the magic that should most be heeded. Debra, this remote girl staring at the prospect before them, can remind one of the Cumaean Sybil. The same snub gaze, out of the mosaic that restricts it. Lately she's been filling out, as women and sybils do. But she's not Duccio's Madonna yet, nor any. She's some other legend, and still in the drawing. Yet one that belongs to us all.

What a fool I've been, as Peter perhaps knew—knows. She doesn't have to answer our questions—she is belief. I didn't need to whisk him to far places to see its embodiment. As perhaps he saw, even in his clouding, or because of that.

Her tragedy has the smoke of older dreams behind it. She's the folklore, come to stand in our midst. According to what the old wives first taught me, and the doctor too, that blacky damp under her eyes and tautness of cheek is called "the mask of pregnancy." Too late for her to have conceived. Surely I've seen contrary bathroom evidence? And for such a mask, which comes in the last month—much too soon.

But too late and too soon—that is what these particular people are. Too soon gone, for the world's grace? Staying on too late, for this world.

Debra has followed the bellhop. Turning, she beckons Zipporah on.

That's what they all do, when they like you. Leading you into their jungle, their island, their sequestered sea. Once you've laid your weapons down. Harmless, dangerous. Beautiful to begin with, in time eaten by civilized woe. Gripped by ceremony, yet waving you goodbye with the most casual gesture.

Scholar of them, why didn't I recognize her? Had Peter?

She was our primitive.

"I n one's life," Zoe says to young Bertram, "or in one's life story"—for everybody believes he or she has one—"the hardest to talk about is duration. Things you are expected to do, day to day. Even those who discover continents. Or the great artists we imagine as from dawn to dusk only on their projects. Everybody has that other slog also. But we don't talk about that—we wait for events. Like with the sleeping beauty. Everybody's hanging around to watch her wake up. We don't ask what she's been dreaming on. Day after day."

He doesn't seem to think it strange she's chosen that example, though she doesn't know why she has.

They're in his grandfather's study, which is exactly as it was during that lifetime.

Bert's classes at the seminary are teaching him to get to the point. Or rather, the spectacle of those who don't, or can't bear to—faculty and students alike—is warning him. "You mean about death? We don't talk about it until it happens to somebody?"

His grandmother rarely looks at him with impatience, as she does now. "No, Bert—I mean exactly the opposite. We all know we're going to die—it's the one great event we can count upon. Yet we go on wag-wagging through life like metronomes who never heard of music; it's the purest bravery I know. I'll admire the human race forever, for that alone."

His grandfather's desk is over there in the corner. The person who used it is one of those who has done it—died. Everyone is able to, even the stupids; it's like being born knowing how to drive. And it's part of why he doesn't now think of that person as Peter, Gramps. Who has gone into that territory of awe.

Bertram puts the tips of his fingers together. "So?"

They both burst out laughing.

"Just because you're at the Theological, must you talk like a stage Jew?"

"A lot there aren't just onstage. And it's catching." He leans forward to pat her cheek; he's never had trouble being what the family calls "demonstrative." "So-o—Missus Anti-Semite?" Meaning like his mother? *Don't talk with your hands, please. We're not that sort.*

She smooths his cheek in return. "If I can't have Peter to talk to, you're the best."

So they've mentioned him. Even with Bert coming here once a week, as they've settled down to on her return, that hasn't been easy. Especially with his secret, that as his lawyers have informed him, his grandfather has made him a bequest of certain manuscripts under the condition that the bequest of these and their contents not be immediately revealed.

She too is looking at the desk. "Like in the other fairy stories, any of them. As a kid, didn't you wonder—I did—why nobody went to the toilet in any of them? Or later, in the great books? Joyce maybe, or Shakespeare, a reference. But not generally . . . Like you ignore. But not for any heroic reason. Like you're ashamed of such daily things? Or that you have to display more than just what everybody does. In order to excuse your life . . . Oh Bert—what am I going to do for the next thirty years of mine?"

And barring accident, he thinks, she will have them. What can he say?

"We take those for granted, Ma. But I see the prob."

He can't. Nobody that young—what is he now? Barely past twenty?—can. Or who hasn't . . . done things. And then come to a plateau.

"I appreciate it," she says. "Now tell me your prob. With my son Gerald for a father—who'll want you boys to do him credit, but in his own footsteps." And Kitty for a mother, who thinks she's managed to keep from the family what her real first name once was, and maybe the last name too, but lay off that. "And with your brother already deep in a lifestyle that sends Gerald wild." She giggles. "'My son, the surfer. With all the investment I've put in him.'"

"By's just—sure of himself. Every time he drops in from Cal, I envy him. And we get along fine, we always have. He even keeps me from—being a prig?"

She smiles. "And me—if I saw Byron more. He's like his name-sake, that's all. He'll swim some Hellespont, someday. Though maybe not in a wet-suit." She squints. "And what's this about you being a prig?"

Before he answers, she says, "Save it for a beer. Let me show you what I've done to the house." Immortal phrase of women. Sometimes the men borrow it, in the suburbs: "Let me show you what we..." Peter never. And traveling as she had, they'd never had that other conversational mainstay of people like them: "Yeah, we have a second little house. On the Island, Keys, Cays, Capes, or South Of."

Lucky they hadn't, or she might now have retreated there? It's maybe good not to have observed all the routines.

In the living room: "Yeah, got rid of those heavy decorator drapes. And valances. When I began here, I just followed suit for what I was told windows like these should have." Now almost bare except for a slight disguise, the view is half in the room. "And more seating, but less chairs, if you know what I mean."

He does. The large double room has been unevenly but prettily sectioned, though that's maybe not the right adjective. "You've gone modern. But not so one notices."

"What a tribute... And same with the cuisine... You know Jennie's moved next door. Norman's not too well." She'll spare him Jennie's further confidence: "I think the Jewish part of me has riz to the top. . . . And I know a nice black girl who'll clean for both of us. And nobody dare say nothin'. The live-in maid's room I'll have to myself is practically a suite."

"I heard. One of them's had a little heart trouble; one's had a change of heart. Hard to know who is which."

"Bertram!" If he's his Gramps to the life, she won't burden him with it. But at the end of the tour, when they're back in the study, she says, "If you can see your way clear to using this as your office, go ahead. I know what it can be like in a dorm." And Gerald's investments are not what they were. Though he himself would never let on, the grapevine is still functioning. "Maybe you'll want to wait to do that until I'm away. No far places. No cruises. But widows who can afford it travel some at first. I can see why."

In the kitchen, so can he. The old cookie jar is still here. These are the corners where you most feel people have been, and might come in again. He prefers those to the view.

Though give thanks this one is still available. She hadn't had to send out cards to notify she was keeping the place after all. Everybody had telephoned each other the details of the deal, step by step.

He gets himself a beer. How can he confess that what he loves is sitting like this? Feeling the slog. Dreary Sunday afternoon, when the unknown one still to be met might be, must be, somewhere. Or the one you have met.

"Where'll you go, Gran?"

"Cold countries. Lapland, Iceland. Where I've never been." And where I have no authority. Or name. Though the "Zoe," no longer needed, is lapsing. "And you?" He's due to finish at the seminary this year. "Where'll you?"

"Last summer I worked a movie house, a pet shop, a coffe bar. Did okay. Summer before—Dad's office. Did okay. Learned a lot, each place."

"Like what?"

"You want to do bad—you have to have an in. Want to be a good boy—you have to have an in."

What's good, what's bad? She can't ask. But they can look at each other, heads cocked.

"I still want to be a rabbi. But I don't believe in God."

When she is silent, he says, "Sometimes I turn that around. Like—'So you don't believe in God? Even so, you want to be a rabbi.'"

What can she say? She answers like a mother. "Go look in the cookie jar."

When he does, shying at her the same as her kids used to do when she did something they were loath to credit adults for, he crows with joy. "The same ones!" Jam centers he'd always made a beeline for.

"She still fills that jar, Bert. She knows you come. She made Norman put in a new oven over there." It's still next door, but now feels more like over there. "Go pay her a call sometime. But don't say I said."

They half-smile. These small family conspiracies, old habits, old recipes. Jennie knows what the bedrock of family is. To keep things the same.

So Zipporah is not surprised when, standing up, giving her a quick smack—he has a class from three to five, he says—and twisting a foot on the doormat, "You ever hear—from her?"

She accompanies him to the elevator before she answers. She often follows visitors out these days. "No, Bert . . . I was hurt at first. Now I've accepted it. I think—we needed her worse then she needed us."

The elevator comes up. He lets it go back down again. Gangly young men, "just filling out," look exactly that. Six-foot vases, frail at the neck, the verdict still out as to how much they contain. But the voice often unexpectedly baritone.

"That's not tenable."

He's quoting his new guru, the Dr. Jacob Moorsohn who was once plain John Moorson, and now a convert, and the seminary's new infusion of faith, and commentary.

When the elevator comes up again he takes it, with a hug but without another word. These days she's left standing there by even the kindest. She used to think she gave them wheat; now perhaps they think all she has to give is chaff. Or it's the elevator. People who have to use those have intervals of remorseless meditation unknown to those who step straight out into the day.

Especially so when the cage is empty, often both up and down, as in her building, until toward nightfall.

During the next ten years she will visit Lapland and Iceland, see reindeer not on postcards, and acquire volcano sites to haunt her head afterwards. She will find small good as a nonprofessional traveler, yet still take off, ever more conservatively, to where most people go. She will accede to keeping tinted the crown of hair that for so long had stayed aggressively black, to going to the park low-heeled and solo, to entertaining new friends tenaciously made, to reading more widely, to attending theater and concerts on her own, and to circling her life within these ravines. So doing, she will begin to accept that persons continue to die, sometimes her intimates.

But these long moments at the elevator will be the real tenor and rhythm of the first ten years of her widowhood.

Meanwhile, early on, young Bert has decided to stay on an extra year at the seminary, emboldened by longer conferences with Dr. Moorsohn, D.D., L.L.D., Ph.D., who had acquired these advanced degrees while undergoing protracted treatment for lymphoma also diagnosed as advanced, and not curable, though it has since been arrested. Under which treatment he has acquired an advanced faith. "Things go in threes, hah? Maybe I'm waiting for a fourth... But, yes, why not stay on, Bert. It'll give you a chance to become more unsure of yourself."

Like many good teachers, he is waggish, but he can rein it in. Unlike many of the faculty and male students, his beard, in spite of being light-colored, seems to belong to him. Occasionally he has shaved it, only to let it grow again. "Any new physical achievement adds to my energy." This is his only reference to his present state of health. Nor is the legend—or myth—of his conversion through healing ever discussable. But "energy" is a big word with him.

A teacher around whom a clique forms may find that the rest of the faculty finds him unreliable. Moorsohn doesn't appear either to chafe at this or to acknowledge a student's admiration, but commentary is his life and he can be amused at too rank an imitation of him. When Bert confides, with the same stately air with which Moorsohn can hint at the psychological value of metaphors in the prophets, "I'm going to fund my extra year by working in my father's office. That way, Dad can feel I've compromised. And he'll think better of me," Moorsohn bobs with unvoiced laughter, then is serious. "And you can afford to love him?"

Moorsohn has of course been made party to Bert's dilemma of belief. "So far as I know, you're the only holdout in a class that last year could be a *schola cantorum* of doubt. This shows real persistence. And is not to be despised. But there's a solution that often follows. Tantamount to a conversion, one might say." At such moments his singsong can sound like the Beatles; though Scottish, he had been for awhile in Liverpool. Full of good hard-shelled Jews, he'd said, including a woman doctor he'd followed to Israel, who'd monitored him in a hospital there. "Who ate doubt with the devil's own long spoon." One advantage of a conversion seemed to be that Moorsohn's references could come from anywhere, often seeming to fly in from whatever he'd been converted from, and as quickly returning to base.

"So, Bert, *mach shabbas gemit.*"

He loves to fling such phrases in the face of the liturgy so solemnized here. He forgets that Bert, as the occasional student who may be two, three, or even four generations away from the *schtetl*, or even not so descended, may know few of these adages which straddle a Yiddish-German-Hebrew patois, beyond those few terms like *Oy veh* and *schlemiel* which are New Yorkese, and comedy.

"So make a holiday of it, Bert. A rabbi who is not sure he believes in God? You could be acting from the deep sincere." He puts
a hand on his Adam's apple, as if sincerity is a tumor there. "And—
maybe one day—God will come to believe in you."

So sustained, Bert will eventually complete his studies for the
rabbinate, though it may take another few years before he "allows"
himself to be ordained. And is allowed it. Meanwhile his energy,
the use of which is what he too has learned best, will detonate in
enough socially worthy jobs to attract government interest, so far
defused. He keeps his own interests close to the vest, one of those
sloppy antique ones that, worn under a bomber jacket and over
jeans, will hope to conceal the "privileged" class that nurtured him.
In time he will outgrow the vest.

He isn't passing the girls by, nor they him. In his grandmother's
intervals home he'll bring the current one to one of the Sunday afternoons. No production now, a limited gathering, and thinned by
time, but one that he takes for granted is still the same. Nice Jewish girls, as the saying goes, bright and brightly dark-eyed, with
positive goals toward the good life—they always blend in. At first
waiting, then wistful, finally they evolve off, then marry other
men. Who Zipporah hopes won't turn into those negative husbands known in the heart as "not Bert."

"What's he want?" his father, Gerald, finally groans to his own
mother. "You were away for Lil's funeral. You should've seen him
officiate." Lil had been his wife Kitty's aunt, exhumed not from
Finland or elsewhere "in Europe," but from a once Lithuanian
street in Hamtramck, Buffalo, and sent on by a social worker so
that she might die in her successfully errant niece's house. "We
gave her every comfort"—eating tray meals, while wrapped in
Kitty's negligees, her name transmuted airily from Leah to Lil.

"Bert would drop in to see her, just as if he still lived at home,"
Gerald says. "Maybe she thought he did. He'd even dig out what Lil
meant in her Polish, which Kitty didn't know anymore ... Anyways, a pity you weren't at her funeral, just to hear that eulogy of
his. The assistant rabbi of our congregation comes up afterwards,

invites him to give a sermon—they don't call it that, at our younger group. They allowed me in . . . And afterwards, that rabbi button-holes me; he's leaving to have his own temple, they're looking for a replacement, should he put up Bert's name? I say, 'You better ask him'—at least I know that much. From that day on I never hear a thing. But of course I have outlets. And what do you know, they investigated, they offered. Our congregation, imagine, who can have the pick. And when he turned them down—they think maybe because of my position there, a father and son nepotism—they are decent enough to tip off another top congregation, I won't mention the name, who is looking. This one wants a man already married. Most do, more mature—and otherwise the scramble among the congregation girls, well. Anyway, they put out feelers, one of their younger members, who even went to school with him. Not the seminary, from before. Who had even double-dated back then. So the guy asks, on the side, like do Bert and his girl of the moment have intentions? And Bert says—"

Gerald at last stops. There's a change in his face, maybe paternal? Ever so often, maybe once in five years, this happens. A big-headed man who looms with his opinions as much as with his weight, he much resembles an uncle on her mother's side called "Aaron-the-joiner," whom the teenage Zippy last saw in the street at a Masonic funeral in squared-off lines of men, each reading from a book and with something on his shoulders, maybe a shawl. Gerald, in a crisp business suit shawled only by his "congregation," is her uncle to the life. But now, that tender pursing of the lips is Peter's; those jowled eyes are his father's blue. His voice is oddly small.

"Bert tells him, yes, he often has the intention. But the girls always turn out to be too young for him somehow, even when they're of an age. Maybe it was the effect of the seminary, he tells the guy. Such a serious place . . . So, no, he wasn't ready yet to lead people to God."

Whisky is at hand. Gerald pours himself one. "So. I have one son who barrels along like crazy because he knows what he wants,

worse than he should. And one, his education costs me thousands—" He hunches so over his glass, she wonders. Nobody in
the clan is ever a drinker. Something to do with their Jewishness,
people have always said, about Jews and drink. But Gerald is only
half. And the whisky Irish. "Thousands I could make work otherwise. Not so's I could find out my son Bert doesn't know what he
wants. Maybe never will."

Suddenly he chuckles. Not the whisky, or not only. Gerald is always cheered up by a conversation with himself. "At least we know
he's not gay. Kitty barged in on him and a girl once. Not in the
apartment, he never brings them there. In last year's rented summer house; she wasn't familiar with the layout yet. And woo-oo—
she got out quick. . . . I guess he doesn't have them just for show."

"Bert doesn't do anything just for show." Not with that mother
about.

Gerald flushes.

Brought up in a bailiwick he clearly thinks dowdy, what if he
had fallen for "show." Maybe too much of it. In temple, in his congregation, he can resolve all this. Where he belongs there are few
dowdies.

"Gerry—"

At once he alerts. She sees how seldom she calls him that. "Not
marrying. And not believing he should have a congregation.
Maybe they're—connected."

She kneads her hands as if working dough, which she has
never done, but always wanted to do. Seeing it as done in Zambezi
firelight, with the flames speaking in all the river's tongues. Or in a
mesa's icy dawn that miraculously does not chill the yeast. A
knuckled dip-and-pull she's come to think of as how we knead
principle—until it is ours.

"I think Bert may know what he wants. Until it hurts, maybe.
And knows he doesn't have it yet."

You can't assist a grandson at that. Or advise this, to a son.

Maybe he does hear, what she can't say. As families from long
practice do.

"So he helps people personally," Gerry says, staring into his glass. "For what they want. As he did with the old auntie. As he did last summer, with me."

The word "help" rings in her ears. Of course, of course—dip and rise. As you knead.

Wonder of wonders, that old Gerry—as his mother, to her shame, often has referred to him—would be the one to make her see how she can best help Bert. But what's a family for, if not to ring with all the intonations of that word?

Gerald seems to think she's been of use to him. He wipes the whisky breath from his mouth with the back of a hand, but still finds to kiss her now too indelicate. He's always had dainty physical manners, a man with maybe a fat personality, but who can step lightly when push comes to shove. What accolade will he give her? One's children sometimes give one the oddest.

He puts a hand on her shoulder. "Thanks, Mother." Shakes his head from side to side, marveling.

"You should invest."

Bertram and The Shine are walking toward the seminary, along the street outside its walls. Shine is merely making use of the research library. "To find out what my confidences are." Bertram is a matriculated student. "Though they don't seem to use that term much here." Anyway, he has decided to "go for broke." An odd phrase for someone wanting to qualify for the rabbinate, his first interviewer had said stiffly. But the Torah studies he'd done while in preschool had weighed in. "Particularly in that fancy prep school," the second interviewer had joked. Had he felt himself to be an ambassador to the Gentiles there? "Oh no," Bert had answered innocently. "We'd already had an ambassador in the family once—my mother's side. They were the ones who had the dough."

Finally he'd written a letter, as they'd asked. "I know I could be

a scholar. But I don't see how one can be a Jewish one without believing in God. At present my most religious moment is when the
rabbi blesses us. To be able to bless persons, maybe anybody, not
like you own it but like you're charged with it, that's what I would
look forward to." He'd got in. Now and then when he passed the
admissions guy on campus, he'd been awarded a squinted smile.
"But I'm not sure he voted for me," Bert said.

When they get inside the walls they'll put on their yarmulkes.
As Bert says, "A matter of reverence. And of manners. I suppose
I'm a prig." Shine says, "Looka me. F'rall I know, I could be anti-
semitic in my bones. My mother, she didn't have an anti in her
whole body; that's what got her in trouble when she was a member
at the U.N. But a black woman from Sierra Leone; unbeknownst to
her, she could transmit me a gene."

At the entrance, they are as usual accosted by a Yeshiva guy
selling discount flights to Israel. He won't take their "No, thanks"
for an answer—don't they want to see the homeland? "I do," Bert
says. "But it's not my homeland." Shine says, "A God who gives dis-
counts worries me." But the guy won't leave it alone.... They are
not students, then? "From in there." He points a long fingernail.
"Just started," Bert says. Then where are their—he points to his
head. "We like to keep it loose," Shine says, lackadaisical. "In *this*
country, you don't got to signal what you are." He pats his cheek.
"More than what you are."

"*Loose,*" the Hasid says on a long, holy breath. "So *that's* what's
inside there. Like the Menachem tells." A string of language from
him, in which they can catch the guttural Reform. He flaps his fist-
ful of travel throwaways in Shine's face. "What you mean this
country, *schwartze*? I come from Bennet Avenue."

They leave him picking up the printed sheets that have fallen
from his fist. Walking inside, Shine is as slit-eyed as Bert has ever
seen him, but his voice rolls out as cool as ever. "Was he the same
one as last time? Can't tell one of those from the other." When
Bert doesn't quite smile, he hisses, "Told you maybe I was. Anti."

Reaching in his pocket he pulls out his yarmulke. Pauses over it. Drops it on Bert's head. A minute goes by. Bert pulls out his own yarmulke. Which Shine, after a minute, bends his head to receive.

"See you after class?"

"See you. After class."

When they meet again, "the Duffy," as Shine sometimes lightly alludes to him, is aglow. "That new man. The one whose class I heard, was so—he's something. They say he's a convert. Big *shlimazel* when they took him on, but they did. Anyway, I'm in. I been nagging him to let me in. The class is not for first-years. But I'll bet you also could."

"I'll take a rain check," Shine said. "Maybe on the whole establishment."

"Ah, c'mon."

"We got to talk."

They settle on the stone bench along the outside wall. A relic of quieter days, it has been so battered that one corner is broken off down to the pedestal, but this has made it a boon for privacy, restricted to two.

"We the assimilators here, Bert; that's for sure. You got it more in the head, me in the bones. No, I got to find me a job takes me out of myself. No travel I see can do it. Isn't any travel any more, right? All down the same tube...Maybe I just need to assimilate faster? Silverstein and Sierra Leone all under one cap?" The one he's wearing does make boys verging on manhood look naive, and little boys look like men. "I don't see that puttin' me in the happy-time phone book though, huh? Where the demograph say we all gonna be at leas' caramel."

"It would help," Bert said, "if you didn't talk like you never went to Deerfield."

"Only a year. I only agreed to do it because it sounded like hayrides. You far worse off in the demo bit, Jewboy—you all white. 'Less out in the Zambezi Zipporah took herself a fling."

"Think I have some hope there?" Bert says with a grin.

"Nah. That dame would tell the world. She always at that."

They contemplate this truth.

"She met my grandfather not far from here. Over by the Alma Mater. Lost the heel of her shoe."

They laugh. "Those heels," Shine says. "But she sure keeps trottin'."

"How'd your own father and mother meet?"

Shine's dead father and his stepfather had been business partners: Silverstein and Thorvaldson. When Shine's mother died of cancer, Shine stayed on. Now his stepfather has a new wife. Who is white.

"My mother met my own father at the U.N. She told me, 'How could I resist a man who sells flags?' My father told me, 'A woman who can carry a bundle on her head? Only problem is to keep her at it.' They kept the insults on top. Worked out fine. . . . My stepfather and new stepmother, they're very polite."

"You expected home tonight?"

"Yeah."

"Me too."

Doesn't matter which one says it first. They've been to each other's houses; they know the score. At Shine's, where he is the adored son and only, Bert, focused on as winsomely as his sidekick, sinks under that wattage. "What color bathing trunks did you boys buy?" maybe—as if he and Shine shopped together like girls. The Thorvaldsons are generous and tolerant; he thinks of them as very high types; it's just that their eagerness to know is like a warm bath. After the one time that Shine insisted on seeing Bert's folks, during which Gerald had been full of an article in *Barron's* on Shine's stepfather's historic and thriving business—"Won't go corporate, eh?"—and Kitty had chimed in, "Oh, so you weren't at Deerfield on scholarship," Shine had apologized. "I only wanted to be sure it wasn't me you were ashamed of." "Come with me somewhere, Sunday," Bert had said. And he had.

They watch as a car stops at the curb, picks up the beard selling Jerusalem, and deposits another in his place, the driver and the other two exchanging words which make their beards, all cut to the same length, wag in concert. If I had leaflets to strew, Bert wonders, what would those say?

"I'll tell you what, let's really assimilate each other," Shine said. "Introduce our families."

"Which?" Bert says tersely. "With Gran and Gramps gone? She and your Mom would have got on like a house afire. They almost did meet, remember, that protest outside the U.N.? Zippy's not political, she always said, but she did that once." "It gets mixed in," his Gran had said.

"Yop." Both are silent.

"Anthropologist" could be a dirty word in educated Africa, according to Shine's mother. But she had never heard one she could hate so fondly.

Bert is recalling how Zippy said of Shine's mother: It must be hard for such a go-it-alone lady. To have to apologize to herself for being in government.

"But the dads."

Who said it first?

"Never—" both say.

"Mine doesn't know I feel sorry for him," Bert says.

Okay, keep it that way, Shine thinks. You can't stand to know you can't stand him. "Me too," he says aloud. "For mine." He loves his stepfather. A six-foot bald innocent whose ninety-five-year-old mother had refused to accept his visits to the fancy nursing home he kept her in, unless he divorced that nigger woman. Who had conveniently died.

They get up and start walking, toward the subway station.

Shine's stepfather still has the venerable inherited business that sells flags. His father and Shine's grandfather had first founded it, and he still keeps the name Silverstein on the stationery. "That's right, flags," Shine had said, taking Bert to the corner window on lower Madison where one was always displayed, usually a museum piece. "I'm the natural offspring. Dad talks flags as if the world and his wife are standing at salute. He says my own father was the same."

Bert's father's sympathies are all corporate, even if there's no telling what he owns. That world has no use for flags, except maybe when they're marketing some franchise?

"You heard from them, him and her, lately?" Shine says delicately.

"My grandparents? She writes faithful. She doesn't say much."

They have come to the corner where they usually part.

"Are you really figuring on going rabbi?"

Bert shrugs. "Are you really considering going into the family business?" Shine's stepfather has a heart condition.

"The older generation—they're failing us," Shine says.

When they pass the girl's college, a group of them is flushing itself out the door. That's the rhythm. The two stand at attention to let them pass. They do.

"Some girls are like flags—noo?" Shine says. "Some women."

Each gives the other a sharp look.

"She still with them? That Debra?"

"So far. In Italy."

"Ah, Bertram—" Shine drawls, in the style of their least favored teacher at their old Hebrew school. "You and I will just have to grow."

Even after Bert is out of the seminary he keeps up with Moorsohn, who when Bert turned up again said tartly, "You want to be like those psychiatrists who check in regularly with their psychiatrists? What they call a 'control'?" But for many his office alone is allure. A renegade library of pro-and-con publications from within and without Israel, it's haunted by browsers fearful of stumbling on some anti-religious shocker, yet unable to resist, and buoyed by Moorsohn's silent, permissive salute, since they suspect he considers such students to be the best.

As the months pass, it is Moorsohn who needs to be energized. One must ignore the hectic flush on his cheekbones, or that alternate pallor one doesn't want to know the reason for. In his feverish scrutiny of how the current event and the historical matrix extrude into one another, he has even come across that old review of Zipporah's book, his teasing comment being, "A Zangwill, eh? In high heels," then with a fisted thumbs-up for her detractors, "God bless." But his obsession, now more than ever, is with "What makes Jews"—being naturally concerned with what has made him one.

In one of his classes audited by Peter, in a lecture hall necessitated by the crowd of academics and others, not always Jews, who seek either to ratify what they are or to transcend it, Moorsohn says, "We discover scrolls five thousand years old in a cave, maybe shaking our Bible wisdoms like dice, like in that leather cylinder I saw a croupier use at Monte Carlo. And the reaction the world over is still that it's only a local quarrel. Ours . . . What kind of a Jew will this make me—if I'm a person living maybe in Brooklyn on Mulberry Avenue? Or in France, where I am almost all French? Or on upper Broadway, New York, where I am everything at once?" He tells them. Maybe, as with the most sought-after lecturers, what the seeker already half knows.

What makes a Jew seem always in the balance? He and they ask it together.

One later day, scanning a Tel Aviv newspaper among those worldwide weeklies racked up in a corner of that office as in a café, Bert will spot a notice that will ultimately set him off on a hegira of his own, to Israel. Half able to do so quietly—he is now after all conspicuous as part of the system, if not of their most favored sector, the Orthodoxy—he may take a job that would allow him to appear there under other auspices, if not quite casually. And perhaps (as he will in time learn to accuse himself) in order to put roadblocks in the path of what is surely a fool's errand, first erupted in the heart, groin, and yes, faith, of a sixteen-year-old boy?

The job, as head of a very small foundation modeled after a huge, and to his mind lazy, giant of an endowment for international peace, is of course billed as apolitical. In the mind of the spirited Maryland philanthropist, one of the globe's greatest, who funds it, it's certainly intended to be so. But what Jew doesn't harbor, in his soul of souls, the verdict that any peace maintained for him or against is always political? What kind of Jew doesn't see how, under the iron of the religious, peace itself can become an Inquisition?

"Gerry says the salary isn't too bad, for one of those do-gooder outfits. But to be sure that I let people know I'm not a volunteer," Bert tells his grandmother. He first-names his father quite easily now. Gerry calls him "the reb." Bert still calls Kitty "Mother." "Because it's good for her. Who says I'm not a prig? . . . But I made up for it, didn't I? When I introduced her to a friend of mine as my half-sister. Mother's still telling it. Because for half that Sunday afternoon, my friend Dorrie believed it. And made like she couldn't believe otherwise, when we busted the joke."

"I liked Dorrie," Zipporah tells him. Not that such sweet-talk will get her any further with Bert. "I've liked all your girls. Women," she adds lightly.

"Thanks," he says. "So have I."

She gets off that topic. Her status with him, as a noncriticizing elder, is precious to her. "Anyway, I commend our Maryland friend. Whom I've heard of. Though I've never met him. Will you get to travel a lot?"

"My choice. A lot can be done from here. But I get to choose where we need to go. If I go." He has three months to decide.

"Rabbi Duffy—" she says; never has she said that until now. He'll carry it off. His is not a poker face; it can open up or be reserved, with the shift not assumed. He has a good sense of direction, if toward people rather than scenery. He's clean-shaven, but you don't miss the amplitude that might go with a beard. Only one dangerous quality in him, as far as she can see. His willingness, toward those who he sees need succor or who apply for it, might convince them that the world-at-large feels the same. "Well, I can think of some places a Rabbi Duffy won't be incognito."

"So can Moorsohn. He advised me not ever to wear anything green."

When they laugh like that there's often a commemorative pause. Neither of them believes in life-after-death. But one may suddenly realize that one is smelling the odor of cigar.

He wonders whether to be fair he should tell her about the notice in the Tel Aviv paper. He may not go on any such vague search. Meanwhile, she might spot too keenly, perhaps better than he, why he wants to. Why he balks at sliding too comfortably into the spiritual profession for which all his schooling and background will give him such greased ingress—if no passion for it.

Why, above all, he feels himself to be in essence a family man—yet is single.

In one of his talks with Moorsohn, who if found dismissing a young conferee may introduce Bertram in passing as "my oldest living grad student," he does ask Moorsohn's advice on the probity of keeping to himself what he has begun to think of as his two secrets. He asks first about the bequest.

"Diaries, are they? Or essays?"

"Haven't read them. But Gramps's publications are considered to be somewhere in between."

"And the terms of the bequest?"

"Actually, the lawyers balked at writing it up. I was to hang onto the works for 'a number of years,' read or unread. The discretion being left up to me. Okay, they said, but legal it wasn't. Or hard to pin down."

"Ah—" Moorsohn had said after a moment. "He was really bequeathing you—his trust."

"You knew about him," Bert said, staring. "About like—his memorial watch?"

"I know nothing about him beyond what you've told me. A scholar-philosopher. With a rep, I gather. But I like what I hear." He leaned forward. "It's you we're both interested in."

"You make it sound as if he's still alive."

Moorsohn shrugged. "As one gets on, the gap gets narrower. One isn't dead, but—loosened. To imagine that state is no longer tabu . . . I'd say he was leaving you—your discretion."

"I thought—I might leave it all be, say, until I was thirty," Bert said with an embarrassed laugh. "Pretty literal. But that isn't too far away. And right now, I just don't want to be in lockstep about anything. It's just not me. It's the way a lot of us feel."

Moorsohn had nodded. "Go with that, then."

Bert is left with a grateful warmth at knowing two such men, both impelled some toward him, as guardians. Yet so differing. Peter would never have converted to anything; he was his own man, as much as a man can be, yet would have a lifelong tenderness for others' convictions. Moorsohn wants convictions that can be sold and delivered. His state of health being more in-between perhaps than most.

All this will occur toward the end of the first decade of his grandmother's widowhood. Ten years after Peter's death. This is the way she records her life.

She is grounded now. The roseate flame of sex is now gone, but she can remember it well. Celibate herself, she has men friends, generally drawn from the companionate shapes men can fall into, temporarily or permanently, when they are single. Confirmed widowers tend to be boring, the confirmed bachelor almost vestigial, often out-of-date in ways other than sex. Both types tend to gravitate toward her. She will tolerate them, even to the point of pity, if that's needed, for a time, but in the end grow impatient with those, with them all. Let them find another woman to bond to, or even live with. Some do.

Then there are the gays. A gay man can be a fine friend to a woman, regardless of the age he may be, such mutuality having nothing to do with groupie fixations that enshrine a "queen bee." Gay couples may be less personal, as with any couple well wedded, but can be great and satisfying upholders of the conversational web. As a network both she and they may especially need? She will not spoil her pleasure by further defining it.

Women who come to the house may be of any category, including mere gender, this alone of course being a ticket of entry, at least at first, just as being a man is that kind of ticket among men, though not for the same reasons. When asked about her feminism, which seems to come from her vitals—either the stomach or the womb; she hasn't localized it, but knows it precedes mere education—she answers, exactly as she does for her religion: "Non-orthodox." Though in either case she has no sense of being personally "reformed." When pestered further she says, "Women are an inclusive enclosure. Men are an exclusive one."

Some of the women who visit or phone, or in some way wish

for allegiance, are leftovers from the constrained domestic years of her close-together pregnancies, some now the satisfied help-meet of a successful man. "We are the most ignored group in American sociology," according to her old classmate Mary, a most intelligent specimen of that breed. Others among her women friends consider themselves to have "broken out" professionally or personally, and mostly have. Her own professional connections, while secure, are now mostly on paper, and have never been genderized, likely due to the nature of anthropology rather than to her.

Her own daughters' friends sometimes frequent the house, if only as adjuncts, often eager for dropped wisdom or else prepared to shy away from any homily, all of them unaware how they themselves instruct.

Of her sons, Gerald and Charles are still married to their first wives, Gerald inured to Kitty's excesses, sometimes suspectedly sexual, by their shared social ambitions; Charles transfixed by a devotion he believes returned. Gerald no longer drops by with the colleagues from the office or the gym with whom he used to turn up; Charles can no longer send professors either to meet his parents or have the elder Duffys put them up. This change-about she accepts, as owed to what age solidifies. Or fragments.

Zachary, who likes being the family eccentric, perhaps in compensation for being by default the youngest, has always come alone. As with Nell, one doesn't always know when he is married, divorced, or just living with, though he has been in each of those states from time to time, if at a less exaggerated pace than his sister. Nell likes to keep the family apprised of her current status. Zachary can be referential about the past, so they know what he has been up to, if not accurately; but about the present he's inclined to be mum, so that though his loft is always open, even at times primed for exhibit, they never quite know the status of the woman met there at any one time—except that she will be one more caretaker-curator, devotedly engaged. As Zach was once overheard saying to Bert, whom he considers unduly tied to family constraints, or else repelled by his parents' version of marriage: "Sometimes she sleeps like with the place, sometimes with me. With both—it can be a real high. You got your own place now; give that system a try. What's with these Sunday girls? They know the score?" Bert had replied firmly, "They do. And I try, Zach. But you made your place. They always want to make mine."

Zipporah had then had to move on, while they were still talking seriously. Zach and his crowd usually didn't bother with talk, even if capable of it.

Later, saying goodbye to Zach, she said, "I heard you—with Bert. Some."

"I love the guy, Ma. Summer his junior year, I was in France too, took him to Mont St. Michel. That rotunda where like the whole human race is carved in stone, pint size? I see him looking at it. Same way he looks at Gerald, Kitty, lots of persons here. Not his brother usually. Not you. I hope not me. I get to thinking, though—we're his congregation."

Zach scoops up a handful of nuts from a platter on the dining-room table. He's no longer ashamed of masticating life, but his fingernails, once boastfully grimed with art, are now scrubbed. "Same with Bert's soccer team, high school, worst in the league, who can they get to be captain? You got it. I saw those games. 'You're just wacky responsible,' I tell him. 'Come off it.' And maybe he does, with those girls."

All the time he's talking at intervals, Zach is absent-mindedly rearranging her. Her scarf is loose, fronting her blouse; he ties it Frenchily in a neck bow, pats her hair upward, even centers her belt buckle. The way he shows affection; who minds?

"Thanks, Zach," she says when he's finished. "Now I'll go for my screen test."

A laugh, the hug he's worked up to. With a mother like her, even a Zach can be shy.

"I'm his favorite uncle, Bert tells me that summer. I say, 'Why?' He says, 'Because you ask.' I say, 'Smart-pants.' He says, 'Okay. Because you're really feckless. And I'm really not.' I say, 'Screw that.'

He says, 'I'm sticking at the seminary. I know you thought it was
the wrong judgment in the first place.' I say, 'You already got judgment.' And there we leave it."

At the door Zach says, "They'd hire you. The film people. A
character part. Want to bet on it? I have connections."

She shakes her head. "But I know I have to—break out."

He nods. So maybe they've all been saying that. "Meanwhile,
finish up about Bert."

"Haven't I?"

"Not when you give me that kind of lapful. You're working up
to something."

He tweaks her ear. Says it softly, already half out the door.

"Don't let him be our token Jew."

All her children are verging on their fifties now, or else are there.
The elders of that thriving clan whom Peter knew, including his
sisters, are gone, Agnes in the smoke of a high mass at St. Patrick's
Cathedral, Theresa in the car accident Aggie might have saved her
from, could she have been backseat-driving home from her own
funeral. Nettie's relict, the squashed lady companion, now in her
nineties—"Older than Nettie was, imagine," and released by blindness to chatter—is the darling of the nursing home and currently
being visited by one of the grandchildren, Charles's Annie, just out
of grad school, who is recording her stream of priceless anecdotes.

Only the grandchildren bring home to Zipporah her own age,
particularly those young women dotted on the living-room chairs
like fresh flowers resurgent from their mothers' wedding bou-
quets. On that sofa, the belated youngest, a nine-year-old with that
same slightly pistil nose which Freddie, against all her principles,
had had fixed. A year after her boss's death she had married a
French count, a famous art auctioneer, widowed, charming, and
blameless, whose dead wife had been American also—only to hear
at their wedding reception how much her and Freddie's noses re-
sembled. "How was I to know?" Freddie brooded on the phone.

"None of her pictures are in profile . . . And who can bear what my new mother-in-law said to me? 'Her nose was the best-known one in Cleveland charity.'"

How familiar the little granddaughter's nose is, *au naturel*. Or one can note that Charles's adored wife has given Annie the same autumn-colored, leafy hair. Among the young men are several who, if Peter had been here to foster it, might have been as well known to her as Bertram, or else perhaps By. Some come from a distance, dropping in irregularly; some who live near turn up, at about the same intervals. They all are—if gently, and with manners—the latest generation, no longer intimate in the old clan's ways, which no doubt they would find airless. Yet if needed they can be somewhat depended upon, like money stashed in a sock, but whose value hasn't quite kept up with inflation.

"This house is like a big bosom," Zachary had said, at the birthday party Nell had given herself here this April past. "It's how Mam herself avoided giving us suck."

"The new reticence," his mother had responded to the not-at-all shamefaced table. "He didn't get it from me. And I did nurse some of you . . . And we're a party-giving crowd."

Zach did give parties, but unlike the rest of them, not using the ancestral house for the largest ones, family or not. All the Duffys, including him, had at one time or another attended private schools that saw their function as interceding for the arts against parents too monied, social, or bourgeois. Each of the Duffy brood had dabbled in the artistic, but only Zach had stayed on and succeeded, making flash money in some film area equidistant between performance and design, and working out of a huge loft filled with trapezes, old orgone boxes, a trigonometry of ladders, various illusionist materials, and the solid "wife" who dusted compliantly. At the moment she was Ernestine—"I keep marrying women for that name," the current Ernestine his second of that name and now approximately his "fourth." Both of those named Ernestine have borne him male twins.

In the center of his loft, attempting to divide what was clearly not divisible in their lives—day from night, work from play, and among the kids, insult from injury—a glass wall had been installed, ceiling to floor. On a recent visit, as Zipporah was about to walk through it, Zach had pressed a button, whereupon the great pane, now seen not to be mere reflection, rose into some orifice on the floor above. "Your father would have relished that," she'd said, in slow rhythm with it. "I know it's the fashion to make a virtue out of dreck," she'd mused, looking toward the loft and truly impressed by the huge pentagons of spatial light, marred for the moment by hoisted cash registers, the dotted and wired insides of transformers, stacked television units, and other industrial objects that parodied themselves, all in a setup that was to be installed in a corporate mall. "But this wall is sincere." Zach's face had fallen, into the gloomy chaps that maybe art had made of it.

To see her offense had taken her a while, and some brooding in her attic room. Now seldom raided, it could have used an Ernestine; even perhaps reassures her. Here every object was graspable. In that loft, where art was to be pursued but never grasped, "sincerity" was a word one must never say. I'm getting mean, she thinks. One doesn't need to say everything. Until one's old.

Her own habit of consulting Peter had not lapsed. Over tea, she charmed him back. Master of the in-between, or its suppliant, he entered Zach's loft, as an illusion firmer than any there. The glass wall, descended, was again in place. "Ah, Ernestine," he would have said, "you dust too well." He hasn't aged.

But Zach's dinner-table comment, on how the big apartment of their childhood had served her own selfish need, had been sharp enough to stay with her. When, not too much later, one of its non-family frequenters sighs to another habitué, "What would we ever do without Zippy's salon?" she sees that her easy decade is done. She is seventy-five.

When people die in the newspaper it's different from when they do so next door. Yet Norman had been their newspaper in a way, their

media connection. Slipped near the door every evening, not can-
celable. His illness had been brief, consciously mortal, and politely
endured. Through the gross of opinions that had sifted from
Apt. 11AA to Apt. 11AB over the years—the lettering signifying a
strong, front-corner purchase by each of these residents—a few
very special legalities now glittered, via Norman's will. As Charles,
who had a law degree in a side pocket, and, deserting the planet, is
now a judge, said: "It is perfectly possible to live on after death, if
you choose your parentheses with care." Executors, he'd added
modestly, were often a problem, "I being one of them." Serving together with the bank that housed Norman's "alarmingly large"
assets, and with one of the nation's great philanthropists. "In his
seventies, it seems, which is old for an executor; but the money is
even older, and very hale. So is he." A man who was rumored still
rides to hounds in memory of a mistress, and maintains a chapel in
honor of an early wife, all within his estate, in his native Maryland.
A good third of which state, acquired by land grant, the wife's family once owned. Should the main legatee of Norman's will agree to
abide by the deceased's expressed desire that she establish a foundation with the monies left to her, this man is prepared to match
that sum, so doubling that endowment.

   "Not an executor's usual role, believe me, Ma. But he let me
know that he admired Norman immeasurably. 'To the hilt,' he said.
'For always getting something for nothing.' He, of course, as one
of the world's richest, has always been expected to pay for everything." Charles, solemn Charles, has turned out to be the family
wit. "The bank and I thought of giving him a medal at least,
should you and he work out Norman's suggestion. But Tiffany and
Co. says that fourteen medals of their make are already on record
as having been awarded him."

   "He used to collect primitives," she said. "But bidding through
brokers is said to have disenchanted him. No fun—and if left on
their own they lost out by not bidding enough. Now I hear he goes
to auctions but just sits and glowers, never buys. He lost the second
wife too; I'm told they were fond. I've never met him. But he once

asked to buy something I have. Through an intermediary, of course . . . And yes, Charles, I'm going to do what Norman suggests."

"We're still using the present tense for Norman, and performing the giveaway he couldn't face up to. Do these old boys never die?"

"They sometimes last forever," she said. "If you know them well."

Her tremor alerts Charles, who takes her in his arms. No one does that anymore. She is filled with joy.

S o you didn't go to Israel first thing," Moorsohn said shrewdly. Most seminarians did so, had they the chance. "Or maybe you won't go at all, looks like. Whatsa matter, Bert? Scared of finding out how Jewish you are? Or how half-Jewish you still are?"

A red scar shows up on his temple when he chooses to be what he calls "bloody." The face can't pale further; the stubble on his scalp has grown back into the fawn fuzz that was once red, and may be so again; nobody underestimates Moorie, a nickname its bumbly users are careful to keep out of his hearing, which is acute, as much as for what is not said as for what is. He has never brought up Bert's bio before.

No need to answer at once. Moorsohn, like any practiced sermonizer, is setting up his text.

He has as many as there are psalms. No matter which text he chooses, the elucidations will resemble one another, like casts of a sculpture by a Rodin. As he wastes under intermittent bombardment from chemical or ray, his intense blue stare, rising and falling from above the lectern, draws every listener, each of them a catamaran bobbing on the sea of that gaze. They are aware that the miracle of his recovery may have made him its prisoner, for he will voice only the upbeat. If you want practical, gloomy, Jewish advice, you go somewhere else.

Of this, Moorsohn is proudly conscious. He will even tell you so. He can be caught musing. "A cawnvert to Canaan's shore? Who better to let out how it was with Christianity back there? With a Trinity—you always have to be explaining, defining, celebrating? Instead of the One. Plus of course a heaven, to keep you interested. And under its thumb." He concludes with how lucky "we" Hebrews were and are, without an afterlife to count on. "What can a man do, except become master of his own fate?" An appropriate hush. Then: "Not that he will."

Bert's habit is to drop by Moorsohn's office after seeing his grandmother, just as he had done sometimes as an undergraduate. It had been a way of joining the two parts of his life, the home background and the intellectual one—a separation that a new collegian sharply feels. Moorsohn is always receptive to hearing about a student's other life, and must have dozens of such bios packed away; he differs from the usual prof in that when a former seminarian drops by, perhaps to discuss his future, chances are his old mentor will remember the visitor's past. It has crossed Bertram's mind that for this sedentary man, half suspended in the medical, such interviews may be a form of travel, and for those who revere him, an obligation. So over the years he has told him of Peter's death, his grandmother's return, and now his prospective job.

But what Bert hears, as he sits musing while Moorsohn deals with a student who barged in for permission to take his class next semester, is what this boy will be witness to, if his registrar's slip is properly signed and returned. A ticket to a conflagration in a classroom which can draw, week after week, a bunch of standees outside its open door. Like most beginners here, he looks no more likely to become master of his fate than any other. But if he gets into the class—and Moorsohn stretches an academic rule for most—he'll learn that even he is at least a candidate.

Some matriculates can't stay the course for the full year; some "auditors" do. In Bert's time there had been two young orthodoxers from a yeshiva who, sitting in the rear like two black notes on a musical stave that had no "accidental" notes, had never spoken, yet stayed to get their money's worth, then vanished.

This boy is getting in. Or staying in, for what Bert realizes is a second semester about to begin. Moorsohn is no thunderer. Rather, he is polite, confident that Adonai is a standee there also. He will be telling how a Jew can become a little godling on his own—if he's careful to remember the human tin in his mixture. "To be one's own Messiah—that's the message." The voice will be level. "And why the Jew is known, and hated, as the God-destroyer."

It will be then that you can hear the pins drop, and noting that Moorsohn's hair is once again growing, must tell yourself sternly that we Jews have no saints.

"But the Jew is that much nearer the godhead," he'll say quietly. "Because he knows the world ends—with him." *Each time.* That will be that peroration. Moorsohn's mouth rounds for it. "Each time a Jew dies, he leaves behind him—the One."

"Marvelously subversive, yes," the aged head of the seminary will be reassuring the jealous. "A convert wants to make his own mark. Bear with him. And a little high-tone subversion—Messiahs yet—may be good for the school." As everyone knows, the head has no interest in becoming one of those Messiahs. Over ninety, he phones his internist every other day to go over his bowel movements with him.

The air in this rear office backed away from street noise is fresh from the river, complicated with a library smell from an ell stocked with hundreds of books, many of them rare. A bulwark, a leathery nest that Bert thinks their collector assembles as an antidote to his blank, irradiated intervals. Any caretaker of this much accumulated testimony, all of it Judaica, and rumoredly not in any way inventoried, has a responsibility; he can't yet afford to die.

Two girls are in the ell, prying along the shelves. The seminary, so far not bending to any pressure to admit females to qualify as rabbis, does allow them in for "research." Once within these walls they seem to travel in twos or more.

According to his Aunt Nell, they are merely misguided or over-hormoned feminists. "The true feminist acts it out in her life." Meaning sexual life. "The made feminists always travel in groups.

Those at your rabbi factory, Bert, they're just looking for a holier way to get back at God. Midwives to the laity is all those bozees will ever be." When Nell fumes, she emits slang like spittle. "They'll never get in the vestry where the boys hang out. Monotheism is always male." When Shine, who always sat at her end of the table, and frankly "wouldn't mind getting in those pretty pants," asks mildly, "What's a bozee?" the table laughs, Duffy close. "Female of bozo," his grandmother said. "A pejorative coined by Nell at thirteen for the girls in her confirmation class."

"What's a 'pejorative,' Bert?" his date had whispered when they broke for coffee. "Is it me?" A teacher in English at Riverside, in her native California, she surely knew its meaning. A week later, on Easter break, he'd flown out to go on a wine trek with her in the Sonoma, and a hill hike after. Sitting cross-legged opposite her at their campfire, he had felt close enough to her to talk about Moorsohn, which he'd never done except to Shine. "Is he married?" she said. "Huh? What do you mean you don't know." She'd poked the fire up with a smile. "The saints are always solipsist."

She'd had several bids to teach in the East and was likely going to accept N.Y.U. In the airport, he asked if she did, would she want to live with him? "We're both a little bit in love," she said. "Have you noticed it?" And when he'd nodded, "And we're both half-and-half; that's supposed to be a good start." But the answer was No. "I'd only get in deeper. Marriage is on my list, Bert. I want that kind of congregation. You don't." She'd smoothed his shoulder. Was he taken aback by her using that word? "Not at all." In the age of proto-self-analysis, any fool knew all refusals were connected.

"I get to the brink," he told her. "The family brink, that propelled me in the first place. But then I pull back." It wasn't fair, to a girl like her. "Oh come on," she'd said. "I knew your previous." That girl, married herself by then, had introduced them, in the brokering way brides act toward those left behind. "You and I go for those who are safe, Bert. Who'll give us an easement to duck out. I don't know why you're marking time. But I know why I am. And I wasn't straight with you. I want to marry like crazy. But I haven't your principles. My mother's a doll, lost in the wrong neck of the woods. But I can't stand my father's family. I could never marry a Jew."

When she came to New York they tried to sleep with one another again, and finding they couldn't, had reacted in mutual cruelty. "Get the synagogue," she said, "Maybe the sex will work out." He'd said, "Get the Gentile."

She had. Some names, that well-known, are not anonymous. Nor is a wedding at St. Bart's.

"At least I found out I can be cruel," he'd told Shine. "You like helping people, you can get stuck with wondering whether you're a wimp. And whether the world agrees with you."

Oh, everybody was stuck with his own company, Shine said. "My relief is, I get tired of Shine, I can be Silverstein. But even if you smacked her—did you really?—you wouldn't have done it on your own. You did it for the Jews."

Moorsohn has finished with the student, greased his bio out of him, no doubt, with that oddly pitiable vanity which doesn't mind others watching him do it. There is no privacy here. Perhaps the convert must be forever public. The student lingers, dazed at his entry to this elite brotherhood.

Moorsohn, once again energized, leans forward robustly. "So, Bert. What about her?"

He knows Bert will have come from Zipporah. But he may mean Jennie, who had endeared herself to him when told of her recent baptism, undergone to see how it felt to be Christian, "You joins the circus," she'd said, "They dunk you. But it don't feel right to me, being that limber." He'd been entranced too, to hear that she spoke perfect English when she felt white. Since he neither visited students' homes nor had them in his own quarters, he has never met either her or Zipporah. "To be *gemütlich*"—like other faculty he could mention—"is not my province." But in the province you came to know as his, a man frontally suffering, never mentioning it, his facts are so plain that you are happy to let him worm out yours. "I'd like to meet her."

"*Her?*" Bert says. "Which one?"

In the ell a book drops, then another one. Mumbling "Sorry," the two girls, slinging on their shoulderbags, tiptoe out, but not before giving Bert grateful, over-the-shoulder smiles, as if in thanks for a pronoun not too often emphasized there.

"Your grandmother, who else?" He sighs. "Such a career!" Here the word for any success, within the rabbinate as well as without. "Such a dignified one, from what one hears." He knows of that book, those reviews, but evades saying whether he has read them. "You are right to reverence."

Rising, he peers into the ell. "Ah, gone, are they. Hard-working, both of them, But women's voices, when they argue the Talmud, it's like geese cackling...No, hens. Geese honk...Anyway, we must watch ourselves. They say every Jew, a rake or a religious, is a misogynist at heart...And with reason, the old teachers say. God stole Adam's rib to make a woman. And when the rib talks—*Oy*—the hole hurts." Moorsohn starts gathering his papers. End of conference. But first, the homily, Moorsohn rocking over his desk in a kind of absent-minded wool-gathering, picking up each sheet, envelope, or pad with a quick look, rapping it onto the pile.

You stand on one foot, not released yet, waiting. This is the other part of what you come for, to this dogged, out-from-modernity, into-eternity—non-heaven.

"When I was converted, Bertram, my beloved wife asked for a divorce. She said now that I was a Jew too, she'd lost her advantage. She's a born Jew, French, a doctor in the hospital where I was at the time. We ended up having two marriage ceremonies—once at the *mairie* in Lyons, where her foster parents still lived, and one by a rabbi, to satisfy her own mother's grave. All the more because they were supposed to have been lost to the death camp; there's a record of them getting there. Though her father, a doctor, survived and

had been returned to his town. So on the divorce too, we compromised. She got a *get*—you know what that is? On the grounds that
she'd married a Christian . . . We keep up the civil relationship."

"A *get*," Bert said. "Yes, I know what that is. A religious divorce,
right? . . . Like in that news story about the reb in Tel Aviv."

"Ah, you saw that, did you? Saved the clip to show my wife—
she knew the woman, young nurse during a war. Rum case, that
one. Woman sued rabbi who wouldn't divorce her, claiming herself a whore. Got the Jewish divorce, the *get,* on that ground. Now
the reb's second wife is suing him. Claiming that there's more to it
than that—or less. You saw? Rum."

"What happened to the first wife?"

"Who knows? Ten years ago, or so. According to Elise, who
still hears from her hairdresser back there, the woman just came to
Israel—and went."

Bert lets down the other foot.

Bertram Duffy and The Shine are having a meal at the Afghan
restaurant on Ninth Avenue. Ever so often they meet to catch up
on their destinies. Always at an eager distance from the neighborhoods that made them what they are.

"This place started as a bakery," The Shine says. "Bread only.
The guy put in a huge iron oven—in a storefront. Illegally of
course. He must have just come over, big tall guy with a beard like
a prophet. His kid, who could speak English, used to help sell the
bread. My stepmother used to food-shop Ninth Avenue, stocking
up the car with all this ethnic stuff; she's a woman has to have an
intimacy with food. I used to come along for the handouts. Cookie
the pastry shop, slice a salami the French butcher, nip a mozzarella
from the ravioli man. Nothin' here. But the kid son, working the
customers on the double—he was the same age as me."

Now the place is a hangout for cabbies; they can park. Shine
had done a summer as a bright young man on Wall Street, then
had gone shares on the medallion you had to buy to own your own

cab, worked a year, then sold his half of what they'd paid to his partner, though the price has since skyrocketed. "You don't ask around why a medallion in the first place instead of just a plain license, less you crave to end up in a garbage can, your shoes sticking out." Shine had quit the seminary just before certification, his account of this being, "Blocking the tendency. Anytime it might cross my mind again to be a *schul*keeper."

But they both want to do good. That is their generation.

"'Do money good,'" Shine says, gloomily for him. "We're stuck with it, Jews like us. Only we haven't got the money yet. So, earn a life in the market? So's to make a big payment, the next-to-last day of our Atonement? And a big spread on the obits page?"

"Know what your motto is, Shine?" Bert is gobbling the skewered meat, flat bread, and side salad with gusto. He can scarcely wait to leave his mother's gourmet home dinners for cheap, real eats. "One word, man: 'SO.'"

"So what?"

Their life is with friends.

"So here you're getting a real cushy—what d'ya call it? Not just a job. Like the old poop, head of my step-pop's law firm—can't make him retire—says when they made Pop a senior partner: 'I congratulate you, sah. On your preferment.' Why, you could coast—like to Illyria." Shine acts off-off theater now and then. Shakespeare even. "On that job alone."

"The peace endowments are like old clocks," Bert says. "You wind them up every night."

"So now comes Grandma Zoe, with an extra foundation to run. All the money ready to outlay. Courtesy that Norman, what a guy."

"She's back to being Zipporah," Bert says. "Since Peter died. First thing she did when she came home."

"She came home, yeah. I would have predicted—like the Trobriands? Like—Outer Mongolia? Stuff like that."

"She found she was too old for it, she said."

The family had bought that. Kept their mouths shut. No

inkling of what he's sure was Peter's true disease has ever leaked. Thinking of Peter's bequest, he hopes to keep it that way. He has put the "bequest," which he still doesn't think of as mere manuscript, in a new safe-deposit box of his own, along with the Italian death certificate alleging heart trouble. Zippy had ceded it to him without a word between them.

"My grandfather left me his diaries, or essays he didn't finish. Or didn't publish. 'Fugitive material,' he called it."

"So what was he running from? He didn't strike me as that kind."

"He wasn't. He didn't. Maybe he just meant me to follow up on it. He was his own guy."

You bring your own beer here. They lift a glass to him.

"And one for Norman," Shine says. "Who gets even the final honors for free."

They have to laugh. That note to Zippy," Bert says. He's read it to Shine, along with an account of the full testament, which is not much longer: "I never could make myself give more than peanuts, on my own," Norman had attested. "So do it for me, now that I won't have to hear about it."

"What a chance!" Shine sighs. He drums his chest.

"To organize—an organization."

They eye each other. Time to enter life formally. They both know it.

"Ain't funny though. To be handed it."

Bert tosses him a squeezed, "Nope."

"Pick your own issues then," Shine snorts. "Don't have no clocks . . . But allow me to pontificate, this once." He leans forward, imitation boardroom. "Management of foundation's portfolio—already formed? I figured. I approve. But be sure to keep a few Christians on the board. After that, lemme give you my little rundown on how Jews here made the money. First—the real estate. Always, the market. A little bit—the law, like him, Norm. And the movies, for art's sake."

"Norm did sneak in a little personal item," Bert says. "His

mother, Sophie, did come from a little Austrian town—so maybe send the mayoralty there a small gift in her name. And his, of course. His father, a gambling Litvak, we're to ignore. And remember whatever is given, be careful. Whatever we give out, Jews will get the credit for."

"We?" Shine says, slowly sliding his palms to the table. "So?"

"Have the dessert," Bert says. "It's very good here." They laugh. Shine said that, the first time he brought Bert here.

When it comes, kind of a tapioca cream with Middle Eastern overtones, he answers, spoonful by spoonful. "She'll need somebody, besides hired staff, to let off steam with... The best for that, she says, is family... I could learn philanthropy... And what better, in case I do go for God and country, later on."

Shine, saying nothing, matches him, spoon for spoon.

Bert's finished his dish. He says rapidly, "Meanwhile during the year they're setting it up—it's maybe to be in the two apartments, Norman's and hers—I can travel, like young men used to do. There's a German name for it: *Wanderjahren*. To find out their temperament." He grins. "Mine for sure she already knows. She's just handing me a decent excuse to—get moving. And a salary to do it with."

Shine has left himself a last spoonful. "And me maybe? To move in?"

A moment of sheer happy silence. No toast needed.

"How'm I to present you?"

"I been present, no?"

"Yeah, but officially."

"My coloration—what else? And my good Jewish name. Duffy and Silverstein on the staff here, come in, folks."

They dream.

"I'm not always... prime," Shine says.

He so rarely expresses doubt; Bert's affection swells.

"But I pontificate well."

Two glasses are tapped, for the waiter. They'll have seconds.

"We won't have to travel to Afghanistan for it," Shine says.

"No."

"Where will you go?"

"Zipporah may have an errand for me. Hasn't said where."

"Your cousin's cousin going along?"

"Where you been? That's long over."

"I been here, mister, right here." Shine has long been smitten with his stepfather's second wife, married after his own mother died. "Too young for my father, too old for me," he'd say. But she made all his girls look too slim, in body and mind. "It's over too, Bert. It never really began."

Two more desserts come. They eat.

"Mmm."

"Mmm."

Twinspeak. They've always been good at it. Those at a near table find their speech hard to differentiate, it comes so fast.

"You realize we're leaving our youth here, Shine?"

"Two desserts? I do, and I'm about ready for younger chicks."

No answer from the blond boy. Late twenties, one would say, both of them.

"Hah, Berty boy, you'll come to it. *Ciao,* anyhoo. Travel well. Never know who you'll find."

They pay the check.

As both a domestic woman and a demi-scientist, Zipporah suspects that most pursuits depend on some variant of housekeeping. In the household of the sciences there was constant seepage from such archive to the realm of ideas. Facing the most accepted tribal facts, one learns to watch for currents flowing that preempt the visible, that must have always been there. One's own "culture," a term arrogant in itself, is often merely a screen through which a supposedly neutral observer sees darkly, or squeegee, or not at all. In the role set for her by the bequest, she must hold onto these caveats as to a set of household keys.

Norman's nest egg, dependent like any other on investment income and the value of money, is expected to remain fairly stable. Based on canny purchases in bear markets, what he bought had rarely declined. Indeed the Duffys had now and then heard him declare—with small reason to, considering their lack of millions—"If I'd been around and with full pockets in the crash of '29, I'd have bought damn well." It must be assumed that in later downers he would have done just that. She can understand why he wouldn't have told them of his intentions, which the will, though new, refers to as "long-nursed." A next-door friendship has to be a wary one. Whether Peter had been named before his death she will not ask. But in any event, why her? In the financial world the only category she fits is "widow," the classic target of rogues. Philanthropy either has causes or is led to them. Norman's convictions were mostly negative, and he would be the last person to be led. Perhaps since she and he had always argued so freely, he depends on her to be the same?

He has left her own apartment to her, free and clear. All his other personal goods of any note appear to have been assumpted into the Foundation setup, including his own apartment, as its possible headquarters, or to be sold. "Conservators," or those who are to manage the endowment monies, have been named, though this is susceptible to change, as will be such boardroom advisors as she may choose. For though counsel is to be at hand, in the event of differences her discretion is to be "absolute." This is the language, a style she hopes not to be thinking in for too long.

Little market talk had gone on at her and Peter's table. When tipped to academe of an evening, world topics had been its gist, if scattily, since so many of their professorial intimates had but one string to their bow. When surrounded by family, the children had been its arteries of talk. At her parents' table, discussing money hadn't been considered polite or wise, if only because money was both business and highly personal. But in the crony corners, a city's gossip could be heard to marvel and cluck. Small family "foundations" could be devised to hoard one's own assets. Others actually dispensed, honorably, perhaps memorially, but one saw them as rarely able to escape the attitudes of nineteenth-century charity, in effect giving cash instead of baskets to the disabled, the poor, or the less fortunate—and always to the "worthy," but at least with a direct path, from giver to taker, that one could still fairly see.

If one could afford at all to contribute on one's own, and often even when not able, one gave "something" in whatever proportion: religiously, civically, "music-wise." That was the Jewish style. Volunteering could bring status, but was obligation as well.

Her mother's more monied clan had even had a scrum of retainers—no return duties much expected, some old, some merely "tragic," even some "schnorrers"—all of whose continuance had somehow to be guaranteed. "Just enough to keep their heads above water," was her mother's phrase, clearly a quote from way back.

Only when Zipporah was in college, and "broadening," as the fond or steely family glances put it, would she realize that her father's brother-in-law, no relation at all to her mother's side, or to her father except by marriage—a swollen-lipped, limp-handed man with no vices or talents except his eagerness to please—had been one of those. "But Joe Weller, Mother—he's not even your side."

Though there were no feuds between the families, the word "side" was taken for granted, as between two opposing creeds. The credo of that remote "Brookline lot" was never "to display." Which could "reflect" on what they were as Jews, or were not. The Zangwills, in a comfortable but too "new" apartment near Commonwealth Avenue in actual Boston, had yet to worry either about keeping up or being too conspicuous. Her father's law practice had earned him respect and acquaintance among "prominent" Gentiles; his own earnings were merely gentlemanly, as one of the Brookline side had once conceded. "You're lucky, Zangwill, you could take the kids to Europe even, as each graduates. It would never look like you were doing it for show."

Even from the grave, where her mother is—"I'll want my bones with me"—she spells things out. Destined all her life to live under the dual pull of her intelligence and the duties of her marriage, she had scraped up the tremors of humor that can come of this. "Joe Weller? Yes. He's one of those who knows where his bread is buttered. And doesn't mind telling by whom—though we Meyerses never would let on. We do it because he helps hold up a standard. Below which we mustn't let those near us drop. Joe Weller doesn't work three months out of the year, but doesn't let his wife work either. That's class, isn't it. And he's too close to us to let him stumble." She leans forward. In memory, she has kept the bones, and her voice, not roughened by time, is tender for both sides. "Listen, college girl. Your father had to work his way up, from his father's two-bit dry goods store. So did we once, we Meyerses, though long ago. But what one keeps too long in the vault can harden the—" What had she meant to say, instead rubbing a forefinger against a thumb? Charitableness? Judgment? Not the arteries, for sure; like her, the Meyerses all lived long. When she says it, it does come hard. But she says it. "We don't have their *gelt*."

Nor, marrying a poorer man, had she brought him any, from their vault. In the end, he and she would die only respectably. Joe Weller had picked his allegiance early, and well; richer folk might have tired of him. "Your father does what he can," her mother says, leaning back. Acerbity was her pride. Listen like a cat, or a college girl, and you can hear the acid tone lighten, with what must be love. "He is in fact known as 'a soft touch.'"

One remembers those men: uncles, fathers, visitors, with their kindly, cleanshaven jaws, the faces more or less Hebraic, a signet ring here and there among them, mouths hitched in pomp around a cigar. Often clubbable, belonging to those they could, in innocent wistfulness. Men who were roguish or mild of wit, lively or dull, ambitious or not, talking of percentages, or of articles by the gross, but with not that much wealth at their command. All of them subscribing to a heritage whose exact details might not be known to them, except in the stern, trickled-down sense of "responsibility"—which must carefully not be attributed merely to race. For no one quality may be safely said to be solely theirs—because alleging this is how history has dealt with them.

See them in those living rooms in Brookline or on Commonwealth Avenue, or even around the poker table, their collars open, cheeks flushed with the gamble, though the stakes are never high. Somewhere, certain stakes still are. What do the lamps reveal, what do the reflective shadows on those unbearded jaws assure? A collective tradition they may fail at, but must sustain? A watching girl hears their exchanged whisper, that sturdy phrase echoed among them, on anything from a stock tip, to a loan, to some humbler connotation that might not at all concern money: *You can bank on it.*

And on them, mother?

The dead don't shilly-shally. Or Zipporah's don't.

"Always, and not always," comes the odd answer. "They're human beings. Or as your own boys say in one of their jokes: 'human beans.'"... The dead see no age groups, or else see the whole span; talking to them can be wonderful... "And I remind you, don't ever talk of the Jews as having only the one quality, good or bad," her mother says with a sigh. "From that corner blows the wind of the Holocaust... Ah, excuse... when I'm tired my verbs tend to invert. I'll lie back now." The voice grows fainter. The living, who must hold up their end at such visitations, cannot believe in them for too long.

Yet her mother persists: "So I've evened things out for you, haven't I? The separations among us? Even among us middle-middle, who were called Reform. Don't be fooled, baby, by the accents. By us Meyerses, Germans forever, who had never spoken Litvak, not ever. Or by your father's second cousin once removed, Simon Zangwill, born Samuel, who claimed ancestry from a French soldier of fortune called Angevin, and has grammar-schooled himself free of a tongue once as cockney as any in Shepherd's Bush... Ah, but I've done it better, kinder, deeper, haven't I, than my cousin Charlotte, that snob supreme? Who, though childless, is said to have been prepared to greet each of her babies when they first said Mama, 'Darling. Don't talk with your hands.'"

That tremor of a laugh, then, with which her mother always changed the subject. But she hasn't succeeded on this one, never will. Born in America, alumna of a kindergarten full of pinafores from the Back Bay, taught cuisine, or its proper elements, from the *Boston Cooking School Cookbook* in the public high school her "advanced" parents sent her to, student of classical Latin for two years at Barnard (having been admitted under the quota then existing for the "chosen"), her speech was mildly New England American, its contours pleasantly blurred. But some slurs do not assimilate. How had she referred to it, that identity tag round the neck, yellow badge on the tongue? Hear its bone-clack:

"*Gelt.*"

The bank and the lawyers inform Mrs. Peter Duffy that with luck, and of course their careful stewardship, she, that is, the Foundation, may look forward to a disposable income of approximately two and a half to three million a year. From their spokesman's polite manner, marred by a certain impatience, she suspects that while this is small pickings to him, he's sure she's about to insist on some starry-eyed scope for it.

"Thank you," she says. "I'd best talk to Maryland."

The eyebrows go up. His don't yet qualify him as a lead fakir in the influence trades. Not bushy enough.

"If you are thinking of changing the fund's investment house, Mrs. Duffy, I wouldn't recommend it. Or did you mean Delaware?"

So they're already calling it a Fund, are they? She gives to several formerly modest charities, who have swum with the tide. "No, no. The man who's just offered my grandson a job. He's in the deep-pockets industry. Thought I might drop in on him."

"Deep, er—," he clears his throat. Thinking she has stingray depths perhaps. Or wondering whether they should sue to put her away? This is how her elisions used to affect professionals of his ilk, when she herself was being "funded." But how brisk, to be back in action! Why had she ever stayed away?

"Young Bertram's phrase, really." And Shine's as well—or his to begin with? You are never sure with those two. But it's bracing.

"Ah, young Duffy. The boy in that odd bequest."

"You mean my husband's watch? Oh, the bequest wasn't odd, but the watch certainly is." She smiles in retrospect.

The man coughs, turns red. "We've handled your husband's affairs for so long. Yes, that must be the bequest I mean."

She glows at the man's being so touched. "Not a boy anymore, Bert. Not far from thirty. Just that generation. Either they take everything on slow consideration, or—" She shrugs. Or they take everything? Some of them. Not him. "He's put the watch in the vault. Mine, as a matter of fact; they don't bother with them. He kind of likes to put things on hold; that's why I thought this job might be . . . Though when he did wear the watch once, I heard his girl give him the razz. That year's girl." A twinge suggests she's betraying Bert. "After all, though, a wristwatch that says 'Trust.' " Her eyes water. She doesn't do that. It's the combo—Bert and Peter, how it was—that stabs.

"You're young for a grandmother that far on," he says. "Not just in the face. Er, after you talk to that chap down there, whoever he is, maybe give us a call?"

Nor just in the legs? she thinks willfully, though he hasn't glanced there. Where she sometimes thinks her naiveté most clings. "Mendenhall? If you say. He's one of Norman's executors."

He sits up. The syllables traipse out slowly. "Foxy Mendenhall?"

"F. D., the initials are. I thought maybe—Franklin? Many got named after him."

A head shake.

"Ah, you've met the man then; I haven't. . . . Foxy?" She thinks of Bert, tangled in wiles he shouldn't be. "A nickname?"

"The man was christened Foxy. By demand of a great-grandfather, still extant at his birth, who conditioned his inheritance on it. Railroad tycoon, up from nothing, who saw himself done in by the August Belmont crowd or the Harrimans, but had snapped back the best way, by branching out. Land, oil, natural gas, chemicals, armaments—you name it. Quite a story." He is savoring it. "Rest of the family wanted the babe's mother to ignore the old chap, for dignity's sake, on the grounds that they all had enough. But she'd been a showgirl, and she hadn't. They'd have sued, of course. But the old man called in the experts to verify he was thoroughly competent, which he was, and did the deal while he was still alive."

"That's the way." She hopes to do the same. But maybe shouldn't say so to this nice, suddenly wistful man who spends his time executing other people's wills. "And has the old man had his revenge?"

This middle-aged one shrugs a lot, perhaps a work-related trauma. "Who knows what he wanted? There are billions, if no longer in what the holdings were originally. But with that much,

hard to go wrong. They're out of munitions, for instance, long
since. But so are others. All you can say is that with the best intentions, modern money has a hard time scrutinizing its sources, Mrs.
Duffy. Unlikely one man could manage that."

"Has the name made a difference?"

"From what? That would be the point, wouldn't it."

How careful these men are with difference. Or with hers?
"You've met him?"

"No chance to. His estate intentions are unknown. He must
have his own law firm."

"He's certainly accessible. They wrote me."

"Everybody wants to be open, these days. Have to be. You're
not being seen, you drop out."

Brr-r. What this man's trade has taught him.

She gives him a smile. "Like me. I've popped up again just in
time. Thanks to Norman."

"You have an appointment down there, I hope?"

"Week of the seventh. Drop in any morning, Monday through
Thursday. He'll make it a priority to see me. Should he by any
chance be occupied, somebody in top authority will."

"You don't say? Former junior partner of ours dropped by
there once unannounced, now that I think of it. On a dare from his
wife. Never got past the gardener. But somehow got tapped anyway. Left us, to do pro bono." His mouth purses.

"Ah." She stands up, shakily.

"My dear lady—you all right?" He gets up, taking her elbow.

She has just heard Peter, in the light, precise voice of his middle
years: We dead can't do all the pro bono. Keep helping us out.

"Perfectly, thanks. I must have missed lunch."

Leaving the ring road around Washington, she almost misses her
turn-off; she hasn't driven in these parts since her friend Dana,
whom she used to visit, had moved away from D.C. Since then,
Erika, when in town, has now and then said, "Come on, Mother,

let's see what the Hirschhorn's not adding or lending; the widow's gone strict on that. And Philip Johnson's glassy bit in the woods—delicious, but no museum should be all see-through. The Smithsonian will bring us back to basics with a thump. And lastly—Heaven. At the Freer."

Standing in front of the quasi-Oriental Whistler room there she would mutter, "When I can't sleep, in Paris, I put a compress soaked in Guerlain's Mitsouko on my forehead, and dream myself here." But that was before the nose. Now she is likely to say, "Philippe says he's sure that Whistler had some Jewish in him. . . . He's being rather heavy on compliments." And the first wife's photo had disappeared. But Erika, the most complex of her children, is also her curator of the visible. Now and then, she hands her mother, without comment and refusing to engage in any, a slide, bearing in some medium—marble or wood, terra cotta or fresco, cuirass or necklace—an Eye.

Dana Guilder, a decade older than Zipporah, was her first adventuress, though she might not now qualify. Entitled to more than one art-illustrious or bank-solid patronymic, as well as income from several, toward the end of World War II, she'd been one of those glamour *journalistes* who flew with generals; her accounts of near-fatal Atlantic flights, with some of the high brass "down on their stomachs in the aisles," had been hilarious. None on her stomach, of course, though in her day she'd been attractively WASP in its female meaning: White American Sweetly Pretty. After a blighted marriage to a childhood friend almost a brother, who had refused to remain that while her husband, she was now married to another who declined to be anything else, and has "put an end to all that." Transported always in jets or hired cars, she had perhaps never learned to drive. Pictures of her "not far from the Maginot line" and in "a *poilu's képi*," that French line-soldier's cap, were jaunty.

When last met, nibbling at the vegetarian meal, as specified by her, that Charles, happening to be in town, had agreeably taken them to—she saying of it, "A double whammy, girls and boys, since the meal neither hurts the animals nor heats the blood"—she had become an endearing, or frightening, storehouse of her era's daintier slang. Living in the apartment complex carefully identified as "Not Watergate, the other one," adding laughingly, "I'm a life-long Democrat, couldn't have lived there," she had kept her well-ordered clothes silkily on view in the half-open slide closet, as if still on the ready. Greater Washington, spreading for miles beyond the glass wall opposite, was "the view I feed on now." She never went out in the evening. The "inner city," a term first heard from her, was now too impossible. "Ah, look at your mother, Charles. She won't go near that window wall. I was always fearless about heights." They had left her there. "No, I won't have you go by public transportation at this hour; a man along doesn't mean anything to them," she said at the door. "Let me try for a cab." She was pitiably triumphant when none could be got.

"She seems not to know anymore what a man might mean," Charles said in the elevator. "Honestly—she was your first adventuress?"

"One should never tell such secrets to one's kids. It boomerangs."

"You didn't tell me. Erika, who met her, did."

"Or your kids conspire together."

"Don't look so rueful, Ma. I'm getting the same flack from mine. They sound off earlier than we did."

He and she were on the metro by then. Everybody was indeed black.

"You were our adventuress," Charles said. "Still are."

As they walked to their hotel, he said, "Your friend has that accent we prom studs used to track. Spence, Miss Whozit's classes, Cathedral school here. Nightingale Bamford?—nix. Brearley—some. . . . Very beguiling. Prim. But wore the shortest skirts." He snickered. "Met those dames at crowd-pleasers the school cooked up for us boys who were unattached. To 'society,' that is. Those who really were, of course, didn't attend. Nor the real debs. . . . But maybe you and your sidekick at school—you remember Barney

Bernhard, Ma?—met a couple of dazzlers who'd broken out, or thought they had. Their brothers went to schools like Pomfret, or the Hill, if the family was from the Main Line. 'Not the big open schools like yours,' one little Susan says. A warning, but we'd fallen for their lisp. And maybe got a hand under the skirt. So, prom time you call her. But get Pap*ah*—accent on the second syllable. 'Ah, yeff—' he says—you know that ess, only the lower lip meets the teeth? 'Ah yeff, Fooven did fay. Fee's not available at the moment, Mifter—Duffy, is it? Fo forry. Fee and her mother are off on a little vacation. I'll tell her you cawled.' Which he doesn't, of course. But later, a prefect who just happens to come from her hometown kind of leans on you, a word to the wise: 'You don't want to mess with Sue Chester, kid. She's pretty fast track.' He wasn't being snotty. Called me Chuck. Because maybe he knew she and I already had messed. Plus what I didn't know. Years later, Barney met her side-kick at the Vineyard. Seems the vacation had been a little abortion in Puerto Rico. But I'd never heard from her again."

"Yes, I remember Barney. Matter of fact saw him on the telly just the other day. Economic adviser to the government, isn't he? Scarcely recognized him. Lost all his hair."

Charles grins down at her. Still handsome, as a young man he'd been the family knockout, a Peter turned halfback, with her dark hair and who knows what genes colliding in an "American" face. And a chieftain's height. "My brother, the half-breed," Nell used to tease. "He slays all the young squaws."

"We never thought—" she says, looking up. "When you got that scholarship to Exeter. We never realized, what else we might be launching you into."

"All of us. Broad waters, you and father launched us on. But it's worked out . . . How else would I have recognized your Mrs. Guilder? I doubt she's ever had to resort to an abortion. But an ad-venturess, you're right. High Gentile style."

"Charles." She's never felt easy with that classification. Nor with any, really? And nothing to do with anthropology, per se. "Ah well. All over the dam by now." What one said when one saw quite well it wasn't. They were at the door of her room by then. "Want to come in for a nightcap?"

"No thanks." He'd had his confidence. Or had he? "That Israeli girl, Ma, Lev's wife—who turned out not to be. Ever hear from her?"

"So that got round, did it? I don't have to ask via whom? . . . For a lawyer, an *attorney,* as he likes to call himself, Norman has the loosest tongue."

"Come on. All the men in the family were kind of gone on her. Gerald even. Wallie. And Zach for sure, who even made a play. Even old Methuselah, your cousin Eustace, who guested me to that Connoisseurs du Vin outfit when he'd come down. But it wasn't only wine he wanted to talk about. As a student in Germany he'd hunted bear, and that could put you in a rutting mood afterwards. 'For a Jewish girl, to have been in an army,' that old gink said. 'It was like she'd been involved in blood sport.'"

"No, I haven't heard from her," she'd told Charles. "Not ever, in all the years. Once I bumped into a doctor at Mt. Sinai, a neurologist; I asked him what hospital a nurse like her might have been stationed at. He told me, and I wrote there. And indeed she had been, but only way back."

"Well there you are—" he'd said with a huge yawn. "She's adventured on."

"My sons and daughters," she said. "They'll never know how they've educated me."

A few years on, Charles, after a hair-raising flight into La Guardia on one of his unacknowledged-as-routine trips to see her, had said: "Whatever happened to your Mrs. Guilder? The one who chronicled all those happy shoestring flights when she was a news correspondent?" He had dipped his smile to hers without further comment at her answer:

"She lives now in Palm Beach."

As other comments on their lives as children stray in from her adult brood, she has taken to tallying these, neither for number nor for import, one by one, but each as an element in the extraordinary thicket of freedom into which she and Peter, and thousands like them, had more or less calmly released their young. Her and Peter's children have liked their early life, even though, as Zach says, "pushed towards discussion almost before I took my thumb out of my mouth," they share a largely unsentimental view of it.

Almost all their comments are positive, and when not, only tepidly general. As when, bowing to the social guilt one must express at having been "privileged"—which all but Gerald genuinely feel—they raise their brows, give a shrug, even spreading their hands in the gesture utterly safe now, agreeing, "After all—Central Park West." What else could one expect?

Nell has a special tenderness for the place that allowed her all sorts of teenage satisfactions, from the bicycle lodged in the backhall niche, to the admiration of neighbors when she wore a new outfit in the elevator, to having six best girlfriends within a range of ten blocks, all able to walk back and forth alone, from doorman to doorman, and to charge cosmetics at the drugstore round the corner that called them each by name. "While the boys of course practically owned their corner of the park."

She'll pipe up: "A lifestyle which down to the last cookie we adored." To which Gerald may add, "Except for me—the religious split. But I surmounted it." Which he has, nowadays referring to the synagogue as "our house of faith."

At which Zach glints, in the hippie sincerity he will carry to his grave and has mulcted millions from, "Oh, we were tough babies all right."

Erika-Frederika (who on her professional stationery is now Fernande as well, Philippe having taken a mistress again) is now perhaps the toughest of them all. Half out of rancor perhaps at what her rating here used to be, and her rep as an arbiter of the style so lacking local definition that it must be termed international, she says, "Oh, *vraiment*. Zach in his leather, Gerry in his shoulderpads."

So, *bump*, they're back to the basics. Even if, Jennie having vanished, though not far, they can't always pass around the chocolate chips.

But the tribute is still in order. "How you two ever did it," they say to their mother. How had she and their father slipped them so handily onto and into "the American scene"?

For in their clarion voices, from male alto sax to female second violin, it's clear that they think their country wonderful. Though they must be careful to call it merely the U.S. now, not absorbing the whole hemisphere. And with its once so coveted European gloss not rubbed off, but counterparted—the way you replace silk with polyester, knowing the odds, but for the long pull. Because they can give their country hell is precisely why they have a passion for it "in spite of everything."

What's more, their passion for their nation goes hand in hand with their admiration for the grace and courage with which their parents had managed their own entry to its benefits—as well as their children's lives. For the question already burning at their napes—in a country always "a-changing" (Zach), a "positive cauldron of take-overs" (Gerald has gone biblical and upscale simultaneously), "a supermarket" (Nell, who between love affairs and court cases, never enters one)—is their grinding, tumultuous, outraged, love-dewy plea: How? How will we do the same?

Now that they are all so—child-blessed. Threefold in some cases. And under even more flags. Charles's new wife, Zipporah suddenly recalls—she has lapses keeping track of all their spouses—is Chinese. And the very new twins adorable. When asked where the beloved other wife, mother of her leafy-haired granddaughter, had now gone, he had said gloomily, "into society."

So, to voice their worry, Charles is prime.

And fresh from his galaxies, more or less up to it.

"So, brethren and sistern—" Peter's little phrase, at which all bite their lips. "In the thicket of opinion, confusion, diffusion, and downright exclusion that is now our America, how will we interface them? Our kids."

Their faces screw; his vocabulary will always be ahead of theirs. "Particularly the youngest," he says tenderly. All the older ones being presumably lost, or saved? "Your pre-pubescent little charmer, Nell." Actually a Romanian adoptee, affronted by the manners here. "Your trapeze artists, Zach." Both of whose main paramours have been brought to bed competitively, of whom Zach is already calling his "big and little apprentices." "And finally, Ma—" They all know he's made a special trip for this. "My own new pair."

Gerald hasn't liked being left out. "Make them assimilate," he says, hissing it for irony. "In what our rabbi—you should really come to hear Eisner—calls 'This whirlpool of sensibility, our land of the free.'"

"Ernestine heard him for me," Zach grunts. "She says he's full of it."

Erika pouts her new mouth. "Well, we aren't France."

Zipporah's call for directions to the Mendenhall estate is answered by a polite if strangulated woman's voice. They will be happy to send a car. To the airport? "To New York—and return." Zipporah refuses, with a careful thanks, nonchalant. She has now and then similarly turned down offers of rides in private planes. If on business, you arrive already in debt. If social, you may be spending your weekend as the target of more perks, and more high-altitude conversation, bound to be remote from ordinary concerns, than you may be ready for.

"Thanks, I may be coming from elsewhere. And it's lovely weather. I'll probably drive." At once a robot-voice comes on, re- peating airports and roads inclusively until she hangs up. The switch is unnerving. Suggesting a routine coolly perfected—with no doubt an alternate recording for those who accept? And in the dispatched car, a robot chauffeur?

The estate—the voice had merely said "we"—was actually as near Virginia as Maryland could get, and the approach along those roads that, leading to and from Washington, always seemed nationally familiar, whether or not you had previously traveled them. What stays with her is the woman's voice, oddly modulated, with a kind of phlegm, or catch, of the personal.

A long drive is a monologue. So is a long life. The first educating of the separate psyche is performed by the family. Her young do support her loneness now as she and Peter have taught them: to join with the single and the singular whenever one can. She must hope that at the last, they will still surround her, a talking bouquet.

She and Peter had never denied their own monologues to each other. Instead they had breasted that double stream hand-in-hand, sending out the bulletins that love takes to be confidences. Later learning to surf together the crests that may mask the undertow: Children, Work, Catastrophe, in the way grandson Byron, Gerald's middle son, surfs the ocean waves.

He's getting on for that, she thinks, and may be poised to settle in—to exploit the financial wit that has kept him afloat since his schooldays at Wharton, and to stop depending on Bertram to keep their father from knowing that he is gay. James, the eldest son, not seen since what is now referred to as her "name-party," had quit M.I.T. shortly after, for a high-paying job in Saudi Arabia. He is reported to have married a rich Iranian, rumored to be a convert to Islam, and known to commute mysteriously between Middle Eastern ports and embassies. On the basis of several phone calls from him to his father, two years back, in request of certain documents—his old passports, his birth certificate, and most queerly, an account of his mother's family genealogy—and each Christmas following, huge, identical baskets from Harrod's (the card enclosed bearing Holiday Greetings From Our Offices above a polyhedron logo, and on its reverse side a faintly penciled *Order no. 124*), Gerald has taken to referring to him, touchingly, as "Our colonial."

It's possible—even probable?—that Gerald has no inner voice.

Flexing the car expertly onto the first highway, she feels she can return to her reflections. She's been driving since she was sixteen, having practiced for her junior license on her father's old Packard tourer, on those unrestricted corners in Waltham which were every jack rabbit's dream, meanwhile hoping vainly to use the old boat's legendary fourth gear, which would haul it out of a ditch.

"People's cars are their psyches," Zach had pleaded morosely to Peter at fourteen, having just rebuilt an oldie almost from scratch. "You going to make me wait to run it 'til I'm legal, you'll stunt me permanently." But the family rule had been upheld, and Zach, whose innards had always been more or less identical with his outers, had profited wildly from the suppression. By age eighteen, having stalled the renovated old Reo in a deserted car barn, he'd there embarked on those almost still-life tubulars, modulars, and polymers, on exhibition of which he had vaulted at once into the art of the visible, in designs that, in compromise, moved grudgingly, if at all.

Some men and women like to chat their inner voices constantly at others. A clan like the Duffys, Sunday habitués becomes resigned to this, its members even interested in each others' continuities.

Her cousin Eustace, a remnant of the Boston contingent who has kept up the connection, is occasionally present. One of the last of the real bachelors, and a sublime chatterer in his time, he has recently all but lost his actual voice, now reduced to an axle-creak, or to the wee hiccup, perhaps, of those unborn babes in pursuit of which his mistresses had one after another deserted him. A long gangle of a man, buttoned up in a bow tie and an initialed belt buckle, and confined mostly now to listening pop-eyed, he reminds her sharply (if she shifts his skin from elderly yellow to an onyx past its prime) of the Nigerian, once reputedly a "bearer" on certain intrepid but illegal safaris, who in his decline, hired on briefly as houseman, had served her with that same gaze. When Eustace does manage to squeak out one of his wine soliloquies, he is Kwa to the life—the village desperado whose gun hand can no longer be trusted not to shake.

It's Bert who, after his evening out with Eustace, recalled what Mickey the sage had once said about the old boy, when "Eus" was "only sixty—and still going strong," as he liked to quip, though by then one was never sure which part of him was meant. That time he had brought along a lady, to indicate. "Pompadours with busts, that's what I like," he'd confided without shame, from behind a hand.

Bert knows she would rather have Mickey quoted than forgot. She sees again the mischief with which a smart kid brought out his silly coinages. "You all call Cousin Eus 'an oddity.' I think he's a *sad*-ity."

Dear Bert, who's too young for his age. Which may be good for a man well on, but not for one on thirty's cusp, by which time the personality should have swollen along with the biceps, to welcome opportunity as well as obligation. When it is time to stop being the elders' "dear."

Cousin Nettie, always hostile to the family young fry, whose outcome she would never get to measure genealogically, had lectured Bert early. "Jews specialize in good-natured family schmucks. Don't overcompensate." He'd just volunteered to take her to the oculist, in order to give her companion a day off, against Nettie's credo that "Mariella" would only lose status by being treated as an employee. And had been shocked to hear Mariella agree.

"Heard your gramps telling you about Sutton Hoo," Nettie'd added, tweaking her new hearing-aid triumphantly. "Those Celts—no schmoos from them about underdogs. Go take a look."

Bert's mother, when he'd first declared for the seminary, had shrieked, "Some Jews are too Jewish. Don't start that."

Countering the verdict of the small visitor from Framingham—daughter of Charles's old buddy at prep school, and contemporary of whichever young Duffy had held a pajama party in the attic the night before. They had decorated it with an arbor for the feast of Succoth, but neglected to explain to her that on next St. Patrick's day they might deck it with shamrocks and have a fake beer brawl. Next morning, thanking Zipporah, with the little curtsey that had never been protocol here, the little girl had suddenly keened, "Oh I wish, I wish *I* were Jewish!"

"She loves the world you brought me to," Peter had said later. "So do I."

One can't help loving Bert for embracing it. Even while seeing what might happen, down the line. For his sake—and for the family's—he must not become their "schmuck."

"So you're going to play matriarch," Erika said, when her mother came to borrow the car.

It's a proper car to do that in, this old Citroën Philippe keeps over here, now that he's at the U.N. But she'd better stop to check the oil.

The garage rest stops along the way have begun to be cleaner where franchised, not always so when single-owned. Either way, the boss, if there, is white, the helpers black—though in the back country occasionally, the po' white kid fumbling for the car's radiator, scratching the mousehairs on his long, sallow chin, is likely bent under the weight of knowing the world calls him "trash."

One can anthropologize her nation in terms of its rest stops, or lack of them. California, whose toilets are already the cleanest and most smartly maintained, shows signs of projecting its heady ethos on the nation at large, "cleaning up" in money as it goes. The semi-rural Midwest is clean in a sectarian way, like churches. In some Eastern states, "rest area" will be found to mean an idling space only, mostly for truckers, with no place except the bushes to urinate. In general the East Coast, supposedly the font of humanism and social grace, is the least hospitable. And dirtiest.

Here, in the semi-Southern way that would deepen, were she going farther, the courtesy that links black and white more than either will admit has begun: both address her as Ma'am.

As destinations go, she too is divided. She knows where she is going, but is ignorant of the details, a suspension that has been useful for most of her life. Whether that's been so as well for those involved with her, she can't say. She knows her own character to the point where it bores her, but no longer dares to judge it. Her era now babbles its life in "value judgments," a tautology that must freeze the shade of Aristotle in its tracks. She agrees with Charles on the confusions that beset him and his heirs, but is surprised that a man born into the middle age of a great national experiment— or what she hopes is its middle age only—should be so surprised. She can never know whether taking Peter abroad was best for him. There hadn't been time to broach that with the one possible judge.

But Charles, and Gerald, Nell, Erika (in all your versions), Zachary, and Mickey—my beloved heirs and audience, there are some certainties. Mine cannot be yours. Some will say that as half-and-half you're under a double indemnity. I say that all birth is indemnity, and whether or not a God exists to justify either side of your inheritance, you yourselves have that chance.

Swinging onto the road again, she smiles at herself. An atheist, full of nonsecular answers. One thing she does know, warming her like a hot nugget placed in her mouth at birth, is that her tongue will never evade the term: Jew.

But she will strive, has striven, never to have all her judgments stem from there.

This landscape she's traveling... Though she's no longer barred from its hotels, and the area is not as piercingly spired to Christ from town to town as New England is, in its semi-rural style, on the road now running under the wheels, it does seem very much a Christian landscape. As she verges toward the estate area, where so much green, in lawn and in money, has been imposed on the native dips and swells, it will seem more and more a Christian-empowered one. And may be predominantly so inhabited.

Any census will find such territory all over America. Roadsides in upstate New York, where a farmer places a text from one of the Apostles on a placard attached to his mailbox, and the newspaper of record interposes Bible texts between its news columns indiscriminately, or as clincher opinions, full stop. In summer, the village streets may be sprinkled with what the permanent residents tolerate as ethnic exaggerations, but in winter, whoever passes will match the snow. And local religion will be as monotone.

"Upstate" always hates the city. Not only for its filths, from rats to art. For its multiples. And from the mountains to the bayous of "America" there will be "upstates" everywhere. Many miles, perhaps, between the synagogues, though always some college not that far. While the highways, Thru-ways, though used, are chastised not because they poison, or as in her home state because one must pee and eat chained to the chain restaurants' weird commonplaces, but because roads are "government."

Jews too can fear or disdain the multiple. In her parents' day, the socially rising used to refer to themselves as "people of our *persuasion,"* as if the Adonai himself had had to go down on his knees to get them to join his club. But their abstentions had been merely interracial, Sephardic against Ashkenazi, "German" against "Polock." That self-choosing—was it always geographical? Which means nowadays what Debra told her and she cannot forget. It has to be—where there's war.

The Citroën coughs. She has to laugh. *Pardon.* She's been feeding it high octane, from the driver's seat as well as from the tank.

The car purrs on smoothly under her hand, maybe sniffing out, in this rolling sward and incline, a hint of the vineyards that had nurtured its French owner, Philippe, who alleges that there is no better training for diplomacy than the cultivation of the grape. Who, when house-hunting among the chateaux built by industrial wealth in "rural" Connecticut, accelerated with a shiver, saying, "We French are more like the English. We keep a little back-country near." Philippe kept getting tickets, Erika had reported, after settling with a grand sigh into the city. "He kept going faster and faster through so-called good neighborhoods, everywhere."

Perhaps he and his car will jog better here, in this terrain that was once land grant and was fed briefly back then by the adventuring franc. A near-South, where the whites know how to appear rural—and that it is not mere husbandry which keeps them so.

Stop the anthropology now, which grows amateurish, like any profession left to silt. Time to get out the map. Yes, this is the right road. A turnpike that for once looks worthy of the name, being followed on either side by weathered houses that would once have been lined up to the post road, the way cows line up to drink. A few of the houses are of the rough stone that predated sawmills. Then come the clapboards, or the board-and-batten vertical style, always stiffly superior. No cobblestone, as on the shore of the Great Lakes. Here and there a house of that bluish "Pennsylvania" stone which may be as old as the Liberty Bell, but always makes a house look upstart, and cautiously square. Whatever, this is not "estate country," like that thrust of it she has just left.

She knows nothing more of Mendenhall himself than what the lawyer told her, plus the two brief letters offering what Bert calls "the peace job" and the long-ago quirky handwritten note to her, showing a snapshot of a group of children in her attic, not saying how he had come by it, and asking if any of the objects surrounding them were for sale.

Why meet him? She's not eager to do a monograph on billionaires. She merely should hear further his intent on the two foundations, Bert's putative setup and the matching of Norman's bequest.

She had, in fact, almost decided not to come. To be totally businesslike, according to the financial pages, one seemingly meets one's partners or competitors on the contract page only, never engaging in the face-to-face that might spark sympathy, or shock. But nothing she's ever done even domestically has been merely business. Neither buying stockings—which can call up that charmed day when, due to some chemical defect the first nylons kept disappearing from their wearers' legs, nor paying the rent, at first such a whack for two academics that every month she had to summon up visions of her brood singing for their good fortune, like carolers. When you're young you either want to be like nobody ever, or to blend in with everybody. At her age you can seesaw at will, providing you are still able to climb back on.

"Sure you want to drive all that way alone?" Erika had said. To have her children worry about her pleases her now rather than irritates, awarding her that sense of dynasty which even the lowliest, "any crumb-bun," as Nell used to say, must crave. She enjoys using their old slang now and then, the more so when they themselves have forgotten it. "Did I say that?" Nell the civil rights lawyer had groaned. "I couldn't have."

But it's equally energizing to get away from them, back to a monologue still strong. And still private, praise the Lord. And "pass the ammunition"? What was that song?

Here, come upon without any warning of hedge or fencing, is the "estate." To all intents and purposes, it isn't one. No gates. Not even that aloofness which comes merely from wealth attending to its roadside chores, while withdrawing at a significant distance. Instead, up a normal incline, one of those sturdy eighteenth-century houses with more than one chimney, a fine line of crenelation along the façade, and an elegant little emblem over the door. The kind of family seat commonly built by many a comfortable farmer of its day, or a village plutocrat whose heirs had in time lost their acreage. Some new owner, perhaps of the nineteen-twenties, had put a "sunroom" on it. To the rear, other side, is a large bricked enclosure, windowless, neat, not drear, but a contractor's effort rather than an architect's, the kind of extension added when the owner has the price.

The clapboard gleams white. Such owners have their particular—and very similar—prides. Shutters original, dark green now; a more stylish taste might have returned them to their first putty, or black. Houses of this era chose their inclines with a sensible regard for road access, along with for where the dowser told them to dig the well, and if possible, to provide a sunset for the wife. Barn behind, tidy, but plainly no longer a working one, neither spilling hay and machinery nor yet "restored." Altogether, some good citizen's home, not a "second" one. Trees have been here a long time, in this area not unusual.

One gesture is.

From where she has stopped the car, aligning it with the low wall of inset stones that often brims a terrace and backs its mail-box, the "lawn" is a garden of many plantings, beds, bushes, and shrubs, not all blooming but sedately trained and cared for, and ex-tending more than an acre, surrounding even the barn. Not eccen-tric, but certainly individual.

As she stands there a voice calls from behind her, "Lady, lady," and a young woman runs from a small, gray stone house across the road, opposite. Next to it, out of all proportion to this little house, which might have been an inn once, and "Revolutionary," is a big, formally graded parking lot.

"Oh sorry. Should I have—is that the gatehouse? And do I park there?"

The rosy young woman has a ponytail and friendly buck teeth. "Was that—the old gal and my dad's time. Now Adam and me owns it, free and clear. Yes, please to park there. Town ordinance, account of the traffic we have here. New York, are you? You'll be who they're expecting. Just go right on up to the house and press; Adam put in those chimes. I got jam on the stove." She vanishes.

After Zoe parks, she stands irresolute. But admiring. Maybe she has come just for the drive. And half intrigued by that strug-gling telephone voice? According to Peter she was always inter-ested in the women employees, or what girlfriends, which style wife—"It must be the feminist in you." No, she'd say. "Merely the womanhood." What kind of tycoon (ugly word, mooing its pre-tensions, but what better?)—one as active as Mendenhall must be—would anchor himself, and the details of his empire, behind such a response? Produced with such difficulty, almost pitiable, yet challenging. The answer must be here, in a gatehouse gone to pri-vate ownership, the security guard busy at the stove, the traffic or-dinance, the chimes anybody may press. With a village girl to answer those for him, and whoever is the other half of "they." And in that cap up far ahead, passing through the hedgerow, some local who makes his living going roundabout with the clipping shears. Who in the spring will rouse from his arthritis to plant "as no one else can," calling on a kid nephew to do the dirty work with him, for those who can pay without looking at the bill. And dying a beloved local character, with an obit from all his best customers.

Cousin Charlotte would be awed at the scale of this unpretentiousness. With the timeworn qualification. "*We* of course cannot afford to be quite that—conspicuous."

That decides her. She's sick of the Jews' tendency to pull every situation through the slot of their Jewishness. Testing their propriety, or the impropriety of others, like storekeepers ringing coins on the counter for the silver in them. Doesn't she do it herself, under the anthropological cover? (What's in a landscape?) Every "ethnic" or once ethnic does this; why else are the two leading black professors she knows sociologists?

She's going to walk up that long handsomely fringed path, not noticing whether it's common privet or rare box that scratches her, but because she has business to transact. And because she's had the sense to wear flat heels.

As she approaches, the gardener working mid-row pays her no mind. On hourly rate; Brookline was full of those, they want no talk. Like Charlotte's "old Arthur," tending a Victory vegetable patch leftover from World War II that still earned her praise at the Garden Club, plus the flower beds without which he wouldn't come. He'd had a soft spot for Zippy, a city child who'd had none. Nip a pod from the trained-up sweetpeas though, and he'd have your head. "Here, chew this: sourgrass." Since the Duffys are city also, he remains her only source of lore.

As she passes, the man is bent over a yard flower common back then, stem high as hollyhocks but the bloom a fat pink disc. "Pie-faces," Arthur used to call them.

"Late for that one," she calls.

The answer comes just as with Arthur, from under the cap. "Hybrid. They're sturdier. But a mole's got it."

Almost at the door, she stops, not sure why. Something about that door; is it already cracked open an inch? Or about that man down there, tying stem to stake with practiced gentleness, his words only the gardener's gruff.

Or, ten days ago, the lawyer's offhand comment on the junior partner who interviewed here. "Never got past the gardener." Anybody's phrase. But the man had got the job, later on. "A pro bono," said with scorn.

A tickle in the blood, muscles lifting in her ears, as in the jungle, at the nearness of an unseen animal. "You funny good for you," Kwa had blurted, adding a glottal quickly suppressed. "To feel what's coming—where you learn to do that?"

From that racial apprehension she scorns the nervous Charlotte for? That crawl of forearm sensation at what may be being said behind you—what else?

Beyond the house, way back, she now sees a magnificent line of firs, surely planted when the house was built, their black-green fronds interlaced like fingers that cannot break their clasp.

As she wheels on the path, a stone under her right shoe gives it a twist. Nothing much. But what if she called out to the cap there, "My good man, I've sprained my ankle. Would you assist me to the house?" As she nears the gardener, he's still fiddling with the plant . . . Hibiscus family, old Arthur grunts. Hooked it from a greenhouse; don't grow outdoors this far north, the tab said. And now look at it . . .

And now look at her, grown so impudent with the years. Assisted as she is these days by all the spectral voices. As she nears, the cap doesn't lift; she can't wait to see the face under it. She extends her hand. "How do you do—Mr. Mendenhall?"

Not a pie-face, no jowl. Strong nose and jaw of a size suited to each other, the eyes narrowed, maybe from squinting over gun sights, real or imagined? Or from ancestors. She's seen such faces in the Piedmont; hunters, rather than hunted, unlike their seedier kin in the Blue Ridge. A face good enough to go public, both easy and feral enough. Capable of being haunted, mostly by itself?

It's letting her look a long enough time. Because it is looking at her. When the cap is pushed back, not doffed, the hair shows more black than gray, like hers.

They're linked at once by mutual amusement. But will he acknowledge what he's been up to—that he has been? Not masquerading, quite. What? It even crosses her mind that the voice on the phone, produced with such effort, may have been his.

He's clipped the big pink bloom, is handing it to her. "How do you do."

As he escorts her up the path she sees that the collar of his wash-faded work shirt has been thriftily turned.

At the door, now closed, he thumps the knocker that must have come with it, rather than its new brass bell. A woman in a wheelchair opens it, then propels herself back, with the joint-thickened grip that those so immured often have.

"Zipporah Zangwill—Katrina van Tassel."

The rhythm is lively, as if tried out before. He must be one of those enlightened husbands who, like Peter, introduce their wives by their own, and usually professional, last names.

"Just got back," he adds, laying a cheek against her left one then the right. "You were at your nap. Had a swim in your pool. Couldn't wait to get to the garden. Useless to ask Adam to have a go, isn't it."

If he's aware that queries pose a difficulty for her—as Zipporah sees immediately—he ignores that. It may be that he is schooling her, with a kind of therapy on which both have embarked.

His wife has one of those faces whose beauty of bone is taken in all at once instead of by angles or features, though those well compare. The ripe mouth moves like anyone's. Perhaps the long eyes have less than normal mobility, or is it the neck? Her trouble, as with all suffering from multiple sclerosis or some such, as she must be, is in the advancing inability to articulate. "We have a new garage door. S-sh-shouldn't be . . . s'prise if it . . . sings. Anything . . . to keep Adam building." Then, with a rush that exhausts but firms her, "You know . . . what Adam wants."

The voice is of course that phone voice. So that answering, if maybe at intervals, the incoming calls for a man whose interests are worldwide is her therapy? No time to marvel. The room they enter is silked in taupe and mauve, lemon and gray, and other reticent stuffs clearly Katrina's palette, her delicate pantsuit and leather brogues echoing its walls. A profusion of crystal objects take the light.

Once they settle, Mendenhall lounges on a sassily curved sofa with hugely triangular pediments—surely Belter? He is too well-mannered to sprawl, but still in jeans, he has dropped his boots at the entry for slippers now sliding in comfort on the pale rug, the ancient kind that only the museum-trained can mend. On one wall, a small landscape, so resembling the tiny Renoirs in that collection—the Barnes, at Merion, Pennsylvania—that it must be of that artist's same period; or perhaps it is on loan? Erika has told her of the latitude quietly given certain large museum benefactors, of whom Mendenhall might well be one. She feels the breathy exhaustion one gets in homes of the acquisitive rich. Followed by a relief, that one's cultural savvy is abreast of what one is being commanded to see.

Impaired musculature can make a face like Katrina's less expressive, giving its owner the same advantage as sunglasses. She enunciates carefully: "The orchids in the sun room do well." The guest is being bidden to go see. "The door . . . to the left." Zipporah goes.

The room must have been preserved as was. No decorator could achieve this comfy nullity of stuffed couch and two easy chairs, box radio and grass rug, between the chairs a tray-on-legs, holding the set of six striped ice-tea glasses, acquired one by one, that garages used to give out. Somewhere will be the house pitcher, of wedding-plate, that the aunt and uncle who always had this room, relatives one must visit, but not intimates, would surely have. The pitcher would be still in the kitchen, perhaps, on the counter, under wooden cabinets, and in a moment to be brought out.

This room has the stasis that still expects the old inhabitants. Except—on window shelves that once would have held ivy or spidergrass drooping like the sag of the ordinary—orchids, orchids,

orchids, and on the floor, where the dog's bowl used to be, more, their heavy, gathered presence like wax on the skin. One could faint, or get the message. Luxury, side by side with—the gardener?

She goes back in, dividing her nod between host and hostess, the latter first. "Yes, the orchids do very well."

"I wrap them in pliofilm, if I'm to be away, and set them in half-dark; that way they survive on their own moisture, even a whole winter," Mendenhall says. "Though I'm never away that long...But when I come back, I go sit in there. To decompress."

"And...to get himself...in tune."

Her pauses are to be hearkened to as much as her words. But what's the code? Though hers and his may not be the same?

With him, you dare, Zipporah plans to tell Bert later. *Lucky I caught on to that. He kind of dares you to.*

She is sitting down again, this time not on the pouf. On a frowning stiff-back. Parlor relic maybe of the mayor's invite for coffee after a grange meeting at his newly built house. Kind of chair that would keep a townsman at eye level, and forced to feel his buttock bones.

"What do you decompress from?" She smiles with it.

The slippers slide. And the smile. "Money, and its uses."

A maid enters, to announce lunch. A very small maid, the uniform very pink, frothy collar. She purses her mouth, like to whistle. "Lunch reddee."

"Why, that uniform—Spanish, isn't it," Zipporah says, when the girl scoots off. "I brought one back for one of my granddaughters; she works in a coffeehouse."

This uniform was a present, also. She hears that Adam and the young woman, Sue, are the Mendenhalls' couple; the small maid is Sue's younger sister. Who wants it known that she's on a job. Not just a member of the family.

"Se-ville," the voice says. "We got it...in Seville. She wears... the extra uniforms...to...the movies."

Katrina wheels the chair herself, into the dining room. Phyfe chairs, eight of them observing from against the wall, four set at the table. One picture only. A Soutine, brooding hangdog from on high. All his pictures being self-portraits, of his starved, devoted life.

"He still looks hungry," Zipporah says, sitting down to the soup. Served by the young woman, Sue, who will have finished her jam. On her way to the kitchen again, she sets the fourth chair back against the wall.

They expected you, she'd tell Bertram. *And of course will from now on, I'm out of it.* She's already sure of that.

Neither asks why Bert isn't along. This man would be the sort to want a first look-see. Whatever Katrina's profession is, or was, she must now follow his. However you would define that.

Katrina, it seems, has been everywhere with him. "Until recently."

He pays that no mind. Between courses served, Sue has helped her feed herself.

Zipporah, watching, knows well why he abstains from doing that. Already, she and he are aligned. Though Katrina's disease must be of longer duration.

"I love this chair," Sue says, patting the wheelchair in passing and meanwhile pushing buttons for the foot pedal, the armrest, and an unseen hitch, perhaps the lower back? "That old one gave me the pip. Bet this one has a switch somewhere, climbs stairs."

They have an elevator, a central one. "Getting old too. Adam says—spare parts, you just can't get 'em." Sue's chat may be over the line, but her feeding is delicate; is she a nurse? They have to be allowed, sometimes, to go over the line. Zipporah feels the familiar sadness. All intimacy is a web. A lost one leaves a hole.

The camaraderie here interests her.

At the dessert Zipporah asks, "What does Adam want to build?"

Sue's spoon stops halfway. After a minute she leaves. Katrina progresses slowly, finishes her meal.

Once Sue is gone he says, "An old story. Adam's great-grandfather is said to have been in grade school with mine. Became his major-domo, died about the time he did. When my mother inherited this property, along with the guardianship, she of course had her own staff. When I inherited, at thirty—not twenty-one, my grandfather had his, ah, prejudices—I was away at war. When I returned and had a family, three sons, two girls, even then, the house was too big for us. And my mother, she'd been a show-man; her favorite word was 'splendiferous.' Those times were gone, but we moved in. And Adam, he'd be the third one, he reap-plied. He knew all the stories; he'd grown up with them, all the ones I'd never heard. Been here ever since. Sue's much later, May and December. And not his first."

Nor is Katrina. Not merely younger, though not by much. This woman, would she ever have had five?

"Grown are they, your family?"

He nods. "Well on."

"So are mine. Two girls, four boys."

He's not surprised. Already knows?

"Re-ally?" Katrina hadn't. Why does her face light?

"One died. But still—this house would never have been too big for us."

"Oh, not this house," he says. "The other one."

"The big one." Katrina is managing to twirl a spoon like swizzle stick; is it an exercise? "And Adam wants...to build it again."

"Of course, of course," Zipporah says. "That's what would have been behind those great trees." What happened to it?

"Douglas fir, odd for here. Always wondered who Douglas was; never had time to investigate." Mendenhall got up, crossed to a table with some of the crystal objects on it, and sat down again, rolling whatever he'd picked up in his palm. "My grand-father liked windbreaks. Both in the railroad market, and on the homeland. But the day the house went, the wind was blowing the other way."

"I...was in Bangkok...my first...big job...Helping a silk merchant...design his...new house. We came back...we thought I had—" She stops the spoon. "Polio."

Why is it embarrassing to hear cripples say what we all see?

"Fires," Zipporah says, she hopes tactfully. "And empty old houses. Used to happen often in Brookline." *Though not to us. Our houses were always fully occupied.*

He's looking at the sphere in his hand, a big old marble, with stripes blown in the glass. "My wife died in that fire. She would never let me wire the old joint, the way Katrina and I did this one. She was a stickler for old paneling."

He puts the big marble on Katrina's tray. "Ever play marbles, Miss Zangwill?"

"My boys did. We had one of those."

Fiercely contested. They took turns for it. *He had the immy,* the loser would kvetch. *So he won.*

The walls here, yes, they're silk in this room too.

"Hand-woven." Katrina blurts, watching her, "Goes on fine."

They are at dessert.

"Sue's crumbcake." Not an easy phrase.

"That's why we're working on the telephone," he says. "Katrina's speech improves with strangers."

And with triumphs revisited?—Zipporah wonders, lowering her glance. ("Your mother's face shows everything," Peter had reported, after a stiff elevator ride with the couple downstairs.) "We're soon not going to be able to take her anywhere."

Katrina is squeezing the big marble, spreading the fingers, squeezing again. Her mouth struggles, shapes. She is still beautiful. "Coral...didn't mind our...threesome, not when we were at home, here. She just wouldn't travel in it."

Sue, coming in to clear, says to Katrina, "Mind if I ask the lady is she staying to dinner? Or staying over? I ought to red up the room." *I can't wait all day for you to say,* is what she means. At Zipporah's refusal—"Thanks, neither; I've a stopover on the way back to Washington"—she wheels her charge off. A bumpy threesome, in which the chair is not the least willing?

"Sue's motto these days is 'I've got to run,'" he says. "It's really her protest at what's happening to Kat."

"Kat has—fancies?"

"No, Katrina's never done that." He leads her from the table. She sees now that the rear window has a view of the back hill. Or would, if not for the grove. He cases a brief glance at it. "Neither did my wife."

"What's happening to her?"

"She's on her way out."

What does that conjure—perhaps a canoe?

"Is Sue a nurse?"

"Practical. Adam won't let her study to be an R.N. Before he came here he was an orderly. So we three will be adequate. There'll be no hospital. And I have a doctor in tow. Sue's sister can cook... Now come in my study, and we'll talk philanthropy."

The study is sandy bare. Those two chairs would hobnob finance, that couch snooze on its results. Here and there a touch too leathery?

"Had it catered. Then I threw some of it out. This office, and house, was the overseer's, in my mother's time. Or that's what she called him." He places a box of chocolates, water jar, sherry bottle and glass, and biscuits next to her chair. An electric kettle and the makings for tea are at his side. His chair's head-and-seat pillows are threadbare; hers are not. There can't have been too many conferences here.

He sits, crossing his legs. "And no, he wasn't her lover. She said, 'In my heart I wanted slaves by the dozen. But with that kind of money and living in a mirror-box, you daren't. So I settled for one.'" He settles back. "When she found out my great-grandfather had long ago changed his original surname, listed only as 'Unpronounceable,' to 'Mendenhall,' after a small town in Pennsylvania that he'd never been in, she kept mum. To me she said, 'Your parents a showgirl and a so-called playboy—he wasn't, but who died in a crash? Ideal for a philanthropist. You got to have something that eats you, in your background. I'm going to dump the main money on you. So get ready for it.' She was a showman, as we both knew. At first the old place was kept high-style circumspect, 'so that you can look over the heavy givers.' Many of them neighbors or their visitors. They didn't visit us. Until she switched styles. 'No, I guess we have to be a little wrong for them,' she'd say. 'Nothing risky; they live too near. Six-day bicyclists. Pop artists. Maybe a few real artists, but risky in the lifestyle. So our neighbors can bump into something loose, and still bring the wife. These people are bored out of their skulls with what they are.'"

He offers the chocolates, takes one himself. "That's what I was never to forget." When still in his teens, he met some of the kind he was destined to be: billionaires of good intention. He saw their collections—"Destined for a museum, of course," they'd say. Or he saw the long, ancient lemon-colored Silver Cloud whose owner had had himself analyzed so he could bear the guilt of being driven in it. "Or my mother would inform me with a giggle, 'From now on we get our cream from Pierre DuPont. Oh, not him personally. His dairy. The one they think they run.' I can't know yet the hundreds of fakey down-to-earth operations like that, which I'll have to applaud. Or avoid later. But I'm already flush with seventh-form history. She sent me to boarding school—so's I'd be equal. So I say, 'He think he's Marie Antoinette?' And she says, 'What are they teaching you up there? Nah, everybody here's so straight they can't bend.'"

She'll have tea? Good. He plugs the kettle in with zest.

"I like your mother."

"I meant you to. Can't tell you what to do with the money, you see. Can only tell you what I'd do. And she taught me it."

"I'll have only a few million to dispense," Zipporah says. "Not your—billions. And none of it mine. Still, even to talk in such terms makes me—" Why does a phrase of Jennie's come to mind? "Makes me come all over queer."

"I promised Norman I'd brief you," he says, smiling. "I see he knew that it would take. And what I've learned, maybe it merits passing on."

"Maybe," she says, smiling back. "It was a good lunch."

The kettle steams. But he's forgotten the tea. She pulls the plug.

"My mother started early," he says. "Not only with the money.

With herself. 'I could send you to a psychiatrist up there,' she said, when I went away to school. 'So you won't stay in love with me. But you'd only end up falling in love with yourself. You can do that on your own. I did, boy—no one else being inclined to help. Or so I thought. But your grandfather's will, what do you know—that turned me around. The old bastard, maybe I'm showing him up yet.'...When I was thirty, and by the will's terms, due to inherit, she having been provided for, she handed me a document. 'I paid a professor to research these philanthropists, from way back. He'll make a book of it; he says there's only one draw bigger than sex: money.'

'You're wrong, professor,' she told him. 'It's sex with money.' But to me she said, 'He didn't find out anything I couldn't have told you from meeting those tycoons—live near enough D.C., they all drop by there to pay their public dues.' And more than a few were our neighbors. She'd had a rep as a hostess, long since. 'It's called a *cachet* if you handle it right,' she said. 'I'm studying French for my old age.' Which was always looming but never quite arrived. 'And to talk to the chef,' she said. 'Otherwise, they cheat...Anyway, I didn't have to read the book,' she said. 'He has some cockamamie that they all choose their causes opposite to where the dough came from, way back. Like Mellon's, the fortune that was aluminum, so natch, he chose art. Maybe foreseeing, the professor says, that one day aluminum would *be* art...Or that poet whose stash came from stocks and bonds and a brokerage—anybody who watches the Dow move his stake would want to write his own prospectus for sure.' But when it came to railroad barons: 'Those were left-overs; they didn't have it that big.' So they went in for government? Which in Washington could mean good wine. And women at your elbow...Had Adam ever told me that story about Harriman?... He had. She and I laughed a lot. As she always does when she gets to the crux."

Mendenhall stops. "Sorry to be so long-winded." But there's a crinkle of mischief in him.

"I'm ready to laugh."

He snaps in quick. "She only knew the American philanthro-pists, she said. 'Call it a four-syllable word or a cop-out like "planned giving," she said, 'it's still charity. And like any inheritance it will take over your life, Foxy. Unless... unless you do like me, sonny. Have two of them.'"

After the pause, Zipporah says, "I think I need tea for that."

Neither speaks further until it's made.

"I already had a wife and family," he says. "We were living in this house, my mother up there. The day I came into the money, she left. It may have been with the chef. She knew early that I hadn't much liked living in the big house. 'It was the house where there was no father,' she said. She also knew that my wife, Coral, would make a beeline for the place. And that, sooner or later, with the options crowding in, I would remodel this one. For somebody."

Tea is for revelation; she might as well dare. "And the children?"

"As long as allegiance isn't required, modern children do very well. We may have been ahead of the trend."

"Or throwbacks?" She can't resist. "As with—royalty?"

He rocks. Until now she hadn't noticed that advantage. Kennedy's rocker wasn't only for the bad back, Peter and she had agreed. A rocker both saves you from response and gives it.

"I see why Norman," Mendenhall says.

"Ah yes, Norman." And did Norman get the two-house idea here? "How did you and he meet?"

"At Belmont. The track. We had the same bookie." He grins. "He mostly bet more than me. I mostly won. He never got over that."

"Norman never got over anything. I suspect that's why I'm here."

"Not entirely. When I first started out—I found out pretty quick that charity takes convictions. Other people are born into those. I wasn't. The money was like a rock I had to melt. With any flame I could find. Now, of course, the causes roll in. I don't net-work. But it's leaked that I've a project I want to staff young. In

fact, that is the project. And given its nature, the professors do recommend. Political scientists mostly—a profession we all have reason to mistrust. But this guy—" He picks up a letter from his desk.
"Theology's his game. He recommends your nephew. Says: 'He resists God in a very religious way.'"

"Grandson," she says. "But yes, that's Bert."

"Ah. For a study of whether there are ways toward assisting international peace, that would seem sensible. Up to now God hasn't
been that cooperative." He refers again to the letter. "Grandson
that age? You don't look that old?"

"So I've been told. I don't always take it as a compliment."

"Some women take compliments hard."

Are they flirting? Well, that's one way of sizing him up. "Like
with orchids?"

"You spotted that, eh? No, those weren't started for Kat. But
she cherishes them. They remind her that some women are only
annuals, others are perennials." He grinds back the rocker. "I
wasn't square with you about my children. Their reaction to how I
live. As an only son I'd have been pleased to establish a dynasty.
Money makes that easier, as perhaps you've noticed. For that one
result I wouldn't have minded what I'd been saddled with. But my
children . . . They didn't give a damn about my domestic arrangements; half their schoolmates commuted between houses. But
they objected strongly to having their own numbers increased. So
the—the person those orchids weren't enough for—she left."

Eustace, she murmurs, fascinated by the conjunctions that can
occur.

He leaps on it. "Useless? Not at all. Nothing is. Otherwise—
everything would be."

"I'll subscribe to that." She's amazed at how much of him there
is to subscribe to. "No, a cousin of mine. With somewhat the same
history."

"Ha. Do I know him? What's his beat?"

"I doubt it. He likes them with big hair. And big busts."

A booming laugh. The kind men cede you when they think

you're being one of the boys. "No, I meant—where's he give out the shekels, what's his field?"

"Oh, some on my mother's side, they dispense. They're what's called 'substantial citizens.' Half-millions. I doubt you'd have met up with any of them; they never made it to the big time. And Eustace was only what's called 'a big spender.' These days he scarcely has a dime." She amends that from her dark knowledge of those who don't. "Relatively speaking." Because he does talk of dropping what he has on Byron or Bert.

Mendenhall reddens, some. He's not one you can cut down to size, and she hadn't meant to. If he were an ordinary man, or had ordinary wealth, or even none, how would one judge him, in the human scale? The point is you can't separate him from his money, double or nothing. And he knows it.

She leans forward. "I'm learning a lot. At my age, you have no idea how good it feels, to learn."

"Likewise. We're the same age, you know. I looked you up."

She wonders how much he's looked up. "And your mothers still alive?"

"In Paris. Has a salon. Much visited by former lovers. She sends me lists of them, for possible bequests, should she not survive them. She's ninety-five."

"So was my mother. Though she was older than yours would have been—when they had us. By the way, what was that story that Adam leaked to you?"

"Oh, that. I'd been away—at college by then. At one of her receptions, it was, somebody brought a Mr. Harriman. By then she didn't have to hostess much. And she dressed quiet, much quieter than some of her guests. 'I grew up in nightclubs,' she'd say. 'Hooters like Texas Guinan. Now I don't need to dress like a chandelier. And I don't hoot.' But she could still sparkle. Even standing in a corner. And he came up to her. 'Lovely manners, he had,' she said. 'The way they do. Only so smooth, it can get under your skin.' And she knew he was between marriages. So he crosses the room to her and says, 'We must have friends in common.' And she says,

'Indeed we do, Mister Secretary'—he was Secretary of Commerce at the time—'Indeed we do. And practically all of them are here.'"

They laugh. It's so good to laugh like that, with someone of your same era. "Distinguished old coot," he muses. "Met him later. Hey. So did you, eh?"

"No. But wait 'til I tell my daughter Nell; she worked in Washington as a young thing. A very pretty young thing." She links her hands, raises them above her head, stretching up. "It's been a long drive." Her hands drop to her lap. "Women have dynasty." The three words come like chords. "Anybody can. But I'm just beginning to appreciate it."

They are quiet. So much has been said. But not too much.

"Would you like to swim?" he says.

She would. And knows better than to gawk that she has no suit.

In the pool house she finds a built-in with all that's required, including a black suit in her size and Japanese tabi-style sandals. Nothing here has been mended. Luxe is in the small things, for which "outlay" is ever ignored, Peter said—"and in the large, so large that only luxe can make a habit of it." His own ambition, he would joke, would be to fly the Concorde over and back within as near to one day as the schedules allowed. So he could meet himself coming and going. "And if so—would I bow?"

The pool, built for Katrina, for exercise, is freeform, after one in a famous Bangkok hotel. That has made its execution in Western materials even uglier. In the center is the supporting cage in which the patient "swims." Made of light wood or reed, balsa or bamboo, it floats tenantless. Katrina's chair is here attended by Sue's sister, in her wet pink suit a sweet, almost androgynous child. In a daily ritual, she swims before her duty here. Katrina swims only in the morning but likes to feel that she is "at a pool." Once a week they open it for schoolchildren. When Mendenhall uses it is not said.

Is what Katrina would have brought him, maybe still does, a sense of indulgence? Tamed perhaps, so that practice of it is almost a routine. Now that she is ill, almost a religious duty, even akin to those indulgences issued more formally—"granted" by a priest, though the pair here are more likely Protestants. She, it develops, is from Kinderhook, New York, of yeoman stock, "impeccable," Mendenhall says with a grin. But never with much land. Her aunt, who'd inherited their farm, went to college in New York, then returned, as last of her line, to manage the farm until her death. The church it had been bequeathed to immediately sold it off. "Not directly for development," Mendenhall says with that grin. "But to someone who could on the double resell. A second party, whom commerce would not affront." Nothing much had been left to Katrina.

How they must love their stories here! Which the neighbors already know?

"Money's little hedges plainly amuse you," she dares.

His riposte comes like a tennis stroke. "And the more so if the gentry is involved." Is it possible he has done all his self-analysis himself? In his quick way he reminds her of Peter, but not enough to confuse.

They have been talking beyond Katrina's pace, and suddenly, by mute agreement, slow down. He perhaps does this habitually. She, geared to years of children, of suiting her pace to the deep, earth-bonded rhythm of the growing, can also listen—and answer, slow.

Katrina is still reestimating the pool. One senses she may do this for each new visitor—as some housewives explain, and excuse, their decor. Searching for the builder, should they have checked Delaware? "Yes . . . Delaware."

The word hangs, voweled on the moist, almost dank air, a word from a riverbank sneaked into this hothouse. "Delaware," Zipporah repeats. "The lawyer, Mr. Waring, assumed at first that I would be seeing you there? He didn't say why."

"Companies used to incorporate there, for special tax breaks. Perhaps they still do, can't say. Law offices, with no activity in them, but on the walls, one great industry after another, lettered in gold, on the whitest white." He has garden gloves on, removes them, stares at his hands. "Our school played Wilmington once, the Town school, as I recall; their team captain's uncle had such a setup, gave us the tour. Those days, it was a wedding-cake state. Drink laws in the bars, like the English. But for the known customer, the barkeep would line up the drinks just before he called time. I once saw a man with four martinis in front of him, each with its napkined stem in a bowl of ice. The name of the first family peppered everybody's talk like a part of speech—and the lowliest could twist their tongues around the Frenchy first names of the fief's founders: Irenée, Eleuthère. You went to the right parties, nobody with the company's name might be there. But half the men would have it for their middle one."

He bethought himself of something, rose, went into the pool house, brought out a pitcher of lemonade apparently already there, handed glasses all round, including the maid, and sat down again, looking into his glass. "And every other girl there was a daughter of one of those men . . . You saw a dog show in Wilmington; the select people didn't use handlers; there was pedigree on both ends of the leash."

His voice was like chorded in thirds during that speech, down down, down, and up again, for the dogs.

"It was a strait-laced kind of wealth I'd never seen," he says, draining his glass. "But the hobbies could be wild. Collections so chilly exquisite they froze into museums. And gardens, with blooms hanging so swollen and decadent it could be Babylon."

He slaps the garden gloves together. "That side of it took, you might say. And the parties—I married one of those girls. But you might tell Waring, next time you see him, that we—my interests—have never really incorporated in Delaware." He's still molding the gloves, readying them. "Had my way, I'd never have incorporated anything. Nor let the existing ones lie. But that wasn't possible. Not if I wanted managers."

She finds she's deeply thirsty, holds out her glass. "So's you yourself could duck out?"

Katrina answers before he can. "We've . . . been all over."

He refills Zipporah's glass, saying nothing.

Next move hers? That's the sensation. "Driving down from Washington, once you get off the highways . . . I'm used to New England's spires. Less of those here. Or less prominent. But still the landscape feels very—" She finds she can't say the word, right out. "Founded by Anglicans mostly, wasn't it? And French Catholics, around Baltimore."

He tosses the gloves in her lap. "Nobody founds a landscape. Not even with these." He retrieves them. "The land takes what it can get. Some places for so long—China, India, Valley of the Niger—that it fools you. So you don't see they were once colonized too, like all the rest." He stands up suddenly, stretches. "Tell you where you can see that best? On television. No matter where the camera goes, nor the costumes. Cities, of course, don't *have* land, not so you can see. Unless the bad times come. But with the semi-rural, or even suburban, like around here? Or desert? You can see we just humanize it . . . Like Iran, Katrina? What we saw last night?"

She is able to nod. Doesn't speak. Doesn't need to. Color rises in her cheek. Because he has admitted their travel intimacy?

"Picture of the Shah—screaming crowd. Or spitting—hard to say. But a screenful. Of us—people. Then it shifts, to some flat terrain; can't tell whether it's dirt or sand. One tree. But like the tree knows it's an oasis. Just behind the broadcaster's toupee." He laughs. "Think I'll join you in a swim." Looks at Katrina. "Do I have to change in the pool house?" Whatever her expression, he understands it. He peels the shirt, then the jeans. He has reason to preen, but doesn't. He dives in.

She too would have felt uneasy to have to say "I'll swim now" in front of that wheelchair. But with men of ease, do women too often impute tact?

The water's very warm, as it would have to be. The cage is in one of the scalloped recesses, tethered to a set of steps that lead down.

They swim separately, then in the lane their rhythm makes.

"You have a good crawl."

From many rivers. But she will not boast.

Their swim is short.

"I've a couple hours of telephoning," he says then. "Hope to see you before you leave. Meanwhile, swim on for a bit, will you? She's on a program of muscle flex, in empathy."

Saluting her, he climbs out, lays a cheek against Katrina's, and leaves, this time for the pool house.

Zipporah swims on. The woman in the chair is watching. No movement is visible in her. Not even in the hand. But there is an intent stare. Of the kind even the normal have when their inner organs or bones are making known their presence.

Her own throat swells, with the need to cry, in empathy.

The stare persists.

Lowering her eyes, Zipporah, switching her path from the pool's length to its diameter, and a little nearer, swims back and forth, back and forth, unsure whether she is being watched as a seal would be, or a shark.

When she emerges, the chair is gone.

When she exits from the pool house, dressed again, he is there, dressed, this time in sport shirt and slacks. But there's no debonair hint that he's role-playing—if anything less so than his neighbor males here might, between boots and saddle, cocktail ascot, "smoking" or dinner jacket. Once again he strikes her as a man as easy with his unusual lot as he has schooled himself to be—the fault being yours if you can't help noticing it.

Katrina will not appear. The therapist who arrives daily to help her with the specially designed machine on which she is able to write letters has found her already lying down, having finished the two that Jeanie, the maid, had been rung for, to fold these and mail. She is now resting, and not speaking, which after extra activity she sometimes does.

"So I can't bring you her regrets." It's always worrisome when she won't speak, he reveals. One of these days she will not be able to. Eight weeks ago she was still semi-ambulatory; now she is not. The decline has been fast. "That is how we know."

"How much do you know about me?" Zipporah asks.

The answer is as she expected. As much as a good researcher could find. "Trust funds are not conceived wholly in trust. Foundations must have more than a leg to stand on." When he teases, the gardener tends to show up. "But I know even more, from today."

"I won't cry unfair."

"No, we're both too old for that."

She's pleased not to be called "ageless," which always means "I can see you were once Cleopatra."

"Besides—" He touches the flower he gave her, still bedraggedly in her jacket's lapel. "There's really no referee." He glances skyward.

When you deny God you can hear an absence, like the air-suck from a grand concussion elsewhere.

He catches her looking at the great firs, immobile as sphinxes, up the hillside. "Yes—they're as far as I can—believe."

"You were brought up churchless?"

"The old boy, my great-grandfather—he married an Englishwoman, a Miss Honeyman; how they found each other in Coeur d'Alene, Idaho, is anybody's guess. Maybe his new last name did the trick, with its Britishy 'hall.' Money from somewhere she already had. She kept the high Anglican banner flying; my own father was killed when actually on a mission with a group of young hotheads whose ideas would help found Oxfam, the charity movement. Their truck, overloaded with Christmas goodies, slid off a bridge. My mother, who was very fond of him, tried to be Anglican in his memory, but it didn't work. 'I keep seeing his poor head stuck in a *Buche de Noel*,' she said. 'And the only English thing you get from that creed is the chilblains.'"

"You're making this up."

"No, quite the reverse. It's what sustained me. When she moved to France she vowed to 'take instruction' there, if she could find 'one of those jolly monks.' She did. But when she was asked, by his abbé, why she wanted to enter the church, she said, 'It's the best place to show off one's hats. Except in the hot tub, with a really good friend.' To me she wrote, 'I spoke the truth. But only God heard. Next time I'll do it better.' And she did. 'This time I dressed like a probationer,' she wrote me. 'On her way to a date with the Lord.' And it paid off. 'I had what they call here a *donné*. You say very softly what's in everybody's head. So when the top guy asked why I wanted to join up I said, "Monsieur l'Abbé, it's where the best society is. I just want to be 'received.'"'

They walk toward where she had left the car. The aftermath of a good laugh is a special atmosphere. Lightening the step and the heart. "She was received, of course. Along with a whopping donation for the preservation of Gregorian chant. They gave her a ceremony. We all flew over for it, the whole family."

"Of course," she says, dreaming it as she and hers might have done. "In the Concorde?"

"All eight of us? Or in the private plane my staff is always urging?" Passing what looks to be a bed of herbs, he pulls a clump of weeds from it, not bothering with the glove. "Not at all. Ordinary first class."

She counts quickly in her head. Five children, him. And the two women, wife and mistress. *Well—it was to France,* Erika whispers in her ear.

"Did it to the last, every year. Only time my wife and I saw all our offspring together. And only time my mother ever gave out money advice. 'Give until it hurts,' she'd say. 'Until it hurts those who don't.' And to me extra, because I had the bulk of what she always referred to as my 'birthright'; she'd whisper, 'And you, F. D., do the same. But try never to show your hand.'"

"And you don't. I'd say," she dares. "And I'm here to learn."

"She learned in reverse, she said. From what went on in this neighborhood. That the distance from the government in Washington to private privilege will turn out to be the same as between your own ears."

"Meaning?"

He shakes his head. "Work it out."

She'd had a mother like that. But a father also, not just one by hearsay. "My mother talked like that, but against the family itself. Chipping away at what we were. I'm still interpreting it. Were we good Jews being bad? Or bad Jews being good? Both assimilated."

"And your father?"

He says that like those who haven't had a father do.

"He stuck to his guns. Being the gentle sort. Any Jew was a Jew."

"We still hunt, down here. But mostly among ourselves."

Not since Peter has she been able to talk like this. Dangerous ground with an unknown.

"Driving along here, I kind of figured that. A Christian landscape. Or so it would appear—on television."

The hedge behind them is privet. He rubs a shiny leaf between forefinger and thumb. "It's the blacks who are the Christians. And maybe some of the meeker whites. The rest? Just Gentiles."

Wow, as Nell would say. What would Charles? "My brood think themselves champions at identifying the—the divides. But I doubt they've heard that one."

"Local. A quote from the pastor of our Abyssinian Baptist Church ... We support each other now and then. Against some attempted deals. After which he preaches a sermon called 'Real Estate.' Milks that phrase for all it's worth, believe me."

As they go on down the hill he swings a loaded key ring, with the air of certainty this lends. Mendenhall plants his boots like a gardener showing his turf. At the gate, there's no one to greet them. He shows none of the impatience that some who have constant servitors tend to. Rather, he's taking a jaunty pleasure in unlocking for himself, in the sly anonymity of a man too usually on view.

She has a pervading sense of understanding him. Guarding that, for examination later.

He makes no comment on the car other than to pat its broad lip in handshake and lean on it. "Be looking forward to your grandson and his pal."

"So are they."

"Dr. Moorsohn sent me a follow-up note on him. Want to see?"

"Any grandmother would."

He takes a postcard from a pocket, hands it to her. On it is typed: "The better young take the world as for their beat solely. The best ones are willing to concede that it's also ours."

"He sends these cards instead of marks, their last year. Sent to whoever paid the tuition." Her voice tremors. "Want to hear mine?" A cloud moves across the sky like a grandee as she says it: "Bert wants not to exploit us, but to extend us. May the Lord look after one so full of love; or at least give him errands."

They laugh. She's teary, but they laugh.

"I'll try," he says. "That prof, he's a maverick, isn't he; we researched him some."

"You have office staff down here?"

"Here?" When he's shocked he looks boyish, even naive. "Not anywhere. I use other people's. And go a-roving. Telephone hours from time to time. Mail sifted. Summarized. Proxy answers, but only to the corporate. Not personals; I do answer those. That's holy stuff."

This is so endearing that she has to look away.

"I thought maybe—in the barn." Her attic office, home now and then to wooden fauna in migration, had at times been dubbed that.

"The barn's Adam's."

"Well . . . I must go." She's relieved not to be staying on, pinned down to watch the torturous routine of this house. Yet it's the hour when a landscape, blurred with old yearnings, belongs to no one except those who are looking at it.

He pats his pockets, clearly searching for delay. "Your young rabbi's note. Expressing interest. Lot shorter than his friend's."

They can't quite see each other's smile; no need to. At this hour voices conspire.

"Peter—my husband—used to call them 'the two-a-day: Bert and Shine.' Vaudeville." Peter's voice intrudes in spite of her. "'Like two hoofers,' he said. 'Tricky footwork. Heartbreakingly sincere.'"

They laugh again. Can't be helped.

"A fine recommendation," he says. "Hope it works out . . . He was in semantics, wasn't he? Your husband."

"Why, yes. They only cast him as a logician, he said, because he taught with some. 'And they feel safer having us with them, rather than against.'"

A silence. Peter might be standing here. Had she meant him to?

Mendenhall seems not to mind. "We used to know where to put the money. Science, art, family—done. Now all the disciplines are breaking loose. Merging, even. They all want to be a family."

"I find I avoid making adverse comments on the age," she says. "Because it might be—just *my* age."

Lighting springs on, one of those timers that effectively destroy dusk. Every estate here will have one.

"We're the same," he says.

That's plain to both.

"You've certainly researched us," she blurts, opening the car door.

"It's customary. You should research us, before the two funds merge."

"I expect we will. Corporately."

"Any questions on your own?"

"Thanks. I think today obviates—" Her voice dies. A coupe, open and ancient, swings in, chugging slowly past them. The driver, a long-faced woman with her hair in a bun on top of her head and a cuff of white atop that, waves her glove. Beside her, filling the coupe, head as high as hers, and the long muzzle resembling, is an Irish wolfhound. Standing, of course, being as big as a—lamb? Whatever, the largest breed in the world.

"Our Mrs. Turley. Relieves Sue on the night shift. And on her day off. Came to us from a rehabilitation hospital, in Haverstraw, New York. The job's been a boon to both her and us. Since most people won't use her. She won't go anywhere without the dog."

How the well-to-do prize, even coddle, eccentricity in their helpers. Our Mrs. Turley. Our cook Maggie, who says a Hail Mary before the soufflé. Our farm-produce supplier, who must be paid entirely in coins. The groundsman who does that marvelous topiary pruning, but as you see, only in shapes of birds. In upper suburbia, the nullity of home life craves a more modest dose of "character," if not right in the family. But even the poor somehow pay for it. Since they own no helpers, their eccentric will be right at the home table, or waiting to be hooted at, in a local bar.

"Is the dog let run?" At his nod she can see it, clicking alongside its mistress like a pony. Or one day, maddened by the glare, soaring toward the dog-star, and into the pool?

And Adam will take care of it?

"I do have a couple of questions," she says, blinking up at him. One for each of his lives?

"Fire away."

"Is Adam for real?"

The minute it's out of her mouth she knows it for what she and Peter would have pondered, could she have told him of her day, even hearing their probable exchange: *Crops up too often in the talk, and too crucially.*

"He's real enough up the hill," Mendenhall says slowly. "Sifting our ashes. He thought we would rebuild."

She waits. For this man so accustomed to being waited for.

"Maybe not quite so real—down here. If he saw you, he'd touch his cap. But you've no place in the story he's lived all his life."

Lights have sprung on in the gatehouse behind them.

"He and Sue'll be there by now," Mendenhall says. "Once Turley comes she can leave. It's his signal as well. He picks Sue up at our front door. Which he doesn't approve of. In his day, retainers made themselves scarce. So he leads her round the back way to their house."

He waits. She says nothing.

"Sue doesn't mind, if that's what you're thinking. He's given her a part to play. And women of that class—she was brought up in a trailer—don't want the kind of man who's underfoot. But in the evening, the two of them will mull us."

He's like the star of the cast, talking of the actors who support him. "And you won't mind?"

"It's our story he guards. He married her because she'll listen to it. And how he got to Paris for it, last time."

She turns to look up the hill, at those sentinel trees.

"We heard bargaining for hours, his yells as loud as my mother's. He treats her like an equal, from back when. She's convinced Adam knows who and what my grandfather was well before he became an "unpronounceable," and accuses him of wanting to carry the secret that belongs to us to his grave, "a thief's grave." He answers that until she rebuilds the house, he won't die."

She knows those feuds, from her mother's family. Borrowings that never will be recompensed. Houses of talk, in which nobody will ever live.

But what of this heir? Who can still say "class" so evenly. What's he been burgled of?

"I've gabbled a blue streak," he says. "I won't apologize."

"Don't," she says. "I need voices. Other voices."

Dare to speak this lack (she never has), and it may be answered. Inside her a dark blank forms, the end of her widowhood.

"I have to go," he says. "If she's able, we have coffee together. And I promise never to forget her. Each night of her life. I do that—and why not? She's only had the one life."

"You're still counting?" Why should her horror be for him?

"I don't win at all the auctions."

"So you remembered that." Maybe when Moorsohn circulated his list of protégés? What a greenhorn she is in the world of foundations! "That's why I'm here."

"I made a bet." He jabs a thumb at the sky. "With the resident bookie." So God is a tenant here after all? She won't ask in which house.

"Your second question? Hurry on."

She won't. What's done every night there's always time for.

Reaching down, she searches for a stem to pull, trying for the root of him. "Why did you want the mongoose?"

"Because no one knew what it was. How it was made. I thought I did."

She's raised up, embraced. His right cheek is laid against her left, left against her right. A phrase is breathed against her mouth, not her ear. She senses only its formation. He's gone.

As every traveler knows, the drive back is always different no matter the vehicle. You are weighing what you bring home.

He's not the only one who keeps counting; is everyone around him doomed to the same?

This man doesn't merely remember. He cannot forget.

In a blowy outdoors, a cheek laid against yours is likely chill, but the hands that grasp you body-warm. His cheek—ingratiatingly hot. His grasp—cold. From what it already possessed?

After returning Philippe's car to the garage, she phones Erika. She confides in her daughters separately, if at all. Nell, the rake, but the lawyer also, could be talked to about money. On sex, with and without love, it would be Erika. The children know, of course, about her visit.

"How'd it go?" Erika says.

"The car performed perfectly."

"Come on, Madam. *Sauve qui peut.*" That is Erika's motto, recently. Though it's not clear who is saved, or by whom.

"I got past the gardener," Zipporah said.

Some people toss what they've brought back from a trip into the cornucopia of treasures or oddments they already have. Some hide this keepsake they will not want to show.

She goes into the "attic." Not quite abandoned, each year cleaned out of some of its actual goods, it is now more of a duty than a refuge. Her office, lacking a professional stimulus, is now empty, and less of a reproach. Her desk, chair, and wastebasket are now near the books in the living room, a small oasis she can get to more casually. The stream of packages to be warehoused had ceased when her travels had. All museums have been sent their trove. Even the childhoods have been plundered of their games. Here and there, the detritus of a marriage, in the objects divorced. Luggage mostly gone, with its generation. The beds were the last to go. What backpackers want is a smart folding cot or blow-up; what their parents prefer is a hotel. Who rootles for sheets in a linen closet now?

What's here are the few masks that hang like surviving friends. A mask surveys the ages best of any objects Zipporah knows. Severed from whatever face once lay behind it, it need only contemplate.

In the center, the canoe. Breasting a space now so cleansed, its wooden oarsmen push forward without urgency, on the current of the unseen. They have a willed destination. What's hers?

She wants not to exaggerate. That already baroque story of his, into which she has stepped like a commoner wandered on-stage of an opera house in full cry. There's no chair here; can she sit on the floor? She finds she can, even cross-legged. The posture makes her laugh, it is so appropriate. What she wants to do is to confront that bench. That comfort seat, just a wee stricter than a couch, on which she has lounged in her bathrobe, her right arm on the one beast's extended muzzle, her left arm stretched along the back, the carved curve of the second one's haunch under her elbow, its pointed snout undangerously nuzzling her palm.

Sitting on its slightly hollowed plank in the blind dark, her navel knotted with sorrow, she had led a dead boy on his walk through the shades. Clumsily executed, the carvings are identifiable as mongooses only by a detail here, there; and because there are two, it has been hers alone. One owns a mongrel more deeply because it is irreplaceable; its pedigree is unique. Shuddering, she takes in what the bench is telling her. She can never sit here again.

When the object first came out of its crate, they'd found they'd forgotten how inept it was. All the refinements waiting to be shipped to museums had seemed to be staring at it. Because, botched as it was, it was going to be allowed to stay?

"It's very down-to-earth," Peter had said finally. "The way some folk art is. When it's just looking, not worshiping.... Well, we no longer have a dog." They had never had fancy bred ones. And because she had had to be the more dutiful feeder, all the children's pets had turned their allegiance to her. "I'll tell you what, Zipporah. It's your mutt." When she still stood there, unable to say why the thing drew her. "Except that it has no mystique." He'd left her to it, saying, "Mongooses? Mongeese? Why don't you have a prowl?"

A dictionary prowl is like a minuet, leading you courteously between definitions. And the steps will always be as you recall. From the first time you learn them.

On checking, these are: "A mongoose is an ichneumon, common to India, able to kill venomous snakes without harm..."

"The ichneumon is a small, brownish, carnivorous quadruped, found in Egypt, noted for destroying the eggs of the crocodile, and venerated on that account by the ancient Egyptians..."

"Mongoose is also applied to a species of lemur... *lemur, lemures:* in Roman myth the spirits of the dead... A genus of nocturnal mammals, found in Madagascar. Allied to the monkeys. But having a pointed muzzle, like that of a fox."

What had Peter said when she told him the results of her research? His voice comes faded, faintly vaudeville, the valiant hoofer doing his buck-and-wing. "Ah. Better not let on to that couple the floor below us."

What she feels now, untrammeled, is being alive in Maryland's early autumn, where a hibiscus is being cozened to linger by a man who could afford to import carloads, the trees preserved from a fire stand like accusers, and in the modern confusion of temperatures, a heated pool can vie with an equinox's sky.

And a man's modest wants can be at war with his great grasp.

Foxy Mendenhall, asked why he had wanted her mongrel, had identified it. Shaping against her mouth what he must balk at releasing to an ear. *"It was me."*

"What a tale!"

Erika's black mop is silky, curly at the top, boyish at the nape, and preeminently in style. Like her new temperament, from which the personal embitterment has been barbered. Or else lazy living in the States has given her new targets, like the tame decor of this expensive half-a-house, whose monthly rent could buy a vineyard and whose air seems monitored by one central Jacuzzi before one is allowed to breathe. "We are one of the last of those on what is called 'New York steam.'"

Philippe, flopping down on one of the tan-on-tan poufs, says, "I believe that to be a euphemism for thought control."

His laze is different from hers, in from his hard day at the U.N., which he much enjoys, saying, "We learn the same lesson by the day, by the week. That the world is determined to learn nothing." But he makes friends by the score, sifting their worth to him in the style his French rearing has taught him, and has just asked Erika to add new acquisitions to a coming dinner list. On better acquaintance one sees that his aquiline, blue-jowled, springy good looks are indeed separate from his fine tailoring, to which he occasionally adds "a peccadillo" of a tie. One quarter of him has brought him a noble Huguenot name. The rest is Sephardic Spanish Jew and "Turncoat Catholic." On inquiry as to when his family had converted she has heard him answer, "Morally too early, historically too late." The era being the Inquisition. His paternal grandparents having converted back to Judaism before him, he is entirely comfortable. "Like between two masseurs, evenly matched," Erika says of him, "Philippe knows exactly where he is, as a Jew. Only he won't say where." *"Vraiment,"* he responds. "All the fanatics would shoot."

He and Erika have become what is patronizingly called "a good marriage." They have put their intelligences together. America has even redressed the sexual balances in their union. For Philippe, the delicate art of pursuit does not exist here: "'Unfaithful?' To what?" when mere straying is reduced either to legalized agony or vulgar openness. Meanwhile Erika's hardened guile has made her a knockout (in Paris pronounced "k'nuck-oot"), and here reported as overheard in the men's rooms of highly proper clubs or at the looser loft parties. All of which explains his new style, although the word "husband" still emerges from him with a hiss.

Though he refuses to be interviewed on his personal religion, citing his United Nations responsibilities, his reply to one of his brother-in-law Gerald's mentors has gone round the circuits of more than family. As Gerald had said plaintively, after the dinner party at his house to welcome the just arrived couple, "It wasn't my rabbi. It was the elder one."

Philippe, asked his views on "American civilization," had said, "Ah, the American experiment" and fallen mum. Pressed, he'd explained, "That is my view." But seeing that the manners here required more expansion, had politely enlarged. "Americans won't tolerate a status quo, good or bad. Once they recognize one, they 'ave to change it." The rabbi had been hot on "the assimilation problem." "Our congregation can be trusted," he'd boomed. "They won't let their kids opt out"—this with a beam toward Bert.

Could Philippe give them "the French pitch" on the matter?

"I do not belong to a—a congregation."

The rabbi, a long-lasting sort, had taken this in his stride. "*Liberté, egalité,* hmm." Gerald had interposed, "We can deal with that." The rabbi, excluding him with an arm, had leaned toward Philippe. "Define Jew." His teeth, certainly not dentures, had exulted in the word. Philippe had nodded. "A Jew is a status quo."

Zipporah is still Erika's confidante, usually in the bathroom later—"The smugness of the French is the hardest to bear," Erika giggled. "Because you immediately start to wonder how you can acquire it."

Now she herself is here to confide in Erika, with Philippe a happy addendum. These days, though not confined to the company of women but enjoying it when she is, Zipporah still feels more in the world when there is a man in the room—and Philippe is one whose advices she would mull. Especially those on other men. And on the rich? Born among them, though not at the extremes, a son deferential to his background but not consumed by it, and splashing spiritedly among the arts and university sets where Erika had met him, he may have just the stance she needs, on Mendenhall and the funds. On Mendenhall—without the funds.

She describes that day with every detail she can summon, geographical and conversational, beginning with her drive down, ending with that prolonged interchange at the car. As to her own reactions, to him, to the ménage, to the whole "tale"—if those haven't quite come through the two opposite her, her son-in-law, more wide-eyed than usual, and her daughter, at one point nesting her hand in his, plainly understand why. Zipporah has come to them to find out what her feelings are.

This morning, the minute she had got the short note still in her purse, she'd telephoned here. Saying she needed to talk, and that yes, it was "about Maryland." Privately she wants to hear their opinion. Then she will show them more.

"A tale—" Erika has said, like a coda. Since then a silence, during which she has brought tea, and Philippe has reached out to squeeze Zipporah's hands in his, release them, and refill the three cups, as carefully as if he is pouring wisdom into cups the right size. Perhaps he is.

"A tale," he repeats now. Stalling? Picking up on others' remarks is not his normal style.

"Gothic. All I can say." Erika's a curator, of course. But this isn't worthy of her. Not if it's all she has to say. It isn't, but her husband has cleared his throat.

"We have all kinds of American heiresses in Paris. Texas oil, Chicago department stores, Hollywood film dynasties, presidential royals. A few are known for themselves. Mendenhall's mother is one of those. In part for that music charity, for which I believe she got a ribbon. But really for the salons, since she has two of them.

She lives on the Ile Saint Louis, in a ground-floor flat much too small to have many people—but she has them." He smiles. "But just to be sure, she's bought a flat next door. Very commodious, but on the top floor. And the house is historical; no lift may be added. So she has signified the one salon for her young friends and the other for her 'arrived' older ones. You can imagine how people jump, to reclassify themselves . . . *Voilà*."

"What are you saying?" Erika asks.

"Two salons? Two lives. Money is a gene. When you have that much of it." He leans forward, scanning her face. "Don't look so dreamy."

"Don't look so nervous, Philippe."

They've forgotten Zipporah. Something will come of that.

"I'm dreaming *him*," Erika says. "Poor Foxy. Having to live up to that name. Having not to."

"*Non.* A billionaire has only that as his name. No matter what he's christened. And he can't ever really earn another. 'He had billions' is what the obit will say. And your Foxy knows it. Just like all the other ones do. And no matter what museum is named for them. Before they die . . ." Philippe clasps his knees. "Know what?"

"What?" So soft. She loves having him ask.

"It's the grandfather that interests me. No name can be that unpronounceable . . . I wonder. I wonder if he was a Jew."

Zipporah makes a sound. Those two don't even turn. They know where such a sound is born. For a moment are they all dreaming the same, that everyone in the world is a Jew?

Erika's the first to snap out of it. "Phew. Let's have a second cup."

"Marvelous." Philippe, who had been sent to Britain as a boy to learn English, knows tea better than most Frenchmen. "I'll do it." Perhaps he identifies tea with the domestic experience. He adds a spoonful of leaves into the pot, pours more hot water from the electric kettle into the brew, gives it a practiced stir. "You were very naughty, *Maman,* about that landscape. But I admit I have seen such. All over the U.S. map."

"Coffee made by the farm-girl maid, that you can see to the

bottom of," Erika says. "But served in that china. Wonder how many angels can sit on the rim of a Capo di Monte cup." She pours. The cups are thin but plain.

"Snob." But he is pleased. As pleased as Erika is that he calls her mother *Maman*.

"So am I a snob," Zipporah says. "Shouldn't have told you all that."

Erika has slipped off the loafers with the tiny insignia and scrunched up so that she too can clasp her knees. She looks down at her feet, webbed in silk. "Cripples have power. I was a stammerer once, remember?"

She remembers. She nods.

"You had to give us the picture, *Maman*. If you are going to send the boys to see him, it's only wise." A man's perspective. As Philippe is gently reminding them.

"*Oui. Alors*, Philippe. What of that double ménage?"

A smile. "Oh la la. He made too much of it. As you Americans often do."

They both appear to be conferring with their kneecaps. "Ah. I do find I'm becoming rather American again." Erika spreads her legs, looking at what Zipporah's mother's generation used to call "down there." Just so her jaw retracts when she is called upon to evaluate what her profession deems to be "objects of virtue"— meaning quality property. In her museum office, where she must rule between fake savagery and the truly naive, that hawk-lip may be appropriate. Here the sight wrenches her mother back to that girl who, judging herself ugly, had for a long spell made herself so. And now has reversed.

"*Cherie*—" Philippe says. "Darling."

The knees snap shut. "You have a crystal ball in your office. Given to you when you came on at the U.N. That man's estate must be like that. Only stare, and it spumes images. The money? Off somewhere, breeding. Giving some people a lift. But not there. A staff, reporting in only. The dead founder a historical joke, the departed hostess a society one. A parking lot empty of what acreage lives on—visitors. Or work. A wheelchair's wheel—is enough to turn the air. No pets even because of that hound? And one phone voice answering, for the entire estate."

She gets up to walk, still shoeless. The room's high drab, plugged with soft obstacles, offers no path. A vanished clan whispers at her: *Always so intense.*

"A piece of art is always addressed to an audience," she whispers back. She had got her first job by spotting at a flea market an enamel piece stolen so many times over the centuries that its only provenance pointed toward God.

She finds a path and slips on her shoes. "So is a violence. You were feeling it all the time you were there, Mom, I know you. That's what made you so uneasy. Land—clues you. And people in their places. Or out of them. It's been your life. And helped me to mine."

"Frederika—" A torrent of French.

Her feet bring her to him. "Is it because you're my husband, whom I love, that I hear what Mom refuses to? Or because we're Jews, always between Gomorrah and Canaan? Never willing to define what we are—and thank God for that. But damn quick to lump together all Christians." She turns over her shoulder to Zipporah. "I wanted to put some non-Hebraic in the collection. Next to it. But the trustees said we couldn't afford. Meaning that all old bones are not the same." She smoothes Zipporah's cheek, more mother than child, then turns to Philippe. "Who cares whether that man is rich or poor? Or even—Gentile? A type whose servant pokes his ashes for him. Whose wife, God help her, burned down her house."

When they break from their embrace, Zipporah has the letter in her hand. There's been no one to embrace her, nor will there be. "I stayed over in Washington, as you know. This morning, this came in the mail." She hands it to Philippe. "Read it out." She wants to hear it in a dispassionate voice.

The envelope crackles in his hands, a thick creamy stock that few but ladies exchange. The inner sheet is that thin tissue which used to be called carbon paper, the words on it run together here and there, abnormally spaced. The sender would have pressed the keys one by one.

He reads:

Dear Zipporah Duffy:

My time is short, it's not only the M.S. And no more chemo. So I write. I watched you all day with him. And him with you. You are perfect for him. Ditto he will give you the best life. I saw how you liked the furnishings. Some would not appreciate. And I would not of guessed your age. Be kind—it will work. Keep this note dark. But let me die knowing.

Katrina.

With a phone number, underlined.

"*Incroyable,*" Philippe says. "Unbelievable." Since being at the U.N. he has taken to translating himself. "Is it not?" He addresses each of the women in turn.

"No," his wife says.

"No." His mother-in-law.

He throws up his hands. This is one of the confabulations of women that one no longer mocks.

"Mom—" Erika says. "Is there anything to this?"

"When I was leaving, he came along with me to the car. We talked, for quite a time. They have ground lights; we were in a glare. She could have seen us, from the façade of the house. And yes—during the day I did feel her watch. But I took it for how invalids can be—with a healthy stranger. As for him—I could see I was a break. From the outside. As in a way, he was to me." She takes a breath. "Is."

She can feel their sudden wariness. They've joined up.

"You'll want to know how I've been affected." For the family's sake, as a clan will say of its widows. From their twinge she sees they must have indeed consulted on her, even before this. "And I'll have to puzzle out—my side." For she's been affected; she's far from sure how. "If I can, I'll be my own project." *Oh Jesus, how pompous that sounds. So be it. But see, they relax. As with any technical lingo, it removes their responsibility.* "I could sure use one." She gives a little laugh. "Let's say—I'll scrutinize the very rich. In terms of Norman's bequest."

Leaning forward, is she persuading herself? "You'll both have met some, in your work. In the newspaper, we all now do. We know how they travel a world of another size from ours, with a jet plane on each foot? But you have to see them in their own bailiwick. It's not just possessions. They have their own attitudes like they have their forks."

She leans forward, "I saw that once, in the Philippines. On my way to Mindanao, to study the Islamic Moros. I'd an intro—maybe so that family of sugar barons could study me, for a lark." They had seemed to her made of sugar themselves, in divers costumes and tints. Male brown sugar, the heir riding his acres in last night's opera hat. Women, in cake-icing tea gowns, advising her with a sweet housewifery born of fawning servants that rice water was the only rinse for antique lace.

"At the museum we have the soap-company former American ambassador, for a trustee," Erika says. "He's had a thrombosis, and must exercise. 'So every other weekend,' he says, 'I safari into another mentality.' Last month he brought back some armor; we had to tell him it wasn't for us. Far as we knew the ancient Chaldeans were not known to wear chain mail. But we persuaded him to have his picture taken in it."

"Erika, *tais-toi.* Shut up."

"No, she understands," her mother said. "But I am tired; that's when I run on."

"I have been places where the rich are not just fake diplomats," Philippe says. "They own people. I shouldn't say." He covers the word he mouths—Brunei? "And that premier—pah, dictator—who makes a *palais* an international spa, with the staff built-in. His own family's for generations back—but no citizenship we could find. I was there." He drums on the table. His nails are like opals; they vie with the sudden rictus of the jaw. She wonders what the extent of his job is. "I am so glad to be here. Where nobody is owned."

A moment of "American reverence," as Peter used to call these grateful silences. Though she no longer hears his voice.

Erika flicks the letter on the table. "The lady sure hopes to own you. Take you to the grave with her. Like the Egyptians took their concubines? . . . Think he knows about this?"

Who knows? She makes that gesture. "We—got to each other. She saw."

Husband and wife sit up straighter. On her stiff-necked daughter a suggestion that sexual activity belongs to them? On Philippe, a delighted grin. His own black-haired mother, a tiny sibyl whose circle of infatuated lovers, possible to probable, claims she might have posed for the siren on the Murad box "only yesterday," has his amused approval, his father never being out of the circle for too long.

"Oh, come on. At my age?"

"Mom, you know you'll live to a hund—" Erika claps a hand over her mouth. Philippe obligingly covers forefingers with middle fingers in the sign made when you have inadvertently challenged that fate which should belong to the Lord. Zipporah bows her head. For a minute they're all Jews together. Then Erika gabbles mischievously the formula once current among the Duffy children for such offense, a chiming picked up at one of their Sunday schools and imposed on their parents. "Ibbity bibbity sibbity sab. Ibbity bibbity kinAYbo," she intones, and they are released.

"That bench," Erika sighs. "We kids could always find you there. We never understood what magic it had for you."

"None, except in the midst of all that other magic. Must be why I go there. Now that you ask."

That's it, she thinks. *Why he affected me so. Nobody's been asking. Not up close.*

"You'll see him again?"

Zipporah smiles at her. Such a female question.

"She has to; he's an advisor on the funds. And he will maybe increase those. Depending on your causes, *Maman*—and his."

She tries to project herself back into that cloudy empire. Some concept surely floated the air, to be inhaled even by the servants? Even the garden hadn't seemed to be merely in the earth. "I'm not sure that he has causes. That place seemed to be so built on particulars."

"These days, *Maman,* you have money, you have causes. Else you don't get into society. Or the *terrorista* will bomb you to the bottom again."

"Personal causes?"

"*Personal*—where have you been, my dear?" Philippe comes to put his arms around Zipporah, crooning them back and forth. "Personal is *de trop.* 'Not with it,' as you say. Even dangerous. In the world of causes you will consult your staff. They will consult the polls . . . But I know what's wrong with you, *Maman.* You have spent your life with that man I hear about so much I have been reading him. A man who listened in high places—maybe to the sphinxes and the department of architecture at his university—and consulted only himself."

"Hearken to the house cynic, Mom," Erika says. "You should see who's coming to dinner, courtesy Philippe; excuse it if we preen. By the way, want to stay?"

Now and then she's asked to fill in. But always with pride in her—at the thought of which she swells, knowing the odds in the exalted company here. Her brood inhabits many variants: Nell's Village "parlor floor" stocked from many prior shakedowns and looking it; Charles's professorial mansions, this one in a historical enclave, in St. Louis; Gerald's pearl of suburbia at a canny price; Zach's loft, now grown to a celebrated "complex." She is welcome in all of them.

"Thanks, no. No protocol tonight. I just want to tuck in."

"Philippe's nuts about some of Dad's essays. Only there isn't much. You heard anything about more? No? Well—Kitty opened an official letter misdirected to when Bert still lived with them.

Brother Byron was there with his new friend. She's helping them fix up their new flat. By and his designer friend—once in some sort of sport, and still built fearsome, but very nice—swore to have her on toast if she told. But I suppose it's got round?"

"I don't think so," Philippe says. "Not at the point we were there. I found them the flat."

"We happened in on the three of them, Mom. Just when the pair were giving her the business. Bert would want to be left alone with whatever Dad gave him." Erika has always had a tenderness for Bert. And an awe of what he has avowed. "Mom—" She squints, as if for permission. "I told Kitty if she spilt one word to Bert ever, I'd call up every friend she has on Long Island and tell them she's on her marriage license as *Fegele.*"

"Oh God, oh God, it's good to laugh." She pats Erika. "But it'll keep mum. And now I must go."

"You going to answer that letter?" he says.

It's still on the table. She picks it up. "If she's still on the phone—she was. I'll call."

"You're brave," her daughter says. "I'd've torn it up."

"No you wouldn't." *No daughter of mine,* her face says.

"No you wouldn't," Philippe says. "A dying woman. Call. Then get rid of it. However you'll answer it."

They wait for her to say. But that's what she's come here to find out.

"Peter's voice," she says shakily. "Until now, I could hear it in my head. I wanted to. But all of a sudden, it's gone. Day before yesterday, when I was talking to that man, and needed like anything to hear it? It just—opted out."

Philippe's hand goes to that speckled tie. As if he has stopped crossing himself, just in time?

Erika's not going to burst into tears; she's grown now. But she looks just as she had, wrinkled and red with the failed effort not to, when she'd bawled at the news they were selling the first house, the one that at nine she'd thought hers. Children own you.

"Whatever possessed Norman," she says. "To know such a man?"

"Why not, *cherie*? Surely everybody knows everybody now?"

"But not to trust. With what isn't money."

When Erika's hungry for what she may have missed, she looks triumphant. "Norman was so Jewish," she sighs.

Home again, meeting the long, accommodating halls linking bedrooms always nondescript enough to be shifted, rooms broad enough for the assemblies that have filled them, the apartment seems to Zipporah much too large a stage for the resolution of one person's quandary. Crowded with memorabilia, reverberating with old conversations, it has responded to her, to them all, like an organism. She has stood at its windows trembling her woe, sharing her joy.

Thousands have gazed like her out of such city portholes, battered or magnificent. To date her city has saved her, counseling her not to leave it for the cruise where she will be alone but too accompanied, or for some tropical climate ready to gild her into a golden oldie, so that like the boy gilded all over in the legend, she won't die as entitled—with all of her span, brought to bear on herself and those after her, but as her own fake memorial, her cheeks flushed with Florentine youth.

This place isn't going to let her segue into the widow's aerie. These walls are silent only because they have spoken. Like Peter's voice. In the cynic household she has just left, she has heard the lesson. A cause cannot be counterfeited. It must come from the breast.

Ah, you've hit upon that, have you? You and I did not congeal our opinions, nor bring them to a boil, for public show. We put our modest convictions on the table, for the children to nibble. Or I floated those from the classroom bubble pipe, for one student to pop the fragile nothing, another to blow the beauty on its perilous way. If you live out your life span, Zipporah, you'll have twenty years more of such possibility, and will have lived as long with yourself alone as you have lived with me...

For you know what I am, the voice says; you have your own ashes. You've known for a decade that I am not the dead returning. I'm one of the saner tricks of love. And I have spent my span.

Though the man she had derived that voice from had believed that while alive we exist in a constant realm of the in-between, he wouldn't deny, she thinks, that the dead are fixed. While by the will urged on me since birth, I believe in the constant resurrection of the living. And that is my voice.

In the kitchen she finds herself very hungry. As a lone person she's careful to stock the refrigerator with some anti-depressive treats, which sustain the illusion that she is being catered to.

As she eats her herring in wine, followed by see-through morsels of prosciutto, she's amused; is this "assimilation"? She's never had relatives who observed the dietary laws. How far back they and she would have to go in the family history on both sides in order to find out when either last kept kosher has never come up, though they have masses of other data: pictures, letters, and passports from the various eras, beginning with the early nineteenth century, when members on both sides had begun to arrive in the United States. Yet there are other monitors.

No Jew she's ever known has been able to say the word "Christian" without somehow marking it, with either emphasis or diffidence. Most avoid it, maybe for its religious overtone. Yet with "Gentile," which can be made to sound more sociological, they are uncomfortable still, and not merely because its use can sound somehow lower class. (Is it admitting what you yourself are not— and on a less heroic scale?) But clearest of all is how except from the pulpits, or matters directly organizational, political, or historical—in ordinary converse, that is—the Jew has trouble saying the word *Jew.*

Perhaps enough of the pejorative clings to it so that it can never be said impersonally. She has heard blacks address another black as "nigger," in either a flat-out, cards-on-the-table basic, or else taking somebody down. To where "we" are? Recently a letter to the *Times* by a WASP decried being called that. In Philippe's "experiment," everybody here is pretty recently from somewhere else, one's origins dangling behind, sometimes touted if possible, rarely concealed.

Meanwhile, each of her children has linked her to the world by his or her string. Charles to that academe his beloved first wife could no longer bear to "traipse about in" as he rose—a world of limits, attitudes, and duties that his Chinese wife adores. Zach "the giant killer," whose mission is to annihilate classical art, trudges her around the world of visual manifesto, to shows and loft parties where the color-flights and talk-shapes can briefly persuade her she's once again on site. Somewhere. Under a similar "native" pressure to sit cross-legged, sup on sheep's eyes, and view your own mirror image, escaped from the laws of perspective and warped anew. Nell, whose latest is "Skin is what's really in," or going to be, is still a vestal virgin of this or that ideological flame. But it's always after Zipporah has been with Erika that she best sees how far that little *Jahrzeit* candle of a three-letter word casts its shade. The "chosen," they have no choice. To say *Jew* is to declare.

How Erika and Philippe assert or subtly fail to acknowledge their Jewishness (much less work at it) may depend on their circumstances as a very special couple indeed, but in the general ruck of how assimilation happens will not distinguish them. All cases of assimilation are special. That, Zipporah reflects, is what distinguishes us from the orthodox.

A crackle from Katrina's note, waiting by the telephone. Crushed in Zipporah's purse, then freed, the heavy note paper asserts itself, a leftover from the era when ladies-to-be in their teens wrote "mash" notes to real actors, graduated to tea dances, and after marriage conducted a major part of their lives in R.S.V.P. responses on such stationery. Often inspiring tender provincial imitators who would make their note-paper debuts at the five-and-dime.

This note is like a plea from another era. Whether the woman who wrote it had been born into such customs or acquired them, she had existed in their thrall—as one more evidence that no time is wholly of itself. A state of being that any person like Zipporah herself, whose years more or less parallel a century, had better not ignore.

Will she herself marry again? No. Never. Not because she has seen too many travesties, or in spite of some gentle joggings that could be a pleasure to watch. She has had her full life, in retrospect as sweet and round as an apple eaten, the parings still red on the plate. Since then, as a widow, she has been paired at dinner parties, in good intention—with widowed bankers and college presidents, often likable, and a maverick artist once, with a portfolio of talk.

But there is now no enclave that she can see herself entering. Any marriage suitable to her age would entail that. In contrast—since she's by nature, and now somewhat by intent, what is called a "social being"—at the parties she herself gives, smaller now and not so rife with relatives, but with old and young, from anywhere in the large circle of her acquaintance, including the enlarging world of the widows, at her table none are paired. Surprising, how this can invigorate. And how the separate strains of the city can toodle off, regather, entwine. Here, not so many years ago, Zach met his current Ernestine, known to him long ago at Cooper Union, by now no longer interested in fast cars, a social worker eager to focus her warmths more specifically.

"Brought by some dame who was really tagging after someone else, so latched her onto me; she won't say who," Zach had said with suspicion. "It wasn't Nell, was it?" Mired at the time in one of the depressions that zapped him after a big commission, roundly paid for, reminding him that he could no longer qualify for the avant-garde no matter what the work was, he had once before suffered—or gained?—from Nell's astute finagling. For someone still on the sexual cutting edge to have to be fixed up by one of the family!

"Nell's still in Cuba," his mother had said thankfully, for indeed she did suspect her younger daughter's plotting.

"Is she now? How'd she get there? Don't tell me." They'd grinned, in the mutuality of those who knew the ropes. "If she needs to be hauled out of there, I know a guy," he'd said. "By hydro. Not air." Then he'd patted his mother's cheek, and stood back; he was going to say something. Judgment from a son is always welcome; it means he's looking at you as more than a mother. "*Mu-mu*—why don't you take a lover?"

He likes to shock her; this time he has.

"At my age?"

"C'mon. You're only as old as you look."

"An uptown remark," she says. So it is, for a man who, dealing in art all over the map, hadn't felt free to abandon his "downtown" pigtail until his forties. "But I'll remember it."

And so she has. It strikes her that Zach may be a better guide than Erika as to what her own proper sexual conduct should be. Women more often hobnob with women friends on that score, but she never has. Never has needed to. Until now?

Of all her children, Zach is now as well the one whose inflections and responses most closely match hers. Were she to tell him how she has lost Peter's voice—no, how she had kept, and then in one rash or idle moment had lost it—Zach might well understand. As the inheritor of Mickey's place, and so the new "youngest" who, through no fault of either, could never hope to equal what his dead brother had preempted, he'd had to live with such a voice. Finally coming to his father about it. Who had come to her. "I can't keep on being him," Zach had said to his father. "I want to be me." "We won't stop remembering Mickey," Peter had said to her. "Never. But perhaps we can cool it for a while. In favor of the living. And we'll stop calling Mickey our youngest. Maybe that'll do the trick." Something had. Maybe their forbearance, which Zach might have sensed was for him. Who from then on, as the other sons had learned to protest, was in turn subtly their parents' favorite.

In favor of the living. Not a voice. More a churchyard motto. On a stone that is now a stone.

To telephone the dying, who have you in that power, one must know exactly what to say. It will be what I cannot write. What must not be found among the dead's effects.

"Turley here." The nurse. "Ah, she's about as expected. She refuses the oxygen tent. Hanging on for your call. The doctor is here." The nurse's whisper is like a preacher's, meant to be heard, above all, by God. "Ah, wait—she wants the room cleared... Even you, doctor. And you, Mr. Mendenhall... Only me. And my animal. What can she be wanting, for the love of Christ... Ah, see— *he* knows. Sit, Billy boy. *Sit*... Here you are, Missus. The phone, dearie. At your ear. He and I'll be at the door."

A chafing sound. The phone must be on the pillow. She waits.

"This is Zipporah."

A wait. A gurgle. Finally... "S-peak."

"I thank you for your note. I regret I can't comply."

In spite of her resolve to be grave, the words come trippingly.

A sound like a violin string, scraped. "Why?" It comes again. "*Why?*"

Spit out the truth. And be gone.

A gurgle. "Tell... me." A thrum, improved. "I'm... going."

So am I. So am I. The strong, released by the weak. Or the compliant, released by that demand. The truth flies from Zipporah like a bird unhooded—a falcon, not a dove.

"He resembles my husband. But not enough."

On the other side such a fell silence. Has she murdered? Where are the others? For the life of her, she can't disconnect.

So she hears it. Small, perfect, toothed like a smile.

"Bitch."

Before she hung up, she heard the dog howl.

This is the Sunday on which nothing much happens except the petty details. Not even a bullet.

"Stop calling them 'the boys,'" Gerald is saying grandly of his two younger sons. "They'll be pushing thirty before they know it, our Bertram and Byron. When I was a boy, that was a man."

Shine and Bert, hustling to welcome people already trickling through Zipporah's front door for the fund's open house, don't respond to a remark addressed to the air, as many of his are. If he can only express pleasure negatively, well, that's his way. Shine's canny bid for his "organizational" help on soliciting publicity has grossly pleased him.

Gerald has finally done well enough in the world of leverages and other gray numerals so that he can wash his luckily thick hair in kindred silver, and scale down his midriff by playing squash, joining those end-of-day venture capitalists who look as if they labor in Valhalla and are groomed between mergers by its manicurists. In spite of which, Byron says, when his father walks down Southampton's main street in a new-resident's shorts bought at that pale, lemon-painted nearly windowless emporium which looks almost reluctant to sell you all the clothes you must already have, "His kneecaps still look like yesterday's muffins."

Kitty has reacted to their very modern villa, which is angled three-sheets-to-the-wind, elaborately empty and meant by the architect to appear so, by a spell of shoplifting, unfortunately pub-licized. Their neighbors, however, new like them, have been very kind. Living as they all do on a peninsula billed before purchase as "the last undeveloped shoreline," a mansion having been razed to make it so, they can sympathize with Kitty's rage to possess. Mur-muring "klepto," they've assured Gerry that when he and Kitty come for bridge, at which she's still a whiz and a coveted partner, "Don't worry—we'll check the knickknacks afterwards."

"Shit, she was always light-fingered," Byron is saying to his roommate, Lucas. "When we were kids, Bert and me, tagging along to the butcher's, the counterman, seeing her come in, always scrambled to pick out her order from the packages lined up on the meat case and hand it to her, otherwise we'd see her make off with an extra. She forgot our heads were only counter-high. But what's really different is she used to be the holy terror in our house. I al-ways pictured my mother, when she was changing for dinner—we all had to, even for cold cuts—as reaching out for a handful of thunderbolts before she came downstairs. And therapy has taken away her malapropisms. Now, poor dear, she's no fun." While, thanks to her "cure," which is to buy one article per week, paying for it at point of purchase, their house is filling with objects far more disassociated than the ones she stole.

Byron is trying to put Lucas at his ease. This is only his second time here as Byron's mate. The first time, rather too many of the older men had buttonholed him, with some version of "I just want you to know that I—," meaning they were taking it in stride that he and Bert were gay. Or had admired his suit—"Esther thinks I need sprucing up"—while the women had signified their extreme interest in home decoration. Lucas, a Milanese trained as an archi-tect, now exhibits handcrafted desks, bureaus, tables, and storage chests inspired by the loops and droops of his former profession, basketball, and touted by some as falling into the very net of art. He is always at ease. It's Byron who's nerving himself up.

"Cool it, By. The crowd here today is mostly downtown. And much younger. What's your grandmother do, call it in shifts?"

"Happens naturally. Or almost. Though this is not her do."

As for the clan, it does remind By of that giant squid he'd seen once, on a deep-sea dive. Floating serene, seeking food, its tentacles ribboning. He knows there's no real analogy; as a writing-class prof had once told him, "Must all your images be about water?"

Byron had let the family think him a surfer long after the medals stopped, never telling them about the commercial diving, after Bert, sounding out their father, reported Gerald's "Going to be a frogman? Didn't know our Navy had them." Now Byron, retired from active performance, shares in a company that raises wrecks, which has made a lucky strike, photos of the loot appearing in the media. "My son the archeologist," Gerry jokes, but the hand on Byron's shoulder is warm. "In the end," Byron tells himself, "water always accepts me." What he would like to tell Lucas is that this is a house where all the personal accounts that belong to each member seem to dovetail. Yet never wind up.

"While you were in Rome, Lucas, Bert and Shine went to town on their foundations; sewed it up with that guy in Maryland. He sent a limo for them, there and back. When they arrived, nothing spared." A phrase Byron has been reared on, along with the early implication that in his case the largesse might be undeserved.

Many of the children he'd grown up with had been on trial that way, the sons especially, and the more so when of fathers on the rise. He's not sure that this is specifically Jewish. More likely American? His own father, Gerald, wasn't pressured so by Peter and Zippy. But when Jews pressure their kids for success—as the Japanese do, and maybe the French, and who else—it's more noticed.

Lucas has noticed it. "It's carried over, By. Emotionally. You've kicked the success bit. But you put us other people on trial. As to what we feel for you."

It's true. Like: Rome is a city where "nothing is spared." Imperial habit, alongside the looser habits they got from the Greeks. Prostitutes of both sexes lurking under the hundreds of niches of a cynic church. Lucas's family still lives there, his father a merchant, his sister secretary to a cardinal; no one intimates that she is more. But the family enjoys the fallout. Lucas himself had been named Vittorio, out of respect for the leftover king Victor Emanuel, but had sharpened his name for his American career. He goes back to Rome ostensibly to visit his family, and Byron, ensconced in his own, cannot charge him that other reasons intrude.

But Lucas was bisexual once.

From across the room, Bertram is regarding his brother. Yes, people would say By's shallow, if to be charming is merely that. And so is Lucas; they match. And how hard they are trying! No one must ridicule that flat of theirs. Each chair Lucas brings in is like a jewel added to their union; the very stepladder is modeled after a design from the notebooks of Leonardo. Each piece is a donation sanctified toward their future, the dining table a marvelous floating disk, yet sturdy enough for the banquets they love; the bed simple, if not too chaste to be wide.

Kitty, whose help they tolerate, is mad for that table, their joke being that at least she can't sneak it off. "Let her help, By," Lucas whispers. "She reminds me of my mother, who any minute I expect to yelp across the Atlantic—'Vittorio, answer the door for your poor mother, you lazy bum.'" He is mad for Zipporah, whom he calls Super Gran, to her face. "Every mother reminds people of every other mother, but you I exempt." To which Zipporah answered, "You're wrong."

Gender discussion may seem rampant in their crowd, but by now is convention. Shine says, "Our elders mistake our verbal freedom for license because it's no longer based on Freud. And they think that anything we talk about, we must do." He and Bert, for instance. "In the early days, even your Gramp thought maybe you and I were a pair? Me sporting I might be going gay, while all the time I was yakking to you about my pash for Arlene, and worrying whether even mental sex with a stepmother wasn't incest? And you off with the cousins? Hot damn."

"Hot ziggety damn," Bert says, to remind him to get off his Harlem kick, which was mostly from bygone white authors anyway, nineteen-twenties tales of Sugar Hill, or Shine's favorite down-South character, a rogue named Florian Slappey, from a series of stories unearthed in a pile of old Elks mags in Shine's father's stock-room, under where the duplicates of former flags had been stacked. "We used to read them like gospel, my mother and me," Shine said. "We didn't know any American blacks."

Meanwhile Shine and Bert had recently learned a lot about their own "prep school poof" from Lucas. Who and what is "fra-ternal"? he asks. In those schools, or among men? For Lucas all that is old stuff. Yet being a Catholic, gay or not, without believing in Jesus?—not possible. How come a Jew not believing in God, even a rabbi, is still a Jew? "Like Jesus would be, if he were here today," Lucas says, squinting sideways at his own profile. "Though that is maybe only my opinion."

"Did Jesus believe in himself?" By says. "I always wondered." For an older brother, he was always naive; he's learning to be sly.

"The son of God does not have to fuss about his ancestry," Lucas says.

Leaving them, Shine had said, "Those two have a lot to work out."

But today, plying from group to group invited here, Shine's as serious as he can allow himself to be, a catalyst, bringing all here a tested purpose in life that they can painlessly espouse.

"That's what a nonprofit org does," he's saying, going from one bunch to another, some earnest, some dallying. "It gives you a cause. And relieves you of your burden of proof."

They love this wry talk, most of them brimmed recently from the colleges, now out in a world where labor unions mix with church groups, who mix with professional charity, who mix with medicals, who mix with civil libertarians—a dose three parts en-ergy, one part hope, and to be taken night and morning. Then hit the subway—at least in this city, though transportation is vari-able—then on to one or another of those shifting centers where good is presumably done. Be sure to protect your heart.

Most here surely won't yet need to. Their teeth flash; their skins pearl; their beards, Afros, and silky "falls" sprout like animal hair. Many carry tokens of who they are at the moment: a camera, a book, a guitar, a gym bag, or even a sling with a baby in it. These evidences may or may not have to do with what they expect to be.

At her old lookout in the kitchen, Zipporah stands for a minute, watching. The kitchen is bare, except for a few bowls of peanuts, granola mix, cans of soft drink, bottled water, like those already set out in the front rooms. She feels the life-shift that comes even in kitchens. Same place—maybe your own house. Yet bowls of food float in, settling everywhere, paper crackling open on smoked fish. What's that? Kreplach, I think, has potato in it? That warm brown stuff—groats. And those darling macaroons. Chink of cutlery. Peal of light voices, here and there a baritone trying its worth. Whatever the delicatessen was, it would be fallen on. Turn and you will see girl ghosts with necks like grails, smiling at gawks sporting their first shave. Those were the young...

She feels shy in this crowd now streaming into her own living room. The program devised by Bert and Shine to drum up volunteers is already what they're calling a "blast." A few no doubt will suit, and some out there, though younger than her grandson, are like him, her blood relatives. But they are all his and Shine's "element," their brand of strangers.

The shift that we hide from ourselves has taken place.

These are the young.

If a house like this is only a receptacle, then as people pour in, it warms well to its duty. Crowds buzz here mellowly, heads lift, cock, bend, in poses a photographer would want to catch; bodies doodle, or spurt an antic arm. The room gains from its own length; movement in it is progressive, rather than on the square. Facing east, it gets a morning sun sufficient for early bustle, giving it a competent look, but no invitation to bask. As the day advances there can be an incomplete sadness to the light which the residents of the street do not admit, but is shown in passing on the faces below. Traffic helps, with its livening explosions and blamable dirt. But the big façades here, built for splurge, some with columns like Knossos or turrets like chateaux—why don't they polish up? Is it that they haven't the flat harmony of a dull street like Park, or are too tall for a street with only one side?

While the trees that wander its other border are perhaps not equal to what once was expected of them? That low stone curb edging their trunks all up the avenue was built when love of the city was sturdy; but the wall that must have come with the park now survives dimly; few award it a glance.

Some resident, ruminating every day at a window at this hour, might advise you on what's happening: "The powerful East Side tends to drain off the golden afternoons." Depending on where the year is, surely? Maybe, but the park gets bushier over there and full of performance, and you can't blame the sun for favoring those flat façades, with here and there a mansion, gone to diplomacy, and with windows deep-skirted, but roofline still with crenelations to be scanned. You want a heady sense of all's tidy and somebody paying for it? Walk there.

The pre-evening on Central Park West is another kind of classical. Over east, the past is always much the same, a multiplication table of caste, bank vaults, good schools that do their best with rogue blood, recognized frills and earnest napery. This West Side street is forever on the rise. Here the past was always a little in the vulgate. Money that could be funky or else in too seedy a trade, romance not quite ordinary, theater people that came and went, names curiously shorn to one syllable and at odds with their bearers, artists' widows, too long-lived. Yet down at the bottom or at the top, as you choose to see it, solid family comfort—with sofas maybe too plush, but ethic strong. A professor who lived here once, wearing the seat of his pants shiny working at paradoxes, said: "This street is solid with change." And the adjectives reversible: seedy rich, strong romance. What's magical about it is that because of the trees, straggly ones likely cleft at the heart, the air is always sweet in rain.

If her broad windows had blinds she could stage old scenes in shadow-play on them. Instead, it is that inner-outer moment before the lamps, which has both yearning and possibility. To which is added, as one lives, a playback of such scenes as have carried one forth. In Zipporah's case with her sack of hope. One is reminded both of what one wants and what one has. But cannot quite pin either down. Or why that opaline light so tentative at her windows, a gentle compromise of New York's striving reflections, should this minute be the same glassy medium invading a *pensione* in Venice, flooding the room's tinge of traveler embitterment with the radiance from religious barges floating on old water lanes, in a region where water is still queen.

The crowd at a corner here, meshed close in the dim, could be that same fuzz of figures outside the dining salon, just before the signal table lamps are lit. The three are still in the room upstairs—where their images will be eternally? Even though she knows to where two have actually migrated. The third person is mentioned now and then of a Sunday: "Where's that girl nowadays, the one who . . . what was her name?" Somebody will say it. "Debra." With the stasis peculiar to the unseen, after ten years she is still a girl.

"Penny for your thoughts."

Zachary, at her elbow. He's the one who monitors her most these days. Nell and Charles remain loyal, but wandering their professions. Or have their own versions of Sunday. Erika is fixed in her life with Philippe. Though of course available. Zachary is also the one Zipporah talks most with; as her youngest, she and he have come to it late. He jokes that they have an affinity: "As the two Zees." The truth is that while Gerald by convention treats her as old, she sometimes feels he's older in that sense than she'll ever be. The others hold her in cherished abeyance. Zach remains interested in her as a person still ongoing.

"Memory," she says, looking up at Zach's black-haired girth. Hair like Erika's was once. "His hair's so modern," his current in-house Ernestine has said. "Practically a performance." Living with Zach, the second Ernestine has acquired humor—and perhaps permanence? "I was thinking, Zach, how memory works by mixed clues."

He gives her a squeeze. "That's what you think you were thinking about."

Just then the lamps go on, all down the room and into the hall. In his early pure-machine obsession, later to segue into art-machines, Zach had put the electric here on timer for a parental anniversary, but spending his life since in works billed as "time-cure" and in "visual telescopings" he's probably forgotten that. "Anyway, your parties, our Sundays—give you credit—were never just memory bashes. Ernestine's family association last summer in Michigan, they wore identity cards and checked each others' noses, but they all had down pat how much better hand-turned ice cream used to be, or who pee'd in bed 'til they were in sixth grade . . . And your Sundays, we always had people outside the genealogy . . . look at it now."

For the khaki bomber jackets, "body" dresses, sweats, camouflage outfits, turtlenecks, and T-shirts that are here, a painter would not need to use his full palette. But his brush might take off for the chignons, topknots, and pigtails whose heads are unlikely to be in Leonardo, or in Gainsborough either. "Wow, that pair, Shine and Bert. Mean that prospectus of theirs for real, don't they? Look, it's almost all *downtown*."

She has to laugh. He intends her to. In youth their family butt, Zach is now their comedian; his work has saved him from the fear of being original. "Hey, they're setting up the video. The second twins helped them with it."

He barges off, without excuse. As a father of two sets of twins, by separate mothers, he must feel partially explained, needing less excuses than most. To his credit, he exploits advantage of course, but not people. As she watches his progress down the room toward a big screen being erected in front of the windowside, ducking to a "Hey Zach," scooping a shoulder here, patting a cheek there, with a

"Hey!" of his own, she exults in how her children are bearing her into the modern world. The others—Charles the conservative, saving his opinions but not his first marriage; Erika the quick-change actress; Nell the over-reliable petition-signer whose sex life gives her a tinge of the camp-follower—they are mostly unaware of how she's watching their own dealings with their children, and with all else that in turn is becoming modernity for them.

Zach is aware. "In New York," he's said, "our crowd's elders are either like Gerald, plain hostile, or they so want to be with it—half the very people who collect my stuff, for instance, see only fashion. But out in Michigan, and the neighbor states those families come from, it's been an eye-opener to me. They sow their own seed—biblically. More to do with agriculture than church. They know how weather can go wrong; they absorb the accidents. Ern has a baby sister who's really her eldest sister's by-blow, brought up without question—and not the only one around."

Of commanding size, he's nothing like Mickey, who would have been one of those middle-sized men whose spry wit makes others cede them poise. Yet Zach, when talking to her, nuzzling her with his observations, reminds her of him. "I'll tell you what," he says. "To those farmers and their neighbors, the young are a crop."

She's an Easterner to her foot soles. To her, "down on the farm" is mere ditty. But what he's confessed places her too in the scheme of things. None of her children ever derides her as passé; there are even quick spurts of like opinion between her and them, if tinged with "Oh yes, you taught us how." Affection between the generations can't avoid that glister of patronage from either side—between "How we did it" and "How we do it now." But Zach isn't just tenderly watching her. He leans to her, as to another confrere in the world they both observe. Deferential not to her, but to their joint obligation. He was the one, she now recalls, in whose quicksilver, increasingly adult company she had first felt the motherhood lift away. He had relieved her of it. Now he helps relieve her of her elderhood.

She feels blessed, but guilty. Now that Zach's father's voice is finally gone, subsumed in the vast gap between the quick and the dead, she can admit what all in the family knew but never discussed—that Zach was never swayed by that voice, perhaps had a contempt for its charms. Always a polite audience, as his father's adages, puns, and pronouncements fell, he merely blinked, or held still. His tense posture, which one saw he couldn't change, was his only comment, though there were other hints that he was immune to his father's mystique.

When Peter's professor friends came to the house, Zach opted out. "They're like Nettie's pianola"—which as a boy he'd wanted to take apart. "The idea keys go up and down of themselves." And unlike his brothers, he never fell heir to the cult of cigars, though like all the siblings he must have smoked pot, if never in the house. Peter, used to being rated less of a scholar's scholar because he was both popular with the young and could calibrate them, had said, "If it's the dither between the art and the academy, then every reason Zach shouldn't dog me." And didn't Zipporah suspect that her affinity with the primitive had influenced? "Look how Zach's known the provenance of every piece in your attic since he was ten."

She can't quite see how the great warpings and illusions of Zach's stagecraft tie in with those testimonials she had continued to bring back, ferrying them to any museum that would accept, this trove she'd had the luck—and some wit—to accumulate. Any artifact is routinely described in terms of where found and how acquired, but in her breast all objects in her trove have the same non-Western provenance: "This . . . is not us."

Same with this crowd now even temporarily taking over the venue of her old Sundays. Little or no genealogy that one may scrutinize, the sole relationship being time and place. Only the one huge provenance. The new. The next.

No wonder the old are angry, she's thinking. And don't assure us these here are only temporary. So were we.

"Who are these kids, Zach?" She knows what she's saying.

Smiling down at her, so does he. "Good Joes, most of them. The kind who turn up. When the word goes round."

"Word of what, precisely?"

Those big shoulders shrug. Is it ever precise?—they're saying. "A job? A cause. Maybe even both together."

"Conveniently?"

"Come *ahn*. Haven't you always had a job with a cause? Or a cause that got you one? So've I. I'm sure there's conviction here . . . Look at my own kids. But today's the opportunity."

The second twins, freckled boys just in their teens, who spend their summers with their mother's family, are kneeling at the base of a large screen. Puttering there, they could be farm boys milking, the screen the cow. Looking up, they catch Zach's gaze. Pride is exchanged.

She finds her middle right-hand finger rubbing at her left hand's diamond. A widow's habit. Must it stop? "Your father—"

"'A man between'—Peter said so himself. When he used to prate so, I couldn't stand it. Now I know—it was just his—"

"His what?"

"Funk."

"Such a word," she says in a whisper. But she reveres Zach for it.

The screen's now ready. The two boys scuttle off, knees bent, each to a side.

"The first twins, they're all city," he says. "When I make a fuss over all that money, they think I'm nuts. These two—they know what's earned. And of course the four are forever at daggers-points. One day—the house won't hold them."

She finds it hard not to smirk. "You don't say."

"We five didn't leave because we fought."

Six. But let that be. "No. But maybe there was too much . . . fealty."

A nod. "Family. Eventually you want out. No matter how good it was. Out." He's looking at the crowd. So is she. "You and he were such a strong couple. We're a different generation."

All of sex is in every generation. Like birth, like death. And not really talkable, though the gab never ends.

She takes a deep breath. A familiar one, throughout life. When you are about to break one of those conventions that pave an easier path. When you oh-so-carefully speak as a "civilized" primitive. As a White, of the nonwhite. Printing it in the mind like that: uppercase, lowercase. Or as Jew to a Christian, delicately. When you speak as a Jew to another Jew, that doesn't help. We know our own kind, mutually. She considers herself to have a decent record in those other directions.

But when you speak to the younger, abandon all tricks. Especially if you've given birth to them. Or at any subsequent age you find yourselves. The grown, to the further grown.

"No, Zach. You just have a different sexual history."

"You never gave us those little talks."

Is he smiling? He is.

"Except for Nell. She came to enlighten me. Complaining that sexual freedom was now part and parcel of democracy. It confused her that Peter and I weren't holding up our end of it. I said it was a pity she'd waited until college to tell us, but maybe she should also consult her father. She said he might think she was propositioning him; that was what happened to her friend Helene."

He snorts. "I hope you—"

"Oh, I gave her what she wanted."

"What was that?"

"A little talk."

A tap on her cheek. "And is this mine?"

She wouldn't dare. "I like your screen," she adds quickly.

Its pediment rears high above the cluster of onlookers.

"Film doesn't have to be encased on the square. Found that frame in the old barn down there. Mirror in it once must have been for a duchess. Or a nightclub."

"Down where?"

"I hitched along to Maryland with Bert and Shine because their benefactor owns an early object of mine—in fact the earliest. His collection's been mostly dispersed, now that the estate's going to public use—his neighbors are having fits."

Maryland?

She makes herself ignore this. She's staring at the crowd, this
cohort which has invaded. Almost an infantry, if at ease. "Touchy-
feely" had been anything from a manner to an ethic during her
girls' twenties. Now the style seems to be to drape themselves toward each other merely, in magazine postures—a generation
meeting, even mating by photograph. "I love to watch them," she
murmurs. "They don't anger me, as they do some of my contemporaries. But a house like this is a structure. See how they convey
the age gap. They do it by ignoring my chairs . . . What did you say,
Zach? Public use?"

"A park."

"Aha. That figures. But why the upset?"

"Scientific gardens. Born-again fields. Human manure, treated
of course, is rumored. And scores of young people will be working
there. Fits right in with what the old guy's putting Shine and Bert
up to. On the way down, hearing them gas, I confess, I thought it
was for the birds—Youth Philanthropy. With the staff the same age
as the beneficiaries? And the whole op to decompress their tenth
year, and start afresh? Crazy . . . You know about it?"

"I approved it. Some. I've left the rest to the—Bert and Shine."

"Minute we got there, those two head off with the overseer,
Adam his name was, to see what's doing. I follow. 'Field of buckwheat,' he says, 'going to be behind those big firs. It'll be the front
lawn of the restored house. Ever see a field of buckwheat, in the afternoon sun?' No. But I'm thinking: they want youth-managers
down here, maybe I'll send the second twins, these here. The first
are already over the hill."

"You're all zany enough, looks like." She smiles.

"Huh. And where do we get it from? . . . Anyway, he points me
to the barn; what I've come to see is in there. You notice that barn
when you visited?"

"Saw it from the outside."

"Mansard roof, slate. Walnut siding, rare now as old wine.
Eighteen-eighty, thereabouts, bastard North America. But with a
pitch to it—there's barns in Washington state with that Scandina-

vian kind of roofline squat. On made land though, and dedicated
to the vegetable. So I opened the barn door. And there she was, my
old vegetable. First thing I ever made. She'd been in Barcelona, on
show, next door to Gaudí's La Sagrada Familia, my favorite cathedral in the world. They're marketing replicas of his furniture designs and had assembled suggestions of the period. And there she
was. My period. My youth—in mint condition."

"What was it, Zach? I never knew you to—do sacred pieces?"

One of the tables with soft drinks on it isn't far. He comes back
with two bottles of ginger ale, unscrews the cap with a talent-
worn fist. "The Reo."

She recalls those necessaries of childhood, neither toy nor icon
merely, fiercely demanded at bedtime or toted during the day. Belonging partly to some need of the body, or prescribed rite. Gerald's battered pewter mug, not to be drunk from but finding its
uses. Erika's blue blanket the same color as her one confounding
beauty, her eyes. Nell's homespun cat pouch with its whiskery
smile. Charles's miscellany of small objects which he marshaled
and graded. Mickey's Davy Crockett fur cap with swagged fur tail,
placed on his pillow at night while he buried himself undercover at
the foot. Few objects either received or lived with had satisfied
Zach enough to choose; he'd lived rather in a whirlwind of es-
pousals. A glass peered in, while pennies dropped, as if into a kalei-
doscope. Papier-mâché twisted, but not into a fan. Toolboxes
plundered, and nothing ever finished in the sneered-at class the
school called "Shop."

"The Reo." What a bedtime story!

Only last year, when Zach got an award, he'd been asked to explain his work. "Secrets," he'd said. "That I want everybody to
know." The warehouse hours, while he rebuilt that ancient car,
must have been that, but nobody had bothered him.

"At fourteen, I couldn't even qualify for a driver's license," he
says. "But I always intended to drive it. For it to be a purpose. Not
just a dream. So one night, I did. It was during when you were
sending us to St. Boniface's Sunday school, remember? Those

Catholic boys were already gut-busting on whether to wait to
marry—to have the holy sex. It was a Sunday night; I sneaked away
from the family. Just the right night for it. And it warmed up, the
big beauty I'd made. It started. It went. Holy sex."

"And then you sold it. We wondered."

"After that once, the baby wasn't any longer mine . . . 'Scuse it,
I'm wanted at the video screen."

The end of the room where Zach has gone is weighed down with
sympathy and its many attitudes: pale hair and paler lips, jazz-burst
heads and blackberry mouths, rag-and-bobtail effects too scrubbed
to be real. The hat worn in the house is not ignoramus but savvy, on
well-cut young men whose sole wish is to blend with one another,
accent to necktie to shoe, all having attended the same schools.
Among the routine "laid-back" ones, as she has heard her middle
children describe themselves. She sees also some "Spanish," as the
city calls its Puerto Ricans, sometimes lumping in too the Haitians
who began arriving in the Depression's great welfare rise. The
slums were the first to become aware of this great migration. Others would later note this first by the rise of Puerto Rican busboys,
and in time by an echo from the barrios. Peter had early known of
the influx through a couple of cousins still in "city jobs"—firemen,
bus conductors, living in the "better" side-street tenements of the
West Forties, once "Hell's Kitchen." These had warned him: "Spics
now, all along the avenue tenements. And spreading."

Bert is once again at her side.

In spite of Bert's history at the seminary, which had made his
fellow students uneasy while he was there and had further chilled
when he refused a plum rabbinate, there are quite a few yarmulkes.
That must be because of Moorsohn, who has had further correspondence with Mendenhall. His verdict, reported by Bert:
"Mendenhall's a *mensch*. But he suffers from the money. Watch out
he don't beg your heart?"

"I think Moorsohn's having it hard, healthwise," Bert had mourned. "These days all his sentences end in questions."

They are readying the video now. Zach and his boys—these real boys—must be behind the screen. The crowd is scattered all along the avenue side. Bert and his father are at its tail, standing against the side wall, near the mantel. His father has his arm around him; Bert seems not to mind. Her eldest son's face at last outshines his silvered hair. She apologizes, silently now, for having fallen out of love of him.

Shine is the spokesman. Near him is a group of black girls and men. He has a Harlem network of friends from "Hunn Twenny Fiff Street" to Sugar Hill. Sundays, when Shine brings such friends, he tries hard to help them mix, wants them not to buddy him close. "That's what we do, as much as the ofays," he'll nicker, waving the "young uns" toward each other, escorting their parents with stately intros. Now, raising that handsomely planed head, he buzzes at two men who are very tall, "Come on buddies, don't clump; this not basketball. Work the crowd."

The video is short and modest. Shine, though clearly braking, is not. "Our aim is the young, but old enough to know they are. Bert and I are mid-twenties. You might say mid-perspective—the limit we intend, for both staff and those we help. But give us five years on our own, after which we leave." They aim to show that philanthropy isn't just to be exerted toward the end of life.

Suddenly, he's jazzing. "Take thuggery. Some think its a talent of the young. Or a privilege. And I don't mean just low-class—you know, uh—like muggery?... No, real high-tone, uh, skullduggery." His glance wanders upward and suddenly focuses down on a man and a girl, two other men with them. Sleek, expensive sharpies, all white. Dressed up too early in the day—and their day not ours? Not ordinary gangsters—or any sort? Though they give off a sense of lone purpose, like a single glove flaunted in the hand.

Nell had had an early lover who'd looked like these—an indolently sinister man, patent-leather handsome, who had either aped the British upper-class rotter type or else had come from it, and after marrying a deb and helping her blow her money had taught her to partner him at playing cards in elite gambling clubs or private yachts, where he and she entertained their hosts by teaching them how to cheat—while earning their own keep from a percentage paid for what they brought back to their patrons in little vials. "Such people have a sense of violence that can seem like a divination," Nell had said many years later. "You can mistake it for the divine." On a voyage to which the couple had invited her, the wife had gone off to multiple beds, at which Nell's lover claimed to be incompetent. "In bed he was single," Nell said. "On his own. Smelled like a civet-cat." But the virtue of yachts was that one could get off, and at Gibraltar she had fled. "Back to my innocent youth hostel." She'd had pictures of the pair and their friends, and here, decades later, their zombies are. Youth is a crop.

"And where's the money to come from?" the older of the two extra men asks, profile to the air.

The crowd seems to be holding its breath, in quietus to something warily recognized.

"Just getting to that," Shine says. "Park your guns." Calmly, he first details Norman's bequest, "Small punkins, though he wouldn't like to hear that," then the "adjunct for peace" which will have a little help from "a larger agency, of the same interest." In neither case does he mention sums. "Our friend Duffy here, he'll integrate. Horn in on The Hague, and the U.N., see if there's a wee place for us. You hear the physicists are studying on chaos, and turbulence? But they're safe in the universe; we got this planet. Any reason folks, we young-uns shouldn't have a stake?"

For the first time, applause. Scattered, almost shy. Then stomping.

Under its cover the strangers ooze off, both the girl and her escorts bowing sardonically to Zipporah as they pass her on the way to the hall and the door—open since these proceedings began.

"Who were they?" Gerald is heard to blurt.

"Nobody you want to know," Shine says to an uneasy ripple of assent from the crowd. "And now a little intermission."

When Shine is disconcerted a flush steals under his caramel skin, turning him oddly roseate; is it the white in him coming to the fore? At the same time his nostrils swell, widening for more than air. Under the adopted thorniness, that division in himself, to which he's always calling your attention steals to the skin, sweetening him. This time he's abashed because the crowd, inured to film noise, is ignoring the video—from behind which the hard-working twins are evident—preferring to listen to him. Tough operator, "but Shine's a softie for righteousness," Bert often says of him. "It's he should be the rabbi."

Down the long hall leading to the front door, does she hear the front door close? Leaving the room to investigate, she is pleased by the bottle-clink behind her, as the crowd swarms toward a number of small tables she'd placed according to her usual strategies. No matter that some of the nibbles are still in the packet, as dumped by eager volunteers used to that ticket of entry. She likes her house to swarm, no matter what crowd.

This long, long hall in the larger apartments is the very mark of the West Side, in contrast to the savvier, squared-off or side-winged floor plans of the buildings across the park. Is it that the builders here had had the railroad-flat tenement style still imprinted on their consciousness? Along with the European's lesser need of sunlight? Or even that rooms budding off a single stem could be more flexibly rented out? Here a family, able to string out each member in his or her or their doubled-up room, yet encounters endlessly in the hall. Across the park divide, floor plans are tighter, squared off to side-wing privacy, even if the "suites" are small and gather centripetally, toward the breakfast news. Less casual immersion in one another's presence, for ill or good. Divorces perhaps more likely? More chances of politesse. And standard over there, "foyers" in order to "guest" people as should be done. One great East-West similarity in the better older residences is in the maids' rooms, which are cells—and the kitchens in which the families don't dwell. The Duffys' is no prize. Still, they have dwelt in it.

Once, in her fifties, discovering the peasant-born philosopher Bachelard's *Poetics of Space,* his exhaustive mapping of how a living space dictates the life, she had for weeks moved about as if the mapping of her own consciousness had been discovered, from the grosser housewifery to moods more delicate. Long since, that home geography had been lost to obsession with the city—gone, as it were, into real estate.

What's the occupant to do, then, with this long stem of hall studded with door after door, until its end—where a slightly larger door concedes to the greater outside? One hangs pictures all down the blank side. With constant passage, they'll become as blank as the wall, and long since have.

A far glance, to the front door; yes, closed now. Then a shocker, stopping her in her tracks. Frame to frame, from Italian Renaissance prints to French Empire, and not all of them repro, then that spate of Piranesi, a last resort, and the pastel of Cornwall that fits just above the light switch—all tilt awry. For a minute she thinks of sonic boom, even earth tremor, to which one has been told New York's mica-schist base is not immune. No. All have been pushed.

She can see the girl and her three men making a game of it, going down the line, fists gaily rhythmic, biff, biff. And in the wallpaper above the switch, a signature gash: *Once over lightly, folks— fuck you.* A curdle of laughter. *Shh. Don't slam.*

She hasn't time to set the pictures straight. Let the crowd leaving think their own shoulders have displaced them, while entering and in passing. Now go back in there, not asking what Shine knows may have riled that set—for they'll have been a set of some sort. Pranksters whose jokes have turned bad. No guns, or Shine wouldn't have twitted. Thievery? And her house disappointing them? A house with a dowdy lack of valuables worth lifting, of a scandal to squeeze. Scorn.

Passing her bathroom she starts to duck in for a pee, and a

touch of its pink-lit calm installed by the girls, along with three housegowns, hers and their two, hanging sentinel. *Leave the light on,* they'd decreed tenderly. *For you and us—wherever we are.* And so she mostly has. Now the transom's dark; some thrifty visitor has stopped by. The switch is on the outside.

Yes, girls, it's been used. By a male, eh? Endearing, really, that even the best of them—but do we want them further tamed, these shoed creatures, already so short on spoor? She puts the toilet seat back down, and sits. Thank the Lord for the human functions; her body is a chariot she yet rides well. "What if *we* were all plastic?" Erika had once asked, brooding over an angel-doll won as a birthday-party prize. "You burned a finger, you'd stink like industrial waste," Zach had chortled. Lately he had shown a piece, *Erika as Plastic Toy,* of which she is proud. Nell had clamored to be done. "It'll depend on what you think you're made of," he'd said.

She smiles, looking up. The bathrobes hang high on the opposite wall. Three white Turkish-towel bathrobes. Each is stained down the front, collar to hem, with a wet, dark-red smear.

In the bush, a cheek scarified with incisions seeping fresh blood will heal. The half-scraped skull will mummify. The disemboweled animal is ritual. Once she'd vomited, told that what she had chewed, a kind of pemmican, had been cannibalized.

But these bloody smirches, lurching down at a repeated angle—done it once, do it twice, make it three—are what's called "gratuitous." An act without reason, with no merit, making no claim. Thrilling most to what is committed casually.

The towels on the rods are fresh. Nobody was wounded here. That blood, any woman would recognize, thickened with maybe the month's cast-off endometrium, its glisten already browning the robes' cotton. Same as with a sanitary towel, those custodians of one of the body's secrets, too gross for some, or too pitiable. Secrets that combine toward a woman's otherness. First mothers, noodling awed over the baby's first feces in the diaper—a mustardy life-force she has never forgot. Holding a child's head as it retches—that grasp punctuates the years. And the smile we hide—semi-Medusa, Demeter—jumble all the classical and catch its rictus in your own mirror, as you pretend not to see the new teenage underarm or genital fuzz.

What was this girl's rage, or graffiti need? And what tool did she use, for those down-strikes? Here, a step-on can, opening its maw. Yes, there. A tampon's capsule, smeared.

And the men? Not types likely to wait at the stage door. End-of-the-road heterosexual chic, imitating the gay?

The mirror, maybe harrowed by what it has witnessed, has coiled her hair into locks. Three men and a girl, constantly triangulating? Or two couples, interchanging. The men complicit. Invited in to applaud.

Tearing down the three robes, one by one, she stuffs them in the bin.

Hunched over the sink, will she heave or spit? She sobs.

Cleansed, she goes slowly down the hall, setting the pictures straight after all. Her house, functioning with her for half a lifetime, has become her mediator. With the patience of the inanimate, it has waited to tell her what she ought to know. Her sobs, hiccuping to a stop as she nears the swarm, are for what has vanished from her own body. No charade is too far-fetched to remind one of how it is—was—to be in heat.

Bert nips her into the big room. "You just missed Norman... Whoo, don't look so dazed. Though it becomes you... On the video. The tribute. His law firm had photos from way back. We ran one of him in a yachting cap, and then that one of him in his office, he sent all his friends. And Shine explained why we can't locate here. Whatever made Norman, real estate to the core, think a coop with residence rules like the eye of a needle would let an organization in?"

She has to dig for an answer; she's still in that bathroom, which may never again be hers as was. "Remember what your grandfather said about him." Let others quote Peter from now on. She suspects he does remember, but Bert balks at anything harsh.

"I remember," Zach says over her shoulder. "He said, 'Norman bulls his way through life. Because he can't face he's a back number.'"

"True, Uncle, but didn't he add, 'Norman's real woe is he's too smart not to know he is one'?"

Tall as she is, the two heads loom above her. The Zangwills have always been maybe a little too proud that they make Jews who are tall. Whatever, these two are looking at each other like brother gladiators who find themselves on opposite sides.

"What's with 'Uncle' all of a sudden, Bert?"

"Sorry, Zach. My father's just been telling me, once again, that today I'm a man."

"He has to. You turned down the official bar mitzvah. He's lucky you had no input the day you were circumcised."

They're laughing, like sons free of their fathers. She's never before really let herself see that about Zach.

Enough of the dead. Speak good of them though we may, or try, in the end we murder them. For not being alive.

"Did you circumcise the twins, Zach?"

"Of course. Both my wives being health nuts. They'd've had the briss, the whole circumcision rite, if I'd allowed it. Any excuse to have a party. Fact, both are here today." But he's smiling. Father of the family, no matter whose?

She smiles too. "May what I've engendered always amuse." She doesn't have to pull punches with him. "I better go say hello."

"No, wait—" Bert says. "There's to be a tribute."

"Another one?" She's near enough to see the video, down which a long list of names is running. "Those the credits?"

"No, the social welfare organizations that are sponsoring us. Not with money, of course. But we'll interact. Take some of the youth load off them."

Zach squints forward, reading. "The Community Service Center. Catholic Charities, Jewish Board of Guardians. Childrens Aid Society . . . and so on. Sounds like my morning mail . . . Hey. The Young Composers League."

"Shine circularized everything in the phone book beginning with 'Young.' Then he found out that the usual prefix for service agencies is 'Youth.' Youth Services, Pathways..." He sees their expressions. "Pull down your eyebrows. Want to know where we got the idea? Shine and I, skiing once, Canada, coming back. Toronto, I think it was, we saw a storefront agency, a state one it must have been. All done up like any, only for kids to come in without their adults. Only admitted alone. We went in to ask details, but none of the social workers had time to answer—place was full up . . . That's our model. The Peace project is for the older ones out of their teens—we'll set the age limits when we're into it. Or maybe never set them. And he and I—after six months we'll alternate going abroad."

As Bert speaks, she is seeing his lineage in his face. At the poker tables of her childhood, watched for a moment before she was patted and told to run along, those faces had divided along a line already accepted by her. Even if the players' joshing hadn't kept the division in sight, gossip would feed it at any family gathering. Those finer faces that still haunt her, good kind ones planed with humanity, often had their destiny also written there: those were the business naifs. Or failures. "He's a prince you know, give you his shirt. But it's hard for Minnie. He doesn't rake in the chips." And should a proper man be that domestic? Especially a Jew, of a race all too often kept from the manly arts of field and sport—and war?

As Bert darts off to the center again, she and Zach exchange shrugs. "These are his congregation." He waves an arm. "For a time."

"Bert always did have to help," she said. "Only it used to be one on one." There's more than one vision to a bathroom. Float a girl in the tub again, white body, in pure white grief, and that sight may destroy the other. As the real violence outlives the fake?

"It's Shine who's the heavy peacenik," Zach says. "Time youth had a voice at the conference tables they die for, he told me. Says he's sick of seeing those peace conferences on television. The British with a patina to their heads like inherited silver. Middle Europe with gray lamb-curls to hide their horns. In the diplomatic, he's noticed, the ones who rise seem to be those who have kept their hair. Like in the United States, the corporate execs. Though the Americans at the table as usual could be anything, a few even bald...I told him, 'Shine, you're in the wrong field; you could do visual. Come to the studio, you can like make your own tables. Better still, life-size images of the people who sit at them.'"

"Table?" a pretty middle-aged woman with a nose tip-tilted by surgery says at their elbow. "You don't say you got one of Lucas's tables, Zipporah?...Hi, Zach."

"Hi, Aunt Kitty."

"A big guy like you, calling me Aunt."

"You been saying that since I was twelve."

"What's a young woman to do, all the kids in the family attain their growth."

"No, I don't have a Lucas table, Kitty," Zipporah says. "Why? He need customers?"

"Him? He only makes one-of-a-kind. For that you have *patrons*...No, I see it wouldn't do, Zippileh. You only furnish schmaltzy. Like I did before I decorated. So I'm going to ask you a real deep favor. I'm getting my kicks from helping those two fix up, when they allow. The doctor says, 'Kitty, from now on you don't acquire; you only adopt—and never without asking.' So I'm asking."

"For what, Kitty?" Zach says. "If it's all schmaltz?"

"I wan' look in her linen closet. I saw what came out for the girls."

"And what they turned down?" Zipporah says, laughing. "Feel free."

"After this riffraff goes, huh, we'll take a peek. There's Gerald giving me the high sign." She dips her head in its harlequin collar, like a bird in its ruff. "I come from the doctor, hubby always wants his report...You know, psychiatrists. Be vicarious, the doc says. I know he means about—this." She flutters out an ivory, coral-tipped hand. "So I do that, at Lucas and By's. But turns out extra, Gerry and I are having a golden-years affair. Right in our own establishment." She skitters off.

Zach is shaking that head of hair which would have done well in the diplomatic. "Know what, though? She always did have beautiful hands."

"A tailor's daughter. Never allowed to lift a needle. Peter and I met the besotted parents. A dear couple, saved from the Holocaust, *schtetl* honorable. Made you weep, for the lost strain of Jewish tailors. They came here a few times; everybody adored them— even Nettie said it: 'The real genealogy. Even though that girl made them change their last name.' Kitty was—tolerated for their sake. The mother said, 'Fegeleh—excuse me, Kitty—she wants me to have a permanent. But I tell her—I already am.' The father said, 'We are so lucky. Gerald too. That he got her before she went on the stage.' Actually Gerald paid them off to live in Florida, at Kitty's insistence. They found out."

Zach stretches his height above the crowd. He slumps only at work, where if you catch him inspecting the bases of his latest constructions, he crawls and hunches, a giant crab. "My poor brother. He just has to be sure to keep her at his side—and what happened to them, that pair?"

"Thought you weren't listening."

"Didn't use to. Listened to him." He has never called his father Peter. "Then I'd find what you said sticking in my mind. When you came back from your travels, mostly. From those people—and their images . . . So give me Kitty's parents."

"Two little brown half-walnuts. Burnt themselves to death, nearly. They wanted to come back home, but more than once a year she wouldn't have them. During her parties they kept themselves upstairs—though that I can't think even Kitty made them do. Last time I went up to see the mother, she was lying down. 'A *shezzah* lounge, my daughter calls it, see how my Fegeleh takes care of me. Look at this quilt.'"

"She did keep them upstairs," a voice says behind her. Lucas, a tall man, at past forty still sapling thin, always takes height's advantage. Inhabiting some tight corner even Bachelard maybe never came to, he spirals furnishings from it. "By told me. The grand-mother tried, but to her Kitty was a stage name. And in the end there was a big fight. The father yelling, 'So I sneaked in a little tai-loring, first class. And your big friends in the Florida area, they found out.' And Gerald shouting, 'You sent them your business card.'"

"And what happened?" Zipporah said. "I never thought. But we'd lost touch."

"They never came back. Not even by telephone. By kept up with them, when he could get there. And Bert, I think, when he was old enough."

"Bert—" she says. "He never said. Not a word."

"*Niente.*" His grin is too gargoyle for pleasantness. "You were the main family."

"But that's absurd. It's just that we were large. Everybody was always welcome here." She all but spreads her hands in the way early cautioned not to—as too "immigrant."

"Sure. My mother had relatives in South Italy. Farmers. Every other Saints' Day my mother sent a blessing. At Christmas, bundles. They'd send photographs; we sent snapshots. But new clothing. During the rest of the year, she could send whatever we had outgrown. So then they sent snapshots."

Peter had had second cousins through his dead brother. They had come once or twice, not again. Agnes and her sister had been chill; she never knew why, and if Peter had, he had never said—or much cared.

"Every family has it," Lucas says. "Whether you are the domi-nant or the lesser one. One doesn't reach out, the other can't, or won't. Either can fade."

She remembers tag-ends like that in Boston. They brought candy when they came, like guests.

"A funny thing happened, though. Because of the snapshots. 'If they don't begin as hunchbacks, they end up that way,' my father said, peering at a print. 'The fields do it.' His family was all doctors.

Come up the hard way, the first one, then not. My mother got guilty, picked out a girl who looked into the camera straight so far, and she was sent us." He grimaces.

"And—?"

"'Agrippina,' what a name. But in school she was stupid. Not retarded, just not bright enough. 'Like a lot of them,' my mother sighed, but only to me. 'Nothing to do but make a maid of her.' Agrippina, she got—what do you say?—knocked up, by a delivery boy, took him back to the farm. He was a city kid. In love with the country, not her. But they did okay on the farm. And when the old guy died—the *padrone,* my mother's kin—what had he done but left her a legacy? 'For her kindness,' he wrote. 'And the presence of family.' My mother spent the whole afternoon in tears; we didn't know which kind, gratitude or shame. 'There'll be no more bundles,' she said—though by that time Agrippina had kids. My nasty aunt said, 'The amount will pay the priest for a mass or two. Or buy you a hat for the Tucci wedding; you could certainly use one.'... My father kept her short. And the Tucci were snotty rich... So she crossed herself, and went out and bought the hat."

Lucas has been eating a handful of peanuts, an American delicacy he adores. "And you know, By and I are going to be fools for family all over again? I can't say it'll be one of Agrippina's descendants. But we're going to adopt."

Lucas's stories are always consciously Italian, spread out like antipasto for the American taste. But today welcome, suggesting however sentimentally a sturdier world.

"Oh Lucas, God bless."

During the telling, Zach has retreated. As he returns, Lucas departs.

"He sees you can't stand him, Zach."

"Oh it's not him I mind. It's the furniture I can't bear," Zach says absently, as if everyone lives, like him, in the likelihood that their works precede themselves to the seat of judgment. Is that why he may have felt the need to be freer in his private life—or falls into those special arrangements that both suit the artist's life and advertise it?

All she knows, from the rush of feeling spumed straight from the other of the two graves she carries ever with her, is that the boy-mentor, whose sayings she's so hoarded because he would never have his full share, is now releasing her. Mickey's voice can now stop. To be remembered, only as one places a flower on a mound. In favor of his siblings, that phalanx which stands with her.

Zach leans forward in the heavy-shouldered way that reassures his children when he coaches them in downhill skiing, reminding them, craftsman that he is, that the trees along the path will have the last word.

"Speaking of chairs—" he says. "Look who."

The crush ahead of her is parting.

"A wheelchair coming toward you always looks so baronial," Zach says softly above her head. He squints one eye, a lens habit. "Poor guy, he isn't liking it."

Now she can see. The chair is being maneuvered past the raised level where the piano is. Kids always take over those steps, curly-heads nuzzling in a party of their own. From the line of young persons squatting there, two yarmulked, plain-clothed young men rise to their feet, then two more near the wall. These four stand quietly, their reverence plain.

The chair's occupant's head is not quite naked. A fawn aura with bald patches fuzzes it. He winks at the pair in front, owning up to them, grants a nod to the eager two at the wall. Teacher style, surely. Bravely. For no, he isn't liking what comes with a chair.

"That must be Moorsohn; I've never met him."

"Bert took me to, a few months ago," Zach chuckles. "'Freak uncle,' he said, introducing us, '—meet freak prof.' Moorsohn must have been due for hospital again, though it wasn't said. He wasn't in a chair."

An orange-and-blue ascot tied around Moorsohn's neck gives him the air of having chosen the bandage under it as more dashing than a tie. The chair's handler is a short woman with an apple-cheeked smile. Under her cardigan she wears medical whites, a doctor's jacket or nurses uniform. They might be on a boardwalk out for the stroll.

Bert comes up from behind to take Zipporah's hand and lead her up to him.

"Grandmother, the mentor I've told you about for so long."

"Zipporah Zangwill. Who believes in God—as the Eye." His voice is a rasp just above a whisper.

So he has that annoying professorial habit of presenting you with what you are, does he? Granted that only the special ones can carry that off. "I merely record those who do, Dr. Moorsohn."

He nods, as if the territory of his acceptance is wide. "My wife, Dr. Elise Weil."

Zach and Bertram have pushed seats into a circle. The wife, murmuring, *"Enchanté.* So pleased," is apparently bilingual. Her small feet, elegantly shod, just graze the floor. Underneath cardigan and jacket, a black dress, half-hidden, peeps with a verve surely French. The hands, blunt and scoured, poise on her lap like instruments. Bert reports with awe that Dr. Weil, war heroine in the battle zone, later clinical professor in a Tel Aviv hospital, is said to have performed all Moorsohn's surgeries.

"I could never accept a God with any body parts," Moorsohn says. "That's what got me into trouble. Mary Mother-of-God's babe, with its pushy little pre-Renaissance belly? The stigmata, appearing like bruises, for all our sins? All of it too human. Meanwhile the bargaining, so much for this sin, so much for that—like trade, on a bourse. A stock market in sin." The last word erupts with a liquid timbre as if from behind the bandage. When the doctor puts the flat of her hand there with a *s-s-st,* all near enough look into their laps or away. This is a man's illness, saying more than it should.

The "opening," as Shine and Bert and their few hardy recruits have referred to this day during preparation, had started just before dusk. "Like a gallery opening, only we'll be the pictures," Shine had said, prophesying correctly. "And no real food. Fizzy water? Too dignified. And costs." People entering have caught that tone from each other, standing about in that aloof forbearance of a gallery show, or greeting aficionados.

The running video is being frowned upon concentratedly—in case its authors are near, or wandered by, opinion withheld. Near the windows are die-hards who will linger to the end. Among them, a foursome hunches like crap players, humming in the absent way of those brought up with each other's songs. The crowd is becoming few enough to form those hugger-muggers in which the best parties prolong.

"Aah." Moorsohn rasps. "A *feste*. Even the best causes turn into them."

"*Chut!*" his wife says. And in undertone, "*Calme-toi*. One can't allow you more codeine."

The tall video screen, now seen to be on a cable yards long, is letting itself be slowly be guided, with a grudging rumble, from its platform to a reasonable distance from Moorsohn, facing him.

"A mirror?" he counters. "Or Leviathan?" He leans forward, kicking out a foot. "Hah no, I'm seeing double." At either side of the grand frame is a twin. "Of course that is how one sees the newest generation." He twiddles two fingers at them. They respond casually, as workmen would. Zach and the Ernestines apprentice their kids early to adult interchange.

Shine appears. "To some of our begetters. A small tribute— nothing Shakespearean." Perhaps he's never quite got over his theater spell.

There follow three simple but graceful statements of thanks: "To Zipporah Zangwill Duffy, our hostess"—this drawing surprise from many, turning on her the sweet wide-eyed stare one's juniors award when you haven't made too much of yourself. Or enough? "To the donor to the peace project who wishes to remain anonymous," provoking a ripple of "Who?" "And to Gavin Ahimilech Moorsohn: for ideas, ideals—and eleven volunteers." The wordage and the sentiments are undoubtedly Bert's.

She and Moorsohn are clapped for. One of those at the window, a contraband bottle in hand, says, "Who's Ahimilech?"

Moorsohn, about to say, is stilled by his wife. He waves a summoning hand, skinny and bleached, at the nearer pair of yarmulkes.

"Ahimilech," one spouts. "The priest slain by Saul for helping David. As in the text: Samuel, one to nineteen . . . Doctor took his name when he became a Jew. Maybe the same as Ahijah, Hebrew for brother of God."

"You see I was modest," comes from the chair.

"And put the 'aitch' in Moorsohn," the other of the pair says slyly.

"That is uncalled for, Joseph," the first of the pair says.

"Not at all. According to the Law—"

Both pairs of elbows are up. Not to tangle, their identical smirks say. To expatiate.

"Dr.—" one of the pair in back says. "Allow us—"

His echo: "To exercise . . . the theology."

Every yarmulke begins to gabble. *And are they well prepared, God? Don't worry.*

From Bert she's heard about divisions among the seminarians. Some come straight out of a lay college, entranced back into religion by the state of the world, or by their atheistic upbringing, or even by a fashionably revived interest in mysticism as a state of being. Some will be children of parents who had perhaps intended to immigrate to Israel but had never made it. Some would be "the immigrants," a few really so. But to say so is one of those harsh class estimates that young slang feels free to make. Many students are merely emigrants from the ranks of the poor. They would work as hard at religion as their peddler predecessors once toiled up the social staircase. Or do so honorably, within the great framework of belief. Bound to that biblically, or scholastically, with a passion that Bert admires. "It's like Grandpa, only what they believe is opposite." Those who hadn't yet been to Israel clustered around those who had. "Hungry for the hot Jewish stuff, like—like it's porn," Bert had erupted. "Sorry. Or they're worried they can't speak modern Hebrew. The ones who have been over there? For them, Israel's the holy land. The world is all Jewish. Except for 'the terrorists,' as Israel calls them. Some still within Israel's borders." As he speaks, he grows more downcast. "'Even the children. Any child can pick up a stone,' this Kalman said. His uncle was a hero of the Six Days War. Why's the guy a student here? 'To help lobby,' he'd admitted. But the rumor is he'd been in an unsanctioned scrap. 'We're not Sabras anymore,' he said. 'We're Jewry.'"

And what then, Bert had asked him, are the American Jews who help? 'Yeah, from a safe distance?' he'd said. 'I'll low-down you. In Talmud, every two-man joke has a patsy in it. That's them.'"

And Moorsohn, hearing of this tidbit, had responded, "Kalman's right on target. So is his uncle. An eye for an eye is good business. A tooth for a tooth, dental surgery—expensive of course. But can we let them speak for all Jews? We must help our God to be even more just."

Bert's smile reporting this had had a wolfish curve she had not seen before. "Helping God has never occurred to them."

It's never occurred to me either, she wanted to say. But maybe this project is Bert's rabbinate?

Moorsohn has been looking about him, which the bandage allows. At first sight she'd been tempted to see him as in those paintings of the Deposition—a man upheld by his wounds. Instead, he reminds her of a bird brilliantly pecking at the terrain still allowed him. "In this room you see the real religion of your country," he says, looking about him. "Democracy is secular prayer."

"And what's the prayer?" Zach asks.

"That the plate glass which keeps the rich safe from the poor will hold . . . and as long as the poor believe in it, it will."

"You are always so pompous when you come out of surgery," Dr. Weil says. "Gives you the right to your opinions."

"When I come out of anesthesia, I keep hearing church bells. Who hears those in New York? I came here to be free of them."

"You hear them every time, no matter what hospital. Mt. Sinai, Montefiore. The only place you didn't hear them was in Tel Aviv."

"Naturally. You were wearing the rubber gloves."

Everybody in the circle is smiling. It's taken them a minute to catch on, as when a comedy team first hits the ear. What they are hearing is the persiflage of a brave marriage.

"This time you outdid yourself. At the top of your voice, the 'Our Father.'"

"That's an interfaith prayer."

"Not in Latin it isn't."

Bert cannot resist. "What's wrong with the Lord's prayer in Latin?"

Moorsohn whispers. She answers. "Because then it is the Paternoster. Which is an act of worship." She sits back, happy. So is he. There is a space around them which is their own.

"It's not so easy to become a Jew," she adds. "The Lord God is not exactly shopping around."

When Zach, Zipporah, and Bert stop laughing, she says, "We are on our way to France. My ninety-six-year-old father is doctor in our village town. When he was released from the death camp where my mother died, he went back into practice—and ever since. Now he should step down—the hands shake, he can't read the chart. He still fondles the women, which the older ones always looked forward to; he's a fine figure. But now he mistakes them, and it shouldn't happen to the young girls. So the mayor, and four others I grew up with, have written me."

"Comes at the right time," Moorsohn says. "Look at her. Clinical professor, they call her. Because they don't know what else to call a woman who served in the army with a record they can't ignore. But now she's being made to leave their hospital, and others in Israel will close their doors to her also. Want to know why?"

The doctor puts out a blunt hand to stop him but, he won't have it. "Because she'll authorize care for anybody. Scrap from the streets, loose women. But worst—people picked up from the other side. 'Traitor almost,' they say. 'A whole channel of cases right in our fine hospitals.' She has no faith, they say; she'll serve anybody. And true, Elise has no politics . . . They want her to."

"Tais-toi," she whispers. "Be still."

"No," he rasps. "Wail, rather. There's a wall for it." A quaver comes from behind the white bandage, wavering, gaining power, "Oy-y, Israel. *Shema, Yisrael.*"

No one pays him mind. Perhaps they think he sings.

"Why—I know who you are," Zipporah says, leaning forward. "You're Doctor Elise. From the woman's army unit. I knew a girl there. A woman. A nurse. Maybe that battalion wasn't all women, but she said you made it so."

The blunt hand turns palm up, then down: she knew so many.

"Her name was Debra Cohen."

A movement on Zipporah's right. Bert.

"Ah, we had a *douzaine* Cohens. Shorty Cohen . . . Cohen from Galilee. When you are that busy—and under danger—you don't stop to see who."

"Tall. Beautiful. A psychiatric nurse—or studied it."

"We all studied it. Also the surgery. An opportunity, the army meds say. One sees the bowels. Brains. Thorax. And repairs by flashlight."

Moorsohn says, "Shh, Elise. Better than the camps."

"She'd been a hairdresser."

"The one married to—? *That one.* Of course. The one with the history." She half smiles. "When Moorsohn turned Jew, we too got divorced. Only a civil suit—in the religious one, the woman is humiliated, no matter what." She looks over at Moorsohn, who is now dozing as a child does, half blinking. "He thought I grudged him being a Jew. But a good hospital is not a sieve. Arabs on our wards? They knew what I was allowing. And didn't want to catch me. But Massad was watching us for plots; Jew against Jew can be the worst. And now he was one of us."

"And were you on both sides, Madame?" Zach, who would know how that is.

Grasping the wheelchair, she stands up, weighing on it. Moorsohn's head has fallen on his chest, mouth open, breathing. Short as she is, their heads are almost parallel. "We must go now." In passing she touches Zach's shoulder, the curved dress slightly showing. "*Sickness* is a plot."

Bert, standing up, bars her way.

He's not that boy with his gramps anymore, golden with mischief from the mouth, soft with family at the heel. He's had his own bar mitzvahs.

He's going to ask. He's going to ask what I wanted to, in the months after that last day in Rome, but buried away. Do I want him to?

"Dr. Elise?" Bert says. "Have you any clue as to where Debra Cohen now is?"

The doctor hunches herself. Everybody wants a piece of her—one recalls Debra herself saying so. "Ten years since she left Israel, maybe more? A nurse could be anywhere." The doctor is very tired. But relents. "You could try London. One hospital she talked about, I visited it. A long way out on their Metro. They permit dogs to ride on it. And wine could be bought in the hospital shop."

Moorsohn is awake. They exchange a practiced look. "Madame," she says to Zipporah. "Your W.C.—*pardon*, bathroom?"

Zipporah leads her there.

Zach is staring at Bert, one eyebrow up. Bert stares back.

"Such a dumpy little soul," Zach says finally. "And so complex. So—devious."

"He's the innocent, Uncle. But manages to conceal."

They grimace at each other. "Think the Israelis got on her tail?" Zach says.

"Who are the Massad? Their FBI?"

They consider. Neither knows for sure.

"Are women devious by nature, Uncle? Or does their history make them so?"

"Both," Zach says instantly. "Took me two Ernestines to find that out."

Shine comes up behind them. He tends to avoid Moorsohn,

saying, "His pitch is he sees down to everybody's socks. Half of me starts an argument. Half of me moves on."

"The crowd's thinning," he says now. "Got a message I want to send them off with; it'll spread. Our new location. Got a still I want to show. Quarter of an hour or so." He moseys off.

The wheelchair returns; behind, its handler.

In an hour the chair's become ordinary, it no longer cuts a swath, Moorsohn is once again alert. The straightened band around his neck might be some ecclesiastical collar, freshening him. Elise perhaps dosed him in the bathroom.

Bert's never seen Moorsohn in a crowd. Until now he'd seemed hunched in that chrysalis which a professor can carry about from office to class, its glassy innard hung with old tags, vanished student faces that repeat. One of the essays Bert's grandfather had left him—that he has begun to pore over—has noted this.

"Witness the undertow changing of the guard," Moorsohn declares, peering forward. "Harder to see that, in this country. Empires are where you watch the uniforms unravel... But where's your grandmother? We must say—" His pale cheeks screw, haunt past Bert. "Say good-bye."

The mentors, why do they die so young? Both of them around sixty-five. Bertram grates out, "You'll need a car."

"No, your peacemaker, he came to see us," Dr. Elise says. "Your donor? He and Moorsohn have been corresponding. He came to where we are in Moorsohn's little apartment behind the college. I think the college must own it. So many bookshelves— and a kitchen that has never learned to cook."

"Elise thinks your peacemaker wants to know about war."

"They always do, the peace men," she says. "Like we in Israel want to know about families like this one." She stares up at the high ceiling, a hand arrested, then down at the pouf Bert has brought her to sit on. As if she cannot quite let her weight down on it. "Families behind the lines, all their long lives."

"That's not fair, Elise. Bert and Shine have both done their military service."

"But their country, it has never yet been bombed. Not the farms, the family furniture. And God knows, the cities. A country that has been to war, you can measure it later, in the citizen's bones. And in the bones of those who have not been. To say nothing of the eyes."

"Such clear eyes, that billionaire has," Moorsohn says. "You want to cast a hook in them. Many must have tried. But take note of that last airy syllable, Bert. These men are like pockets of air moving between the continents. Wanting to be here, right with you, in the bed, the domicile. They themselves have the children that money procreates." He shifts his collar. "But wherever they are, they are only there for a time."

"*Oui.*" The doctor's *oui* is like a small hammer. "In the wards, after a bombing. *Les gosses,* the little kids, they hang onto the pinkies of these rich visitors. But they are always given the whole hand."

"Nothing about the body escapes her," Moorsohn says gloomily.

"Well, your billionaire, he'd heard you were *hors de combat, cheri* . . . And Bertram—you don't mind me calling you so?—he brought us such a car. He was in New York to drive another car to be shipped to Europe, but this car a courier drove. A car built for wheelchair. His mother's—a horse once ditched her, smashed the leg. 'She wanted to be Sarah Bernhardt,' he told us, 'maybe even to play *L'Aiglon* with a wooden one. But the leg healed.'" Elise pauses, but not for breath.

A Frenchwoman never needs to, Shine has told Bert. "If they wanted, they could all be coloraturas."

"Your billionaire has humor, he has many things, *non?* He has even a mother?" When the doctor smiles, the cheeks apple. "He didn't want to give us her car. Only to lend. But tomorrow we leave. So he picked us up himself and dropped us here. He does not want the ceremony; he is shy of those, he wouldn't come upstairs. But he will come. He insists that we wait to be picked up." She sighs. "That car. What a hospital would give, to have it. What a village would, eh?"

"Near Aix," Moorsohn says. "My father-in-law holds office around the corner from the Aix market, near the pay toilets. In his day the doctors dispensed as well; he still does." He looks up at Bert. "Near the vegetables there's a bronze boar I'm in love with. I'll station myself next to it and drum up a constituency."

He's drowned out by loud voices in the hallway, men's, and then a woman shrieking.

"*Nom de Dieu.*" She has put her hand on her big purse.

"*Calme,* Elise. This is New York."

A pint-size woman erupts into the room, followed by a man, thickish, also in evening clothes, and behind him a man in a doorman's uniform. "This is outrageous!" she cries. "What kind of business you doing here? We warned. Crowds in the elevator; this is a residence. Blocking the stairs. Who are these people?" A doll-size version of a man's black opera hat rides undisturbed on her high, canary-bright hairdo. "We demand to know." The man beside her concurs silently. "And what was that mammoth vehicle barring the canopy? We called the police."

Bert recognizes the couple from many rides up and down in the house elevator. He has now and then, unthanked, helped them unload the plants, small tables, and boxes of glassware they are always loaded with. Before he can speak, Zipporah strides through the door.

His grandmother isn't fazed. Silent but flushed with action. After so long? That's a story the family is used to. Widows, widowers, Cousin Eustaces. Who travels shakily from Boston to warm himself in a haze of "recollection" he wants Bert to confirm, his last bosomy lady having—decamped? "No. Bert, she's down under. But I'm looking about."

So is Zipporah. Swanning about to catch every glance before she gives tongue. "Ladies and gentlemen, meet our good neighbors, Mr. and Mrs. Alter, from the apartment below."

In the quiet, a titter, as the boy with the bottle lurches forward from the group at the window, swinging it harmlessly, in pace with his shambling gait. "Who are these people?" he singsongs. "Pee-pul. Nice peepul. Me. Hah, Professah?"

"Yes, Yehudi; Yehudi is a fan of the seminary. A loyal one."

"Hah, Shine?"

"Yes, Yehudi. Who are you being today?"

He pulls out a yarmulke, slaps it on his head. "The twelfth-th volunteer. Yay-y-y." He shambles off. As he goes, two of the yarmulkes trail, obviously to see him safe. They may be prickly with Talmudic word-splicing, but they have a sweetening of the righteous faith; they wear it now like a domino.

"One simpleton is good for the seminary," Moorsohn says. "God usually provides."

"Seminary?" The man of the couple says. "Like who, may I be so bold? I'm a part-time member of the Council. When business permits."

"Oh, indeed," Zipporah says. "If I'd known your interests I'd have invited you today." She addresses the woman. "This is just a reception, I assure you, Mrs. Alter. In honor of donors, and spon-sors, like Dr. Moorsohn here. Our offices will be located elsewhere. Like yours is, I presume? Except maybe at Easter . . . er, *Pesach.* —Sometimes?"

"We give heavy entertainment, we notify Lester here, like the house suggests," the woman says sullenly. "And a compensation don't hurt. That way, he monitors."

Lester, the man in uniform, lounges so successfully that one can both forget he is the house doorman and rely on that, so he is a party to much, which, as a treasurer of house lore, he will often impart to Zipporah at length. Here since many of the tenants were young family, he has taught Bert how to shoot crap, set him straight on the Caribbean geography of "the islands"—and cau-tioned them all to say "Bajan," not "Barbadian." Once he and his wife took Erika to visit an "island" family who had brought in artifacts, pre-warning that she was not to favor any one object aloud; else they would have to give her it, in deference to him.

He considers it his obligation to help the children here to go beyond the paucity of their white lives. All his own grown children are educated, some now in government and medicine. He is a testament to the underground action of cities, even here in edifices lukewarm to that, and columned like Luxor.

"Oh, I take care of Mrs. Duffy's Sunday since Hector was a pup," he says. "She pays a lot more than some." As he leaves he says to Moorsohn, while nodding to his handler: "Your car's in a garage, sir. Driver confirms he'll pick you and the lady up soon as parking regulations go off; that's an hour from now." He speaks to Moorsohn as if to a man standing on his feet. When the lady, making a French noise, signals her charge that she's going off for a minute, Lester, taking this in with the back of his head, says obligingly, "Right down that hall, Missus, that pretty door with the brass knob."

When he's gone, Zipporah says, "I always see Lester as one of those orchestra conductors who do so while also playing the piano. Down on the left hand, and the brasses come in. Up with the right and it's the violins. And we are his instruments."

Bert is thinking: And you are so graceful, Grandmother, making neutral conversation, so that the Alters may take themselves off with dignity after their snit, and with the least pain to all. But this small ooze of good manners, issuing from the ribbed rock of his grandmother's "background" and era, seems to elude them.

They are now among the few strangers left in the room. The Moorsohns, as honored guests, not counting as such. All the others, Gerald and Kitty, Zach, Bert and Shine, even the twins lolling meekly on the floor and staring into their sneakers, would be known to the Alters as family or close, from encounters over the years. Do the Alters by any chance assume, against all the strictures of apartment-house living—the brief nod, elevator silence as if rising doomed to the gallows, strangulated blurt on the weather—that

since they eat, fornicate, and grunt their gut confidences to one another in the space just below here, they are at home?

Allowing Mr. Alter to smooth his bald crown, reach for a nut,
and issue a sigh? Mrs. Alter, with a butterfly shake of her garments,
coyly pats her tiny hat. They are prepared even to be winsome.
Their outrage, projecting them onto intimacy, serves now as social
connection.

They move toward the wheelchair, following their own snouts;
Mrs. Alter's profile has been nipped to a kind of llama indentation
recognizable as an early nose job. Zipporah often wonders what
Darwin, if he could have met such but had been left in the dark,
would have said of such profiles.

"Dr. Moorsohn? Honored to know you, sir. Herman Alter,
tourist agency, sometimes working with the state of Israel. May I
present my wife and colleague, Judy Goodstein Alter; she is also
known politically."

Moorsohn is asleep. Or shamming. Even shamming death? On
the edge so often, why not try it out?

"He only sleeps four hours at a time, sometimes in a whole
night," the doctor says. "But always when we are waiting somewhere. Airports. On his feet even, waiting in line...Even in
schul—he says faith is a wait." Her chirping medical voice has gone
drowsy. "A good health habit." Her eyes half-close. "Excuse." A
whisper, "...I have been on call forty-eight hours."

"Waits are difficult," Zipporah says. "You're remembering all
the other ones. Like waiting for a lover once—when you're only in
line for the washroom."

A blurt from Zach. *Bravo, Mother,* his look says.

"A lover?" Judy Alter says blankly. That must not be her style of
intimacy. "Once I'm hauled out of bed like today, I'm a goner for
good." She preens, a person happily afloat on resentment's salt sea.

"Oh?" Zach's patience is reserved for what he makes—art. And
kids. "Does your husband sleep in his dinner jacket? Thought you
walked in on our rumpus from some—soiree. Maybe with the
mayor."

The current mayor visits some tenant here privately. No one knows who. Encountered once or twice in the elevator he was thought afterwards to have been a look-alike, those who rode up with him later regretting they hadn't noticed the floor he was bound for. And of course he could have trotted up or down a flight, using the stairs. Now Lester must conduct him through basement and back elevator. But of course will not say.

"The mayor and I have brushed elbows," Alter says. "At the Harmonie." He titters. "I must say—he looks just like his look-alike."

All this time Mrs. Alter has not sat. Short as she is, she strives. That glare, so hostile to the tall, must come from constantly looking up. "One flight down, we are hung right over the canopy. That monster of a car. Then the crowd, such a motley; even over on Columbus you don't see such specimens. Barefoots. What is this, Lourdes? And a noise from the lobby like bees. So Herman rings up Lester; where is all this coming from? And Lester answers, 'Charity.'"

In the silence, Herman Alter says, "Judy is sensitive to this house in every pore."

The miniature opera hat quivers. Her cup of injury is full. "You make an honest complaint, you don't do it in your bathrobe. You prepare for a contingency."

So, coddling their outrage to a boil, they had dressed for it? She motions to her husband for them to leave now, but clearly he wants to delay. Even met in the elevator they are social climbers, fawning small talk at the penthousers, ignoring those who live below themselves. The tenants who issue like rabbits from the tiny flats on the ground floor would be beyond the pale.

As for the Moorsohns here, who are royal enough to doze off in company? "Europeans," Alter mouths, waggling an eyebrow at Zipporah. "Well, turns out we're even-steven on receptions, hah? Come Sukkoth, Judy makes the living room a real autumn bower, grapes on the vine, by invitation only. Drop by, meet our crowd from Paris." He extends an arm to his wife. "Come, my bride."

From the niche where the piano is, a suave baritone.

"Why, I thought I recognized you." Gerald's voice.

Shameful, how she continues to forget her eldest son's presence, the very importance his siblings concede he has to have. "Find him amusing," they had long advised her. As a fat-cheeked infant he had been. The absolute pomp of Baby, prideful even of his own stool. Giving the hint that when a man he would still be wont to detail that trustworthy timetable? She's had to accept that her firstborn doesn't get the rest of the family's jokes. Worse to witness that he is one of those. Worst would be to find that he knows how she feels, while refusing to pay the cost of endearing himself to her? But Gerald's ultimate virtue is consistency.

He rises now from the small settee where he and Kitty have been sitting, he by her request, holding her hands, this lending them the devotional air that Kitty claims for fact. "My mother and father are having an affair," Byron has said. "They're forever at Bert and me for not giving them grandchildren. Maybe they mean to produce one?"

What is Gerald saying, his expression bland?

"You're Hyman Hugo Alter, right? Holy Land Tours. Last year's pledge dinner, the United Appeal? You pledged big."

"Herman Hyman Alter . . . It comes to mind."

"I can assure. I'm treasurer."

"My partner here, she does the accounts."

"Of course wartime, even a short war, the enthusiasm runs high," Gerald says. "Not like ordinary years, when some who just want to show don't come through on their pledge. This year people fell over themselves to signify. I kid them the generals didn't consult our dinner committee. But over there, they are tops at the short war. So I push: You want to show solidarity, better pledge now . . . And—we set a record. Millions received . . . Only three pledges not yet honored. One, bankrupt. One staff error. And yours, sir."

The Alters move into a separate box of air, heads lowered at each other.

"You didn't send?" he rasps.

"I didn't send."

"You know what this does to me, my character... The business."

"And to me, nothing? Soon is Shavuot, comes the Israel crowd like clockwork, to push for the handout, like nothing is too much to sacrifice for what's going on with them. So we wine and dine, we take couples to musicals like it's us who want something from them. And to temple, where the rabbi apologizes it's only money we give. And over there, only Jewish bullets are pure, everybody else is a terrorist."

"Tell me this at home," Alter says hastily. "Say good night."

"No. I made a mistake maybe. But let them hear."

From the floor where the twins are stretched out, one says, "Pa—can we go now?"

Zach says, "Where?"

The other twin sits up. Raised in an atmosphere where art is the fiercest controversy, their domestic life is mild. The two Ernestines, flower children in the sixties, had baby-sat each other's twins, and still talk sororally every day.

"Someplace else," he says, eyes lowered.

"Home," Zach says. "Take a cab."

"Nah, the subway." A protest against their parents' looser "uptown" habits. Their hyphenated names are Liam-Abraham and Terence-Saul, to give each of their bloodlines an equal chance, but they are known as Abie and Terry, according to their own preference. Their grandmother, though quick to tell them apart, won't reveal to them why, for fear of embarrassing them: it is in the distinctly different way their freckles pulsate, the one in a tawny standout, his brother in a sneaky, almost merging pallor. She secretly thinks of the twins, born of a half-and-half father and a wholly Christian mother, as the triumph of assimilation. Abie, whose spots quicken faster and deeper, veiling him with a subtle, foreign tinge, has the Jewish edge.

"Nah, we won't duck into the toilet. Promise. And we'll stand well back on the platform," they carol wickedly, in a unison too absolute for mere pitch. Zach packs them off, with a practiced double swat at their neat behinds.

Mrs. Alter has waited. Bert sees a resemblance to a cousin on his mother's side, of whom it was said, "Marion is the kind of guest can't leave. She only knows how to arrive."

"You want to know why I didn't send in, Hy—ask your teacher friend, Pocker."

"We were boys in the yeshiva is all, Judy. Leave him be."

"Is that Pocker, the authority on the five books of Moses?" If Jehovah could have been shown to be first and foremost a scholar, Bert might have less trouble believing in Him.

"You know him?"

"I heard him lecture once."

"You play poker, you can hear him at our house. He says—the Pentateuch, it teaches how to bluff." Alter is cheered, less stiff, his tie askew. Mrs. Alter has removed her dark glasses. Her eyes are bright, round, and blue—the kind, Zipporah thinks, that so often end up executive.

"Small world," she says. "Especially Pocker's. I have dozens family pictures on the piano. My four sisters—pregnant all the time, they compete. Pocker goes to the one tiny shiny card, from the old country, a little girl in a pinafore. I love that picture; she is still in Russia and only five. Who is she? My mother. 'But she has a cross around the neck,' Pocker says...So it comes out. I am only half Jew. Through my father, I say. Two lonely Russians, they marry in New York. That church with the onion on top—she never went back. Any boys they had were to be his, to be Jewish. But after five daughters only, she gave him us girls. She went with us to synagogue, belonged to the Sisterhood. Anybody wants to be a Jew that hard—is a Jew...But Pocker says no. We are not Jewish at all. Not in Israel. It goes by the mother. 'That onion,' he says. 'A strong vegetable. But nothing compared to us Jews.' 'That's my mother,' I say. 'Leave this house.'"

Her hands are clasped stagily at her breastbone; is she professional or amateur? No matter. These are the women who spawn comics, Yiddish version or any. From clotheshorse to home, actress is never far.

"So you're my better half," Herman Hyman says. "Come along downstairs. Leave these fine people to their business."

He's ignored. "Allow me, Herm . . . So Sulamith and Aaron, big *machers*, every year our houseguests, they're off to L.A. the next day—to lobby the benefit there. They have the usual good-bye call from Pocker before they go. She has already taken my measurements for the swimsuit, the Goretex she has their factory custom-make me for a thank you, every year. 'We pinch every penny, now there's a war,' she says. 'But it will come to you like always, in time for Florida. Shalom.'"

"It came," he says. "The night of the appeal dinner. You opened the box. I saw. Stunning like always. But down in Florida you never wore."

"It came, yes. The factory must already have cut it. So she sent. But like routine. No thank-you note. And on the box, an invoice— to pay . . . So I should send them our hard-earned money?"

"So for a—a bathing suit you let me welsh on the pledge? It didn't fit?"

"It would fit like a dream, I could tell. Like a dream. The Christian half of me said 'Pay.' My mother never left a bill hang overnight. The Jewish half is more cagey. It said: 'So you're not that Jewish, you're excused.'"

Zipporah is always astonished at the fine sense of drama the most ordinary women display. Adding the kind of finish to a family scene that a craftman might suddenly apply with skill. As a child she'd witnessed when an offended aunt, not usually clever, had said what had suddenly aligned every person in the dining room in their proper place in the family queue. Among Orthodox women, would such a talent have come from being always in the balcony, while the men meditate their godhood on central ground?

She has a sudden vision of the women's section in the synagogue in Venice: two lacy iron fretworks flung against the wall— had these actually existed? If so, what would she herself have seen, if, reentering the great doors after her shopping walk, she had climbed there? One present bought for Debra, which she still has, cached in a cabinet back of the family silver, never unwrapped.

"Excuse me—" the woman now falters. Is she aware now she's destroyed that nullity which every apartment dweller had better maintain—else how to continue to say good morning, while a neighbor's real story silently crashes in one's ears?

"No, no," Gerald says, coming forward. "Being half-and-half never leaves you, I can tell you, though it can smooth over—like cream into whisky. Or energize you—right on the floor of the Stock Exchange. Shah, look at those two now—" Shaking his head he points to the Moorsohns, nodded quiet, heads on breasts, like a pair of birds. "Who can sleep in a public place like that except the saints, in their niches? I had an Aunt Aggie, may she rest in peace as she never would in life, who almost made me a Catholic. It was my mother here who must have saved me, Mrs. Alter, without any conscience she was performing for the Israelites."

His great fair face bears down on her, beneficent. This eldest son who, if not named Gerald for a father's dead brother, might have gone surely and proudly into the role that drapes so awkwardly on Bert? He flings up an arm—casting off a prayer shawl?—and strides up to Mr. Alter. A palm an Alter's shoulder, bonding man to man. "I hereby release you from your pledge . . . Not a word now. I insist." Which draws a split apology from the Alters.

She: "I thought it was one of those snobby Jewish committees maybe starting down here."

He: "Most of our hard business is done in the mother country, sir. We're the social end. More than one of our prominents lives partly here." He plans to give a donation a little later. "If convenient. Our tourists are all devoted. To the history. Plus the climate, the beaches, the fruit. A fine mix—but for Americans don't add a bomb." He expands. "Soon as that war ended, though—people wanted to see the sights like crazy. Then what do we do but put ads calling it 'the gentle country,' which fed right to the guilts. So the rates going down, the French came. You never make money on the

French. And their Jews are not like ours—they're as French as France will let them be." It is apparent that he is a tired man.

When you mix business and religion, Bert thinks, you must become weary of one or the other. But Alter will not let himself know which. He loves the wife, though; she'll do what he won't—and merely be thought kooky for it?

Alter makes a move to go. She nods abstractedly. But they don't move. Thanks to confession, they now belong here.

In the room at large the buzz of many has dropped to the low groove of a few, blending into one conversation seemingly available to any ear.

"Half-and-half, this is sure a halfway house," Shine mutters to Zach. "That's how I bonded, way back." He's fiddling with an old machine for camera slides. "Found this in what they used to call the attic. Man, so empty now it made my stomach warp . . . You feeling down, Zach boy? Why?"

"Lately, when the boys go—just anywhere, I feel, mmp, diminished. Because I know they are, *mmp*—going." He dawdles a finger along the edge of the slide projector. "Brother Charles brought a girl home once; she had slides she wanted to show. Turned out to be the porn circulating her high-class school. He palmed her off on a classmate—or they shared her, don't know which. The other guy married her; the child of their divorce came here once overnight—kept saying she wanted to be a Jew."

"What was the porn like?"

"Almost art. I hated it."

"What brought that up?" Shine says. "You thinking of marrying again?"

"God, no. Though we get along. Ernestine's a doll. They both are." He slaps the machine. "Never felt this way when the first twins left."

"Because the second crop were coming up. Whyn't you have another set?"

"How could we be sure next time would be a set? Besides, this Ernestine won't. The other, she still might."

"You could make a harem. Those girls already always in each other's hair . . . Or have a third round. Then do it."

"The Firsts are already in love with their stepmother—my Ernestine."

That's how it was once, at Shine's house, though Shine does not remark.

"Anyway, I come here to have my mother buck me up," Zach says. "She thinks I'm doing it for her."

"You know, Zach—you're the only one of her Duffys who's not a half-and-half. You're all you. Here. Lemme show you a couple of slides." He jams one in.

Shine's a photography buff, veering dizzily between the underground and the antique. He believes that photography is the underground of all the arts. Even music. In his huge new loft, which Zach helped him find, the cool, blank walls, opposing and succeeding each other like the plane geometry of an era, are slowly filling with his collection, which includes a huge black-and-white of the score of a composer who has musicalized the sounds made by whales, the notes now appearing to issue from the shadowy hint of a maw, this managed in the darkroom. There he has an archive, barely glimpsed by Bert, of shots of all the Duffy Sundays Shine had been to. Plus studies of Zipporah—including a shot of her legs that Bert is relieved to see is not scurrilous. Prints from Shine's own home life, "when I get one," are to hang on the "antique" side, which he claims everybody's home life in the end turns out to be.

The black-and-white slide he first shows is one Bert's seen before—of the building, located on a northwest corner of lower Fifth Avenue, and recently inherited, which once housed the flag business and because of that figures modestly in New York's pictorial history. Bert has often been there. Framed now by Shine's hand, here's the big window on the Avenue, circa 1915, in it an explosion of fanned flags, the array continuing around to the window on the side street. The colors of the flags selected would have been bravura to the eye: hot reds, yellows, cobalts, along with striped or starred flag patterns. Often the window arrangement had been a sly allusion to the news—just short of controversy, Shine had said. "They knew where their bread was buttered." Shine can identify the flags of the first Allies: England, France, Russia, Belgium, Japan; Serbia and Montenegro, although in the conflict, are missing. "If they'd had separate flags, we'd have had them." Though in 1915 not yet born, Shine always says "We." "We had a window decorator won awards." The line of flags marching within, curving around the corner, and ending with a huge question mark, shows what the decorator must have had in mind. "We weren't in it yet," Shine said. "The war."

So the future is still in this shot, Zach thinks; then why does it look so stilted?

Bert, who has come up behind them, says to himself that the minute a print parts from the negative, Time, the silent assistant, is there at hand. He agrees with his grandmother: Death is the collaborator in every photograph. She doesn't fault them for that. "The life they show *was* glorious," she once said of the photographs on the mantel. "Even if the 'was' strikes to the heart."

"What I like," Shine says now softly, "is when you can put just one object in a window. We did it the first Armistice Day. One flag. The other Allies were there, but only in the back. Back then, the U.S. wasn't considered arrogant. Second World War we went a might fancier. Smashed pieces of a big swastika were still in the basement when I was a tot; I used to sit on them, until the iron was sent for scrap. Gratis, my stepfather told me much later. It had been a real one. They couldn't bear to profit by it.

The slide shows the warehouse entry, down the side street, through which the big parade floats emerged and returned for storage.

"We used to wheel in a float a couple of days before a parade. For Armistice Day, 1919, year after the peace treaty was signed, we hauled in an ambulance surrounded by the flags of both sides— that's when the plate-glass was first smashed. Did the same every

Memorial Day after, until the smashing stopped. We—" Shine
pauses, then says in a reedy voice, "They, the company, thought
they'd finally won the anti-war argument. But it was only that the
flag business had begun to fade. People no longer knew which flag
was which, my stepfather said. Not like they used to, same as they
knew popular songs. And the ambulance, a small French one, had
gone to rust."

Bert has listened deferentially to a plaint heard often. He marks
how Shine's account grows more accomplished with each telling.
The first time, after Shine's mother died, it had come out rough
and squeezed, yet pointing to something he could hang on to. As
Shine's stepfather had proved to be. And at the time Bert was being
squeezed too.

Zach, who has never heard this tale, is wondering traitorously
whether Shine, too, who so brazenly exploits his outsider lack of
niche, will unwittingly find one, becoming merely the man who
has lived to tell the tale. All the tales.

"This slide's for you, Zach," Shine says. "Don't bother to put it
in the projector; just hold it up to the light."

The light is soft, evenly shedding. Same building, same corner.
But in the window—"My God. How did you ever?"

"Better than an ambulance, huh? We stored it for Mendenhall
overnight. Due to be shipped back to Spain the next day, a garage
would have been iffy. My idea to put it in the window. 'Our new
Fund's location, why not,' I said. 'Maybe it could be our logo. I'll
take a shot of it. And you know what he said? He doesn't have that
nickname for nothing... 'Sure, why not,' he said. 'Flags are not
strictly for peace.' And the way he helped ease that thing into the
window. 'You been around cars?' I asked him. 'I race some,' he
said. 'Nothing fancy. I like to keep it dark.'... I liked him. He's a
man coming out of the dark. But what's he want with us?"

Zach leans over the slide. There it is in the window, bold as
brass. When he began restoring, the chassis had already been
painted over, more than once. The manual had named the colors

this model had once come in, but hadn't shown them. Finally he'd done what he yearned to: long brown fenders forging ahead, the chassis cream. "Hail and good-bye," Zach says to it. "Or I'll see you in Barcelona." He pockets the slide. "Thanks a million, Shine. Or a billion. Hey—he drove it, hah? Son of a gun."

"I took this shot the next morning. The sidewalk was already crowded, had to shoo them off. One little kid wouldn't shoo. So I let him stay."

And there the kid is, the back of him, looking up as if he had grown there and has decided to stay.

"Good omen," Zach says, wondering if Shine will ever have children. "Hey. Looka there."

Moorsohn is rising from his chair, hands braced on its arm, forearms trembling. A man of medium height, standing tall once on his feet, confronts them. Clockwise from his left, a circle of four: Gerald Duffy, Kitty his wife, Mrs. Alter, the husband.

"A miracle," Alter breathes at Moorsohn. In his business one has to hope for those, perhaps.

Two female noses in the middle, one tip-tilted, the other sloped, manage to agree. From the chairside, Dr. Elise, her mouth quirked, regards them, maybe reminded that not all females in the world are the same. Or maybe are? Shrugging off her coarse medical whites, a petite, ever-in-black Frenchwoman emerges. The folded jacket is slipped into her dun carryall. Neither doctor's bag nor mere purse, simply a *sac* large but not sloppy, it accommodates. Even to the gloves, not rubber, extracted from it, and the muffler she wraps around Moorsohn from behind.

Gerald hasn't moved a muscle. His face shows nothing, which is not its wont. If he's being consistent, his mother can't surmise how. To her Moorsohn is heroic, to her son perhaps only acting as a man should. And his "lady doctor" according to role?

"Lend me a hand," Moorsohn says to Gerald, in the clearest voice yet heard from him. "I must do this once a day." Gerald extends his arm.

The room watches. Once away, Moorsohn confides. "And before I'm stowed in that car. He means well, that chap. But his goodwill can be a monsoon."

At the window he stops to rest. They are alone in the bay; the crooners have gone. "Rooms like this, the periphery never ends; we could go round it forever. I knew it would be like this from Bert. A clan house. Elise's family house is the same, far too big for the three of us, but we'll stay for the old man's sake. He was invited to Israel for a death-camp survivor's honoring, and housing in case he would emigrate. He turned them down in five languages: French, German, English, Russian, and Hebrew. He's pissed that they are monopolizing the Holocaust. 'The Holocaust is like medicine,' he said. 'It belongs to the world.'"

Gerald grunts. "My son Bert says I'm like a convert to Judaism. Like I got it twice as hard as natural. Did you tell him that?"

"As a convert myself I would have, if he'd asked." Moorsohn squints at Gerald. "But I suggest your sons want to maneuver for destiny on their own."

"The same double-talk I get on a bonus from my wife's shrink. Like—my sons, they're not the ones rejecting; I am?"

Outside the window the street is both lambent and murky, in that dusk beyond dusk, light before evening, not yet wholly nightfall, for which some absolute term should be coined. Moorsohn's collar bandage shows ghostly white. A man wearing that may perhaps speak more freely. "Bert brought your son Byron to class, to show off his artifacts. We were discussing the sea versus the desert in biblical lore. He said he was named Byron—picked as neutral, neither too Irish nor too Jewish. But for him the poet's swimming the Hellespont was a sign."

"That's just like him."

"And when Bert was out of hearing, your other son said, 'My father should have been the rabbi. Not Bert.'"

A blurt. "He got that joke from our rabbi. When Bert was ordained. The one time By went to temple."

"A good word, temple. Biblical. But not on par with synagogue."

This time Gerald stops. "Excuse, professor. *You*—are telling a Jew how to be a Jew?"

"A Jewish characteristic. I try to oblige." Moorsohn, leaning against the wainscoting, seems glad to rest.

"But with not one drop of the blood—maybe from a grandmother, let's say?"

"In Caithness, Scotland? Not likely. But a county very semitic in style. Rigorous coastline, yet plenteous fish. No trees to speak of. My idol was Thomas Carlyle, because he'd walked to Edinburgh, to attend university. I didn't; my folks weighed the cost of shoe leather. And in time he became too German for me . . . But Elise did walk, if not so far. Because even after Vichy, and suing for the house to be returned to them, though her mother could not be, some of her schoolmates disdained to ride with her. . . . We met when I fell ill on a lecture visit in Cairo, and the deputy ambassador's sister-in-law, with the same trouble, advised me to go to Tel Aviv to a specialist there. That lady too is still alive. . . . Why do you smile?"

"Lady. Girl." Gerald says. "My sons kid me. You are supposed to say 'woman' now."

"Two fine sons. They will keep you abreast."

"Three."

"Three? Bert has never said."

"My oldest. Put himself through school because he disapproved of how I made money. Left years ago; Bert would scarcely know him. Or By . . . Jacob Ezekiel. Named for my wife's father, little guy I liked—she'd been the apple of their eye. The little grandparents—they were both tiny—they called the boy Jakie. My wife had a fit; she called him James . . . I hear on the Street he's in oil. North Sea Operations, managing for private interests; his cut must be in the millions. His brothers say he won't communicate because he doesn't want to eat crow. I say that kind of crow I could take—and wouldn't he know that? Once a year, Christmas, a present, nothing personal, a secretary must pick—I always respond. 'James,' I wrote, 'you're our colonial.' But he hasn't written back."

"I'm supposed to go on walking—" Moorsohn says. "But right now I have to sit."

They sit on a long overstuffed sofa, flanked by matching armchairs, a plump seating common in the ads but the only of its kind here. One sinks down, beyond comfort, to a persuasion of what those ads pose comfort to be.

"When I was a lad—" Moorsohn says, "pardon, a boy, the houses where there was time for indolence were considered aristocrats, whether or not born to it. Time for ideas—though it would turn out it wasn't always the aristocrats who had those. In Edinburgh there were Jews; I fell in with a couple of their students. Poor as me, their household still had that Jewish tolerance of ideas, even could be cursed with it, a peculiarity that they themselves scanted in favor of getting on in the world. I thought it was because they lived by the book—theirs. Yet at Caithness, so had we— by our dour, once-over-quickly church services that we'd have felt it vanity to stretch, as did the Anglicans. My two Jews, Aaron Levey and Isaac Fitzmorris if you please, hooted at me for romanticizing them: 'Comes of our not being admitted, or worse,' they said, 'this messy innerness you call "ideas."' They never said 'persecuted'— that whiny word we Christians loved . . . And indeed the ideas do come in part from the bitterness. Though not the full spirit. 'We can be as hearty as any of you,' they boasted to me—and I could see that with all my talk of what I found at their house beside the hospitality, their touchiness believed I was putting them down for it . . . Yet their hospitality kept on; that was their pride . . . And the pride, that was part of it all too. Food and ideas—one pride excuses another . . . and that's the quality of the true Jewish household, kosher or not. When I eat the bitter herb at the feast I always think of it. And when I converted, that's what I converted to—not their God." Moorsohn tugs at his bandage, then stops himself, the way a person stops scratching. "That's what your Bert may learn for himself. Must. I can't tell him so. Not in a seminary." He smooths the pillowy sofa engulfing them. "Are we sinking? I'm not sure I can get up from this . . . Or want to. Though I apologize, for the talk."

"Don't," Gerald says without thinking, "you were only praying. I mean—just saying that prayer."

They sit, in sudden awe of each other. Of having found each other.

"How did you make your money?"

"The stock market . . . And you—what do you lecture on?"

"Philosophy. Nearest I could get to religion, at the time. Nearest a lot who stop there can allow themselves."

They smile. At what, neither would be able to say.

"This suite," Gerald says, patting the sofa. "The family—some of them—banded together to give it to my mother. Because our chairs were too bony. And there weren't enough of them. My father said that only bores would sit here. And for a while that was true. Then the suite melded in, like everything else." He glances down the room, checking. The men have bunched together. Kitty is talking to Mrs. Alter. "Like even the Alters meld, those two. Like even them."

"Some Jews are said to escape the touchiness. Or conquer it. Elise says not. It just goes down deeper—and shows itself by class; she has a whole scale for it. The Alters, they'd be just 'thick'—she uses the English for it. 'They'll see insult in every incident, or not at all.' At the top of her scale are the *elegantes,* who either fall short of so-called Jewish characteristics or else work at it losing those. 'With them, the fear of being tapped as merely Jews or really Jews escapes through the scalp,' she says, 'lingering in the air like a fine hairspray.' The main loss of body heat being through the head . . . In the middle are the too-loud ones—who never stop telling you what they are.'"

Gerald, after a marveling headshake, says, "I think my touchiness is Irish—I think."

They both laugh. After which Gerald is able to say easily, "My father was the scholar, Peter Duffy."

"Oh? What was his line?"

"You'll have to ask Bert that. I was never—up to it."

When it appears that Bert has never mentioned his grandfather, even that Moorsohn, oh so apologetically, has never heard of him, Gerald is freed to wonder aloud what he often has in private. "What would it have been like, I wonder? To grow up without everybody knowing—the people who were 'everybody' to us—who my father was."

Moorsohn's reply is slow—and when it comes, cautious. "Like maybe—the same as it would have been, might have been, for your son?"

This sofa muffles, Gerald thinks. Nothing detonates. Instead you see what you see. Saw. In the long baseball afternoons. Or that last time Kitty let her parents come up from Florida. *Zeke, Zeke,* it went—and from their daughter, *James, James.* And the poor culprit, the little tailor grandfather—for the blame was his surely—staring from his corner at his namesake and replica, nose for big nose, height for probable height. For Jacob Ezekiel, already sixteen and fuzzed on his upper lip, could still fit into his last Little League uniform. "Ah, look at the two of them," Gerald's mother-in-law said, gazing with the fondness of a lifetime at her little tailor husband. "Look, Fegeleh—excuse me, Kitty—your Zeke is my Zeke all over again."

"It wasn't the money." Gerald's voice is bright with declaration. "It wasn't the money he was running from. It was the way he looked. His size. Next to his tall, handsome—and younger—brothers. If he'd waited around, he'd have seen other Duffy grandchildren to come. My siblings' bunch, in all sizes. And colors. But he didn't wait around. He did remind many of my younger brother, who was also shorter than the rest of us, though not that small." And had had the same quick wit. Mickey hadn't waited around either. "But that brother had died. And hadn't the same hair." That Brillo which Zipporah says must have sneaked in from the Pharaohs, that Jews sometimes share with the blacks. Who can get stomped for it also, by their own kin. Their own mothers. Though never by Zipporah.

"He was a ringer for my father-in-law, except for one instance. Maybe he felt that our genes, mine, were playing the fool with him. My father-in-law, whose physique was almost tiny, had a bush of hair black as the ace of spades and almost the same shape, and seemingly one third his height." Gerald pauses to swallow. "He wore it like a helmet. Under it, a nice ordinary face, but with a quality expression. My son—well, maybe he would grow up to that. Meanwhile the size, and that bush, which sprang back from any haircut. But it was blond."

He sees Moorsohn's eyes close. "Ah, I'm a bore."

"Not at all. I am seeing him. The classic 'little Jew.'"

"Shall we move on, then?"

"Complete my periphery? Right." Moorsohn is about to get up when Kitty sweeps past them, motioning to Gerald that she is going to the bathroom. Then detours back to them, hesitantly. "Dr. Moorsohn...I just found out who you are. Last winter I played bridge with two rabbis, from your seminary."

"Those two? You must play champion bridge."

She nods. "But I could take pointers from them. Real sharks."

"It's rumored they are revising the Prophets, according to the laws of chance. We tremble every time they open their mouths... Who won?"

She leans forward, the purse that Gerald will check before they leave swinging on a shoulder. The face was "quality" once. There is now that imbalance which occurs when the ethnic has been interfered with—so that one glimpses the animal. "We tied."

"Bravo."

"But that's not what I came to tell *you*, Gerry—Zipporah's about to open the linen closet; I'm so excited. It hasn't ever been emptied. They keep the regular linens in a cupboard off the kitchen for convenience; Jennie started that. For years, that real linen closet, it hasn't even been used."

Gerald has the languid male response to such talk. Then he remembers his role. "That closet? Dumped at last? What do you know?" He pats Kitty's cheek. "Don't worry. I'm sure she'll give you plenty. I'll be back in a minute there. Just want to—" He gestures toward the hall. "And here's your wife coming for you, Moorsohn." Gerald heads off to the left, presumably to another bathroom, she to the right.

The doctor looks with distaste at the pillows in which Moorsohn is ensconced, but does not assist him. Once he is in the chair, she says: "Our benefactor phoned. A thousand apologies for the delay, but he has to find the driver. His 'manager,' he called him, remember? One can't think for what, unless for business. I don't see anyone managing that man—except possibly a woman. . . . Why doesn't he just drive us himself?"

"The parking, *cherie.* Anything that happens in New York, in the whole U.S.—murder, bank robbery, divorce—you just say 'the parking'—and it is at once explained."

"Oh la la." Expertly parting the front of his bandage, she examines his throat.

"I will survive."

"Ah, *oui.*" Swiftly she recloses the bandage.

"*Ah, oui.*" His tone is precisely hers. "But let me rest a second. Don't move the chair." She obliges.

"I am looking forward to Papa," he says.

"*Moi aussi* . . . And I am thinking . . . you would not believe what I am thinking."

"Of the hospital."

"*Non.*"

"Of—how we did not have children."

"Not quite."

"What then?'

"Of how Madame's linen could be like my mother's—before the Nazis."

"Elise, ah Elise. So stay for this—auction?"

"Madame would not do that. I watch. She is very *compliqué, non?* I think she does not know how *compliqué.*"

"None of them do here. It's what Jews get, for turning into Americans."

"*En avant,*" she says, in the voice he hears each time he goes into surgery, just after the injection that will put him under. "Layt's go."

So engaged, they haven't noticed until now the Gerald Duffys, met together again at the door from the hall. The Moorsohns' salute is ignored.

"No one goes off to the toilet here without embarrassment," he says as she rolls him along. "And some lame excuse. Even in Caithness, we took it for granted. Is it the animal in them they can't get used to? Or being really civilized?"

"You will lecture about it."

"*Entendu.* On how the toilet-shame connects with the bomb-shame. And of course the sex. One does it, but must deplore . . . They would eat that up here. They love shit-*analyse.* Not so in Aix."

"Of course not," she says. "We have the bidet."

When the Moorsohns rejoin the others, Shine whispers to Bert: "Look at them. Enter laughing—that's their credo? Anything I grudged him—I take it back."

At the door from the hall Gerald waits, as his wife, who must always prepare for scrutiny, pats her hair, sets to swinging her shoulderbag. The left shoulder always, the hand curled protectively beneath.

"Kitty, what's that in your left hand?"

Already she has shrunk from him. "Something I picked up from the floor. I swear to you."

"Give it here.

The hand uncurls.

"The mezuzah. My God."

"I couldn't have," she says. "Done what you think. It was always hung up high, over the molding. How could I? . . . I found it on the floor."

"It's wet," he says.

"I washed it. It had blood on it."

"Bl—?"

"Slimed on it. Like somebody wanted to. Who knows what

riffraff they let in." Delving in her bag she passes him a Kleenex. "That doctor you sent me to, he says I have to get in touch with my own violence. Diplomas on his wall from Connecticut, Albany, and—*mach Shabbas gemit*—a certificate from Mt. Sinai Hospital. What does he know from violence? Maybe they should send me to a woman?"

"*Mach*—what does that mean again?"

"'So make a holiday of it'... The parents never spoke Yid to me. Only to themselves. A potential for the Academy of Dramatic Arts shouldn't have such an accent. But I didn't get in anyway. So maybe I had it."

"My father hung this, Kitty. And told us what was in it. He spoke beautiful Hebrew."

"I know. Everybody in Duffyland knows that story," she says. "Maybe next time get somebody who knows Yiddish to hang it."

When Gerald first brought Kitty to the house his father had said, "Beautiful. And with a tongue. The Queen of Sheba. Only she's not sure of it." Gerald's younger sisters, Erika and Nell, who communicated in a needling back-and-forth to which their own carcasses were immune, were instructed to lay off, to be kind to Kitty's pretentions. Even to mull them, Peter said, for the social keenness they might contain. "The Grand Concourse," to which the tailor had recently moved them, "may indeed be the Fifth Avenue of the Bronx... But she's not sure that West End Avenue should be their next move—she said maybe it's only the Grand Concourse of Manhattan."

Shortly, as Kitty veered off into her spiral of non-Jewishness, the family, not finding that worthy of resentment, had merely adopted old Nettie's shrugged judgment: "A loose connection, that girl." Meaning both that Kitty was zany, and didn't count? Gerald's religious zeal had amused them on other scores. "He looks too Irish for it," Cousin Eustace had decreed. Byron's actual life had eluded them all, even Gerald, under the general umbrella of hippiedom—and the diving profession. Too weird, for either a middle-class boy or an East Coast one.

... And if Bertram the good hero, the clan whispers, comes out of all this (if as yet unsettled as to his mission, and light-handed with the princesses so far offered him), then consult the folklore ...

"Duffyland?" Gerald says. He has put the mezuzah in his pocket.

"Lucas's name for us." She is looking at the pocket. "Maybe Lucas could hang that thing. Or the family could lend it to him and By. To start their new life."

"Lucas is Italian."

"The Italians don't have Jews? Even Jews who cross themselves—he says it's a national habit ... Everybody has Jews ... No wonder they get sick of us."

"Go to your auction." But he knows he will follow her.

Meanwhile, downstairs in the lobby, Lester the doorman is admitting that pair again, the very big man and the smaller one, owner and driver respectively of that health-car. A Mutt and Jeff, as he would term them. He nicknames much of the human traffic he must deal with, as a way of keeping tabs on his multiple responsibilities: door, house telephone, tenant identity. Also child care (whether or not the parents are aware), doorside chats with the housemaids who seek advice on their romances—all these merely a pennyworth of what has to be kept in mind.

This pair had let him examine the vehicle, an account of which will be the centerpiece at his own family table. "Almost as many of us as you Duffys," he has teased Zipporah over the years. She and he have what he calls "one of my best working relationships." And some late night, nobody but them in the lobby, he will tell her all of this.

To the vehicle, after standing rapt, he'd said: "Custom job, are you baby. Nothing like it." His own uniform is that, and in sweetness of fit and fine woolen, fully equal to what the two men wear, though the big man has been careless about made-to-measure. The small man wants not to be dandified. One can see this by the common cut of his blazer and trousers.

"A Mutt and a Jeff they were," he tells his own dinner table that night. "Like in that old cartoon, the tall one being the Mutt. He's the one who tips." And plenty, but not with an air. A somebody, but not in any of the magazines. Lester has the house porters save him from the trash.

"It was the young one I was sure I'd seen before. Gave him the test—put him back in knee pants and with past-and-gone families, but no dice. Anyways, my old kids, they come back grown, they sing out. And we gas. So I figure he never lived in the house. But my eye tells me he must have came.

"Just today again, they delivered a wheelchair person. I was on my break then, but I was there when they come back, before I go off at nine. The little guy wanted to stay in the car, not go upstairs, but the Mutt was insisting. They weren't loud but it was serious—and I felt it was my duty to overhear." (Laughter from Lester's home table.)

"'No, you promised, Jeremy,' the Mutt says. He doesn't really look like a Mutt; he's smooth and I gather he's the boss. So the small guy is Jeremy; I've never had one of those. He does have a Jeff attitude, cocky but a kind of resentment, lordly to a six-footer like me, and especially doormen. 'No, I'll do it someday. Change back. But on my own. I have to live my own life,' he says. And the other one says, 'Aren't you? Head of our North Sea Operations, a big man in your own right?' He shouldn't have said big—but maybe hasn't much people experience."

(A mutter from the table, and a shush.)

"'You stay away from your own kin too long, Jeremy, you'll never get back to them,' the big guy says. 'Yet you don't go for any other. Live in Dolphin Square, when you could afford a real place—I'm not pushing a mansion, I wouldn't push at all, Jeremy, but I know what it's like, to live under an alias. When you choose it yourself, that may be different. But not that much. You're not much past thirty, Jeremy, you could end up a freak.'

"The other says, 'Half my family already are,' and the big guy: 'Sure, but not in hiding,' and the Jeff says, 'You can hide right out in public these days. Haven't you?'...

"And I think, me, Lester: he says that to a boss, the big man'll hit him, but the boss only goes sad...I could work for a guy like that. No wonder this Jeremy is affected. And that leads me to what I wasn't sure. That little guy, his head's been—not shaved like a punk, but close to it, and not yet grown out. The Mutt's—an older man—don't show it so much but it's longer, maybe he got out sooner?

"They been in jail, folks, that's it," Lester says. "And not small-time, not safe-crackers or even con men—what is a 'North Sea Operation'? So should I let them upstairs, like last time? The Duffys been there since Methuselah, the Missus a Jew, the Mister as Irish as Maureen here, but he didn't seem to mind...Like I don't mind an off-island daughter-in-law, long as she'll listen to me." Lester smiles at her.

"And the parties those Duffys have had. Even a parcel of bare-foots once, from Africa. But no more trouble than those creeps we have in the penthouse; she goes after him regular with a shiv; the blood to the ambulance twice ruined the elevator carpet; management hints maybe next time go slow on the ambulance call, let him bleed upstairs. Or the pot in 14G—you got to call the firemen, even if they break down the door and are too quick on the draw with the water hoses; smoke is smoke...

"But then the little Jeff, he says, 'The guy we're picking up, a convert. Isn't he in hiding?' And the Mutt says, 'If you were in that sort of hiding—would I carp?' And the Jeff says, 'Those head-hunters who found me for the post at North so quick, you must have had me on your agenda, I'm no fool.'... Those were his exact words, but to be sure, I scribbled them on my pad. Which I do ever since that police case I was involved... And the big guy, he's sharp, he sees me writing, he says, 'You won't need the license number for the cops; I've a mechanic in the car, he'll circle the block if we have to.' And to the other guy he says, 'Your name came up as a prospect. Once I saw the name-change, who you really were, I picked you, yes. But I wouldn't of hired you unless you were tops.'

"All the time of course, I'm letting other people in the door, packages, you know. So I don't hear consecutive; I don't have ears in the back of my head, no matter what you boys think. So I miss some. But maybe they need a push. So I say, 'Shall I announce you, sir?' to the big guy. And they look at each other, those two. Then the big guy grunts, 'I'm bringing you back here, you're bringing me in. We're each other's excuse.' And the Jeff says, 'You're giving them money. Why else would you be here?' And the Mutt says— now listen to this—he says, 'It has to do with a mongoose.'. . . And the little guy—he says . . . he says . . . like in such a voice, 'Ours?'

"And I'm looking at what the big guy all along's been hanging onto. A metal box, screening at the top; there would be air; there could be a small animal in it. I've known cats to be that quiet, even dogs. I don't know what a mongoose would fit, but I know it's an animal, and not a common pet-shop one. So I say, 'Sorry sir, but no animals allowed. Except domestic. We had a monkey once, got out. And the Cushmans, he's that scientist; they had to get rid of their snakes. He sued, but they had to. Sorry sir, but it's house rules.'. . . But then I weaken."

There is a snort from the table. To which Lester says, "Okay, so he's a tipper, the kind that might even come across with a grand, like that mob guy I didn't accept. But I have you boys' education to consider. One of you could be a super. It's not pie-in-the-sky anymore."

They stare back at him; they know the score. Supers have to take courses for it now; he's made them do that. "Building engineers," they're called now—and that they can do. But the hierarchy is still on hold. From way back, supers are Irish or German; it can go from father to son, yes, and often has. Mere house staff is going more and more to the spics. And there have long been some from the Islands—like them. But a super, call him whatever, has to re-side in the house. And like a tenant, not in the basement anymore. His kids would even ride the elevator—he has to be white. And with Maureen being wife of the middle son, Frederic—their father dreams too hard over what having an Irish daughter-in-law might do for them. She and Fred, who met at N.Y.U., are taking courses that have nothing to do with building management. But the old man has brought them where they are. The least they can do is to listen to him—maybe even learn how to dream?

So when he says, "As you all know—and I've brought you up to know—I only weaken so far," there's a kind of Amen murmur from the table.

"So I say to the man—if he wants he can leave that cage in the package room for while he's upstairs; I'll watch."

"Oh Les," his wife moans, "sometimes you do dangerous." But they both grin. She's only waiting to see how much of the tips she can snag from him. And he only regales them with first-class stories, the ones that work out.

"So the Jeremy guy—he's been like as gloomy as at a funeral— he all of a sudden laughs. It lights him up; he's not a bad little egg. 'So show the man,' he says. 'So go on, F. D. Show him your little pets.'

"F. D.—I'm thinking. That's corporation lingo. Do I know any-body in the mags with that moniker? I don't. What I do see is this Jeremy looks up to him like a father. And I don't blame him. I'm seeing the big guy, the way he was with the wheelchair patient, and that hell-of-a-nuisance car. And I'm thinking how the supers here, the watchamacallem. 'building engineers,' except for one stinker, I always get along with them. But it's not like having a real boss, where you're on your own.

"So the big guy—I'm not calling him Mutt anymore—he opens the box. And in it—well, what I've seen delivered in there in my time come from the best in the city, and fit for a queen. But I never seen orchids like those.

"'Ga-ahn,' I say. It's the old island way, come back on me. 'Fancy those won't bite.'

" 'They almost will.' he says. 'If you don't pay them mind.' He
closes the box like he's tucking them in. Then he looks at his watch.
'I'll just go and see if the garageman's had his supper.'

"When he's gone the little guy says to me, 'He drove back a
hundred miles to get them, because I'd forgotten to put them in.
He said orchids were like women, you couldn't desert them. Never
said a word of reproach to me.'. . . Funny little skink, the way his
front changed; kind of a likeness to that Duffy boy died.

"When the big guy comes back is when he tips me. (I already
been to the bank, Fiona, hah ha . . .) When I thank him he says,
'Thank *you*, Lester. I hear from my friend here you're quite a character.' How'd he know my name so quick? I say, 'You'd make a jolly
good doorman, you ever buckled down to it.'

"Just then the house phone—they seen the vehicle from the
front window. They have something going on a little longer, but
whoever's manning the car is welcome to bide a bit. It's Mrs. Duffy.
I look at those orchids. She don't need my approval, but she has it.
'Hold on,' I say. I give those two the message. The little guy says,
'Maybe I should ask Lester here. Whether I should go upstairs.'

"And I'm thinking he's got to be one of my kids, he's in the
range. But I get no impression. And who'd know if he belonged
here better than him hisself?"

At Lester's home table he gives a tired shake over what he must
report, but doesn't quite know the meaning of. Such gaps are why
he's only a doorman, with an agile brain bent on the details of
what surely expands in the upstairs regions of the house, but remains outside his ken. Still, his audience is listening, as if they too
are pondering hard, and will put their education to work on it.

"So the big one, F. D., he says soft, 'Jeremy Durfee. You want
them to recognize you? Or not? Nobody else can help you decide
that. But if you don't go upstairs now, you'll never know. . . . As for
me—I release you,' he says. Just like that. And he lifts the orchid
box. 'I come this far. I'll deliver these,' he says. 'And I should do it
on my own.'

"Meanwhile the house phone is squawking in my ear. 'I gotta

answer this,' I say. Time and again, people downstairs not sure
what'll happen upstairs; I get the nod—or the no-no. This time it's
the nod; first the big guy, the tipper, then the other one. 'Name?' I
say. But they wave it off. 'Coming up,' I say. 'Coming right up.'"

The linen closet, alone in its short passageway, is in the east center
of the apartment. All these years, going to and fro, she's subconsciously acknowledged it. Inside there, the past of her family
gently recedes.

When the group gathers there, Kitty is out front. Gerald's arm
is around her from behind; Dr. Elise, standing oddly away from her
charge, is blocking the chair's view. The Alters are rooted in their
inability to leave. Shine's the farthest away; distance is precious to
him. Bert hovers to one side.

Zipporah unlocks. Revealing merely linen inside there, neatly
piled, kept almost dustless over years of housewifery. Yet as she
opens the door, the present is falling in fragments, each of those in
front to be allotted the shard that is due.

Kitty, grabbing, at first held back by Gerald's arms, finds her
long fingers clasped by Zipporah's.

"I'm not sure where the banquet cloth has got to, maybe way in
the back. You look, dear." She has never before called Kitty "dear."

As Kitty burrows, her frilled cuffs breasting like a swimmer's, a
dry aura spreads toward them, the odor of the domestic order of
things, coming to the fore.

From what used to be called "the household gods," Zipporah thinks,
watching her, noting each of the persons standing at her own elbows. *All of us like figures ready to be turned to stone by some doom we
expect. It's greed, yes, but for what destiny? For the signs and markings of
that slow unreported life at the center of things?*

Kitty, deep in the lowest shelf, is pulling forward a white
weight, swathed in tissue paper. *Never put in anything else,* the early
voices remind. Oilskin would yellow them. "Plastic," that world of
wrappings and substitutes, being yet uncreated.

"Ah-h-h!" Kitty cries, palms pressed together in prayer, staring at what she's clawed free. "There are two of them. Two of them." Reverently, in a two-handed rhythm, she begins to unfold one of the cloths. Far too long for one person's armspread, the cloth confounds with a will of its own. Her chin set like a contender's, she seizes the cloth by two of its corners, pulling it toward her. "Here." She thrusts a corner at Mrs. Alter. "You boys take the other two corners." Shine and Bert obediently come forward. "I'll pull it out carefully," Kitty commands. "You two catch." Once managed, the four stand gawkily, the cloth taut between them. As if ready to catch someone, Zipporah thinks—an angel maybe, or at least an ancestor.

"I know that cloth by heart," she says. "My mother used to show me. Stored linen needs to be refolded now and then; I'm afraid I haven't kept up the obligation." Indeed, it has creased. "The linen's heavy, but I never thought it fine enough for all the work expended on it. Sometimes more than one person worked on one of these, doing the scalloping, the buttonholing, the fringe, and so on. But my mother's mother's is hers alone. Is that the one? It had insertions on it—they bought those ready made. Lace— with a Greek-helmeted woman in profile, embroidered on it."

Kitty leans forward. "This is it."

"Thing is—" Zipporah is trying to be matter-of-fact. "My mother used it as a grand bedspread once or twice, for some occasion. I doubt she ever could have borne to expose it to food. Even if we'd had banquets." She wants to make light of this, to modulate Kitty without making fun of her. The four of them holding up the cloth look as if they are about to folk dance. Yet this ceremony is somehow not ridiculous.

"Bedspreads." Dr. Elise's voice is a groan. "Ma mère. That is how she and her friends use. But they buy in the village, they do not make for themselves. She buys one for me. For my how you say—for dot—my marriage."

"Dowry," Zipporah says low.

"The young men—they are gone. I have no fiancé. But she

buys one anyway for me. Lets everyone know. So when I am sent to England like for a visit, but to be safe *actuellement,* they think I will come back. So I did."

"And then the Nazis," Moorsohn says from behind her. "And to the camps. Her father survived. Doctors were used. He's never said how. Until now."

"Surgery," Dr. Elise says. "Yet he is not a surgeon."

"But Elise will take care of him," Moorsohn says. "Her mother—whom she never saw again—would expect her to." He looks over at Bert. "That's why I'm leaving the seminary, Bertram." He touches his bandage. "Not because of this... To go home with her. To help my wife take care of that old—reprobate. In that long-lost house. The people who occupied it?—A large family, and related to the church; he could never get it back from them. But he has survived even them."

Kitty's restive, even sullen. The weight of her Jewishness is so intertwined with her ego that she cannot tell which is which. In the lingo of her doctor she has "internalized" it—as if everything mental is not.

"Fold up your cloth, Kitty," Zipporah says. With the wickedness that her daughters-in-law inspire in her, she adds the shortened locution that New Yorkers have adopted from the immigrants. "Enjoy." But Kitty is already head-deep in the closet, scrabbling for the second cloth.

Billowing around her it emerges, seized one to a corner by the obedient Mrs. Alter now beaming with social duty; by Bertram, to whom any family role or chore is nourishment; and by the wry observer Shine.

This cloth is yellower than the other, perhaps from storage farther back in an airless cupboard. Or perhaps it is older. Kept too long from human admiration it has jaundiced, as old fabrics do. If it were silk it might have rotted like flesh, in the sympathy that silk has. But no, it is linen, coarser than the finest, not royal, but spun from a wheel in some human corner. Of Europe undoubtedly, as all the good household linens of its era were.

Dr. Elise, her crumpled medical smock held on one arm, is regarding it. Done for some young woman's dowry, it may have striven to be unique, but it will have the same stitches, the little scattered dots each made by winding the thread round and round the needle's point before plunging in. And whether the lace insertions were fabricated in Belgium, France, or Germany before being imported to America, or whether the inserts bear helmeted Athenas or cupidlike angels, the cloth's message—"This marks and sanctions the riches of a household"—will be the same. Whether the young woman in question was a Christian or a Jew.

"Dr. Elise...please accept this one? In—" *In place of the lost one?* Just in time Zipporah saves herself. "As a—token from us." Not a remembrance; one can't mention that. "A parting gift."

Dr. Elise steps forward to the cloth now held for her by two men and two women, for Kitty, in a rush of benevolence, has seized one of the corners held by Mrs. Alter. She holds it up higher than the others—as a custodian.

Bent over the cloth's center, the doctor's figure is shorn of its French style. One sees only the hump of shoulder and neck, hears the heaving, sees the dumpling cheek shake. If the pattern of the cloth isn't the same as others, perhaps its power is that it can't be. Or that its folds billow with the air that the mother in the camp was denied. The gut noise rasping from the doctor, not a sob, is nameless.

Moorsohn starts up from the chair. "She never—"

"Let me." Pressing Moorsohn back in his wheelchair, Zipporah grasps the doctor from behind, the way one holds a vomiting child. As the dry gasps ebb, the body in Zipporah's arms relaxes. Zipporah looks up at the men in the room, numbering them—Gerald, Alter, Zach, the two younger men who still grasp that cloth. What are they thinking—what can they think?—of this display? Of these acts allotted to the household and its goods, flowing thousandfold between the birth sheet and the winding sheet, meant for the duties of the bed only, or the table. What do men think of the embroideries of women?

She's forgotten her call downstairs to the doorman, made out of worry at how exhausted Moorsohn must be. Interest appears to sustain him. Plus his addiction to what he can find of the godly in ordinary life. Dr. Weil's medical method smacks of a religious nature also. Zipporah, helping Gerald to settle the doctor in a chair, is admitting to herself what her own sector of the century barely concedes—that religion is more than opium.

Dr. Weil, once calmed and seated, will not apologize. Rather, with a hint of the old Talmudic habit, she will explain. "I saw her, you see. Gassed, but still breathing. Under the sheet they bundled the bodies in. If they bothered to. I saw the breath puff. But I could not operate."

She's fighting her own breathing. The wheelchair moves to her. They clasp hands. Gerald and Zipporah still hover. Regaining her breath, the doctor says to him: "What's that in your hand? Ah." A small object to dedicate what it does, but she's used to them. "A mezuzah?"

Gerald looks down with some surprise; he must have forgotten he was holding it. "Take it—" he says to Elise Weil. "Hang it in the new, old house." Mute, she returns it. Looking past her, he catches his mother's glance. "It fell," he says. His glance flickers at Kitty, who, commandeering the four pairs of hands again, is making them stretch the cloths one over the other, comparing for size. He coughs. "And I was planning on stealing it."

Zachary, motioning to Elise that he'll relieve her of handling the chair, is standing ready behind it. Moorsohn and Elise are softly exchanging. One might think her the patient, him the doctor.

Zach is staring at his mother. She's looking at Gerald, with love.

Two men walk into this tableau.

The tall man is expecting one of those rooms full of intramural chat, grave or cozy, fed by frequent meetings, close ties of blood, and the staginess of back history. He knows whatever is publicly accessible on this family. From his day with Zipporah he has imagined little more. To fabricate around the exploits of such a woman would be useless. He dares to hope that he will hear of those gradually, sifting through future days. He's glad she has had children. His own wife, the heiress, born into a ruling enclave, had had theirs almost impersonally.

Otherwise, he's lived with women who, whether willingly or not, had been childless. He knows the limits this imposes, both on physicality and ego. Or the excesses. That gothic swelling of the imagination, into witch-dreams that can smear any perceived corner of mortal action with the blood they themselves have not expended in giving birth. That he himself had once refused a lover a child has been his own anti-mortal stinginess. He knows his own limits like a terrain which with effort can be extended into ordinary range, watered where dry. Such blooms as may come of that are his personal money—earned.

From the habit of dispensing, he has learned also. A big man, he doesn't loom. Though not what the lingo calls "withdrawn," he stands to one side, ready when needed.

The short, younger man is so focused that at first one can't tear one's attention from him. His intensity is like glue. And like glue, irritates. His trouble, as familiar to him as a pool swum in daily, is that he can't separate the uneasiness he causes others from his own. Yet out of this he can often make whimsy as endearing as a Charlie Chaplin's splayed feet. The women he most satisfies tend to be charmers themselves, but he cannot long tolerate these duets. Rather than abandon, he drifts. Work is his constancy, his drug.

He anticipates this room they're about to enter the way a former acolyte recalls his Bible. In those days, old stagers here would remark on his resemblance—"except for the hair"—to Mickey, his grandmother's youngest—to him an odd uncle, permanently age twelve. To exist in her aura, if only to observe, had put life at home in perspective; he had never hoped for more. As the eldest he'd borne that brunt. Bert, who as Gerald and Kitty's youngest might have slid by, but instead had knuckled down as the family go-between, still has his love.

He tremors with respect for this man who's brought him back here—the only one who could have done so. Not only because he happens to have discovered that Jeremy Durfee was once Jacob Ezekiel Duffy—in this volatile world of acronyms, slogans, and personals shouted in drumbeat, surely no big deal. Yet he's so interested, this boss whom both a Durfee and a Duffy can admire for the way he accedes to his lot in life, yet does not. Most of all, Jeremy is here because this man, who should need no excuse to stop by here, seems to require one.

For himself, why had he demurred at coming upstairs? Or has all these years kept away? The fracas at home had indeed become unbearable; this had unquestionably helped him to leave. But to abscond as well, from what? That's always been the question. Near to agony once, now close to tiresome. Certainly he has dealt with that confusion, if not solved it. He is weary of it, and too canny to engage with it once again. But now he is here and the question is the same: Will I be recognized or will I not be? But as what? Smart? Ugly? Jewish? Legitimate or bastard? Classy or cheap?

He is five feet three inches, in a nation where, thanks to diet, plus a brash mixing of genes and the inherited pomp of being American, the males verge toward six feet or more, and some of the women also—and in his own family of two brothers and a father, this is the case. Farther off in the clan it's much the same; his Uncle Charles, the giant, is six foot five. Since he himself came to puberty and full stop, this table of measurements has been ever with him. On the clan's Sundays, an invisible tape measure had run above the assembled heads, his father's own parents presiding, that kingly pair.

Into this happy assimilation his mother's parents had briefly been inserted. "A sweet little couple," as the clan dubbed them, the male the epitome of "little Jew," with tightly curled Phoenician grizzle, the female emitting "Fegeleh-Kitty" like an unhappy bird.

To the clan's credit, it had disapproved of their later exile. Gerald, his father, not protesting, had for a while lost face. But the virtue of a clan is that, sooner or later, "There was once a little something" is said of most everyone—and that too is the tie that binds.

No one knew that his mother had once taken him to Harlem to have his hair straightened. The first beauty parlor had refused, alleging the process wouldn't work for whiteys—or they wouldn't? The second, a salon that did actors, had obliged. But only the little pair, his grandparents, had noted his lank pompadour, ascribing it to the diving, at which his little grandfather also excelled. "That pool, it has chemicals? But why only for the boy?"

He had fled to London, finishing his degree at a Polytech, where his fancy prior schooling made him a star. The colonial polyglot of the students—Paki, Yid, Cypriot, West African, Cockney shrimps to grammar-school dropouts gone punk—had elevated him to a temporary norm. He had got a good job almost at once, his study specialty being oil, just at the time when Britain was elated by its North Sea oil wealth.

He now pays his tailor as much as some Americans pay a therapist. To this expert man, a paragon of sartorial sympathy—and of course, Savile Row lore—he had said: "Just see that I don't look as if I want to be Napoleon."

The woman who has been as steady as any in his life is a long-legged demi-blonde beauty born of a county family of whom she says, "We run to rotters." She herself had served a year's sentence in Holloway prison for forging checks. She had since progressed from croupier to manageress-with-a-share in a chic gambling club he now and then frequents, where the stakes are not always large but a certified bank balance of some million pounds sterling is required. "You and I match, Jerry love," she's said, lying beside him and stretching to a length which exceeds his both at the head and the toes. "It's our psyches were born runt." She keeps affectionate tabs on her ruined family: the gigolo brother who has twice been left a sum under dicey circumstances, the mother who wins at bridge "rather too regularly."

He himself knows nothing of his own respectable clan except what has appeared in the news: his Duffy grandfather's death, which had occurred not long after his own flight. The family's diverse reactions to how to dispose of the body, reaching him by new account after the event, had convinced him that for a scientist, which his geophysical studies will qualify him to be, such zanies might well be dispensed with. Living in a country that prizes its eccentrics has tempered this—though he lacks the stamina to become one.

As the two men arrive outside the Duffy door, the short one says, "I'm afraid I'm going to turn tail." A box the size of a carrying case for small animals is thrust into his hands. "Hang on."

The door is open. The big man pushes it in. The smaller man submits, entering ahead. His companion follows, taking the box from him and setting it down just inside.

They stand in the dim hall entrance to the living room. Unseen themselves as yet by the persons gathered around the wheelchair, they are looking in on a tableau.

Older New York apartments tend to frequencies of light and dark that can affect the pace of the life there. Meditation breeds in shadow. The word "reflection" acquires a double meaning, quasiphysical. One becomes accustomed to seeing one's family members portrait style, in the dim from living room to corridor; and where a room fronts the street, even from as much as fifteen stories above, there is still the awareness of people below. There is even a conservatism of light, which tends to patronize as newcomers all who choose to live in the sharp blue glare of a high "modern" view, all their ambitions revealed. Each style of residence avers it owns New York. The Duffys, proud of their city brats, have taught them that both do.

Lucas, vaunting, "We Italians adore our sunlight but know how to hide from it," has chosen Byron and himself a skylighted, southern-exposed loft, whose dazzle he has then cloaked. For a house present, Zach has made a nameplate, "Chiaroscuro Corner," painted in the light-and-dark masses to which that term refers. Caring visually for the work life only, he lets the currents of food, sex, wives, and kids shape the rest, exempting his aquarium, the studio, which he regrets must have walls. Yet when he comes here his eyes—and maybe his understanding—dilate.

The house entry has been left open again. He feels the breeze at which his parents and Jennie must have thousands of times called out to kids coming in, going out, "Shut that door!"

Recalling that louche threesome who were in here early on, he is about to check the door when Shine glides in beside him, taking hold of the wheelchair's bar, hissing, "Let's get this guy on the road Zach. Here Bert, give the doctor your arm. And who's that out there." Shine's full of the loving impatience this family inspires in him. "And turn on some li-ight."

"Hold your horses," Zach mutters amiably. He reaches under the bookshelf for the double switch he long ago installed. One controls the overhead chandelier's glare, one the soft side lights in the hall. He flicks both.

Living room stares out at hall: at two men who would have the stance of portraits in brown-tone, were they not shifting their feet.

Hall stares in at a living room shocked white, the domestic tangle gone awry. Each knows the score. There's always this tussle. A visitor, no matter how welcome, is outside energy, invading. Those receiving are the discovered—at what?

Gerald, basking in his mother's overdue love, yet feeling its heat as overweening for a man who wears double-breasteds with vests, is the first to shake free of the tableau. Pressing the mezuzah into her hand with a murmured, "Get one of the grandchildren to hang it, eh?"—a duty cannily shed because as yet he has no grandchildren—he advances on the tall man, whose picture in an old issue of *Forbes* had been brought to his attention by a partner.

"Ah, the benefactor," he booms. "Let me introduce myself." They do shake hands. But he encounters a stare fixed beyond him, on the guy's handsome, slightly-more-than-life-size face. A hesitance. What resistance can this power of a man possibly fear?

Gerald sees that his mother, on whom the man's stare is fixed, is returning it, instead of attending to her hostessly duty. There's such an unfortunate bias against money in this house. He beckons her forward. "My mother, Mrs. Peter Duffy. You may know of her as Zipporah Zangwill, the anthropologist. Your hostess." A bit heavy, that. He lightens it. "And our dowager."

Why does the man color? Is it with a repressed laugh? Son Byron, who, interviewed by a sports magazine, had said obscenely, "No, I was named Byron after the guy who swam the Hellespont because when I was born the water broke too early," has in turn warned his father of like family references By considers unseemly, though unable to explain why, except with a soar of those ever-expressive hands. On which, cautioned early on by his mother not to speak with his hands "like some Jewboy," he had retorted, to Gerald's mystification back then, "No, Mom. It's to show they're empty."

Zipporah, eyes big on the guy, though not what you'd call polite, says, "Welcome, from her."

Almost a whisper, but they are both smiling, so Gerald's done okay? His parents were always being praised as sensitive observers; he claims to follow their path as he can. "Yah, but it's like you're dyslexic at it," By would say. "And will you stop referring to us as 'son this, son that.'" Bert, ever the peacemaker, had quipped, with an Irish lilt: "And why not? Here's Himself. The Dad."

The second man, depositing a box at their feet, shuffles again into shadow. A driver perhaps. Or a valet—the exalted gays of Gerald's world sometimes have those, as rich women have their chauffeurs. Or some nowadays their pilots, though trysts must be harder to arrange... He reminds himself not to see gays everywhere, which he has, since By came out to him.

His mother bends over the box. "Your cat?" Because of her updo hair, which Kitty has pointed out as new, Gerald sees that his mother's ears have flushed bright red. He makes a note to see that she checks her heart.

"No," the big guy is saying. "Orchids. You don't have to keep them. But they could use some north light."

Gerald risks a joke. "Orchids. You must want to stay for dinner." He laughs at the joke, knowing better: *Do it deadpan, or not at all.* "And who's your friend?"

Zipporah too, gestures, murmuring, "Won't you come in?" but the other man, raising his head briefly to cast her a brief look, as if to see her before she sees him, shrinks back. Just as Mickey used to do, before he said, "Boo." She sighs, recalling how only the short can say Boo.

From behind her Kitty cackles, "Zipporah? I was only trying to pick Mrs. Alter a couple of tea-towels 'fore she went, and the whole closet did a dump. All those old linen goods on the floor, but like they wanted a show." She giggles. "I must of leaned on a shelf. Come see." She hares off gleefully.

When Zipporah turns around again, the second man is gone.

"Your driver, eh?" Gerald says. "They must have taken the wheelchair out the back way . . . Let me introduce my wife."

When she giggles, you see a look of By. "Nobody has to le-et you, Gerry . . . Ah d'ya do."

"No, he's the manager of a British operation of mine. Guess he's on his way. Back."

I can smell he's being careful not to tip me off to what that operation is, Gerald thinks. He hasn't that nickname for nothing. Remind me to dig out what his Brit holdings are.

He looks up to see Bert and Shine returned. "All stowed away, are they?" Has he said something indelicate again? He has. He rebels, "Son Bertram, sir. Our youngest. And—" He can never remember Shine's full name.

"We've met," the two chorus. Bert's hoarse. His face is raddled, like a man who's wept. Or has held the tears in.

"Ah, Bertram," Gerald groans. "Bertram, my son." It strikes

him that he is embracing a rabbi. He wishes he knew the Hebrew for what he's just said.

"You have other sons," the man taller than either of them says. Though he's looking down, it's not in judgment, surely?

"Three in all. One who's just come out to me as gay. One— who I've not seen for ten years but who keeps me on his Christmas list. And this rabbi, who can't bring himself to be one."

Gerald emits a laugh. "I'm the prodigal father."

Zach's watching the big man's face, in odd trio alongside his brother Gerald and his mother. Having ceded the wheelchair to the two young men, though not cold-heartedly, he's keeping in the background.

Moorsohn's chapter in the history of the family is over. Though all the Zangwill side of the family have snatches of photo-nostalgia or proud reference, as attached to what kind of Jews they had been and where, Zach knows himself to be the only member who sees them without racial prejudice, as mere people. Zipporah has professional flashes of that. Everybody in his family is an observer; that's the kind they are—or maybe all families are, each to its degree. But to take Zipporah's account as the main one would be like having the heroine of a film thrust her head out of the screen to say, "This is a history."

Charles will certainly write a book someday; he has that aura, even if the book's subject isn't yet visible, even to him. He now believes his main concern to be what he calls "jurisprudence"—the study of law. Zach, watching his more beloved brother, hears what their father might pun: "Charles is a prudent man who acts imprudently." Like replacing his "lifemate," that sinuous lovely who wasn't too content as a housewife, for the chilly-sweet Chinese student with whom he deludely feels just as permanent? What Charles really sees himself as is the first Supreme Court Justice from science. To whose life the family will be peripheral.

As their only visual artist, Zach feels he sees them in that third dimension which only his art contributes. Yet he would never humiliate any human being by casting their replica in, say, plaster—to the end that, bumping into one, the verdict would be *Absolutely.* (Plus the bump.) His talent runs towards the surroundings in which humanity hovers. That's his doom, which he happens to love—doomedly. But at least when I watch them, I know that we're all caught in that thicket of life—locality.

What Zach just this minute saw—is almost certain he's seen—is his elder brother's oldest son, James. That head, always seeking the—dim. Shorn now of its usual proportion: that rise of frizz hair which Zach's eye has however at once added. Unmistakable? No. But that posture? Never quite out front. As his too-knowing aunt Erika had once remarked: "James is being 'not Ezekiel.'" Gerald's oldest was said to resemble Mickey, but this Zach can't say firsthand. Why he goes about almost shaven could be merely fashion, the "punk" skull, freed of all ancestry except bone?

Would I swear it was he? . . . Zach straightens, as to some patron questioning his measurements.

Float as you will, nephew, in the North Seas. Each of us joins up as he can. Some can't deal with the mass membership. Or not as themselves.

Zach is newly proud of his older brother. Whom he almost hadn't seen through in time. As is their mother, whose guilty sense of taste Gerry offends almost every time he opens his mouth—she has patted his cheek. She's kneeling over that guy's flowers, the box just opened onto orchids of tinges Zach has never seen, pale browns and faint lime. None of those mauve monsters. A hedge of greenery, studded with buds, lines the box. "Miniatures—" she breathes. "I—*adore* them." A word Zach has never heard cross her lips. "They remind me of portulaca."

The donor bursts out laughing. "Usually it's the other way around."

"My aunt in Brookline had a gardener. He felt sorry for the little city girl. Who had no flower patch. In a rainforest, sometimes

I—thought of him." She smiles, into the buds. "But it was our Lester, the doorman, who brought me some of these—once. She glances at Zach.

"A condolence call," Zach says. She didn't want to say. "When he heard that my father'd died. Lester dressed in his civvies for it."

"Lester grew up in Barbados, worked in a place had whole hedges of these, he said—called Highclere."

"Highclere?" the man says. "Why, my mother and I were there; she knew the pair who owned it back then. They served us a sweet drink they swore had no rum in it but a Bajan specialty, I can still remember the taste of. I was nine . . . Out on the lanai, though they don't call it that. I guess they don't call it anything there. Because the whole coastline—I never forgot this—is free to the population. You can't rope it off."

"Fre-ee, tothepopulasheeun." Shine grooves up to them, exactly like Zach's older twins do. "We lookin', to name the Fund, our side of it." He clucks his tongue. "But I dunno if that hits. "

"It's what my older twins think an allowance is," Zach says.

Zipporah gets to her feet. The man helps. Yes, she's flushed. "These need water. Maybe they come from Highclere?"

"No," the man says. "But their ancestors maybe. Our greenhouse, we're emptying it."

He and she are like a couple of teenagers, Zach thinks. Finding out they might have been in the same classroom, first grade.

Gerald and Kitty plod in from the center of the house. Her arms are piled high. She's puffing but gleaming. "I stood still, while Bert stacked these. Breathe on me, I'll drop. Wanted to skip with that other cloth, Zippy, but Gerry laid done the law." When it's family largesse, her habit can be a joke participated in by all the women. In Zach's youth, packages had gone to and fro as far as Boston—exhuming nineteen-twenties bloomers, lost wedding dresses, and once, from an Idaho stray: "Here are six of your greataunt's salt dishes. She gave them to my mother on impulse, when we moved. But without the spoons." On impulse *indeed,* Cousin Charlotte had said.

"Bye y'all," Shine blurts. "Gotta check on the new office. Hope y'all enjoyed." He salutes the big man. "See ya on the barricades." He has fled.

"Thank you, mother." Gerry is the one who has consistently called her that. He slaps his jacket. "That stuff's dusty.—Where's Bert? He was going to help us to the car."

A natural sequitur, Zach thinks. Where there's dust, where's Bert?

"Wear it in good health," Zipporah says mischievously.

"That's for clothes," Kitty manages over the pile under her chin, but in spite of this peasant echo, she's pleased. But does almost lose her load when her husband and mother-in-law embrace. Once again, Zipporah strokes his cheek. "Jesus God," Kitty mutters, "we better take that magic mezuzah along."

"I could invite you all back to the loft." Zach includes the benefactor with a broad smile. "The Polish restaurant sends in. Also of course the Chinese. By which time my two wives will be home—and they always splurge first at the French bakery." All the plenty at his house is crowd-sufficient—like here.

"Two—?" the man says.

"Present and former. But they bond."

The smile on both men is collusive. Oh, it's going to be all right, Zach says to himself. Whatever she and he are up to.

Nobody takes up his invite—an honest offer, but he's not surprised. Spontaneity's not the tone here. "Well, I'll split then." He swats Gerry. "G'night, prodigal." He's not being any meaner than the brotherly spiel allows for. "I better get home and find out what my sons think of me."

Zipporah lays a hand on each of her son's cheeks. "Don't fight, boys."

Even in your mid-forties, and with Gerry past the half-century mark, that's what a mother can do to you. But deep down the boy in you is mollified, could almost weep. It's like hearing old music.

And here comes Bert. What's with him? You forget how commanding that tall blond ascetic Irisher, with the hooked nose that could as well be Plantagenet, must seem to outsiders, and when he's not with family. That fair skin of his can go dead white with some injustice. Zach well recalls the day his nephew was hit by an intentional foul ball, and the fracas that followed post-game. One broken nose—not Bert's. What's wrong?

"What is this?" Bert's holding out to Zipporah a small dun-colored bag.

"Oh tha-at," Kitty says. "It fell out along with the other stuff. I thought maybe extra hookles for the shelves . . ." She shrugs briefly, always relieved when it's nothing to do with her. "It has *Moth Balls, Do Not Open* crayoned on it. Don't Jennie know moths only eat wool?"

"So it does," Bert says, looking down at it.

The bag looks like it belongs with the gear-pack that used to be issued to Boy Scouts. Too big for your soap, or your spare eye-glasses. Not as heavy canvas as the bag for the canteen.

"All of us kids knew that closet was the only one locked," Bert says. "And rarely opened. So whenever it was opened we used to toss small treasures in the back. Next time open, Jennie would clear them out. Saying, 'Fascinating. The junk you kids save.' And it was, after maybe a year. Your old joke book. Or Lincoln pennies. Or the yo-yo you gave up, as kid stuff . . . I picked this up, I was wondering what—and which of us this belonged to. But it has an envelope tucked in the flap. One of the ones the bank gives you for your safe deposit key. Nothing in it. But there's an inscription on it." He reads from the small tan envelope, his voice shaking. *"Property of Levi Cohen. Held at Lev's request. For his heirs,"* He gulps. *"At their majority."*

Has he held it out to Zipporah before she put out her hand for it? It's a draw.

"Lev gave it to me one Sunday. The year before he was shot—in case anything happened to him. He swore it was nothing of in-trinsic value. 'No diamonds?' I joked—since that was his trade. He did give me his wife's solitaire to dispose of as I saw fit. I thought this was probably mementos of Laura—something both could share. He cornered me at the linen closet, you see—how all women were linen freaks, we joked about that. And—didn't joke...So I tossed it in, the way you act when people as young as him...mention their death."

They are all stock still. Including the man behind her.

Now comes the hard part. She sees Bert tensing for it.

"You remember Debra?" A silence. They do. "I think I did tell her early on—that I had it. But it was no time to. And then we were in Italy. And then—Peter. And then I lost track. I wanted to. Lose track of all deaths." And all who might be concerned?

Ask me something now, Bert, anything. But he doesn't.

Gerald says, "That stuff must weigh a ton, Kitty. Give here."

"I let go, I'll drop it all. Let's head for the car."

"Excuse us then, Zippy? Can't wait to hear what you find in there. But have to take a rain check. As you can—see." This last hissed at Kitty, who doesn't always escape venom. "Thank Mother, will you." But she is already past the flower box and the man. "Well—" Gerald nods, circling. "Zach—see you in Jerusalem. Mother—know where I'm going to hang this mezuzah, with your kind permission? In the new house. First one ever, I bet, that side of the Pond."

And bowing to the benefactor: "Shalom."

"These need water." The box grinds when the big man shifts it, heavy with earth. He lifts it easily. "And so do I."

"Down the hall." Zach follows him. The house door is now closed; Gerald must have shut it. Most of the crowd who'd entered it during this protracted "open house" would likely be the door-open crowd, a policy governing even their personal lives. The unit of privacy is everywhere melting. His own loft is a kind of passageway. Though still locked at night, keys given out only to family, at mealtimes to after-school hours the gap between those who live there or don't tends to shrink. The first Ernestine had turned in her key the day she left, to indicate where she would draw the line. This to display the good manners in which both her mind and handsome body will forever be stuck. Her twins, skinny-dipping in mags they call shallow and books they deem profound, wonder if the two Ernestines aren't having an affair, but can rest easy. As churchgoers from rival sects, they have merely been named identically, for Zach's eternal delight? They're even faintly homophobic, though as readers of the *Nation,* this they would hotly deny, and are always asking Lucas and By to dinner. The Ernestines are in a pact to keep his life-style familial—at least until the boys leave home. "All your other women thought they left you," his current legal wife has confided. "Pooh... and don't call me, don't even think of me, as E TWO. Doesn't tickle me that it reminds you of Einstein's formula for the fourth dimension. And in this one there'd be only three. Or were."

She's a "Village Jane," the kind that since the nineteen-twenties has been seeding lower Manhattan from all over America, many like her with high cheekbones—whether Swedish, Czech, or any kind of Indian or what have you, Jewish, Irish: American. Talented, though rarely to the top, they make the best wives for artists, since they've spent their youth among them.

The two of them must have left early, after seeing the second twins in action, which could be why they came. Though they also have volunteered to help the funds behind the scenes, they know how to cut the mustard. "Give me a sociological entertainment like this afternoon's," he'll tell them, "and I know better what I've got."

In the toilet, Zach and the other man take turns; then he leaves the guy to his greenery, saying, "Don't disappear."

"Oh, I don't," the guy says, kneeling to work a minute spray-gun he's taken from a pocket. "I'm an artifact." He sprinkles the blooms with powder from an envelope. His jeans are the kind sold for gardeners. "You recognized him, didn't you."

Half out the door, Zach opens his mouth, closes it. "*Now* I do, for sure."

"That man—your brother, I gather—is his father?"

"The oldest son, yes. Gerry refers to him as 'our colonial.'"

"So he is. It's what's called a 'mindset,' I suppose. When he agreed to come here with me—because I needed a bit of a push myself—he showed me a photo. Not of his parents. Yours. His grandparents. Fond of her, isn't he, in his reluctant way." He's tending one of the orchids as if diapering a newborn. "He knew, of course, that I'd already met her. 'A Sephardic queen, isn't she?' he said. 'But with Gentile gams.'" He moves to another bloom. "I'd thought of transferring him back here; North Sea oil won't last forever. But he's better off—anywhere else... Don't you think?"

The thrust is so quick, Zach nods. Feels as if they've sounded a knell, but there it is.

"Oddly enough, the father would have made a good manager."

"How come?"

"They never lie to the boss. Only to themselves." He lifts his head, still kneeling to the flower box. "I'll hang on here a bit. 'Til your mother and Bert finish their business. I understand he's shortly off to The Hague. But I'll want to see him before I go." The head lowers like a bull, but he's smiling. "If I'm told to go."

Curiously, Zach wants to ask this man, who can answer straight or obliquely, what normally the man might ask Zach. "Think my mother will open that thing she was trusted with?"

"Never. Guaranteed she'll find some other way. Looks like Bert's the unknown quantity. But that's not my business."

"The unknown quantity," Zach says. "You've hit it. That's our Bert. Look—I'll put you in my father's study. Bert sometimes uses it."

They leave the orchids for Zipporah to find.

Once in the study, Zach sees how full it is of his father's quirks. Stocked and furnished with those, from brass inkwell to photos of all the Duffys, arranged like a genealogical tree, to books still open on the desk lecterns he collected—"So that I might see what books say to each other," he'd said. Adding that there was never a better way to find ideas than staring in an inkwell with no ink in it...

The dead can hypnotize you with their absence.

"I'm taking advantage of him," Mendenhall says, looking hard at the study. "But then—you already know that."

Walking back to "the big room" as it has always been called, rather than the living room, Zach finds himself approving of apartments—as if he's ratifying his past. They are more circuitous than houses. In those on a single floor, which most are, and if generously halled like this one, one can live almost simultaneously in all rooms at once. With the family brazier burning warm in each.

Bert has gone. No sign of the treasure, if that it is. Zipporah is alone. At Zach's step she startles eyes wide, even shamefaced. She questions. Yet won't ask, not she. He sees very well what she may be getting into, stepping out of the narrow widow's walk that the world, and the clan also, have consigned her to, along with her assent. That man's range will spin her off, even if she herself doesn't move an ankle. Against it are the photographs of the clan, on the mantel here. Add the mulch of the years, at the roots of the family tree. Her garden.

Weigh those. Against the music of a single automobile horn tooted all the way from Maryland.

"I put him in Dad's study," Zach says. "Go for it."

Nell is a person best known through her men: lovers and friends, often identical, and in a sequence that can sometimes repeat. Sex with affection, plus a piano accompaniment of discourse both timely and political, is required. Naturally these can't always be found in the one man, or if so, perhaps not all at once. Her female friends are of the same sympathies, short of any sex among them, which never enters her and their minds. Often their conversation is about men, though never exclusively. That exchange they consider mere chat, almost on a par with swapping recipes, children's habits, or where to shop for what. It goes without saying that, given the serious world they inhabit, some of their lovers will have been the same men—though decently never at the same time.

Nell would be shocked to hear she has requirements. She has *standards*, which include one man at a time—so that in case of negligent ecstasy, or accident, you would know the father of your child. Meanwhile she practices birth control, since, though you are in favor of abortion, you yourself would never abort. She maintains that the several times she has conceived have been by intent on her side, and with the assent of the partner; she would never do it on the sly. None of her lovers has been polled, but what man would regret having it known that he'd agreed—and indeed all but one of her birth children and their fathers are on intimate terms. Once her little adopted Romanian became vocal, Nell, calling all siblings in for a conference, informed them that in a sense all were adopted, perhaps a trifle more so on the paternal side. Since she lives in that world of social justice which either favors or permits to others much that it would not permit itself, she must responsibly keep her kids alert to her non-standards; this has entailed a lot of family conferences.

And how is all this possible, in a world of conventions she may not share, but functions among quite powerfully? Listen to a cocktail party at which she may or may not turn up.

"Nell's no classical beauty," one of her admirers says. "If she were she'd be dead. With all of us laid out like at the siege of Troy." A second espouser adding, "Besides—she works." A local feminist, far more orthodox than Nell, is moved to say, "She has no self. She considers the institution of marriage just a puddle you step over. As for equal pay—skip it, boys and girls; I went to grade school with her. Academic brats just rise above all that. The rest of us have to care about money. Otherwise, all political issues connected with it just slide."

The espouser asks, "What school was that?" and when told "Little Red" says politely, "Little Red Schoolhouse? That was a Village landmark for smarts." Adding, "And Nell works like crazy. At everything."

The siege-of-Troy poet says, "It's all very much simpler. No, Nell's no Cleopatra—but who wants a royal, around here? Watch any man in the room, should she walk in. If he's new here, he won't believe his eyes; if he's a former, he'll remember that he can. My Russian friends swore she must be Russian, an early bluestocking. The Austrians claim her for Vienna. She's like a period piece that fits anywhere we are, whoever we may be. I myself used to think of her as Mrs. Keppel, that astute mistress of Edward the Seventh, who still could be invited to the best houses, and was. And accumulated a fortune. At a noble profession, for those times. And for more than equal pay."

He pauses, for breath, or the iambic rhythm. "What Nell is—is just: deadly pretty. And since she can't help that, or get people to admit she has a non-foolish head on her shoulders, she'll take on some attitude of the era as if she's taking the veil. Each time."

He stops short, aware that he isn't making things simpler. "And she's faithful." A hoot from the feminist, but he persists. "She may drop someone emotionally, but still invites you to dinner—if you can stand that unholy shoeful she rules like Mother Goose. Who are even allowed to join the adult table talk, just so they think they have something important enough to say, and don't interrupt." He laughs. "Which at tables running to eighteen can usually take care of the matter. But the point is: She defers to the *persona* in you. She never disregards."

A new man in this crowd that must think it is such a woman's only one says, "Pity she couldn't come to this party." She'd invited him, by phone: "A friend of Daryl's, are you? That should be fun."

"Nell's absences aren't always reportable," the espouser says. "But when they can be accounted for, always interesting. We miss her at my firm. But I was at her table only last Sunday." He chuckles. In this corner of what is rapidly becoming the Old Village, gossip, being nostalgia really, can be pursued without blame. "That bright fourteen-year-old boy of hers says to me, 'You're an attorney-at-law?' and when I answer in the affirmative he says, 'Then what is an attorney-*not*-at-law?'"

The poet, who is the father of the boy, beams but holds his peace.

"I'll tell you the difference," the lady says. "If you're *at* law, you think of yourself as answering in the affirmative; if you're *not*-at-law, you just say, 'uh-huh.'. . . But I can tell you where she probably is—still in court. My outfit—we have an *amicus curiae* brief she's advising us on. Pro bono—she won't profit. And can't appear in court for us, of course. But gives us a lot of her time."

The lawyer says, "Latin is so equalizing, honey."

"Why can't she appear?" The new man has a face on which eagerness can look like innocence. He's a stand-up comic from a Chicago group with not much rep here, but on the loose for mate-

rial. Whoever said the Village was so sophisticated? Give him the
Second City in the raw, any effing day. That's a British word, he'll
say, "for social intercourse." He wonders whether these jerks realize they are pimping her. The whole scene would play—but he'd
like a look at the girl.

A babble from all three.

"She's an assistant District Attorney for New York."

His head is already ablaze with gags. "Oh really. Does she wear
class-action suits?"

Grrr, says the crowd.

"Where you from?" says the feminist.

One of Nell's lovers had once written at length to his successor:
"Nell isn't untidy or scruffy. Neither is her house impeccable. It's
rather that domesticity seems a little inflamed there. Tropical? Not
in any 'Madame La Zonga' way—Nell's New England pretty with
a slight fever—or a Renaissance Madonna, who's been out for a
run. As for the house—milk sours quickly there—she does love
peppery food—and there's always some cooking. The children
charm you, no matter how many are in the house. A male visitor is
important to her, acceptable. Nobody's pressured, though. Everybody itches politically—even the ten-year-olds have a stance about
something—an insistence maybe on cocoa-colored buddies. It's
become moot which kids are hers, which adopted. A nest. At
nighttime, as soon as able, off to bed they go. Ethnic foods slide
in—local delivery boys are her slaves. There's music—pop to
Pachelbel, softly on. Sometimes even the silence is—softly on.

"You don't feel any pressure to go to bed with Nell. Yet you
wouldn't be surprised. She's an excellent lawyer. Yet anywhere she
is, the furniture is warmer. Turn her corner and maybe, if only in
your head, a band of *putti,* those fakey boy-angels, are jacking off.
Her world is full of human rights. Feel free to leave. You often do.
Return, and it's still vanilla. How is it you never feel her emotions

are too loosely tied? Because they aren't—it's you who are wavering. After sex, you feel like your skin is full of little paper cuts, an
irritation you'd like to keep."

Nell has not been in court. Either that day, which was yesterday, or today. Last week and this she's had to excuse herself twice
on medical grounds, first for the X ray, then for the results. Since
she looks as healthy as a—how much healthier than other animals
does a pig look?—the judge sitting on the case, a man not by any
means a crony, no doubt thinks she's malingering. She has friends
at court in both senses, but he's a judge before whom neither female counsel nor a prosecutor likes to plead. Yet she'd been looking forward to doing so. The case isn't much—fraud and mayhem
in a Brooklyn laundry—but with both accusers and accused being
suspected of gang connections, it is utterly *mach*. Just doing her job
in that venue may brace up her feminism. She was raised so freely
that she hasn't the proper resentments. And is known to be griev-
ously soft on such matters as a harmless bit of slap and tickle, or, if
it will keep its distance, other people's porn. If she wants to keep
abreast of the times, she'll have to earn more respect.

Tonight. Midnight of result day. She's in a cab, going to her
mother's. When she first moved to the Village, cabs were not only
too costly, but also too adult. Grad students ganged up in old jalop-
ies—the word itself now almost gone, as used cars turned over
faster, and her own city-bred children scorned cars, or had no place
for those. In her day, out-of-state students mostly had those old
cars, causing many interstate romances, and even marriages. Now
and then a suburban guy had a carefully waxed, ancient family car,
never turned in. Clear evidence of the gap between the city and its
neighboring counties, or those of its boroughs where there might
still be backyards.

"We have the garage meditation," a guy from her N.Y.U. law
class had said to her darkly, a frown pursing his forehead. She
remembers thinking as he kissed her that the deep forehead cleft
would be handsomer on his chin. "Don't you mean garage men-

tality?" But he hadn't, and he is now a politico often mentioned for the lieutenant-governorship and owns a house with at least a three-car garage, in which his children, a large Italian brood bumped into once with him in his station wagon, no longer meditate?

Cabs came with her professional life. Until then the Village's habit had been the subway. Even the buses were considered too stately, as on the upper East Side, where filled with middle-aged women going to doctor's appointments. Or else on Fourteenth, too jammed with the poor, and as slow as their hopes. On the Thirty-fourth Street crosstown you met those citizens doomed to be clerks or some other nine-to-five, many of them tunnel-bound to Jersey. On the Forty-second you might meet just anybody, whether or not bound for the Port Authority—once her own father's editor, seated and calmly reading page proofs in a mass of standees juggling their loads above his head.

Only yesterday she had bumped into an actor-producer not seen since her twenties, he then thirtyish, who'd latched onto their young crowd in a coffeehouse where more than one of her buddies had served nights as waitress, or manned an espresso-machine built like a wing of the Vatican.

"Let's get out of here," he'd said back then, "and I'll buy you dinner." Two bad clues with older men. "Watch he can still chew," a sidekick had hissed at her. "His teeth are capped." But in those days she'd been a pushover, not so much for sex—though that could happen with friends—as for what she and they'd dubbed "glow." Meaning the nimbus of a future not yet theirs.

He'd fed her a "Reuben's," a sandwich named after a haunt of her mother's day. "You were really hungry," he'd said, then led her to a downbeat warehouse section she'd never heard of. "It's the Village-to-be," he'd said. She not picking up on it until she saw the loft, its sixteen windows griming on a cloudscape running three sides of a vast rectangle of flooring that glared with the insolence of a new life. No furniture except an under-the-counter-to-be refrigerator with a leatherlike grain, and a quite ordinary wooden kitchen table and chairs. "We're going to *warehouse success* down here," he said so intensely that she saw it, a hugely lettered SUC-CESS blazoning from the yellowy floor.

"Where you from, ladybug?" he'd said, in the faked drawl people had once lifted from crooners but nowadays were getting from the rockers who had done the same. "Missour-uh." Showing she too knew how to pronounce it, she came off hip, meanwhile signaling that the odds were still out on whether the evening would click. He'd said, "So'm I." It was understood that you were both role-playing, a hot psychology Zipporah said had in her day been called "having a line."

The table in the loft had one of another kind: a trail of white hieroglyph, alongside it the little spoons. "Who's 'we' here?" she'd said. The caps pearled his smile. "Nobody steady . . . You still hungry?" She can still hear it, that voice of all the seductions. Smiling, he'd licked a bit of the white powder on his tongue and bent to a grainy French kiss. There'd been only one door to that place, mercifully unlocked. Skidding across the floor, she'd made it out.

Hunting down a deserted street for a subway station is a waking dream. A city can drop you into those without warning, some only half-a-block long. Waking toward a job, a lover, a doctor—or away. To halt the dream, one rides. When a taxi came along like a fairy-tale rescuer she hailed it—her first.

Boarding an M104 bus twenty-odd years later, she is now one of the cognoscenti. Four-thirty P.M. is shift time; all cabs streaming either way have their Off-Duty signs on, or flash them at the sight of a putative passenger. But board an M104 on Madison, and you can still get a seat. The Grand Central area has few doctors, but once out of the hospital blocks north she has walked blindly there. At Eighth Avenue she can transfer, maybe get a cab, get to that party after all.

A man bends over her, tall enough to hang onto the overhead

pipe. Good raincoat, chin bearded in the short clip now in fashion. Hair speckled, salon-silked.

"Nell Duffy, by God. You look just the same."

She sees he has that same mouth, the tongue sly on the caps. By now she'd expected he would look seedier. But cannot summon his name. "Have you still got that loft?" she counters.

"Loft? . . . Oh, that . . . We must have sold it."

"But you're still in the theater?"

"So to speak," he says after a long pause.

"You were going to warehouse success. And have you?"

He's staring at her, amazed. People nearby are nudging each other; perhaps she's spoken too loud? No, they're looking at him.

"Buses," he murmurs at her. "Don't know when I've last been on one, can't really afford to." Then he puts a fingertip on her lips. Stagily. "Scarcely a wrinkle. Just one between the eyes." He flicks it. "Still that bee-stung mouth. On the Coast, what it would cost you . . . You still in the Village?" and at her nod, "Ah, that's how it's done, eh? You don't move on." Bending low he hisses, "You haven't got a prayer, have you? Of who I am." Straightening, he checks his watch, the same one, advertised magnificently and singly in the paper, that Erika last year gave Philippe, causing a family uproar.

"Get you a wrinkle or two," the man in the bus says. "It's time. I'd drop this watch in your lap, if it wouldn't cause a stir." Then as the bus jolted to a stop, he gets to the door, people craning at him, and swings off.

"Who was he?" a mother whispers to her daughter. The daughter whispers back, but Nell doesn't hear. Maybe one of her movie-freak friends will tell her who.

By then the bus is at Eighth Avenue, where the M104 turns up and off the cross-track. No good for her transfer. She walks the long block to Ninth, a down street, and hails a cab. She is always lucky on cabs.

Riding, she can readjust who she is. *I have four children,* she could have said to him, *and my job.* Or better still, the job's title. On the Coast, children are maybe not that weighty an emblem. In any case she doesn't have to know his name to know who he must be. Granting some talent, he's what you can be if you'll move on willy-nilly with the times, and agree to be warehoused on the way. So that you can be a buzz on the bus.

Last night she had got to that party after all, straight from the X-ray place, who would call her doctor the next day. As for dress, she isn't dowdy, but her social occasions aren't formal; "black-tie" is a term that used politically can still draw a smile. Conversation, rising by degrees to "discussion" and a "final" analysis, takes the place of combat. The kind for which to dress would have been absurd. Only recently, when sister Erika had attempted to scold her for a lack of interest in clothes, Philippe had been most tactful. He would never of course hint that Erika had been—at least formerly—jealous of Nell's looks. When it was actually Erika's envy, translated into a love of appearances, that had made her fortune. "Oh, Nell's opinions are her uniform," Philippe had teased. "She'll wear it for life."

At parties Nell often finds that one man, if she reveals she thinks him simpatico, will likely take over—or is she allowing him to? Her brother Zach, some of whose arty circle intersects with her wide range of acquaintances, had initially been rude on the subject: "It's like the mating dance of the birds." But with age, he's mellowed. "Ah, Nell—both of us have been left with the eggs."

At last night's "do," which had been a mannerly drinks-and-nibbles not rising to any brawl, the man from Chicago had been quite delightful about being from "the Second City," very receptive of her "New Yorkiness." So that she could explain it was so much more than merely growing up there. "Our family feels itself to be part and parcel of the city. Oh, nothing snobbish; every resident claims to be that. But where there's a clan, it can be so obvious . . . No, nothing to do with community service per se—though we might serve, we're not obligated that earnestly . . . No, it goes deeper. From the first I knew, without having to be told point

blank, that my life, the path that I pursued, would be—all part of
the city's lore. . . . Yes, you could say that. I do live in the Village. Yet
all of the city, and all that it means to the world—is in effect my
home town? You put it rather well . . . No, not on Barrow, tell the
driver," she'd said. "But near."

What better lead-string to bed than swapping such dossiers—
after which a one-night stand, if it was likely going to be that, would
be a kind of public intimacy, even a tribute to that? His own bio—
as a neo-political comic—had been fascinating (meaning different
from hers), his body clean, adroit, and for the night, close. Her one
disappointment, quickly over, had been his flipping of the mags on
her coffee table, the sacred *Nation,* especially. Saying "They diddle
piano on your vertebrae. Playing scores you already know."

She had given him the good breakfast she never ate herself.
"You weren't fooling about your background," he'd said. "Shirred
eggs!" A term he'd never heard—and she could see he'd been a
mite shocked when the two children not that day at school had
joined them. But as a thank-you he had performed a short spiel for
them. Plus a promise to her: "Free ticket, whenever you come to
Chi." Nothing gross, just one of his jokes.

What was new was, she'd never before taken a man home in
order to delay the morning.

Cabs are her city's lore, she's thinking. Waves of immigrations can
be clocked by them—almost no Italians anymore; the few remaining, as one had told her, have likely put their all kids through college. The Irish, always fewer, tend to be sullen or zany leftovers
whose more stable cousins had gone into the bus or subways systems. Though they do know the city like a book, likely having
grown up in Hell's Kitchen, the West Forties, or maybe even the
Village, their white status only works for them in a cab. So, keep off
any talk about the new Africans, or any blacks, or you get a blast.

For, noting a driver's name, she always talks to them, often in
any patois she's onto. Jews are rare also; they organize the car

services now, since the cost of a medallion to have your own cab is now a subject for sociologists. Though now and then she's drawn a Russian one, not too forthcoming, who turns out to be from Israel; how and why eluded her until one said, "We came to Israel for what we didn't get." Equality? Religion? What would a Jew from Marxist Russia want—if he could say? She gave him a whopping tip.

Tonight it's all down the drain, or soon will be; she hasn't even looked to see who's up front; he seems to know where he's going. The worst is what would normally be the best: it's spring break and the two older kids, good students both, are coming home for what normally is a jamboree—home parties that even her mother often comes to, with all levels free to join in. If there's some pot circulating, Nell will at least have her "youngies" under her. And none of hers has ever needed drug rehab, or an abortion, whatever her own life. No "peer pressure" affects any of them, much. Though she hates these slogans she has to notice them, like everyone else.

An X ray can be like a slogan come true. Furtively she cups her breasts, small neat ones, and not too slack. Not those big boobs, whose flesh ought to be the most ambivalent. One breast, she's been told, has a nodule merely "the size of an olive pit," if as dense. The other is the prima donna. Though she wasn't shown the X-ray plate, she can visualize that star-shaped invader. "Both should come off," is the oncologist's view. Should Nell want a second opinion, make it fast; every day counts.

No extra sympathy because the doctor was a woman. Perhaps less? She'd listened impassively to Nell's tale of the recurrent cysts she'd had for awhile, when younger, whether after she'd had a first child or before she couldn't recall; she has never clued every sexual fact to the primary one. She does recall how the gynecologist, every time he plunged in that large syringe toward a cyst—"Aspirate, as they call it?"—had mumbled something, and when challenged had smiled, the old sweetie. Saying, "I'm Catholic. I pray that the syringe will go in." But meaning—no cancer. Just a cyst you pop, though Nell would not look. "These are not that—" the oncologist had said merely. But now, in a hurt inclusive for all women, Nell thinks: maybe, after I left, that doctor woman, she felt her own breasts? Maybe she has to do that each time one such as me leaves. And that's what I'll tell Mom.

"Central Park West, miss, your number." He waits. Then an irritated, "You wanna get out?"

Once inside, the night man nods. She has her own key. Though she hadn't turned up for Bert and Shine's big day, she hadn't been much expected to. She'd opened up plenty beforehand, on whatever metropolitan advice might be useful to them. And of all her siblings, she's been the one most absent on the Sundays. Nor would they assume, on any weekday, or any daytime hour of it, that she was necessarily in court.

"You're Dad's favorite," canny Charles had once blurted. "And the family flyaway. You get away with it—no, not murder, just your willed way. And why not? With Dad—and maybe with all of us now and then, except Mother—it's because you do what we'd like to do, and he certainly would have." When she'd asked what that might be, Charles, patting her lightly, though she was nearer his height than most women, had confirmed what her airy carriage half-displayed. "You opt out." Oh, nothing disloyal, he's assured her. "Only for yourself."

Standing in the hallway she takes deep breaths. The house is enfolding her like her girlhood come again—or never left? The apartment is dark; her mother asleep, after the big do. Somebody's cleaned up. But not too well.

The apartment smells like humankind. Soaks people up, Jennie had claimed. "Day-after smell always take two whole days here to get rid of. This place don't want to. This place don't want to," Jennie said. "Your mama done trained it. To assept." *Accept*, somebody had corrected. One didn't correct Jennie. "Nix, 'assept' is more silly-ass. Which is what you folks is partial to. I hold with Mister Norman there." She so often had, with him; had she been trying to tell them something? And had their own father really wanted to opt out? Zipporah hasn't needed to.

What I want is to lay my head—on that surely accepting breast.

Such a house doesn't worry about smelling of widowhood in any papery, lavender-y way. The layout itself is a family diary and map, ever updated. All the bedrooms except her parents' debouch off the hall. The first two (nearer the kitchen for scavenging) and the attic (to quell noise or scuffling) were brother territory, shared over the years in a variety of moves. Her and Erika's room, later more hers, is at the top of the long hall. A smaller *T* of a hall intersects midway, holding the big bathroom belonging to the girls, and one end leading to both the whole back end of the house and up a small one-step landing to the front of the apartment, which forms a *T* with the hall. On its left is her father's study, then the dining room and living rooms. To the right, on its own small hall, with a door that separates, is "the master bedroom suite," as the real-estate ads tend to say—her parents' bedroom, with its own inner bathroom, and opposite its door another "half-bathroom," presumably the "master's." With so many kids, the door separating the suite, had been a boon to all.

The boys' rooms have become guest rooms, done over for adulthood as her brothers peeled off, to school and then to girls who had or had not become wives. Babies, nooked in baskets and cribs, had been encouraged to the attic as soon as decent. None of the do-overs has ever been optimum; one still senses the skeletal originals.

She tiptoes up the long hall to the farthest room at its left, a room long since hers alone. Actually a second "master," too near authority for real hijinks. But it also had been nearest the mystery of her parents' sexual life—of which the boys never spoke, at least around the girls. In their teens, as she and Erika lay in their twin beds late at night, the door to the suite might suddenly be softly shut; sometimes they caught a glimpse of by whom. "Was it her— are you sure?". . . "No, it was him," would be breathed from bed to bed. They lay there, imagining the heat behind that door, or not able to, quite. Erika, in those days the more vocal, had finally said, "Do you think they really do it?" Nell, who by then almost had, kept mum. If they "did," the image repelled her: two stale older bodies who should know better. But once she had done it herself, she had felt generous to all the world.

Confiding in Erika has long since ceased; for years their choices have so diverged. If Erika is jealous of anybody, that horizon is blotted by Philippe. Nell is sure he does stray, though that word doesn't occur to her. Once she had so intimated to her mother, who had quickly cut her off with a rise of the chin as holy pompous as a priest's. "Our mother's conscience is as strictly laned as a bowling alley," Nell had teased. Tonight she is deeply glad that Zipporah does not gossip a son or daughter's secrets to another. Whatever she decides to do, she wants no one to bother her, unless she fades enough for the concern of all. One thing she's already sure of. Now or later, she's not going to let the doctors alone decide. But she'll tell Mom. Breast to breast.

She keeps night clothes here, but is too tired to do more than slip into the chair by the door, the silly "sweetheart chair" with indeed a heart-shaped seat. A relic too of their teens. Yet when she recalls what has most tired her physically of the last forty-eight hours, thank God she can still smile. Soon as she's settled her future, maybe she can make it her business to drop by in Chi? Depending on what she must decide medically, and how soon—how much of life is still allowed?

The door of the suite is rarely closed nowadays; the last time she recalls is when Charles's babies had been in the crawling stage. Zipporah is now free to wander a domain wholly hers, though not as likely as Nell to wander it unclothed. At a certain point most older people seem to enter memory as into a lock-up, from which monologue trickles. Her mother's not even nearly there; her sense of the world is thoroughly alive, if no longer fed by an expanse still widening. Some of the cronies who stop in for tea or drink, maybe before they and her mother go to theater or to dine out, may cede her their confidences. Her mother's professional life may be in abeyance—few articles about her, none by her, and life in the bush as she knew it decimated, when not by commerce, by television and war. But people now go much to the social scientists for guidance, as focusing everything—medical, scientific, psychological—in one batch. At times almost derisively including Nell's own specialty, the law. And of course, theology. "I'm not sure," Charles has said, sardonically, "that if Bert is truly seeking a religious path he ought to chin so much with a Gran so experienced, and so much of that in the raw." But Charles always has second thoughts. "A habit encouraged to a fault at university," their father used to say. "But good for Charles, maybe. A bit of a change, from us."

They all of course take extreme effort to be with Zipporah at holiday time, though it worries them that her own clan interest, at least "the party push," has slackened. Once met, they do confer. The verdict being that their mother isn't lonely in any prime or dangerous way. Merely lone, in what a widow has to expect—and they can be proud, even exult, at how she's dealing with that. "And don't forget, since she's still living here, we're like personages, still present in the house, at all ages," Gerry said. "You can tell that from the way she keeps reminiscing about us." (Since Kitty's debacle, Gerry is rather over-exhibiting his new sensitivity.)

"Gerry," Zach said impatiently, "Mu only goes on like that to please us."

Charles said, "Don't you think it's time to stop that juvenile 'Mu'?" thus expressing his conviction that all art is slightly childish.

Erika, addressing her Chanel shoes as usual, smugged, "Sometimes Zipporah confides in me." But wouldn't say about what.

Later, Nell tackled Philippe. "Was Erika speaking the truth?" She has to admire his supple evasions, one of his degrees being in jurisprudence. "Erika lies only to herself, *chere belle-soeur*. She leaves other lying to me. At least over here. A question of language. Most people here think a Frenchman speaking French is automatically lying, *n'est-ce pas?*"

And have reason to? Though lying may vary internationally, every time Philippe calls her his dear sister-in-law in French she's rather sure he's making a pass. She's feeling a bit restored now, possibly as much as she's likely to, from now on. What's more refreshing than a bout with ultimately dear if fractious siblings? Who with time will become to her also what Gerry referred to as her mother's "personages"—vibrant and soothing when not even there?

Correction. She likely will not have that span. She's an expert on witnesses. How they manage to say what they do not. What's a doctor but a witness eternally, of a race run every day? And not from a boudoir chair bought when one was fourteen.

Looked at straight, the day has seized her, not she it. Results aren't received in a single session. Doctors aren't always obtainable on the do-re-me. When finally seen, they can be as exigent as they are kind. A pair seen in a "consultation" that both her internist and the specialist must have devoutly not wished for, yet had moved quietly to achieve, has an inquisitional power. The surgeon will have already exerted his technique on others that morning; the on-cologist has learned the morning's statistic in the hospital. "We can fix you up for today." Was that a command? No. Of course not. "Day after tomorrow," both mouths said.

And after that, some exemplary torture. To keep your example alive?

She has slept, no matter how. Perhaps reverting to teenage years can trick the body temporarily. Across the hall the intervening door leading to her mother's bedroom is ajar, and probably the door to the room itself also. "Wake us at once if there's anything wrong" had been the parental rule. With that many kids, there often was. Down below, in the child's world that in spite of benevolence is al-ways culprit, the rule had been otherwise: If you're in trouble, don't wake them yourself. Get the others to tell on you. As when Mickey's baseball scar had alarmingly festered. Or Erika, too bright not to trip up teacher and wrongly accused of cheating, had been discovered packing her bag in shame.

Nell had once awakened her parents by herself, late one Satur-day night. Walking to the Catholic Sunday school she had been at-tending—it had been when they were each at separate ones—a man each week accosted her, saying dirty words. She already knew what was meant; that was the trouble. But this was not what she was going to tell.

That same week, assigned to read up about Spain for Columbus Day, she'd come across Torquemada, the Inquisitor for King Ferdinand and Queen Isabella of Aragon. "He was also their confessor," she'd told her awakened drowsy parents. "And—he was responsible for the expulsion of the Jews." She wanted their permission to stand up in class. "Stand up for Jesus. Who was a Jew. Maybe even stand up in church." It had been bothering her all night, she said.

Her father's eyes are what she recalls: bleary but squinting to clear. "Chip of the old block, are you, bunny?" Her mother had been sharper: "Is that the only reason why?"—but hadn't pressed. "Stay home with us, tomorrow," Peter had said. "The Holy Father won't miss you." Her mother had said, "And then?"

She'd burst out crying. "I want to be expelled."

In due time, after several boring Sunday mornings at home, and a new spring outfit beckoning, she'd gone off to synagogue, with Zach.

She and her siblings had no one strongest faith to pass on to their children, but each had reacted. Gerald bounding into conventional worship—because he was the most conventional? Charles into the academy, where all spiritual idea was examinable, and he and his crowd the heirs. Erika had finally married a Jew. Though she and he were not specifically religious, it was plain that any offspring of these two curators, Philippe diplomat of countries and their sorrows, Erika guardian of objects prized for their holy existence, would be fanatically pure about something.

Zach, casting his works upon the waters, thundering, "This is *my* faith," should have spawned either artists, craftsmen, or derelicts, or all three. Instead, the younger twins, already priests of the new computerdom, are burning with a pure mathematical ardor to serve mankind—and yet sweetly not averse to helping with their father's eternally mobile props. As for the first twins, both jazz musicians of talent, they're scouting. Buddhism isn't their ensemble; they want to hear many hands clap. They are pals with black Muslims, but Islam's females, whether black, white, or escaped from Araby with clitoris intact, don't allure. Currently the two are attending a seminary—Protestant, since that faith seems most in need of revving up. Asked further, they say, "We have faith—in faith. Just like Ma and Pa."

Nell has been the worrier. Her children have been given her precious trove: her attitudes. Handed on with some trembling, but empowered in the end—as she agrees that all faith should be—by her own acts. Plus her causes, for and against. While the fathers, half anti-enthusiast, if mostly against marriage, half, as one said, "ever on the loose for some *idée fixe* to be pro about," have helped coach the kids to a fine balance. "Just like in their own babyhoods," Nell's mother had commented. "*Their* fathers would have taken them to the swings."

"I don't mind amusing you, Mother," she'd countered. "As long as I'm approved."

Her mother had reddened, surely for both of them, with the impatience that empathy can bring. "Oh Nell. Stop trying to be the dumb blonde of this family."

Right enough as to hair color, with all the distinctions that implied: between whore and wife, the mousy and theatrical, down to the dubious aristocracy of the beauty salon. Relief had flooded her. This was the only time her mother had ever said: Stop.

Nowadays it is Nell's children who say that to her, sometimes mutely, often using visitors as their sounding board, or in their own smarty answers, taken to be supercilious, when they know they themselves are being used. Brilliant as their schools admit they are, their elders, whether Nell's crowd or its opposites, are alike in warning them that intelligence is heartless. That without some "belief," it will not carry them through.

"Or not in America," a guest husband said, is always saying, meaning not as sufficient antidote to "the American way," that

sneaky outmoded norm. "But of course it needn't be a formal religion, kids. Just an ethic of one's choice." An advertising guy, weekend essayist, and the acknowledge father of Thelma, her elder
daughter, he can both pay her college fees without fuss and brood
paternally over her sex drive—though Nell reassured him, "She's
no flower-child. Those lassies aren't getting preg for the sake of the
universe. Like us. Na-a-ah." When he said, "Nell, you sometimes
sound as Irish as paddy's poke," she could counter, "That's what
working in Brooklyn does for me, Irvin. Acey-decey on the am-
bivalences. Have a nosh?"

But it was Derek, the fourteen-year-old, who shocked them
one and all. Chided for his age group being hooked on video
games night and day, he'd retorted, just a wee too sullenly for fun,
"I'm looking to join a real war. Not just pretend, like around here.
With guns, like the Civil War. Or like World War II, bombs. Some
war I won't have to conscientiously object to. Got any to
recommend?"

"Christ, he really means it," his father said, when told this on
the phone. "We shouldn't have sent him South. But it was my
school. Wish to God I could see my way clear to acknowledging
him. Beef him up on what really matters." Derek's father, a university poet who could use a touch of the bohemian, is also a married
poet, with a range of legit kids poised for all the expenditures and
a strict wife, half-owner of the brownstone, who would most certainly "strike up the Baptist rage. She'd have my head." For the first
time in her life Nell had said, "I'm almost tempted to." That's why
he doesn't come to dinner.

But in the end it is the kids who hearten her. Thelma, who
adores her half-brother, and had saved the little adoptee (who at
first was mute) from being fashionably diagnosed as autistic—"I
just bought a Romanian songbook and sang to her all day"—is the
peacemaker. Of course she has the advantage of having a famous
grandfather, whose portrait of her at age eight was in the *catalogue
raisonné,* under the surname he'd also bequeathed.

Flying in suddenly from Oberlin for the weekend, to meet

whom and on what funds she hadn't disclosed, she'd sniffed at the table of tabouleh, macaroni and other salads, kosher salami, squares of curd, and one oven-roasted deli chicken, brown as a cow's eye, for those who'd gone back to meat. "We seem to eat our politics," Thelma said. "Derek may not really want a war. Maybe he just craves a square meal."

Unluckily he'd been the one to witness Nell's adieu to the guy she'd brought home. Tecla, the adoptee, snatching one of the buttermilk biscuits that had been languishing in the fridge for a dog's age for just such occasions, and saying, "Gee, Mom," like any normal girl, had been picked up by her bus. Derek, already late for school, had lingered, surveying Nell and the guy—and the breakfast—like the man of the house. Had she been too chatty about coming to Chi? Saying farewell ("Fare thee well," actually), had she too openly assumed the pose—head cocked, palm under chin, fingers curled—that a photographer of note had told her would elongate the neck? (Who when he left permanently for Rome had arranged her so—"Let me remember you this way always"—and had shut the door just as delicately behind him, so that it hadn't clicked.)

Waving a good-bye from the upstairs parlor-floor window, mightn't one fall quite naturally into that posture?

"Grow up, Mom," Derek had growled. The door banged.

Consulting Zach—always fruitless, but he did have boys of that age—she'd sighed: "It's so lovely when the fathers come, of a Sunday. It's so sad when they can't."

"Come off it, Nell." Zach, the best of brothers, likes to act older than she, rather than younger. Yet he'll not topple her dignity by calling her Sis. "I've heard that from you just once too often. Lovely and sad is how you like life to be."

"I hear you," she'd said. "Once too often." Is that what they think of me, the flyaway? And in her mid-forties. Come off it, Nell. Forty-eight.... "A dangerous age," the surgeon had volunteered.

The oncologist had given him a dirty look; maybe she disagreed. No, Nell, don't get carried away . . . She just hadn't approved of his saying it out loud. But maybe at this point everything should be? She herself had felt that an exit line was called for. "I've always been at the dangerous age," she'd said.

But now it's not friends and relatives saying it . . . It's specialists. In her head she hears the end of her conversation with Zach. "Nell—you're a slave to your empathies," Zach says.

She's hearing two conversations at once. If the acoustics are good enough, people can. But scary if the only auditor is yourself. Maybe she's really sick, coming down with a virus. Not just cancer. Can cancer come from too much empathy? Or from all you haven't dared? From the shadows of some room that Derek, the son a father won't acknowledge, must always have had by himself—a room not half the size of this, a room still a childhood's—he sticks out his tongue. There's dope on it. And none of the others have reported him.

Such a roaring in her head.

Mom. Stop this roaring. Mom.

She wakes and is about to slide down from the chair, already feeling herself clasped in Zipporah's arms, when the door to the master bedroom opens. Does a mother always hear her child?

A figure looms in the doorway. Tall for her mother, but the chair Nell crouches in is low. I'm seeing her from below, the way we children used to, before we could look her in the eye. "When you can look your father in the eye," Gerry said at fifteen, "you're a man . . . Peter was expounding something to me I couldn't make head or tail of—why does he always choose me?—and you know that ridge he gets near his right eyebrow? I saw I was looking at it on par. And our eyes too. On a par—" "It can happen to girls too," Erika, the shortie of the family, said. And praise us, none of us snickered . . .

But why is Mother standing there? Does she see me, the way she used to see us through the closet doors we thought we were hiding behind?

Then the lamp in the suite's bedroom is turned on. The lamp by
her mother's side of the bed, where she still sleeps. Only her mother
has ever turned it on. A wedding present from Cousin Charlotte, it
had been sentimentally—and stingily?—offered. "I'll love seeing it
in your house"—being clearly not austere enough for Charlotte's
hopefully non-Jewish one. Product of Limoges, her mother had still
vowed to smash it, once Charlotte's home visit, threatened yearly,
had occurred. In forty years or more, it never has.

Shaped like a rose—"No rose looks that absurd," her mother
learned to say fondly—the lamp sheds a dim, pink light in which
their father had claimed to feel foolish. Later, Zipporah, in her
brood's adulthood, had qualified slyly, "Has its merits. It's a lamp
made for monogamists who wish to feel adulterous."

The figure is a man. Tall as her father, it can't be him. In the
dim light from behind it, she can't see more.

Though he can't possibly see her, she shrinks even farther back.
They mustn't see her. For he's no marauder. Her mother had
turned on the lamp.

Have they sensed another presence? Or is he merely on his way
to the "husband's" toilet opposite, whose switch is to the right of
its door?

He has found it. In the flash of a hard single-bulb light as he
swings the door wide, she sees him. Taller than her father, he has
to dip his head even more. Peter, mocking the fashion for the
parental nude—"I like my pajamas"—had in the end seemed more
natural. But now and then when she and Erika, if not exactly in
ambush, had glimpsed him cross to the half-bath with nothing on,
their interest had been otherwise. "So they peel when they do it,"
the two sisters had agreed. As for their mother, the two had assumed this. The difficulty was rather in ever imagining her as coy,
under cover of an inflammatory dark. "She's not a negligee person," Erika had loftily said. "You hope," Nell had replied.

This man is naked, and in the caught flash of him, a real specimen, with the off-the-scale look of those men who, whether or not
the handsomest, are accustomed to having women's eyes follow

them—and have a powerful stride that eludes. Or chooses? He has reminded her. Not of any of her children's fathers. Of such a man, more briefly in her history.

When this man comes out of the toilet he stands there, a white man, tanned but not tropically. Stretches arms above head, lazily. Drops head and arms between the spread legs. Likes being naked; she can tell. She knows their bodies. He's younger than her mother. Or else young for his age, like her? The watch he wears is nothing special, maybe a Timex—what's his bag? And is this after sex, or before? The calculation shames her. And how's she to get out of here, noiselessly?

As she watches, he wheels, no longer facing the bedroom. Is he peering into her dark? No, he's staring down the long hall as if in reflection, a smile playing on his lips. The face is hewn now, probably more so than once, when it would have been a good-looking young man's, on his way to a squaring of the jaw, to cheeks pummeled lean. A face of the kind, falling short of any one ethnic identity, that's more and more being called "American." But what's it staring at? Nothing down the long hall but what leads to the kitchen—has her mother cooked him a late supper? Or to the "guest" rooms, where he's obviously not staying—but if he has family himself, he'd be interested in the Duffy provenance? So finally, on to an "attic" scarcely deserving of the name, now that it's been stripped of all except clothing and trinkets nobody can yet bear to say are rubbish, and of what that little tyke of a genius-to-be, Mickey, had dubbed "Mama's existential bench," though he couldn't explain why? Not the sort of thing you'd bother to show a lover.

Yet that this man must be. As he turns from the hall once again to the bedroom door he has that grimace, of yearning mingled with apprehension, which one learns to recognize. So, the act is still to come. It may even be the first time. Whether or not, he's turned his back to her, standing in the bedroom doorway, looking in. Pray God he closes the door. So that she may safely creep away.

But he leaves it halfway open. So she sees the light lower, but not vanish. To children allowed now and then to turn the lamp's key in the slow inching that effects this, that rosy veil had been magical. They had watched their own faces achieve mystery.

Nell's on the daybed now, pressed against those pillows, many of them mottoed "From Your Best Friend" or covered with autographs, that Jennie used to punch and air, muttering, "They still smell of girl." She's hearing nothing from the bower across the hall. Not always a bower, when and where that clutch-and-glide and hump occurs. But she has to bet on this one—that in the slipping and lipping going on in there, something of good order is being conceived.

The hoarse intake of breath is her own, seesawing in time with what she doesn't need to hear. Behind her, that can't be Erika, breathing, learning how it is done. Leaning into the pillows Nell bears down hard, pressing her breasts, those best friends not yet lost, into the girlie pillows' buckram and velveteen.

From that door across the hall, so trustingly ajar, a man's groan, justified, and a woman's silvery answer.

"I feel like an orchid," her mother said.

Lucky Nell. Once again she's caught a cab, a night-shift going off-duty, and the Village on its way. "Thompson Street, yeah." The driver is a woman, to whom Nell can find nothing, absolutely nothing, to say.

Getting out on the sneak had after all been a breeze, soon as it hit her again how her brothers had done so. Eager for at least some espionage in a house where parents were not enemies, they had made a great thing of how, coming in later than expected, you avoided the front door—which did not creak but somehow might vibrate to that open bedroom door. "We were the only kids I knew whose front and back doors opened with the same key," Charles liked to reminisce. "Dad initiated the change years ago; I recall him saying 'I have no idea why the front and back keys of a house should be different.'. . . Of course we boys roomed nearer the back anyway. We had our fun."

Home at last, she tips her hand in salute to clan intelligences. Whether her sister had ever needed to sneak in she can't say; their paths had been so separate, outside that room. Erika could be a prig; her Paris lover had gone undeclared until just before his death, and her inheritance. Perhaps the love-of-one's life, as he clearly was, lasts best undeclared; Nell herself can't say. Never has had one, not her style. Nor her style to sneak. Left home early, soon as she would have had to.

This flat of hers has only the one door, to which each of the kids, never "latchkey children" in the city's phrase for the growing legion of those left to their own devices, had been given an "emergency" one as soon as pockets could be trusted. And their heads, of course. Once she had thought of doing over a loft, but that kind of restoration intensity required a stable partner, the school districts weren't viable, and she'd been intent on climbing that other stair, the law. "How very legal you are!" Derek's father had sighed. "In all but one respect. That does confound people. I suppose it's the Jewish side of you."

"*What* confounds people?" she'd hissed. "My Jewishness? Or that my kids are not what you'd call 'legit.' Though only one is fatherless. For a poet, your grammar is not that clear."

Derek is home. His new black-and-white sneakers, size twelve, groomed like pets and indeed suggesting a brace of spotted coach-dogs temporarily off lead, are unaccustomedly not inside but sniffing in front of his door.

Sneakers as a signal, God love him. That he's still home safe. And apologizes for what he'd said.

She never wears these "athletic shoes" so called, loutish footwear in which half the young women of the city now clump. Up the steps of the courthouse she minces, in shoes with heels of one inch to three—depending on whether she's most upholding the dignity of the city, the law, or herself—but always with pointed vamps. After all, in spite of the slimy compliment tossed at her by a movie star on the M104—walking away from the bus she'd seen the poster—she is a person of a certain age.

What if Derek could have seen her sneaking down the hall in her stocking feet, key in one hand, in the other her three-inchers worn all that day. In her view, hospitals require a show of contradictory health, even of arrogance.

Sitting down she takes off the shoes, stretching her tiny, still admired toes. "Do what you have decided is right and would harm no one else," she has always taught the kids. This to be preceded by consultation with such elders as you respect. Of course the language the elders had better use if they have the luck to be consulted across the kitchen table, or in a gabfest on the big divan, is much simpler. Sometimes advising merely what they have watched you children do.

What would Derek have done, had he come upon his grandmother and her lover? His school is near; he borrows books from her. Once or twice he has stayed over after a late game and with an early class impending. "Don't wake her," Nell herself had said to him. "Here's the key."

"I was so proud of him," Zipporah had reported. "He walked in on a little supper. A British don, who used to be practically an emissary without portfolio in Washington at one time, was there. Quizzed the boy British-style, almost to the point of dressing him down. Derek stood his ground brilliantly. Like he'll do at your table, if pressed. By his elders. But somewhere he's learned not to talk about himself."

Who are the elders? Nell goes to the mirror to find out.

When next she meets her mother, though she'll bide her time before calling, she'll want to take that dear, naive fount of wisdom into her own arms, holding her—against these breasts even, but keeping mum. As I shall about what I saw tonight. Today will be my secret, for as long as I can keep it. Tonight was hers. May it be forever in her keeping.

In the mirror behind her, she can see Derek's coach-dogs. She resists an impulse to kneel and fondle them. For I've decided. In the consultation room you are merely the suppliant, presenting your two little bags of flawed flesh. Here you are in the womb-nest you and your children have made. To which the rank of fathers is allowed only to accede. If there had been only one father it might be different, but that was not my choice. I'm not a wife. I'm the favorite.

Operation chop-chop? It's too late for that; she heard that in their voices. One doctor's sweet, false mucous, the other's dry rattle. They'll be doing only as they think they ought, and are trained to? Tossing one more test-rabbit into the annals of medicine?

In the mirror she can watch herself cup her breasts in her hands. A mirror has always been her ally, why desert it now? Behind her, on either side of the old-fashioned double doors, she can see her books, shelves and shelves of them, if not always read. The doors have rested for years in their pockets, waiting to be slid out for some need for privacy not yet arrived. Beyond, as prominent in the room's other half as a ballast weight, is that long table, for those valiants, bores some of them but loyal, who believe that food is merely the ally of conversation. The habitués of her village, to whose number she has ever added new recruits. Her joy being like her father's, to see them swimming like tadpoles in the realms of talk.

In this room all her attitudes are simmering. Neither of her born children were bottle babies. These breasts had fed them. What's nature but a household with double doors?

She's given away as many pieces of her body as she'd cared to. Or was obliged to.

I've decided, she thinks—to decide. Her mother has shown her the way. Whatever Zipporah does, she does in her own house.

When Derek wakes, stumbling into the room blind with youth's sleep, she speaks to him through the mirror, shyly, still staring at her own face, that fortune. "You don't have to go to war. I've grown up."

Bert's on a steamer that ferries from the Hook of Holland to a port in Britain—Harwich? From there he can entrain for London, where he's never been. The glassed-in deck is empty. The hardier tourists or Hollanders are gathered at the bow, the less so at the stern. Except for the sight of a deckhand passing outside from time to time, he might be entirely alone.

He's never shared his brother's fishy empathy for the sea. The one time, several years back, that By, booking him as his "assistant" on a group trip prepaid by some surfer fans, had that first morning cajoled him into one of their finny second skins, he'd managed to stay vertical much of the time, even enjoying his black emphasis on the sunny air. Watching, he'd seen his brother's face, triumphant on each wave-crest. Each gliding swoop down is a prelude to the next eminence, atop of which By, catching Bert's glance, proudly lifts his chin. Dotting waves like a school of trout risen to some universally cast bait, all the others of the group appear to be shifting face like By. It's a muscular response, Bert tells himself, stifling the hunch that the looks of triumph cast toward the shore of this famous beachhead might just possibly have to do with their being gay.

"No sport for you, is it?" By had said to him at morning's end. With no double meaning. By has little guile, though a strong appreciation of those who do. "I'm getting out of it. Lucas likes the underwater stuff." He gazes fondly at his new friend's dot of head, now and then emerging to blow off and sink again, in its own trough. "He says it must remind him of treading water in his mother's womb. Desperately trying to get out through the back."

Bert was able to grin. After all, he and By have that same mother. But By is never fooled. "Try to like him, Bert. It's going to be a long relationship."

"Oh, I will." They never lie to one another. Having so often had to lie in tandem. "And the furniture's wonderful."

"If I can ever persuade Lucas that the only really steady market is in replicas, he jokes he'll call the line 'Exaggerations.' He says Americans don't go all out for genius until it's one-upped. But that if he'd wanted to sell his soul, he could've done that when he was a sports star. . . . So—so far, I haven't been able to persuade."

Good thing. Because that might well end the relationship. Whatever the value of Lucas's soul, he has to feel he has one.

At The Hague these past months, as auditor without portfolio, Bert's quarters, booked by whoever handled such for his sponsor, had proved tactfully moderate. Still, he's relieved that the expense-account dignity expected of his sponsor's representative can now be shed. He wishes the same could be said of the wing-tipped shoes he's staring at, and the glumly unoriginal suit, toward which porters gravitate.

"Take Lucas shopping with you," By had said. "On Europe, he's infallible. He says: 'You go to conference in a Peace Palace, you don't dress for it. Not for such a cause. On the other hand, you won't want to look too American.'"

Scanning Bert's wardrobe, thumbing past a scarcely worn navy blazer with gold buttons—"Gerry made you buy for his country club, right?"—Lucas had okayed a few sweaters and pants. "Take a pair jeans, so you don't get homesick. But for god's sake, only wear at home . . . Or else sneak some time in Amsterdam, where anything goes . . . No need for the black-tie; in Europe what you rent can be better than what you would buy."

In the shop, he'd stayed Bert's hand, about to stretch toward the very dark day-suit that diplomacy obligates. "You want to be taken for a Russian?" Bert was urged to choose between two suits of unobtrusive cloth, one with a faint understripe. "The Hague is what? Just bargaining. You want not to look naive, but not too smart-aleck neither." Surprised that Lucas had nosed out his own very intention, he'd laid his hand on one of the suits. "Ah, the stripe—good," Lucas had said. "That way, you'll be more or less invisible." Had Bert disappointed, or been approved? Settled, when Lucas added in a plump voice, "Just like a good serving table." On their way out, he'd seemed to weaken toward an Italian sports jacket, smooth as brown sugar. "For the cock-a-tails? Where you carry off the head envoy's wife, to at least a dark corner of the conservatory . . . No?" He'd shrugged. "Okay. Take her to the woods, then. Even in that flat country there must be some; The Hague was once a count's hunting lodge. You might wear the jeans."

The sea the steamer is traversing is a dull gray perfectly allied to the sky, a low country's sea. From centuries of dealing with it the Dutch have managed a phlegm from which an edgy apostle of the Americas is expected to learn. Yet Bert's sessions as an onlooker have stirred him to arousal, rather than calm. The Hague has seemed to him a vast hall of dictionaries, formed out of its successive roles as Tribunal, World Court, and International Court of Justice, to whose "definitions" countries can bring their minor squabbles, all the while sidestepping that one grand definition, a word the seasoned crowd there is almost afraid to say, yet constantly invokes.

He had indeed been all but invisible, a part-time state of which he's already known something in his role as family ombudsman. But at those conferences, trials, and tribunals, there has been such a taken-for-granted company of invisibles as he might never see again—all entranced by protocol. While the international will-o'-the-wisp they're purportedly after, squeezed from one "local" conflagration to the next, takes refuge breast to breast, in silent populaces that cover the world.

"Oh, you can now and then see the big cause get an assist," Mendenhall had said, at a little send-off just before Bert's leaving— only him and Shine, and the "manager" who would be Bert's liaison for any need, a young man about Bert's age, last name Thomas, to whom he might also report any observations he wished, though under no obligation. The young man had been un- happy with the "office flat" they were in, ground floor of a brown- stone on Manhattan's upper West Side, which someone else from Mendenhall's outfit had found for him. "Garden looks like shit." Mendenhall had been amused at pretensions for the boss's sake that the boss didn't share. "That's what I specified. But they might have briefed you." Saying good-bye to Bert, he'd repeated his warn- ing. Maybe out of his sense of obligation, to this new recruit? "The Hague? *At worst,* what countries have tried 'immemorially,' as the saying goes. Sad word."

Over their handshake, Bert had flicked, "Or, 'at best'?" Such a family-style retort. Blurted because Zach, that summer in France, had once said what seemed akin. They'd been confronted by that great stone circle of human variants at Mont St. Michel, figures smaller than modern persons but recognizable in every grimace and plea of limb. "Who doesn't want to join up with the human condition, Bert? At the same time choking on how far to break away? Maybe that's why I can't bring myself to work in the figure."

You would do well to listen to Mendenhall with the same care.

The American vice-consul, who'd insisted on driving Bert from The Hague to the boat, had tried to pump Bert on his "con- nection." As a grad student, the consul had interned at an endow- ment for international peace, and his ambition to move from his present post back to better-paid civilian effort stood out as awk- wardly as his ears. "Underlings of too many nations here seem to have those ears," Bert had written Shine, his safety valve. "And our boys tend to hiccup 'State' every other sentence (for the 'Depart- ment of,' oaf)."

He's been advised that everybody there travels trains second class. "Only the blimps go 'first.'"

"State knows your guy's infrastructure pretty well," the vice-consul had continued. "He's tight on everything *except* money. And nobody's ever met him. Even his minions mayn't, I gather. Have you?"

"Couple of times. Maybe three? Nothing formal." But you would count up. Not that you would tell this guy.

"What's he like, personally?"

Tell me what a man's like impersonally, consul. Maybe I need to know the difference?

They were at the ship by then. At a gangplank, taking off, one feels generous. "He's no blimp."

But Mendenhall has a way of removing himself from the scene.

They'd met only once with real purpose, in Maryland—Shine and himself, and their ever lively cargo, Zach. The estate, on that bright day, had seemed to feed them impressions in triplicate, behind whose screen their host could stand back. Talking business. The three of them would later agree, in some awe, that they had done most of that. "He's the one giving," Shine had squawked. "But you feel like he's the one receives. Jesus, do I sound like some ministers?" When Shine answers his own questions you can almost see trains of thought inching under his scalp. "He must go to the black church."

Zach, still brimming over, said from the rear seat of the limo returning the three to New York, "Gifts that aren't money. He's had to invent. He understood I don't want the Reo. I just wanted to see it, existing still. He might even understand how I can let my own works go. So much money as he has, able to buy anything? It could make you a kind of artist at *not* owning. I'd like to make him something he'd want to keep, couldn't buy. But most art you can. Certainly mine." And for the rest of the trip he'd lapsed into that gloom.

That last Sunday at Zipporah's. Not "A last act," as Charles had called it, phoning around from out of the guilt of not having been there. In his communiqués from China, where he and his new wife and family were spending the academic year, Charles continues to

bring that up, as if the family must now accede to a finality he now
wants of it. Bert knows that monkey-on-the-back feeling quite
well, as far as his parents go. But even "Central Park West," as the
Sunday outer fringe has always referred to it, is no longer Elysium.
That would take a first cast, immortally never dying. And an audience never changing. Which he has had, elsewhere.

Saying good-bye to Moorsohn, Bert had knelt at the wheelchair, an action met with the occupant's gruff "I don't give bless-
ings," but a protracted grip of Bert's shoulder. Returning
wet-cheeked from that, he was noticed only by that Mrs. Alter,
who'd pulled in her lips with a kindred headshake. As if to say:
"Today nobody leaves here unscathed."

It was then he must have bumped into Mendenhall and his
buddy, one of his "managers" no doubt, standing over a box on the
floor. A Mendenhall with a stance on him like some extra who'd
brought in an unscheduled prop.

Was this before or after Lev's long secreted packet had turned
up, followed by his grandmother's lame explanation? He no longer
recalls the sequence. Under that rain of linen, who would have? He
recalls only a powerful sensation of inner events merging with
outer. All hinging on a thimbleful of circumstance? That's just one
of the soppy remarks that comes later. Like that yenta, his grandmother's friend, Ruth Halle, nosing out his phone number to call
him late that same night to say, "I can't get over it. I *knew* Lev."
Who'd told her? And then, in that insinuating voice which implies
an undetected spot on you somewhere: "I'd invited your grandmother to spend the night with me. To get out of that mess, until
the cleaning gang comes tomorrow. She didn't say yes or no. But
she didn't turn up, so I phoned. No answer. This late? So I phoned
Erika. 'I keep trying but no answer,' I told her. 'Your mother's always there,' I told her. 'I wouldn't worry, except that was no kind
of crowd for a lone woman, to be left with its dribs and drabs. But
your aunt has always had a mean streak.'" What had Erika said?
"She said if she were me she'd stop trying." He'd fobbed Ruth off
with "Thanks, I'll take over"—which of course he hadn't. But it

had been his first brush with the veil of extramural gossip, concern mixed with envy, that must surround such a family as his. Or were these calls merely the widows, networking the night?

"Intrusions. but no conclusions," his grandfather, met at the door of his study after a day when the phone had too often rung, would sometimes welcome him with. "Got any conclusion on you, Bert?"

Over the months here he's acquired some, if not the one most craved. This steamer, plowing on with a deep engine grumble satisfyingly in step with his pulse, may be carrying him closer. Under the seaworthy plank bench he's sitting on is his sole piece of luggage, a heavy leather affair snagged at the last moment from his grandmother's attic after that ass, Thomas, handing him his plane tickets, had said: "That all you toting? A duffel? That won't do. Customs think they mean dope; you'll spend hours on the open-up line. Get yourself a nice elderly Hartmann—you know where there is one? Okay." The barrage of phones on Thomas's desk was an array Bert had never before seen. Thomas stood behind it erect, sauntering in place. "The help has to uphold the standard here. We can't all be gardeners." He actually winked, a comic "out" that marked him as from somewhere else—maybe the deep South or the West? There was no real malice in Thomas. Just one long candy stick of ambition. "Keep in touch, Bertie." The plane tickets had turned out to be for first class.

Shine and he had met for breakfast at the usual coffee shop; their apartments were still accessory. "That crazy, absurdist open house," Shine chortled. "Like a scriptless theater-piece you improvise. And the drama sticking up all of a sudden, like a chicken bone in soup. We got eighty volunteers, fourteen will maybe show up for school, maybe nine will hang in. Arlene, who does groups, says that's the energy average . . ." Arlene is his current girl. "You going to your grandmother's before you go off, give her my love. That lady still simmering, God bless her. But I got a prickle. That was a heavy Sunday. It'll be the last." His hunched shoulders, in the shrug he called his "Jewish" one, hinted it was time. "Well, gotta go, it's flag day every day, with us now. Your uncle's car is gone on to some

Valhalla they keep those jobs; a movie lot wanted it but he said no,
you put an old horse out to grass. He sent us a whopping check, by
the way. Made out to me, so maybe you wouldn't have to know."

They'd embraced. Whether they would keep up by phone or
by letter, as well as by the faithfully mimeoed office memos that
Shine's new secretary, a bright, handicapped young man, was already sending, wasn't broached, from a hesitation newly come between them. An ebbing of what had once been so natural—but
why hammer it in? Bert, for all the fuss, is only loosening his tether.
Shine is being launched.

A day later Bert dropped in on his grandmother, not seen or
heard from since that Sunday. This day, midweek, has been one of
his Manhattan favorites, cool, sunless, even dull, with the brisk of
activity only glinting, relaxing in answer to the least hint of climate, as only a city day can. A faint trembling excitement is in the
ground, more than traffic vibration, far less than quake. Like the island is being lifted on its own hawsers, into a latitude deserved.

He was admitted to the apartment by a buzzer newly control-
ling the front door. Walking down the hall, a gallery he would
miss, he came upon Zipporah and Mendenhall sitting with drinks
in the bay fronting the Park. Rising to kiss him, she said,
"Spritzer?"—which they were having—and went to fix him one
without another word. "A drink she's taught me," Mendenhall says.
"Takes a bit of doing."

Outside, a dusk already mulls, as always at windows facing so
uncompromisingly east.

"What a town!" Mendenhall says. "So much on the square, it
fools you. So high, newcomers who can afford to are deuced into
thinking that's the only view to have. When the city is the street—
the talk, the people. Whose first taste isn't always for—glare. When
I see a man too proud of an office lookout that gives him the city on
a platter, I kind of wonder what his mind lacks in grasp." He sips.
"And all the whirring that keeps New York in action." He chuckles.
"My new little place, still in the nineteenth century. But flush the
toilet, half the time you hear a plane answer, from up above."

Bert nods. "I grew up here." That sounds too know-it-all. "I guess it all connects."

Mendenhall sits back. When he regards you, you know it. But to buck up straighter is not demanded. "Been reading your grandfather. You remind me of him."

When Zipporah comes back with Bert's drink, Mendenhall rises to go. Not a huge man, but a presence. He must always leave rumination behind him, among those left. "Got to plant my fig tree...Don't smile, Zipporah...You pot them." He nods at Bert. "Give Thomas something to do, if you can. He wants to put his best foot forward...Call you, Zipporah." He's gone.

When she comes back she remains standing. Waiting.

"He seems enchanted with New York."

Her face doesn't change. That's not like her. "He's buying a second place. Across the park. So his children will be encouraged to visit him. The Maryland place was never their dish, it seems. He's deeded it public, as you may have heard. Gardens—which pleases him. And a Museum for the Decorative Arts. Which he hopes will be their speed. So the one son and daughter who've shown a mild interest in the public, and are the more competent, would serve on its board."

An explanation almost in her old anthropological vein, at table. The family verdict, on the likes of the family she's described, would have been unanimous.

His face, has it betrayed him, as the saying goes? That's usually what his face can't do. "Oh Bert. He's—as loving a father as he's allowed. And they'd have been brought up to—estimate. Not by him."

"Doesn't every family—estimate? Don't we?" In his case (for he too, has one, he thinks half jealously), wasn't it Nettie, though long since in the genealogical earth—in the coffin she and the companion had comparison-shopped for—who still sets the tone? Like she had about his scar?

Suffered when he'd thrust himself between his parents in one of Kitty's eruptions, when she'd said the sexually unspeakable. She'd blamed Gerald's wristwatch, afterward. The cut, at once streaming blood, was more likely from her diamond wristband hitting his forehead. His father, pulling her arm down by the elbow, had further dragged it into the flesh. The scar had been attributed to a neighborhood stray. "Never feed a dog that comes from nowhere," Nettie had barked to him. "I've no doubt you do."

A teenager's rankle. "I still think of Nettie."

His grandmother sparks. "So do I. You know Nettie thought my going to college was déclassé? Until the debs started doing it? Ah me... You know your Uncle Charles's elder girl, Annie, who taped Nettie's companion's recollections before she died? Well it seems Nettie was buried with her genealogical chart. And ours. 'I'm including them all,' she said. 'One day, they may thank me for it.'... Ah, Bertram." She rarely calls him that. "Families give one a character. Even instill it. Then censor you later, for what they've damn well collaborated on."

She means him. Reasons plain. Byron got out of the nest his way, James by another. And me, through hanging in. Shine always said, "You got like a miner's lamp on your forehead, man. Just show you a needy glow, and you dig." And warning that being ordained wouldn't take care of it. For either of us.

"Shine sends regards," he says.

"I'll miss Shine, while you're gone. Though he's invited me to the new office, to help him choose which flags. He plans to plaster it with them."

"He's on a roll. He says, 'Doing unto others is everybody's burden, man. And every country's. Not just some holy man's kick'"

"I sometimes think—he's had too much influence on you."

"Ma-am. It's we who had it, on him. We're his family. And that's what we were taught: Leave it loose."

"Ah. Were you."

"Anyway, I shouldn't need an office for quite awhile. F. D. says since peace efforts are always 'premature,' and always merging, better not to be entrenched. I'm only to be an observer anyhow."

At that, she'd looked at him so quizzically that he'd stuttered. "In my schnooky way."

He'll remember the sound that came from her. Not a sigh. Not quite a chuckle. Not surely a giggle? "Well now, Bert, there are two of us."

"You? Come on. Who in the family was ever less of a schnook?"

For some reason, new to their confidences, neither of them had excepted Gramps.

"Cousin Charlotte thinks otherwise."

"The legendary? She's real?"

"Enough to come down from Boston two, three times a year for any shareholders' meetings, held here. She buys just enough shares in corporations she considers important nationwide to qualify her to express her opinions. The only modern way, she says, to register those with government. She doesn't expect to affect policy. She simply wants them to know that not all Jews vote as a block. And sends her record to the *Globe* and other papers afterward. She doesn't want to be, as she says, 'lumped in.'"

"But she's still Jewish."

"Oh, profoundly. Her category being 'some of us.' Others, not to be identified with too closely, tend to be called 'those.'"

"Ah—*those.*"

"Right. Charlotte's mother was exactly like mine. Careful not to say 'Polock' in our hearing. Only laying on thick their own delicate pronouncement of where our kind had come from: *Mewnchen, Fronkfoort, Bair-leen.* And a Vienna that did baffle us: *Veen.* Or a London long enough inhabited so we needn't wonder where we'd been before. Otherwise, no prejudice. Unless one of 'those' came to be 'just rolling in money' and showed signs of intending to become 'Some of Us.'"

When she adds, "Oh, it's an old story," he laughs dutifully, sad that his vibrant Gran may be more and more harking back.

"I sometimes think I relish it too much, Bert."

Only love keeps him from agreeing. "There's always Mordecai's letter," he says.

Brought out and hung in the dining room whenever Charlotte and her mother's touting of their superior German ancestry got too much for her spouse. "That frame I had made goes so well with your mother's dining-room chairs," he would twit. She and her daughter never knew when they might look up, after an unlucky dinner-party reference, to see hanging there a letter from a collateral relative of Mordecai's, head of a family of Spanish Portuguese Sephardim long resident in South America, but still accustomed to vaunting its own exalted heritage. The letter being replete with snide references to the Ashkenazim, the German Jews, and warnings to their own more newly arrived cousins in North America. Since willed to a museum for its other historic value, it was not usually exhibited.

The South American relative, after detailing some early history, had been cautioning Mordecai's parents on his marriageable sister's visit to Germany:

> The mark of an aristocracy is that it can breed great eccentrics, who bring us fame even if we ordinary ones do not always agree with them; think of our Spinoza, that lens-grinder who became a philosopher. Our Jews have always tolerated their lens-grinders, but over there in Deutschland, they must have learned to goose-step. Daniela, my wife, insists that for one of ours to marry one, even of their orthodox, runs a risk beyond—

He had used a Portuguese or Hebrew phrase presumably to do with religion. The blot had perhaps been intentional.

> She says she would not dream of allowing one of our daughters to marry even a merchant prince from there— though because of our pampas a number have come calling. Their Berlin villas have velvet over the dado in the salon, we hear—and some of our Spanish plates hung. The dietary laws? Oh yes—kept. Where to tell you the truth, we often fail. But Daniela reminds me our young men still are born with the royal hook to the nose from their forefathers. And our women the same face oval (we

enclose a cabinet study of our Esther, now fifteen). Of course our girls ride, and our very language is more aquiline. In Germany a girl our darling's age (three years or less than your Mordecai, and as you see already into her mother's shawls)—she would be called a *Backfisch*. We see only the young German hopefuls, the heirs: Hamburgers, Berliners, the Bavarians the worst. Keep your hands in your pockets. Not for the money, the dowries they offer are as high as ours and as solid, but their hands sweat grease. Is it the pork-eating breath of their neighbors that gives those Ashkenazi bourgeoisie such a resemblance to the *echt Deutsch*? Think of the grandchildren of such an alliance. Cheeks like bladders. Back of the head—flat.

Gran always enjoys that last bit. Since she was born only a few years into the century, it's not hard to keep track; she's in her mid-seventies. Is it age that makes her dwell more on her background, even while she derides it? Yet a tendency to place what people are comes from her profession is not a ploy.

He reminds himself that being a Jew isn't just a background. "Who were they?"

"They wanted to dissuade Mordecai's parents from marrying him to Lottie—the 'Charlotte' came with the marriage. They were the DeSolas of Brazil. The Pools, Mordecai's lot, were more Western by then—England. Daughter Esther de Sola did marry Spanish—Sephardim of course. From São Paulo . . . Gold and diamond mines."

Will she broach what he must own up to before he leaves? Or must he?

Diamonds. Some Sundays stand out. In the long chain of those woven by family hands, that one black-market link. Against all scripture, a man is shot because his business is honest, aboveboard.

The Homburg, belonging to who knows who, had hung in the front hall like it was waiting for a *minyan,* that early morning meet when six men crouch under God's hat. You had clapped it on your head like a seventh man, aware he is only the substitute...A morgue is like a hotel. For one-night stands. When Lev's body came down, hung behind the glass like a turkey in a storefront, you held the hat crossed at your chest, as you had seen the elders do for that other salute, the Pledge of Allegiance. She at your side hatless, in her own uniform, the hand with Lev's diamond at her throat. When the two of you went to the sergeant's desk to identify, you laid the hat down on an empty chair, vacant like no one wanted to sit in it, that headed a line of chairs occupied by others come to identify bodies. When you and she turned around, the shock of her "I am not the wife" newly in you, Lev's body had been hauled up out of sight, unclaimed. You pretended not to notice that the hat too was gone, on into the house of who knows who?

The steamer he's now on plunges ahead like an unfettered house, some passengers at its bow, some at the stern. "Big families can be like prisons, Bert," the girl who would later wed at St. Bart's had said to him. "Why does yours seem such a Jewish one? When you're like me, half goy? Better get out, Bert, into the big blue yonder."

And so he has. Out of the loving prison. Not without one small crime? Confessed on leaving.

"You once said you had an errand for me, Gran."

"To deliver something, yes. But you already have it now, don't you?...Ah, I figured. I even got Jennie to hunt with me. When I was straightening the linen closet again, just the other day. 'Seen it ever since,' she said. 'First off, wouldn't touch it. Mr. Lev's bad luck. But all that white goods maybe sucked that out. Soft, it was. Maybe something good luck for his boys. Maybe a lock of their dead mama's hair.' Jennie even suggested, 'Maybe it went out with what Mrs. Gerald Duffy took. Closet's half empty.' Funny—Jenny always pooh-poohed when we used the pillowslips. But hated to see the stuff go. I didn't, I can tell you. I offered her the rest, in case she's staying on in Norman's apartment. She isn't."

The phone rang just then. When she came back she'd said the one word that had always signified that legend, and in the same tone: "Charlotte." Then everybody could resume.

Zipporah had, looking straight ahead of her, taking up Mendenhall's emptied goblet, revolving it in her fingers. "I didn't come clean, Bert, about not remembering. Lev's packet. I did and I didn't remember, off and on. Because to deliver it, one would have to find the recipient. And I would have to live through again that scene in the synagogue. With her, *her,* bent over him. When I should have been the one to be there."

He sits with her, seeing it. Seeing Peter die.

"Sometimes I dream Italy," she whispers. "Then I want to find her. Then I wake up—in America. And I don't."

When she stands up, she's still the Gran his school friends found formidable. "But you had it in your hand when you talked about the toys you and the kids stashed in that closet—and took out the following year? So I figured—you have it." Her eyes veiled, broody. "Maybe that's all our silly housewifery—scalloping, French knots, hemstitch—is for. To stash. Maybe that—was his idea."

In Bert's memory she seems to him like a sibyl, offering her oracle. "So, you go. Yes, you."

To hide his own feelings he'd begged off to the attic, to get a suitcase. Two Hartmans had long been there, borrowed and returned. Only the smaller, not enough for his needs, remained. A stack of outmoded leather ones nearby. He'd chosen the most serviceable of those, neat enough inside, actually quite handsome enough for first class. When he returned with it his grandmother's eyes widened—at a choice so unlikely, no doubt, but she said nothing. And nothing here was ever begrudged. "Thanks," he said. "And for not—begrudging me. About the other."

She'd gone to the elevator with him, carefully leaving the house door ajar. Zach had put in the buzzer, she said; Shine had asked him to. Some unsavory persons had wormed in with the Open-House crowd, the kind who might get a kick from sneaking back. And Lester's relief man was only half his worth. "And I'll wait for Charlotte." She can laugh; she'd recovered herself. "Charlotte is always imminent. But more so than usual. She's never before come here—'Over West,' as she's wont to say. We have a brief tea someplace like the Pierre, where she can more comfortably express her opinions, and how mine are not upholding the family. Her usual opening gambit being, 'Zipporah— Boston is not that far.'"

Before the elevator came she embraced him, less tentatively than since she'd been alone. As if he was now the one who more needed the hug, the warmth. Freeing him, she'd said: "Shalom. One of its meanings is 'Peace be with you,' isn't it? Funny thing to say to somebody going to The Hague."

When the elevator passed them, going to a higher floor, her heel-tapping showed she'd meant that to be her farewell. When it still hadn't come down, she muttered: "Thursdays. There's a whole Scout meeting on the top floor." Then said low, "Let me know if you find her."

A gout of hope went through him. He has it yet. "So you think I will?"

She fiddles with the buttoned tab on his old military-style rain-coat, which he had refused to give up. "Because you nicked it. Which is not your style." A startled look on her, as if an echo has lodged in her ear. "And because you've had the grace not to open it."... She gives him a stricken look.

"What, Gran?"

"If you do find her. You will decide. Whether or not to give her it."

A noise of shoving and hoo-hoos from the floor above, the sound of the door slamming, then the slow, imperial whine of an old elevator in an old house. It hits their floor with its usual slight tremble. The door slides open. The cage is indeed filled with boys.

They grin, she smiles; they know each other. "You devils," she says. "You been, or you going?"

"Going!" they shout.

As he presses into the car, she holds the door for him. "Take care—" she murmurs.

"Oh it's aces all the way with F. D., they keep telling me."

As the doors inch to close, her smile from the other side is brilliant.

"I call him Foxy—" she said.

Port is called.

Bending to part the straps on his one piece of attic luggage and press the center lock which opens its jaws, he slides the zipper on one side of its lined interior, a process at which he's now adept, and finds reassuring. He takes a long, thin company envelope from the zip-pocket, slips it into a breastpocket recommended as deep enough for those passport wallets which accommodate travelers checks as well—one reason he is wearing the suit. Inside the envelope is Lev's keepsake.

A sailor is walking along outside, rapping at windows. A megaphone calls the docking time, translating sea hours to shore time.

Bert goes to the bow, to join the brave.

In the connecting train, which is scheduled to wait for debarking passengers—presumably those who have reserved—he settles into the seat the ever-fussy and persistent Thomas had perhaps for that reason provided him. The compartment is empty, but he's early; Customs had been a breeze, and perhaps not merely because of his business connection. Or The Hague.

Ahead of him had been a little Englishwoman, speaking what must be cockney and nervous about a bundle, patently a half-ham, which she obviously feared inadmissible—as meat? "Smoked," she said. "I was told that if it be smoked—" The customs officer had lifted both hands. "Don't tell me, luv," he'd crooned. "Just don't tell me. Pass on." To Bert, whose "purpose of visit" slot read as advised, "Business and pleasure," he'd cracked, "The Hague, eh. Ah, now you can have fun." Yet in the line to their left, a dignitary clad in what the consul had described as "full morning-dress, some still oblige," was being required to open every sleek piece in his pile. "Going to a wedding, are you sir? Kindly let me see the presents." And had not been passed on. If he himself had been asked what was in the pouch in the envelope, what could he have said?

He's been to Amsterdam, savored the eels then in season, admired the canals for their neat compromise between the dreamlike and the practical, wondering if this caused a laissez-faire understated by the Dutch themselves. And so oddly neat, all the way down to the mound of bright orange dog turd often at a pavement corner—and respected as the national color? It had been a relief to go from The Hague's formal receptions, swollen with after-hours protocol, a further lesson in the intermediary European craft of getting nowhere too fast, to stark late-night bars where tables could be suddenly upended, as either the start or the finish of argument.

He had strolled down the not-to-be missed approved attraction, where the prostitutes sat behind plate glass, their tidy, plain quarters without frill, at least on the stretch he saw. "One of them was reading a book," he wrote Shine. "I had a strong urge to go in. To find out what she was reading." Nowhere would he be solicited to buy available dope, the hard stuff, whereas on a New York street he might have been—Madison for "uppers," amphetamines, Harlem for "downers" of unknown extraction. He had left that city of median indulgences without allowing himself any. To date, whatever he'd practiced at home had been considered mildly negligent of the letter-of-the law, as befitted the American sense of where the serious freedoms lay, but not loose. For his errand, no aura of "weed" must cling.

Back at The Hague he'd been cautioned, encouraged, or even gender-queried, and finally instructed, always by foreigners of whatever nation, on the sexual freedom of the ordinary Dutch female. This often via the standard joke: Young man, American: "Care to go for coffee?" Dutch girl: "Sorry, thanks. I have my period." Took him awhile to see that the real butt of the joke was the American, still Puritan to all Europe except the Pope—and other diehards of the unreformed.

"They're all so pretty," had become his standard reply. "It's been hard to choose." The vice-consul, here on a repeat tour, had provided himself with a pincushiony wife from Amsterdam, whose sister lived with them. Pressured to dine, Bert's "I'm expecting an evening call" had to be politely taken as indication that he was, as later intimated, "Already fixed up?" From his mother, Kitty-Fegeleh, Fegeleh-Kitty, he and her family have long since learned that to the accomplished liar the most successful fabrication is half-true. Though to puzzle out which half is which can keep the liar heartsore.

But this too may be salved, at least temporarily—during the college years, say—by a little twist from what his grandfather had called "the great American screwdriver, social analysis."

For those born mid-century, or like him just before, the sexual thread twining his life and time has become its own ethic, taking over the moral, in a way new to the Jew. Annexing the spiritual, all but displacing the religious, it has created its own commentary— and appetite. No wonder the Orthodox rabbinicals, permitted to prowl the seminary library to see what reforms they were up against, sat with their yarmulkes frozen to their pates. Their loins no doubt as hot as Beelzebub's?

> Manna—that's what all commentary is. Including mine. . . .
> The food miraculously supplied the Israelites during their progress through the Wilderness. And pharmaceutically classified as "gently laxative."

So is inscribed the notebook—on a first page otherwise blank, undated but evidently kept over the years, coffee-stained and

faintly tobacco-y—his grandfather's bequest. Which he has here
on his knee.

Nights at The Hague, solitary after days awash with dialogue,
he sits in the room whose tidy propriety reminds him of that
street, whose visitors must—like the whores, no doubt?—be registered. Do his colleagues mark that he has not been? He reads, and
is solaced, amused or immersed in Peter's repetitive prose, exactly
as once. The notebook, tied where the binding is by that string Jennie trussed fowl with, a ball of which Peter filched now and again
for his study, is a semi-private inheritance—his own name,
Bertram, even penciled here and there in the margins. One life addressed to another, trussed for him, in annotations so shaky they
must have been made near his grandfather's own end. The diary
(begun, from occasional references to where Peter was at the
time—Cyprus, New York, Bari Translation Seminar, when he
would have been about Bert's age) proceeds to the first family
years, West End Avenue, then is interspersed with all the domestic
cities in which he had been an esteemed circuit lecturer, and
dawdles finally to the crowning "CPW." Central Park West.

This is its only narrative. Nor are there "personalities," except
where the vis-à-vis in a discussion is identified; this is not a memoir. Though Bert, in an act of faith toward jottings that seem to ask
to be followed consecutively, has not scanned to the end, there appear to be no allusions to family; the Duffys have not been spied
upon. Even the paradoxes, adages, stately or mocking allusions,
though recognizably Peter's, are not what they would have heard;
this is not Gramps . . . What it is, Bert can't yet characterize, except
that in spite of its many public allusions, it is private. Meanwhile,
the diary has given him company grossly needed.

Waiting for a call to tell you that someone being looked for has
been found, and where, is a limbo, where an accessory memory,
one even blood-related, helps keep the balance. These pages are in
fact searching too. Not for a woman, already so ripely alongside.
Nor for an "insight" on what Moorsohn had called "that trumped-
up quandary of the psychologues: 'Not being *in touch* with one-

self.' Which, whether you slam the door on it, or cough just subtly enough to let us hear, you always damn well are." Or when like Moorsohn himself, Bert remembers, you choke on your own conclusion: "What we religious want is confirmation from on high."

Well, Bert has got that now, if only from the exalted empire that keeps in touch with its interns—this sign that the gods may have been watching him. He had given Thomas something to do.

"Oh, a nurse?—You say she was. That should be easy; they're registered." Thomas had sounded disappointed. "Not your old nanny? These days they scatter the earth. Maiden name? Cohen? Too bad. That won't be much help. Age? Approximately—mmm. Not to alert the Israeli authorities? Got you. Nor the British? Hmmm. Nor the person herself if found? *When* found, pal; we hit pay dirt regular. But what are you and the boss up to? Hits me a rabbi, not too smooth but not wet behind the ears either, could be one *sweet* cover. Sorry . . . Keep my trap shut. Not to F. D.? No one? Gawd, that is a responsibility." His next was a squawk. "No reports? None?" A whisper. Gotcha. Not the phone? . . . We've an anti-tap gadget here . . . No? Okay. Nemmind." He'd rung off.

Three nights ago Bert had got his evening call. Whether Thomas had found his assignment easy or hard, or had wanted to stretch his task to some dimension, wasn't to be told him. Thomas is showing his mettle. That romantic tenacity, perhaps, which Mendenhall, reputedly fond of staffers with uncommon quirks, had maybe hired him for? As with Bert.

"Sweet bird found," Thomas says. Then a tussle—of silence.

Wish I knew the next line, Bert thinks. There must be one. "Thanks. Enormously grateful." That Thomas can't see the rush of wet to his lids. His throat contracts. "Keep it under wraps."

"Details—at the dock." Pause. "And regards from F. D." A snigger. "The old rip." Click.

He'd had the wit to guess that the consul's insistence on driving him to The Hoek was connected. At the gangplank he was handed an envelope. "Came in the pouch," the consul said. "If you know what that is. Of course we don't actually use one, anymore." He'd watched with interest while Bert eased the slim missive into a jacket already bulked. "Our life is in envelopes," he'd sighed. "Discarded the vest, have you? I do the same." Gabby—but he deserved something for his efforts. "Letter I shouldn't wonder from my grandmother," Bert said. "Been the target of some notoriety. Been suggested she should marry. Er—again, that is. She won't." A dubious squint from the vice-consul. Then a respectful salute. "Good try."

Actually, he'd blessed the diversion increasingly hinted at by Erika and Zach in the news from home. Possibly serious? Zipporah, normally his delightful correspondent, was keeping absolutely mum.

Zach's outrage had been the funniest. "We're all being written up in the papers as a family. Sociologically. In terms of what we are, and what we are not. I had no idea how demeaning the social sciences can be. And how racist. The Jew part is what interests them. Like: 'Not the Rothschilds—just middle-of-the-road bourgeoisie.' You can imagine what that did to me in the arts pages. Tabloids go for 'Abie's Irish Rose—in Reverse.'" Zach had ended up laughing at himself. "And when the ball got rolling—the scholars. On Peter: 'A Hebrew Mind, an Irish Pen.' The Jewish *Forward* you had to admire. A retro on our possible Zangwill ancestor. Seems he didn't only write classy, on the ghetto. Also a play called *Merely Mary Ann*. A copy in the British Museum to be assessed next issue . . . Then a neat dip, from the *Forward*'s Kultur mix—on mixed marriages . . . But Charles is enjoying himself, via the Supreme Court Justices who were Jews. Cardozo, Frankfurter, Brandeis—how would a half-Yid Duffy go? . . . Your father, our Gerry, denies 'this billionaire rumor' bothers him. And looks smug . . . As for you, kiddo; keep a low profile."

Shine has sent on an article, "Half-and-Half People, Our Theology," mailed him by its author, a former history instructor who had gone back to her profession, as the bio said, "after a marital gap." At the top of the clip she'd scrawled, "Show this to your buddy." Bert's name is not mentioned. She merely wants him to know she's divorced.

Erika, on the phone after an aside: "God, are you easy to reach of an evening—are you always there?... Seems Mother and a Man—spell that with a capital *M*—have been spending theirs at a funky hideaway, the Roseland Ballroom. But seems the Man dances the tango divinely... *Entre nous*, Bert, you either do it that way, or not at all... The Roseland emcee, an old-time nightclub guy, asks where he learned; he answers, 'My mother taught me.' He's what—seventy-five? Comes out, his mother, who hostessed nightclubs, is still famously alive... Now, at Roseland, a couple's anonymity is respected—especially if they're nobody. But they've even more *tendresse* for the elderly, which is big business there. So when the owner hears who's tangoing, he says, according to the reporter, 'Keep it in. Just enough so it gets out.'

"Which, if you ask me, Bert, is just what Charlotte has done.... The Man? Imperturbable, one hears. I find most attractive men are... At least to begin with... But with him, it's said to be a lifetime accomplishment."

She'd had a fit of coughing then; he'd been chary of asking after Philippe. But that had been her third phone call of the week; either she felt it her duty to give him the news, or had some of her own to tell? He hadn't pressed; she may have thought him oddly remote. Never detached, though. Surely never that?

"Gee, thanks, Aunt Erika." Unlike his mother, she likes to be called Aunt. As a tribute to her wisdoms—which she needs to be sure are there? "I had a card from Nell."

An alto cough-groan—the kind that's been in waiting? The phone, as he's been learning, already strips one naked, in a way. "So did we all, Bert dear." The next comes with the usual venom. "You don't get a leave, that job of hers; you'd have to quit. But she's sweet-talked as usual; they've let her take sick leave. I told her: you want a total lift, these days the chic route, and the best, is that miracle man in Argentina. Ginny Kemper came back looking like an ingenue—even on the beach. But Nell's card is a one-liner, wouldn't you know? I have it right here: 'In Switzerland, dear Freddie, the

trick is to keep one looking like oneself. Love, Nell.'...Matter of
fact, Philippe saw her there just before...He's on the Wallenberg
search; that quest never stops. Said she was blooming; her cosmetic
need was all in her head...But that's what he—what he says to
me...But enough of that...How's The Hague?"

"Oh—itself. For what passes for eternity...Matter of fact, I'm
on a sort of hunt. Nutty. But keeps the yo-yo bouncing." A relief,
to let it out.

"You could use a little 'nutty,' nephew. Good luck."

She's always bracing, and they'd exchanged their "matter of
facts"—a phrase Moorsohn had said was always symptomatic,
"like 'Matter of fact, I'm Jewish.'" As for Nell, the family "dizzy"—
who had once said to him, "I'm their token for that, m'lad"—she'd
endeared women to him early, if not toward her type. Her card to
him had read, "I'm having an affair with my body. Hopefully not
blighted." Signed, "X X X. Our Nell."

His grandmother and Mendenhall? He can't face it. Doesn't
have to. Let them.

On reflection—forty minutes of it by the vaunted British Railways timetable, at the start of which this train, stock still on the
track, should have departed—he's exhilarated to be following
those two, swaying in their wake. At any time a new life-course can
beckon. Whether by land or by sea.

Another passenger has entered the compartment. Acknowledging
Bert with a blink, or rather Bert's possession of the seat that will
face forward with the train's motion, he considers the adjoining
seat, faced in the same direction and involving a possible intimacy,
but settles for one of the backward-riding seats opposite. This gives
him the window, and since Bert's seat is the inner one, near the
sliding door, the most privacy obtainable. He hangs a raincoat on
the hook above.

Months among all nations have given Bert his own assessing

blink. A "gentleman," this guy, though these days not necessarily from birth. Fiftyish, bulky but not stout, florid at the cheek but not the nose, from climate perhaps, rather than wine. As to clothing, suited up much like Bert, until you take a second look. Nothing this man wears has ever dared to be new. Nor would he ever be caught fitted out "from top to toe." A dun vest peeps. Weather-taming, not a match. No hat. Hair that sardine-gray, madder-brown mix which seems to favor the peoples of northern Europe, clinging to the scalp, and if it lasts long enough to speckle, not deserting. Like this man's, usually barbered conservatively, according to what the skull has asked of it. A faint curling at his nape, upward of course, may indicate long-ago attendance at a public school.

In Paris, prowling the main drags, Bert and Zach had played this identifying game—his uncle haunted maybe by the affection for the humans he'd banished from his art?

"When the Young Brit goes mod, Bert, he can go vicious. And she. Look at that one, buskined like a medieval cowgirl down below, her mouth like she's been strung up for the hangman's crowd, and bloodied afterward. Next to *Angleterre,* the French, with their pinched little harlequin or de Sade fancies, are just paddycake. What the French do for us is to keep Western dogma chic—just shift it to some other ketchy corner. But never forgetting the real cathedral...Ah, look what's coming toward us. There's a traditional Brit for you, or thinks he is: City of London man, not a high-flyer, maybe one of the banks? Civil servant? Maybe even Scotland Yard, computered up to know everything, and keep it dark? Those boys don't mind looking out of date, even court it. Young or old, rich or poor, every Brit keeps another century in reserve."

About America, Zachary Duffy will never say.

Outside the window, what one can see of the sky is brewing like tea in a pot. The steward will bring you a pot of your own; the word here is "cozy." Man across the way has no luggage, no umbrella, no reading matter. Doesn't need any of that. He's at home.

Bert, over-clothed, weighted with all of that, feels vulnerable.

Traveler's weather, blowing hot and cold in the glossy salons of "abroad." Where schools of fish swim past him, none his. Where the thrill of the new can fail, without warning. Or the wonder of his job humdrums.

He knows what to do. Think of the errand. The one you took so long to realize you harbored. Such an errand is like a waiting arrow, its bow flexed. The archer kneels, in an ambush not of his making. The target? What has brought her to where Thomas has discovered her to be? Not to hide. To hide would not be her style.

How does he know her "style"?... Four hours in a morgue. Then—a one-sentence revelation at the police sergeant's desk. "I am not Mrs. Cohen." The voice neither belligerent nor meek. Merely proclaiming what she is.

A long cab ride then, your best friend chattering away between the two of you. He casting you a speaking look, whenever the dim scuttling light—under a bridge, over a causeway—will allow. Then at last subsiding into what had maybe never silenced Shine before. Awe.

Next: a funeral, as long as a pine box. The two friends see tears in each other's eyes. None, in hers. She stretched herself on the box before it was let slide—as much of herself, brow to waist, as she could. You thought of the rest of that long, slim body. Of those parts left for her to keep. Not for you. For the man in the box.

Ten years and more on now, she may be in a new tangle of what life offers. Lovers? Marriage? Work? Thanks to Thomas, the work is all he is sure of. The rest he will—risk? For what? He has only these images.

After the shooting, a trail of time while she'd stayed on with his grandparents until they left. Intermittent glimpses, behind the screen of family company, and their estimates of her, overheard. They had made strong images of her also. By then he was into manhood, that burgeoning which no bar mitzvah will fully dictate.

What age she is now he doesn't know. Their circle never knew her age then, though the family gossips had nudged each other,

"How old is she, do you think? Younger than poor Lev was—we can be sure of that." Or they'd counted back to when Lev's first wedding was, to how old that bride was, and when she died. To when that was, in Lev's life. "And the boys?" To when he died, a Sunday in their own lives. "He would've been forty-two, forty-three." No need to be accurate. That's what Bert thinks each time he sees a rabbi giving the funeral oration and specifying, from notes, the fine-ground meal of the Lord in his mouth, over a person he's never met.

One is said to dream that persons not seen for a length of time will look the same. Bert hasn't really dreamt. Now and then has a girl reminded him, without his noting this, and so been chosen? And in comparison, so been put aside? He can't say. The images remain.

Time to read in the notebook. The brief part about the profs maybe—any former student can't help relishing when those are mocked. Yet his grandfather had included himself.

The essay at the diary's end, on funerals, he has so far avoided. He had been a pallbearer at Peter's. A high Mass, in the cathedral. How many dispensations his Aunt Agnes had had to obtain for that, he wouldn't know. She had been disposed to argue that he not wear his yarmulke, until he shut her up: "Oh no, I wouldn't, Aunt. Not until they show the Christ wearing one, on the Cross."

At the Mass itself he sat with the other bearers, men he didn't know, recruited for his aunt maybe by her Monsignor. Or even professionals, like the Jewish watchers for the dead? As he sat, wrapped and soothed in a liturgy that ascended with the incense toward that graven plaster Jesus nailed there, his flesh yearned to migrate toward it, to help make that body real. When thousands yearn with you—or six shouldering a coffin, or a minion bearing along what stays forever disembodied—is that faith?

He'd wanted not to be excluded up there on Gethsemane, and for the aisles of people bowed with him in the sweet-smelling clouds to be included among those addressed by Moses on Mt. Nebo—in that joint peace which will never come from The Hague.

He hasn't worn his yarmulke since that Mass. Not that he's

abjuring his bit of cloth; it's needed elsewhere. Until it rises with
the smoke and settles on that bent plaster head, he is ceding it.

FROM PETER'S NOTEBOOK:

All serious scholars worked under an aura we understood. In
any discipline, each scholar's work being a kind of carapace—
like the shell of a beetle or turtle, formed gradually, and sustained throughout life. Those whose shells were the most individual might be at more risk, but in the end—i.e. during a
lifetime—might attain more renown. Communication criss-
crosses between or from under such shells, and this worldly
union of identity never stops. If the messages to the outer
world were not entirely understandable, this could make for
reverence—in that the work under these carapaces was distinct from daily life.

For some scholars this was a plus, though some held an
opposite view—and hope. Such aspiration was not unlike the
lyric in art—sometimes vilified but always on a pinnacle.
Scholars hold it a virtue never to quite achieve, so leaving
room for the next. At one's death or gradual demise, the carapace is stored on a shelf of history, always open to reference.

He is reading this when the train jolts, shoving with a back-and-
forth motion severe enough to make the diary slide from his grasp.
Already too thick for the leather cover it came with, and temporarily out of the secondary wrapping in which the bank had made delivery, it also here and there holds personal cards that must pertain to
those alluded to. Some of the cards are loose, some still attached to
the relevant pages with dried-out tabs. Some have scattered to the
floor, though not all. But Peter's allegiance to the random has been
demonstrated. Were there no railway carriage, we'd have gone on
to his further interest: chaos. Bert starts picking up the cards.

The other passenger doesn't help. He senses I'd find that embarrassing, Bert surmises, remembering Gerald scrambling for
Kitty's pearls, tugged at too demonstratively in a theater lounge.

But a few of the cards have landed on or near the stranger, who solemnly hands them back, one by one.

As he does so, the train heaves again, and they are both jolted to the floor. Unharmed, their hands braced on the floor, they stay so, while the train, gathering with the familiar grooving sound, settles into the greased lickety-lickety-split all rail passengers trust. Both men stand up, brushing themselves off. "British Railways prides itself on meeting its schedule," the stranger says. At the window the landscape is fairly blurring. "I rather fear they will."

Bert feels at home with dry wit. "Customs had ahold of a man when I was coming through—maybe that was the delay."

"Work stoppage, more likely. London, the union likes to turn off the lights just as Mum goes to make supper." This doesn't seem to irritate him.

"Maybe there was a roughhouse?"

"Doubt it. Not since the coal-mine troubles. Mild as lambs these days, Labor is." It's not possible to tell on which side he may be. "Different with your lot, is it?" Does he hope?

"Same."

"Ah."

Bert is inserting the cards where they belong. Here's the Roman architect's card, marked in pencil "Cyprus," and under that, "Plums." Eating them? Or perhaps some insight, specially rendered? Here a card whose jokey significance he does know—the French couple who were researching Maritain. It's marked "Beds." The Hague has meanwhile shown Bert the diplomacy of the monosyllable. Phrased early on by Shine: "When I don't talk, 'at's when they listen."

The stranger hands him a last card, lodged in his seat. A Japanese one, issued Peter by the State Department for a trip under their aegis, it has his name, address, affiliation, and even honorary degrees, English on one side, Japanese characters on the reverse. The man can't help staring with interest at it, and at the notebook and portfolio on Bert's lap.

"Diary," Bert volunteers.

"Um." Plus that chortle-choke The Hague has taught Bert to recognize as endemic to the British. The odd sound they make when, against training and perhaps better judgment, they're going to break down and speak, possibly even chat with someone to whom they've not been introduced. "We're, ah, a nation of diarists. Quite ordinary pairsons." A second sound, the one that telegraphs a witticism about to arrive. "Perhaps you get it from us?" At least he hasn't said 'you people'—meaning of course, you Americans.

"My grandather's." Bert gets an elbow-dig from home. *Yes, Shine, I will, thanks.* "Er, we have those also."

A sneeze? Cough? Their repertoire is endless. Anyway, a smile. "Thank heaven for normal converse. I've been at sea four days."

"Not on that boat."

"Nor any . . . An oil rig."

"One of those platforms? Where they monitor? Or dredge?"

A keen estimate—from the eyebrows. "More or less."

But when you've scored on this kind, they pay up. He's an oil specialist, Bert hears: methods, finance, history—the lot. First for the Dutch—Shell, for thirty years; then "our own people." Latterly a consultant. As expert witness. He has often testified at The Hague. This time his final one. "They gave me a send-off . . . Our trade, one doesn't retire. One at least writes a book. On what, though?—there's been such a slew of them on oil rigs, I told them. 'By an expert who's never been on one.' Neither had they. Experts don't swab decks. I'd always wanted to. So they arranged for me to join the crew of one, as a parting gift. From my friends, or my enemies. Not simple. Clearance, transport, accommodation for six days? I'd have lasted. But on the fifth day, a severe storm coming up, the crew and I agreed I wouldn't get off otherwise, until who knew when . . . The wife's a good sport, but I was due home . . . So here I am. Made the train by a spot of someone else's bad luck, eh? . . . And the research done. Hah. My whole carcass aches from it." He settles to his window again. Talk's over. But as the car rocks, he smiles.

So that's how it looks, when one's dreamt well?

This Brit won't ask what I've been doing, never fear. But it's owed.

"Oh, that lot," the man says, when Bert has identified his mission, and its sponsor. "He does his bit for the world, no doubt. His managers run a very tight ship, though. I've dealt with them."

He leans back without further comment. At his side the window darkens. From Bert's angle there is no landscape, only a cocoon into which all on the train with him are traveling. "Train must be half empty."

"Always. The neutral nations are seldom crowded."

"You're right," Bert said with surprise. "Four months, and I never noticed that."

"Diplomacy can puff. Has to. How would you rate us there, one to the other?"

Us? Is he with their Foreign Office then? At home, "oil" is all business.

"The Dutch are the most up front. I liked that." Though it had made him feel devious. "The French? Huh. They make legal lace. So you won't notice what's most to their good . . . As for the U.S., everyone accepts we come on too hard." He feels he's done well. Yet maybe an addendum. "The Swiss? Maybe—just too clean."

"And us? No need to be polite."

Teach me not to be? This guy seems up to it. "Any of you I got to listen to—each Britisher seemed to be a committee all in himself. He hearkens to all their views, before he speaks."

A slap of water at the window, then rain drumming. The light blinks, then blacks out.

The voice opposite says merely, "Better hold onto that notebook. Here comes that storm."

The train runs on, eerily with less rocking. Could an increased speed be why?

I have a flashlight, Bert remembers. But why? The wheels' grinding resolves to a high whine. At intervals, they skip.

"My wife's great-grandfather kept a diary," the voice opposite Bert says into the dark. "He was a circuit preacher during the

Luddite riots, when the workers were smashing the new machines. He agreed with them." *Steady,* the voice is saying, actually. Then a laugh. "I agree with him."

Bert's turn.

"My grandfather...was a lapsed Catholic...He kept...talking himself out of it. Or still looking? Hard to say." But has he willed me that?

That creaking must be the window.

"Double-glass, this car. One hopes that all of them."

Is that the dark speaking, politically?

The car, chilly to begin with, is now icy cold.

"Layers we wore on the rig; couldn't half tell was I hot, was I freezing. Kept wondering how armor reacted, in weather. History books don't say."

Bert has a vision of ranks of schoolboys, pestering their tutor to find out. All of them in thick sweaters. Like the one in his own bag. "My New York liaison rang me early this morning. Dawn, in fact. Likes to show he's on the ball. He's made me an appointment to meet with their London manager; they'll pick me up. And warned me, to wear a suit."

"Ah, that manager. I've dealt with him. Little Jew, smart as a whip you'll find, short of his telling you so—what *is* his name... not the one he was born with, I fancy...Ah, names are the first to go..."

The voice has gone wee. As if suddenly alerted, even in this dark, that somewhere along the line it's gone wrong. Bert's encountered this before. They know, yet they do not know.

Such remarks boggle him. Is he to counter, seizing ridiculously on whatever small insult: "Some of us are *tall*"? So casting himself in with the Charlottes? Or will he ignore, with no one to applaud his own loftiness, and the offender unscathed? Thump him, or her, to a friend later, and you may risk: "Oh, you're too sensitive." Too stubborn to admit that in any of life's trade-offs the gap between the uncommon and the common remains unbridgeable—and the insensitives will hold the cards.

His teeth are chattering, or is it the carriage's side-to-side rocking? Cleave your tongue to your mouth.

A gray streak at the window. The man opposite is peering at his wrist. "Luminous dial, my old watch. Radium, but I shan't give it up." Small houses are blurring past his head. The light has lifted, on schedule. He gives it a nod. "You're going to make it. We're on time." The wheels too have muted, to that syrupy glide which intends destination. "Nasty little villas," he says, lifting his chin at what is now passing. "Build them inches away from the hoardings, they do now." But his tone is affectionate. "Well-l, we're out of the weather." The train now and then gives a comfy shunt, as if it too has changed temperament. "Twenty minutes, I'd say." Halfway through he snaps his fingers. "Names are the first to go, alas. But that manager's a betting man, it won't hurt you to know. So am I. Wagered him once how many barrels in production in a given month ahead—both of us were wide of the mark, of course. But I was nearer. He paid me off with a pair of tickets to the Test Match. Won from a lord at a gambling club the night before."

I'm out of my sphere, Bert thinks, happily. His whole body smiles.

The rain has stopped. Shortly the train does, without any bustle he can see. The stranger—he's that again now—shrugs closer into his jacket. Bert does the same, as if by now he knows what weather to expect. In the long pause before the doors open, a tickle from the business cards Thomas had ordered for him, from the "correct" stationers. At The Hague he'd learned the protocol for cards—and the smarts that underlie: Exchange those freely with persons you will likely never meet again. With some countries the exchange is like a tic that everyone has, and must exert. Or when two or more from anywhere intend to huddle for mutual future benefit. But once over the border into the personal—nix. A brief sympathy? A search for a paper scrap better shows it, and perhaps the favorite pen. An action extra but still loose, and the other's enthusiasm better gauged.

This stranger and he have grazed intimacy. But only by reason

of situation, weather and transport being obviously of the com-
monest. And by chance acquaintance several steps removed: the
"random" his grandfather had touted. And not forgetting that nice
touch—diarists. He'll bet—beg pardon, wager—this guy has a
wallet full of cards, but would never even consider proffering one.
Nor will he. Though there's that urge simply to know *whom*. What
kind of person has shared a possible danger with you. Whether he
is what you assume.

"Cheers," the man says. A nod.

No handshake, of course. Too, too American. Nod back.
Done. Very mannerly. Come on. Chuck him a fare-thee-well from
our camp.

"Have fun," Bert gulps.

A wheeze, unclassifiable.

Gone.

He's not met, but is paged to the stationmaster's desk, where the
telegram, from Thomas of course, reads: "Proceed to hotel. Manager unexpectedly called to the continent."

Split Thomas down the middle and you would find old guide-
books full of such rheumatic phrases, plus clips of the very latest
advises in print, including magazines for the coffee table and those
better stashed under the rug, in case your visitors are not as "into"
as they should be. Thomas, Bert suspects, merely has one foot in
the door, and the average man's desire to go no further—except
up, within the empire that has hired him. As an aspirant in "publicity," his mission is to catch "the total tone of things"—after "a
horrendous spate" as a political speech writer, "who only catch
each other's." He had come to Bert's plane bearing a gift of some
old Hachette guides, ranging around the world. ("I have duplicates.") On the top one he'd lettered: TRAVEL IS KULTUR. As to
the nitty-gritty details, he has the certitude of the scholar gypsy
who has never been anywhere, so can't prove himself wrong.

This telegram further reads: "In the future, should you want to meet a manager, better check." What sauce! It was Thomas who had set it up.

The telegram also repeats the hotel address. "Just in case. Any London cabby can get you there. They're the Talmudists of their trade. Don't over-tip."

He hadn't been aware that Thomas knew he was a rabbi. He expects that will always follow him. *Be sure you have the calling,* all acolytes are warned. His mistake had been to declare too early and in public. Keep it private, as he's almost certain he will, and he may better discover who and what gods call.

"Be sure to ring me," Thomas had said at the plane, "whenever you arrive." The words with a softness perhaps special to the tongues of those haunted by what will always be for them vicarious. Yes Thomas, I'll phone you. But how can I tell you how fully arrived I am?

In the huge Victorian shed of what must be either St. Pancras or Eustace Station—he can hear Thomas's correcting mutter—he stands stock still. Glass and metal is all it is, the air stained to that smoky tobacco-chaw effluvium of all stations; maybe there should be spittoons for trains. Or maybe not. Bathe in this dusty anodyne. Underfoot the same terrazzo dirty enough to be marble, or wood hardened to stone, which persuades, forebodes—that one is going somewhere, or has gotten there. The same ant-people bobbling their appendages as if a leviathan toe has just stirred their nest, scurrying them to the ends of their Hymenopterous earth. He is at his end. Above him is a great, soaring archway, strutted with metal but prismed with sky, whose sentimental era might well have labeled it ABSENTIA. He can still hear his family at their chattering—a distant aria. Those voices may swell to opera, now and then. He's no laggard; he may answer. But they are no longer following him.

Outside is a street rutted with promise, to be fulfilled maybe only skin-deep. A street as reserved in its way as a compartment, but with tickets available to all; the snub buses meek as oxen, bridling in impudent red—in tribute to history's gore? Boarding one, the accents fly behind him like campaign hats; he's ignored the queue. He sits, jaunty, in the fudged silence possible only to a nation whelmed in talk. He's lost his manners also. "Charing Cross," he says when the conductor comes round, though he knows it to be in the opposite direction to where he's bound. He wants to savor that too. Primed since he was knee-high by the Anglophiles at his grandparents' table, he hears again old Isaac, the college's language overlord: "The Norman Conquest was an absolute boon to them. They have as many vowels as they have vegetables."

What better place to declare, to dare what under the obeisant "we" of the clan he never has. Nor as amiable second-guesser to his dearest friend. "I am an I."

Possibly each one of this herd of mutes sitting two by two is saying the same. The more so if he or she has an improbable errand, worn close to the heart. But beware, now, of extending sympathy. Be selfish.

At the next stop, though warned it isn't yet his, he is the first to swing off. Wherever he may be, everybody there, the whole of London, seems more ambivalent than he. Umbrellas, though there's a glint of sun on wet cornices. Shop windows breathing forward to be noticed, in the sudden rays. A girl passing, sleeveless. An odd fizz in the air—of spirits determinedly high? Two matrons in raincoats. No men in those. He takes his off. He has no umbrella—advised that the kind purchased here lasts for life. He walks on, envying the cyclists, who have a lane, their faces raised as to a chord of music. No opulent clouds—as in the colonies? Up above, a brushwork sky, changing palettes. That's it. This sky is holding conversations . . . It rains.

He hails a cab. Nobody else has run for one. Slowing, it waits, condescending. A nod from the cabman, at the address. One adage. "Mind the head."

He rings Thomas.

Thomas enjoys apology. It allows him to ramble. "Sorry. Slippage of authority, top down. See it all the time in L.A." Son of a

Texas couple who'd both worked without luster in the studios, he'd attended high school with some of the children of the directors, even of the stars. "F. D.'s in the office, he always stops at my desk, to read my postings. He's kind enough to say they educate. Sees your schedule, goes to the phone himself. Must have known the manager mightn't be there. He wasn't. Maybe later, F. D. says. But I'm to run any meeting through him first. Such an easy guy—but you never know when he wants to be hands-on. Anyway, I was to head you off. Your ferry'd already docked. The Railway just gave me sass. Seems there was weather, heh? But I was able to pull rank...How's the hotel?" He doesn't wait to hear. "That whole block off Sloane Square's what they call 'maisonettes'; you don't like yours, switch. Let me handle, huh?...You going off on your own now, we can still accommodate. Had my way, I'da put you up at Brown's for a night, for the experience. When he was younger F. D. himself used to stay there."

Bert's about to ring off, with thanks, when the hungry monologue returns. "Got time for a story?"

Shine and Bert had met a couple of the New York managers. "Benevolence can be hard as nails, at the bank," Shine had whispered. "Sure, they bow and scrape to the big guy. But you and me, we're not pay dirt." Exiting, at the sight of Thomas grandly semaphoring at them from his cubicle, he'd added: "That T. T., if we're all he's got—he won't last long." And Shine has long since left Thomas behind.

"Okay. Spill."

A preempting cough. "London in the fifties, F. D. was staying with his wife. Cocktail parties, the top guys at the BBC, Commie sympathizers more than one, wearing fancy Chinese-silk embroidered vests their wives had bought or made for them. She bought him one, buttons all down the front. He's standing in the lobby waiting for her when an American guy, loaded with suitcases—big crowd, bellhops all busy—says to F. D., 'Here boy, take my bags.' So F. D. clicks his heels, hoists up, and shows the guy to his room. Gets a tip from a wallet of bills the man don't look too familiar with. 'But this is a five-pound note, sir,' F. D. says. The man shakes his head. 'You people, your lousy class system. You'll never make the grade.'"

"Ah, great."

"F. D. once said to me: 'Don't wear too many buttons, T. T.' That's how I heard the story. He had to explain."

"Ah."

"Keep in touch."

He will. He still has this urge to follow up, come what may. "By the way, what's the other T. in your name stand for?" In case Thomas is eased out, as is probable.

"Thomas."

Takes him a moment. Thomas Thomas. What the elders can lay on you. "Wow."

"Used to hate it. But it distinguishes. If you can live up to it."

A fraternal fear steals along Bert's arm bones. Maybe that's all his own sympathies are. "Well, thanks again. For that other— project."

"Mum's the word . . . Tell you the truth, why else would I put you in that kind of hotel?" His voice has dropped, though the office may have given up listening to him. "Keep too low a profile, there's a heap you'll never learn . . . Ta."

Though it's damp here, his breastpocket is like burning. When you're feeling the "I" raping what you thought you were.

After two months of hoarding what he didn't want to meet until he could take action on it—her address—he opens Thomas's second, smaller envelope.

On the Underground he sits opposite a blind man who smiles sightlessly, lifting his head in greeting to all, and his lead, a German shepherd, who will meet no one's glance. Cautioned to save his ticket to give up at journey's end, Bert has, but how did the ticket-seller know to inform? Or are they trained to clock any too-impetuous stride?

At Hampstead, the high stairway to reach the outer world pleases him, a glass mountain he runs up lightly, hearing his steps clack. The streets unwind just as mapped. All small façades here, likely not single-owned, but he has whatever a frog prince must have; here's the door. *Ring basement bell.*

A merry-faced woman with her hair wrapped in a towel opens up. "Ah yes, we spoke. I'm Val, Deb's landlady." A flirting survey of him, sideways. "And friend, more's the pity. What a surprise! Do come in. We're giving her a moving-day party; anybody who gets away from us deserves. *Do* mind the step." He barely has. She watches him survey a gloom brightened with easy chairs, plop cushions; a cookery alcove behind Asian hangings; a desk at either end, one piled with books, the other with newspapers; Oriental rug far too big but rucked up to fit. "Happy untidy, that's the ticket here." Her face, upturned, isn't yet wrinkled, but pouched with what those batting lids surely want him to see as cycles of love. "Upstairs flat rents unfurnished. But the jumble sales roundabout are glorious."

"Val, you're outrageous," a man detaching himself from the eight or so people in the room says, his head bent for the low ceiling, as is Bert's, who is nodded at. "Howja do . . . Val—you know my sister's first in line."

She wags a palm between them. "Neville's our resident government architect. Presently on a university dormitory—looks as if it'll house only wheat . . . This is Debra's friend from—ah—outer space; we've always suspected she had one." As the two men mutter names, she grins. "Outrage is what I do best, Neville . . . Bert, wine's over there. For every two loads carried down they're entitled, but for guests—on the house. Debra's upstairs, going over the last of it. She should be down directly. Meanwhile, join the fray."

"I'm not in the market for a flat," Bert says.

"Good—oh," Neville says. "So many of us are. Wasn't really worried though. That flat leases to a woman. Val likes to be fair. And have at least one tenant long-term. The neighbors grouse every time there's a van." He jerks a thumb to the trundling up above. "We load and unload from the front, and in the passageway to the proper front door. The rear's on a grade."

"What happens to the other flats?"

"Ah—those are the decoys. Move in down here, it's pleasant enough—and bide your time for an empty. Or lease upstairs, later find you can economize—and down here is warmer. Val's circumspect. No swaps. And no sulks—when you move out."

Two men come in and move to the wine. "Easy enough, there isn't that much," one says. "Not a parcel to what it would be down here..." The other snickering, "No fear of that. But woof, everybody has china; I had a barrel." Two young women entering join them at the wine. "And what did you two dears earn your drinks with?" the other man says.

"Oh, Val wanted us to see. Her friend has beautiful things. But not too many. We took care of those."

Neville is still hovering.

"These are not Debra's friends?" Bert says.

"Oh no, her crowd, if she had one, would be all healers; they'll be still at the hospital." He jerks his head; it must be near. "And savers, no doubt. Swotting double time, for the sake of humanity. But if Deb's had to scrimp to buy that cot she's going to, or just lives plain, one can't say. You meet her in the States?"

"If that's what Val meant by 'outer space.'"

A rumble. "Val's phrase for what her fans might not find affordable. She writes a travel column, tipped to what's mod, but not pricey. And if she's pressed, she'll sound off for a fee in the Woman's pages. Though she doesn't approve of those."

"I agree," Bert says gravely. "Men should be treated equally."

Another rumble. As if at a bright child.

Catching Neville's gaze, he's suddenly aware the man is tipsy, even possibly a drunk?

He's always been slow at identifying those. Jews of his grandmother's kind and era—after all, the most influential household in his upbringing—simply hadn't had those; they themselves tended to wonder, self-appreciatively, as to why not. "*Säufer,*" they might joke at one another if at all tiddly, but never drinking because of liquor itself. Out in the college world, encountering a teacher always late for his summer extension class and brilliantly wild when there, he'd had to be told what was amiss with Professor McGill. His own Irish aunts, loudly teetotal "because of Dad," had been induced to a nip when in their brother's house. "In any misalliance such as Zipporah's and mine," Peter had remarked, "the Jews tend to prevail."

"You in the market for Debra, you'll have a long pull," Neville says. "Join the club of those who've tried."

Dizzy with the happy ache of what he's learned in less than an hour here, he says, "Think I'll have some wine." He makes for it.

Neville beats him to the glass. "Ask you something. About her." A gulp, the long nostrils sniffing—a hound at the behind of another, who may have the scent. "What's she doing here, a princess like her, one of theirs? Who won't give any of us the time of day? And in a house like Val's." He's not too pissed to give Bert the once-over. Fallen dead as a stone on arrival, Bert has showered and changed, into his own armor. "Expect you've not seen much of this yet, your age—the stink of middle-aged sex. Nor run across a house like this, where you come from."

He's weary of hearing where he comes from; he may no longer even be from there. But growing up in a city can school you early to the sight of people's power comforts, their small, fake Edens. Looking about the room he sees the same mix of quasi-professionals attempting various ages or concealing those, a few of them men like him in sweater and jeans, the women in no special plumage, except that each will sport what she considers—has long considered—to be hers. Hang about their conversation and an aura can indeed steal on you—the sexual afternoon, still proving itself, and only semi-ruined. And of no special faiths. Except perhaps the lack of them.

He can remember such a place. Nell's—the furniture sparser, but with the same ideology—thrift-shop luxe. And here comes the woman Val herself, tripping through the door, clothes-laden. She holds up a long sweeping duster of a coat with leather on it, trailing from her short arm, and plops a silky clutch on top of it. "Have a look at these glad-rags, will you. She's never even let on that she has them . . . Ah, we've all had them, haven't we." She gives herself a shake, with that same poignant bravado. Not in my first youth? Watch my act.

"Oh, I dunno, Neville—if I can call you that," Bert says. "My youngest aunt's been desperate to be a whore all her life. Without success."

"Silly ass." A paternal hand on his shoulder. On second glance Neville's not that old. Nor that drunk. "Look yonder."

She's there. The image. Tall enough so that the dumpy Val, in front, comes just above her breast. Slowly she emerges from the alcove he's kept her in. The mouth-curve. Faint smile that has no dimple in it . . . The family curator, his aunt, decreeing that until you see Etruscan in the flesh—the deep-holed eyes that appear never to blink, the span between brow and chin—you're not disposed to believe that those craftsmen culled from life . . . "Can it," Wallie had said, "she's a *ballibusta* any guy would recognize. Plus extra, being from the holier side."

She hasn't seen Bert yet. He is catching up with all he hasn't remembered.

"A toast to the foolish virgin who's leaving us," Val cries. "Van's packed."

A clinking, a "hear hear," a few limp huzzahs. He can tell without turning that Val must be a bit much for some of them. But not for her. That long-fingered hand presses Val's cheek. Even in a basement, with not too many lamps challenging the drear, the diamond flashes.

Wheeling, Val's seen him. "Oh, good grief, I forgot to tell you, Deb. A beega surprise. Over there."

She's seen him.

"Not foolish, certainly," Neville mutters behind him. "Our Val makes free with the biblical. But so do we all, eh? . . . And the child? A love, however she came."

All her history is being fed him. He moves toward her, with

whatever freight. Does she still see him as he was? Will she see him as he is now? He wants both.

"You?" she says. "You. Bert."

People aren't regarding them. He's lost Neville. There's been a toast. A van waits. Val is off again, in a free-and-easy beyond tact. In this house people stand back.

Debra. He can say it aloud now. He thinks he has. They clasp. "You come from Zoe?"

So she still thinks of her that way. What a lot he'll have to tell. "I have something from her, for you. But I'm—on my own."

"You—always were."

That smile. He only saw it once. At some quip of Shine's.

"I always see you coming in with that hat," she says. "The one that was nicked." Her shudder isn't for him but to cast off all they're not to mention: the Plaza, the morgue. And to say she's "seen" him, since? All these months he's thought of himself as searching a history, not bringing one. He touches the crown of his head. "Wore another one for awhile. But discarded it." Before he can tell whether or not she gets his meaning, she's called outside. Everyone in the room follows, he with them.

The van is at the curb, two doors down. In front of a boarded-up house with an agent's sign on it. "Nobody here to complain," Val says to the dozen or so gathered. "Pray, all of you, that next-door doesn't sell." A youth with orange and purple hair lounging at the side of the van swings himself up on its platform, goggles at the inside, hops down again, and slams the rear shut, each move spryly elaborate. Just so he and Shine had done in the teens, acrobats showing off their universe. "You let this punk son of mine cadge a ride, he's not to drive," Val says. "God knows, he's been trained to unload." At Deb's headshake, the son gets a motherly swipe. "Smarty-pants." She and Debra hug; Debra climbs into the van's cab. The motor kicks in, idles; she's a smooth driver. Funny, how one can tell. The motor in his chest is savage. Around him people start to wave, even a hankie or two. In front of his nose a grizzled hand, two fingers crossed, slowly expands to a V.

He keeps his hands grimly at his sides. No scenario like this was ever in his dream. He will uphold that dignity.

A head leans from the cab, dark glasses on.

"Bert? Bert. Have you time to come along?"

They're sitting on deck chairs, facing a not-too-broad reach of Thames, on whose other side no houses are visible. Half a mile back they'd passed one on this side, larger than the small spare one behind them, built by the same architect, a Swede. She and he have the exhausted ease of those who have been in traffic. The van, still unloaded, rests outside a garage as neat as a breadbox, whose height, Debra had agreed, the van might just clear, but why bother? A phrase he sees the value of. At his hotel, the woman at the desk, to whom he'd explained he wished to settle his bill, had stared out at the van parked as best it could on the cul-de-sac's angle, and at Debra seated high in its cab. "Very good, sir. Since you've paid for the reserved night. No bother." But when, carrying out his valise and suit bag, he apologized for blocking the façade, she'd gone glum. "Seen far worse." Perhaps apologizing was best left to them?

Lounging now, he stretches to the feast of questions and answers to come. "Good these chairs were right at hand."

"Oh, the punk knows what's needed first in any move. He's had to."

"Doesn't he mind being called a punk?"

"Half of why he does it. Has done, since he was twelve. Nose rings to elevator shoes. The lot."

"How old's he now?"

"Seventeen."

The age he was when they met. Does she know? "Maybe the best way for a kid living in that setup."

Her glance turns full on, then veils. "Neville been briefing you? He can't believe he's lodging so far beneath him. Yet lives in fear of being bounced."

He won't ask on what floor Neville lives.

"How'd you and Val meet?"

She gives him a look. People must often ask. "You mean—why'd I hang on ten years and more? Since I left Zoe in Italy, for Britain, actually."

"She's back to Zipporah, by the way. When she came home."

"I can . . . imagine why. We were close, those months. She was like a—not a mother." Her lips tighten. "Nor an aunt, which I've never had. More like an elder sister. Who's a grandmother as well."

He has to smile. "And mine."

"Ah, that boy's, yes. Same age as the punk." She studies him, her chin set. "Harder to credit now, that she's yours."

Hearts do miss a beat. When one's seen as the age for it. She's dealt straight. Do the same. "And how old—was that girl?"

"Twenty-eight. Pushing thirty, as they say."

"They do." But we're also where we are. "You don't have to tell me more. If you don't want to."

"Maybe more than you bargained for?"

"I'm not bargaining."

"Val and I met on the women's ward. Of the hospital where I still work."

"You were her nurse?"

"In a way we were each other's. We were both patients there."

A bird flies overhead, broad-winged. "Hawk," she says. "I spent hours in bed with field glasses, watching them. And Val in the next bed, making up comic names for them. She's the cleverest hysteric I know."

"Breakdowns?"

She shakes her head. "They monitored us both ways. It's a canny hospital. And the mental unit—I'd trained there—it's tops. They caught onto Val fairly quickly—gave her a D. and C.—dilation and curettage. Kept me wrapped in cotton wool." The hawk's long gone, but she's still following it. "Sorry, I forget, go professional." She leans forward, to the river, not him. "Val'd been afraid she was having a child. By which floor of the house she hadn't a clue. I thought for sure I was having one. By Lev, four months dead."

She sees his shiver. "Men don't want to hear how women's insides work. But it can be like an ark in there. Swelling up on the least bit of treasure passed on. And waiting for holiday." She stands up, brushing off the crumbs from the basket lunch found on the seat of the cab. "So I had her. A tiny, screwed-tight bud that wasn't going to have the wherewithal." Her face pursed, shrank, so that he could almost see the small, withering creature. "Excuse me, Bert, I don't usually—" She's smoothing the belly of her white dress as if birth pangs are still there. "And I have to change."

While she's gone, will he mourn the way she's altered? The brittle, Englishy shrug-and-tell. The tatty devotees? Or when you stumble upon the offerings that an image once adored for its strictness is now accepting, do you too accept?

When she returns she's sniffing into a handkerchief; she's been crying. That too isn't the stunned coolth all had half-admired when she'd lived on with the older Duffys: the middle-aged widows or the deserted, grudging "You have to admit—"; the aunts' "Nurses see everything!", meaning sex; Wallie's "When she's over it, I wouldn't mind seeing what a Sabra has between those legs." Even Charles's quizzical "She does rather hang about the old man . . . probably only the Middle East deference. Which Jews and Islam share, by the way. I should write about that. I wonder—do they *know* they do?"

Bert's had his girls; he wants not to grudge. Nor to pry. And don't comment on the tears. Women either sneak those in or expect you to ask why; she's not that sort. When he does look up—has she read his mind?

"You're wearing those—khakis." He and Shine had taken her bicycling once, to cheer her. Shine saying afterward, "She don't want cheer."

"My old army uniform. It suits, out here."

"Where are we, exactly?"

"Isle of Dogs, it's called. Why, I haven't researched. But it spoke to me. And I'm supposed to have done well. Outskirts. Odd residents when there are any, one grotty pub, one for the families. And one measly bus. But now the Thames has been cleaned up, people have spotted it; there's already a minister from the Home Office, we're building a bank here." She laughs—at ministers? He had never seen her laugh.

"Shouldn't we move the stuff in? Before it rains?"

"It *is* raining, Bert."

So it is, a drizzle so fine it seems merely a freshness on the pores. They laugh together. "If I can't have the desert, Bert—and I know I never will again—I'll have this."

"You won't go to Israel again?" He knows he must be on tender ground, but maybe they can exchange. She might clear up why he too resists.

"No." Her head shimmies, the black hair, bound with a twist, loosening. "Never. I did go back. Once I was able, and circumstances by then permitting . . . That's when Val coped like mad. I'd learned to trust her. In hospital. After she'd left, she'd brought me her cat to visit; they allowed that then. Even the punk helped; he was still Etienne; father was French. He calls pets and babies alike "animalia"; he's going to be a zoologist." Each time she speaks of those two she softens; they'll have been her family.

Leaning on her spread knees, her fists between, she looks as young as he recalls, but in the black locks there's a white hair or two. "I had to go back. I went for a *get*. Know what that is?"

"A Jewish divorce. Orthodox. I'm not up on the commentary."

"You may have mine."

A swallow, before she can voice. Is the river in part why she's moved here? It can mirror memory's stare.

"The pair appear together," she says. "Or we did. There may be divorces in the absence of one or another; I had thought him capable of it. I came back in order for that not to happen. And you might think it would be public—not a courthouse, this was religious law, but maybe part of the *schul*? I see now of course that this couldn't be . . . In the schoolroom, for Hebrew or where the rabbi instructs the bar mitzvah? You would contaminate the children? Or in the vestry, where only the men are?"

There's another bird; she doesn't look up. He holds still.

"You go to the house of the patriarch. Or a reb can arrange. . . . It was a long way out. My hairdresser friend from the old days—she has her own shop now, a strong bold woman—she wanted to drive me. I said no but gave her the directions, for her to wait outside until it was done. I wanted nobody bold there except me."

She stops. "Shall I make tea? The kitchen is set up."

"Keep on."

"Two cab drivers attached to my hotel—they weaseled out. One had to drive his mother-in-law to a service, the other had a business client—at that hour in the evening? They didn't lie well. They didn't want to be associated with such a business. Or with me. But how did they know? The patriarch—he was known to do this. Even a reb can't always command different. Or ask a *get* of those quality friends who sipped his kümmel."

The river gives back her stare.

"So I took a bus. The buses in Orthodox neighborhoods, the women still sit separate. I knew otherwise by then—Antwerp, Rome, even in that holy of holies—and New York. Where Zoe—Zipporah—took me to shop. But riding along, I saw how this bus was better for me. This was how I was born. And the women in the bus, though they saw I was not like, they could respect. I wore this—the uniform." She smooths a crumb from the shorts. "I'd be objected to; I had a skirt with me. But I wanted the judges—they should see." She's stopped again.

"Don't stop."

"Don't look at me."

He obeys. There's enough to look at, though so far no boats.

"It was a slum like I'd never seen before; not with us. I'd never seen it with Jews. Low tenements, huddled around an inner square; they'd remembered the ghetto, or even missed it. Made their own. Stucco fronts, yellowed and spotted, like with liver disease. On one side, a black car parked, a man sitting. I could see the forelock, young. One of his acolytes. The reb, my husband, was arrived. And on the other side, my friend's car." She stops.

"Yes?" He keeps his face averted.

"A dirty room. Three men in it. My husband, last seen when Lev's boys were living with him. A clerk—the scribe; he will write down what is said. The patriarch, so old the eyes are mucoused, near blind. And the smell. A nurse knows all those. This smell is old men, widowers, singles, sitting day after day in the pants they pray in. The women of the congregations feed him, should help wash. But maybe the stink of what he does puts them off. The scribe whispers what I have on. The reb is furious at my shorts. I say, 'He should see. But he won't.' Then I have to 'speak my shame.' Christians have sins; we have shame. I say, 'I confess I am a whore? I am glad to.' Then their words come at me, but like pebbles. Even such a patriarch is civilized; we Jews don't stone. Not our own kind. Then my husband, the reb, speaks, why he wants the *get*—I shut my ears. The scribe writes everything down... Then—the old man yells at me to take off my shoes. And then— to take off my rings."

"Your rings?"

"My friend warned me. Not to wear my good one. But I did. I wanted him there. Lev...I was told to throw the rings on the floor."

He wants to share, to be with her. "And did you?"

"I laid Lev's ring on the floor. I will not throw. There is also a finger ring from my confirmation; in heat it sticks. The scribe comes at me and pulls it off. I think he's going to step on Lev's ring. I say, 'Take my confirmation ring; it belongs here. You touch the other one, I will crack your neck; the army teaches how.' Then my husband speaks, the only other time he does. First to the old reb, then to me. 'They only lie there while he reads you out of the marriage. Then you can pick them up.'

"Only I am to be cast out, is it? So I let both rings lay there... Then it's a long schmoos from the blind reb, on who the husband—who is granted grievance—should marry. 'Is this one tall?' he says. The scribe answers yes. 'Marry short.' A long ramble on wives who will obey. 'This one is handsome...Ah, I thought so.

Choose maybe a widow, not in her prime. The marriage broker will have dozens. And when the husband is the reb's age, money hurts less than youth.'" Debra leans back. "So some young fool with an ambitious mother will be saved, I think then—and I was proved right. But the reb—that's another story."

"I know. Read about it."

"You saw? A lot did, I guess. But that was all—some time ago."

"Yes. It was." How much he has to tell. "But—finish up."

There's been a change, as swift as the weather here. A sense that those stories are past. A calm.

"I did," she says. "I picked up my rings. I kind of had to—scrape them. The floor was—viscous. But I put them on. Then the patriarch chanted. Maybe not a curse. An absolution. For the reb, against me. He joined in. I was wearing a headband. The scribe tore it off. And then they shooed me out the door."

"They what?"

She made a pushing, with her hands. "Or like—if they'd had mops. And the door slammed behind me. Then it opened again, and they threw out my shoes."

He takes her hands. In the last light, Lev's ring doesn't sparkle much. The second ring is gone. She draws her hands away, washing them together, turning them palm up. "Outside, there she was, my friend. I got in her car. We don't speak. She doesn't start up. 'Where's your headband?' she says. 'And what's that smell?'" Debra got up from the lawn chair, lifting her palms to the drizzle. "'Vomit,' I told her. 'Probably female.'"

Summer days in the north of Europe are lengthy. But they have exhausted this one. "Let's empty the van," she says. But as yet they don't.

She's at the river's edge, looking skyward, arm stretched. "Sun's coming out. You watch."

Not what would be greeted as "sun" in North America, but as if tints are seeping from above. A scaly fish-gleam in the water, a rosiness on the new tile roof. Her voice comes distantly as she walks the edge. No, there would be a man here tomorrow; he'll help them unload the garage. "Teaches at that modern school you may have heard of." The name escapes him. Turning again to face him, her smile is wide enough to pierce the dapple of ray, gleam and cloud. "And bringing me some important baggage." Her natural voice is alto, often a darkish almost monotone, but this last is softer. He has a glimpse of what she might have been with Lev.

She's seen his thoughts. Some of them. "He's Val's friend. Currently in her basement, whenever he's in London. Though he gives signs of wanting to be permanent . . . Why Neville is so bleak."

He watches her. The shorts make her stride; in a dress a woman thrusts the legs side to side more alternately. She can be chatty now, though still lapsing into the remote. He pictures the society he's seen her in. Not one class, rather sororal and fraternal. And sexual? Weaving in its strays, as only a city can. According to Shine, whose stepmother had one night come to his bed, you put a woman on a pedestal, it's you who can take a fall.

She's enchanted with the new house. On the way here she'd described how she and its architect and his wife, friends of Neville, had stayed here in its last stages, adding the "built-ins" she craved. She's prideful on "the technicals"—like whether a sump pump would be practicable, at so low a level. Now, as she wanders, he sees her circling the house perimeter, with babbles of startled admiration, kneeling to a cellar door as if it has mushroomed. Yet even Zipporah, worldly wise and formidable in her sphere, can wax into this other focus, spinning a haze of domestic needs, goods, comforts, toward which the very walls of her house seemed to lean, helping her to compound. He's seen Peter stand there, endeared, then throw up his hands and tiptoe away.

"Let's just take out some of the boxes in the van," she says. "Get those stowed away? Behind those there's not much that bulks. Gresham and I can swing it tomorrow. He plans an early drive."

The teacher. Her lips quirk when she mentions him—why?

Some of the boxes they remove are see-through plastic. Towels, blankets, and quilts—ordinary. One box of fine lingerie, folded and tissued. He's seeing her history. Sewing kit, picnic basket. "Ah, the thermos," she says. "And look, they've packed us a feast. I better trot it in." She goes.

What looks to be another basket is carefully shrouded, maybe more food. Leaning into the van, he pulls it toward him, uncovering. A baby's basket, underneath it the neatly collapsed legs on which it would have rested. Inside: tiny shirts, coaties, smocks, gowns, a frilled cap. What's called a layette. A baby's life. Quickly he covers it again, with its piece of torn sheet.

Helping her stow away what they've unloaded, he has his tour. Wherever possible, what's built in—slat-beds, drop-leaf table—is also movable; that's the architect's idea. "He says it's his ideal house." There's a center pole at the top of the stairs. She grasps it almost ceremonially. "So this will be mine."

Downstairs, the leafed table swings out from the wall to accommodate two opposite each. She divides the food, poring over each allotting. Fruit, cheese, a tube of salami, boxes of wafers, an avocado. There are spoons, a knife. Slicing the meat, pouring oil on the avocado from a small cruet in the cupboard above the table, she motions him to eat. He sees an open bottle of wine in the cupboard, holds it up, questioning; she nods. The glasses are not yet unpacked. They drink from the bottle. No crusty loaf. Otherwise the spread could be in New York—the upper West Side, the Village, Brooklyn, other places where he and his friends had started out, or still were. The wafers, one thick, crenelated kind, one feather-thin, are the kind you find in airports, hotel restaurants, commissaries where diplomats gather, the "convenience" grocery spots dotting highways, USA. He tears open the packet of thins. "Unleavened bread; now you can get it anywhere."

He's not sure she gets the reference. Why should she? Jews in the desert; the two of them are not that. Her glance, cozy between him and the food, urging him, averts. He's not so sure she hasn't understood what he meant.

She points to the "Made in England" on the packet with a long, pale polished nail, the same that traced Lev's name on the list that the desk-sergeant, a sober look on his black face, had offered her. Unforgettable, his features. His protracted look, as from a kindred desert—that a sergeant on such duty was able to award each suppliant.

"A seminary reference," he says. "I should stop making those."

She is still regarding the packet. "Marks and Spencer. The girl who sold in the hospital shop taught me to say 'Marks and Sparks'; cockney, everybody does... So you did go to the seminary. I remember there was talk." She's still tracing. "And that Shine—did he go along? Ah, no, eh... Why do you smile?"

"Because everybody always said 'that Shine.' Not so much now." He tells her what Shine is now up to. And what he himself is doing.

She hasn't asked why he might want to stop "talking seminary"—a Moorsohn phrase. How will he ever tell her that though some think him semi-defected, he is a reb?

"So you do good," she says. "That was on the charts." Her lips purse. Food doesn't vulgarize them. "And the others? The old Nettie—I suppose not still in this life?"

Her cadence is so biblical he answers, "Shalom. No. But still with us. She took us all with her." He explains.

"Ah, she reminded me of old women in Tel Aviv."

What's suddenly sobered her? She'll have her references. None so mild as his. "And you remember us, so well."

"And why not?" She can flare. "Those months after. When they took me in. You never wondered maybe—that first Sunday—how I knew you all by name even, by face? *He* had told me. And how he would show me off. On our—first Sunday."

They are silent. The phrase has such a sound. Such a picture. The last one you see, before the amateur screen clicks off.

"And he kept describing to the boys. Year by year, so they would keep up with their mother's family. All of you were tangled in."

And we never noticed. We were the hosts. "How are—the boys?"

"The older one is in business. His own. Not the gemstones. Accounting, advertising?—something with an *A*. They start early

there, and can go like lightning. Once they get out of the army.
And the business left here gave him a stake. I think, too, something
came from Boston."

Of course. That would be Mordecai.

"And the other son?"

"The younger one. My little Moshe. He was killed in the Six
Days War. He was just old enough."

She has risen again. His image, the round eyes, lit from behind.
The long sculpted neck, nurtured in outrage. The hairdresser doll,
buried in the marriage midden, but rising again, monocled with
history.

Alive—a double beauty. Long nails, glistening in this ascetic
overhead light. Under that khaki the long white body, lying in the
bath, eyes closed.

When he'd brought her back from the morgue, after reporting
to Zipporah, he'd had to pee. He'd ducked for the bathroom at the
head of the hall, the nearest. Opening the door, he couldn't close it
at first; for a minute he'd thought—another body, not trussed. Her
eyelids fluttered. Not at him. In those days he took only showers.
No baths since he was six. Now he saw how in a bath, you floated,
in rhythm with the earth. He'd lifted the heavy door by its knob,
easing the hinge so when closed it wouldn't creak—a trick you
learned if you had girl cousins, and had stolen away.

A body trussed like a fowl in a window, you don't forget. It
hangs behind its glass, shifting into sight now and again with
sneaky ingenuity. The other vision, half-confirmed when he began
with girls, gradually vanished. Or he'd thought it had.

She's bending over the spread on the table now, hovering for
choice. "Food is food."

He can see her as an old woman, still saying that, casting the
spell that works for her. He'll want to be there.

"Have a nosh." She slips a thin round of salami in her mouth,
holds a slice toward his; he parts his lips. Chewing, heads cocked,
yearning slowly, they kiss. No umpire could say who kissed first.

His valise is at the top of the stairs, waiting to be allocated to its bedroom. She catches her breath, they've run up fast, hands linked. "Got it from the attic," he murmurs, at her fixed stare. The old family password, said when one of them chucks you a grin, having recognized what you're wearing, or carrying. She nods; she's remembered that too. She hunches, brushing the old leather. "They sell these in Europe. Many people buy." Motioning him to put the valise in one of the other two bedrooms, she leads him to hers.

In bed he says: "There's a painting of you. A woman floating, in the bath. In the Louvre. Or the Jeu de Paume. I could not buy." They have yet to embrace.

"I saw you, Bert. Your face, in the crack of the bathroom door." She doesn't whisper. "You've like—stayed there. All this time."

As they grip he hears against his chest, "We're like tangled, Bert, you understand that? You were there with me. You saw."

She's so tight he could think she never has had a man before. Being a whore, behind her own window? With luck, they may touch on that someday, jokey. In the confines of love.

For awhile, there are three in the bed. Then there are two.

At the breakfast table, where she's preceded him, the bread and butter laid out, the jam, even oranges, she greets him so touchingly, so suddenly the good consort, an air he knows isn't adopted. Seated, the two of them looking out at the river, she is calmed, queenly, in the way women are when all has gone right. He pushes aside the thought of breakfasts he's used to. All with coffee. But he can like tea.

It's late; that should make them smile, but she's restless; the teacher-chap is past due. "Couldn't I bring in what's in the barn?" He's discovered she calls it that. Already he's assembling the homely facts.

But she is vague. "Not much that bulks, true. A few pieces to set me up at Val's, when I first came. Bought on the never-never.

That's what they say here when one pays by the month. I had the money, but calling it that seemed to suit; I already knew I was in for the long haul . . . But no, let's wait for him."

He marvels that she can refer to those months "in cottonwool" with such nonchalance. But she has been in waiting for so much of her life. He doesn't quite match her there. But they will fall into step.

Suddenly, she's chatty. The school the guy comes from is a marvel for Britain, he hears. A beacon in the educational world. "Children from every corner. Including, well—the wrong ones." A quick glance at him, almost humble. Is she referring to what he's told her of Shine's new project, in part his?

"Gresham could teach in a public school, but he's not having any. He says where else could he teach both history *and* plant life? Not all the students are super-bright. But all have passed their A-levels in worldly ways—before they were out of training pants." It's clear that she's quoting. But her voice is shaky.

"A-levels. A kind of test?"

"Some here see it as the dividing line, on more than brains. Class. Nationality."

They are still looking at each other across a divide. He must take that into account. Is she testing him? How? On whether he'll root here? As she certainly has. Or can they do so together anywhere?

It occurs to him, with a sinking, that she may mean kids. She's thirty-eight. And there's that grim layette. Is she asking him whether he can do without? Or whether he needs for the two of them to try?

"Training pants," he says. "Two years ago, Christmas, Zipporah's spare room, made into a nursery, fairly stank with those. Charles has new twins."

"Ah, he does? You must bring me up to date." But she's looking out the window.

"The mother's Chinese. They tend to win out. You find yourself dandling two Buddhas. Named Duffy." There may be one

thing above all she must be told plain. "Generally we do the absorbing. We Jews."

It's still dazzling, to see her smile. She leans to him, rubbing
her hands back and forth on his knees.

"And I'm all for taking what's offered," he says. "If it is."

"So am I—" she says. "So am I."

She's looking at her watch. "That whole school's off time.
They make a show of it. Go there, you won't know whether you're
in lesson period, or a recess. A troupe on the hillside, girls and
boys, doing mime. A sheepdog herding in a prize ewe. Or a senior
lab experiment—of such medical interest that a top journal, the
Lancet, has been alerted." Her voice is amused, even tender. "In the
kibbutz, that age, we would have danced for joy."

"You go there often? As part of your job?"

"A kind of job, yes. Not my hospital one." She stares at him as
if to evoke a response. Like the interlocutor, in a charade. She
wants him to ask her something—what? Out of the fund of those
matters she herself won't phrase?

In New York her aloofness, poise, had at first been ascribed as
natural to her situation, even to be admired. Later it had been a
little blamed on her country. "Those Sabras I deal with in the market," Gerald had said. "What chutzpah. They let you know they
come from pioneer, you betcha. And believe you me, businesswise
they can carry a short knife. Not that this girl, of course. But it carries over." Wallie said, "Not only their grandees, who I meet in the
campaign. The young ones, they let you know who they are. Ask
you for money, they still patronize. Like in army camp, you are the
tenderfoot. And even if you wouldn't be them for a million—that's
what we are, hah?"

The women of the family, awed by her situation, a trifle romanced by it, would have gathered round her in harem fashion, but
found her standoffish. Erika, who had been to the Middle East as
part of her art training, said: "They're all like out of the ages there,
Jew and Arab both. Know-how as to what to do—like archaeology
is just part of the family. I've a friend, a lawyer in Tel Aviv—you

would think her so advanced. But there are some points we are
agreed not to discuss. You think a Jew is a Jew? So be it. But there is
always—'the foreign element.' The Israelis are that—to us."

He, Bert, had still been young enough to be allowed to stay in
the Sunday discourse, yet be ignored. His grandfather, listening to
what he called the men's "mantelpiece yak," had said to Zipporah:
"On that score I'm not qualified. On who is a Jew. Or only a Jew-
in-the-rough. But you know who Debra sometimes reminds me
of? That Irish woman, Erin, who nursed Mickey at the end. That
impassivity they have. Like they walk around in ordinary life,
knowing our intimate flesh. Every time I see a painting of the Deposition, the body being lowered from the Cross, I think—maybe
one of the waiting kneelers is one of those."

Eustace, the childless rake, wanting a young male confidant,
had said, "That new young woman at Zipporah's"—all the young
ones appearing new to him—"she a nurse, eh? They can be the
sexiest."

Outside the window this morning the river, gray-green,
doesn't assist. That's the virtue of a river, even when city-tamed. To
the right he can see the path, branched off from the road to London, along which the teacher and his load will come.

She comes to stand at his shoulder. Their fingers link behind
him. In bed she has a tender ferocity, ministering to the rules of the
body, yet giving him his personal due.

"You haven't yet told me. What the new job is." He turns to
her, palming her face. Add a veil and she could have been one of
those kneelers: young Jewish nurse, in the year before the Lord.
"You still nurse?"

She stiffens. Like an applicant. "When I came back here, I
wanted to. And when I myself was in hospital. When I get out, I
thought, that will be—our support. The hospital was delighted.
I trained there, you know. But a week on the ward, and I knew I
couldn't. Shouldn't. Someone like me shouldn't be personally responsible. I trained in a war, I told them. Where you must some-

times cross the line of duty allowed a nurse. You are advised to. But later—it's you who are left on the battlefield."

He takes her in his arms. What visions she must have had, may still have! While he was deciding whether or not to believe in God.

"So they offered—" she says, muffled, "to train me back."

He can only hold her until she breaks away.

"I have many friends there," she says, standing tall again. "But of course they wanted most to help because of the child. So that's where they send me first—to the children's ward. To learn again the war that is in any hospital. The small ones there, with the brain tumors? After the chemo they wear turbans. The girls look like little mothers, the boys like pashas. After that, I go through the wards, one doctor says, 'like a dose of salts.' To pay for my keep, I go where I am sent. One week to watch operations. The next, to serve in the gift shop. Where they sell wine, imagine that. I sit as administrator, behind desks. And stand out front, waiting with the patients who have no rank. On the hospital budget I'm an adjunct fellow. Because, they say, they learn from me."

"So have I." So will I. "Debra—what is 'crossing the line'? Is it—helping people to die?"

"In war it is permitted—not frowned on. In peacetime—not." She says it first in English, then something in Hebrew.

Is she telling him she did both? What Hebrew he knows is ancient. How the modern might phrase its Talmud he can't say. The Hague has taught him only so far: that a nation and a religion are not the same.

"And you told no one?"

"I did what I did alone. I must be judged that way." Her head bows to that rhythm. "The hospital was very fair. The British are always trying to be. Though they are not very Brit anymore." She looks up at him. "They will never ask me. But like you—they have guessed."

So he has his reply. A Talmudic answer is always half from your own head.

"They did ask—did I want to return to Israel? If so they would help me get a post."

"And would you?" His lips are stiff but he says it. "We could perhaps go together?"

"You have not been?"

"I should've. No."

"I will never. A person does bad, maybe it reflects on the country. But a whole country, when it lets itself do injury? Its own children will suffer bitter wounds." She tugs at her hair, now in a pony-tail, as if it's indeed a rein. "Mr. Gresham, Alec, he teaches that one must endure history, but live it too. He told us about the Children's Crusades. Who were lost to slavery. So I decide—where people try to be fair, and where my child was born—I can build a house?" Her eyes fill. "Crazy. To talk so quick, after years. But I want to tell you this, before they come."

"Sounds like the whole school is coming."

She smiles. "In that place, one scholar with enough push can be the whole school. But Alec may have one or two hanging about extra; they like to ride in that car. And of course they're welcome."

In the house where the child was born? "Debra. I saw the basket in the garage. With the baby clothes. So—neatly folded...I'm so sorry."

When her mouth falls slightly open is when she looks as Zipporah once said. Like a sibyl who doesn't know she is. "Oh. Yes, the basket. I would no longer do up the clothes, actually. But that basket gets lent."

She's brushed past him, to peer through the window. Is she sobbing?

"Don't waste your pity too soon, Bert." She's rubbing the mist from the pane. "That car of his. It is hardy. One still sees them about. And on the telly. An estate car once, he says. Given them. Now it's a family member. The school calls it 'the last aristocrat.' But an owner of a fancy shop on the corner down from our shop in Tel Aviv, he had one. I see this one, I am there." A plaintive glance—is she half laughing? She's at the window again. "If they aren't here straightaway I shall have to phone—and get nowhere. It's like phoning Bedlam."

What so infuriates him? He can't tell whether she's sobbing or laughing; can she herself? He's sore with change, hearty with sex, wanting her to stay in his life forever, yet with the foreknowledge that in her peculiarly dictated way he and she will be separate. Can he withstand the burden of mystery she imposes? Of which, he would swear, she's not aware.

"'Straightaway,'" he snarls. "You've sure passed your A-levels on Brit lingo." The rush of blood in his ears stuns him. Does the franchise to be nasty come from ego pursued?

She's turning to him, radiant. "I have to keep up, yes. And look, look. They're here."

He's pulled by the hand to the outside. The car is a lulu, a vintage tourer, some native brand with frets and angles that half proclaim its affinity to carriages; one can almost picture it hitched. A lanky man gets down from it, and a chunky child, a girl in the middy and plaid skirt of school photos any time, everywhere.

Any boy who has attended a good school, the kind that if public can yet reverence its pupils, and if private may overdo, will recognize Alec. He is the beloved master. If Debra has said his name too often, this is because in his purlieu his name is a fixture on every tongue. His face, shriveled by teaching, wary yet trusting, remains young, from immersion in generations that don't age. To "knock you into shape" would be anathema to him; he'll tease the too poetic scholar toward sport, and ply the shot-putters with classical analogy. In the end, their generations have shaped him.

He and Bert shake hands; the girl and Debra kiss—so they've met before? Debra, laughing, attempts to swing her around but the girl's too heavy; she must be nine or ten. So Debra has a protégé. Maybe her "program" at the hospital is involved. The horror he'd felt as she told him of the sweet thrall of being needed is a mix he won't soon untangle. That meekness of hers, like an animal capable of telling you how it is being trained up. That power, beyond frankness, of the blunt.

She is bringing the girl over to him, to present her. There's an air of that about both of them.

"This is Cicily."

One of those solemn little owls whose stare can put you on trial. Thanks to the Duffy clan's habit of breeding, one or more of these now and then crops up ("Seen Nell's newest? What a sober-sides." Or. "Watch that quiet little minx of Erika's. She's got us all down pat."). These kids stare at one like intruders. He was once one of those himself; he thinks he knows how to handle this.

Smiling faintly, in effect raising the newcomer to your grown-up level, you return the stare.

Cocking her head slightly, as if to balance the tiara on it while holding him eye-to-eye, this kid slowly bends the knee.

Alec sighs from behind her. "A new fad. Broken out like a rash, all over campus. Even the boys are doing it. Telling us whether or not we pass muster."

In turn does a curtsy help tell the court who you are? The girl's face is a familiar aquiline, big orbs above. Part Jewish, surely. Maybe all. He always feels queasy making the Jewish diagnosis. You slap shoulders in an Irish bar—"Ah, Duffy, is it!"—and you're merely identified as a kinsman. But recognize a Jew, even inwardly, and it's a racial remark.

Debra has her arms around the girl. "I named her 'Cicily' in thanks for being helped so here, to have her. Sounds well, don't you think?" The two faces do blend. "My baggage—" Debra says huskily. "Cicily Cohen."

A stammer comes out of him, like at The Hague when he'd been addressed in a language new to him.

"Oh, I know who you are," the girl says. "Mother made me a list. And we have snapshots. You went with her to see my father. You're Bert."

A week later he and she are walking the river edge where they can. They do this daily. "To find a hill," she'd said, the first time. "Down here, they're hard come by." He likes tempering his stride to the clipped accent just above his elbow; in the week he's stayed on here she seems to have grown. She's well aware of how her mother strives to imitate her. "Oh I natter; that's what one does. When I was at Val's, I trotted alongside with whoever was talking; it was like being on the tram. At school, some are quite posh; I can do that." She purses the lips with a richer curve that may someday be Debra's. "Too-*oo* fearfully twee!" She giggles. "And sometime I've done Mrs. Willis, our char."

But she's stopped that; it isn't "demo." "Alec says one makes fun only of one's equals." Or, even more to the point, one's betters? All the teachers concur, except for the despised one sacrosanct in any proper seat of learning. "A horrible" dubbed "Miss Fuzz."

In course of "giving you a tour," she and he range from sedge to grass to street; climb steps only to be met by barricades, or "No Exit," veer more or less toward London, next day vaguely toward Greenwich, but never really on target, under orders not to go "too far." It's he who usually terminates the walk with a "Let's bumble back home, shall we?"—a quote, the girl's own, so appreciated that the owlish grimace makes his heart stop. Of course he no longer thinks of her as "the girl."

It's then, at a walk's end, that her prattle subsides into one of the conclusions he waits for. "My mother does her best," she'll say. "But she can't really chat." Or: "Debra is not really too strict a mother. She's ace about letting me wander. 'Too far' means I'm not to press you about us." But daughter has her ways. Complimented on her growth, which at ten going on eleven is not yet in tow with either her fellows or her ideals, she had kicked loose a stone on the hill they had finally found, from which vantage they could glimpse the Tower of London. "It comes from having a man in the house."

She's on school holiday. Debra, this week finishing up at the cardiac unit, where she'd been asked to assist in an emergency and had done so, has returned home in a glow irradiating the house — and them. She's been offered a post on the hospital staff, as assistant

and "ethical advisor" to the administrator of her old bailiwick.
"*Cor!*" Cicily had chortled, so breaking her vow not to "send up"
Mrs. Willis, whom he has now met. "Is that the Mental?" Assured
so, though cautioned not to employ that term, she'd countered,
"Well, it *figures*," this throwing Bert a sly credit by quoting him.
"After all, you've done well enough with me." Adding, as she pat-
pat-pats Debra's cheek: "And if some of our 'ethic' can be tended to
outside this house, I would really welcome it."

By sleeping in Debra's bedroom without explanation or apology from either of them, is he helping there? Also, his presence
while Debra works means that for "the hols," Cicily won't have to
go to Val's. "It was okay there early on," she said. "Little darling,
being passed from hand to hand. And my being there kept Mum
out of the sex bit. Even so, we did have to kind of crouch at the top
of the house. And though the punk is my ideal brother, having a
female punk is not my mother's style."

How much she knows of her mother's public history is taken
for granted, he gathers. All. As for private confidence, there are
confessions one must not—need not—exact.

Though any thoughtful man will see "the land of Canaan" as a
blessed illusion, he's resolved to take the lure. If she and her owl
will share his life, or he may share theirs, he will stay in Europe—
if that proves to be her only choice, or the best. Strange as that hegira will seem to the home folks, on second glance it may be the
destiny they expect of him: their schnook, with a dream wife and a
ready-made child.

When Alec left, after helping Bert empty the garage, then
breathing in the cups of tea that revived him like air being delivered to a wrinkled balloon, the three of them watched the old car
flourish itself off, a dowager performer lifting her skirts to dance.
And to fart.

"Some parents object to his driving us," Cicily said. But the
school argues it is teaching them to risk. "Since most of us are at
risk already. And we'd better learn how to manage it."

He's heard that approach. At his own school, when he was perhaps two years older than she, the math teacher, also the sports
coach and no fool, had complained to his well-fed team of cool
suburbanites and the supposedly city-stunted, "What kind of Es-
peranto you guys swapping? Do you have to sound like adults trying to be kids?" Expecting no answer, having met too many
parents doing the reverse, he'd growled: "Knock it off, huh? Won't
get you anywhere in basketball."

"And does it work, Cicily?" He savors her name. "About the
risk?"

A nod. "I only get romantic when I walk."

One morning, days after Alec first brought her there, Debra, a
housewife he's come to respect, had gone into the garage, which is
tidy now, only a few boxes remaining—plus the basket.

"I tried to tell you," Debra said to him, when she returned with
the basket.

"Tell him what?"

Swapping glances over Cicily's head—which one of them will
answer her?—he takes up his parenthood. "That bassinet looked
so—folded away. I didn't only think she'd lost you. I thought she'd
had you, but you'd died."

She does remind him of the new ones at his grandmother's,
the wide-eyed "Raphaels." They know they will never die.

She shrugs. "It's supposed to be nice inside a mother, getting
born. I don't remember it." The basket is to go in her room, to
house her doll.

Upstairs, her room is strewn with clothes and other regalia,
shoes, rubber boots, books all over the floor. "Put the basket
there." He manages to. "Nurses are so tidy," she says, looking
down into it. "That's all it was. But that's my scourge."

A Madonna he recognizes is tacked on the wall facing her cot.
"Hideous, isn't it. That babe could never cry. She had it hung over
her bed, in hospital. I put it up to remind me not to be difficult."

He helps her open the crate containing the doll. A porcelain beauty, with those parted lips. When he was Cicily's age, a sidekick whose sisters had such a doll had once urged that they poke stuff down the hole.

"Hannah. Hannchen. The grandparents in Israel sent it. I guessed it was hers. But no, the great-grandmother's, my mother says. They kept it in the safe, her father's shop. We wrote a thank-you note. I signed." She rubs her nose, pushing it to a snoot. "She can be difficult."

The doll is laid in the basket. "She's German. I try not to like her, but mostly I do. Partly she gives me the shivers. Want to see why?" She inserts a hand under the red velvet collar at the back of the biggish head. Unlike the Christ child, will it cry?

See what it's doing under Cicily's hand; shiver too. The perfect pink-and-white face is turning, disappearing into its own head. A second face appears, twin to the first, only smiling. A third. On the bisque cheeks there are china tears. "Sometimes I leave it like that," she whispers. "It was kept so long, even before the shop, in the kibbutz; it must be Jewish by now? The punk, he says they don't boil people over there. Or gas them. They only slide them out."

He can't slap her. He can't exclaim her graceful name. Or that the punk may be a neo-Nazi. Or that some of "them," in her mother's province, do cry out. All of which occurs to him. Instead he's silent, all the psalms of his and her joint heritage sounding their grace notes in his ear. But his face betrays him.

In mutual dismay he and she start picking up the books. But there are no shelves. She lets her load slide from her arms, happily. "I expect you read a lot." Is she mocking? "My mother doesn't much. One reads her."

What devotion has enabled her to say that? "Hush, she's coming," her daughter says. She scurries to the bassinet. When Debra enters, the doll smiles.

Next day there's a wild wind-and-rain storm that makes it impossible to walk, though Debra drives off as usual in her craft, an old but still respectable car called a Morris Minor, of which one

sees legions on the road. Whether there is a Morris Major he
doesn't inquire, only beginning to understand that though an
American may be hip to all the clichés of very upper- and very
lower-class life here, "that huge muchness, our 'lower middle,'" as
one of their own newspapers, picked up at The Hague, had referred to it, remains impenetrable. In this extraordinary week of
his own "hols," actually dictated by the child's schedule, they have
seen only the milkman, the postman, and a few tradesmen; no
neighbors are near enough for a casual encounter. There is a pub
where, of a Sunday, Debra and Cicily, down here to watch the
house grow, had lunched. And have promised to take him.

At home, Debra would have been said to be "undergoing psy-
chotherapy." From what he can observe there's been no such, only
an in-gathering of medical experts who happen to be friends, who
exert only that authority, allied to the curative power of the hospital routine. She has been treated as if she has a normal woe. In his
New York life, seen through this end of the telescope, that great
stream of common woe to which all religions attest seems no
longer to be assumed. Instead, there seems a quackery for everything. Or at best a palliative, extending to the very brink of death—
and on the way to reorganizing life as possibly excluding even that.
At night here, listening to the brooding of the river or to its quiet,
holding the sleeping Debra in his arms or disengaged from her, either comfortable, while he and she rest at a domestic distance from
a child nested near them in her own future, is he perhaps being instructed in alternatives? If—if—he can see human circumstance as
the very idea of God, in which we hang illumined in the same purity as under physical law, might he serve as a rabbi?

Next morning he's slept past the birdsong he usually greets
with delight, as ratifying his presence here. Debra is gone; her hospital hours are always too early for it or too late. In a fortnight—
that sturdy word whose brisk punctilio he's begun to appreciate—
she'll be told either to stay on as fully a staff person, or to go free.

Every morning, he wakes also to that looming obligation, the message he must deliver. For surely, whatever it holds, it is that. Why else has neither Zipporah nor he been able to destroy this hand-me-down that can't help but disturb? To whom are we being loyal?

There's a rat-tat-tat on the bedroom door. Closing a door, when one wishes to be alone, or should be, is carefully observed; whether or not the practice precedes his being here he'll not be privy to, nor should he expect to be. If he stays on, such small tokens will be part of a situation he will accept. Mother and daughter have bloodlines he can't share. Mother and daughter, and true father—however remote.

A chortle of laughter from outside.

He's decent. "Enter."

Cicily bursts through the door. "Wake up, lazybones."

They go through this each morning. She's adopted him.

At breakfast, her cheeks chipmunk with the same oaty paste eaten at school; she says: "The wireless says there's to be a big storm, as we had last year, first day of term. Birds blown into the chapel. Wind and water, you couldn't tell which."

Her school is what was once an abbey. What polyglot faith goes on there?

"I'm chicken on walking, today," she says.

"Me too."

She's grateful but doesn't believe him. "Have some of my cereal?"

"Not on your life."

She giggles. A familiar tussle. One will need those too. Some morning he will eat it.

"The first big storm for this house," she says, awestruck at the window. "We're to watch the skylight particularly."

What to do meanwhile? At that age they don't want substitutes like an hour of music, a choice of book, or even the telly—not if you have to. Only action will please.

"You could show me your list." Of us.

The list is so inclusive that even stray visitors to the Duffys during Debra's time there are on it. To match it to the snapshots, where those exist, to check what Cicily knows of each subject, along with what he can add, takes them to tea-time. "The list was made when she was in hospital," Cicily says. "While I was being born. She made it for me. So I would know that part of her life, she says. But I think it was because she thought she might die. And I might not."

No written descriptions are attached to the names. Only who they are, within or with respect to the clan. Except for Zipporah, identified as initiating Debra's stay in New York and a time in Italy, the dates of both sojourns being given.

"Mother doesn't tell much about them," Cicily says. "She says she just wanted me to know that part of her history. I have to pester her for more." Her face is pensive. "But do you think she did the list just in case? So that if I had to, I could—go there?"

He's choked. At the fidelity, that saves, and stores. At the continuity, beyond one person's lifetime, that insists. "It does sound— the list—like a will." Unsigned.

She's saved one snapshot for the last. "My mother is a good photographer. She learned in the army. And she did it for the reb. She left all those photos with him." Her face screws. "And good riddance." Not a child's phrase. What the women of a family may say. Best that she's learned it.

She pushes the last snapshot left. "He's not on the list. She keeps all his and hers in a folder. But I took this one out. See why?"

Lev is much as he last knew him—clean-shaven under the wavy dark hair, the half-smile he gave in greeting that says even to his lover taking the photo, "Dare me."

May his daughter never see the final picture that hangs in my mind.

"Look, look, Bert." She's pushed her hair up behind her head. "See? See? He has my ears."

She may have more than that, father to daughter. Because there's so much of Debra in her, he can't be sure. But if ears are her choice, so be it. The angle of both sets, and the shape, seem merely what one expects. But on deepest scrutiny, perhaps neither pair lies as flat to the head as some. "Yes, I see."

"I had to wear a cap," she says, jumping up and down in glee. "Can you bear it? One ear flopped right over." The picture is much thumbed. "I wonder whether he had that too. We don't know about him when he was a baby. Or even at my age. Only where he was born, from the passport." She smiles, not at Bert. "Brook-lyn, En Wye. That means New York, doesn't it." He nods. '"My brothers, my half ones, when they were boys they lived with the reb; he would know everything. Else why had my father sent him them? But when they asked, the reb would only make a ghastly face—my mother says little Moshe would imitate—and say, 'Because even a Beelzebub remembers.'"

She smooths the picture and puts it away with the others. "I asked Alec what that meant. He says it means Satan. From a Hebrew word meaning 'adversary.' My mother said those are persons who know too much about each other. And that she only knew for sure what Lev knew about the reb. Not what the reb knew about him. But that my father, when he was talking with holy friends in Antwerp, was so brilliant they wanted him to give a talk in the— the place in the synagogue where the robes are kept? And the men meet?"

"Vestry."

"She knows all the words. But I have to drag them out of her."

He can see that tussle. The two mouths are so alike. But he too must drag. "Holy friends?" He hears the edge in his voice. Against a dead man. Or more?

"Why—Jews," she says. As if all Jews are holy, as he should know. "In Antwerp my father's customers. And their wives." She claps a hand over her giggle. "They thought my mother's hair was a *wig*."

Orthodox. He'll leave that word to Debra. "And what did Lev—your father—talk about?" He can see Lev's other face now, the Sunday one, clean-shaven under its fan of hair. In the kitchen would be the spread he always brings. But as they are about to sit down to it, he leaves.

"He told stories. The ones that always have a catch in them?"

She rummages in the piles on the floor. "Alec found me a book of those. An old paper one. He says they fit right in with what he teaches."

He sees a familiar cover in a corner—an old monthly issue of a Jewish Publication Society. Moorsohn's library had had the whole file. *From the Folklore,* this one says. And yes: history—and plant life. And a romp with a Val.

"Parables," he says. From the Haggadah, the more poetic digressions of the Talmud. And yes—always with a "catch" in them. "And did your father go to speak in the vestry?"

"No. He was angry with himself. He'd been *shicker,* he said— that's 'tiddly.' From the champagne they'd toasted my mother and him with. And she thought maybe he was angry with her. Because they couldn't marry."

So she does know it all. The *get* too? He wishes she would giggle again.

"But on the plane to America—she says—" her voice is soft, like for a secret, "he told her that the evening in Antwerp, with her and the friends listening, was to him like a solitaire. Know what that is?"

A diamond in a single setting. "Your mother wears one."

Unlike most Cicily's age, she has silences. The storm is still on, a steady blow, somehow comforting. Reminding that we are all in God's cup, so to speak, though not far from London. The Thames rises, but not that much. Not biblically.

"Will you marry my mother?"

Hold on. Don't get to your feet. To retreat to that sustaining howl at the window. Which is your impulse.

"Are you—proposing to me?"

Her hands are in her lap. She's not saying. He sees how it may be to her, when he and Debra shut the bedroom door.

He does go to the window. The river is whipping; which way does it flow? South, of course. Yet there are rivers on the planet that do not. Has he lost all orientation? The sun will rise on my left—Debra said on his and her first evening here—and go down on my right . . .

"If she'll have me," he says, turning. "And if you will." He's half afraid she'll curtsy. But they know each other better now. There's a hint of a smile; she loves jokes. "But Cicily—there's something I'll have to tell her, first. About me. That I've not been able to bring myself to tell her." To see Debra shrink back, a stricken *Not again!* in her every outline. "About what I am. Or could be. If I tell you, would you tell her?"

Her head is moving from side to side, but not in negation. Like a mother tut-tutting at her worrying child. "If you mean do we know you've been—um—*ordained*?"

Chin forward, she thrusts at him the pug face that kids challenge with. "It was in a clip from an Israeli paper; my mother's girlfriend sent it on. About a famous teacher in your seminary, and what students he graduated that year. I was too young, back then. But my mother brought out the list to show me anyway—I remember that." She picks at a scab on her knee. "Because she had no one else to tell. And when you came, she brought out the clip." The knee scab, a familiar brown crust, is what was called "a scrape." Mothers dabbed it with red stuff, mercurochrome, making you a veteran at the skate crowd's corner. Or if your mother was not that kind, you did it yourself. Or, even more nonchalantly, let it be. That was what he had done.

" 'Ber-tram Duffy, grandson of,' " she singsongs. "Then about your grandmother, who once made a fuss in Tel Aviv. Nothing more about you. Except from Debra. Want to hear?"

When she says "my mother," we are in formality-land—at school, say, addressing a similar authority. Or ratifying her own life, position? When she names her, there's a tremor of power, more than the cronydom or the sister-bit some mothers and daughters play. She, Cicily, is the one who is here to tell.

Not the go-between he should have. "No. Don't tell me. I'll wait for your mother to." He knows what he's daring.

Both her knees are scabbed, both pink-skinned, innocent of any medicament. The mother no longer nurses; her child will be stalwart.

"My left knee is always jealous of my right one," she says, staring down at them. He recalls that intensity of the body newly owned, the tabus it casts, the spells it insists on. But jealousy is new to him. This girl's no Beelzebub. But no fair Alice of that wonderland still maybe classic here, either. The tales she's heard are grim. And her mother's stories, whatever they may be, are hers to tell.

When she looks up at him, he remembers that the Hebrew Satan means "to oppose." "My mother said: 'A reb Bert is not. A rabbi he may be. But—on his own. The person on the list he takes after is the grandfather. I saw it in him from the first. He has an Ark.'"

When he doesn't respond, she says, crabby, "Why are you looking like that?"

"You gave me a blessing. You didn't intend to. But there it is."

By now Debra is late. Whether she's decided to stay on at the hospital or leave, there'll have been a celebration. And there's the weather. Whichever, he won't worry. He feels capable of deciding all issues of domestic travail, and more, and is intent on doing so. "Why don't you go up and bring down the book Alec gave you?" he says, in the cozy tone of parental suggestion. "Read yourself one of those. Or read me one aloud. I'll set the table." She does as bid, but when she comes down snuggles herself in an armchair and reads silently. There's only so much suggestion a self-reliant child will accept.

Religion is never far from food, either its ceremonies or its needs. His faith is bound by it, from manna in the desert and on. Food as sustenance is never far from personal resolution, whether you want to be Orthodox or merely thin. It may not be quite customary for a man who wants maybe to be the rabbi here to be trotting back and forth from store-closet to fridge. But the kitchen-work paths of this sweet and homely establishment have been well designed.

Early in the week he'd helped stock up on food. One way to indicate that he wanted to stay on. The victuals he brought in had been not too gala, not just a guest's house gift, but day-to-day.

As he loads the table, he feels her watching him. This child who can ascribe her week's growth to the presence of a new man in the house, yet craves passionately to be heir to her blood-father's ears. The table he sets is generous with the nibbles and side dishes that she and her mother complicitly love. He has left the heartier daily additions—meat, fowl, fish—to Debra, enjoying her queenly eminence at this. And certainty. Of which, in one respect at least, he has so far fallen short. But there are ceremonies even for unbelievers, and he's been to the wine merchant. Under the stairs there's a small, tidy wine safe, from which he brings out a bottle, nothing Eustace would much applaud, except for its proper temperature. This place is so winning, so modest in color and outline, a true nest on the outskirts, never assaulting the river area, yet with hidden sophistications that console. Indeed an ideal house.

And here comes Debra. She's dripping wet, yet still lively with celebration, with also the briskness common here that comes from daunting the weather. Is her glow merely from that? "I'll just run up and change." She does not run.

Seated again, she's wearing a dress. "You're very posh," Cicily says. There's a sullenness—not to do with him. Her mother gestures to the table. "It's a party. I see Bert has on his jacket. Why don't you run up too?"

While they wait, he pours the wine, pausing at the third glass. "Give her some," Debra says. "Only some." When she comes from her hospital sessions, she's crisper, in charge, of herself as well.

When Cicily comes down she has on the real party dress her age and station wears, a demure lace collar on its ruby red. All on Central Park West would recognize it. She and her mother exchange a glance that doesn't include him. "Ah, you've guessed," her mother says to her. "One can finish at hospitals. I have done." She lifts her wine glass, wooing the array on the table with it, and with a sweep that includes him.

Not a party, Bert thinks. More like the Seventh Day of the week. The light-and-dark here, the amber gloom at the windows even suggests those rooms, bred of a city, that open to the outer air, even to a park's flat side. The architect here, walling us off from the to-and-fro London traffic above, and rightly deeming the river enough of a street, has compounded this. If Debra's list, those who are still alive, could be here, they might feel at home. Some of the dead even more. When it is time for announcement, especially.

"Why are Jewish clans so coy?" his brother James, seated next to him at a feast, had hissed at him like a riddle, under the barrage of jokey plays on the sex of a newborn, the date of a wedding, the kidding of the bar mitzvah boy of the moment, that had erupted with the toasts. "And so sacramental," James whispered. "I can't stand another minute of this *schmoos*. Makes me wanna jump down a hole." Old Isaac, the professor whose wedding to the young secretary at his side it is to be, had snarled across the table, "Go ahead. Jump. It wouldn't take much of a hole." And James had.

Bert's clan. He has a longing for it that no telephone will assuage. They should be here.

"I should be wearing something special too. Maybe an ascot tie, if I owned one." He wants not to be coy. But to announce. "Debra. Your daughter, she's made a proposal—" He wants to get it exact. "'Will you marry my mother?' I said I would, if you'd have me. And if she would... Will you?"

"Ask her." Debra's not fooling. She's not coy. She belongs to the land of the antiphonal, where confirmation is thus exchanged. Where the ritual word, repeated on another's lips, is the seal of both your thoughts.

"I will," Cicily says, eyes lowered.

Debra, leaning forward, waggles a finger, mother to child. "Say 'please.'"

"Please," she says, with a child's impatient shake. "And—is that caviar?"

After a ritual, people burst out laughing, freed. "I hid it in the fridge," he says. "In hope."

"At school, we say grace."

"What kind?" her mother says.

"We take turns. Let him have my turn."

The three of them bow their heads. Upstairs, in that heavy

satchel whose weight between planes he has both regretted and been thankful for, he has with him, tucked near the packet, the yarmulke without which he no longer feels respectful in a synagogue. He could don it now, as a signal—to himself—that these two will be his day-to-day rabbinate. Only three of us altogether, *Adonai,* yet a crowd.

He wonders if the other two see the heft in this room, the congregation of shadowy gray-beards, the striplings who flexed their arm muscles against kings, the pomegranate-lipped women who were begat upon, but in the Bible's list of who fathered who, did not appear. In this room haunted by the Testaments, who will not believe?

"Dear God, thanks," Bert says. "Have a nosh."

Heads raise, his also. Has Debra smiled in acknowledgment? He is not sure. Accept that he may never be sure of her, but left hanging, entranced, as by those tales on Cicily's floor.

Meanwhile, fall to.

As they eat, he notes, as not before, how grabby after food the girl is. In a school like hers, like one or two of his, where the scholarshipers were mixed in, it wasn't the underprivileged who had the worst table manners, but those born to what they considered their due. Born to money, or a special background, focused upon until they were its honed representatives, they reached over, and were fed.

The lashing at the window continues. "Don't worry," he says, as the double-paned windows strain. "We're in the temperate zone," and at last they smile.

"If the house falls in," Cicily asks, chewing hard, "which of us two will you save?"

"I'll give you a seminarian's answer," he says, looking at Debra. "Since Cicily says you know I've been ordained." When Debra nods, slowly up and down, the image of her he hoards is still there. He leans between them in stagy concentration to snatch the last roll. Butters it. The Talmud has its comics, show-offs all. "I will save the one nearest the door."

Two pairs of eyes squint; two sets of teeth show their delight.

Probably their gorgon reb—for he'll have been Cicily's too—
wasn't one to joke? Bertram Duffy the "assimilated"—but never to
that man's grim tactic—can afford to. "You remember Shine? Or
his photograph?" They do. "When people laugh at Shine's jokes, he
tells them, 'You have intelligent teeth.'"

A mouth-twitch on his left. A gleeful howl on his right. At a
round table, one can sit at the head without being that.

Cicily rattles to a stop. "Wait till I tell the punk that." Wiping
her mouth, she purses it at him fondly. "You clown."

So—he'll be that to them as well? It may help.

They are quiet throughout dessert, which he's chosen as if
food emissary from The Hague: figs from Italy, double cream from
here, both native and imported cheeses, oranges from Florida.
Though sweets from Israel had been on the counter and urged on
him by the watchful grocer, those were not his to supply. As compromise, from the Middle East, one of those glazed sheets made of
apricot.

"I'm full," Cicily sighs but seizes it. "Ooh, that stuff; Mom loves
it. Want some? No? Okay, I won't break into it." She has sighed
over every item, like those scavengers in Zipporah's kitchen had,
over Lev's spread. "Last day of the hols," she sighs.

He feels the burden in his jacket pocket. Tomorrow, Val and
Alec, who has been with her in Hampstead, will come to pick up
the child and drive her to the school, somewhere in Cornwall.
They know of Bert's presence of course, and will stay to lunch.
"The first of many, we hope," Val, who had insisted on his coming
to the upstairs extension to be congratulated, had said on the
phone. "Till tomorrow then." From below, Debra's "Weather permitting," then Val's bred-on-the-bright-side chip-chip: "Oh Deb,
don't be so Jewish." Alec, on their extension, quickly interposing:
"As a rebel from a vicarage, Val takes potshots at any faith as her
right."

But it is true; Debra takes for granted those careful sops to the
ever-abiding infinite which were heard more often from the elders
at the fringe of the Duffy household. The habit grew perhaps, with

age. Erika's husband, Philippe, calls it "the touch-wood syn-
drome." Latent in all religions, he'd said, certainly in the Catholic,
where it led more quickly to outright damnation, but in Western
Europe even fading among Jews, the farther they got from the
Holy Land. Philippe has been surprised to find it still in America,
but later revising: "You are a gloomy country, all over really, compared to us. As well as one where European verve, our frivolity, is
translated at once into the titillating, can't survive. Modern plumbing is your true positive. So helpfully anti-gloom." But revising
even that when, installing an imported bidet, he had suffered the
plumber's combined ignorance and leer.

In Debra there is another darkness Bert prizes. It comes from
that battlefield of emotion on which she was reared. That plain,
torn by a history still actionable, is what his father, his cousin Wallie, and their support committees subconsciously envy, while
pulling on their golf socks or riding their cavalry of weight machines. Or in that temperate zone of family, from which he has
come running.

He can't do as his elders have, tolerating new evils committed
under the insignia of the old. His session at The Hague has taught
him why, unable to identify with that Jewry, he cannot preach. Yet
he can love Debra's nation in her, in all its first pro-victim glory. He
can hate what an orthodoxy has wrought upon her. Yet he can see
an old vision begat upon the very flesh of its women, severe yet
honorable, ruthless yet mutable to reason: the Jew, unable to swap
humans for angels, holding the universe to its vow of cause-and-
effect, of life and then death.

What he can't do, won't do, is to love and cherish Debra only
for her tragedy. Yet as he and she sit here, held in the domestic coil,
lolling in its interlude—he maybe at the beginning of his own family—isn't that what he is doing? Clinging like the man who sought
out the oil rig, to a purpose and energy he himself hasn't had?

From across an ocean he sees, as through a telescope, the family he was born into. His grandmother, born not too long after the

beginning of the century, will—if she fulfills the span of her mother's forebears—be at century's end almost identical with it. His grandfather hasn't had that luck, but by-and-large had kept his own private pace—as the academics down the ages somehow seemed to do. What he and she have done, jogging along blissfully unaware of this mismatch to be, is what many like them were to do: to count their history in terms of the wars happening around them, whether they had been in the heart of those, or merely alongside. While for them and their country, religion is no longer a war.

Gerald his father, the happy bumbler, perhaps owes that personality in part to having been just a degree or more inside the fringe. Born after World War II, he had been of an age, though quickly married, to serve in a medical unit that never got across, in what would come to be America's most deplorable "conflict"—as some would prefer to call it. Still, he'd been honorably saved from having to deplore.

Now comes Bert's own generation, already not the latest, and the globe has stretched—or narrowed—on and around it so many small wars, with the citizens still local, even if the munitions are not. So many tribal wars, that at times a biblical age seems once again dawning. Or the globe returning there. So many crusades, but each confined to its allegory. What sensible man can any longer clock his own life by a war?

Yet *over there* (as the phrase always goes in his country), in Debra's third of the planet, this religion that has willed itself into a nation, this fist of energy, is raised.

Across the table is the woman herself. Yesterday, sitting by the river, she had remarked that her friendly healers at the hospital having advised that, if merely to confront where her own interests are, she compile a bio, she had obediently sat down to do so. Only to find her bio already in front of her. "My bio is in my fingernails. In the kibbutz I bit them, to get out. In the hairdresser we had to show them long. A nurse clips them short. Then, in Antwerp, like little almonds. For the American plane, long, long, sharp, eh. So that nobody will scratch. And now—hmm. Maybe like you say over there—'square'?"

Will he dare to bring this life of shifts and climaxes one more of those—in a paper envelope? Or will he be a dropout, and send back to Zipporah a duty arguably hers? Or be rogue enough to destroy? He wishes that he himself were not curious. Or that the accident he'd striven to avoid had occurred at customs, a lumpy "Open that, kindly," or the satchel vanished.

Debra, reaching behind her to a cupboard's satiny wood door, smoothing it, now brings out a box of chocolates. "Ooh, those," Cicily breathes. "From that place in Bond Street." This time she doesn't grab. Offered first, he takes what's nearest. The two of them hover over the box. They are deciding. Two who haven't had much choice, until now.

"He's not eating his," the girl says, leaning forward, tooth-smeared. "What's that you have in your jacket, you keep touching it." At the pocket's level she almost does. "Presents? A surprise?"

A cantor without a real voice, he intones it:

From your father . . . Left with my grandmother to be given to your brothers if anything happened to him. Your mother left without getting it. Zipporah meant to send but did not. Then she lost track of your mother.

Then she forgot. Or claims to.

"Forgive me," he says, the packet in hand, "I could not."

Debra has risen. The chair, a makeshift, clatters back. He stands too, then the girl. "From my father," she says, extending both hands. One envelope, recent, hard to tear. Then a second, a mere scrap but readable. She reads, "'For my sons. In the event of my death.'"

"Moshe is dead. Your other brother does not wish to associate." A battlefield voice.

"May I please? Open it?" This girl who grabs.

"At your peril." An army voice. A nurse. Medical.

"From their dead mother, you mean? The wife? A souvenir? What do I care? *I* was born."

The grand title. Remember it.

The bag is long for its width. No drawstring, or disintegrated. A slit down its length. On an inner slip of white cloth, two twists of black hair. As she unfolds further, two more. One slender pair of the fuzzed black—a young boy's? It must be so. The second pair, thick—a man's.

A woman can cry without blinking. Tears like pebbles. Or like kidney stones. Secreted long since.

"What are they?" There's horror in it.

Her mother whispers. Hebrew to him is a language of answers. Which one should already know.

The girl forms the Hebrew word with her lips, sounds it in her throat. Turns to him.

"Forelocks." He touches the front of his ears, index fingers to thumbs, drawing a path forward and down. "They are worn as a sign of orthodoxy." Who first saw what these could add to the bent cheek, the lowered eye?

"The punk has sideburns," she says. "Yours don't even show." A pinkie-tip delicately taps each pair. "One pair for Joshua. One pair for Moshe. The shorter one. But hair can keep growing after you die, my friend Rupert says; his father does digs. So maybe Moshe can grow his own."

He and Debra can only breathe with her. She's finding her own tale.

Cicily is about to cry. She is crying. "But why did my father give these up?"

Such a wail, like to the marrow bones. Breaking up Debra's mask, maybe beyond repair. "I don't know, I don't know," it keens. "He would not say. Not even the reb, when he got angry with himself for taking the boys, for thinking Lev would let him adopt. Even though he and Lev had been in school in the States together; he would never say more. But when Lev took me away, he cursed at him, 'Your name will be erased from the tablet; I will see to it.'" She covers her face. "And Lev said, 'It already is.'"

"Ah, Mom." They embrace. From that nest Cicily says, "Maybe
my father will grow the forelocks again, in the grave. Tell me what
they are, again—in Hebrew."

Ah, the Jews, Bert thinks. Lord help us. Lord be thanked. We
are grown ever again from your graves.

"Where are you going with those?" Debra is saying.

Her daughter, Lev's daughter, is at the room's door. There the
architect has had to violate his simple intentions, but the clumsy
entry will perhaps serve as anchorage. One way will lead you to
the river. The other will bar you, referring you back.

"Upstairs." Her chin lifts, asserting her world's small dignities.
"To show them to Hannchen. My doll."

The one set of forelocks was maybe from when Lev left Brooklyn, Bert's thinking; the family had always assumed, uncontra-
dicted, that he had grown up there. The second pair could have
been discarded when, in whatever capacity, he left Judah—if you
take that to mean only the *schul*. Many a Jewish family, assimilated
or not, has a leaver, a "colonial." Sometimes, the harshness lasts
forever. Or there can be a trickling back.

Like those "Handle With Care" gift packages, with business
addresses that when responded to had proved dead ends? What signal might James be sending? His father still avers, from gossip
heard years back, that James is doing well. But pressed for detail
he's vague. The pretenses in that household were indeed circular.

So why not intrude? Performing in any case a good deed, why
not put Thomas Thomas on to it? Meanwhile sending him a
progress report, on a grateful client who with his help has intruded
well?

On the way to bed he and Debra pass Cicily's room, now semi-
dark. As parents have been cautioned, her school, swaying from fad
to fad, has recently undergone late-night mummery with candles.
Cicily is allowed two votive candles, the kind encased in glass, for
her meditation, but each night they check.

The two wax stumps in their dumpy red hobnail containers are
lit, each set on the pint-size dressing table he'd carried up himself,

that Val and the punk had given Cicily on her "tenth." In her festive white pajamas, shown him as also from them, she faces its mirror. The doll, propped forward in the basket, sits staring in the mirror as well. Taller candles would give off a more perfect flame, but these nozzles of light flicker back and forth, by convention alternating between what the dead expect and the living can give.

When Cicily hears their step she turns, on her rosied features the smile of obedience. Her arms, bent at the elbow, extend like small wings. Her hands are fanned at her cheeks. On either side, suspended between forefinger and thumb, a forelock hangs, forming her the required pair, and worn at that familiar angle of humility jutting into pride, just below the ear. The doll, set to watch, wears its best face.

The house stands firm. A rattle of hail, slapdash at the windows, is showing what a season can do.

Constant Comment, the brand of tea that Zipporah's Boston had been fond of, may have been blended with a Charlotte in mind, or else some saint of the gossip world, socially avid, part suffragette. Today at lunch, she is imminent.

"She's the family yenta. A family our size, or like the Boston crowd's, will have at least one," Zach says of her. But what she might be saying passes over his head; he's only interested in her bone structure. "She's filed down so stringy she can insert herself between any two on a sofa. Those pipe-straw gams of hers? Hollow, for sure, waiting to be filled. Wonder whether she would pose?" To the hilarity this evokes, where, along with Erika and Zach, the non-family Philippe and the two Ernestines, all of whom have met Charlotte, are also at Zipporah's table, he says: "She wouldn't have to be nude. You don't ask whether or not a walking Giacometti is wearing clothes."

Erika, always ready to join in on art, and a bit show-off because of this special occasion for it, adds: "One leg for her charity malarkey, the other for the real dirt."

The opposite arc of the roundtable—those who haven't met Charlotte—is at first quiet. It consists of two of Zach's sons, one older and one younger, each of the twin sets preferring now not to travel in duo; Charles's college-freshman daughter, Annie; and Foxy Mendenhall, who sits between her, on his right, and Erika.

Gerald, up from Wall Street, and without Kitty, is very quiet today. Charles, nipping an hors d'oeuvre between conferences, has now left. Only Nell, a caroling voice said to be pursuing her ultimate face-lift from clinic to clinic, is altogether missing, having had it, and is reportedly now with a man she will not reveal. "Some European jock, maybe," Erika says.

"Jock O' who?" Annie, the minx, says. When she was three, she was one of the little Raphaels.

"Good God, girl, where were you brought up?"

"You know, Uncle Zach. Winnetka mostly." She turns to the partner on her left, Zach's son, at whom she's been chatting animatedly. "That's Illinois." He nods. "And Oberlin, Uncle Zach. We're more musical."

"She's kidding you, Pop," Zach's older twin says. He is her contemporary, more or less.

"You are?" he says to Annie, a cousin he's never met before. "Musical? So'm I. Who d'ya like?"

From then on, except for the "So do I's," they're unintelligible.

"I'm used to my kid brother being my child's uncle, Zach," Erika says crossly, "but it's a shock to see him also a Pop. And of all things, out of step."

Philippe, always debonair when he and Erika are back together, seizes a chance to undertone to Zipporah, *"Très elegant, votre ami"* — as if these asides sound better in French. Since hearing of his mother-in-law's new situation, he's been chummier, though no less deferent — perhaps linking her with his now-and-again errant *Maman*. Mendenhall, making gentle good-byes but no excuses, had by then also left. "But so quiet. Especially on art *affaires*. Or perhaps your so united family has scared him? If I hadn't been out of the same mix, you'd have scared me."

"Oh, he didn't want to upstage anybody. Especially Zach. He's grown fond of him."

"Upstaging Zach is not possible."

She looks at Philippe. A rake, but aging. The Ernestines, those small-town pretties who were briefly the big town's art-scene lovelies, have the fine weight of progeny on them, an inch or more at their waists, a tenderness in the eye-wrinkles and the smile.

And there they are, those two new light-hearted smarties, Annie and one of the elder twins. Whose cross is that no one dares his name, for fear of getting the wrong one.

"It is now." Zach's kids do it all the time, but what other parent dares to gloat? Nor will Zipporah tell him why Foxy would have specially kept out of it on the "art *affaires.*" He has owned so much "art" in his time.

But that's not what has seized her. "A united family, Philippe? You see us as that?" Late at night, by phone or silently, mentally she gathers in her far-flung chicks. She has them to dinner when they're in town. "You think of us as that?"

"But of course." She has really surprised a man whose job ensures that he not be. "Iron—to iron. Sometimes like magnets to steel. Or like rubber with molybdinum." He rattles off other elements or compounds, whose properties he must have learned in countries where natural resources are of importance to a diplomat.

"But—we all have our strays, *belle-mère.*" Philippe calls her that with relish. According to Erika, he and his first mother-in-law fought "like gamecocks," even her sex being in question during those brawls. "Our colonials, dear Zipporah. If one has had the luck to land in France, like us, one turns those into legend: our great-uncle Serge, who would not leave Algiers when we lost our land there, whose descendants are by now either Muslim or dead—and how had he come to be named Serge in the first place? Ah, one of us was in Russia, possibly as valet with the Marquis de Custine? A bit of Poland? Those would be the ones who were musical. And those would be the legends. Our South American branch, which does still exist, does not speak to us. Unlike us, during the last of the Inquisition they left Spain, rather than turn apostate."

Erika leaving just then to pick up their young daughter at the Lycée—"a wonderful school"—he waves her a formal salute-with-kiss, fingers bunched at the lips and then spread, as if she's a receding country, rather than a wife, and continues.

"We Sephardim spread like fleas—and are not always, hummm, Sephardic. Jews travel. Sometimes a stopover, call it. Dresden, London, Capetown. And some lucky Berliners, still with a Spanish *de* to their name, who fifty years before Hitler discovered New York."

A Gauloise Bleu appears magically and is stared at as if the serpentine griffon on its silver case has produced it. Philippe gave up cigarettes when he left Europe "for good" and violates both vows continually. "So, how am I French? My father's side, we were foolish enough to lend their last king money, so had to stay in hopes of being repaid. Actually, we were never bankers but loyally domestic; we'd invented first a commode, then a chamber pot, then the best cookware—and had bought land. And finally a title, swapped for the debt, that we have the sense not to use. Louis Philippe, for whom I am named, was a great king for business. And bourgeois humor. Our blazon of nobility is a rather odd shape. Maybe for the same reason, the men of our family are careful not to wear bulbous finger rings."

He wears only the wedding band designed by Erika, and identical with hers. "Coptic," he says. "Ah, these insignia." He tips Zipporah's chin with his fingertip: among women of any age he will find some fleshly tribute he can pay. "Ah, *chere amie*—for that is what you are to me—that king had to abdicate to England in 1848. But we got to stay. Which is what a Jew always wants, but can't always do. Your son Charles, the researcher, he told me your people started coming here that same year. From England, or just passing through." A silver lighter, flat as a belt buckle, appears in his palm, as if from his cuff. He could earn his living that way, if ever hard up for tricks. He squeezes the thing as if it may have blood in it. Suddenly he lights it, staring at her over the flame. "And here I am, a valet to the U.N. Of course you are united; we all are, singly or together." He snaps the flame shut, on again, shut. "A Jew is a Jew is a Jew.'"

She's never seen him on such a roll. Or on any.

He brushes invisible crumbs from the vest he isn't wearing. "So I told your yenta, Charlotte, when I met her. Mordecai and I had correspondence, over his famous letter. All very friendly; I dined there. She was hoity-toity about Spanish like us, who once converted to save our necks; she's an Inquisition all by herself. But I told her that all these years, from the late eighteenth century until 1820, when the precise Spanish laws were changed, we—our family and others as steadfast—managed to marry, in the church of course, but only those Jews who had turned, like us. 'But you, madame,' I said, 'One wonders if your own history is so unadulterated: your eyes are so blue.'" He hawks the spit in his throat. "She found that laughable. Yet so chic . . . And Mordecai said to me later, 'Saw you give her a goose. Thank you. She has ribs to spare.'"

He goes to bid adieu to the Ernestines, who are more cushiony.

He has made Zipporah laugh. Yet she wants to kneel to what this sardonic man, so glossed with international savvy, has been able to say. The asides of family talk—do they serve as our confessional? Often she's watched this mute selection of whom you shall sit next to, in order to bare your heart. Or whom you should avoid at all costs, for the same reason.

Are we middle class so united in anything, would she whisper? Except that we're so in control—she would say—so in charge of what we take for our manifest destiny, thanks to our money and intelligence—whichever comes first. We who seem to slog down the generations seeking only the middle path and accepting no adventure except our mortality. Who want only to live in eternal peacetime, watching other peoples' wars. And what has that go to do with our being Jews? You man of the U.N.—was that what made me yawp, throw off the sweet mutuality of suffering offered me, during my three-day lecture-trial in Jerusalem-cum-Tel Aviv? What is our sacred anthropology—and the price we pay?

And why is it that my own race, or the magnificent snarl of faith that comes with it, must constantly convert me?

"Oh, Philippe—" She will tell him how Shine, that rhyming

optimist, greets her when she reports in at his "agency": "Welcome to the tunnel of misery, the funnel of hope." How Shine has affixed a door for unaccompanied child applicants, which he will allow adults to enter only if with one of those. "Got the idea from the children's zoo."

Or she will tell Philippe how when Mendenhall, the royal fox, returns from a day "on the wire, dispensing my grapes," he and she salve themselves from the world's woe. Because these wired days, persons like them are members of that internationale, willing or not.

"Those Ernestines—" Philippe says, returning, "how charmingly they accept. That for Zach, one of them is not enough. And how virtuous that keeps them," he sighs. "Like in the hareem." Enunciating so languidly, perhaps he even knows whereof he speaks?

He presses Zipporah's cheeks lightly, first one, then the other. Being the rake he certainly is has refined his repertoire; he knows what is appropriate.

"Philippe—you never feel that it is not enough, these days, to be a Jew?"

Stupid of her, to ask that of a man who is so many other things? Yet being what he is, he takes women seriously.

He fusses with his lighter. "I did feel that. When I was not married to one. In that, my poor first wife was her mother's creature. In France, ever since the Edict of Nantes, Huguenots have been able to feel more oppressed than anybody. But her family was rich enough to afford a Jew—and she wanted one. For a rival?" The light ignites okay and is quelled. "If I call her 'poor' it could be because she is no longer married to me. Ah, I tease. But with some people, being a Jew among them is hard work."

Is she being taught to dance occult steps she never thought of as being in the Jewish choreography? Or merely learning how to delay a cigarette?

Suddenly the Gauloise is in his hand, lit, in his mouth drawn on deeply, and tucked behind him and out of her orbit—as if a

genie has popped out of him and been put back again, leaving behind a cloudy wisp of shirttail, and an odor of singed boot.

"With Erika, it's another story," he says. "A curator? There is
nothing more Orthodox. That museum, the Judaica, is all the religious expression she needs. But in love you need another kind of
confidence; you yourself are the artifact offered. I—" A thin ozone
of smoke bridles his parted lips, luxuriates on the air. He's carefully
aimed his face another way. "I myself perhaps express myself too
freely there. But when Erika is in Paris, because of the lawsuit over
the collection, and I am at the U.N.—we have to cross the Atlantic
in order to meet—we recover the honeymoon. And catch an
angel—" A puff. "Our little daughter."

She watches the inhaled and expelled breaths come and go, the
veiled eyes of a man celebrated for being always on the jump. She
has rarely smoked, except for a few fags stolen from an older girl's
brother and passed from hand to hand to hand, then the ceremonial pipes met in her travels, and after a spell of dengue fever con-
tracted in Chieng-mai, some opium in a Bangkok dive; but she has
spent her life among smokers. Is all smoking this reminiscent, even
if only of the cigar before the last cigarette?

Exchanging "Good-bye!" waves with the always casual
Ernestines, turning back, she's suddenly enveloped in his cloud. He
hasn't coughed, this man whose opinions and manners are so
evenly distributed you can't often tell which is which. The very
handsome can hide intelligence in their own way. The family men
in particular had at first doubted his. Erika, on introducing him,
had apologized to her nervously: "Philippe tries very hard not to
be a movie star. But he can be very demonstrative." Other women
can wonder how many times a day those powder-smooth cheeks
are shaved—and for what reason? His and Erika's marriage has indeed been classified as "nervous," Charles adding judiciously, "On
both sides. Who'll be suing who?"

But now there's a flush on those suave cheeks. The eyes, behind which there must be a veritable atlas of the world, stare unguarded. Smokers are wafted on a magic flying carpet. Her father,

alone with his cigar at a window, had once said to her, his free hand light on her small shoulder: "I am imagining myself out of Boston." She herself remembers the opium, her body drifting upward, the breathing of other bodies stretched alongside hers, a susurrus of pulling and exhaling, bearing her and them to the farthest east.

Is Philippe about to tell her they're divorcing? That he is flying on?

"Somebody should have told me sooner," he says. "I know of course that her official name was Frederika. She has always presented herself as Erika. Even when we were—fond. Endearments can be such keys to a—to women. But call her Rika, as people sometimes do? No response. You never told me, Zipporah, that nickname she had from her father. And in the family, you are my only intimate."

That last is true. She can enjoy a correctness now vanishing. Though not always the formality addressed to the lady in a woman. But Philippe's elaborations are not of that order. While debonair to the fair sex, perhaps to too many of them, but conceding their intelligence where he finds it, he likes to match wits "up to a point." Watching him and Erika, this has always pleased her.

Her sons, talking Philippe over, react otherwise. Zach saying, amused: "He reminds me of those second-class diplomats I meet on State Department–sponsored tours. Speak to you from aloft, unaware that the tower is leaning." He is proud of those tours.

As Charles's expectations inflate, he's grown more genial in manner, concealing whether underneath he's now less of a prig, having gone through a divorce where the fault wasn't his, or now that he's remarried, more of a one?

"Oh, can it, Zach. One rake merely annoys another."

"But most annoy the faithfully married, eh Chuck?"

Charles explodes. "From you the most faithfully married man I know—if in tandem."

Zach says: "I did do a drawing of him, playing with your two girls and his. Sings them the *roi de leve tot*, claps hands with them, which bewilders those fifth–sixth graders; does he think they're in nursery school? Yet your girls think he's 'cute.' I tell you what— he's a family rake. Oh—nothing untoward, merely understated. Our Eustace's opposite." Who, last seen here at eighty-nine, had arrived with a hefty Swede on his arm: "Let me introduce you to my little Jezebel."

"No, primogeniture is still the European kick," Zach agreed. "They crave heirs."

"That's why you annoy us," Charles said. "You have four."

"Leave it be, you two," she had chuffed walking away. But smiling. They are brothers to the hilt.

"What family members say out of each other's presence is the real *histoire*, yes, Philippe," she says now. "And I am complimented to be your intimate." She too had had to be correct in a foreign country, as each nativity appeared. Do not voice your suspicion that a bargain diamond may not have passed through De Beers but had been excreted, then sold at a pittance; do not ask what geishas actually do. "But I'm not sure I want to hear what's bothering you."

"Bother? I could dance." He kissed her hand. "Our Erika is miffed. She did not plan. But already we know, yes, the test says, we will have a little Philippe." He kisses her other hand. "Why did no one tell me? Call her 'Freddie, Freddie'—and she melts."

A silence. That they can muse jointly has been her pleasure in him. And that he can handle Erika. But not this time.

"You are not happy with me, and why not?" he says, his French lilt returning in force. "Six of your own, I am thinking I can talk about what one finds on the pillow." He has never before allowed her to see him angry. "It was not rape, I assure you; that is the point. What that miow-miaow means to her, *qui sait*? I only wish I had known sooner. So she will be *hors de combat*—like she was with our little darling? But this time—I was not under the necessity to persuade."

Her head's hanging under the barrage, but she hears him smiling.

"In Amiens, our family seat, the *paysans* say a bastard works the land better than anyone else. But even in *mariage* the child conceived warmly is extra blessed with strength . . . So she will have a few more of those stretch marks, I tell her. My mother, who had four of us, remains as vain as any fashionable. And my father has learned to stay at home; so can I. I can swear that now."

Raising her head, she sees the grimace men make when their eyes moisten.

"Don't worry, *ma belle.* International scapegoats we Jews may be. Whether we like it or not. But this grandson will be like your others here. Born in a country that does not send us away. That has never yet sent away a Jew for being a Jew."

How else could he have been informed of the diminutive, avoided by Frederika's father, kicked around by her brothers, finally at her request shelved by all? Except between the sisters, after a quarrel, when Nell, who had no jealousy, who has never in her life been accused of "depression," could be generous. "Nix on gunning for degrees, Erika. Start being giddy Freddie again; you never would give in to how it becomes you." Then day after day, subtle or blatant, saucy but gentle, the pounce at a stray sparkle: "There you are, *eff eff*"; or over a photo: "That's the snazzy one. That's Freddie." How else would he know about this key, or even the existence of a Freddie? Except from the person who, quite without guilt, perhaps even passing a man on or back as is her general habit, is still gamely trying to help her sister feel beautiful?

Stricken as Zipporah is by what else her son-in-law has unwittingly told her, she has to marvel at how blithely he swings between the political and the personal. Sending himself to a neutral country, one where the very altitude will help thin any convictions, meanwhile outlining one's female counterpart in ruthless clarity. These days most anybody is easy to find. Or, as has been hinted to Zipporah, he already knew.

Their mother has never before acted the head of the family. Nor felt so sick of proximity.

"Philippe, damn you. Where *is* Nell?"

Most people as they age grow gaunt, dumpy, or merely small, at least shrink from their original shape, but Cousin Charlotte, once a tall girl, still a woman with "a carriage," seems only to have muddied, held together by her liver spots. As a student at Radcliffe, in an era when all were bullied into acquiring the habit of research, but girls of means, destined for marriage, not "work," had small chance to flourish that expertise professionally, Charlotte had sublimated hers to gossip, in which field she is as well-known a collector as those of her classmates who have "gone into" art. As such, though she might own the details of your lineage, finances, and peccadilloes—in that order—she remains amateur; she does not publish or exhibit—except privately.

Meanwhile, since Mordecai, not rich though moderately well-to-do, has insisted she manage the dispensing of their tithe, her temperament has been further sweetened by years of easy philanthropy, carefully localized. As even a Mendenhall might grant, the art of giving is on its nether side the art of not giving. Public generosity has excused personal stinginess; Charlotte has no guilt. Because of years of not eating too much, her wrists pipe through her bracelets, her neck sags in its gold circlet, but this gives her a refined air. Having blue eyes, as one step toward being taken for Gentile, is a vanity she would never confess. But her need there, being insatiable, is also visible.

Where most non-Orthodox or non-practicing Jews might take
their supposed or real "assimilation" as owed to lapse of time
and/or interest, Charlotte's need—to have all the honorifics of
being a good Jew while never being taken for one—presents itself
so continuously that it is all many can think of as they estimate her.

"If she would only embrace Christianity and have done with
it," some of her and Zipporah's relatives snort—to say *convert*
being still anathema. But they know that for hopeless. She had
wanted to be born so, and hadn't been. The constant pretense, to
act so, has formed her character. In Mordecai's congregation,
where she routinely "observes," she does have a social circle who
see her more tolerantly, as a congregation must often agree to do.
She does them a real service; they keep her around for reference.
"She's *that* type."

As she sways into her cousin's living room, a New England
reed on the high heels donned for New York, a man brushes past
her and out the open front door. She's used to that, especially
among those who will suspect they're in her archives, and down for
having done something wrong. She'll look it up later, in the un-
written memoirs always nimbly on tap.

"So you have a buzzer now, Zipporah. Ah—apartments." She
has a house. Mordecai used to plead, "When you first meet people,
could you manage not to give that slight sniff?"—but had long ago
given up on it. "Ah, was that by any chance your son-in-law? The
U.N. one, the Count? Who doesn't use the title; that's so dashing."
Ordinarily, on tea days, she might well have wondered why he
didn't use it—some attached scandal, or a hitch to the entitlement?
But today she has a powdery meekness—disposed to being favor-
able? One wonders why.

"I've only the one son-in-law.

"But lots of grandchildren, dear."

Some of them not legal, she means. On her, powder doesn't last.

Behind her, the Ernestines peep. On their way out, they've
been unable to resist coming back to meet her again. At home

Zach has made a family tree for their children, on which Charlotte hangs in effigy like the rest, each with some identifying symbol. Hers is slung with a heavy sack, shaped like a six-pointed star.

"I've lots of daughters-in-law. May I introduce Zach's wives. Two of my favorites."

That plural doesn't escape her. Or she's heard? "You two are— sisters?"

Plumply fair-skinned, each from one of those central U.S. states well-stocked with Norwegians, South Germans, and Swedes, their sleek brown hair tinged with a suggestion of the henna that Zach once said reminded him of Egypt—a rite they perform in giggly sessions at one or the other's home base—they do resemble one another. On a sofa you will sometimes find them sitting close, like dovelets, in some sympathy of the flesh they must enjoy. As now.

Charlotte's stare is medical. "Perhaps—twins?"

They break into laughter. Farm girls, bred to every barnyard variation from calving to slaughter, from the gelding to the cow brought to the bull, their Village years as painters' models, gallery staff, coffeehouse waitresses, and helpmeets in general to the ethos of "downtown" have polished them to a sophistication that as women and mothers they perhaps can find best in each other.

"Oh no, we're not twins—though we have them," one says. "I'm Ernestine Jansen."

"Oh no, nothing Siamese," the other one chimes. "Not even sisters. I'm Ernestine Vandenburgh."

"I'm from Nebraska," one says. The other echoes, "From Idaho."

"She's Lutheran."

"She's Catholic."

They both sang in their choirs, they say in a rush.

"But that's as far as it goes."

Rising, they make their pretty adieu, leaving any who know their history, whether the conventionally introduced or their own buddies, in an amiable state of flesh-buzz. These two impish sisters-under-the-skin know what they're doing, what they will tend Zach for, what perhaps all three crave. A relation which they have finally, after a long wait, achieved. On which happy triumvirate the gods, often in a like situation, have rained down twins. Wherever the Ernestines go, they bring farce.

Charlotte, staring into her lap, is as pale as the pearl studs in her lobes, good ones with a bill of purchase tucked in her safe-deposit. Not to "get it wholesale" is part of her character.

To be speechless isn't. Help her out?

Plenty are nasty about Charlotte behind her back—Zipporah has told Foxy. But I'm the only one who's nasty straight to her; even Mordecai dishes it out on the slant—and I know exactly why I do it. Brought up the same, she's what I might have been—and maybe some of our younger fry judge I am? You'd better come by, Foxy, and interrupt us. And she might as well see what she's going to be on the gossip about.

I can't promise not to disgrace you, he'd said. But he'll come.

She and Mendenhall's children, though dutifully met, are not each other's sort. The secret he and she share is that they are never going to be his sort. Though he will do his duty, by making his appearance in their world as they require. He's eager to meet everyone in hers.

"That sniff of yours, Lottie." To call her that is to pick a fight. "Boston must be farther off than usual. Or hadn't you heard."

"Boston hears everything. And has done everything. On the Q.T. Where if anywhere, it should be."

"How like Eustace you are. You both announce a code people usually won't. Though not the same one."

"That old bird? We heard he was dead."

"He was. He had his death announced so his one surviving old flame would come back to get her rights; she's his legatee. He brought her to dinner; we weren't sure he wasn't as dead as printed, but they're holding each other up—as he'd hoped. Charles asked him, wasn't he afraid she'd do him in? He wheezes—you know how he does—'Chuck, you mustn't be ready for the Court yet. I fixed it so the longer I live, the more she gets. Which ain't all.

But that's on the Q.T.'" All the expressions their joint families exchanged; bonds that soften you, though you don't want them to. "What's that mean, by the way?"

"On the quiet, I suppose," Lottie says absently. "By the way, Eustace wasn't—isn't that poor. He still had his gigolo fund . . . You didn't know? Never seen his photos, him bare to the waist in a scull? He had bids for the movies, he says, but in those days it wasn't respectable. It still isn't. What we let our maids see—I can't bring myself to tell you."

"But you see it."

"Somebody has to. They band together to go, Thursdays, their night off. Mrs. Commins—you remember, he's the bond specialist like his father—she and I went. At least you can sit in the back row at a film, even if next to you, you don't know who. Anyway—she and Nate have three houses, a lot of staff, at least one house would be empty, something could be going on; and all white help like his mother and ours had. She's from Atlanta—the new Mrs. Nate—but he says he gives enough to black causes, at home he doesn't have to deal with that particular disparity. Nate still has a conscience; he's famous for it."

If Lottie has grown garrulous—well, so have I. "And was something going on?"

"First a short film, not short enough for my money. Aimed at an all-female audience. The second part—" A pause. "Well, it was live men, naked, and showing off. And hooting and carrying on down in the front row, Mrs. Nate's head housekeeper, an upstairs maid, and one of her au pair girls; she has two. She's Nate's fourth; he's no spring chicken, she's had her babies quick, to get in line."

And yes, some of that had been going on, in the alternating third house. "The Comminses have the biggest home-screens in the congregation. And you can rent films, Thursday nights, the guard told us, when we sneaked out."

"Pity you couldn't stay. For the whole striptease."

"That what they call it, even when it's men? Mrs. Nate, she's a shiksa; she wanted to stay. A journalist needs to be authentic, she said; she wrote Nate's speeches before she married him. So we stayed. Until she said she felt a hoot coming on."

There are two schools of thought about Charlotte's gossip: one, that she's an innocent; the other that's she's a first-class fabulist. Both can be true, Zipporah thinks; she and I came out of the same box. Now she's like one of those antiques that didn't get broken, that are called "mint." Good girls between the two World Wars, good Jewish girls, who qualified for the quotas in the Seven Sisters—the good girls' colleges—Goody-goods. Some of Zipporah's crowd developed a wild humor; Lottie's mother, Zipporah's aunt, was one of those others who decreed Jewish humor was coarse—and part of what had got Jews into trouble historically.

"You've developed a sense of humor, Lottie."

"I have not. Ask Mord... Anyway, Mrs. Nate asks me not to circulate anything, so all this's between you and me." It always was. "She can't fire the housekeeper, who is from forever, maybe from even the first wife, and hires the staff. Instead, the Comminses are going to be careful not to barge in on Thursday nights." She glints. "Anyway, it's Nate's poker night."

"Oh. Well, the help situation is not what it was." When "greenhorns" fresh from war-torn Europe were plentiful, cheap, and you "let" them do only what you approved. If they were docile, you were kind, there could be a bonding. You saw them courted appropriately, married off; they brought you their babies to see.

Drop down a peg, though, and there were the street-corner "slave markets"—she'd even driven past one once when in college—where the Jewish housewives in the Bronx could go to hire a black scrubber to make all clean for Friday eve's candlelight, and for the Sabbath, when one does not scrub. Yet many families, as they went upscale, had relationships with their help similar to hers with Jennie—or were conscientiously benign.

"The relationship between Jews and their domestic help—it's a sociology, isn't it."

"You nitwit." On her bosom the add-a-pearl necklace of Lottie's girlhood, supplemented by Mord, swings forward irately.

"Nate's the one barges in of a Thursday, I'll bet. His and Mord's poker pals will cover for him."

Do they cover for Mord?

"Oh, you were always ahead of me, Lottie." She feels her claws grow. "Remember Senior Banquet? Where the girls who'd got engaged were called up one by one to the dais and given a long-stemmed rose? You sashayed back, stopping to tickle it in my face."

Lottie had tricked Mord into it, with the dainty crudeness she'd been tutored in, by prodding her kid brother to dare Mord to put his hand up his sister's skirt. Mord had—and pronto had been tattled on. Lottie, grilled by her parents as to "how far" Mord had gone with her, had answered he'd been "all the way." With the mental reservation—"up my skirt." Disclosure of that would have come too late from Mord himself. The parents, linked in business, had seized on what they'd been hoping for. Mord, already steeped in the Hebraic lore that can be so dangerous for a layman, had decided, as he can be heard to say, if too frequently, "to let my own fatalism work for me."

Lottie begins to sip and munch. "Why—this here's a banquet. Mmmm." She'll be mum for awhile, in the pleasure of it.

Mord is that recognizable Jew whose gloom is marketable, in the art world taken to be talent, on Wall Street assumed to signify foreknowledge, and in a government job functioning as prophecy—and Mord has been in all three. Behind his coattails, at a platform where he is receiving some service award, which never appears to elate him, "a Renaissance man" is sometimes whispered. When these nationwide fund-raisers take place in New York he invites Zipporah to attend, and she does so, enjoying the tribal flow of the congregations, if mulling as always why she cannot join in—wondering whether this has come of her training as a kind of separatist. Yet there must be many, like her Jewish to the core of birth, bones, and memory, who, rooted in a new multiple life and its educative freedoms, will not turn back. Cannot.

Last award dinner, Mord had induced her to sit on the platform among various divas, theater and film personalities, and "ambassa-

dors from the world of academic excellence," as the opening remarks had trumpeted. The word "academic" still irritates her.
"Wear décolleté," Erika had counseled, "your arms can still go
bare. Carry a stole. And don't go black, not if there's big theater
there. Why not the gray that Roseland photographer caught you
in? Be your kind of star."

Erika, as usual, had been unfair. Out front, the vast orchestra
was indeed dressy, ranging from the blatant to the modestly subdued aged, to those semi-obedient young, bared in their heyday of
sex and beauty, against which religion may no longer intervene.
But it will be taken as hopeful that they are there at all. Up in
the press box is the dowager of a newspaper clan, as usual like
a "Whistler's Mother" gone just charming enough, a black velvet
bow in her white chignon. Though the assemblage is predominantly Reform, with perhaps a sprinkling of "Conservative,"
what's really here is money and/or status, as added to spiritual conviction or displayable worship; this is America. Where the men get
off with black-tie.

First row center, upright among the wives of the awardees, is
Lottie, in a pottery blue-and-white some there would call "Garden
Club." In her mind she would be Charlotte, as, in her stockholder's
navy, she is today, though now she's eating, with the appetite her
legs belie.

"I always look forward to our high tea," she's just said. As Zipporah does, to this reverie, getting ever rarer, which old friendly rivals and classmates can partake of, all true comment luckily in the
fastness of one's head. Her cousin will be tucking in for many minutes, except for a few mutterings like, "I skipped lunch." Along
with her steady inroads on the cucumber sandwiches ("Crustless!")
and the little iced cakes ("Just like in the college parlor"), she now
and then gives an angry shake between bites—she's still brooding
on the striptease. Finally apologizing slyly, "Excuse me, but we
were both brought up never to talk with a full mouth."

Zipporah is back at the awards ceremony, eavesdropping on
two men directly behind her on the dais, listed on the program as

past presidents of Mord's synagogue, who chat in the elevated
voices of those who need or have hearing aids. Mord has just accepted his citation with a few graceful sentences including a standard salute to his "helpmeet" in the front row, this acknowledged
with her blue stare. At the Duffys', there had been a category for
her, reserved for certain wives of the go-getters, or the famed: "Oh
her? She's a 'Without Whom.'"

"Renaissance? Yeh, in more than one way," the first whisperer
answers. "No man has a better excuse. My wife, yours—hearts of
gold. That one—maybe platinum. He paid a high price for it . . .
You ever seen the other woman? A gypsy on fire. You and I should
live so long." And does the wife down there know? "Any dirt goes
on in temple, Mrs. Mord knows—my wife says the Sisterhood depends on it." A joint snigger. "So she shouldn't know her own? But
they say she won't give Mord the satisfaction." A pause. A whisper
unidentifiable as from either: "Toss a coin, she ever has."

Turning her head slightly she'd seen that the one man had a
walker, his neighbor a cane. He is the know-it-all and livelier.
"Know who the other one is?" The walker does not. "His cousin. A
lifelong romance. They say some of her children are his."

Zipporah and Mord have lunch about once a year. What in
God's name has Lottie been circulating? She hears that mumble-
mumble when the old masticate history. "No wonder he needs
the *schul.*"

Among the last to join the decorous file leaving the platform,
Zipporah wanted not to know who those two were. On the receiving line, next to Mord and Lottie, she had come to her senses.
"Oh—you're the cousin," a woman said to her. "The one on the
program." No comment from those two, Mord and Lottie, flank-
ing her. "Yes," she'd answered gratefully. "Charlotte's cousin. Not
Mord's."

Lottie, drugged with whipped cream, moves her upraised palms
in the *kaffeeklatch* sign. She's had enough. "Nice to talk. Family."

By Zipporah's watch, checked for when Mendenhall will come,
they've been mum for three minutes. Long enough to say the

pledge of allegiance, as they had in grade school, or bend the head in honor of the Armistice.

"If only in the head." Half of which family talk is.

"I don't get much of any kind, Zippy, these days, 'less I initiate."

So that's how this gossiper regards it?

"But frankly, Zippy, I wouldn't say to anybody except you—everything up there's at sixes and sevens."

Enough. Resume claws. "Well, for bigger numbers, you can always come down here."

"You mean my stockholders' meeting? Crack of dawn this morning, and no lunch. We showed a loss." If there's been a profit she suggests they go "gala" to the Plaza, though she doesn't spring for it. They go Dutch. "No, I mean like what that shiksa took me to. You don't forget an evening like that."

"Nor I."

"You go to stripteases?"

"Award dinners. Only they overdress for it."

"Shah. Your humor. You and Mord."

"Sephardic maybe—a little, my father's side. Your mother and mine, Ashkenazim through and through. That old letter sure told us off."

"Mord sold it, the minute my mother died, bless her name; she had a habit of pointed remarks."

"What happened to those Portuguese?" She can risk leading up to it. They are safely into the tribal now, that antiphonal of who-what-where is a Jew, in which everybody's a troubadour.

"Still there, hah, still strict; who knows about the money? Esther, the one who they wanted Mord to marry, she married too close, he died young; one of the children is a hemo, like him. Though they say it comes through the mother. She is now almost our age. But if she has *tsoris,* she puts a good face on it. A new one she got in Paris, along with the body. And clothes they give you for discount. Although still "the profile"—which we call a nose. Jewelry they brought over, and have hung onto. We thought aquas and topaz, when Esther came for Mord's brother's granddaughter's wedding. But our jeweler's wife said no, diamonds, canary yellow, and that many carats, some can look blue."

Zipporah has wanted this—why?

A long breath; Lottie takes a last little cake. Mouth full, she manages, "Esther was shocked at our lack of ritual. She cackles the law through that parrot nose in three languages; Zippy, I want to cry. For us. Down there the girls are taught to know it, like the boys. And don't laugh, they keep so strict on Yom Kippur, even the cattle have to fast." She blows her nose. In the alto voice which comes with repressed tears she says, "Zipporah, you married out of line. But the Jewish life, you know how it was. So pure in every detail; if it itched you too much, you knew to wait for the Friday candles, or Sh'vuos. Or when the shofar is blown, when Mord says, it's like blown on your own backbone . . . So what's happened to us?"

The Lotties confuse people, Zipporah is thinking. The canniest assessor will find them slipping through his fingers, his powers failing. They inhabit the odd corners of behavior, unsure themselves from which they come. They rise out of caricature, like small monsters we've birthed, and must hold in our arms.

"Oh, Lottie—" Who is embracing who?

"Stand back, stand back!" Lottie cries, this shrunken woman who spends her life making others' bargains appear as bad as her own. "Who are you to commiserate? Gone from us, but in the infinite ways of our teaching, simchas Torah, we held onto our Zipporah, a role model for the Reform? Turns out now what she's doing? Do it once, do it twice, shifting adoration; like they do now." A rush of blood in the cheeks, her education trying to come to the rescue, if only puckering? A long wail, "Ei, Aye-yah," untranslatable.

"Oh Zippy, what has happened to us? What has happened to us Jews?"

So there it comes. The ancient sleight-of-hand that will ascribe any Jew's private woe to the Jewishness. So somebody's itty-bitty eternal triangle and the trauma of our backsliding become one— the Job suffering. And in our souls, once again—worship. So we survive, at least as Jews. And so will the religion, never fear. Up in all the rejected hills of belief, hear the old gods snickering?

"So I can't hug you?" Zipporah says. "Two who have known each other for fifty years, who's holding who?" She hears her synagogue lilt, persisting, under any language, in any land—and no matter what college. We catch it from each other. Even if, like with orthodoxy, we never had it in the family.

Lottie's still sniffling, like a child who wants you to hear. Poor stockholder, she knows the loss she's really showing, has known, those same years. And will suspect that I've known about Mord and Esther all the time—who would be more savvy than she on how the word spreads?

But something I must tell her. Arrived at me like a quote from the past, of what had never needed to be said.

"Charlotte—" She needs that dignity. "'Adoration,' as you call it—and I can guess what you've heard about me, what you're referring to—that doesn't shift. The habit of loving can." She's teary herself; it's taken her so long. To feel guiltless. "So rest assured, Peter lies easy. Blessed be his name."

That said—that learned, Zipporah can check her watch. "My friend, Foxy Mendenhall, will be here shortly." She sees the name is not new—or odd. "He'd like to meet you. So—" Go fix the face? Lottie doesn't wear makeup. A phrase from that other era leaps to her tongue. Those apparently lurk, waiting. She says tenderly, "Go repair."

In the bathroom, she herself does that. At the moment further makeup isn't really needed, nor scent, except for the delight that comes of having those observed. She pats her face, tendrils her hair. She's showing her years but is persuaded that vanity is what one must keep stalwart. Then, leaving the mirror, she looks up. Since that final Sunday she's never entered here without seeing again those bloody smears. Convinced by now that in the relatively charmed lives of her and her clan, and their crowd, bearing those smears in mind is required. Now even when she walks in her city— feeling it hers as it is no one else's, though she is a bean at the bottom of its towers—she carries that bloody touch-up with her. Or when she leans at her window, one of the lucky thousand out of the city millions with such a calm, unbloodied view.

Waiting for Lottie, she leans there now. These towers that scrape the sky, and at such expense—what arrogance! Rest assured, they will tempt—and not merely the hungry. One generation more, two, and the worse-than-bloody smears will be upon them. Or tomorrow. And nowadays the pride is to gild them. *Gelt.*

Yet if she leans long enough, she relents. Especially so in winter, when her avenue shines like a fake jewel. But looking out from warmth, the heart is still immigrant. Across the park, in the downtown of a city where churches no longer strike the hours, those towers seem to her to be chiming: *Bring us: your orthodoxy; We will; harbor it ... We will also: doctor it ... That is: the bargain.*

Then, she will leave the window, in self-disgust. That's what the old folks used to say: "The meat, the milk, the coffee; they doctor it here." Yet man-made stone does whine at that height, as if at the edge of a continent. Until we can doctor the wind.

But come winter, she is still immigrant.

Lottie's back, settling herself in a chair, prettying her skirt. "Boy, did I have to go."

There's cousinship for you. But watch it.

"So you're seeing someone, ah-hah, dolly." A coy no-no sidle with the head. "Uh uh, Zippy. We heard."

Thanks anyway, for the rose. "Do you mean am I sleeping with him, I am."

"Noo, such a temper. Like old times. And is he willing to marry you?"

Old times indeed. "Ask me the other way round."

"*Gewiss.*" A quirk; the young Lottie used to do that. "That's Yiddish for okay. Who *was* it in the family used to say, maybe one of the grandmothers? Meanwhile I'm learning Yiddish from Mrs. Nate, Lurlene. She studied up on it in order to meet Nate's relatives; turns out they're third generation and don't speak a word. So she's farming it out on me. And for me—it's patriotic." She sombers. "Given the situation. Okay—so are you going to marry him?"

"I am not."

Lottie tips her chin to what is still officially the heavens. She remains fixed that way.

"Who are you petitioning, Lottie? The angels?"

"We don't have them. Except the 'angel of the Lord,' we're not acquainted personally. No, I'm listening to the girls in the Sisterhood. Our age. The new members don't call themselves 'girls.' They're none of them my friends, exactly. But you know how it is—in a restricted community. You keep up with them."

"Restricted? Boston? Even a suburb, in such a—"

"You live under an illusion, Zippy; you lost ones. Every time you tell me about the children, I see it more. What you must think you're all safe from."

Blue eyes have a more fanatic stare than brown. Or simply remind her of Agnes?

"Zipporah." From Lottie's mouth, like her own rounded early to Hebrew syllables they hadn't needed to know the gist of, the name sounds like part of the Sunday-school chant. "Zipporah, we are not just the chosen. We have to choose."

She must have said that before. But like an actor's faded performance, it has its dignity. Do she and all the Mrs.'s—the solid matrons—say it to each other?

"You won't want to hear what those old wives say about you," she says virtuously—and bursting to tell.

"No, I'll tell you. When we were at your mother's knee, I heard them, those sacred ladies. Those are dead now. But it'll be the same." Her mother hadn't liked to go to their meetings, sewing groups, *kaffeeklatches,* but when she was on one of her errands of mercy she would leave Zipporah at her aunt's.

"'Sacred ladies'—that's what your mother used to kvetch. Yet in the end she did just fine."

"Yes, she did. She still does—from the grave." Who'd think that

I would be revealing that to this cousin—yet to who else in the family? One cannot always choose. "So let's go. I'll take five." Zipporah holds up a hand, fingers spread. "Fifty-sixty years those ladies have been at peace, but now at this important news, of what that bad creature in New York is still doing, they wake. And take up their—what? Sewing hoops? Bandages they rolled for a war? Or maybe the mah-jongg set? Anyway, here's the ring leader, Mrs. Edgar: Arlene. The thumb. She doesn't do anything, she doesn't have to." Mrs. Edgar had a voice like a lute, sounding at intervals. "She says: 'Zippy seemed like a Gentile? What would you expect?'... Next comes the forefinger—long, thin—Mrs. Asher something, banker's wife. She says, 'Such influence Zippy could have with him. Not just money, he has. Sheer wealth. You sure it's she who doesn't want to marry? I remember her, none of our boys would do. But now someone should get her to take up that "responsibility."'" Zipporah elevates her middle finger, clasping down the other four. In Italy not a polite gesture, but Lottie's unlikely to know. She waggles it. "Now here comes Luba, the husband snatcher. Sweaters, no bra. Always late, like she's come from an afternoon bed. She says, 'What can he see in her—with his billions, who couldn't he have? I bet she learned special from those savages!'"

Zipporah stops; they're both laughing. "That's it... Oh no, one more. The pinkie. Miss Mary Petty, the head teacher at our school, remember her? The Sisterhood invited her once a year. She says, 'I think you're all perfectly terrible.' But she too is laughing. Maybe at them?"

"Oh, Zippy, what games we played, didn't we. Such imagination."

"You had the most. I just—learned to write it down."

"Did someone actually once say that to you? About the savages?"

"Cousin Nettie... Smart old bird. 'I'm an old maid,' she said. 'But who doesn't know where genealogy starts?'"

"You left out the fourth finger," Lottie says. "Is that me?"

"Could be."

"Come on. Give. This has done me a world of good."

"Me too." Like a ritual bath. She had been to one once, in Iran. And once in Jerusalem. A soaking in the warm inter-female enjoyment. One always learned something.

"What would I say, Zippy? Finish the game."

"You won't like it."

"Let me be the judge."

As Lottie has been, leaving a stain on what lives she can.

"You'd say: 'Six children. Why would she want any more of—of that icky business?'"

"Icky" used to be her word for sex. Is it still? Lottie has no children. The brown spots show up stark and clear; maybe that's why they're given us. What she says is going to cost her.

"Mord has a child..." she whispers. "The hemo. A grown man. But Mord wanted to adopt." Casting left, right, she finds her handbag, seizes it, and crouching over its open maw, starts taking the studs from her ears.

"Whatever are you—Charlotte?"

The studs are stowed, the handbag snapped. In her navy-blue lap, now two inch-wide pearly shells. She lifts them in her palm. A shop here is famous for these, each one a semiprecious whorl of uncanny beauty, ready for an ear.

"I always wear my market suit," she says, dreamily. "It's from a name designer. At those meetings, you want to speak, you better not look poor. But I don't like to wear these on the street." She screws each one in an ear. Too big for her face, they float it between them like two water-wings. "Except on the East Side."

They sit without talking until the hall door is heard opening. No buzzer, a key. Lottie marks that, shifting tall in her chair.

It's Annie. "Oh, it was great, Granma—A tiny place, everybody friendly. The rap songs—like out to kill. But they said, 'Only afternoon stuff, come tonight.'" She's still on that cloud. "So we are. We might get to hear Derek, they said... Oh, excuse me."

"This is Annie, Charles's daughter; she's here during interim. Cousin Charlotte, Annie, from Brookline—Mrs. Mord." She tries not to be proud granny, not to rub in what she's got. Hopeless.

Charlotte is queenly. The lips, slightly rouged now, tuck in. "Nice to meet you." With a funny look, keen though, Annie extends her hand. She and Lottie fingertip, daintily. One wouldn't think an Annie would bother. But she's always done her chores.

"And Granma, we'll be late. I'll just slide my sleeping bag into the attic, may I? I've been in all the other rooms . . . 'night, then. Thanks." Withdrawing, she drops a little nod to this sacred lady. "Your earrings—they're the works."

When she's gone, Zipporah says, "She's doing a paper on us. For a course called Intersocietal Studies. Sociology proper got itself a bad name, with all those graphs. So she's sleeping each night in a different bedroom, to catch our realities. She doesn't use the beds, says being in her own bag keeps the distance . . . But she's catching onto them, all right."

Another key is heard in the lock. A small bulb on the facing wall lights flickers, and goes off again.

"Whatever is that? It went on before."

"We didn't want to have to buzz in the family. But there are a lot of keys to this house. Keys are keys. And Lester our doorman, who knows everybody, is retiring. Zach thought I should have an alert. There's even a bulb at the door, shows up ahead of me if somebody's come in while I've been out." So many solicitous keys to this house. But how can she nullify them?

"Ah, Lester knew *me*," Lottie says. "But I expect you and your boyfriend need the alert."

Before she can box her cousin's ears, he appears. As always, he casts his own light. Today he's wearing what he always does when tending "the patch," whether an acre or the few square feet behind an office, after which he walks up here. The cap is the same. When he sees Lottie he doffs it. He's carrying a plastic bag of what must be plant food. "For the orchids," he says, nodding pleasantly. "Hard to find this brand. I'll just put some in there." He goes off to the bedroom.

Asked whether she would mind having blooms once deeded to another, she'd said no, but you'd miss them, so why not divide?

Half are in the apartment across the park. If he's had more sexual stories in his life than she, she'll not hold those beauties to blame. "They've had more such stories than either of us," he'd said.

"How's the garden?" she says when he returns.

"Coming along, Madam. I'm winterizing. Two roses look hopeful. But you're not to see it until spring." He's amused. If she wants this charade, he'll play along.

Charlotte is bug-eyed. Is he "Foxy"—or isn't he? Some "outside" help, up her way, offshoots or by blows of New England stock, bones longer and heads more comely than their employers' are—according to the neighborhood gazette, they're sometimes beckoned inside.

"Charlotte—this is Foxy." Offhand, the way Annie and her crowd level each other, away from lineage.

"Zipporah has spoken of you. How do you do," he says.

"So she said," Charlotte gasps. To add "and I've heard of you" won't quite do. She ticks a fingernail against the depleted packet he's about to stow in his jacket. "I believe we used that, years ago. Pricey, eh."

"Nothing like it. Ah, you have a garden. You did, eh? Old herbals." He cracks the pack in his fist. "Some young people, trying to bring these back. Tell me—you use it before or after bloom? Two schools of thought on that."

Lottie has the look Lottie's mother had, when lip-smacking guests asked the ingredients of a dessert fabricated by the cook.

"Oh, Charlotte has an elegant garden."

"We always gave our Arthur the ribbons," she says virtuously. "But he won't display them. You remember Arthur, Zippy; he must be almost a hundred. His nephews do the ground work now."

"Under the same salary, Lottie?"

The spots appear. One can almost depend on them. "Time moves on."

"Garden Club—" Mendenhall says swiftly. "A fine tradition. My mother was given a charter membership. After some years... Like to meet Arthur."

"Oh, you can, you can. We give old Arthur a little dinner, these days, come his Yuletide. Get him to bring out his ribbons—in the end he always enjoys—you know how they are." A vagueness seems to enfold her; she gives in to it. "And it gets us over the Christmas celebration—our wee compromise." She looks at him sharply. Mendenhall remains amiably dull.

"I'd love to see Arthur," Zipporah says with passion. "He— treated me to sourgrass. And warned me of hellfire, if I raided the pea vines."

"Ah, she was always a town girl, Mr. Mendenhall . . . But do fit us in to what must be a very—well, I would be at a loss to say. Your schedule . . . I can't promise any of your father's crowd, Zippy. The Zangwills were once so—so prominent. But now, as Mord says, one would think the Jews crossed the Red Sea right to Harvard . . . But for you to come, it would be—" smiling up at Mr. Mendenhall, she swings the handbag inclusively. "Family."

And now she must run, she says. She stands up. "I seem always to be running."

"I'll get you a cab. That new doorman—yes. But he'll get on to it." His tolerance can put Zipporah's to shame. What's he waiting for? For their cousinly farewells?

"Well, Lottie. Charlotte."

Her cousin stands as she sometimes had in the ballroom danc- ing class their mothers sent them to, age twelve, one toe digging the floor she wanted to sink into. Will someone choose her? His smile encourages her. "Oh, Zippy—" she falters, and holds out her arms.

When he returns, they don't at first speak of her. Instead, they embrace. Releasing her, he says, "She took a bus."

So does he, commuting between their two apartments. Having a huge resource frees you to do what you want, supposedly. Reared among the rich, seeing how they were taught their wants early, he's learned to elect these small intense pleasures. Yet remember- ing always that such indulgence is the reverse of what the poor yearn for. "The game is hopeless," he's said. His mother used to tease, "What are you going to be, a money monk?"—but approved. She has read the publicity about him and Zipporah. She receives her admirers at breakfast in the style of a royal levee, "and we discuss the morning. The *Herald Trib* starts us off well." But she has made no overtures. "Over here, Foxy, one can take a new lover without the family having to move the furniture about." Besides, she has a handful, at the ready. But they will all of course meet. "Not just in the hereafter," he says. "Though she keeps an abbé or two on call."

"I have to go across the Park," he says now. A phrase they've settled on, showing them as separate, equal, each in a milieu—and of the age they are? She won't wait in, but will be here; he'll return.

Today his two daughters, both of Delaware, are bringing up their eight-year-old birthday boys for a blow-out. The older married first, as was proper, but they have since worked at progeny in tandem. Their brothers pay this scheduling no mind, but have had compliant wives. The mate turnover has been about average, for their breed. Everybody's standards, of both principle and conduct, have been refreshingly high, considering that there's so much more than enough money for each.

His and her affair will be for life. Because of their age the world tends to take this for granted, but other oddities may keep it from growing humdrum. As a couple, they come from two strains commonly thought opposed, though in the encyclopedias called Judeo-Christian. But as personas they are uncommonly joined. Both have lived much under public estimate, he more than she.

So-called celebrity, even when modest, separates those who have it, in a way she does not define, except that the psyche forms round that apartheid, yet retreats from it. Either fluctuation will affect. He and she are the closer for it. Much, though trivial, does not have to be explained. So they can laugh.

"My family expects that we two freaks will take care of one another," he's said. He loves them, has attended them, but is tangled with their destinies only as men are—in his case, mildly. He doesn't expect them to carry out his attributes. Perhaps he'd like his children to be more unusual than they are. But disappointment is not in his nature.

Her passion for her children comes from the body, exerts itself from that matrix. The cord is cut each time, but as with an amputated limb, the bond of sensation persists. She's tried to bear down on that, expelling herself for them as she has expelled each child. If animals wholly, they would have wandered off. What remains between her and them, between them and her, seems benign. Civilization has done this. Except emotionally, they are not her burden; she hopes not to be theirs. If they fancy she's attaching herself to this man for that reason, they're wrong. Each of her brood will interpret her life in tenor with his or her own—this is the great expectation. "I hope to be around for that as long as I can," she's told him. "With you."

"To wend our way. Between daily life—and the conclusions we form," he says. "What luck, eh?"

"Right." The eye of the future beams on her. "And by dying, we are able to pay for it."

They don't laugh. They don't say, "Stop mentioning that"; instead, they share an uncanny certainty. They will grow more alike.

"I'll be staying the night there," he says now.

"Annie'll be in—late," she says. "About four, I should say, at the earliest. Those clubs don't boom until after midnight. They're looking to hear Derek, songs he writes. Nell's boy."

"Zipporah."

He rarely says her first name. Or addresses anybody so, confronting them with who they are. It's the only hint of how he may have after all found "Foxy" difficult.

"We'll find her," he says. "I've put Thomas, our office sleuth, onto it. Funny—we thought we were going to have to let him go—his excess curiosity was getting into everybody's hair. And one had to satisfy him. But we don't fire people—we'll do anything not to. I think he comes from a rural county where they still hunt and trap, and snare. And the loose way city people can live, shedding identity or scarcely having it, appalls him. Last week he found our Czech cleaning lady's sister, thought lost in that take- over. And some months ago—his first coup—the hit-and-run driver who injured a child, as witnessed by one of our staff in Buenos Aires . . . And the child."

All this time he himself has been patting, soothing her. "I think Thomas may not like to meet people face to face. But targets are an intimacy he craves. And he's developed ways rather expensive— he loves to fly. I think he may never have—first class especially."

Foxy has talked himself into smiling. She loves watching that dawn, as the benevolence he conceals escapes him. "He'll find her. And he's safe, there. Once done—he's lost interest. The outcome is up to whoever set the problem." He blinks, thoughtfully. "And to the quarry, of course." He pats his pockets, filled no doubt for the birthday child. He is always filling them. "Thomas'll be in touch. He does, I'll phone." She and he have a private line, one that crosses the park.

In the hallway she stretches her arms around this rock of a man, cradling him. He may not have had that many lullabies. As they stand so, the hall phone rings. "Shall I answer it?" She nods. Listening, he says softly, "Lottie." Does Zipporah want to take it? She answers in dumb show—no.

"Oh yes, it was a pleasure," he says into the phone, which purrs on. "You telephoned Arthur? How ve-ery good of you. On Varick Street, he says? I'll investigate. Do thank him. And yourself . . . Yes, I'll tell her. She's not available right now . . . yes, I'll ask her to let you know . . . where she gets the little cakes . . . Same to you."

When he hangs up he shakes his head, bemused. "Arthur was quite excited, she said. That someone remembers. But Varick Street, nowadays? Accountancy-land. Garden stuff? They'll have never heard of it . . . She seems to want to ignore that I already have ob- tained the stuff; she wants to babble on about the coincidence . . . I think she felt her call interrupted us in the act. She must imagine that the minute she leaves a couple, that's what they do."

"Cakes," she marvels. " 'The little cakes.' . . . Of course my mother and hers—that era, spent half its afternoons over the coffee cups. Or our kind did. Even the poor."

"Spend a half-hour with your Lottie, and you'll hear it. Sour and parochial though she is. And in spite of the camouflage."

In spite of herself she feels the old, ingrained lip-stiffening. What does he hear? *What, Foxy? Come across.*

"You hear it, you envy it," he says. "Jews are enthralled by circumstance."

Through a sudden convexity of tears she sees that long cousinship, forever circling back on itself. But she's able to smile. "Ah, we just kid ourselves. That we have more of it."

At the house door she says, "What's that you're twiddling in your pocket?"

He lights up. "One of those tin frogs, you press a flange to make them jump—I've had him forever. And two miniature kaleidoscopes, ditto. One for each eye." He's always trying to bring those silvery-cool grandchildren something they don't have.

"Tell you what," she says. "That slippery ancestor of yours. That great-grandfather who thought he had so much moxie. Why not put your sleuth Thomas onto him?"

He shakes his head. "I like him where he is."

When Annie's key is heard in the lock, Zipporah, counseled not to wait up and dozing in the living room, wakes and joins her in the kitchen, where she's rousting out one of her unclassifiable meals. Three-a-day must be unknown to their gang, except when they come home; maybe all the dorms are steam-table now. Scholarship students who used to wait table, serving other students for their own keep, would be out of luck—but so are solved the glitches in a democracy. At this hour Zipporah may look muzzy, but always feels her head is piercingly clear, even if only her own other-generational ideas drip from it, like whey from a cheesecloth bag.

For Annie, "late" as her elders have it is early, "early" is late. She has twice transferred from one very good college to another, convinced that these exist for her, not she for them. Since the age of six, when she announced soberly to Charles her father and Vivie her mother, "I'm not sure there's enough love to go round, here," she must have been watching. Ever since her teens, when school permits, Charles has brought her along on his visits. As if to say in his literal way: "Here's where there was enough." In his composure, so serenely the university lord of two disciplines, celebrated for having "principles," there are crevices the family sees, but never one so clear.

Big-boned like him, Annie may someday be as handsome, but at seventeen passes for ordinary. When she's off-guard, and allows herself to be lazy, it can be seen that she has her mother's leafy hair, and winsomeness. Her judgment of her parents, no longer so sternly personal, has lapsed into the contemporary, along with other children of the divorced. She approves of Vivie's desertion of too mild a marriage—though her mother was the one adored—but thinks less of her father for having allowed it. Though when admitting this to Zipporah, staring between her knees in the unguardedness that eating can bring on, she had had the rueful slump of the one who has been left.

When she comes in with the dawn, energized by talk-music, people in concert, being on the town, and just being, she likes to prowl, going over things. Zipporah is happy to join her. A woman prowls her domestic empire sporadically, in a surveillance of her lot. No matter what else her life includes. That's what Vivie must have done. Annie may be used to these forays. For a young person she is unusually tactful on silence. On the table, culled from cabinet and freezer, some warmed, some chill, is one of her meals tagged to no hour. In amiable quiet, they share.

Last one in, when sated, tells the news.

"Place was super, Granny. Pics of all the greats on the walls, and a hip crowd. Some could even testify. I met one who'd heard

Mingus, imagine." One of her charms is that she spreads her vocabulary—jazz, swing, rock, and pop—broadside, to fan or newcomer, and giving no quarter to Zipporah, who keeps up as she can. Zach's sons, the Firsts, have "a gold-mine collection." On the son who accompanied her: "He's nice, re-ally nice. Only it's so weird there are two of him. He said he doesn't suffer from it, that it can be a plus. She grins. "A plus-plus?" Grows thoughtful. "But between you and me, be-twe-een you and me-e—" Ah, how endearing that soft implication, that they rate equally here—"I think they slip in and out for each other. When he went to the john"—she shudders out a whisper—"br-r-r-r. I wasn't sure it was the same twin came back."

"He's Zach's oldest son—by three and a half minutes. That can affect the character."

They laugh. She's a gift. They are forever laughing.

By then, after stowing away food and dishes in comfortable synchrony, they are strolling down the hall as usual, passing doors that remind only one of this pair of former occupants. Then up and over the jog, at which Annie says, "The attic, I love sleeping here," and Zipporah may say, "I always think of that jog as a stile." And the next time: "A stile is steps. Over a fence. But until I went to England, I didn't know." And the time after that, "A stile is to let one person in at a time. And to keep the cattle out." After that, and their laugh, there had been nothing further to say.

Then always the rite of the sleeping bag, to be spread on the floor to sit on; Annie will do it, no matter what else. In that they all already belong to the same profession: the prowlers. Which can be lone. Here is where all is brought "home" to you. Men, even family men, don't prowl, except in emergency, when they wander what is not theirs, hair rumpled if they have it, piteously eager not to be useless. Or, in a fine rush, they cope. It's no trick to catch this hint of how men and women differ. They differ on what is imperial.

For the moment, in these wakes for the living, all is flashbulb clear.

Assuming the lotus position, Zipporah is prideful that she can still lower herself on her bum, clasping her knees.

"Once it was all beds here, huh? Charles says when you cleared out everything they were all shocked to the gills."

"That's his illusion. None of your aunts and uncles do anything en masse."

"He says they looked forward to seeing it as it was."

That is so. They mourn when you clear anything out. "I say—let them look back on it. Like me." She relents. "Or do I sound crabby?"

There's nothing in the room but the neatly corded stacks of newspapers which Lester the doorman's grandson has inveigled a number of tenants to save, collecting them with a bimonthly truck, whose contents he then sells, "for charity."

Annie: "Those gray papers, brrr—they're like mummy cases, totaling the week?"

"I see them as secreting away all the worldly violences and horrors. That this family has so far missed. Not evaded, you understand. And not fled from. Just—so far—missed." This estimate, unvoiced even to Peter, of the medium she exists in has been with her since adulthood.

She sees Annie's shock. Collegiate disbelief looks the same on all of them—which is its limitation. Such specific is not the way history is taught, merely the way it occurs. "There is always a great swath of people in the world, in a country, to whom nothing much happens except the usual."

This gray locker room, where clothes no longer hang. Where the luggage of a lifetime has been dismissed, and the picnic window, outsoared, no longer has a view. This is where you see how breathtaking the usual has been. The everyday from which each of us, one by one, even this girl here, must in time step up and over the stile. Into that boundless air where no cattle are.

"Gran. Gran—are you all right?"

Summon yourself. "Quite. Just hold my hand, will you, while the ghosts walk in?"

She's admiring Annie's fair cheek, the staunch curve of the mouth, when the African mask flies in and claps itself onto its old place on the wall. In the museum where it now bides, it is compelled not to stare at anyone in particular. For a minute or two she and that heavy-lidded oval commune.

Next, that poor bench lumbers in, tired, irritable, like an ancient pet kept too long. Made of teak—the African kind, too heavy even for most ship-building, Mendenhall has said—it rests now not far from here, in his office garden, where, put out to grass if not to sea, it is weathering. It must be relieved to see her sitting on the floor.

Now—her desk and chair. Retired to the living room, the desk surface scarred with her labors, the chair crippled with her shiftings, they are still extant in their dustless corner, unvisited. They settle in their old niche, creaking inaudibly. Where else can we go, now that we're unemployable?

She won't question where the attic goes, when no one's in it. The problem of whether matter exists if it is not perceived, raised by Bishop Berkeley and never to be satisfactorily answered, does not pertain here. Until the last of a family goes, an attic stays.

That's enough, then. No people-ghosts, thank you. What we have owned can seduce—until we make a museum of ourselves. But the dead visit us more ardently, in a consciousness of flesh once theirs, still ours. Even our dogs frolic there—in between.

She releases Annie's hand. "You haven't said," she murmurs. "And I was afraid to ask you. Did Derek show up for his gig?"

"No," a voice answers before Annie can.

The answer descends from above, not from a mountaintop. Foxy is back. Raising her eyes, she sees from her floor level that Foxy's pocket, the one that held the toys for the grandsons, still bulges. Then he lifts her up, pulls Annie up by the hand and gathers the two of them in his arms, holding them tight. A thrum then comes from his chest, sounding from him to them, on their triangular harp.

"No. He is with Nell."

Thomas Thomas, sandy-haired, nose-tip bent to the wind, is like a photograph of a photograph, retreating from the lens of the per-

sonal, yet doomed to cooperate. The hardest part of his job is to
have to turn up for it in the flesh. Once it's clear that he would
shrink from hanging his successes on himself like a general's array,
and asks only to be projected toward the next, he can fascinate,
with a sleuth's charm. Bred to the chase, whittled by it, once to
every lure, he himself would be almost impossible to catch. Yet,
someone has?

"Concorde's very tight quarters, isn't it," he says, meeting with
Mendenhall and Zipporah. "And the personalities aboard so large."
He sees, or remembers, what Mendenhall is too kind to say. "Ah,
you'll never have been on one. I'll never catch onto you." He hopes
this will endear. "Anyway, 'Spare no expense' is my motto. Ours—
as we agreed?" A nod reassures him, but he takes time to stretch
out. They are in the office-flat; Mendenhall's decor is strictly
daybed, but there are four. "You wanted a quick report. But
some—you can't just phone."

Reports are his apogee. He would like to conduct them
through all the steps in the snare, "the whole imbroglio," as he calls
it. Foreign phrases help distance him from any interest beyond the
professional. "Suffice it to say, that the easiest to find are those
who ordinarily travel—er—with a pack. No intent to insult." He
pinches a narrow trouser leg higher at the knee. "But there it is. I
found her. And when I heard that teasing voice—" He never confronts. "This time—I went."

She is in a small, gnarled inn above a town on the Lake Como
shore. He hands them a picture of it, and the half-dozen or so
women of varying ages who run it and a small nursing wing.
Some are licensed, some not; gossip is that all were novices not
found acceptable, for one reason or another, by any order. "There's
considerable anti-church feeling in Italy. They get a steady tithe of
provender from the town." He had spent some days in the area before approaching her. "They don't know for sure why she is there,
though she came from a Swiss clinic just over the border that
sometimes refers. She sees a doctor there, met through the clinic
but attached to a respectable hospital in Bergamo. He wouldn't talk

without her permission. The Swiss are accustomed to secrets—I could have been talking to a bank. But I had a strong impression there was one. And even banks have secretaries."

He had found out the day she was due for checkup, and had gone to the inn in her absence. "They are devoted to her, and she pays, well, all sorts of extras. But her phoning, all over the map on their one line—she's put in for another, which in that town can take months—is an impediment to their business.

"I located her that way, of course," Thomas says. "The phoning. Easy. When they are addicts."

Even in the foreboding that grips even now when any one of the brood is in danger, Zipporah has to smile, as over a prodigy. "From ten on, we had to phone-ration her. The way other kids are, on sweets." And her mother can wait now, to hear the finality. He's like a chemist, dropping one fact, then another, into the brew. We need him, though he repels.

"Her kids even got in ahead of me; she phoned the son and daughter so faithfully."

Ah yes, that's Nell. If she's a whore she's not an old-fashioned one; she'd never put the kids out to wet nurses. "Thelma's an electronic whiz. And Derek—the father of one of his buddies is the phone company, if anyone is. I thought of it. But it was not my place."

"Right. But it was mine. And I got on to them . . . Your granddaughter Thelma—she's a tough one—going into medicine. She said, 'I'll bet anything she's sick. And doesn't want us to know.' And your Derek says: 'Doesn't want anybody to.'"

"Is she?" It bursts from her.

He hands her another snapshot. When weekending in the country, Nell often wears a riding habit, though she doesn't much ride. Tall, full-breasted, curvy hips emphasized by the jodhpurs, she knows she'll seem extra womanly. Now it all hangs on her. The face? That arrogant pout of the extremely pretty? Gone. Refined to beauty? Thomas evidently thinks so. A mother can't.

"She's thin as a—" What? Not a rail, the usual. A whiteness.

She's not yet emaciated. But a whiteness shines from her, as from the starved. "What's wrong with her?"

"The nurses say the clinic that sent her, which does both general and cosmetic surgery, usually sends a post-operative history and agenda along with the patient. With her—nothing. At first they thought perhaps the face had been done over, being so perfect—and some clients want to hide the fact. But no scars—which they can always spot. They didn't want to go on, but I pressed. Surveillance is their job. And their bathing facilities are—open." He flushes, bites his lip. "There are no post-operative scars. And they say she eats well. But wastes."

So he had gone back to the doctor. "When I told him family was involved—and who I work for—he gave."

Thomas stands up. The expression on his features is piteous. For a sleuth he hasn't a sharp face, rather a laid-back, blunted one you'll see in many a Deep South drugstore: rounded to a pie by the town, but with the mountain squint still lodged. "Can I report to you in private, F. D.?"

"No need. Get on with it, Thomas." Definitely the last name, not the first. Mendenhall can be more of a boss than she has romanced.

"She has a condition. From which she could die." But the doctor is a veteran of youth clinics. "He claims he has seen cases where vanity, if strong enough, effects what most would call miracles. He believes it to be a placebo that works." So he and she have made a bargain. For some months he will monitor. The town pharmacist, a friend, will have a program of pills. "'No painkillers,' he said. Whether the pills were blanks, he wouldn't say. But if the symptoms worsen, she has agreed to put herself in his hands at the clinic. 'A grave risk,' he said. 'But a brave experiment.' One he has always wanted to try."

For the first time Thomas addresses Zipporah: "They took me to tea, her and the son and daughter, the three of them. Coffee actually. In a dark little café." Thelma and Derek had agreed to approve. Though Thelma doesn't agree with alternative medicine, she knows her mother. "'This is sparing her,' she said. The boy said, 'She'll manage. She always has. Look how she's left us to confab . . .' Every day she walks to the café, and if the gate to a certain villa is left open by the gardener, she walks up the hill, she said, 'for my assignation with a certain tree.' She even laughed. After she was gone the boy said, 'Oh she'll manage. But it would be best if there were a man.'"

Then the son and daughter had left him to wait for her. A car was coming to drive them to Milan for the plane back to New York. But they would be back. Bringing their other sister.

"Remarkable pair," Thomas said. "Self-sufficient. And not callous." He looks puzzled. "Like you wouldn't expect."

But then, he said, a strange thing had happened. While he waited for Nell to return, the café had filled. "Wrinkled oldies, mostly. And while I sat there, the waiter, clearing away the cups, crossed himself when he picked up hers. Then brought me one on the house. And when she came back—when she strolled in—it was like she lit a candle. She sat down as if I—" He's feeling something, surprise? "Well, she didn't mention the kids, though when I did she said, 'Yes, they're the best.' Then she said: 'The tree. It's my Loie Fuller tree—the dancer. One arm up, one branch flung out. And a cloudy skirt of leaves.'"

An exclamation from Zipporah. "She has a photograph of Fuller, at home." And then: "Why aren't we calling her by her name?'"

"When we left, one old woman tried to kiss her skirt. They all—like she was the apple. Or a star. She said something to them. 'I have no Italian,' I told her. She told me then, they gave her strength. Only time she ever admitted she might be ill." She'd walked on steadily, only once saying anything; she needed the breath. "She said, 'Miss my high heels.' And when we got to the inn door, the daily offerings were piled high against it."

Until then he'd thought those a tribute to the innkeepers, who served as unofficial out-patient clinic of the town. They were wry women, no doubt sophisticated by the woe daily at their portal.

When he asked about the crowd at the café, two had grinned, one pair had crossed themselves, and the other three had abstained, deferring to Annunciata, the one real nurse, who lends sanction to their outfit. "She is an accountant's niece from Arezzo," he says, referring to the bound notebook whose pages he has been flipping throughout. Not that his reactions aren't real, but need corroboration, like those who sidle through museums with mechanical opinion ticking in their ear. "They are selling her picture, behind her back." They have given him one; he touches his breastpocket but doesn't at first pull it out, then can't resist.

Nell has one hand in front of her chest, one arm upflung, the face in three-quarter view, chin raised, challenging something out and beyond, that the viewer will never see. "The pharmacist kept shopping the word 'placebo' around; he has to keep his customers in tow. And the café owner also. So, the not-so-clever ones, they gather. To them that is the word which begins the Vespers for the dead: *Placebo Domini,* the first antiphon: 'I shall be pleasing to God.'"

Thomas Thomas enunciates that as if it may apply to him, and to the god standing so near, who has so elevated his humble servant. He purses his mouth, suitably, he hopes. Mendenhall's offices are filled with such oddities as he, elsewhere not long employable. Certainly his elsewhere hadn't offered such entrancing missions.

"They think—that she may be a saint. So they don't want to lose out."

He's shocked them. He himself looks whelmed, in what it is to confront.

"And what do you think?" Mendenhall looks weary. Middle of the night, but that won't be why. Brought up to showgirl hours, he'll joke—that's when he feels lean, hungry, and prime.

Thomas looks frightened. The huntsman should not be the quarry. When Zipporah, sad and big-eyed, puts a hand on him, whispering throatily, he jumps—*These people don't observe protocol; they'll stop at nothing,* one can hear him say. But he'll hold his ground.

"When you see her—" he says, "you want to say her name."

There are threads that may each be pulled and examined, one by one, from a long life still intrepidly lengthening. Twenty years later, Zipporah, lying in state—in that state of survival which is in part a dream of dying—remembers that day in every detail, as the one when her and Mendenhall's affair ended, and their happily unmarried life began.

As Zipporah Zangwill, born under that heavy euphony early in that solemnly imposed, temporal arena called "this century," she and it are now in their final decade. Both readying to leave. All around her, people are preparing for the era's interment. Even solemnly assessing its character to each other, in hasty attempts to beat their successors-to-be to the draw. As an early inhabitant of that span, existing almost parallel with it, she has been doing this all her life.

Her father, however, had had a disdain for what he'd called "calendar rot," pointing out that every sector of time, from the era to the hour, is man-made. Time, that slippery element, is more august. Neither he nor any known ancestors had written their memoirs. "Every person is a memoir," he'd said to her on his deathbed. "But particularly, every Jew."

Spoken in that tonal accent, warped by many hegiras and often confusing to semanticists, which many a modern Jew still has. A manner of speech half somber, half taciturn?—hard to tell which. Often sprinkled with a lemon-zest of argot, or inner satire?—hard to tell which. When dying of the "wonky" heart he hadn't told her about, he had however mentioned to his law partner that now and then he had heard a gurgling, "like a pesky third partner—some prospect who wants to buy in."

Her father had died in hospital, robbed of the family-surrounded bed scene he had described with fervor, seen when as a boy of ten he had been brought in to bid his grandfather good-bye. That generation always died at home; he had wanted to. She will. The clan has so agreed, shaking their heads in public but according to her informant and ally, Nell's doctor daughter Thelma, secretly admiring the woman they've never dared call matriarch. Over these last few years she has had a hip that, yielding to gravity, had cracked, then healed, followed by a series of skeletal warnings which have not—"Nothing too messy, so far," Thelma has told them. "With good attendants, we should be able to get by. At home. Give her that boon."

Not long ago, when Zipporah was still on her pins, she had seen a good friend, also in his nineties, all his life the glory center of his Irish Catholic friends and admirers, lying in a nest of plumbing, and wired ignominiously by the nose, mouth agape, as the sole occupant of a special unit at St. Clare's—"Nobody allowed in except by special dispensation," they said. "He's in intensive care." Meaning God's? Now and then, friends had come to pay their respects and a dispensation had been doled; during the last several days, nobody had applied. She had stood at the bedside, willing her consciousness of him toward a core of awareness, maybe the size of one smoldering coal, that she felt sure was there. He had already received "absolution"; what more could his faithful spirit want? He was only absolutely alone.

So, Zipporah has been promised it: born at home, she will die there. Moreover, all family members reachable have been put on notice. A goodly show—even to the fourth generation, among those a Johnnie-come-lately babe-in-arms belonging to Annie—will gather, having accepted tentatively, or sworn faithfully to attend when summoned. This too being Thelma's work. Like many raised in the Village by its leftover, gentler radicals, she exudes an energy in search of a community, while embracing convention with an exaggerated squeeze. Unmarried, having served as a physician in too many harrowing places, she has had lovers of both sexes and feels a medical responsibility for everybody, with an endearing lack of tact. "I thought I'd tell you," she'd said, when reporting these exhaustive arrangements "while you're still able to enjoy."

"Thank you, dear," Zipporah said. "You've saved me from sending out cards."

"Ah, Gran. You're so sharp."

Best not to show that too often, since great age is said to free one to say almost anything. At times she has a wicked desire to do so. That's when one most misses one's like-minded but vanished coevals. With whom one might moan, "What energy it takes, to stay behind the times!" On rare occasions one finds those again—in the young. It's then that she would like to live forever. After the first shock—on both sides—it's like finding she can still skip rope.

Death, that intensive carer, has meanwhile been working on the case. Her skeleton is making its presence constantly known. "Tell them," she was able to say in the interval after a morphine shot, "if people wonder why I'm not in the hospital—tell them I'm half-cracked." A heart makes itself known instead by its absence—of beat. Breathing oxygen, you don't speak. This state has gone on, may go on, for some time.

"She's a tough one. It may even suspend—for a time," the doctor has said. Allotting her what only the very rich can have, or the recalcitrant poor. Or those who've a doctor in the family. A home visit.

Thelma says to her, "You've given birth six times in a hospital—the old Doctors.'" Thelma had been born there herself. "A haven, I'm told. They're not that now. Even for us." But Thelma has seen a monk dream away into death, under no drug except the inward pressing circle of his fellows, who did not touch him. They said afterward that the dying ebb away to a solo of their own instrument, each time heard only once. The last humming of the mind. Their custom had been to form a circle, to lean. Hoping to hear.

So Zipporah is promised her jubilee.

During these weeks of suspension there are visitors, casuals and family, dropping by. The casuals always phone beforehand: *Can she be seen?* Once, urging her arthritic hand to pick up the phone at her bedside, and hearing that sneaky inquiry, she answered fiercely, "She can always be seen," and hung up. "Who was that, Mrs. Duffy?" Nurse McKenzie asked, aggrieved, although as day shift her duty is to encourage periods of consciousness. "Some reporter." Zipporah's voice, often inaudible even to herself, can be intermittently strong. "How did he get on the private line?"

The phone line between herself and her one remaining equal, whose face is ever-present in her sight, whose talk over the last twenty years can still purl, by stops and starts, in her ear. She's increasingly deaf to people in the room, never so to him. At almost a year older than she, he had by his own admission "flubbed" a bit on that long ago day in Maryland, when averring he and she were exactly the same age. He too is still alive, though in some ways not as lucky.

A series of small, cat's-paw strokes hasn't quelled him, but therapists must pummel him to keep him from being as bedridden as she. Another crew is training him to speak again. Sometimes his speech is heartbreakingly that same open-mouthed smear which had emerged from two kids with cleft palates, at her Boston day school.

"Go on, I'm listening," she always said to him, and in reparation, to them. For like that pair who'd had to struggle so for people to recognize that they had their wits, there's nothing wrong with his intelligence. Several times, a new device, still in the test stage and brought in and activated by its inventor, has relayed his bouts of speech to her, too loud but spottily, gratefully, a word now and then plain.

In turn she has a humiliating lack. She cannot always remember her lover's name. She too has devices. Shaming ones. "What are those initials again?" she'll ask, meaning "F. D." Or "What's that nickname of his—what animal?" The nurses aren't fooled, but revealing her quandary brings down her status with them. So when that blank occurs, she now waits for Thelma. "How is he, Thelma?" Who will answer artfully, quite understanding the real question: "Ah, Foxy? F. D.? I'll check."

As for the nurses, with them it is alas wise to play the aristocrat. She is under no obligation to load her brain with their hireling identities. Actually their names, McKenzie and Halvorson, bug her, like some tap-dance team from old vaudeville. So, gleefully, she will address them only as "Day" and "Night." The daytime one, a Swede, pale and calm as so many from the land of the midnight sun, only smiles. "My, we are fanciful," Night says.

She's a good girl and very adept at all the body-shifting and dosing; they both are. But when one is dream-dying, one must fight to keep command. "Not at all," Zipporah said, to her own ear without quaver. "I am . . . merely being poetical."

When Thelma hears this she laughs, motioning McKenzie aside. Both attendants know that doctor and patient prefer to confab without audience, but allege to each other, as they go on and off shift, that it's the doctor-patient relationship here that warrants curiosity. Not that they're attending one of a celebrated pair. This not so for the pair's age, in a country that never pays it much respect, and where such age is getting to be ordinary. Nor even for their duration as a couple, now almost two decades. But when the erotic should be, well, an embarrassment.

Not that they flaunted it. But at the opera for instance, according to one of McKenzie's former patients, even into their late eighties it was clearly evident. Maybe being illegal makes it last longer?

"It hurts my pelvis to laugh," Zipporah says. "But I'll gladly suffer it. And McKenzie is really a pearl. She all but asked me. She's so literal." Thelma is always bracing. Zipporah feels able to ask her own dicey question. "How is he?"

A doctor, even a relative, has to test; she's not being mean.

"You know who, Thelma."

"Of course I do. But I have to get it from you."

It won't come. There's that pocket of space again. She strains.

She invokes. Finally she says humbly: "The—that man across the park."

"Oh darling." Doctor is embracing patient. Not at all suitable.

"Doctor—" McKenzie dares. Patient's wearing a support. The vertebrae."

"Right. Give me a pen. Have you that identity bracelet handy, nurse? The one she came home from the hospital with." Thelma had had to promise it would be only overnight, for the X rays and other tests. When there's that much pain in the back, you have to be sure it's not lung. "Give me the bracelet." She writes on its tag and slips the bracelet on Zipporah's wrist. "There. It has his name on it."

"Thanks. But how is he? You haven't said."

"In a rage. It's not wise."

A rage? "Oh Thelma. I saw that on him once. When they wouldn't let the little grandson come for his birthday as arranged. Just a curt note on Foxy's answering service. Nothing more . . . It's scary. He turns white."

Almost twenty years back and she hasn't forgotten how his teeth bared. "I couldn't understand it. Such an outsize reaction. He'd taken the tin jumping frog from that bulging pocket, let it hop once, twice, down the floor, then crushed it underfoot. He had the two kaleidoscopes in his fists, when I stopped him. 'They've done nothing,' I said. 'And they're glass.' I didn't catch on until much later. That the fuss was about me." And when she had—still didn't understand. A man his age, who'd already had two live-in mistresses—what business of theirs? None of her family liked the "items" in the gossip sheets either.

In the end they were the ones who'd enlightened her, worming out of Foxy what he would never in the world tell her. Zach has elected to. Her youngest son has grizzled early. Physically empowered by the heft of what he works on, as he paces, his gait rolling from box-toed boot to boot, he might be one of his own creations, activated; he's begun working in the figure.

"Ever since the Reo, we talk easy, he and I . . . It's the money, he told me. The Bundle. People who have enough dough or too much, they have to protect that by more. And have hosts of nannied kids, ready for the manna to fall. It's what he's been afraid of being, all his life, and was brought up not to be by that doozy mother. For his heirs—bad enough that the money spills from him like Niagara now. He's like a gambler who knows how to lose. But such fortune grows by perpetual motion—what'll happen when he's gone? 'My heirs are afraid of undue influence,' he said. 'In that territory one sees a lot of it. At the drop of a hat they'll sue. They'd have gone after Katrina, but an invalid?—their own advisors talked them out of it.' But you? They want it clear, if ever they have to go to court, that they saw from the first, that best they never have anything to do with you... 'They're not bad at all, singly,' F. D. told me. 'They're even—winsome.' And he loved that grandkid. 'But it's what can happen to nice people in a war. The money war.'"

...Yes, he'd loved the little boy, whose suave, bland-featured parents had dangled him, then pulled back. "But what has that got to do with me, Zach? I shan't invade that social life. He and I don't ever plan to marry...Zach...You don't suppose—?"

When he stops in his tracks he does bulk. "Ma. They're up to lots of that down there. I sell to them. Dog people. Horse people. Sometimes even art people. And all connected, no matter how many times they divorce each other. Why? Because, altogether— they're money people. And altogether they'll stick." He comes to take her face between his palms, giving it a shake before he releases. "And to them, you're the same. Only from the other camp."

She couldn't believe it. She defended them—their manners. Good breeding tells—a phrase left over from Brookline, there applied indiscriminately. He'd waited, smirking, through all her faltering—at the end of which, she believed him. The word "antisemite" was never said. Meant for pogroms and the blood-fears against the foreigner, it was too strong for the situation. Ought to be another, milder one. For the people who are merely "nice."

"Make me a cup of coffee," Zach said. "Half-and-half." In the kitchen, he said: "Ever tell you I took the family to Jennie's restaurant? We fell on each other's necks. Seven of us, but she got such a kick out of not letting us pay. I don't think she wanted to see you."

"No, not since her selling Norm's place. Some blacks heard about it, and wanted it. But she wouldn't show them it. 'I can't afford the hassle,' she said. I told her the co-op wouldn't dare non-approval, not these days. Not if the buyers were qualified. But she wouldn't believe me. She said, 'Reasons will be found.'"

"Ah, yes," Zach said. "The best people do that."

And then, of course, she had to laugh. "You win, Zach. You win."

"Half-and-half," he said, stirring his cup. "How grateful I am— to be that. Supposed to weaken you, dilute. Not if you watch. And both sides as strong as Peter and you . . ." He stirred so hard it slopped. "Sorry. You know, when Dad used to prate, I couldn't stand it. I wasn't old enough to listen. Now I can. He said once— when we kids were gypsying around Sunday schools and there were a coupla incidents—'Jews are trained to be logical. Maybe *because* they're so mystical. As your forefathers saw, Zach. But prejudice, any kind, is anti-logic. Talking it down is just talking to yourself. Yet the Jew always tries.'"

When this son stares into the past, she sees why they say he's the one who most resembles her. "'*Your forefathers, Zach,*' Dad said; imagine that. My father, who couldn't lay claim to them, giving me them. The beauty of it, I'll never forget that 'your.'" He took a cookie from the jar they all knew she kept filled.

"Jennie's. She wouldn't give out the recipe. But I set the girls to watch. Glad I did."

He took another. "The restaurant's a roaring success. But Jennie, she didn't look too good, even then. Soul food all day long, wasn't really her dish."

He'd waited until he got up to go to say, "Why'n't you and F. D. light out? Go to all those places you wanted to see again, didn't get to show Dad."

She is stunned, but knew they would do it; Foxy would be enchanted. Those islands off shore of the civilized Philippines, or

mechanized Japan, where "lost" tribals still were. The Africa of
that bearer who so reminded her of—who? That tip end of a continent where the fathoms of the sea and its tackle were being paid
their final and blighted due. That farthest northern opposite where
an Eskimo still was an Inuit. And one mountainside where there
might still be some remnants of Hessian-Indian from the time of
the American Revolution—in Rockland County, New York.

"Just the thing," she'd said. "For an unmarried honeymoon.
And before Mendenhall's mother's hundredth. She plans a party—
and a stylish exit, I shouldn't be surprised."

Zach, the devil, had reserved his news until then. "And after—
Bert's wedding?"

But she could top that. "We all of us spoke on the phone. I think
it'll be in a registry office. But anybody around is invited to a party
in Hampstead, afterwards. If they come over here, I'll of course volunteer another. But I doubt that will be—for some while."

"So do I. Bert tracked me down; I was in Paris, flew over . . . I
bought shares in the Tunnel once, but that'll be the day—worth
now about thirty cents . . . Debra wasn't there; she's decided to go
on working at the hospital. May have been leaving Bert and me to
catch up . . ."

"Did you?"

"We're a clutch of surprisers, our crowd. Nobody ever catches
up . . . All? You spoke with all three? . . . The little girl?"

"At length. She wanted to meet me. I felt she already knew a lot."

"She chatted on as if she'd met us daily. All except—Peter."

Ah yes. Debra wouldn't have told her about him. I try not to
think why. "That child. She talks like—like she's in training to be—
one of the Muses; I couldn't think which. Or one of those docents
who take you round museums. Those that haven't yet been built."

"She took me for a walk. 'Why do you call yourself 'Nuncle,'
Zach—is it out of that play?' She's mad for family."

"She'll get one. Or nearly. She wants to be a reb."

Surprises. What would a family be without them? Truth is,
ours looks forward to them.

"Bert's influence?" he says. "That soon?"

Not according to that little voice. "From Lev."

The years pass. Both still hear. That one touch of a violence not theirs. The shot.

"Sundays—" Zach says. "I always wondered how we could bear them, afterwards."

Lev had been given no time to learn to die.

She's been given an indefinite leave, in which to learn that this is a part of life. Whether one whimpers or is stolid is not the question. She is being tutored to exist as: interval. As from some ancient pre-Gregorian score. At first, the body-box feels how it would be if pushed into flame, but prematurely. Then—cry out. A nurse comes who has no face, being only agent, personless. "Won't sting." What spy needle is being applied? Or else the heart chopchops: Let/me/go, and the answer? A tent of air—locked. The hospital has come to me.

Her house has so many guises. For years now, it has been her *schul*. Is that what was wrong with it? Is that what's right? Hush, a house is always in between. Nowadays the charts are simple here: one if by land, two if by sea; expect no reply to your semaphore. Take with you this fathom-line, yardage without end.

Nobody on the towpath, push off. Sail. The oars will not plash.

Those are the deeps. When she wakes she doesn't deny what she found there, in that lucent sailing through clouds that parted to receive her and closed behind her, only to nudge her on. These hours "under" aren't sleep-dreams, playing at parlor games with daytime images, making kangaroo leaps into what we didn't know we were wistful for or hiding from. This is that abiding otherness of dream which must always underlie all meditations and acts. Just as the atom stream, underlying all matter, resides in that night table and the scurf of bottles, syringes, and nappies lying on it—and though

I'll never see that stream of dancing particles, I must believe in them. So I must believe in this other-dream which is carrying me along.

Interspersed, she has hours of cogency, even the whole of a day or a night. Then she will pull a thread from her life and examine it, less often now a strand from the immediate past. Her life with Mendenhall has been no postscript. Rather, a kindling, of what apparently has to be taught again and again—that one must never expect less of any period of one's life, no matter when.

What holds her back from revisiting those years, the way devotees of a warmer clime return to bask in it, is her shivering awareness of the man across the park. Attended and valeted with every paid service, visited by dutiful, even fond employees from his empire, and of course monitored by those sons and daughters who have warily avoided feud, and now even offer him their progeny like tidbits—that man is now alone, in the hospital of himself.

You are right, McKenzie. At times "Mrs. Duffy" is fanciful. For then, by the power of her imagination, plus a cynical trust in what money can do, his bed and all its paraphernalia is wafted here. Over and across Central Park, with all his in-at-the-death followers scrambling behind the ambulance, in a fleet of cars. During his and her years together she has developed a wifely tenderness—the kind that settles a man in a haze of protective husbandry—though she had been careful to look after him openly that way only when they were traveling. Now she even plots how, this bedroom suite being too small, one might set going a double operation in her big living room, their beds to be side by side, with staff housed in the rooms all along the hall. Bathrooms—a fair enough number. And the attic, a godsend for all medical gear and tackle.

So linked, love will speak for him. And death will marry them.

Has she voiced this? At times she can't tell whether. She sees by Thelma's face that she has. "Don't say," she quavers. But Thelma does. "You each face the same prospect that the body teaches. Loss of command. In that you are joined."

At times she hears his voice as last heard—as if through putty, a glottal smear. At times he is at her side, in such wrack as she is. He can still shift his limbs about, but moves little, in order not to lord it over her. She can whisper but seldom does, since he cannot reply. They are in harmony.

They swing now as couples long together, and talking as one, are able, each pulling his or her thread. Whether side by side, or from across the park.

She no longer begrudges him his family. Perhaps he has made peace with them. He has never begrudged her hers.

One night—or morning?—four A.M. or P.M. by the clock she has had hung so she can see, she says to Thelma, who though never seen entering is always there: "He's gone, isn't he? He took up his bed, and walked."

Thelma has reappeared in time to nod gently, one of those mandarin-doll head-on-a-wire nods that doctors give.

"Thelma? How come you're always here?"

"I took leave."

"Ah, like your mother, once. How is Nell?"

"She came to see you last week, Gran, remember? She's a bit frail."

"Ah, yes . . . She came back, didn't she." That little, birdlike woman. But Nell by now will be pushing seventy.

"After two years. She's never admitted she's had the operation—there was no medical history. But she must have. There are no more men."

"Sainthood can shrivel you. Even when it's temporary."

Thelma bursts out laughing.

"You're really here, Thelma? Sometimes I'm not sure. All of you come and go."

A hand squeezes hers. "I know. But today I really am."

"When I phoned her. At that nun place. You and Derek had already got there."

"That espresso bar. She took us there. All the natives hanging

in, buying her photo. Fraud of frauds. And those nuns, padding her
phone bill. Poor Derek, already singing, but not yet making bread
hand over fist, like he does now. But sending her some, every time
he had a gig."

And Philippe, probably. And Thomas Thomas? Her last flings.

"I only recall what she said to me on the phone. One word before they cut her off. Not what I expected from Nell."

The two new nurses are standing by, with this contraption
she's to be in now. The others deserted, just when she had their
names down pat. She won't bother with these. Can't.

"Just one word?" Thelma says "From my mother? That'll be
the day. What was it?"

One word from Dad's girl. But bringing myself home to me.
"'Ma.'"

The new nurses are shifting her. "There you are, Zipporah."

That deplorable convention. "Thank you," she murmurs. "I
know who I am."

"My, we're feeling feisty today."

"Right, Susie. You two will learn to sit me up at your peril. My
head clears."

Nurse and doctor exchange looks. Before the end, is it?

"My mother, and her sister, my aunt, went out that way. All
clear. A kind of doxology."

The younger nurse says shyly, "When we give thanks. You
folks High Church? We thought—" The older woman gives her
a stare.

"Right," the patient says. "Very high. Practically invisible." Her
breath fails a mite during those long syllables. "Thelma, will you
hand round the chocolates?" When permitted, these buoy. And
allow her to appear blessedly natural.

Thelma lingers. "Well, I better be going." She grins. "Now that
I've really been here . . . Derek will come to sing again, anytime you
say. He says you liked."

"I didn't know any of his music. He didn't know any of mine. We settled on . . . calypso. Wonderful."

Thelma brightens. She's an ethnics insister. "Which song? I used to know them all."

Her breaths are her pauses now, but she manages the chant. *"Stone-cold daid in dee mahket, unh! . . .* My favorite."

Patient has blundered. In this chamber awash with tact. "Sorry. Comes from another time. And I can never remember the next line." The nurses, heads bowed, busy themselves apart from the bedside. These wanderings are out of their sphere.

"Derek and I . . . agree. Everybody's a native now. Like when . . . when Foxy and I took that trip. Around my old haunts? All the so-called 'savages.' Who were barefoot in my time? They're wearing running shoes." She tries to sit up farther. Is immediately quelled. "Sorry. But I bet you three are wearing them."

From the murmurs—*Adidas, Nike*—they are, merely different brands.

"You didn't—don't," the younger nurse says shyly. "I saw in your wardrobe. Those heels. Wow."

I'm going to like this one, Zipporah thinks. She doesn't mind using the past tense. "One of my daughters . . . still wears them. The other not."

Thelma's still here. "My mother. Said that to you?"

"Said what?" I'll hear it forever. But I want to hear her daughter saying it.

" 'Ma.' "

More like a wail, it was. But this I won't tell Thelma. She'll find out maybe, in the night silences, where even at ninety-odd, the mothers are invoked. Along with the fathers. But not alike.

A drug is stealing her away. When did they inject? Or some pill. One can't always monitor. "Women have dynasty." This comes out blurred, but it's what she's always wanted to say. Maybe she's said it before? It bears repeating. My, these days she's saying everything. From behind closed eyes one seems able to. One can. She rouses. "Don't confuse it with maternity."

She dreams that she is completing all her thoughts. But if challenged, could not say what these are.

When she wakes, she is in one of those landscapes where people still go barefoot. Where the toucans still flash...Derek. Make that a song? Put this bone-ache in it, seeped from old bruises. Any landscape can bruise. Flesh of my flesh's flesh as you are, Derek, I heard that in your music. Ah boy, my treks were my war. And I have done with them.

As midnight wanes on her luminous clock, all the threads seem pulled. Even pain has deserted her. Sorry, sorry, sorry, she's said all day long. They don't warn one that when dying, we apologize.

In the small hours, as the window lightens, her youth begins to sing to her, a troubadour. All its denizens appear.

Full morning and not a dark one, what's this? Her bed is moving. On wheels it handles easily. Though her heavy lids lift only to a slit through which she sees a white field that must be the nurses' white-uniformed middles, she can hear their starchy jokes. Down the long hall they go. Only one doorway will let the bed through; do they know it? They'll have plotted the itinerary; they negotiate well. One rumble, the foot of the bed lifted, then the head, to a hissed "watch it," and they're over the sill.

No pallbearers they, they have borne her into the light; she's in her living room. The bed holds still; the floor will not open to swallow it. Table on either side hold crystal, metal, bottles, napery—towels, a cutlery of small instruments, a roll of floss—for what bird?—hidden on the lowest shelf, the one essential piece of enamel ware. There are flowers; she can tell, but only tastefully; this is not yet a funeral. Is it a fete?

"Can you hear us?"...Ye-es. "Can you answer us?"... Nnnnnnnn-o.

"Zipporah! We are going to raise you up. Just a wee-ee. There."

Rise, my eyelids...When you don't speak, they don't obey...

"Do it yourself, dear, can you?"

There they are, on their faces a solicitude for which one cannot pay. But what's this? They are walking backward, as one does when leaving royalty, their gazes fixed on her as they ooze away. She's never craved such status, has mocked it. Does dying make royalty of us all? Nurse—I sink. But do not yet blind me. This cadence in my head—biblical? That is what we are honoring.

She understands now, mind humming.

They have all now been summoned, her family. For her jubilee.

Cicily loves to fly. High up in the heavens—which aren't called that anymore. In a winged box roaring loud enough to persuade that it's the bird-dragon archeopteryx reborn. In the dappled light you're a movie-still. Except you're alive, breathing everybody's recycled breath.

Nearing thirty, her life to date has hopped from interval to interval, in a process not quite under her control. She is not sure it should be. Maybe gliding between educations, jobs, countries, is her modern temperament. Mostly self-supporting, though once in a while Debra and Bert, though never asked, find it a pleasure to kick in. Her love life, never merely the one-night stand yet always shy of live-in affair, keeps her out of the marriage and children questions. There have been passions in it, but have these been "love"? And how long does modernity last?

"Having as many talents as you, and the energy to exert them, can be like having too many fingers," Alec said in his good-bye graduation homily. "It can interfere." As it may have for him? Nothing was said about her being too smart for herself. At that school almost everybody was. It was conceded that those few who were more "ordinary" might later have less trouble being "real." Both kinds could be "troubled." As for the thumpingly stupid, they were at some other school.

She has gone student-cheap all over Europe, and some of North Africa, once back and forth across the Channel with a group of Oxford chums, their passage to the weekend birthday party for one of them being paid for by his father, a Paris-based relative of the late Shah. Once with Val and her son, the Punk, to Ceylon, poor Val unaware that this former tea garden of the British had "gone political," as well as dead set against temple travelers like the Punk. That trip, to the border and back, had been all flight. Val, humbled by being so out of touch, had apologized for the disappointment. "Screw destinations," the Punk had consoled. "That old DC-7 was an experience. Or was it an 'eight'?" He keeps a log.

Now, were she alone on this first trip to New York, she would no doubt have been flying coach like those of the unfancy friends she mostly favors. But as Alec, retired but still the family guru, reminds her, even two humanitarians like her mother and stepfather have to do "business." So today, what with laptop and international phoning needs, she and they are flying in that class. Bert's half of her parents' unique agency, being devoted to refugees and the work of getting them out of one country and into another, "is destination personified." Debra, now a valued liaison between the clients of the somewhat debilitated National Health Service and its government, and the sponsor of a prize documentary on a cystic fibrosis child, shunted in with the retarded and later discovered to be a genius—"Well, Debra may seem to have arrived. In demeanor, I suspect she always has. And I understand she does well with the investments, yours and the fund's both. But really all of you are even more in transit than most of us. So it's no wonder—and not to worry—that you still hanker most to be in flight." Being a guru, Alec's style means that while calm is suggested, self-examination is kept at the peak.

Slipping into Oxford with others of that ethic, Cicily had lasted by shunting from the moody-muddy philosophies still in vogue to summer sessions, and later a winter tutor, both at Cambridge, where she could indulge in that tonic breeze which mathematics, ever higher and higher, seemed to bring on. Though she was never to be on the straight-and-narrow which achieves prizes, she'd done quite well enough, thank you, to qualify as a drudge to a member of Parliament, then on to a minister's office. Learning, as already

suspected from Bert's account of his clan, that as with family secrets, "secret diplomacy'" is merely what is never acknowledged,
even if the details have already got out.

By then she was ready for godhead, somewhere in her life. But
no longer convinced that one found that through studying "the
field." School would always be a magnet to her and her kind, as
haunts where the serious hobnob with the juvenile, to neither's
detriment, and where the afternoons, once more the longest, most
fruitful parts of the day, promise eternal mystery, and the chase.
Yet, at a proper university, perpetual discussion is a mandate, and
thereby postponement. For solid belief, you go to a seminary. But
before that—and even demanded, if you come of a mother who
was made wretched by ritual and a father who retreated or was
severed from it—you go to the fount.

Bert would never have got to Israel without her. As it was, he
didn't wear his yarmulke, having long since given it up "in favor of
my gray hair." Now that Debra is a matron, at least in manner,
jokes acquired in the kibbutz can afford to peep. "Carry it anyway,
Bert. Then if manna rains down you can catch. To bring me some
back."

"Rains down anywhere somebody needs a tax break," Shine
says. "But I don't like the taste of it." According to Bert and Debra,
age has much darkened this apostle of their youth, but his opinions
are even more saturnine. Having now melded his own agency, long
a staple in youth care, with a larger community service, he'd emigrated to the Caribbean, planning to enter government. "Bought a
manor farm; I'm calling it that. Plan is to become a dictator, but
legally." His new fourth wife—from her picture, the darkest yet—
insists he must. "That being the tradition among those Bocooks."
It's not clear whether that is her family name or an expletive; since
inquiry would bring on more opinions, nobody asks. When he
leaves, with genuine hugs and promises to visit again, Alec says:
"Why do people love him so, everywhere he goes? I'll tell you. He
gives us a chance to exercise our own tolerances. He works very
hard at it."

"He does always answer his own questions," Cicily says demurely. "Just like you." Everybody laughs. But then was when she felt—I'm not an imp anymore.

"Is it time we all left for somewhere?" Alec says to her later, privately. I've been temporary at Val's for too long, you think? Who knows how long she's been temporary with herself? There's your mother, pushing sixty, and still a dish. Bert pushing fifty, everybody's unofficial rabbi but in his heart a refugee from something—"

"Don't say a word against Bert, Alec. He can't embrace God, it only means more room in his arms for everybody else."

"You don't say. Teach your old teacher how to suck eggs, eh? Val and I go to the films these days. One day they're going to explain all our lives to us. So we won't have to live them. Anyway, it's the villains who show up easy. A good man, you'd have to describe and describe. Takes too much footage. They don't even try." Alec is in no way alluding to himself. His is an ego that exists only to record. "No, honeybun. All I mean is—everybody is pushing on."

Including her, he means. It must be hard for an oldie to say that to a person. A person this young. She pats his cheek.

Debra says little. A powerful swimmer herself, at the beach, watching Cicily in the water, even now she's tense, wanting to swim for her. She's afraid Israel might swallow her up, this onetime candidate. But in that depth she is powerless . . . "Mama, belief is the same everywhere. I'm onto it." Cicily had been thinking of two dons who had taught it, one a thin fanatic whose throat chords worked euphonically, the other a plump man with marshmallow tongue—and how it all came out the same. How when those two had put that Yorkshire woman who was daring to become an Anglican priest through her paces, the two men became as one—steeled.

"We'll take care," Bert says, referring to an old cautioning. "When Cicily walks any river's edge, I'll take her hand."

What they hadn't bargained for was that she had had to steady him.

Had he expected to weigh and answer to himself, like his old preceptor, and in the end be converted? Or like that Moorsohn, find some healer who can blithely squeeze the sac of disbelief? In Bert's case saying, "Walk Israel's neighborhoods, our borders, watching yourself. Peer into a child's satchel, see what obligations he carries, ready to put on. Don't cringe; we don't. Here are a few other prescriptions. If this doesn't work, we'll operate . . . Meanwhile—good shopping!"

"This place is beleaguered," Bert whispers. "That's what we forget. Forgot. They do not . . ." What's this cadence, the singsong one falls into here?

They walk the edge. Some streets were as Western as you could want, or might disdain. Watch your neighborhoods. As for the people—a flaming mix everywhere. But in places where belief is fought over, no matter by whom, bloodying the streets and blackening the sky, there will be where it best flourishes, growing again like thistle, overnight.

They spend a second week with those to whom Bert has introductions from a scatter of sources: the seminary, The Hague, the academia that will dialogue with its counterpart anywhere. Plus two charming merchant sea dogs from Haifa, and via an underground aware of Bert's agency, an Arab doctor and a professor, each with one or two from his novitiate.

So they have met the gamut of responses here, from the heavy political smarm to the defensive joke, Cicily even coining one of these on her own. "Hard-liners all," Bert notes. "No matter how soft the talk—and not much of that." And she, reverting to that pun game never quite expunged from those nationals she grew up with, quips: "Yeah—the dogma dog. Follows one everywhere." Trotting behind the foreigner, nipping at whatever garb, manners, argument, is showing a lack of respect for the forces on high—or worse yet, for the ritual. While invisible amahs shroud the passing foreign female, or spit in her wake.

In the face of such conviction, no matter how terrible its

effects, it becomes hard not to feel the shame of the lackadaisical. "Americans beat their breasts," Bert says. "Brits blink as if they're being caned. Both write editorials." The landscape is the real conqueror. Deserts may be made to bloom artificially, as touted, but when one meets only the wind at work on bare sand, one thirsts for those dunes to bring forth the old inscriptions—as parchment can, when touched by water. Then one can see what the wars are for—and must bow to it.

Meanwhile, as they trek and muse and fall away from talk, their own constituency follows them, Debra behind Bert, ever on the street where she got her *get,* Lev ahead of Cicily, up the one hill she knows to assign him, the address where he had left her half-brothers, "the boys."

At any moment in her life, he may turn around.

Perhaps in the land of those snapshots her mother still cherishes, where the old woman waits for them.

The day before they leave Israel, they finally turn up Leah, Debra's hairdresser friend, in her shop, closed in her absence. The tiny place on a modest side street, under its own arched portico, is high enough for Leah's gawky six-foot figure, but barely wide enough for the assistant she would rather not have. Her clientele, "For *tint,* not 'dye,' please," want their artifice kept secret: "Even from themselves. I tell them, 'you are only a little gray'—and if they come for touch-up often enough and you are quick about it, they can almost believe." And her formulas are arcane. "The French are good, but nasty." An ambassador's wife, provided with enough of Leah's touch-up for a stay in Paris, took it to a salon there for the process, but was refused. "The Italians are the best. And there's something about their water. We have such alkali."

As she chats at them, over the tiny cups of fragrant tea and bite-size cakes she keeps for "consultations," they are momentarily her clientele, basking in that even more precious service she provides—a charmed sinking away, far from that other strict "observance," and from the terrible gamble of the streets. Any "regular" here will have a calendar like intaglio, hiding the hard daily stone beneath.

"Do you have male clients?" Bert says.

"You bet. They need more than anybody—time out. I give them head massage."

The sole missile to avoid here is age. Or so Cicily is thinking, basking too. One can never tell about Bert. Until, with the shop explained, the talk veers as it must.

"We write, you know, Debra and I," Leah says. "And she sends pictures. I have you, little one, since you were two. A file I keep for one day your fiancé...sssh, don't apologize. Girls like you, these days..." Leah has that rebel gesture of the hair-mistress, intermittently raking her blunt fingers through her pompadour. A very high one for a woman who will tower over many males here; she understands how to foster her ugliness. "As for your mother, that mop of hers, whatever she's doing, she should keep on. Maybe nothing—? It could be. She would never have made good in the beauty line. All the jealous women would walk out. And the men? Ooh-la-la." She seizes Cicily's left hand, flicking the bare fourth finger, releases it, flaunts her own bare hand with a smile. "You don't want to settle down, that's your privilege; don't say I said...She still wear that diamond?"

"I couldn't give her a better one," Bert says, smiling.

"Nor would she want, with what you give. She would kiss your feet, if you would allow."

Cicily wrinkles her nose. "Does my mother really write?" Not that stuff, surely.

"I read between the lines. She and I are from way back." She hunches, pointing to the floor. "She had the *get,* I stayed in the car. But I still see that ring, your father's. Not just a hunk of ice. And the *schmutz* it would be laying on. And the smell...We're a clean people. My mother, my aunts, scrubbing for Shabbos like the Lord God was going to sniff the cupboards. And check our meat and dairy dishes separate. But our Jewish *schmier,* when you come across it that thick? From a mile away—like bad pot cheese."

Bert says: "I'll have another cake."

All three break up. It's a relief.

Leah rocks from side to side. "Shah, I can tell. Your happiness is my happiness... Come. I want to show you something."

A rear room, windowless, narrow and high as a shrine, which it may be. Or what in old slides of Val's used to be called a Turkish corner? Two built-in daybeds, rug-covered, one on either side. Two low stools, Middle Eastern, the kind with many cross legs and pieced veneers. A high rococo shelf, dubbing for a mantel, but triangular. Above it, a huge blow-up, familiar.

"That Hokusai—" Cicily says. "*The Wave.* There it is. I know from my mother. That you always meant to have it. In your salon."

A smile like sun on the long features. "She talks of me—and that time?"

"Only you."

"Shah. That's the way with her. Her time in the army, everybody swapping later. From Debra? Like pulling hen's teeth."

Bert is delighted. "I must tell her... uh—do they have teeth?"

"Who knows?" Leah is standing at the mantel shelf. Picking up, unfolding, what must have lain there flat. Cabinet photographs, a boy's head, a girl's.

"That's where I was this past week. At my brother's; he's a grain dealer in Galilee. Where they can be safe. And where if we have to, we can ship them out. He says I'm crazy. I know I'm not. If I am— why can't I get them visas?" She hands Cicily and Bert each a photo. "When he was eight, when she was ten. They're grown up now— like you, dear. But keeping pictures here of them now? No way. I wanted to call this place The New Wave. Even my brother says don't call attention; 'You're a mark—to both sides, you're a mark.'"

She yearns down at the photos. Good-looking, both—with the distinctive black hair and brows, dark eyes, and that unmistakable nose-curve. The whole profile—probably even more so. "They should be lucky they don't look like me?" A shrug. "Not here." The folders go back on the shelf, flat. But she's fumbling. On her palm, tricked there, a flat silver cigarette case, buffed to such a shine that when trembled it casts its own light.

"Souvenir, year I served. After the bombing, for pickings hunt up a jeweler, they tell me. Then you don't have to know from where." She opened the case, which now holds a picture. An ugly man in a fleshy-lipped way, but the great eyes would rivet you; there'd been a man very like him once, at Val's—no, "He was not Hassan, who used to come, but Ahmed," Cicily had heard him say at a party. "To you we all look the same." Val's upstairs tenant, Keiko, had giggled—Debra had later explained why.

"He was here for four years at their university," Leah is saying to the photo. "A journalist. His sister kept house for him; he used to escort her here at night, because my customers wouldn't like... Beautiful hair, only a henna rinse, they do it themselves. But I myself had to give her the cut. She came for the diversion, he said. And after he took her home, he came back, for the same." She twiddles the case. "The first year—I gave him this. He said, 'We dirty Arabs'—that's what they hear in the street, 'we don't smoke.' And I remember what my folks heard in Russia. So I say, 'Neither does this dirty Jew.'" When she laughs, the cords in her neck stand out. How can one lick the lips, blink away a tear and rake the hair, all so neatly? "Sleep with the enemy, Liebchen. Revenge? For sex, there's nothing like it. And maybe love?"

Seeing how stunned Bert is, she gives him what the Punk used to call "the playground snoot." The chin-lift to the weak, from the strong. "Of course, I don't mean Debra and you."

"What about the children?" Bert says. When the helpless are involved, nobody lords it over Bert.

"He couldn't help see, when I was carrying. When it was over, he would come back. I still had the husband then, so I let him think they were the schlemiel's. I didn't want it mentioned between us. And they never were. They are mine."

"Does Debra know?"

"Know? When we went for her get, weren't we both carrying? Only on her, almost nothing ever shows." She chucks Cicily under the chin. "That was you, dolly."

"And then?"

She knows what he's asking. "I sent her only baby pictures. But later, when I am braver—and prouder, year by year—who knows, maybe she thinks—throwbacks? Or maybe—something more. When you live with them, these people, cheek by jowl you could say, you begin to see a resemblance to us—though God forbid you should say . . . She has never commented except to praise . . . They are brought up as ours. The schlemiel—his family made him divorce. So he wouldn't have to acknowledge. My brother takes the risk. The boy works in the granary, like an ox he is, they say. That office—a view like a painting—a showcase, for such a girl. They don't marry yet, they will—what are papers? I had them by a midwife; they pop from me like rabbits. She said I was a natural. I am their birth certificate. I am the mother. By me they are a Jew."

The mantel has its burden again, two photos face down, a case that shines. As she talks she is edging Bert and Cicily out of the shrine, her hand on the doorknob. "My brother, he keeps but won't acknowledge them none. Not for *schul*. He is too prominent, God knows. Not even to send them to college." The door shuts. They are back in the shop.

"The shop is plain, yes. When I started up, a woman could relax in one of my booths in her lingerie, like at home. Now just dryers, sinks, porcelain, like anywhere. And one window, no blinds. So the hoodlums don't smash, like once, to see in. What I offer, nobody else can—you go home with a head like a crown, scissor to tint, to set—no blow dry—and guaranteed for the week. I teach them their own comb-outs?—a little longer. I write everything down; all the formulas in the safe, and lists of my longtime suppliers; the customs should stand on their heads to know where. They don't—they know I am good for this city. An international— you would know the name—she sat right there."

This time the raking sweeps a shield of hair across Leah's forehead—in peroration. "So, when they come—the boy and the girl, to take over—nobody lasts forever—all will be in order. The shop, such an asset even my brother would be a fool to ignore. And they will be courted—like my customers do me. 'Ah, Miss Leah, slip me in an appointment.' I have twenty extra, anytime, if I will make the exception." She hunches between her shoulders like a crow. "But if they soon come and I am still here, what a celebration. Like the bar mitzvah he didn't have. And her, she should marry in every grace. And me, I will give out such favors—" She straightens up, abashed. "*Mir nichts, dir nichts, mein Bruder.* Anybody bothers me and them, to close up? My ladies—wives of ministers, sisters of generals— they would pull down the sky." Breathless with her own cadence, her eyes cross-hatched with the vision ahead, she shrugs to a stop, mouth corners wry.

They are at the shop door when Cicily asks, "What about the father?"

Leah, like Debra, is still a tall woman. "When the two of us were new to the trade, we used to stand watching the scalps on the line of seated clients while the owner went down the line with her tray of dyes, each with its dab-brush." She and Leah had already been made to mix the formulas but weren't allowed to know which was for who. "'Half number Six and half Eight for Mrs. Levy,' we'd whisper. For the sister-in-law, all black, poor thing, like she was when sixteen—she refuses to go light. But that minister's mistress—she knows her business—light brown, with one flick on top of the silver blonde. While one of us would watch the timing—three minutes here, there four." Because one day, Leah would have her shop.

Now Leah, backed against the door of her shop, grows taller, even on a level with Bert. "You come like the tourists, hah, from the States. For a piece of what they call 'the heritage'? My folks, Debra's, all who fled from the Holocaust, they brought that with them. But when a cousin is in *Ah-mayree-kah*—like a blessing on the tongue. Where like her here, Cicily, the kids, ask any question they want. I am in the army almost before I know what means 'The States.' Jews who are born there, and maybe their parents also, they come here just for a look—a country all Jews, we are a curiosity—so then they come smiling, *Schmeichel Katz*—smiley-cat, dolly, for the sentiment. One tells me, 'There you are also highly recommended, my New York salon—and I see why.'" Leah looks in at her shop. "So they come back a second time—after they have been to Jerusalem. And maybe to what they call 'the desert,' as if we here should keep it in one place. For them. They need to look smart again before the States, and we are cheaper—for them. And I hear them talk among themselves." She herds Bert and Cicily further inside. "Come in. Shut that door." Once in, she bends down, arming the two of them close, whispering. "And what they have found out, or it has come home to them—that we are not a country of all Jews."

Once her curved lips might have been her one beauty; now in middle age, lip-rouge mottles, as she keeps pressing there, speaking between her fingers. "And that is what he taught me."

"Ah Leah," Bert says. "Cicily didn't mean any wrong. This is bad for you—stop."

"Stop? Why do you think I tell you all this? A letter? Maybe after Yom Kippur—and between the bookkeeping? Your Debra, my friend, she will never come again to be in Israel. I want her to know—who else can I tell? How I too had my *get*."

She presses a hand on Cicily's chest, a diviner, listening. "You will always want to know about the father. So where he is, I will tell you."

She keeps the hand there. "All kinds of Jews there are—this I knew. All kinds of Arabs—I was learning. He was not from Gaza, from anywhere here, but from Beirut. He is journalist, the sister too. The American University, he studied there. She too." She half smiles. "Everything 'she too'—I think that's why he hasn't a wife. But wrong. He had; she a husband, both killed. 'Who could bear to ruin a city whose people went back to the Phoenicians?' he said. Only their own kind. Also a people from way back. But where he teaches—that school of theirs with the long name—they tell him to keep mum. He teaches languages—French like a dream. English—like you speak it, dolly. They tell him: an Arab opens his mouth too wide in any language, here, they will think he is a spy. He says, the people in his country are mixed like a stew, for whom would he spy?"

Reaching absently, she strokes Cicily's hair. "So one day, the sister comes to tell me they will leave."

Deep in the core of the shop, the phone rings. "Shah—I take it here—" she says. For a minute she lets it ring. "That'll be Mrs. Rosen, one of my old-faithfuls, always Friday, she leaves it late. But I depend on them." Motioning the two to stay where they are, she picks up the extension hung at the door. "Yes, Esther. I get you home in time for the candles . . . What? Your son's engaged—here from Chicago? Ahh, how nice . . . But Esther . . . tomorrow is Shabbos, we are closed. She is—what? . . . *Oy* . . . If it was just me—but the shop's reputation, I can't afford . . . She couldn't have it in Chicago before she came? . . . Ah, he and she were on a hike, the mountains. And Sunday—all the family." In between she is raising her eyebrows at the two of them. "I tell you what. Right now I am socially occupied—friends from America. Bring her tomorrow. Shhhh. For consultation only, you understand? And come by the back door . . . Ah, sweetheart . . . Who else would I do this for?"

There is a bench at the door. They must sit. They do. "What a *mishegas*," Leah says. "Her son's engaged is not a Jew. Better maybe when the girl meets the family she should not be so blonde, nah? But they have been together, a hotel under everybody's nose; there's nothing to be done. Which means Esther and Avrahm—they see they can't do anything." She isn't seeking to hug them this time, rather to formalize. "I'm no pariah here. This is a big town; there's no time. But you don't exist here, without a circle. These women are mine."

She takes Cicily's hand. "When the sister comes to tell me though, what she has to tell me, she reminds me of your mother. 'Every time we open our mouths here,' the sister says, and closes it, 'somebody puts dirt in it. That is the way all like us feel, Miss Leah, not just him and me. Day by day they will put in the dirt.

Until we are filled with it. My brother says we must leave. Or else open wider our mouths.'"

Leah drops Cicily's hand, reaching for Bert's. So grasped, she says: "That's when she was like Debra . . . I wasn't at the *get,* I was waiting in the car. But when your Debra comes walking, she's carrying her shoes, she's in her stocking feet. On that foul pavement. 'They made me take my shoes off, in front of the patriarch,' she says. 'And when they were finished with me, they threw the shoes out the door, then me, and slammed it behind.' Then your mother peeled off the stockings and threw them on the ground. And shook her fist at the sky. 'No more of your *schmier,*' she said when she got in the car. 'The reb's?' I said. 'Thank God, no.' And she said—'Not him. The Adonoi.' I said, 'Never say that, Debra. It's them.' And she says, 'Who knows what to think—look there.' And we see a little girl peering out of a doorway, and running to pick up the stockings."

Bert raises her hands and kisses them.

"So now you must go, I know, I know," she says. "To the States. But first—look at this." She digs in the cashier's desk, holding unseen what she's removed. "The sister said, 'In case we don't see you again. Or you don't hear from us.'" Leah lays a gold bracelet on the cash desk. "She wore it always. Every time she came in." She lays next to it a man's wristwatch, not gold but respectable. "So did he." She slips them back in the drawer. "For the boy. And for the girl."

Cicily stares at her, tranced. "Did she say that?"

They lock glances. Until Leah says quietly, "No. But she does say I will hear from him. 'When he can.' she says. And she leaves. And when I go to my mixing table, where only I go—I find these. But when I look in where I keep the negatives, those photos—gone. Then I wait. So—two months I don't hear. I phone their school. I am too smart to say what she leaves. I say somebody left a fine scarf here, must be one of my customers, the States, but just to be sure I am phoning around. They say nobody there by that name, they will give me the registrar. The sister, she has the same last name. I wait—maybe twenty minutes, longer. When he comes back he says I must have it wrong. Nobody by such a name was ever there."

Cicily remembers the cringing chill that came over her and her stepfather. Coming from Leah, at the phone again, staring at it,

"So you want to know where the father is?" she says to me, Cicily, this time not touching me. "I will tell you. They are in their own dirt. Buried somewhere. In ours."

She presses a vertical finger on the rouge-spread lips. Bert and Cicily are not to respond. They may now leave. At the door, she presses a small packet, gift-wrapped, on Cicily. "Henna. The best. Not from here, from Iran. All the young people who come to me for the cut only? They are crazy for it." Her pompadour holds firm.

When they get out of there, they walk all the way back to their hotel, maybe two miles. Neither wants for the moment to talk to a cab driver. To anyone from here. Though they both know this is unreasonable.

Once in the hotel, "From Beirut, he could have been anything," Bert says, breaking their silence. "A people that were maybe Hittite to begin with, under Ottoman rule, under Roman, Eastern Orthodox. Maronites. Druse. Even Christian. But still an Arab. For whom would he spy? Not just for Iraq, though they are now the power in Lebanon? Maybe not even against Israel, which since their raid exercises border control? Maybe he was here, even in admiration? For a country so new. Yet so ancient that it understands. The art of the short war."

At the airport, leaving for London, they have a long wait. Somebody has left a suitcase unattended, strictly against rule, and not far from them. All in the lounge are questioned by the brusque El Al guards. No nonsense, no matter who you are, as the guilty— two Frenchmen—find. Watching them return, cowed if not pummeled, the two guards slouching, noncommittal, Bert says: "Funny. How we misread the Old Testament. How we Jews still think of ourselves as never using force."

In flight, urged by the pilot to look down on the wonders they're leaving, he says, "Jews shouldn't expect a Paradise, or have an Eden. Only a Canaan, flowing with milk and honey. That's all their own law promised them." And before they landed, while they circle a London airport befogged but with many planes bound for its runways, he says: "God is back there for sure. They've got him trapped. Tied by the leg, leashed. I was ready to make them release, then I saw what a service they perform for me; I no longer need to believe in him." Intoning this, rocking from side to side as much as one can in a seatbelt, her stepfather seems to her all that she would ask for in a rabbi.

At home Debra, staring around her ideal house as if she must never stop measuring it, says, "True? It was in the newspapers long ago. That there was such a man there, then gone. Two persons. But it was the sister who was the better known, for political."

With her mother, to be "political" means to be against, not for—as it would have been in the kibbutz? And in her parents' shop? Leah, listed as interviewed about the sister, had sent her the clip—but without comment.

"I thought it was because of the salon. She always told me about celebrity customers. Yes, she could have been carrying, when I was there. She was still married to—the schlemiel. I met him. Ordinary. But married to her because her parents thought she was too ugly to do better, and she did too; he didn't have a chance. And he was a nuisance to her around the shop. She was a somebody—the way hairdressers can get to be. And he wanted to be part of it."

As for the rest, Leah is her earliest good friend, maybe calculating, but smart. Maybe wanting it known that she has had bliss. "If it's true for her—I don't mind."

"But Mother—she kept referring to 'the boy,' and 'the girl.' They would be as old as me."

Her mother holds her smile long enough for Cicily to see that sometimes she is still that to her mother.

Bert, in the room, has said nothing. What he and her mother may have said about Leah's story has not been reported. What they say to each other—as with what Cicily may exchange with each of them—is never reported. So is kept the privacy of all three.

"Memory is international," her mother says suddenly. "Comes at you from anywhere. You can think it is your own."

"Do you mind being an expatriate?"

In Boston, in that sector which respects those who do good works, Bert, whose modest achievement in that line now precedes him, is often asked this—wistfully? Although that area is proud of its role in the American Revolution, can it be that some are no longer so sure of on which side they now are? He answers non-committally: "Oh, there's so much going on, on both sides. And back-and-forth is part of my job."

As the manager of all Mendenhall's charities, he has long since become inured to the expense-account mode required of those who must labor for the underprivileged on a large scale. He still tries not to confuse the scale with his personal one.

The Zangwill Boston elders, still flourishing, have annexed him, for reasons obscure to them surely. First, since Bert practices little religiously and without affiliation, he is their ideal family rabbi. Even functioning once at Lottie's funeral, as requested by her before. Mordecai, no blood relative but as long-lived, has chuckled to him, "A philanthropist, and not with your own money? The other old leftovers like me can't get over it; one even whispered, 'And you mean he gets paid for that?' For them the ultimate of shrewd, my boy. But for what you did with what Eustace left you—a foundation in his name, so small alone it would be nothing, but under the wing of your boss's outfit—and you don't manage it—*Selah!* Of that they are rightly proud. And so am I."

Mordecai can go overboard, embarrassing him. A passionate historian, if in his narrow Sephardic slot, he can be tetchy about Israel, though in the end grumbling, "Okay—they showed we could be farmers. So why didn't they stay? A modern democracy they're defending? What chutzpah! They want to be the new America, they got plenty Indians." Yet a benevolence lingers on his face, like a father secretly relishing the cheeky exploits of a not-so-bad kid.

What endears him to Bert most, after his stance as elder, is that Mordecai has made it a point to read Peter—"Your grandfather— what a *mensch*"—and is liberal with quotes. In thanks, Bert had given him one of the printouts of the old diary that he had had made for the family, who in surprising agreement, and perhaps re- calling the stir over Mordecai's family letter, had judged that publi- cation of what was neither full autobiography nor polished essay and according to Gerald, "Indeed, outright tatty"—would not add to Peter's already declining reputation, after which the original had remained locked away.

Bert goes to Boston more often than usual just now, always dining on his first night with Mordecai, who goes out quite nimbly "except to funerals" but has a house-man who is an excellent cook and winesman. The first and last toasts are always to "your grand- father, my unmet friend." The quotes that follow are an old story; it's Mordecai's tender choices of these, made with that delicate in- telligence which may care little for philosophies but knows how to keep a man alive, that brings tears to Bert's eyes.

Not to deny that Mordecai is unaware of his effects; that too beguiles. "No, we Jews have no Paradise," he'll say. "That's why it behooves us to keep the dead alive. I was brought up to that duty. A *Jahrzeit* for eternity, the old folks used to say; it does not matter for whom." Then, on the heels of this: "That's what the world has against us. Dead or alive, there are too many of us."

In the somber house, Bert can almost see that array, edged shadow on shadow, back into the dark. Waiting to be called forward by some simple phrase—perhaps when one of the living elders says "the old folk." As the old slyboots watches him, Bert notes there are still evidences of Lottie about, her unmistakable froufrou. Her hus- band has kept up with that secondary command: *No matter who.*

Mordecai always reverts to Lottie's funeral. "Well, we sent her off with all the recommendations she asked for, didn't we. That part of your grandfather's diary—on funerals—he could have tucked Lottie's right in."

Mordecai, if referring to God, does so as to a distant relative, who one day is going to look him up. What might he say to Bert's unholy idea of God-in-Israel; would he smile? Or console, saying what he often does when musing over some misfortune: "Shah— at least one experiences."

The plane gives a shove, reminding Bert that at 20,000 feet up thought aerates. Or makes too much haste to conclude. Each time he leaves the old man he is furnished with Mord's estimate of him. Meant to cheer? Or to chill?

"In a country long enough, Bert, a Jew mutates. Takes no biology to concede. My crowd, we congratulate ourselves we keep close to the original, no matter where. Also the Hasids—though one hates to admit . . . Anyway, from the country of Don Quixote, from Mittel Europe, Russia, comes the irony, even the great comedians? But your family? Excuse me, the Zangwills maybe were not long enough in England, the Myerses too long in Germany—Jewish serious, they are. A Hebrew dignity for which bless them. But to find humor in them—the kind that strikes to the heart of our condition—nah, you should live so long."

Mord squints with pleasure at having nearly done so, and takes another sip of wine. "But then—comes along this Irish wit, this wag. This musketeer who calls himself 'a man between.' Where else are we Jews and our irony? And Zipporah and he, they marry. T-t-t-, our faithful say; one more lost. But what happens? A mix we should kneel down and give thanks for. Your uncle Zach—millions for satire in art, we-ell—I'll take what comes from his mouth. Even your uncle Charles, so pompous you want to stick a pin in him— then peeps out, what do you know, some joke could be only from us . . . and even the girls, I hear, are a little from us. One for the law, is it—always our province. And one has that museum—not for the Greeks, or for only the Gentiles, but for guess who? So altogether— for our side, not bad, eh?"

He's not going to challenge the old man by saying that his family had not been brought up to take sides—or not without examining those. Moreover, isn't Mord's contention just what Jews who accept the birthright without question will never believe?

Still—Bert isn't sure of the old man's game. Once he had met a falcon held on the falconer's wrist without gyve, its unhooded gaze regarding him steadily. Can a bird's stare have irony?

"Here, fill your glass, Bert. I'm going to tell you something. The same Madeira I sent your mother when you were made rabbi. Only older now, like you."

They drink. That will maybe get them past argument.

"And you—what did you do?" Mordecai says suddenly. "You don't want a congregation, we hear. You'll do good on your own. So you're ethical, Bertram, but not reverential. That's maybe—American?"

"You telling me I'm American, Mordecai? That I already knew."

The old singsong, how it take over, both of them, even Mordecai's New England twang.

"Granted. That mix you are . . . And in your personal life independent also. All those girls you had—beg pardon, Lottie kept tab. 'He won't marry a Jew,' she says. 'Wait, you'll see.' And what do you do? You marry not only a Jew—but a Sabra." He smiles into his glass. "She couldn't get over it. A stunning woman, we hear. But that's not the whole of it, I told her. I watched the grandfather. *There* was the irony."

"You saying that half a Jew, not quite a Jew—is still a Jew? That for sacramental wine, a mix is just as good as old Madeira? Thanks."

"Any good wine is a mix, Bert. Eustace didn't teach you that? . . . No, I'm telling you what took me years to put together. When you gave me the diary, I thought of it. How Lottie told me years before, 'The goy—he hung the mezuzah in their house. My cousin Zipporah, that backslider; she thought it was funny.' . . . But me, the pure Sephardic. I begin to think about it."

"Zipporah's no backslider. She's just—on her own." Whatever that is—not for me to say.

"So are you, Bert. Only one half-step ahead of her."

"Ahead of my grandmother? Not me."

"Ahead of me also. If you wouldn't take it like a blow in the face, I could tell you what you are."

He wants to tell me, the way he wants another glass. Give it to him.

"Let's have that last toast, then. And you can tell me." Though what in hell can it be?

No one handles the wine bottle in this house but the host. The hand is shaky, but it pours. Watching his curved glass fill just beyond the half, then stop. Watching Mordecai fill his own, cutting off at the same level with that practiced turn of the wrist, he fancies Mord is pouring his Judaism into each glass. Behind him on the wall, covering the patch where the letter used to be, he has had hung a photograph of the Esther who was his mistress and had given him his flawed only son. She is handsome in that hawk-queen style which some of that tight lineage have. Cousin-to-cousin would be its pride, no matter what came.

Mordecai is lifting his wineglass, holding it by the stem without tremor. "To the man between. And to you, Bert—the perfect assimilate. Honor to you both."

He did not take it as a blow. Instead, he understands with awe the concession that was being made. Though of course he is not the perfect anything, it helps to have his life and his beliefs united in an easy turn of phrase. The wonder being that what he is said to be was not dismissed.

At his side Debra is asleep, lips parted, the breath coming from her still sweet. They have neither tried not to conceive nor wallowed in regret when they hadn't, only going so far as to find out that both separately are, or were—capable. She has had her ewe lamb;

he hasn't the ego that needs to replicate; perhaps a lack? In exchange for not being a match that way, they have kept, one for the other, a certain mystery. She does not question his. He will never plumb hers.

What he remembers best of Mordecai, gone now, is not that verdict, which may have been wilfully anti what "the congregation" was likely to say. What hangs in Bert's mind, like an orb lit from within but unapproachable, is the way Mordecai, a man who had held onto his wits, said "modern." He wonders how he himself will say it, in his time. Until then, he can tolerate himself, without further itch. He is like some keeper of the keys in a great safe-deposit vault devoted to the storage of people in distress, where the keys are not his to issue and he cannot know what each box contains. But must nevertheless nurture them, not as a multitude, for the politic of which he hasn't the talent. But as they and he stumble toward each other, each by each.

Meanwhile, he'll listen to his grandfather's chat, waiting in his lap. "What's see-mantics," he had asked Peter, when in grade school. "Does it have to do with the sea?" Peter's uniform when he was in the Naval Reserve had hung in the attic, okayed for indoor theatrics but not to be worn outside. "Yes, we study the sea of words." Then, reaching to seize Zipporah in the Sunday-noon room that hasn't yet filled with strangers, only with grandchildren in from their morning worshiping at whatever synagogues and churches, and she in turn pulling all of them in, they circle in the sailor's hornpipe, Peter's dapper feet jigging in the one happy practice he flaunts from his Irishness. Only Bert's elder brother James hovers offside. "Come dance the light fantastic!" his grandfather cries, but the sullen dwarf won't be pulled in. Then Jennie appears at the swinging door, smiling her best for this seventh day of the week—any gunshots to report years ahead yet; his grandfather cries, "Children, what is the *gharstly* password to the dining room?" and in one voice they shout—"Brunch!"

And the jigging stops.

Here comes Cicily down the plane's aisle in her restless fashion, not onto the toilets, only wanting to tuck in for a minute, as is the way of ewe lambs, and Debra, waking, reaches up to stroke her cheek. "What are you reading, Bert—oh that—" Cicily says, "You've never let me read it except in snatches." Bert says, "Here, take it, it's open to the passage on funerals, I know it by heart," and Cicily sobers. "Ah, I know, you're on the way to Mr. Mendenhall's. It was big in the papers. Going to be in two places—the family one at St. Bart's, and downtown at that youth place you helped found— and your friend is coming in from his island to speak, and in both places there'll be a throng."

"Yes, go read this," Bert says. "Mendenhall's funeral will fit right in. It'll be that travesty, the very one the dead person didn't want." He thinks of Peter's, a high mass for that apostate Catholic with a Jewish soul. Yet let the censers swing the incense as they do, from side to side; a mass is beautiful. And the Savior a Jew who meant to save all. "They'll say of Mendenhall what they always do on such occasions: 'He was a prince.' And for once it will be true."

"And the lady?" Cicily says. She has always referred to Zipporah so. "What a pity they couldn't be together."

"Oh, they have been, somehow," her stepfather says. "Somehow or other my grandmother would have managed that."

The stewardess tittups along, smiling her message. "A little turbulence. All in the aisles are to return to their seats. And fasten belts."

In her seat, Cicily reads:

Along with the advent of the new century and the threatening rise of an elder population, an obituary itself became a form of art. Surviving elders themselves took to compounding them, often able to enlist recording assistance up to the very moment of "departure"—now the preferred term of those who, like the "morticians" of the century preceding, balked at advertising themselves as undertakers. In contrast now, these commercial assistants cleverly elaborate their functions; you could have a "period-style" attended death, the Egyptian—a "closing show" of you in the center of your own artifacts—being one of the more expensive.

The "art of the obit," now regularly in the culture columns, influenced the major arts, and indeed sciences, about as one might expect—much as the amateur snapshot, a worldwide industry, was practiced alongside the art of photography. Let the common man in and the ivory tower begins to lean.

Biographers became especially bitter. In the twentieth century their works often took precedence over the achievements of those they purported to celebrate—all the more so if the bio could be revelatory or mean-spirited. Now these "arranged memoirs" could show up the bio for what it had always been—secondhand. You could in effect crown your own life, even if you had to pay for it. Critique had rebounded of course in the classic way. "Dammit," two art-judges had been overheard to say from their wire-slot, "such deaths are always amateur."

It's like a lot Alec made them read when he was on that Utopia kick. "Butler, Orwell, Bellamy," he would intone. "The Triple Crown of the Futures crowd. When you yourselves get out on that track, boys and girls, remember them." A racing fan, he had chugged the class to Epsom Downs, that time in a hired van. "My favorite of course is that old environmentalist, Sir Thomas More. *Urn Burial,* that's the ticket." And when they were counting up the day's wins and losses, each of them having been allowed to bet anything under a pound, "Chalk it up to a lesson 'on the track.'"

What Peter's effusion reminds her of most is those folklore mags she used to keep scattered on her floor, so that waking up in the dead of night she could see them. Knowing most of their stories by heart, they made her feel safe.

This old bird—well, she'll take him on trial. Her stepfather adored him. Bert's always been on an elder-prophet kick. When he already is one, to her.

She rolls up the printout, stashes it in her backpack. By the date, that passage would have been written just before Bert's grandfather and the lady, and her own mother, went to Italy. She knows that story down to the ground. "In those churches I'd never been in before," her mother would say, "even then I would have been carrying you."

The lady and her mother had gone to a lot of such churches. "To me she has been an eye-opener all around," her mother said just now, before they left. "In Italy, how she loved that man. Even when he beat her, from the disease. And how he loved her, even then. They were like your father and me—would have been. And yet for her again it happens, ten years later—and the same for me: Bert comes to England, remember?"

With that precious packet from Lev, her father—which Debra does not mention. What a weirdo I was in those days, Cicily thinks, with satisfaction. What a weirdo I still am, thank God—just enough for me to do something special. "Over there," Bert says, "in the job you find, the love you find, you young ones—that's the way it often works out."

On the Isle of Dogs, back there in the ideal house, her mother said: "Bert asked me to marry him. I already knew I loved him— that way. The way I loved Lev. How could I let myself, twice. Was I the whore I got my *get* for? . . . And then I hear. About her. How she loves this new man, Bert's Mr. Mendenhall. And I trust her. Like Dr. Duffy trusted her—you saw that watch Bert inherited, with his grandfather's hallmark on it, 'Trust yourself'? So her news reminded, telling me that love could shift, and still be true."

Her mother reveals herself now and then. People think she cannot. That is not her style. But when she does, she finds the words for it. Maybe in that Torah the lady had been shopping for, as a promise to Bert, and was bringing back with her to the synagogue, that sad day. "I remember how she looks, holding her packages, way down the aisle, just inside the big doors. Always with packages, for other people. And I am holding Dr. Duffy for her."

And he was dead, in her mother's arms.

"So I am going, finally, to America," Debra says. "I wanted not to go again, ever. But the way they say she is dying. With some: they hear what you say, you can tell that it registers. I have seen it, many times. And her doctor agrees with me—we talked. So I am going. 'Only a whisper,' I tell the doctor. 'To say thanks.'"

They were in their favorite chairs, looking out at the river, which for her mother and Bert flows like the abiding flux of their days but is getting too damn tidy, now that it's been cleaned up. Like all of England is for those who've been bred up to their ears in it, like herself and the Punk. Who is already in what he calls "the Benighted States" and reports that just by telling them they are, up-staging them in jobs suitable for that message, he is making a pile.

"I know why you wouldn't ever go there before," she said to her mother. "It was because of—your tragedy." She's always thought of it like that, even as a kid commandeering the Punk to act it out with her, in one of their versions of "playing house": *You be him, the jeweler, I'll be her.* "You practically a bride. In a wonderful new country. And then that. You were strong enough to tell me that story. So's I could share. But who could blame you for not wanting to see that terrible time in New York all over again."

Sometimes her mother seems to her—a foreigner. Whelmed in an upbringing Cicily can only imagine. That half tempts, an idyllic dream Cicily wanted to join. Then, slowly, begins to horrify.

"You think that." Guttural. Not Debra's measured speech, which Alec used to call "statuesque." And not a question. "Bert also. Both wrong."

Minutes go by before her mother speaks again. "It's been my-self I didn't want to meet. The nurse I was then. Or thought I was—before Italy." She bent, picked a stone and threw it into the water, something she never did, and disliked others doing. "The nurse I didn't turn out to be."

"You? Because you work only behind a desk now? And only for children? Must you nurse everybody? And hands on?"

Her mother's hands are a lady's now, the nails curved. Cicily can remember when her mother, denying herself the charwoman she could well pay for, kept those hands raw and blunt, indentured to the house. "Debra—you still yearn for the battlefield?"

A headshake: No. Bert says living in England has cured her of it.

You don't probe her mother, no matter how intimate the two of you, or how loved. You wait, prowling the details of your life together, for Cicily so smooth that few are odd. You can wait till doomsday, while her mother stares at the river like the sybil old Neville used to say she reminded him of.

But the young have the right to be brash, Bert says. As you get older, the questions themselves cloud. There was one Cicily had used to wonder, never satisfied. Never posed, that's why.

Bert's beloved grandfather, Dr. Duffy, whose wife, the lady now dying, her mother had admired so. Thumbing over the hoarded snapshots of Debra's time with them in New York—why was his picture absent from those? And no pictures at all, from Italy.

Bert had long ago told her of Debra's staunch support of his grandparents during that time. "Traipsed with them from spa to spa, while he declined. That must be a woe to watch in anyone. But to see such brilliance go that way. Shine and I, we saw it, but we were in our teens—we thought it was only age. My grandmother never admits to that decline. Your mother did say, 'I grew too fond of him.'" Which Bert could well understand. "But that must be a hazard for any good nurse."

When Cicily, still a juvenile, had declared her wish to be a rabbi, he had dutifully taken her on a round of synagogues. Her mother does not go to those. Cicily had always thought it was because of the reb.

But now a stone has been thrown.

"You had a patient who died under your care," Cicily says. "He died in a synagogue—so you do not go there. He belonged to a family who befriended you—but you couldn't save him for them. So you don't go there . . . Mother. Dr. Duffy's disease, that lady hid it from the world, Bert says. And his grandfather suffered also from the heart. A man everybody loved, maybe you too. He died in your arms. What more could any nurse have done for him?"

Her plea makes her proud, then shamed—dare one exhort one's own mother? Who is not answering. Head bent, like a child waiting for absolution. Hang on too long, Cicily—will you become your mother's mother?

"Debra—" She has rarely first-named her. "If Bert was sick. If I was. We would trust you with our lives."

Whenever her mother moves suddenly, rising from a chaise as now, turning her back swiftly, draperies seem to swirl around her, though she never wears any. What she says floats behind her. "Don't."

It was then that Cicily said to herself, *it's time to leave the Isle of Dogs.* She is seventeen. And she will put being a rabbi in abeyance.

When Bert hears that, he says only, "Well, it wouldn't have grown you forelocks. Already have the ears."

At university, some dons had consoled themselves with a thought-world in which there were no hard-and-fast conclusions. Their opponents had advised her to rejoice in the abundance of conclusions to be reached.

Her parents, all three of them—for that now seems to be the case—seem to have lived, to be living, otherwise. In stages of reality that they bow to, but manipulate as they can. So doing, they seem to be answering the dons.

And what sweeties these two are. Prisoners of what Cicily herself, and the Punk, their crowd, are said to lack so shockingly: conscience. Though the Punk never fails to send some of his pile to Val. Trouble is—it's shock your elders or be shocked. Meanwhile, as this plane creaks from side to side like a rattle with too many pebbles in it, and now and then gives one of those sickening drops, shrink deep in your seat, Cicily, and concentrate on what's ahead.

A family. Royals, whose faces you held in your fist like playing cards. Whose genealogy of mixed fidelity, powerful caprices, and astounding frivolities, all delightful, were recounted as from a chapbook your mother must have somewhere, of innumerable details: costumes, voices, how the rooms over there succeed one another, and the scenarios. The very position of the furniture will be known to you, the way the generations meld in talk, or mill around the eats, the fine Sunday smell. "It's all so much the same," Bert has assured them, with an odd creak in a voice now smoothed to baritone by performance as an adjunct rabbi. For those now dead, whom he has identified, will be there, along with the live.

"It'll be like the dream I used to inhabit just before I awoke," Cicily said, when she joined the two of them at the plane. "They were *my* folklore. In my dream they would wake up with me in the middle of the night. They would fill the room. But they wouldn't be magical. They would be real."

"So they are," Bert muttered, checking their tickets. "But for me, the time in that house is always afternoon." Preoccupied or not, he's always joined in her fantasy on that score—perhaps to sustain it. "Bother—" he says then, "you were supposed to be seated across the aisle." Her mother's so pale. Though pallor becomes her; she looks young. Over the years, she and Bert have merged, she downward, he a year or two up; they now seem the same age.

Nuzzled in her seat, Cicily is happy to be under their wing, yet separate. That's the way to approach a new country. From the apex of all that has reared you, yet alone. Back there, her mother sleeps heavily, as Bert reported she has done the past week, though she never medicates, neither herself nor them. When Bert came to live with them she had jettisoned the little leather satchel, symbol of her nursehood, kept until then in the chill-closet, with the wine. Dumping its contents—old vials, syringes, torque bandages, that

Cicily, fascinated, had never seen before—into a plastic envelope, she'd murmured, "Not the river, no. These last forever," and had taken it to the hospital, for safe disposal with the medical trash. Cicily had wanted the little satchel but had been refused: "It's to go with the bundle for the Sisters of Charity." When Cicily, bleeding too copiously during her period, had had to duck off from school, a chum saying, "Lucky you, your mother's a nurse, I can't even talk about it to the *mater*," she'd had to reply gloomily, "Nix, she won't even give us an aspirin, not without a prescription. I'll have to go to that old fart in the dispensary."

Dr. Duffy? Not a medical doctor, but from what Cicily's just read quite as formidable as some. She has his picture now. Not a Jew, yet a Jew, his voice sounds its familiar bell. An irritable charmer, with the power of the don. Dying in front of Debra's ark. Under the rule-of-honor, rule-of-guilt that the synagogue prescribes. In Israel one entered an air shivering under that ukase, fixing even the gaze of those returnees who no longer felt prodigal. She, Cicily, is able to answer better than most: I swear by the shot that killed my father, that I am, ever will be, a Jew.

And there my mother was, come back to the synagogue, as the bride she was never to be. Holding the patient thrust in her arms like a bouquet. On the battlefield nursehood would not be in question; a cup held to a lip before it stiffens may be all that is required. A presence, leaning over the bright wound. But in the house of the Lord, judgment is weighed. If only by the worshiper. My mother must think she failed him, somehow. She was not the nurse she had been, before Italy. What could there be, that she didn't do? Nothing, but we are not to trust her? She must think that she did not do enough for him. No wonder she can't sleep. Perhaps she dreams.

Several seats back in the bucking plane, Bert watches the two stewardesses seat themselves, primly fastening their belts. Surely nothing can happen while those two blonde coifs ride serene. He thinks of Thomas Thomas's stagily offered advice, "The safest place in case of accident is in the tail." That was in the days of the DC-7s, or even smaller jets, or old Soviet Union jobs still hung with imperial red velvet, or those jaunty mosquitoes that once flew Southeast Asia, all of which "business travelers," whether after good deeds or ordinary commercial ones, had had to patronize. That advice can scarcely pertain to the big jets like this one.

To think of Thomas, which he often does, is to think of Thomas's business—pursuing secrets, and of the particular one, doggedly sneaked after on his own, for which he had indeed finally achieved distinction in Mendenhall's organization. He had been canned.

To date, Bert has never met up with his brother James, though Thomas, having dug out who James Durfee, manager of their London office, really was, and by then hooked on these confrontations, had had an appointment between James Duffy, alias Durfee, long lost brother of new employee Bertram Duffy, gleefully arranged. His mistake had been to post his own schedule, as usual, including a meeting he would attend. "I smelled something," Mendenhall had told Bert. "When Thomas was in New York. He was bursting with something. And I suspected what. You see, I've been your brother's longtime confidant—maybe his only one." Mendenhall had at once phoned James to come to New York. "Over a possibility in Nigeria. They have tremendous oil reserves. Only we've not been able to latch on. You may not know—but James is an authority there."

"I do know," Bert said. "I met a man on a train." He'd explained.

"Commerce is full of coincidences," Mendenhall said. "Some call the phenomenon 'networking.' When you deal with that many numbers, or personalities, sooner or later the information ball falls...Anyway, James won't be unhappy to go to Nigeria. When you live under a mask, being in the one place can weary."

They'd been having a drink at the time. Mendenhall stirred his, the spritzer that Bert would learn Zipporah had taught him.

"Sometimes I play the Fox. Living up to my name. Hoping nobody notices."

Bert had laughed. He'd been young then. "Plain as day."

"That so? Well now. What shall we do, about you knowing Durfee is—Duffy. Shall we tell him?"

"People should be allowed to keep their masks. Unless they do mortal harm."

He and Foxy had been friends since that time. "A friend in power," Shine had mocked. "He want any dibs on dictators? I'm his man." Shine's wives had busted him. "No, but I might," Bert had told him," in exchange for never again having to be a best man."

The newest wife, niece of one of the island's governors, has lasted. "They are teaching me how to govern; I am teaching them how to be nonprofit," he writes delicately. "We both give out a lot of my flags." What one most loves in Shine is not only that he's high and fancy in his see-through-everybody way. It's that he works all that equipment not to depress us, but to cheer.

Mendenhall was harder to give thanks for. There was so much of him. He could balance his billions, and carefully not come out ahead. Zipporah had called him "the shy independent." Though he and she were not to marry, he craved some celebration: "I'm wanting to embrace a union." Foxy gives you all the certainty he can muster. While his own tenses are always in flux.

Bert and Debra's marriage being at hand, he might have scooped up the whole family checkerboard and partied them fashionably in some Eden-for-a-day. Instead he had quietly established "wedding scholarships" in their name. Each guest to have a trip to Paris. "And here's the hitch," his grandmother said, smiling. "To meet his mother." With a wide choice of venues: "Tea at one or both of her flats, dinner party at a restaurant of their choice, one of her concerts, or an audience with her abbé . . . Or they may opt for all four."

According to Foxy, his mother had given out that she was fading, but actually her lovers were. "She wants company," he'd reported. "And can't bear to admit that she would like it to be

American." So for her remaining years she had blossomed, saying, "I have two doorsteps. On one, somebody is always arriving—I have to arrange a welcoming soiree. On the other, somebody leaving. And a bang-up good-bye." At her end, according to her abbé, by then a new younger one, she had been able to murmur gracefully, "Say au revoir for me, from each." But Foxy had no doubt his mother had commissioned the abbé to so say. "She always wanted to give up the ghost with a good quote."

How to mourn such elders? The messiahs, they come and they go. He, Bert, is their *minyan* of one. Enough to say of each: He was. He was once here ... And now, soon, they will say: She.

The plane is now gliding in pattern. Those two attendants sit again, binding themselves sternly in, vestal virgins, at least until they touch ground. The warning comes from the pilot's cabin. "Prepare ..."

"Wake up, Debra."

For now we land.

She's in her second childhood now," Zipporah can hear them saying. True. Here's her mother, in from shopping but still wearing her hat for an hour or more, as some ladies, to show their importance, used to do. Or perhaps because for the moment, more passion is felt for the hat than for either husband or child.

And there she herself is, at the window, yearning down at the flower peddler whose cart, heaped with lilacs, has just halted in front of the next of these new-style houses, a whole avenue of them, which have no yards. Will her mother, who had eyes in the back of her head, say: "Here, run down and get a bunch, maybe two if they look fresh, but don't pay more than twenty cents for them"? And was that for one bunch or two? She herself is not living there anymore; she can get out at any time. She is only visiting, to say good-bye.

And to conclude.

Though not as a wholly selfless act.

She is pruning her life, before nature does it for her.

Peeping in at the family window, with those lilacs for ballast—fifteen apiece, but she'd added a dime from her pocket money and would keep mum—she can see the table. Their table. Though this is no last supper. They are always at dinner now, the heads and figures with a little nimbus, after so long in their graves. Just before they died, they too would have been doing their duty: going back. "Passing on," they preferred to call it. She prefers "Die."

That table, the sneaky inanimate, has somersaulted from generation to generation but remains always the same, whether loaded or bare. She cannot see of what wood it was, or whether its legs were straight or curved, but she knows full well what that linened table-top, and others like it, is passing on. There will be many guests, mostly relatives, but except on mild anniversaries, no especially honored ones—though gossip can embalm in a trice all those of the blood who may be elsewhere celebrated.

Honor is the permanent guest. Morality could be explained but was not lectured on—you absorbed it. You listened, you watched, observing the balances, feeling those seep. There are pariahs, though you will not easily pry out the offense. Marrying "out" would not banish you, as it might at some tables: "We are not that Orthodox." A heavy word, its three o's reaching for your neck like a lariat. When she confessed this to the young father she can see through the window, he eating anything he and her mother desire, except maybe on the holy days, he snorted with approval. "Yes, we labor only under a noose."

You went to the synagogue to signify what you were; you were a race. The ritual celebrated what was meant by "always." Daily morality was the residue, and in the main you brought it with you—silently hoping for the best, or already exhibiting your prowess at it. Religious conduct outside the synagogue, not tied to it, was the point here, and clan conduct took precedence over the private—you had to be good, but were not overburdened with immediate inborn sin. This, not "Oriental" blood, must be why she would not think of sex as sin.

All this surrounds her unspoken as she holds the lilacs, peering in. At ten she couldn't have said any of that, but it was an atmosphere whose terms she already knew. At ninety-odd, she doesn't need to phrase. Memory thickens, like a pudding on the stove.

When she brought in the lilacs her mother said, "Good. Give them to Josie to put in the vase. How much were they?"

What can she say? Her mother minded the manners there. "You said we were not to talk about money at the table."

Behind his paper, her father snickers. "What did you do, embezzle?"

What's that mean? He's the custodian of what she as yet has no words for. "Should I lie?"

Her mother, on the double: "That what she learns in that temple?"

She never attends. Her father: "We send her to imbibe the legends, the lessons?—a pity the reading level is rather low." He goes, but only at Yom Kippur. The rest of the time, does their holiness depend on Zipporah?

"Explain, my dear." When she does, about the pocket money, his mouth-corners turn down, then up. She had such photographic grasp of gesture back then; she can see him grimace while he slips his onyx signet ring from his fourth finger and tries it on hers. She already knows he's the profligate who cancels other people's debts to him. Her mother's crowd are the kind to whom money is owed. "No," he says, shaking his head this way, that. "Doesn't yet fit," and to her mother sadly, "So we can still hope she takes after the Myerses." Bewildered to the point of tears, she had stamped her feet. "Do you have to take after somebody, to be a Jew?"—and the tears came. Restored, leaning against his knees, his one arm encircling, the other's hand smoothing her hair, she said: "I counted how many times you shook your head. Three times sideways. Three times up and down."

She can still count him doing that, though her own lids, leaking granulation, are stuck fast. He's taking her hands, small and dimpled then, now a corrugated blue; he's waggling first the left, then the right. "The left one's the race, the right one's the religion. All Jews come in two parts."

At her bedside—ah, she's back in bed now—there's a moving wad, banded like a package, talking too. "Patient is hallucinating."

That heavenly suspension, exactly the word for it: full of light. "What did she say?"

Who's that? I know that voice.

"Something about lilacs,'

"My God, that story. She's rallied. Nurse, my medical bag's in the kitchen. Get me it."

Somebody smoothing my brow. I smell sweat. Not a nurse; they smell of starch. Who?

"Zipporah. *Zipporah.* This is Thelma. I'm going to give you an injection. If you feel it, open your eyes. If you can't—your mouth?"

Nothing feels, not from the waist down. But open the mouth for her. That monk must have told her. A person in a coma still hears.

Her eyes are being gently washed. She blinks. It's the nurse now. A ringer for—who? Not Aggie. The priest's housekeeper—that day. Life resurges, in its own light. "I'm not yet on the cross, nurse. So don't bother with the feet."

The other woman is laughing. Of course. She's one of us. She's—? "Th-Thelma?"

"That's me."

I can't see. But I can whisper. "That was nasty. Apologize, for me."

"So *be* nasty. Very good for the blood count."

A whisper: *The gran's a corker, isn't she.* Nurse is still there, a broad smile on her. "That's a good one, Mrs. Duffy—all in the church. I'll be telling that one to the Father . . . Well, I'm off now. Nighty-night."

Able to swallow, she takes nourishment. "Off the hook," she snarls to the intravenous feeder and its whorls of rubber line, standing by. She can even say, over the bedside: "So you're a grand-daughter. But also a doctor. Don't waste your time here." And when Thelma, as hoped, only smiles: "What was that story?"

"About the lilacs? You told me, yourself. And how your father gave his legal service for free to a burial society suing your mother's brother, Honig Myers, over a piece of property adjoining the burial grounds of the congregation Honig was president of. A

member had owned it but wouldn't leave it to them, and the heirs
didn't care who wanted to buy it. So when your uncle found out—
'Polacks?' he said. 'And in ten years a slew of gravestones with
names ending with like "ski" and "witz" crowding the good German ones, and maybe not only the dead'—he had a survey made
that said the ground was too porous there for burial. So—"

"Oh, let me finish—hah," Zipporah says weakly. Some of us
have dozens of such stories at their fingertips, but she's had only
a few.

"Shoot."

"So when . . . Judge Riordan asked my father . . . was the survey
in his opinion 'conclusive,' . . . my father said, 'Oh yes, your honor.
It concludes that the ground surveyed is only porous to Poles.'"

When she laughs, she discovers that the brace is gone. Too
loose for her. And maybe not enough bone mass to tolerate the
pressure. She looks down at her wasted limbs. "Which part of me
is the dead half? Anyone asks you, Thelma darling—say it's the
Myerses."

She is faint with satisfaction—and with pure faint. She has
made her last joke.

Thelma is asleep, under slitted lids showing that whitish gleam
which deems itself awake. She has dosed me with some trimethy-
glycero-seconal-latenopro-diazole-clindax-radomontin-fibrila—the
longest word in any language, and the same prescription that with
other ingredients is on all the cracker boxes. Otherwise known as
Hope. The best doctors have innocent eyes like hers, that see beyond the whirling trickery to the *Om* she cannot cure, which has
only the one syllable. She's doing the dreaming, leaving to me the
last spin of the personal. What can she have given me that would
be worse—or better—than this high clarity?

This orthopedic bed, how can it be immobile, yet undulate?
Her pillows support, yet float? Her breath is even, bowels tamped,

the sinuses so clear that their acoustic must be like a concert hall's. She must be in that almost perfect stasis to which only death can add. Landscape after landscape should be passing, to a freight-car rumbling, one after the other fresh as paint, borne along on memory's rolling stock.

Nothing... But be not downhearted—as some suitable psalm must surely have sung. Those traveling years were your Olympiad. Now once again, Zipporah, it is lilac time, but with the city pavement your soil, its windows your weather, the crowd your crop. If you could but resume even for one hour that marvelous ballet: the walk to your own window, the easy leaning there. Then—the pirouette to a lover, as, a star in his own ballet, he strides through the door. With age, as the landscape becomes more the inner one, you move as a piece of it. You are the "native" in your own life.

She picks at the coverlet, inching it aside. They have her in a hospital gown again; she has short ones of her own, but hired caretakers are hungry for discipline. Her belly, strangely round in its pelvic cage, still looks human. The triangular patch below she has to imagine, but not its warm history.

And here come the two men involved. She won't dwell on their practices with her; she never has. We were ordinary, she and they—three swooners shuddering in the drumming glides of the body, belong merely to that sweet paleontology first scrawled in the cave, between the imprint of a roe deer and a bear. All the way on to those rural gawks, angled legs, and wide grimaces inscribed on many a chapel wall. Tie that sexual knot, and the bellies swell, with or without the egg. She'll take no more credit than is her due.

And aren't I doing here what one wants at the end, knowing where the bodies go? I shall bring all three of us together. "Her two Christians," I can even hear Peter say. And the other answers: "She would never allow me to investigate. Where that scoundrelly grandfather of mine had arrived from. For surely he was one of those scalawags who see the grand American design from far offshore, vowing to give it a hard twist, the minute they step on land—nor did I want to run the old fox down, really. The balance was better kept so. As with you—don't you agree? . . . We keep better what is dealt us."

Ah, Foxy, she thinks, you gave all the grapes away.

"But as I've aged, Dr. Duffy—or may I call you Peter?—I've fancied her sneaking looks at my profile. Quite possible that my ancestor had some Jew in him?"

"Ah, she'd prefer the balance," Peter says. "She always did. They're just plain nosy. The smart non-shiksas like her . . . And speaking of noses, didn't she opt for a subject of study that finds both hooks and pudges the world over?"

She hears a sigh. From the one who has the broader world view, along with an abiding shame at how he had come by it.

"She wants us together, Duffy," he says. "But that wouldn't be fair to you. I'm still alive."

Still alive, in his own nest across town? She must have heard wrong.

Or I shall will it so. At our time of life, one of the privileges is to resurrect. Those years so evenly pursued return, with the remembered grasp of a hand. I see him, in his bed over there as I am in mine here; we've kept pace. Although I must speak for him, he can move for me. I can see him, across a park, although I may not like what I see. Last I heard, the attendance there was desultory. One couldn't call it a bouquet. Not without the family smell.

Do I smell that now? Not a raw blast. A silent attendance, of many, through an open–house door. That rubbery waft from wet raincoats, damp boots. A murmurous convergence of breath with airplane breakfast still on it, or even of the mouthwash I taught them to use? Long-ago after-soccer sweat mingling with the girls' dance leotards, and the midnight lamps—that college smell. And would that be my eldest, Gerald, hiding the goat under the aftershave? And the candy-pee from one of the everyday snowsuits? Ah dear, I'm your mother's mother's mother—I diapered her.

Or is it summer? Do I smell the fleur-fleur of patterned dresses? The all-year-round crotch of jeans, washed or unwashed? The other in the family? He of the studio smell covered by Russian cologne. Under both, an international hurry-up from some open-air art-latrine? He's not yet here.

Flesh of my flesh, all of them, I can smell them from a mile off. From this receding mile away.

A whisper to a whisper to a whisper. "She's lasted."

Those tiny, deft hearing aids in my ears—I'd forgotten I had them. When my upper body is lifted, propped up for the tidying—a morning job just like anybody's—the nurses amuse themselves as with a doll: "Marvelous dental work, she has—nothing movable. Fresh batteries for the ears, check those . . . Braid the hair." If they could, they would attach the dollmaker's newly jointed legs to me, pink and mechanized. Or better still, plug in my own limbs, for an electronic twinge.

As it is, let me dream away, hearing the last rites.

"Yes, as you say, we could put her in hospital," Thelma is saying to someone. A visitor? "When the heart is that good, but everything else going. There are routines. But she made me promise, Mrs. Magafy–Ilonka . . . You want to, you ring for an ambulance. And bug off in it."

Thelma, God bless her . . . My heart's that good, is it? Thunder—then a hiccup, a scary stop, like it's pondering—that's a good heart?

"Call off your mistress, Gerry. This is our mother." Charles. Let him swagger. In the nick, he's always there.

That fake ice-queen, Ilonka. From Bloomberg Financial News yet, "a systems analyst." She won't get mine.

"How could you, Gerry? Bring her here." A chorus.

Ah, they don't remember. What poor Gerry always could do: "He has Agnes's digestion," his father said of him. "He can swallow tacks."

"She's a former," he says.

Wish I could laugh. Can't. Can hear. How they are settling in. Seen so many of these previews, semi-wakes. But this is mine. Am I rallying?

A whisper in her good ear. "This is Thelma, dear. I have to go now. To another—patient. In hospital. Sorry. Nurse Conlan should be here at six. They're on strike, you know. But she'll come. Soon as I can, I'll be back . . . She'll sleep now. She's had an 'up.' There'll be a down. Here's another half-dosage. In case I don't get back—anybody know how to give this to her?"

A silence. That must be what Thelma stuck in my thigh. She had to pull up the skin like . . . crepe-de-chine . . . Is anybody going to volunteer?

"I can. I will."

Know the voice. Who?

"Annie."

"Yes, Dad. The year my mother was dying, I learned how."

Charles's first wife. That girl with the wreath hair. I saw her—a crone, thinned to a leaf. And Annie will not forgive him. Nor blame her.

When silence is general, funny, how you can tell.

"Good girl," Thelma says. "And while you're at it, Annie, when she wakes up, sponge the lids. All on the table there."

A cheek against hers, a kiss. My last? No one else may dare.

"Hang in, Zipporah. Back soon."

Keep naming me. Tell them to. Helps.

She dozes. Dreamless. Instead, the undercurrent, no rhyme or reason to it, that signifies a house is full. The cast settling in rooms. Kitchen clinkings. Forbidden games of innocence—a six-year-old rising at dawn to grind down the long hall on his first roller skates, and pulled to earth with a sleepy father's "What the devil," but no slap. An eight-year-old girl, found reading by flashlight under the bedclothes, is mother-snuggled with: "Shhh, what's that you're reading? My old Sarah Crewe? Let me in." While under the blanket, toes big and small touch . . . Go even farther back. Who knows the Edda saga of a nursing mother, when a house—not this one yet—is stilled? . . . All houses with children in them are at times the same. The villa will smell of gravy, the hut have an arch.

When she was lowest in spirit, sitting with Mickey through a night when his swellings threatened to choke, and she would hyperventilate in an effort to breathe for him, they would play word games to get them through their panic. She consoled herself with words that when she was little older than he had seemed to float beyond the domains of language. *Halcyon*—signifying that heaven which could never be achieved but must always be imagined. *Diapason*—to her, that expansion of the universe which occurs as in music, from a first force grown infinitely wider with distance, until it is out of hearing. Yet we know that it never dies.

What had he said when kept in the hospital week after week—because when there is nothing to be done, you must still do it? "The sicker they say I get," Mickey says, "the more my brain—like shines." At twelve a master of evasion, he'd never before admitted he was "sick." Who was she to carp? The brain is held not to have sensory reaction in the usual way of the body; is in fact deemed to be numb. What if a brain's thoughts are its "feelings"? What if a dying, when sufficiently protracted, is like a musing, phrased or not, according to what each brain can assess?

Mickey, already a declared candidate for zoology, along with other lab enthusiasts, had witnessed and partially engaged in the classic beginner's dissection—of a dogfish. And later of some earthworm she cannot identify, though she had seen slides. So—half sitting up on his many pillows, no shine visible on that diminished face, had he been already in research? Secure in that death corner which no scientist can get to, except under his own scalpel?

They won't believe it, out there—those "dear ones" gathered here for me, sitting on their bums in actual chairs—that dying is a kind of last knowing. Only give us time, hedged though we are, and all our persona will gather also.

Dearly beloved—will you pause to study with me here? The way the scholastic monks studied the Existence of the Soul. Far excelling the rest of us, because they already believed.

Who am I kidding? What am I trying to share? The trajectory of a fly, already flown?

Pluck at the cover. That's what we do. Do I want to hide this fading they will all come to? Or caterwaul, "Save me—ye who cannot be saved?" Neither? Am I skirting "the intense inane"? Whoever coined that one? Someone like me. In a last reverie, intensely sane.

"She's breathing hard," Annie says. "But it's not the death rattle. I heard that once . . . Here, take the baby, someone—you, Dad? I better check her heartbeat."

"I'll hold him," Charles whispers back. "My first grandchild from you. Four months, is he? Aah . . . cootchee-cootchee. Mike."

A heartbeat, in this shrunken chest? Who will find it?

"Tough, when nurses strike," an unknown male voice says. "Un-fort-unately—they too deserve."

Erika bends her head in distaste. Her son-in-law, Ralph—Rachel's husband. The two met years ago at "L.S.E.," as they often chirp. Two economists who deserve one another. Shipped off to the U.S.A. as a kid during the blitz, he'd returned to Oxbridge to rescue himself, becoming later an "American adviser," long in Lady Thatcher's pocket, first dubbed a baronet, then an earl. Not upper-class, as most of the little Brit emigrés had been. Philippe's Gallic scratchiness had sent him up the wall: "No economist should have that much poise." Philippe's estimate had been: "He does so want to be called 'Rafe.'"

How she misses Philippe, dead in a public service he wore so lightly. When she'd let her hair go white, in misery as his going approached, he'd teased: "Ah, but now Fred-dee, you are wise enough to be matriarch." During one of their separations he had acquired a farmhouse outside Washington, installing a private staircase he dubbed "my Thomas Jefferson," in the event of her return. She had. How she wishes he could too. So that they might have a few more years, happily not getting along.

A rasp from the bedclothes. Not a rattling. A groan—almost a growl.

"What's she saying... what... what?"

Their susurrus is like a scurrying of mice. Her hearing is so keen now, transcending that prompter in her ear. Their feet shift, a cup is set in its saucer.

She says it again. "Baby."

Repeated softly, ah-ee, vining the room with its tendrils, it could be a spell. People still cast those.

"'Baby,' she said, Mom. She wants to hold it."

Some ten-year-old? Sounds like. Going straight to the core. So—they too are here, as I craved.

A giggle—from another. "She wants to nurse it."

So I do, darling. From these dugs. Once called nipples.

Huusssh, the parents say, or the grandparents, as some will be. *Shhh.* But a light rocket of laughter follows, pop pop. Vibrating in the old furniture, felt in her pillows. Coming to a stop no doubt in that overstuffed gift-sofa, more like a caravan that had foundered. Where once had sat—just as predicted—only the bores.

A bundle is held to her. She can smell it, acrid, restorative. The odor that is never a stink.

"My grandson." A cough she would know anywhere; Charles is correcting himself. "Your great-grandson, Mother. Not your first, of course. Needn't open your eyes."

Almost can. Someone gently dampening them. Bleared. But that's Annie, all late-mother pride. "Don't strain, Gran. He looks like they all do."

She strains... Another rocket of laughter. They have heard her. But what could she have said? An echo comes. *Unn-uh. Looks like us.*

And now, raising up in this living room of a bedroom, she can see them all. Two of the anonymous young, tapped for the honor, come forward, solemn angels, to hold her from behind. So that she may see who have gathered here. So that they may see her. Death has sent out the cards.

She can see them clearly now, her holy family.

The wars they'll have been to. The small wonders they've found. See that bundle, being walked around the room with such pride. See the circumstances of the hegira, bred again and again in these faces. Rest assured, such faces will never quite meld.... I leave our secrets—such as they may be, such as we've shared—for your disposal. Whether a people so scattered share more secrets than most, or only the habit of those?—we have them. This I bequeath. As has been bequeathed to me. And before me. Remember this, when you judge the scattering...

Put her down now. It's too much.

No, no, hold me. In your midst, I'm released from the drag of my own bones. You are my consciousness.

...Look at my face, please. Born early century, almost parallel with it. Greedy specialists in mortality that we both are, might we still talk a bit? I'm awake...

On some cheeks, tears. On others, a stony awe. She is laid gently down.

"I apologize for this protracted—afternoon," she quavers, in a voice they can hear.

"Ah, what manners they had, didn't they," a voice says. "That's what she'd say when I brought her ice cream."

Not a family voice. Nor Jennie. No, not she. Let us all remember what happened to her. Jennie, achieving her restaurant, sailed in it like on a lighted barge, packing in a crew of husbands. At fifty, a child emerged from her, like a welcomed stowaway. She is gone now, but for me her barge sails on. If I said her name she would appear, flinging back that swing-door, memory.

"There you are," Zipporah says.

"Yes, dear—" a daughter answers. "I'm right here."

"A gormless crowd—" Agnes says. "Bent on fulfilling their obligations without rule. I was obliged to monitor them."

The Agneses are always with us. If not one's own sister, they can amuse.

"I prescribe for her reward—a holy torture. She is the mistress of a cardinal," Zipporah mutters.

"Is she wandering?" someone says.

And of course she is. But only a nurse would say it. The kind one rents now.

"Not the Sabra—" comes from the bed.

"If she means Debra," a man says, "she and Bert are flying in. Should have been here by now."

But do we want her to reach America? Did we ever?

"She comes from Jerusalem," the bed says. "Not really from Tel Aviv—which is more like us. That's why she obeyed the rabbi for so long."

"No, Mother—" Gerald says. "They've lived near London for twenty years now. She never would go back."

England, the great compromiser, does for her. And Bert's inner wars are maybe enough for them ... Would he have wanted to come back here, if on his own? But he has never been on his own. Should anyone be?

She cannot raise her head to look around her. But the answer is No.

"Old Rabbi Eiseman, remember him, Mother? Retired years back, to write his book. He was only seventy-five, the temple would have kept him on for years yet." Gerald speaks with the firmness of a man only seventy. "He was already Senior when I started there. We had him to dinner, remember? He came to my service anniversary the temple gave me, just the other day. Still hale and hearty. Everybody's boosting to the nineties now, you don't have to feel alone."

Gratitude floods her. Gerald, the booster, may still be the family butt, yet this most literal of her sons—determined to keep her "in the real world," denying that she is ever "out of it"—is the one who can pull her back. He still believes his own platitudes.

Watching how he marshals those likely to tease her back to intelligence, how he has developed a healer's intelligence of his own, she dissolves in tenderness. How can she refuse to be the cogent mother, on whose existence he insists?

It's a lie. I'm... stuttering. Like—a whole diary is at the base of the tongue. Clogging it. A roomful of people listen courteously. With half an ear. While exchanging tidbits on being alive. Each of their bodies proceeding like an equipage that needs no coachman. While I can't get past this great blockage. This rush of all past waters, at the small spout... Do the dying not have landscape? Only these stops and starts. And language itself the barrier? I speak at a podium over which no one presides...

"Has the rabbi written his books?" Charles says, with the fullness of one who has. Expounding the art of physics—once a science—and the dilemma of the artist-physicist, to the common lot. "I fell short of proclaiming us believers in God. Had I done, I should have made a mint at it."

"What kept you back, brother?"

Zach. He has arrived. He's always doing that. Born last of the brood, arrival is his schtick. Which he doesn't deny. His attitude is: Artists are cupbearers. Here. Wanna spit?

She's laughing. Or her belly is. All her parts are on their own now. Actors, extemporizing one by one, before leaving the stage?

"Ah—Zachary. Asking us how to avoid making money, are you?"

But she can hear the two of them back-slap. In what is called brotherly love.

"No, Chuck. Just wanna know what's the latest in scientific pursuit. Like to keep abreast legally."

They respect one another. Zach's taking his hat off to him, really. Though he never wears a hat. And Charles will be putting his fingertips together, in one of those pyramids university men used to make. Long since gone out of style. But shaping yourself any which way will always win my Zach.

"Well, I'll tell you, Zach," Chuck says. "I believe the Divine should be a neutrino we all pursue."

... How odd that of all Peter's brood, he's the one who has most kept faith with being in-between.

"You asked whether the rabbi has written those books?"

... That's Gerald, wanting in ...

"Matter of fact, no, he hasn't. He's too bitter. He'd planned a commentary celebrating the alliance. But their Jerusalem is not his anymore."

... She can hear-see Gerald's headshake; his pauses are so obvious to her. And by now, so dear. He visits her every day. Now that Kitty/Fegeleh is gone, he can afford. That Home for the Aged wasn't cheap. But giving recitations, dancing with the livelier elders, she'd been the star of her floor. Until the hip broke again. "She's soured on the place," Gerald had said. And on him? He's never credited that anyone could.

"Why—we'll take her," Byron had said. "Give her dinner parties to the end." His helpmeet Lucas adding: "On that cloth." Compared to the horrors some of their friends were undergoing, Byron said, "What grace it is, to die of a hip."

... As who has better reason to know than I. High-heeling it almost to the end, only to drop, decently fading, in one's tracks. One's animal tracks. Kitty's legs and mine being much the same. ...

As, when admitting her true history, she'd pointed out.

Two years on, the obit had fallen to Gerald. Who has such a knack for them. "Lucas always sort of stuck in my craw, Mother. But to the end I treated him like a son." An irony that escapes him. As so many do. "I spend considerable worry now, on Byron." Later informing her: "Byron was like me, thank God. Just in time, he turned celibate." That did throw her for a loop. "Gerry—were you ever gay?" His answer had been simple, unaffected. "Oh no, Mother. I always knew what it was to be a man."

Byron, who visits her bedside en route to dying friends he now attends full time, says of his father, "He's so true to form, it's practically an artistic experience." Lucas may have taught him what those were. But the remark was not a quote. He'd have said so. His honesty braces her. He tends some of the dying at home checks some in the hospital, all the way to burial. "I'm clean, myself, yes. But I get the bends, every night. I come to you for my dose." He grins at her bewilderment. "Dose of cheer. You're dying so naturally. At least, what used to be 'natural.' And with such a clear head."

"Oh Byron—" she hears herself sigh. "I go in and out. Sometimes I'm even with *my* mother." He'd laughed. "Feel free." She can see what a tower he must be at those other bedsides. What a boon—as he kneels, bringing himself to her level, saying what she cannot think he says to them. "You're dying such a good death. Thanks for the dose."

Not even Thelma has been as straight with her.

The hardest—she will tell him next time—is this living double. Or with the brain's devilish variation. Zooming out of blankness to almost uncanny intelligence. Down again to the slight indignity of hearing herself sigh.

What he may mean, she thinks guiltily, is that I am dying without pain. And no machines. Only this winking out, cell by cell. This draining down, in which one addresses nothingness, almost sinks there, and is dragged back. She has had relatives who clocked every organ's slightest failure, and did this verbally, often finding some other crony in the family with whom to exchange. And at her Sundays, certain characters were not to be asked too sincerely how they were. "They will tell you." And the more religious they were, the more hypochondria mewled from them. Perhaps every Jew has a little Job in him. Or even more prominently—in her?

She may live until Byron comes next. She has cheered herself up.

What is this hullabaloo? Raise me up. Surprisingly, they do. Is it the next day? Are they not dressed the same, this circle around her bed, all of them staring down?

Now, the heads swivel. Like in that ballet, "The Green Table." She can't see where they are looking. They are staring away. Do they want her not to identify any of them?

Muted conversation has been going on, for hours certainly, maybe for years. Are they discussing their symptoms? The tidbits that keep them alive?

Give me a tidbit.

But nothing is put to her lips.

If she could open her eyes, perhaps they would.

Somebody's plane has made a forced landing?

"They will be late. Perhaps too late."

The son-in-law. Nobody's agreed with him. Does he feel the chill? Sons-in-law can have a hard time in this family. He's no Philippe. Who led us by our noses like a smart coach-dog, showing off his spots. While he and Nell...

Since I'm at it—let me tally up the secrets for once and all: Peter, hiding his illness from me. I hiding it from the world. Nell never telling us—or anyone?—whether or not those two modest tits—she always padded some—are still real. Byron, for years closeted. His brother, James, absconded who knows where?... No wonder Lev gravitated toward us. With whatever that packet hid. Had to be serious. If Bert's never said.

Debra.

When she came to us fresh from Lev's murder, I thought to myself: This girl is like a tall spearhead, never yet aimed. Never likely to be? She does not hide the reb, or that she is not Mrs. Lev. Merely—she does not speak of it. Later, when we parted, she did not say to where... Child of the kibbutz, beauty-parlor sibyl... diamond mistress, drudge to the wounded.

None had the face of the figure I saw down the long aisle of the synagogue, Peter slumped in its arms. There's often a figure like that in a Pietà. The one that holds the dead Christ tumbled from the Cross, its own face flattened with agony received.

I was holding the gifts I had bought at the shop that stocked Judaica. The book for my grandson. "Ah, he respects ancient editions, does he?" the shop-owner said. For her a necklet, formed of tiny notched and stamped dangles of a blackened silver that he warned me must never be polished. The circlet came with a matching, pointed headband—neither piece to be sold separately. The set was ceremonial, to be worn only once; did I know that? I said I did.

So there I am, in the Venetian sunlight, standing just inside that huge synagogue they leave unguarded. Which needs no guarding, admitting you at one push to its dark theology. Ahead, the long aisle. Down the years, my dream-steps will flit along its length. Debra is always at the end, arms holding up her gift to me.

Burials like that one was can numb. Multiple voices on the phones, fretfully stating their rights. Official papers, too plump for their envelopes, but narrow with stipulation, when unrolled. The hotelier's grateful assistance, so that our gloom might be distanced. And finally, the very soil of a watery city that can scarcely bury its own.

On the road to Rome, to which all roads are said to lead, meditation was thrust on me. As can happen in hired cars, with unfamiliar creakings. In the dilapidated ones, the drivers take refuge in speed. At every rut, the coffin in its trunk had slid forward. Such a slight rasp, humble. Reminding me, in spite of itself, of a terrible compliance that at times had seemed to be demanded of me. That I could not bear to give.

In the mountain ranges where tribes toil to the apex with their dying, leaving those to freeze in the beneficent snow, a lesson had been posed me. And once again, on that sterile plateau where I had watched the man encased in his own leather walk in his own cortege, a helper with a sac of arrow-poison trundling alongside. We go to anthropology to learn our own. I could not have joined the tribal procession on that alp. I would not have walked at that man's side. I could conspire only so far. To Italy perhaps, to the hidden journey. But I was too weak to end another's most desperate journey by my own hand.

In that old jaunting-car I had time to reflect on the nature of those who might be more capable. And on the nature of gifts. I saw how she fended off the advances of that slimy salesman with his portfolio of Duccio and porn—the six-inch nail file pointed at him like an épée, she not even looking his way. Such a victim draws no pity. The witty art of the épée is not to touch the body. I could even smile.

But as the man, unreproved, thrusts the folder of Duccio prints at us, she has her arm around me. The man gives us time to study it. The folder's cover has the Deposition. Christ's body is being brought downs the ladder, a bearded man encircling the breast from behind, a young one grasping the thighs. Christ's left arm is stretched on the black robe of the woman receiving him. Her red-sleeved right arm emerging from the robe crosses his, her hand is laid on him, thumb at the chin. Their faces almost touch at the nose, his death-colored face seen almost in full except for the right cheek, hers in massive profile, rosied at that same cheek. One might draw a vertical from the Christ's death-slitted eyes above, to the woman's wide, live scrutiny below.

Debra passes it by. Also the small repro of the black-winged Satan in the Temptation on the Mount, though for a second she studies it. Also a detail of the right arm of the Christ on the Cross, the arm impossibly long, angels covering their eyes floating above. I feel her tension as we stare, a release as she again passes each by. We are going through this together.

When she halted at the Madonna, this woman so unused to the pity to be found in churches, who must be seeing that, I had to break away from her. This girl whose life was like a page torn from the Law, was she answering what I dared not ask? I couldn't stay any longer under that arm.

On the steps of the Inghilterra, I explained her to myself. Excuse being not in question. I stand by that description now. The gap between the civilized and the primitive is closing fast, true. But it's only the locales that are shutting down, in ozone doom. Among peoples, one sees the primal stare any day, always trying to date it, all the way back to the animal orb, soft or fiery, in its frame of furred bone. I tried to think of hers as pre-Etruscan, that round, remote gaze.

But when it beckoned me from the top of the hotel steps, I found I could not follow, motioning instead that I would go straight on to my plane. As the bellboy went by me with his luggage cart, I glimpsed the zipped sling in which she kept her "extras," and had kept Peter's. We had picnicked from it. When a wind came up brisk she would pull out his muffler or knitted vest. The sling looked empty enough for good-byes. I slipped the necklace in it.

As one's body fades, does the inborn monkhood of the spirit re-assert itself? Acquiring just before going that quiet overseer—the Third Eye. Goal of scholars—even one like me, who could never separate herself enough from her own wigwam. Or grail of artists like Zach, forever trying to make one shard of the world stand still? Maybe the "Third Eye" is even what the cult film-goer is after—those who must "see"? Funny, if to acquire it one has only to die? As we rot, do we purify?

I see whom Debra pitied most. To her, patients were an old story, she not to intervene. She was offering him, peaceful now in her arms—to me.

The long living room is empty again, except for the furnishment it has always had.

"We had to shift her," Thelma is saying to Bert and Cicily. "This space—she wanted it. But it couldn't be organized. At first I'd thought—well, it's nearer the kitchen—and we so wanted to oblige. But the nurses were trotting miles. One does need a con-centrated space. Outlets for plug-in, and so forth. So we removed her to the bedroom again. Had to get rid of that bloody lamp—re-member it? That rose-colored job. She didn't seem to mind. She's in a—" when a doctor shrugs, it's a sop to what the universe won't give in to—"not too special a state. We see it, now and then. When there's a strong heart, that doesn't want to give up. And maybe a brain?...Zipporah goes in and out, you might say. It's certainly not coma...But when she responds—well, I suppose you'd call her 'conscious.' Hyper, actually. At first we thought it was the stimulant. Given that up... and oh yes, Bert, in case you're wondering, we've had to exclude the children. Some of the parents thought the scene just too startling. I hated to. Know how she used to tell us about those she'd been at—China, the Andes, Africa? 'All the little angel-faces,' she'd say.

"'All the little Raphaels,' yes," Bert says. He can't help looking down the long room, now so bare of people. "Whether she was telling us about the Congo, or—or French Canada."

"The hardest was to explain to the littlest ones," Thelma says. "Why they had to—leave. That was a surprise. 'Too crowded' was our excuse. But my brother Derek's youngest—she knows all the tricks; she travels with his band. She said, 'But you were letting us in two-by-two.'"

"Ah, cousin," Bert hugs her. "You've had to deal with all the family excuses. No wonder you look beat."

"Tired of *not* dealing with some excuses," Thelma says grimly. She taps her cell phone. "Our own, all morning at the hospital. Medical ones."

"Can't be easy. For a medic to buck those."

She does a two-step. The other Thelma peeps—"I'm my mother's child."

"We saw her."

"Gone tiny, hmm. Some do. The heels help. A tradition she keeps up. And her salon. Our raunchy dinner table, Bert. That Derek and I grew up at—and the adoptee we bewildered so. She went to work for the U.N., found a Romanian to marry, and zoomed back...You remember that table, Bert? The transients, who were treated like habitués. And the half-time fathers, who she kept on the move? Remember?"

"I remember."

"She tells herself it's a ringer for your Sundays, I imagine."

Cicily, shrewdly watching, gets the picture. Two people, a man and a woman, remembering a cliff from which they didn't take the plunge? She's been through that. She's more interested in this long-imagined room. Not at all with the luxe she'd equipped it with: draperies sweeping profoundly to a floor walked on by New York shoes, all trim. The air meanwhile would be a myrrh of that history too many Americans lacked. This "living room" (a phrase that used to magic her), a period decor, for sure. A double "lounge," middle-middle, from some store like London's Heals, supplier to those who dearly hoped to be bourgeois. Yet spawning what she's just heard? "Your brother—he has a band?"

A laugh, obviously from a duet those two know. She must have forgotten, too, how smart they will be here.

"Cicily's pals were either brought up dockside, or in ancestral homes they couldn't wait to trash," Bert says fondly. "Nothing midway." He looks around. "The place does have that—terrible stasis. When all it's been, all that it still is—is waiting to slide." He chokes up. Recovers. "Cic—it always looked like this. She's kept it up. Renewed it—though you wouldn't notice. We rarely did. But no more than usual. We had more money than most, admitted. Though we were far from rich. We were educated better than most. Otherwise—nothing here was ever meant to be grand. Those sofas, the chairs—look at them. They look the way they always have. Expectant. Waiting for people to shabby them." He blows his nose.

Thelma says softly, "I suppose. I did see this house as—where one could be different. Yet they would take you as you were. But I never got here much. Nell was so fierce on our side, like we were parts of her. But always busy being herself. She's a mother who's always had a mother. That can be strange. A mother who's a child? Like she was acting it out—ahead of us." Thelma hunches. No belle. But a woman who knows her own sturdiness. "When she got to be a saint, that time? That's when Derek and I found we could scram. And what do you know—she'd fooled us, down to the ground. She'd made us competent."

Thelma pulls up. "Well. I expect everyone's in there who

should be. I phoned around . . . One doesn't always get the chance. Great age, no pain, just an—ebbing. The vital signs—respiratory, excretory, vascular, and on up—not failing really. Just—bowing out? If we could record that—what wouldn't we know."

"Medically—" Bert says.

"Ah you. You always wanted more," she murmurs. She's hustling off her white jacket. "I wear this, for the nurses. Otherwise, I confuse them. Am I the doctor in charge? Or just a family member. Right now, that's what I'd like to be." She smiles at them. "Glad you got here. And you too, Cicily . . . remember your father."

"You do? . . . Were you—here that day?"

"No. Just something nobody else might. Lev used to carry rock-candy in his pockets. For us kids. I would have been about eight. And old Nettie—Bert'll remember her all right—she horned in for some. Just as he was giving me mine. And I said, loud as I could without yelling—she was stone deaf—'It's got a string in it.' And he said, I can see Lev saying it—'She knows'. . . Well, I better get on."

"Zach's somewhere here," Bert said. "He subbed for me, at Foxy's funeral. And there on his own, of course. They were great friends."

"I had to tell her," Thelma said. "About Foxy. One doesn't spare Zipporah. Maybe because she never spared us—what she thought we shouldn't have to wait for . . . I wasn't sure how she took the shock. That age, the face doesn't have much expression—except age. But she—took it . . . Well, Bert . . . *Ciao.*"

"My mother's in there," Cicily blurts.

Thelma wheels. "Is she now. I wondered whether. Under sedation, people say lots they haven't let themselves hear. We always thought neither she nor Debra wanted to be reminded of that time with my grandfather . . . But I'm glad your mother felt she could come . . . When they're dying, they want to be reminded of everything."

"What a trump she is," Cicily says, when she's gone. And when he merely nods—"Your family owes her a lot."

He no longer ripostes at once: "Your family too, Cicily." That malarkey she has at least rid him of. How can she be "theirs," and Debra's too? All she wants is for the snapshots to be verified—whatever remains of those. Not to belong. Bert, the old sweetie—here is his rabbinate.

"Fancy her remembering like that. She's a duck. Bert. Was she ever your girl?"

He pulls back. "You're only romantic when you walk—you once informed me. Keep to it."

"I *am* walking. Hear the crinoline? This place is Nostalgia Park. Okay—I'll be crude. The Punk says that's the only way to stay young. You and she—were you each other's firsts?"

No reply.

"I like Ferdinand," he says. "When are you going to break down and marry the guy?"

"You call him that, he'll commit thuggee on you. Indian strangleholds. He goes to a gym where Whitehall practices how to, quietly. Karate yells being so old hat... Can you see him and me tootling down some village High Street behind a pram?"

"So he's on with those politicos, is he? It's the status quo they're needling—you Brits do that better than anybody, when you put your minds to it. He gets too good at the silent strangle—he'll find himself in government. And you? Swanning behind the nanny who's behind the pram. Wife of the first punk to be in Parliament."

He's answered her question—by refusing to. A denial would have come straight.

"O.K., Bert. If you would only sermonize like that somewhere—" Cicily cries. "All our crowd would sign on, I swear."

"He learned it from me," Shine cackles, entering from the front hall, Zach stomping a cane behind him. "Only, this house, they urge you follow your natural bent. I had to learn how to go to the dogs on my own. Hi, Cicily. Long time."

On his yearly visits to the Isle he'd avoided the kid whose skewed questioning of the conventional had made his seem labored. Since then they'd rarely met. He is swart, grizzled, wearing skinny tropicals that suggest the sophisticated tea-planter in town for his annual flutter—with maybe something to swap? Though all on the level, which he would prefer not to display. Charity is so aging. He's clutching a roundel of violets in a silver-paper frill.

"Sprained my Achilles tendon climbing up to check one of my installations," Zach explains gruffly. "In Athens, matter of fact. They thought that hilarious. The gods resent sculpture that moves, apparently...And now this funeral...Longer than Napoleon's. I'd've left, if I could've without noise. All Mendenhall's world staff is there—an army. Next to me an Episcopal divine. His cane is malacca. He admires my briar. So much less showy, he says." And here Zach sinks in a whelm of snorts and hoots that hack into what might be laughter. "That round-collar, he says to me: 'America has no native wood suitable for canes. That is our strength.' Then, when we're greeting the minister, the family surrounds me—the young ones. They're nice. Mendenhall must have got to them. They are truly sorry the family never got to know my mother; they think we're the nuts, obviously. They all seem to be newly married, introducing like mad; one of those Anglo-blonds is even married to a black girl. A real one, dark as Sheba, not like this cappuccino at my elbow...And a couple the young grooms, they might even be Yids. Smoothies of course, stockbroker variety."

"You better watch out, talking to a man of color like that," Shine says. But his heart's not in it.

"I do," Zach chokes. "I only insult the Jew half of you." A coughing fit subsides into a handkerchief. From its depths, his hoarse whisper comes, agonized. "How is she?" He shakes his head at the reply.

Bert has observed these bouts of hysteria at other obsequies, usually where the dead or dying are being truly mourned. Among some simple people, as his kind would term them, an exchange of grotesque humor could seem ritual. Among the men, that is, the women ducking away in the fake shock that manners imposed.

Zipporah herself, once showing him her store of "ceremonial" pictures from her travels, had commented on how religion was down the ages served by the grotesque. "Or by what we no longer think of as grotesque. Check any cathedral," she'd said. Reliquaries with bones in them. The two-foot-high canister on the archbishop's head. And of course, the gargoyles. "American Jews get more embarrassed by religious emotion, the higher they go in the—hmm—*socioeconomic* scale," she'd said, impishly mocking that lingo. Her own mother had warned against being "too demonstrative." That had been the catchword used. Well—it was understandable. "You don't go rending garments on the upper East Side. Or on the West, either."

Chuckling, they'd improved on that: imagining Zipporah's friend and scourge, Ruth Halle, being assisted out of her limo by her Fifth Avenue doorman, naked except for her torn mink. Or Gerald, ripping away custom-made layers, while shouting near-invective at what sounded suspiciously like the Adonoi. "I don't think, though, that he'd sacrifice his Swiss underwear," Bert said. She'd confessed to an impulse to raise her arms and yearn in unison to the sound of the shofar, the ram's horn being blown. "I do think," she'd said, "that no God worth his salt minds being chided. It might even give Him a rush. And if you're going to personify the Deity, you had damn well better keep on being personal."

That had been the one time his grandmother had opened up on that score. He'd have been about sixteen, just when he and Shine were milling it all over. Once he was in the seminary, both his usually opinionated grandparents had seemed wary of expressing any, as well as restricting language, more usually impious, that might now seem to blaspheme.

Since living in England, his business relationship with Mendenhall had become an education, and a joy. Though Foxy talked only moderately, and never vaunting, any chance reference might amaze.

He had been everywhere—and his empire has been his encyclopedia. Physically powerful, he had early practiced sports without being more than amused, once saying slyly, "When I got tired of wrestling, I fished." He was no muscular Christian, except in wielding his money dead-on, to whip opportunity into other people's lives.

He had matched his mother's singular love and energy without being daunted, had apparently been both naive and regal with women, but hadn't needed to reject—perhaps they had rather exploited him. With his children, he had resisted being powerful, though well aware that the good of this could be questionable.

When Bert dined with him and Zipporah as a couple, usually the day after he saw Mordecai, Foxy often remarked that when between London and New York, between any two air destinations, but most on that flight, "I'm always a blur." He was appalled at all that time lost, which might have been spent "studying." What would this man of so many experiences and seasoned conclusions be cramming up on?

"Why, the possibilities are endless," he'd protested. The blithe stupidities resorted to in order to push conversation could make him uncomfortable—especially in company he revered. "Including—why am I a blur?" Asked years later what his conclusions on that were, he replied: "Periods of psychic rest, I'm afraid. Pompous of me."

Being the head of so vast a number of individuals had weighed on him morally. He had never absconded in the ways that money could. His qualities and intelligences always struck one as oddly mixed; one was tempted to say that he was as simple as he was wide, as fair as he was bluff, as kind as he was tall. In his company it was you who rested.

Surely his and Zipporah's years together had been golden. Yet women who have had a house always theirs may have a certain cruelty. It had pained Mendenhall to live divided—a man whose husbandry would have flowered like his garden. Worse for him, as one impelled to share to the nth, was to see that she could not share. But this too he had accepted. As he had accepted his name.

Bert has it otherwise. Debra, still remote, is the faraway princess, possessed. Reared as she had been, her house is utterly his. But the house itself, being "ideal" in the modern way, half urges one to dispense with it. Her past is like the clothing she cannot give away: the army shorts, the long coat. When Cicily asked for that still handsome garment, she'd handed it over with such a scared look that he'd later mentioned this to Cicily—who said, "Oh that's the way the mothers always look, when they hand you their luck."

Hearing this, Debra said, faintly bitter, "Will you wear it to Israel?"

Cicily, pirouetting in hand-me-downs, was what parenthood asks of their young: touched by what you've brought them, but with just enough modernity to haul you along. "Oh no—" she said. "It's for *America*." Brit to her bones, born there, she says that word, so old-fashioned even to him, as if it is still a talisman. By now, her modernity has gone on rather too long? Perhaps she'll shed it in the States, here. Or more likely, it will be outclassed.

Meanwhile, he does his job well, and relishes it—if in the abashed way one must, when succoring the tortured, the patronized, those so lightly called "disadvantaged," the bleeding poor, all that tower of adjectives. If war had once lurked in his family background by its absence, he now attends it constantly, as one of those civilians "with connections" who may be rather more exposed than the generals. Tiring of the Rabbi Duffy jokes, but needing to formalize his infrequent but continued functioning in that line, his travel papers now read "Clergyman." He and Shine, like many of the advantaged, had been made well aware of the lifework visions that haunt some, and as with Zach, become destiny. Envying, they had at least sought vocation, hoping secretly to be swirled away. But he knows well what has happened to him. Nothing but the commendable. Like so many of the "dedicated" he's fulfilled that role which the clan, ignoring Nettie's warning, had gone on benevolently fitting him for. Like at the seminary, the grounds cop's seven-year-old, proudly goose-stepping, already knew his lines. "Tell 'em what you're going to be, Kevin . . . 'My Dad's putting me in for the force.'"

Upscale, it occurs more subtly: *Bert's so responsible.*

And his job has been his luck.

He has thought of bolting. Whenever the goodwill crowd

sticks in his craw. Or when the blood, stanched today, on the morrow resumes. He is Mendenhall's designate-to-be, though not his heir. Informed of Bert's wish to leave, Foxy will quote his mother, something appropriate. Like, "Our Creator does botch. Let's give him a leg-up."

His mother had been his stooge, the office parlance for her being MOM—Mother of Managers.

"Those aphorisms—" Bert had said, "whyn't you put them in a book?"

"Oh I did. She gave a two-story party for it. Want her autograph?" With Foxy the jokes were what was sacred; they kept the balance. The founder of his line had intended him to be one.

"What's a two-story party?"

"Newspeople on the ground floor, priests on the *premier étage*."

Bert has stayed on, of course; he can't bolt now. In the world Mendenhall had brought him to, where to change oneself to suit the money is the norm, Foxy had accepted him as he had himself. As if acceptance itself is the vitality.

Chairs have been arranged in the hall to accommodate those waiting. They sit in them. Zach's hands are folded on the crown of his briar, his chin on the hands. The cane is making him old. Or helping him to show that he is. "How to mourn a man like that" he grumbles. "A prince, they said? He was a commoner—God knows how he managed that. I told him once, 'You're a designer, Foxy. Specializing in sculpting humans.' He made me into a friend. My mother—he let be. And she him. They didn't tinker with one another. That could be on their headstone ... To mourn him—and then come here; it's too much."

Excess is not what Uncle Zach usually complains of; he's usually urging one not to toddle in place.

"You already got yourself so much muchness," Shine grunts. "Ought to be able to handle this much more."

"Oh. Shine. When are you going to stop trying to convince us how callous you are?" Zach stomps his cane. Unfortunately, on Shine's boot.

"*Ou-ouch. Ha-ahr-r.*"

Cicily widens her eyes at Bert—Up to now, wasn't sure I was acting properly, she mouths. He doesn't want that confidence; he looks beat.

If they only could have waited, she's thinking. These people I so wanted to meet, but held back on, on account of Debra. What she wouldn't do, how could I? But if only the woman in there could have waited . . . I saw the picture. A grandmother, whose history would be her very breath. A woman fit to be my mother's mother . . . How could that cipher in Tel Aviv have bred Debra? Sending word, when news of Debra's arrival for the *get* had reached her: "Your father rolls in his grave. You have no brothers anymore. I have no daughter."

According to the Punk, who was not a satanist but had a witch friend, a fuller malediction might have read: *Accursed be the fruit of your womb.* Cicily had been fourteen at the time. "So, you're safe," he'd said. "You can hang loose." The curse had been handwritten with flourishes, evidently by a scribe, though the sender was not illiterate. In her own hand she had added a postscript: *Out of shame, I have closed the shop.*

At thirty, thirty-one, what kind of fool am I—still waiting to be recognized?

Shine is soothing his instep. "You lucky, Zach, I wasn't wearing my loafers, you could have broken my toe." He eases his foot back in, pulling the long tongue, wiggling into the pointed leather. "Eh, eh, —eh, there."

"Knockout boots," she says.

"Baby crocodile. Belonged my former wife. She had feet like plantains. Had to wear a man's."

Zach turns his thick neck slowly. "Feet like—?" He considers. The shape of anything is serious, not to be too lightly invoked.

Shine ignores him. "My now wife is daintier, she's part Anglo. Though that native snotty Island set, they don't like to admit. You ought to come down, Cicily, brown yourself a little, metaphorically speaking. We give you a hot time."

"A 'now' wife?" Zack says. "What was the other one—a 'then'? . . . And how long would a plantain be? 'Bout a size ten? . . . And what's that ribbon in your buttonhole?"

"The rest of her was not so explicable," Shine says. "Except maybe in a graph. She was a government type."

Bert is choking. They have to slap him. His face isn't red, but his cheeks are wet. "Sorry—" he wheezes. "I saw the feet."

She slips him a tissue. He'll get away with it, she thinks, until she clues in to the posture of the other two. They all want to huddle in at being men together. Who don't cry.

Shine straightens up first. When he'd first visited them, Bert had explained him to her—his two accents, the clothes that had to distinguish him, his quick look-see at the pub, to sniff out what was being made of him. "He can't stop wanting to be the foreigner. When we were college smarties—that could be king-of-the-mountain. He taught me a lot. At our Sundays—it used to kill me; anytime we got too inbred, we could depend on Shine. But nowadays, everybody wants to be a professional outsider. Or else doesn't have to profess."

"My buttonhole?" Shine says. "What did you think it was, the Legion of Honor? It was the smallest flag in our inventory—don't ask me what country." He sits, with his head between legs so long he can address his knees like intimates. "Goes down okay in the Caribbean," he says to them.

Cicily watches . . .

The Punk is getting very tired of being their generation, "Like—every play opening with *our* music—even Shakespeare?" Or like Val's vet—who early on attended wine tastings so that he and his wife could upgrade socially, only to find out the gentry is serving plonk. And calling him in for their alley cats. Instead of Siamese. Or Manx."

Bert, red-eyed, gives her a smile. "Not to worry," he'd assured the Punk. "You'll be moved on." Bert looks as old as her mother now, sometimes older. The Punk and she are closer to the same age—and have known each other for most of it; how can she marry that? Debra is no one to ask about marrying. Bert said, "I don't fancy that would give trouble—you both seem bored by everyone else. But then, each of you is the smartest person the other knows. That may." When she asked again, after a spell of adventuring which had left her low, he'd said: "All this fuss about marrying. Are you two sure which generation you are?"

Shine says: "Penny for your thoughts."

She shakes her head—hasn't any. "Except wishing for a clock that would tick." These days you're left to suffer time all by yourself.

Zach's cane lies on the floor, where it can't harm. He loves silence only when he's making something. Otherwise, fill it. Don't let the universe get away with more than it deserves. Four people here have tried their best. How many already gathered in the bedroom? All of us listening for what? The rattle that will sound the disembodying? My mother wants us here, not by whim. Some parting hunger that must strum in all of us. I even teased her: What would she want us to say?

He had done what she had asked him to do about Mendenhall, neither of them conceding what that nineteenth-century tribute might entail. She hadn't asked that he do the same for her.

"I can't stand this, any more of this," Zach says. "Shall we wail?" He digs the air, up up—the way a choir leader asks more of his choristers . . . but these here are dumb. So is he.

No. Bert is going to try.

"That's right, Bert. You could be a cantor, your voice."

"No—I heard it in Jerusalem. You were asleep, Cicily. I went early, when they allow, at the Wall. It's not a song." He opens his mouth. What comes out is not loud. It hangs in the air, slowly comes down. And again. And again.

Thelma opens the bedroom door. Not to scold. Brushing past Zach's outstretched apology, to embrace Bert. "Fine. But better come now." She numbers them. "Bring a couple of chairs." At the door, she leans back against it, spreading her arms, protecting the treasure in the room behind. "She's awake—and she isn't. So slight—maybe only a rictus. A gape. You can speak. She can't be hearing much; we had to remove the aids. But the vibration, it could be soothing, who knows? Wallie—you know how loud he is—I thought she smiled. But one imputes—what may not really be . . . She can't see—that I can assure you. I had the oculist in, to check. She's such a canny bird, she had us guessing. But there were hemorrhages." Thelma's hands clasp in front of her. "How long? I've sent the nurses on. That about says it." The hands tighten on some nugget. "I hope you'll stay." She smiles. "Toilet across the hall—being plenty used, I assure you. If she lasts the night—we can send out. Take sleep shifts. I've already had mine." Can they credit that, seeing her fatigue? But she is still physicianly cool, neat. "This house is made for—for vigil. Wish I could show the hospital. Maybe all houses are. Anyway, we're giving her it."

As Thelma cracks the door, Cicily says, "Can she speak?"

She is hugged like a cousin; does Thelma know her story?

"Zipporah mumbles to somebody," Thelma says. "Maybe to anybody."

She holds the door wide, they file in. As Bert passes, she says low, "I think she did hear—you." Zach follows, limping. Then Cicily. From behind, Shine hands her the violets.

They have been sitting, whispering-talking, mulling—waiting for hours on end. Arrived one by one, at dawn, noon, dusk, they are now united in dark. The avenue windows are velvety with sconces of light. This is a corner room; on the side street below are the faintly drawn windows, seen through their curtains and these, of two brownstone façades and above those, their black-shadowed, blank roofs. Thanks to the tracking back and forth to the toilets or the kitchen, nobody has a particular chair, other than the armchair ceded to Annie and the baby when she is there. The room she is occupying, "the girls' room" once occupied by her aunts, is near, just at the top of the hall, but she does not leave the baby alone there.

When she is not here, the aunts take turns in the armchair, two frail women in whom the sister-resemblance, a matter of bone, has at last emerged. Nell is still assertive; when her back is turned, a stranger hearing that she had been an attorney, a district attorney, would not be surprised. But that this lady with the sweet, blunted *moue* had had such amours—"And did you say—beauty?"—might well bemuse. The difference between beauty and a deadly prettiness is impossible to assay.

Erika, who will advise you in her still seductive alto, "I am known to my friends as Freddie, do feel free," is most distinctive— a little black-and-white-garbed Punchinello, hair a frill of white, feet not quite touching the floor. Nell has the bygone aura of a woman whose worldly functions have been put in lavender. Even her assertions are mild, if continual. Her day-help, a savvy elderly black woman, once her client in a discrimination case, keeps Nell's apartment—the same one, just untidy enough to comfort the old habitués, including a demi-husband or two who now and then visit. The maid knows how to keep Nell's foibles going; their client-lawyer discussions still smack of the barricades. Derek, the bandleader, supports his mother's ménage; Thelma monitors when she can. Nobody mentions the saint.

Erika, by contrast—she's not averse to pushing that—has the power presence honed at committees and by the attentions of the auction houses who quietly vie for her private collection of Judaica. "Those vultures might as well fall on their swords," Charles likes to crow; as president of his university he is a master of the mixed metaphor. Whenever Erika refers to the collection he calls "her Hebraica," that heritage flashes from her to him; his sister helps keep his faith warm for him. He looks forward to a retirement during which he must do "something on that score."

Nobody here from Boston. Nobody much left. They had not reproduced well. As Zipporah said, exhuming their photos from way back, when she began distributing things—"As you can see by the features, they are free from foreign taint."

Every now and then something she's said crops up, or those waiting see to it that it does. Hard to relate those sayings to the small mass on the bed there, but as the hours have gone on, a kind of formality in these quotes has developed—an antiphonal, in which nobody has to lead, and anybody can revel. Nobody's praying. They are interceding for her—with whom or what need not be clear. Bringing her good qualities to the fore. Bless her, for having had so many. You intercede for someone, your quality is on the table too.

Annie, who sings in oratorio, a kind of answering in chords to what one wouldn't ask alone, knows what this signifying is. Her crowd has grown up with the urge. They here are being communal, whether or not aware of that. For these moments, she and they are in communal love. She intends to bathe the baby in that, every chance she can. Charles's monologues have practically taught her how to research; she's been in libraries since a tot. An expert now in her family's history, maybe a mite disappointed at its narrow breadth, one day, like from a blow on the head, it came to her that she needn't only read about it—she had been (and was being) on the spot. She thinks she can discern which side of the clan has sort of engendered what—of course not scientifically, but Baby will be interested. A single mother has double obligations. She has a whole box labeled "Zipporah's Lore."

When Cicily enters looking modestly for where to sit, Annie, baby on shoulder, taps her with her free hand—"You're Cicily— I'm Annie"—pointing to a hassock next to the bed's footboard. "She used to call the youngest grandchildren 'the little Raphaels.' I think she hoped some of them would be here. Right there, where she could see . . . But we're really grown up and scattered." Like the jean-girls and tennis-whites Annie used to bump into here. At thirty-eight, refreshed by the baby, sometimes the dates confuse. But she can see very well what's wrong here. There are no such drop-ins anymore.

"Baby's too young for it," Annie says. "Don't think I'm crazy. But the youngest here could maybe be there for her. At the footboard. And you're it." She speaks in a normal voice, nothing fey.

"Thanks," Cicily says. "It's welcoming. And you're not crazy. You—like went to my school." She sits. The footboard is too high for her to see over. But in this lull, caused by their entry, she is near enough to hear what is coming from the bed—not a rattle, not a snore. A heavy breathing. Laboring. The kind that would be put under oxygen, but is not. She saw Alec there, in his tent, hiked at an angle, the nostrils stretched wide for the clamped wires. She had wanted to reach in and stifle him.

From where she sits, on the right Zach is at the headboard, looking down at the person in the bed. The occupant. A person who is dying is not a patient, not anymore. Next to him, sloshed in a chair half-facing away, fingering his watch—that's Gerald. Bert has kept updating the snapshots. His stories do not change. Gerald looks as he should. The two sisters next—how they've shrunk! Can they contain all the personality she's heard about?

One by one they had nodded at her, or tiptoed up to press her hand and return to the bedside. With a little extra marvel, they'd proffered her mother the same. At times they speak to a neighbor, the men particularly, in subdued voices, but not whispering. Once in awhile they get up to wander, even stretch. Otherwise they sit with heads bowed. That big man, dressed like a clubman—would that be Wallie, the family joke?—has nodded off. Ever so often he heaves, and subsides. There is the kind of peace that encloses a room when there is a ticking clock. But there is none. Then it steals over her: the woman on the bed is the clock.

Bert has found himself a seat at the other side of the bed, opposite Annie, at the base. But where is her mother? Ah, she knows, guesses. At menopause, in some protracted even to the late fifties, the flow can start up, even where there's nothing wrong. Plane travel can affect it. Sure enough, when Debra reenters, she has switched slacks, with a fresh blouse—so no one will notice; Cicily knows that trick. As her mother passes they exchange that eyebrow lift, almost a shrug: *we are what we are.*

There's only one seat left, center, the other side. Debra sets herself there. At her arrival, Wallie blearily wakes. Mutters to Bert, "Hi ... Y'all staying here?" Her stepfather nods. "Debra and I in the boy's room. Cicily in the attic—she can't wait."

Wallie clearly has no clue to what that means, or who she is. "This here gets too much, man, Bernice and I glad to oblige." He lapses again. Maybe tight?

Dr. Thelma, returned, has been pacing the room. At a mumble from the bed she pauses, stops there. Shakes her head. "She's holding her own."

In the sickroom, you should call even the very sick by their names; you never "she" and "he" them. Debra is tight-mouthed on her past training, but at Alec's bedside, her sharp reproof to an orderly had taught Cicily that.

Thelma is wavering on her pins. "I have to have forty winks. I'm in the maid's room if needed." On her way out she stops at Annie, who, deep in the chair, is breast-feeding. "That's right, Mother," Thelma says. "Gee, not a peep out of that happy child."

When Thelma's out of hearing, Annie grins. "They call you 'Mother,' you can be sure they've never been one." She sighs. "Wish Zipporah could see Baby, just once. And vice versa. What a great person." She aims this last at the bed.

"Thelma mightn't call you that—if you stopped calling it 'Baby,'" Erika snaps. Her children have turned out worldly enough. But not to her advantage. "What is it, anyway?"

"Don't fuss with Annie, Erika." But Charles waits for his daughter to say.

"We have gender classes now, Auntie, where I teach." Annie smoothes the tiny head. "Of course the dear thing shows evidences. But I'm told to be careful not to predict."

"Come off it," her father says. "What are you going to name him?"

"I'm thinking Emmanuel. That's in an aria I love. And isn't it one of the names for the Lord?"

"No—it's for the child who was to be a sign of Judah's deliverance." Charles is ruddy with pleasure. "I didn't know you were interested in the divine."

"I'm not. I'm interested in arias." She relents. "Want to hold him? He's probably wet, but when isn't he?"

"It's Hebrew for 'God with us.'" Bert is standing by the bed. "Hey. Did she say something? I could swear."

"She mumbles." Gerald is rolling a cigar between thumb and finger, though he no longer smokes. It's that or worry beads, he'll say, if anybody notes. "I'm here steadier than anybody. But I've never been able to catch what."

"Thelma is dedicated," Nell says. "We owe her. But she knows too much. Like all of them. The ears were inflamed, yes, but Mother put up a fight when they took the aids away. A choking, blind fight. I had to get out of the room."

Annie is laying the sleeping bundle in her father's arms. They all turn to watch. To Bert—the immortal gesture, that will never come his way. Charles has had two sets of children, but his receiving arms are still tentative. Annie, his first, must have been just such a bundle once. Now, like her grandmother, she is on her own. It's good to have the span of life presented; if only it didn't have to be in such a harsh way.

Zach, the only one at the bedside, notes again the slow majesty that the breath of the dying can have. At home, he should watch himself more; time after time he'll stumble into some reference belonging to the Ernestine who has gone on, not to the one who has survived. Luckily, his pet name for their privates had always been the same.

To him, the spirit of a person, whether or not it survives, must be paid homage. It is the art of the body. Who can separate? He leans over his mother. Whether or not she can see with the eyes, he is careful not to shadow her. He's respecting what has been there to listen, building up to what hearkens now. "I did what you asked me, Mu. For the Fox."

There's a smell of coffee. Nell says to her sister, as if scared, "Who's that in the kitchen?"

"My Melanie. I've been sending her in, when I can spare. I thought there ought to be some help here. Who you can trust."

"Ah, your French wonder." There used to be no one Erika trusted, outside of the family. Not even Philippe. And with reason. They have never mentioned it. And within the family—maybe only Zipporah. With reason.

"Freddie—" Nell whispers. "Let's sneak the hearing aids back in."

All that lacy black-and-white foof on her recoils. But their old pillow-name—that's the trick. Sends them both back.

"Where are they?"

"On the table."

Shine sits cross-legged on the floor, expecting to show off muscles prepped with shoreline walks, to these suited men who at best ride fake bikes on indoor paths—yet toward a horizon he still calls "the continent." He is posted near the door, ready to spring himself, if need be. Revolution shimmers, if behind him; he still hears its call. His buddy Bert—they both know he'd never hare off that way, but Britain has kept him fit enough. And marrying whom he has. Who, laying her almost-as-was cheek on Shine's right cheek, then his left, has only now terminated for him that long-ago cab ride. That girlie over there—though counting up, she can't be. Daughter of a Debra. Time like this, how can she doze?

Gerald, never one for babies—not until they were old enough to listen to you—is glad to be pulled off into a corner, even by Wallie, though any time they meet, he'll be dogged for not any longer "giving the Fund the benefit of your experience." Synonym for not contributing more.

Wallie, now president, would have a fit if Gerald thought to run again. On the perils of dealing with "the situation," meaning Israel, he, the incumbent, is careful to lecture Gerry. Also, though not of the wit to be what the city, careful to pull its punches, calls "a developer"—"Catch me, running with those leeches"—Wallie has parlayed the family residence he inherited, once a four-story limestone white elephant his father had turned into apartments, now a very minor embassy, into what he calls "holdings," though he tries not to hang on too long.

"The bedrooms, these old Central Park West joints, they can have it all over those on Park. Front ones of course, like this—look at it." He squints. "Eighteen by—I'd say—twenty-seven; with the dressing room, even more." A hiss. *Look what it can accommodate.*

They glance aside. The women, eyes downcast, are mourning appropriately. "Fine women, your sisters, my cousins." Bent over the bed, the two are tenderly regarding what can't be easy on the emotions, to say nothing of the digestion. They are doing the honors for their tribe. "Olden times," Gerald says huskily, "immigrant times even, the women of the family—they used to wrap. Once it was over . . . Excuse me, Wallie. I should be with Zach."

Zach, away from the bed now, seems to be having a bad time. "Let Bert."

Gerald has the feeling that he has too often "let Bert." His mother, once applied to, had said: "If you mean, did you let your youngest put his neck on the block for the rest of you—not quite. No, it was more subtle. You let him be the peacemaker." But what was subtle about it, she hadn't said. She never will, now. One doesn't have to be at a bedside, to mourn. A son wants to remember a mother like she was, almost to the end—it's no sin. Even backdate a little. "Know what, Wallie. Years ago, my secretary telling me she saw my mother dancing at Roseland, I almost fired her for pushing that gossip—I didn't believe."

"I saw, yes. I saw he passed on," Wallie says absently. "Big bucks." He nudges Gerald. "Look at her up there. Your Bert's wife. Sitting straight as a statue. Classy. But the only time she's been here since the Duffys took her in, that sad business; I bet you hardly think of her as your daughter-in-law. Mother of that *hübsche Mädel* over there; they could be sisters—but still she don't mix. We heard since—Lev left her some, but back then—like an icicle she was. We thought it was grief—and being out of her culture. We used to call her 'the Sabra,' remember? I asked her once, she should speak her experiences at the Fund campaign—boy, did she give me the aloof. And all the time our quiet Bert must've been carrying the torch for her." Wallie shoots his cuff to check the watch. He always times his lead-ins. "Gerry—"

"Wallie. Whatever it is, another time... What are my sisters doing over there?"

"Expressing devotion. You'll have time for it, I guarantee."

What won't he assure? "You have an in with God?"

"Not me, Gerald." Use of the full name signals *we are serious folk.* "But maybe the Fund. And the Fund wants a favor, Gerald. A favor so big, it could be your sole contribution." Wallie's voice drops—a salesman's confiding the discount he'll give only to you. "Old man Elias—we want you to go talk to him... Okay, okay, you gave up the house, you don't live out there anymore. Maybe you don't know how out of touch you are. He was going to leave us the whole kit-and-caboodle, he hasn't a soul else. Big bucks—I don't have to say. Living next door, you told me yourself what a privilege; over coffee you used to listen to him talk while he shaved. But now not a penny for us. He's cut us out; he wants it known." Wallie drops the voice. "We think it's a case of undue influence. Where else could a man ninety-four get such opinions? You ask me, it's those young lawyers, junk-bonders, who crammed out there, the eighties, bought those gray environmentals, looked like seagulls were nesting. You build nontraditional, everything else follows." He leans, speaking from the side of his mouth. "He says—that old fool, I hate to soil my mouth—he says, 'A state religion they have—so we should make them honorary liberal Americans?' He says did he fight in World War II—to save the Holocaust only for them?... So help me, I was out there to see him myself. 'You been giving since 1948,' 1 said. 'When we crawled there on our knees, you gave. Now we stand on our feet, you stop?' It's my speech; it always brings in."

"I know it well, Wallie." But you can't nick this guy anywhere.

"So the payoff. Nothing for us? I don't give in easy, Gerry; you know me. I say, 'Elias, who's been getting at you?' He says, 'Only you. And my reader from the temple, who comes every day with the paper; she didn't read me the bad parts. But now the. cataracts are off; they gave me a lens, I have an appointment to the Inquisition every morning.'"

Wallie rocks on his heels. He always catches them in the end. "*Oy,* yes. This man who still runs his own firm? So I say ve-ry cagey, 'Toom who, Eli?' And he says, 'To the Inquisition in every Jew's blood. Or that ought to be.' Ve-ry lofty. So then I know what I'm up against; this is not unique. I say, 'Did I hear a dirty rumor, you thinking of going over to the other side?' And he says, that *schamus,* '*Is* there another side?'"

Bert has come up to them, after whispering to Nell, "I see Wallie's on a spiel, I think I've never left." She answering: "He has all the time in the world. Other people's." Ordinarily Wallie would ward Bert off; he's been known to do that to two prospects simultaneously, a mitt on each man's shoulderblades—until he crosses the finish line. Today he hasn't the gall. Or he wants in? Gerald says, "Is it—don't tell me?—"

"Zach's talking to her, Dad. Nell and Erika were trying to put her ear aids in but were afraid they might hurt her. She can't be hearing much, if at all. But he thinks she's pressing his hand." Bert is pale. "I came away. What's going on is private."

"I was just telling your father—"

"Don't bother to clue me in, Wallace. Just carry on."

"Right. A day like this... So, Gerry. To wind up. On the train home, all of a sudden I illuminate. That old fart, who made his pile sitting on the fence; maybe he's fallen off, hah? He was always overhungry to let us know what he was leaving us. Maybe it's taken a dive... And you can find out for us. Who else can play so intimate?... Not while you have this sorrow, of course." He glances nervously at the bed. "With him it's not so imminent... So you'll do this for us, Gerry?... When you can."

"Sure, sure ... If it wasn't for—for this, as you say, I'd go out there tomorrow. Give him a shave myself."

"Ah, come on. I just mean—when you see your way clear."

When a Wallie doesn't get answered, two of his relatives standing there, a father and son, it can induce rage. "So I made a boo-boo? From only a manner of speaking? You people don't understand the strain. What you put on us. Bernice said it: 'Other families receive civilized, afterwards; my family has to receive before? You go, Wallie, pay our respects. I'll go later, to the chapel.'... She can't stand the strain ... So if you permit ... I'll go pay our respects."

They watch him walk the bedroom's length. The same pace as when he goes down the aisle with the collection plate in temple; certain members are naturals for that chore. At the bedside he measures himself a place behind the sisters, and stands there.

"Our cousin Bernice, she was over two hundred by the time she was sixteen," Gerald says. "The family couldn't blame her, for marrying down. So we got Wallie." He rubs his lip. "And I suppose we should say—he got Bernice. He's always congratulating me these days, for living in a hotel. 'You don't have to go outside for it,' he says. 'You're already there.'

"*Shh*—" Bert says. "Look."

Wallie, scrounging in a pocket, has found a yarmulke, is sneaking it on. Their congregation does not wear them. It is Reform.

When he comes back to them, at that stately pace, he is still wearing it. He puts his hand on his chest. "They have her on a monitor? That thump-thump you hear from her. It's like you hear the approach."

They don't answer him. Two animals, meeting another of their kind, yet so foreign, so other, that not even a fight is possible. Bert has never felt so close to his father.

"So I gave offense." Wallie has an air of knowing what to do. "So I spoke normal at the wrong time. So I spoke money. While a beloved mother is going. You don't think we all know how you idolize? Would I bring up even for your own good, this place, it's top of the market? You're going inherit, you should offer for two million, not one, maybe settle one-five? Did I even ask—that man, he didn't live with Zipporah—did he at least leave a token his regard? . . . No, I make a single request. I want we shouldn't backslide . . . Sorry. Inconvenient." He stabs a forefinger at Gerald. "My folks. Fourteen weeks. One in Mt. Sinai, one in Memorial; I learned something. It goes in stages. You don't want them to go. You want to help them to hold on." He stands back, thumb brushing the invisible from his forefinger, not quite snapping them. Such a soft confession they almost don't catch it. "You want to help them go."

Three men, heads bowed. Who's saying?

"Wallace—" Bert's never spoken for his father. He can feel the surge of agreement at his side. "You better go."

"Don't you 'Wallace' me, you—what should I say? We know you since Hector was a pup—part-time rabbi. Fallen on velvet—a cushy charity that don't discriminate, not like us." He swishes the worst in his teeth; spits it. "Married to Miss Coldbottom there; that keeps him kosher?"

Father and son pry each other off him.

"I should cut off my tongue," he says, enunciating carefully. Maybe to show himself what he would lose? "Night after night Bernice has to run in from the spare room, where she has a double bed; she's too heavy now for the twin. I am groaning, rocking, beating my chest, fighting for breath. And always for the same outcry—*Israel*. And again. *Israel*. Why? I was born here. Right here in New Rochelle." He has the shiny air of the vindicated. "And in the office, out with clients—even worse. I am saying exactly what I feel. Try that at a business lunch."

They are too fascinated to comment. The family's stuffed shirt, coming out at the seams? "She's afraid I'll maybe end up exposing myself—maybe I should sign myself in that fancy shrink outfit in Connecticut?" His laugh is hollow—perfected? "I say, 'Wait awhile; maybe they'll put me away for free.'"

Gerald gives him a shoulder-grip. "Go. Go take a leak."

———

It has been an interlude. They're unaccountably refreshed.

At the other end of the room—that charade they must return to, at the heart of it the weeks-long woe you wake to, each morning. They return to it with heavy step. "He spoke normal," Gerald said.

Annie is at one of the side-street windows. It is still night, but that pre-dawn in which there is a kind of city precipitation, as if a great egg is breaking. "I'm showing Baby the two old rooftops." Low-lying, with what must be water towers on flat planes, they're a black geometry not meant to be visited. "Zipporah used to love to pretend to be walking on them." Annie says softly to Bert, "She said it was like being in a child's dream." She's moving with that almost imperceptible dandling mothers have. The baby's eyes, slitted open, show that glassy violet which may or may not refract. Annie is unaware of that other rhythm proceeding in the bed; rather, she seems to be sweetly offering what she holds. He sees how restoring it is to be that kind of acolyte. At the bedside again, he wonders what his function can be.

Zach has replaced the sisters, who stand by. His long deft fingers, used to every anagram posed him by the wood, glass, plastic, or zinc of "installations" ever in performance, are fumbling at the ear of this near-corpse, in which the bulge of the forehead and the upper jaw already project the skull. Yet someone has tended the hair, which spreads as if the head has will. The mottled hands rise and fall, whether too fast or slow is not in his ken. The eyes are what stay him. As with the old, the shrunken lids show their pale edges. The pupils, once a fine brown, are now dun. They too are remote. Yet there is something they see.

He should feel guilty, staring down at her details as if she is already in a satined bed; instead, he is heartened. That stubborn arrangement is asking to be scrutinized.

"I can't... seem to," Zach falters. "Why'n hell she didn't settle for one of those wee plugs. These clumsy drape-jobs, you need a sturdy ear."

Hers, always neat, are larger now against the lessened face, and thin as shell.

Debra has swept to the bedside. Almost as if she has leapt
there. "I am a nurse."

Bert has not heard her say it that way, ever. Regret turns its
flange in him, for the children they hadn't had. The long, volup-
tuously curved but tintless nails slide under the hair, expertly fiddling. "Nah?" Then, bending, in slow syllable, "Zipporah, this is
Debra." Placing a hand behind the neck, in practiced extension,
she eases the head up an inch, keeps it there. Slight as the weight
may be, that takes doing. On both their parts?

The lids quiver; yes they do.

A sob from Nell. "I knew she was there. I knew."

One of the mottled hands rises. The light has been lowered.
Long ago Zach put all the apartment on rheostat. A ray of day-
break is caught in the blinded window. The silver bits circling
Debra's neck have intercepted it. She bends to let the hand touch.
"Yes, the necklace you gave me. You were bringing me." She clasps
the seeking hand, pressing it there. Then lays it gently down.
Crosses her lips. Her long, pointed fingers, shivering in the air, she
asks them to step back, give the patient air, quietly dispersing
them; a nod assures them her charge will rest or sleep now. All
without a single word. Circling the wrist, she clocks the pulse, before she herself steps aside. Bert is proud.

They all find chairs, not too near, not too far.

"That's Venetian work, that necklace," Erika says after a while.
"A wedding piece, isn't it?"

Seated near the headboard, Debra nods.

"We have several, at the museum. Meant to be worn only the
once, they were. Then handed on, to the next . . . They usually
come with a headband."

At the footboard, Cicily, awake now, leans on it. "I have it.
Mother gave it to me." She sends Debra an impish smile, received
in kind.

"Wallie's gone, I see," Nell says after awhile. "What was he
going on about, back there?"

"His holdings," Gerald says.

"And about holding on. Not necessarily to those." Bert has seated himself next to his wife.

"Well, good riddance, I should say. Or sad."

"Sad?" Erika says. "That's not like you."

"If he's sold short again, Bernice has to step in."

"That's how it works, Nell," Gerald says loftily. "Borrowing. In the real-estate field especially. Unless Bernice is just making herself big."

A general titter, quickly suppressed.

"A case came over the D.A.'s desk, years ago, brother. Wallie'd dipped into funds he had access to. Done it before. That time, took too long to pay back in. The accounts showed up. She took care of it. So it never got out."

"Jesus."

"Joined the church, Gerald?" Nell almost had, once. He'd cracked—"Seeking her niche, I suppose?" Somebody had snitched it to her; guess who?

"You two," Erika sighs. "You practically cancel each other out."

"So we may," Gerald says comfortably. "Leaving you to be the perfect religionist among us sibs? Not that I think running a museum quite takes care of that." Formerly slow at repartee, being at Zipporah's elbow, and subject to her lively tongue, has improved him. Even in the early years, she had never let the others make him their butt. His throat contracts, at what he is going to lose.

"Please—" Bert says. Remember who you are. Where you are. These are his elders, or were once. When he was young, in the eddies of his parents' rage, he'd had to say more. He hasn't come back to be the ombudsman, ever again. But he's afraid—he wants to be glad—that his grandmother can hear. So he says it again. "Please."

... Not to worry, Bertram. Thanks ...

This is the yap and gabble of family, in which she thrives. Throve. The past hoards old-fashioned verbs. The voice of the house dove is saying, "Peace, peace." While the meanest of them shrieks the nightmare of what he does not want to flee. She heard him.

A smell of coffee, coming from a kitchen once hers. A *femme de ménage*, imported, makes the best. Or a woman of the household, from anywhere. They walk toward her, past her, with her. Images of what she was once. At times princesses with Egyptian step, bearing the impedimenta of how we must live. At times only sphinxes, with blunted profile.

. . . *I know where I am going*. That was a wartime song. We hear it, dulcet, in the movie we maybe didn't get to see. Oblivion? It's the soap that washes one well, for where one does
not need to be clean.

Before I go, I am listening. To what I leave . . .

"Where's Charles? He's wanted on the phone."

That's Nell. She's always the first to answer it.

"Dad? He's in the kitchen, feeding."

Annie. They laugh with her . . . That son of mine. Six-and-a-half-footer, who must constantly be stoked. I would laugh with them. If I thought they could hear.

"Sit in the big chair, Annie. It must be more comfortable."

That's the new girl. I saw her. Before my eyes closed.

"Thanks, Cicily. Yes it is. He's such a bundle."

Ah-h-h. The bundles . . . I rocked . . . And rocked.

And rock.

Zachary leans over his mother. She's not the woman who wore a mumu, but that is what he sees. "You asked me to do a death mask of Foxy Mendenhall. I've done it, Mu. It was the hardest for me to do, ever. You're not supposed to put your own heart in it. In the end, it was the easiest. He had done all the work it should have."

She had been shifting from side to side. When he spoke, she

stopped that, but she is still breathing. He stood up. "I wish she could see it. I hope she heard."

Walking as far away from what's left on the bed as he can, he circles the footboard to the other side. Plumping himself in a chair next to his nephew and the wife. "I had all the materials in the station wagon. I thought—maybe for forty seconds, that I could—do the same here. I know a photographer who's seen the process done in Paris, many times. He swears the face sets itself. But when I came in here—that's why I broke up. Waiting. Confronting. All the stuff I do—all the art anybody does—it's just memory that waits?"

Debra reaches for Zach's hand, then Bert's; covers them with hers. On impulse. Bert has never seen her do that before. Never felt so near Gerald. So many never-nevers. Maybe that's the way we all buy.

"Memory just waits, yes." Debra says it clear enough for the bed to hear.

Cicily and Annie have found each other. Annie thinks she would like Britain. Cicily's been told about Annie's mother. "Your dad's new wife isn't here?" Not new, Annie says; the two Buddhas, as her half-brothers are called, are getting on for grown. "No, she's a scientist; she's training to be an astronaut." She giggles. "She's fond of him. But he's such a high-class yakker. She has to put space between her and him. So do I, between Dad and me. Actually, I'm learning it from her."

"That's some space."

"Mmm."

Annie hasn't heard about Cicily's sex life yet. Not sure she wants to.

Cicily hasn't asked if there's a husband. Maybe they'll come to it.

Annie tries to get up out of the low chair. "I have to burp him. Goes better when we walk. Here—would you hold him?"

Cicily looks down at the bundle in her arms. "Such a good baby. Doesn't he ever cry?"

Annie looks down at her. "Not all of them have to." Lifting the bundle, she presses him close. It's like holding the world.

Charles hurries in. The phone call has been the most important in his lifetime. A Supreme Court Justice he'll never be; he hasn't been on the straight legal path, but there are other jobs that rank—not elective, rather those like this, for which one is tapped. He'll get this post if he wants it. He's never embezzled, borrowed, nor fornicated, beyond sleeping with the new wife before he stopped sleeping with the old. As his rival for the university presidency had quipped: "He doesn't knife you; he filibusters you until you may wish he had." Adding further, "This time, as a Duffy he will please the cardinals and their entourage, both here and abroad. Of course, as a half-and-half, if he chooses to turn the screw a bit, he could be called the only Jew who has ever held that job."

No cynic, Charles cheers people. As he enters, a banana held at his side like a sword, their spirits lift; they all suspect what the call concerned. His grave nod tells them that he will accept. In fact, he is needed at once. But he has never failed an appointment with his mother, and he will not do so now.

As head of the family, he kneels.

Is he going to pray as well? Bert wonders. For who? For Zipporah, the fearless? Who could say to Gerald's rabbi, "I'm not an agnostic, Dr. Eiseman. I simply feel free *not* to believe. Or not in tents . . . Eh? . . . Oh, you know—arenas. Palladiums. Odeons." (Has she known she would sound blasphemous to more than the rabbi—whose ego, elevated to prophet in any argument, brought this out?) "I guess that's why I have to go abroad for my—togetherness. I'm very affected by religion in the open air, rabbi." At her own table, which he patronized freely in order to exhort, she hadn't felt free to bait him, but they were at Gerald's. "Oh, I could never follow a god," his grandmother had concluded. "I would expect him to follow me."

Gerald had been very upset; this was no way to entertain a rabbi. Peter, who'd had his own congregation, one without a *schul,* in which even the rabbi would be laity, had risen from some bottom of reflection to fill the silence. "Not to worry. He'll never catch up."

Bert intrigues Annie, always has. In his way, hasn't he been a rebel, like herself? On this solemn occasion, what can be making him smile? Having Baby has made her less shy; any venture is for him. "Bert," she whispers, "what's Charles praying from?" To her, prayer is a general repository, into which people dip—as in music, when hunting for a song. And Bert, in his field, the trained musicologist. But he won't say.

"You ask." His Uncle Charles is that mystery—a simple man? Or one who thinks he is. "I wouldn't dare."

She grins, squeezing the baby in response. "Dad? . . . Why don't you pray out loud?"

Her father raises his head, stares at her, bemused. "She'd kick me in the soup. I'm listening."

He crouches, laying his ear to what ground? Faintly they hear, scarcely a voice. A sound you may think you hear—a body creaking along, the bedclothes murmuring. A consciousness, trapped.

"I think she may be numbering us. She can't see us. She must want us to—declare."

In the classrooms that are Charles's life, that's reasonable. For any of them here to pose his or her life to the intensity raying from there—that's brave. His finger summons them.

One by one, as he names them, they come forward to station themselves closer to the bedside. Charles, still kneeling, is at his mother's left side. The sisters inch up behind him; in such a devotion there is no rivalry. Bert and his father are at her other side. The young women lean on the footboard. The bed is a mahogany one from an era of solidity, the model called a "sleigh," the headboard a thick but modest curve. Debra, who has not moved, is already there. At the last moment, Zach, wandering confused in some spatial measurement that doesn't fit his usual command, inserts himself with a wild, "Room for me?" between the two at the footboard. Shine, summoned, declines, with an outsider's politesse. Tall enough to see over everybody, he leans against the wall.

They stand. Each can see a part of her. A tattered persona is receiving the responses of those who have known its perfection. They themselves cannot help being whole.

A buzz at the head of the hall, just outside the bedroom. Someone is letting himself, herself in. Zach's shoulders lift. Poor old wizard buzzer he'd installed to keep this family abreast; the wiring ought to be looked at, but it still works.

Byron walks in. The circle wavers toward him, recognizing, but mum. Tired standees, they deserve interruption but do not know how to step down.

"She's not—?" he asks. No. Ah.

All in pantomime. People don't always need speech.

Byron does. "I was afraid I'd be—. Got your message, Bert but I was—" He wilts.

They know where Byron must have been. The old ones are maybe a bit bleary on the details of one of the few endings not usually theirs. Night after night the messages pile up at his answering service; he won't have a machine. A human voice can lure a man to wait, to expect, even to hope. Some messages for him are from dunners. Though he keeps his credit cards sacrosanct, emergencies are routine. He sells Lucas's works one by one as needed; they have come to be coveted, now that the artist is gone. Ordinarily a sale might keep him long-term, far more comfortably than he actually lives; could he save, he would be provided for life. His other source of income is their former apartment, owned but rented with all its glitz, which can involve repairs he himself performs. These activities are his work. What he "does" on the side—with no possible schedule, but surely twelve or more hours out of twenty-four—no tax man can name. Zipporah had been an authority on what he does. And sometimes a source.

He goes at once to the narrow space next to Charles, who has stumbled to his feet.

Byron's body language can remind one that he was once a diver. His sense of target, how long he must stay, how long the trip will last, is said to be acute. If he sags, one guesses that though never underwater these days, he is still subject to the "bends."

They here have their daily life. People are taken; sure, that's the other side of life, a prospect for each new one, even for the baby here. But one does not brood; one half forgets. For the special loss, as here, one rallies. While secretly, all the clichés of feeling come to roost. Is it desertion, for instance, to sit while she, maybe at this very moment—? One visits the dying. At the very moment of death—one must stand. Paying attention. Helping to usher out, into such eternity as one acknowledges will be one's own.

The division in the room is clear. One by one the elders sit: Gerald, Erika, Nell, then reluctantly, Zach. The two young women stand, Bert with them, though not as young. Debra sits; her attention is of another sort.

Byron is the expert. With what grace he lifts Zipporah's hand! "Zipporah?"

One hears how a three-syllable name may be the more useful, in such a summoning. He says it again. Very direct. All his actions are. As if this is a process he and she are both engaged in. "I see that you can hear," he says. "You don't have to answer me. Though you can if you want to. Maybe press my hand. Anyway—I feel that you are listening. You know how glad I am to be with you."

They are awed, Bert sees. All of us. Glad. We never thought to say.

Will he name us to her?

He does not. It occurs to Bert that this anonymity is the way one might want it. The core of a person—being spoken to, by another core. One other, no matter who. Byron couldn't have known all of them.

Holding Zipporah's hand, he is faced toward Debra at the opposite side of the bed. Sitting close. If she leans forward, she can take the dying's other hand. She does not. He does not ask her to. She and Byron have met, in her house. He knows what her past work had been. "Debra," he says. Nothing further.

Slipping an arm under the body—or is it still Zipporah?—he does not raise her, so that they might better see. "It's hard going." He does not whisper. "It's hard not going...So they say." "They" are his authority.

Charles mentioned me, Cicily is saying to herself. And will say my name to others of the family later. He mentioned me.

Weird, Annie says to herself. I just wish Baby were old enough. She cradles him. So you could say you saw.

Byron has tensed. Good athletes seem to, before the dive, the slalom. Though to Shine, overlooking the pair as he can, she is the one who looks most different. Is it the last change?

Byron leans over her. One must have strong arms to both hold and lean. "You're seeing—" he says. Even now he doesn't say "she." Those whom he attends, who may have gone blind or nearly so— "They often do see," he will say later. They may even tell him what they do see—if there is time. "What they see is never the same."

Debra is looking at him, her hands fisted, her eyes wide. He nods. "I'll fetch Thelma," she says, and runs.

Thelma comes swiftly. Behind her, Wallie; he hadn't left. Though it wasn't anything he would want to go through again, he said later. "I had that living room all to myself."

Thelma stands by the bedside. She is tall enough to lean over, to share Zipporah's weight—"Ah, that seeing effect?" she will say later. "Maybe. Medically, we judge it perhaps some somatic change—soma is the flesh—that relays some image to the brain. Some image it held dear...But my monks—they don't agree. They say, 'What is seen is seen.'"

But just now, Thelma steps back. "Say that for Thelma," they'll say later. "She takes over. But she knew when to step back."

Bert takes Thelma's place. "Come," Byron says to him. "Share her weight." This time he whispers. "She is still here."

What a smile he has! But it is not the last she hopes to see. The Eye of God will be as bulbous and long-cornered, or as slitted, as need be; it can serve for any race. How this was designed must be sought in some telescope yet to be . . . The orb is the color of atmosphere. The pupil can be seen through, like rain. The aspect of eternity is such that it cannot be said who is looking at whom.

In all her images, the Eye is open. Say something to Me, before you go? Up to you.

She says something. The Eye shuts.

They wait, hearing their hearts thump. Byron signals. She no longer hears hers.

Gerald, as the oldest, has the honor of breaking the silence. "She said something. She was talking to somebody. Who?" Does he mean himself?

Zach says, "Look . . . Her face is making its own mask."

Daughters Nell and Erika have clasped four-handed, as was their habit when waking in "the girls' room," to all the ghouls of sex, men—life. What they said then they will not repeat. But they are sure that their mother spoke to Dad.

Wallie says, with the proper hush he hopes will redeem him, "She spoke to all of us. Even to me."

When Byron sees that no one else will speak, he says to his brother, "Please close her eyes."

"You do it, By." This man from the sea, his brother. "You're our real rabbi."

Byron would rather not have his work referred to—not in terms of himself. But his dead deserve their tribute. "There is a— what I say for them. Since they cannot. But like only they are to hear." He bows his head over hers now. "I am told it's from the kabala." Let them wonder how he would have come upon such an inscription. Later he'll tell them—among which mollusked brass instruments, in which sea. He had said it over Lucas. Only silently, Lucas being so hard to please.

. . . The world reveals and makes visible the Boundless and the concealed of the concealed . . .

Each time he says it to himself, Byron gets his thanks.

"Now, you, Bert," he says. "You do the eyes." In his protocol, using *the* instead of *her* is proper now. "Then the last words—if you want." He is never sure they are meant for us.

Carefully Bert pulls down the lids of those staring eyes. He knows what he heard. She said it for herself, but it echoes for him. And Wallie was right; one mustn't begrudge him that. This woman who spent her life stirring the midden, poking there, she spoke for all of us. For Norman, Nanette, and all the other cousins and barnacles, long since gone. For his own mother even, "the fecklessly fashionable Finn," as the vanity press had called her. Who could not bear to be Fegeleh . . . What would Gramps—who by leave often spoke for both of them, who saw through that sad maneuver of Zipporah-Zoe—what would he counsel?

Say it, boy. One must always say. But stand on your own two feet while doing so. She knew that. May the Lord make his face to shine upon her. On her terms. Any God worth His salt will know what those are . . . It's between Him and her—whatever she saw . . .

As a rabbi of these times, ambiguities surround him, breed in him, leech from behind. No harm in one more.

So he says exactly what he heard her say, as—sightless, surely—she stared upward. But says it, near as he can get to it, in the Hebrew none here will likely know.

Then, having satisfied that depth, he says it in the language to which, escapading through history, he was born. Not as if in translation, but, hand raised in benediction, exactly as the woman on the bed, dead in her ninety-sixth year, has just said, her wish to die with nothing said denied.

" 'Don't think, Lord, that I'm only here because I'm Jewish.' "

On the Hebrew, his wife Debra has moved to him. By some prism change, no miracle, she has lost her mystery. Though no less dear. She is like him—ordinary.

The baby cries.

FINIS

READING
GROUP
GUIDE

READING GROUP GUIDE

The matriarch of a diverse, dynamic family, Zipporah Zangwill prizes sincerity far more than tradition. Role models for the art of exuberant living, she and her husband watch their children discover individual ways to love, develop their talents, and experience faith. With wit and candor, the characters in Hortense Calisher's *Sunday Jews* raise universal questions about the true significance of cultural ties and legacy—particularly when a tragedy fatefully unites Zipporah's family with a young woman from Israel.

We hope that the following topics will enhance your reading group's discussion of this captivating novel.

1. What distinctions do Zipporah's children make between their father's Catholicism and their mother's Judaism? In what ways do their maternal relatives, as remembered by Zipporah, and Peter's sisters, their paternal relatives, differ?

2. Hortense Calisher made several subtle choices when creating the novel's cast of characters, including the mention of a child who succumbed to cancer at a young age. How does Mickey's absence affect the family?

3. Does each Duffy child reflect an aspect of Zipporah's persona? Or of life in general? What about Zach, the artist? What about Nell, as a rebel, an activist, and a mother?

4. Discuss the significance of Zipporah's decision to change her name to Zoe, along with the fateful events of her "naming party" hosted at the beginning of the novel. Why do you suppose the author varies the names she uses for this character?

5. Does the murder of diamond broker Lev Cohen—a man of integrity—bring about a shift in Zipporah's life, or does it instead enhance her immutable identity?

6. In what way does Zipporah's stance on Jews around the world echo her work as an anthropologist? What does her friendship with Debra reveal to her about Israel?

7. Besides her practical assistance as a nurse, what does Debra provide Peter and Zipporah that their children could not?

8. What makes Italy such an appropriate backdrop for Peter and Zipporah's final days together?

9. The book's title is discussed on page 135. In light of the definition given there, is Zipporah indeed a Sunday Jew? Who would be a Saturday Jew?

10. Page 135 also includes the following sentence: "And the children, riding in buses with guards on them, seeing lush foreign movies in the meantime, could scarcely be blamed for assuming that among those Sunday Jews there must be a lot of Americans." In what ways is the family distinctly American? In what ways are they atypical Americans?

11. Explore the author's style in writing dialogue. How does she evoke distinct voices for her characters?

12. Examine the profusion of symbolic elements that accompany Peter's dying words on page 221—the Ark of the Covenant, the spirit of Lev, the synagogue itself, the wristwatch designed by Zach. Do you agree with the assertion that he has been a guest in his own life?

13. Does the inheritance from Norman create an entirely new chapter of Zipporah's life? What is the significance of money and death in *Sunday Jews*?

14. How would you have responded to Katrina's plea that Zipporah marry Foxy? What does Foxy represent in the book?

15. The Duffys honor a fascinating range of immigrant orthodoxies and new-world philosophies. What is the expatriate folklore of your family?

16. What makes Bert a better match for Debra than any of his brothers?

17. Zipporah dies surrounded by many generations of relatives, including an infant descendant. What can be expected from these future generations? What do you imagine her legacy will be?

Reading Group Guide prepared by Amy Root